Also by Jo Amdahl

The *Empire of G*

Foundatio

Jeremiah I, Prince of Babylon

Jeremiah II, Emperor of Babylonia

What Critics are Saying:

In the introduction to *Empire of Gold: Foundations,* the author asks, "Who said history was boring?" And this book takes away any doubt, dramatizing history with solid characters and full-bore action. We follow Jeremiah from his youth through the final scene as he is told he's the prophet to the nations. The reader ends up caring about him and what happens next. The author does a good job of weaving biblical events, historical facts and imagined events and dialogue. The book brings the stories alive and is a page-turner.

—Judge, 2nd Annual Writer's Digest Self-Published eBook Awards

What Readers are Saying:

***** 5 Stars!!! Superbly written and researched.

This is a book I would recommend to anyone. It makes the era of the Assyrians, Babylonians, Egyptians and the Israelites come alive. You will get to know the kings and leaders of these great empires personally instead of as just historical figures. Great book! J.S.

***** 5 Stars!! An Eye Opener!

The story is fast paced, very interesting, and I could hardly put it down. I would highly recommend it to anyone with an interest in ancient history or biblical studies. O.M.

***** 5 Stars!! A Great Read!

I found *Empire of Gold: Foundations* to be captivating AND informative AND a page-turner. Can't ask much more than that.... I'm actually anxious to read the next books. B.B.

***** 5 Stars!! Political Associations in Founding Empires.

With conflicts prevalent in the Middle East (Syria, Iraq, Israel) a very interesting look at the rise of the Babylonian Empire thousands of years ago, that highlights the political associations that arise when powerful leaders look to allies to build their empires. Jo has written a great Foundation. I'm looking forward to the next book. M.A.

EXCERPT:

Topheth, the place of burning, that was what they called the fiery altars of the Baals, and the unquenchable flames of the garbage heap of Jerusalem had appropriated the name. It was the picture of eternal damnation to the people of Judah.

Tongues of fire flickered before the prophet's face, casting eerie lights across his visage in the shadows of the city wall. The flames burned, attempting to devour the rubbish of the city which fed them. The rejected and outcast broken remnants of society were consumed here forever amidst the swarms of flies and the scavenging creatures which tried to gorge themselves on their share of the refuse before the flames could claim it.

Jeremiah faced hell and knew it could be avoided no longer…

—*Empire of Gold: Jeremiah I, Prince of Babylon*

EMPIRE OF GOLD: JEREMIAH I

Prince of Babylon

By

Jo Amdahl

Publisher's Cataloging-In-Publication Data
(Prepared by The Donohue Group, Inc.)

Names: Amdahl, Jo.
Title: Empire of Gold. Jeremiah I, Prince of Babylon / by Jo Amdahl.
Other Titles: Jeremiah I, Prince of Babylon
Description: Second edition. | Byron, WY : Shoshone Publications, [2018] | Includes bibliographical references.
Identifiers: ISBN 9781736280911 (hardcover) | ISBN 9780997675535 (softcover) | ISBN 9780997675542 (ebook) | ISBN 9780997675559 (audiobook)
Subjects: LCSH: Bible. Old Testament--History of Biblical events--Fiction. | Jeremiah (Biblical prophet)--Fiction. | Babylonia--History--Fiction. | Prophets--Babylonia--History--Fiction. | LCGFT: Historical fiction.
Classification: LCC PS3601.M43 E462 2018 (print) | LCC PS3601.M43 (ebook) | LCC PS3601.M43 (audiobook) | DDC 813/.6--dc23

Second Edition
Copyright © 2017 Jo Amdahl.
Shoshone Publications books may be ordered through booksellers or by contacting:
Shoshone Publications, PO Box 125, Byron WY 82412
shoshonepublications@gmail.com
All rights reserved. No part of this book may be used or reproduced by any means, graphic, electronic, or mechanical, including photocopying, recording, taping or by any information storage retrieval system without the written permission of the author except in the case of brief quotations embodied in critical articles and reviews.

Cover art by Aaron Amdahl,
Adapted from Jean-Honoré Fragonard's
Jeroboam Offering Sacrifice to the Idol, 1752.

This book is a work of history told in Creative Narrative. It is fiction only in that some gaps in the historical records or specific personages have, by necessity, been imagined and inserted. Unless otherwise noted, the author and the publisher make no explicit guarantees as to the accuracy of the information contained in this book.

LCCN 2017903754
ISBN: 978-1-7362809-1-1 (hc)
ISBN: 978-0-9976755-3-5 (sc)
ISBN: 978-0-9976755-5-9 (ab)
ISBN: 978-0-9976755-4-2 (e)

Printed in the United States of America

Remember the wonders he has done, his miracles,
And the judgments he pronounced.
—Psalms 105: 5

CONTENTS

Introduction ... xv

Synopsis ... xvii

Part 1:610 BC The Daughter of Egypt ... 1

- Chapter 1: Invasion ... 3
- Chapter 2: Hostage ... 12
- Chapter 3: Peace ... 31
- Chapter 4: A Marriage of Convenience ... 34

Part 2: 609 BC The Year Peace Died ... 39

- Chapter 5: Betrayal ... 41
- Chapter 6: The God's Wife ... 52
- Chapter 7: War on the Horizon ... 60
- Chapter 8: A Messenger ... 66
- Chapter 9: The Death of Peace ... 71
- Chapter 10: Royal Prophet No More ... 81
- Chapter 11: Jehoahaz ... 85
- Chapter 12: Troops and Mercenaries ... 94
- Chapter 13: Preparations ... 103
- Chapter 14: A Betrothal ... 117
- Chapter 15: The Fall of Carchemish ... 124
- Chapter 16: The Priestess of Sin ... 132
- Chapter 17: Princess of Babylon ... 143

Chapter 18: Jehoahaz's Sin ... 153
Chapter 19: Jehoiakim ... 160
Chapter 20: The Median/Persian Empire ... 164
Chapter 21: The Fan-Bearer to the Left ... 168
Part 3: 608 BC Idols and Desecrations ... 183
Chapter 22: Anathoth ... 185
Chapter 23: Military Training ... 198
Chapter 24: The City of the Seven Walls ... 210
Chapter 25: Amyhia ... 219
Chapter 26: Uriah ... 234
Part 4: 607 BC Prophets and Politics ... 249
Chapter 27: The Last Emperor of Assyria ... 251
Chapter 28: Rab Mag ... 256
Chapter 29: The Murder of a Prophet ... 261
Chapter 30: Topheth ... 264
Chapter 31: The Feast of Weeks ... 271
Chapter 32: The Great Council ... 282
Chapter 33: Progressivism ... 287
Part 5: 606 BC The Signs of the Times ... 291
Chapter 34: Domestic Bliss ... 293
Chapter 35: Setbacks ... 298
Chapter 36: To Save Harran ... 302
Chapter 37: Taking the Reins of Power ... 306
Chapter 38: The Procession Bark of Bel ... 309
Chapter 39: The Tablet House ... 316
Chapter 40: Growing Up ... 321
Chapter 41: The Tumilat Canal ... 327
Chapter 42: The Wisdom of the Ages ... 330
Part 6: 605 BC Nebuchadnezzar Comes ... 333
Chapter 43: Seventy Years and the Cup of the Nations ... 335
Chapter 44: Last Chance ... 345
Chapter 45: The Price of Obedience ... 355
Chapter 46: Egypt's Defeat ... 362

Chapter 47: The Faithful ... 375
Chapter 48: The Unrighteous ... 384
Chapter 49: A True Prophet ... 390
Chapter 50: Consequences ... 397
Chapter 51: Chaldean Recruits ... 408
Chapter 52: The Choice of the Negev ... 413
Chapter 53: Sharu-lu-Dar ... 420
Epilogue ... 432
Endnotes ... 435
Appendices ... 475
Appendix I: Who's Who in Prince of Babylon ... 477
Appendix II: Time, Calendars, Measurements ... 499
Appendix III: Gods and Goddesses ... 505
Appendix IV: Map ... 511
Partial Bibliography ... 513

INTRODUCTION

Babylonia, the queen of the ancient realms—the *"Empire of Gold"* spoken of by the prophet Daniel had such power, wealth, and splendor that its legend lives on in the imagination of the world today.

Egypt, realm of the Nile, great in glory, with a tradition of power that stretched back into the distant mists of time—the Upper and Lower realms were reunited at last. Egypt was whole and determined to conquer the world.

Media and Persia, the first of the Aryan Empires, was now pressing into the Middle East, desperate for coastline territories and Mediterranean trade.

Judah, the tiny remnant of the chosen people of God, found itself caught in the middle of the struggles of its titan neighbors and the Prophet Jeremiah struggled to understand God's plan amid the chaos.

War consumed the world. Everything changed, politically, economically, and religiously. It would never be the same again, and the events have been recorded for us to learn from them.

This story is true. It is a historical work disguised as fiction only in that it is told in the form of a series of novels, and so there is a greater allowance made for inferring the reasons behind the facts.

Empire of Gold is a chronicle crucial to both Christians and Jews, of great interest to historians, and just a good story for anyone else. It is a story of the supernatural and of God's grace in unendurable trials. It is a story of power, war, treachery, and romance, all in epic proportions. Even better, it actually happened. Who said history was boring?

SYNOPSIS

Foundations

Jeremiah, a 12-year-old Judean boy, is appointed Prophet to the Nations by the Lord of Hosts. He bears witness to Judah's sin before King Josiah. The king yields to the divine directive and eliminates idolatry from the land, cleansing the Temple and bringing the Ark of the Covenant back to its place. Though invasion from Assyria seems imminent, Josiah is promised peace for his lifetime.

Nabopolassar usurps the throne in Babylon and conducts war on Assyria, forming a Coalition with Media and Scythia. To cement the Treaty of the Coalition, the Crown Prince of Babylon, Nebuchadnezzar, is betrothed to Princess Amyhia of Media.

Nineveh, Capital of Assyria, is wiped out by the collapse of a gigantic dam. Assyria moves its capital to Harran, but the Coalition soon conquers it too. City after city is swallowed by the Coalition, and ultimately all of Assyria falls.

The Scythian's uncivilized ways and deeds render them odious to their allies and ensure the future doom of their chieftains at the hands of Uvakshatra, King of Media.

Babylonia, aided by Scythia, defeats Egypt and invades the Egyptian capital city of Sais.

The Prophet Jeremiah, grown from child to young man during the reign of the good King Josiah, takes on the mission of collating and canonizing the Scriptures. Life in Judah is good, but the prophet knows it won't last. The Peace of Josiah will end with Josiah's death, and Jeremiah will begin his true mission as Prophet to the Nations.

PART 1: 610 BC

The Daughter of Egypt

The daughter of Egypt has been put to shame,
given over to the power of the people of the north.

—Jeremiah 46:24 NASB[1]

CHAPTER 1

Invasion

Sais, Egypt

Ra shone down hot and bright in a sky hazy with dust from the deserts. The heat was severe as the young princess bathed in her private inlet of the Nile. The calm, tranquil beauty of the day was hers by divine right and Amun-Ra watched over her lovingly from above. What had she to fear from the god? His fire would never harm her. She was the chosen of the god's wife—soon she would *be* the god's wife!

The still, translucent water was warm as a bath, and she dived under, swimming right to the bottom. The pure water soothed her and embraced her brown-toned skin.

Princess Nitocris, daughter of Crown Prince Necho, was now twelve years old. Yesterday had been her birthday, and it was time. Queen Nitocris of Thebes, God's Wife of Amun—the princess' aunt, for whom she had been named—had traveled from Thebes to see her adoption sealed.[1] The queen had come to collect her adopted daughter so that the princess could begin her training and duties in Thebes. When she became a woman—when her cycle started, and she was ready to wed—the daughter of Psammetik would step down, and the daughter of Necho would ascend to divinity. She would become Amun's wife, his representative on earth. With that office, she would also become the source of divinity for the entire royal family.

Religious aspirations aside, Nitocris also looked forward to inheriting all the lands and wealth of her aunt. This was vitally important. Of all the people of Egypt, only the priests owned land, the rest were merely tenants, working the land for pharaoh. Only the priests were free. When Princess Nitocris would become the god's wife, she would be a land-owner, no longer a slave to her grandfather.

The princess and the queen were to leave Sais for Thebes within the ten-day.[2]

The girl kicked off the sandy bottom and shot back up again. Breaking the surface, she found her three handmaidens standing on the multi-colored tiles of her patio, right where she had left them. Except now, they were staring round-eyed in confusion at an officer of her grandfather's army. This bizarre apparition had somehow mysteriously appeared in her private court. His presence was so impossible that at first, she doubted her own eyes. Treading water, she blinked and looked again, but no, he *was* there; a tall, dark man in a light-weight overskirt and linen loincloth, sandals, and wearing a captain's helmet.

Outraged, she brushed off the water still clinging to her heart-shaped face. "What is the meaning of this?" she shouted at him. "No men are allowed here!" He averted his eyes as she quickly swam to the steep, tiled side of the pool and climbed out.

Her maidens hastily wrapped her in a linen robe and set a short wig upon her close-cropped head. The wig's hundreds of tiny braids chimed with the miniature golden bells woven into them.

"Lowering your eyes won't help you now," she snapped at the intruder. Shaking with anger, she stamped her delicate, perfectly shaped foot in a small puddle of water. It made a slapping sound. "You commit this sacrilege, and then you don't even bow down before your princess! I asked you a question! What are you doing here? How dare you?"

The officer turned back to her with anxious eyes. "Highness, I have come at the bidding of the god's wife, your adoptive mother. Though you are the undoubted glory of the Two Lands, we have no time for formalities, and I apologize for my lack of praise.

"You are to come with me. Now. Sais is under attack. The Babylonians are upon us, and you are the heir of all Egypt. You must be seen to safety, even if we lose everything else."

"What?" Such an announcement was entirely outside her realm of experience. For an instant, her self-confidence wavered. But it was impossible. Such an occurrence was beyond her conception of the universe. After a brief moment of indecision, she dismissed his statement as non-consequential, and her anger returned. "Before evening falls, your head certainly will," she declared. Then she frowned, wondering, as the sound of distant shouts and screams reached her ears. What *was* that?

"I don't have time for this," the officer muttered. "I will rejoice, O Scion of the Gods," he told the astonished child, "if my head falls this day at your command and not at that of the Babylonians." He scooped her up and tossed her over his shoulder. Then he turned and ran as fast as he could out of the small enclosed garden, encumbered by the princess.

Bouncing up and down on the captain's shoulder, Nitocris kicked and shrieked. She caught an upside-down glimpse of her maidens, standing in shock and dismay in the midst of the pile of her clothes and jewelry. They stared after her as the soldier carried her through the garden's gate.

Turning right, the officer headed for the docks.

The princess scratched and bit at the sacrilegious tormentor who dared treat her so. "I will have you flayed and quartered! I will nail your skin to the city gates!"

"If that is your will," he gritted, rubbing a bleeding ear, but he never slowed down, dodging some panicked citizens and elbowing his way past others.

In short order, Nitocris found herself unceremoniously dumped into a small reed boat. The officer, still unheeding of her threats, removed his helmet and threw it into the Nile. He was an officer of the Saite dynasty, and the Saites loved the ancient Egyptian heritage and customs above reason or common sense. As a result, they fought almost naked. The officer wore no uniform. The helmet had been his only identification as a captain of pharaoh's army. Now, with the helmet sinking to the bottom of the Nile, he was indistinguishable from any passing peasant. The officer jumped into the boat, next to the outraged girl, and pushed off.

Released from the hold the captain had on her, the princess leaped to her feet, nearly upsetting the skiff, but she didn't seek to escape. As the boat rocked dangerously under her naked feet, the "Scion of the Gods" attacked the unfortunate soldier with her bare hands, clawing at his face.

It was the captain's turn to be astonished. "Girl," he exclaimed as he caught her slender wrists and flung her back down again, "look around you! What do you see?"

No one addressed the heir of the god's wife as "girl." It was such a towering impertinence that it stopped her cold for just a moment. That moment was enough for her to actually take in her surroundings. She now realized that the yelling and screaming she had noted in the back of her mind were not the cries of citizens outraged at this treatment of their princess. The dock area was in a panic. She watched the last of the boats cast off from their moorings. It seemed the entire population of the city was attempting to head west, downstream to… what? Her anger was replaced by incredulity. "Where are they going? The Fortress of the Milesians? The Great Sea? Why?"

The Fortress of the Milesians, the home of Ionian mercenaries, was not far, nor was the sea. Sais was on the Canopic, the western, branch of the Nile, just south of the reed marshes of the delta where it opened to the vastness of the Mediterranean.[3]

"We are under attack, Princess," the officer explained. "I have been trying to make you understand. The Babylonians have come! It is a complete surprise. King Nabopolassar should have been heading back to his city. His men need to tend to their fields and families. Since ours do as well, our army has been dismissed. Other than the Milesians, all our mercenaries have returned to Ionia for the year. This city will certainly fall."

"That is ridiculous!" She snorted, and imperiously bobbed her head. But a small, unfamiliar chill was starting to crawl up her spine.

"It is the truth! Princess, you must be kept safe at all costs. You are Egypt's future. We will attempt to make the Great Sea and the Fortress of the Milesians. From there we can find passage to somewhere safe, perhaps in Ionia."

Leave Egypt? Finally, she began to understand, and she felt fear threaten to overwhelm her. But she was a princess of Egypt. No, she was the princess of Egypt! Her training came through, and she regained her composure. "I will allow you to escort me to the Fortress of the Milesians," she declared regally. "And I will reconsider the matter of your beheading, at least for the present."

In spite of the situation, the officer grinned briefly, his white teeth flashed in his dark face. "I am greatly honored, My Princess." He took up the oars and began to row west, downstream. "It is good to know that I may yet live to see the glory of your reign."

Nitocris decided she actually liked him. "Perhaps I will have you transferred to my personal guard in Thebes."

He glanced around nervously and rowed harder.

"Have you news of my father?" She needed information to decide what she should do. Her father was vital. Prince Necho, First Prophet of Amun, was a handsome man in his forties, strong and capable. Nitocris knew that he would prevail in any battle, keeping her secure.

A panicked paysan swam up to the small craft and tried to board, perilously tipping the boat.

The captain beat him off with an oar. "He rode with pharaoh against the invaders," the officer explained as he splashed at the water with the paddle. The boat rocked dangerously.

"And?"

"I have heard nothing more."

They outdistanced the swimmer and merged with a group of vessels frantically trying to evacuate. The banks were lined with screaming people; some pushed into the water by the panicked masses behind them, some jumping in willingly, trying to swim to the other side.

The girl ignored the peasants and paused, thinking about the officer's tidings. Her grandfather, the pharaoh, was old; he should not be riding to war. But her father would protect him. "Any news of my mother?" Chednitjerbone was a Cushite princess. Nitocris' beautiful dark complexion and black eyes were an inheritance from her mother, but it was almost the only thing she had inherited from her. Chednitjerbone was docile, tractable, and almost certainly hiding in her rooms.

"No, Lady," he responded, confirming the princess' opinion of her mother's character. Panting with the effort of hard rowing, he continued, "But your adoptive mother sent me to you, as I have said. Queen Nitocris rules Egypt at present. The Queen of Thebes will not leave the throne, so it is crucial that you, at least, be evacuated." Princess Nitocris felt reassured that the government was in her aunt's capable hands. Things were under control.

"Of course. My brother?" Prince Psammetik was a young man in his twenties. He was almost as handsome as his father, and he was as dark-skinned as his sister. The princess adored him.

"Prince Psammetik rides with the chariots, but your aunt, the God's Wife, means to see him to safety as well. She has dispatched men to have him intercepted. He is to meet us at the river's bend, where the Nile turns north again—if he can."

"It is well."

But it wasn't. As they passed out of the capital with the city walls behind them to the east, the officer gasped, and Nitocris turned to follow his gaze. She did not see Prince Psammetik and his entourage as she had expected. Instead, the banks here were littered with the dead and dying.

Strange men with white skin and clothed in gleaming scale armor were riding hairy ponies up and down both banks of the Nile. Yodeling, their high-pitched vocalizations were clear and loud over the screams of the people. Laughing, the barbarians were killing or capturing everything that moved. Their skin was covered in bright tattoos, and they bore long braids of gold, red, or brown hair. Their ponies were wrapped in colorful war cloths, embroidered with yarn, and dripping with mud and water. They were the most alien and uncouth beings the girl had ever seen.

"The Babylonians!" she cried. For the first time, the seriousness of the situation struck her.

"No Princess," the officer corrected and rowed faster. "The Babylonians march or ride in chariots. They could not have reached this side of the city so soon, not with the Nile cresting and flooding the plains. These are their allies, the Scythians. They are barbarians from the far north, and they ride, so they move very quickly. The mud doesn't bog them down. But they would not be here either if our army remained on the other side of the city, still to be conquered. They have fallen so soon? The city is defenseless!

"Get down! Lay down flat in the boat, and we will attempt to pass midstream..." His voice was cut off as an arrow struck him in the throat and in a strange slow-motion he fell into the Nile. Nitocris screamed and reached over the side of the boat to try and catch him, but the current carried him away and under.

And then... then a Scythian warrior, with eyes the color of the sky and skin like milk, astride a swimming pony, collided with the boat. He grinned at her and grabbed her arm, yanking her overboard. She clawed at him, but he laughed and threw her across his lunging pony's neck, babbling at her in what was undoubtedly his vulgar and crude language.

They swam back to the shore. As the shaggy brown pony climbed, leaping and scrambling, up the bank, Nitocris decided that she was having some bizarre dream. This was not real! It couldn't be. Nothing like this could happen to *her*. But if she was dreaming, could she be thinking she was dreaming? Could the horse and the man both smell so of sweat? Could she feel so wet? Would she hear the river splash with the plunging horses and struggling people? Would the screams and cries be so piercing? She felt her wig slipping again and grabbed it with both hands, straightening it and holding it in place. Somehow, it seemed important that her tresses remained properly on her head.

Another of the northerners galloped up on a tall bay stallion. Unlike most of his men, he wore plate armor, and his breast piece was completely covered in gold. It was detailed with an absurd mixture of scenes depicting fantastic, Greek mythical creatures cavorting among common laborers, toiling in their fields. He was a huge man, and his long braided hair was a ridiculous bright orange, the color of poppies, and his ruddy face was covered with a ginger beard, also braided, and riddled with gray. Unlike many of the Scythians' mounts, the stallion was not hampered by a heavy, wet and soggy war cloth. It wore only its bridle, saddle pad and a matching hood and saddle blanket, embroidered with gold, not yarn. Beneath the fanciful, encrusted hood, its eyes rolled wildly, and its nostrils flared red. This enormous apparition looked as if he could have ridden right out of one of the imaginative paintings that covered the walls of the palace and she realized his appearance was meant to strike fear. It succeeded.

The unlikely figure of the northern barbarian was accompanied by a shorter, chunky man, astride a sleek gray mare that also had no war cloth. This man's skin was tan-colored, much like that of her father's kin, the Saites. But he was no Saite. He wore his brown hair curled and down past his shoulders. Like Nitocris' people, he had no facial hair; but his smooth skin declared he did not shave. He was obviously a eunuch. He wore different clothes from the barbarians too; a long robe hitched up around his thighs so he could sit his under-adorned horse.

The northerner with the gold armor and reddish hair chuckled and said something utterly incomprehensible. Nitocris' captor laughed and answered, jerking her face up and holding her under the chin so that the other could see. She tried to bite, and they both laughed. Golden Armor said something else, shrugged, and began to rein his leggy stallion away.

Did he dismiss her so easily? Rage coursed through her veins. "Amun will curse you and this ruffian for daring to lay a finger on the heir!" She spat at him. "Ra will condemn you to burn forever for looking on his chosen! You will suffer horribly in everlasting fire for this, and your names will be remembered no more!"

The eunuch's eyes went wide, and he spoke for the first time, laying his hand on Golden Armor's massive, hairy arm. The redheaded chieftain pulled up and looked sharply back at her. His eyes narrowed. He frowned and carried on a brief conversation with the other two.

Nitocris saw her chance and shook her head free. She bit her captor on the hand, and almost managed to jump down off the wet shaggy pony before she was brought back, struggling and kicking, under control. Her barbarian captor sat her upright in front of him, sideways across his mount's neck. She glared at him.

"You are of the royal house?" the eunuch asked her from the back of his tall gray. His accent was thick, but she understood him perfectly.

She glowered at him. "You speak Demotic?"

"I am Chaldean," he explained with a deprecating shrug. "It is my function to interpret. In this capacity, I am on loan to his Majesty, King Arbaces of Scythia, Chief of the Royal Scythians." He nodded at the warrior with the poppy-orange hair. "The king wishes to know, are you truly of the Royal House of Sais as you claim?"

"I am Nitocris, heir of the god's wife!" She dug her heel hard into her captor's shin. He yelped but didn't let go. "It is I who will determine who will become pharaoh in the circles to come, the royal status of the House of Sais will hinge on me! And your lives are all forfeit for your sacrilege." The interpreter translated this, and another brief discussion followed.

Then Nitocris' captor reluctantly lifted her from his mount and seated her astride in front of the Babylonian eunuch on his gray horse. "You are to be returned to the palace immediately," the Chaldean told her, speaking in her ear.

CHAPTER 2

Hostage

Sais, Egypt

Nabopolassar, King of Babylonia, was a man still in the prime of his life. His black beard, carefully curled, showed no trace of gray. His wide-spaced, light-brown eyes in his narrow, long face made him look even younger than he was. His saucer-shaped battle helmet with its wide metal brim sat firmly on his head. His black, square-cut bangs peeked out from underneath the golden helm and thickly covered the tan colored skin of his brow. He was the hero of countless campaigns, and yet he was, first of all, a statesman. His intelligent yet compassionate gaze inspired trust in almost everyone he met.

The king stood tall and straight in his chariot as he rolled to a stop between the massive brick gatehouses of Sais' eastern city gate. It was good construction, vividly painted with exploits of the Saite chiefs, and Nabo approved. But the gate was not good enough to hold court. He was going to need the palace, and soon. Sais must be secured, as much for the Egyptians' protection as the Babylonians'.

The city and most especially the Temples of Neith and Osiris were going to need protection, and the king knew it. The Scythians had a well-earned reputation for destroying everything they laid their hands on, including temples. They had managed to despoil two very famous ones in as many years and alienate most of the civilized world in the process. That didn't bother them because they cared very little for civilization. But for the moment, Nabo's barbarian allies were occupied outside the city walls, and that gave the king the time he needed.

The Provider of Marduk deployed his armies rapidly. Before the Scyths tired of their sport on the muddy, water-covered fields surrounding the walls and turned their greedy eyes towards the city itself, preparations must be made. Nabo meant to see that Babylon's elite were stationed at all the gates and before every important building. The king jumped down from the high bed of the massive war chariot and began issuing orders to his officers. "Arioch!"

"Great King," came the instant response. The Captain of the Daggermen—Nabo's imperial guard—had been trotting along behind the chariot and came instantly to his lord's side.[1] Tall and lithe as a dancer, Arioch was a man in his early forties and like all the daggermen, fanatically loyal to his king. He briefly bobbed his head and crossed his arms over his chest, snapping his fingers.

"Take twelve of the daggermen and a battalion and secure the palace. Place the occupants under house arrest. No harm is to come to any of them. See that the throne room is readied and my field throne established in the place of honor."

"At once, Great King." Arioch bobbed his head again, clapped his hands, shook his fist in the air over his head twice and trotted off. Twelve of the guards peeled off from their places to follow their captain. Arioch's whistle flagged down the commanding officer of a nearby battalion, the Anshars, and their sixty men fell in behind the daggermen, jogging smartly in step towards the palace, their sandals snapping a staccato rhythm on the brick-paved street.

Nabo turned away and motioned a scout forward. "Where are the rab mag and rab shaq?"

The scout, newly arrived and still breathing hard from running messages, was dusty and scuffed, but he brushed himself off, bowed deeply, and held his arms straight out before him as he snapped his fingers. "Great King," he answered, straightening up again, "Rab Mag Nergalniari sends word that he had reached the Nile on the west side of the city and that most all of the enemy have surrendered. Rab Shaq Belshumishkun has taken a regiment of the chariot core and two battalions, as you have ordered and he has secured the

Temple of Neith and the Temple of Osiris. He reports there has been no damage to the structures or the temple grounds."

Nabo watched his men disperse on their missions, beginning their house to house search. He nodded and dismissed the scout as he leaned back against the nail-studded wheel of his chariot, relaxing at last. Then he started to laugh.

"Great King?" Nabo's driver and spearman were both watching their king, puzzled over his mirth.

"It's over," he explained. "The war is over! We have peace!" He stopped and thought about it. "I've never known peace before," he mused. "I wonder what it will be like?"[2]

"None of us has ever known peace, Great King," the driver smiled down at him and shrugged. "I'm a chariot driver, so I suppose I'm out of a job. What will I do now?"

Nabo laughed again. "It is in Marduk's hands."

By that evening, Nabopolassar moved his base of operations into the now-secured palace's throne room. Captain Arioch had Nabo's field throne placed upon the high dais and moved the gilded throne of Egypt, with its embroidered web seat down to the first step.

Despite the rows of windows high above, it was hot in the thick-walled throne room. The efforts of two frightened-looking fan-bearers—one Saite, one Cushite—moved the stifling air around the suzerain as he mounted the dais. As always, Nabo was surrounded by Captain Arioch and twelve daggermen and accompanied by the king's annunciator and the king's scribe.

Nabopolassar was still wearing his armor and the short skirt of battledress as he sat down and surveyed the room. It was large and rectangular; the brick walls plastered with dazzlingly white gypsum. The two side doors and the entrance were secured by daggermen. The colorful paintings on the white-washed walls and the four massive sandstone pillars of the dais portrayed over-sized images of the chieftain, Necho I, and his son, Psammetik. These were surrounded by even larger images of gods and the tiny figures of their citizens and their conquered. The pictures on the walls of Sais' throne room reminded Nabo of the boasting of Nineveh, but the figures here portrayed were stiffer and far more scantily clad. A canopy of vivid blue accented with purple, black and gold embroidery was stretched from the brightly colored pillars. It sheltered the suzerain like heaven smiling down on him. The canopy's golden tassels—long as a man's forearm—waved gently overhead in the sultry breeze of the huge fans made of long poles and ostrich feathers. The Sacred Pool—knee-deep and filled with water from the Nile—stood in the very center of the room, forcing any petitioners to skirt it before approaching their pharaoh.

Nabo signaled to the daggermen to allow entrance to his officers and men. For nearly a half-beru, the Provider of Marduk struggled to bring order out of the chaos of the invasion. He listened to status reports, gave orders, and finally accepted a small meal. The Egyptians brewed an excellent honey beer; he was pleased to note.

During the pause, Rab Shaq Belshumishkun—Nabo's new cupbearer—brought him pharaoh's son. Pharaoh Psammetik had been killed almost at the start of the fray, but Prince Necho, the grandson of the Saite chieftain of the same name, had been captured.

Nabo took a large gulp of the beer and handed his cup to the newly arrived cupbearer.

Belshumishkun accepted it without a pause and took his place behind and to the left of his sovereign.

The suzerain studied the prisoner standing before him.

In his mid-forties, tall, muscular, and more handsome than any Greek statue, today the prince appeared as ordinary as a peasant in the marketplace.[3] The First Prophet of Amun stood in chains, trembling with barely contained anger, before the suzerain. His royal kerchief with the symbolic braid was missing, exposing his shaven head which was smudged with mud. Barefoot, the heir of Egypt wore only a soiled and tattered linen skirt and loincloth. He should have been utterly humiliated, but no one had informed him of the fact. Necho was physically unharmed—not even a scratch. His almond-shaped eyes blazed and his perfect, sculpted nose flared in rage. He was obviously unafraid.

"The prince is not properly grateful for your mercy, Lord," the rab shaq muttered in Nabo's ear. "Actually, he behaves more like a wild ass than a prince. Not a likely candidate for an heir."

"That's Egypt's problem, not mine," the king answered, eyeing the bedraggled and furious figure before him.

Egypt's Problem spat on the tiled floor before Nabo's feet. "It is well that you brought your own chair, for if you had defiled my father's throne by sitting on it, we would have to burn it!"

Nabo leaned aside and drawled to the rab shaq, *"Aiyah!* He speaks Aramaic!" The king was pleased with the development.

"He speaks it too well for his own health," Belshumishkun growled.

"Both my father and my grandfather were generals in Assyria!" Necho returned hotly. "Of course, I speak Aramaic. When Babylon falls under Egyptian heels, perhaps we will allow your sons to become our generals and have the privilege of learning Demotic. High Egyptian would still be too good for you!"[4]

Nabo laughed. "You want us to come live with you and have you risk catching our fleas?"

"I am the First Prophet of Amun, Heir of Pharaoh! Your fleas would die before touching me! My grandfather was the Great Chief of the West and carried the blood of the Libyan pharaohs from over 300 circles past. My grandmother was the daughter of Ethiopian kings. My father is… *was* the son of Ra and the Nile, Pharaoh of Upper *and* Lower Egypt. My mother was Mehtenweskhet, the daughter of Harsiese, High Priest of Atun at On. My sister is the wife of Amun-Ra himself, and my daughter will be his next wife. *You* are the son of a lesser son of a lesser son of a defunct house, and your wife is a harlot from the streets of a minor city. That is not really your fault since all of the women of the land between the rivers are harlots!"

Nabo caught his breath and held out his hand, restraining Belshumishkun from rushing forward to strike down the prisoner. From Necho's perspective, the women of Mesopotamia probably did all look like prostitutes since they all did service to Ishtar before they could be married. "If you wish to equate religious devotion to promiscuity, I suppose," he allowed, his voice hard. "But I have only one wife because she is a woman the way women are meant to be. I need no other. How many wives do you find necessary, Prince Necho?"

He turned to Shum, "Have him returned to his family under house arrest until I am ready for him." Once again, he addressed the prince, "You should go and thank your gods that it is Belshumishkun who is your jailer. He is new at his posting as rab shaq. I left my former cupbearer to be the Commander of Carchemish. Belnasir would never suffer a slur on the name of his queen, and my command would not have stopped him. If it were Belnasir who stood here now, you would be dead. I'm not certain that if there were to be another such incident, that my command would stop Belshumishkun either. Think on that as you go.

"You are a strange spectacle which has sprung from a strange people, Prince of Egypt. We will speak again once I have had time to properly assess the situation here."

Necho's guards pushed and pulled the struggling and kicking prince out of the room. He shouted back outraged insults in Egyptian at the King of Babylon as he was dragged away with a total lack of dignity. The annunciator declined to translate, and the sounds of the scuffle faded down the hall outside the throne room.

Nabo gave his immediate attention to other matters as his officers once more began to solicit his orders.

For a quarter-moon, the Suzerain of Babylonia listened to his officers and the results of their questionings of local inhabitants. Nabopolassar took notes and learned. Slowly, he came to better understand the current political climate and realities that ruled Egypt.

Egypt was a land like no other, alien in every way. The people shaved their heads—and then made themselves wigs to cover their skulls. Indeed, where in every other country in the world, the priests recognized shaving to be a symbol of mourning and so in holiness let their hair grow long, here, the priests refused to wear even the wigs of the general populace and walked about completely bald. The men—considering hair to be a source of uncleanness—

shaved their faces. Perversely, their king—recognizing a beard to be a sign of masculinity—donned an obviously fake beard for state occasions. Daughters bore the responsibility for caring for their parents, leaving the sons free to pursue their own interests.

And the system of inheritance was utterly alien. Egypt, like most of Africa, was essentially matriarchal. Apparently, a man could not be confident that he *was* the father of his wife's children—therefore, his closest certain heirs were the children of his sister. This explained why, historically, many Egyptians, including their royals, married their own sisters!

In practice, the Saite pharaohs—with their Libyan background and training in the courts of Assyria—were patriarchal rather than matriarchal in heritage. Although they tried to uphold the ancient Egyptian customs as much as possible, they still preferred to see their sons—rather than their nephews—inherit. They, in conjunction with their councils, had generally mandated which of their children would be the heir. But the right to succession could not be passed directly from father to son. It depended upon the blessing of the god's wife, who must be daughter or sister to the pharaoh. Fascinating.

Finally, the king satisfied himself that he understood the people and the land. Early one morning, he sent for Prince Necho, heir to Osiris Psammetik.

A half-moon had passed, and Prince Necho had had time to reconsider his position. The anger had not left his face, but the prince of Egypt grudgingly acquiesced to all the demands of Babylon. He placed his thumbnail print in the pair of wet clay tablets containing the new treaty of Egypt's subservience to the Babylonian Empire.

The crowning of the new pharaoh took place the next morning.

Nabopolassar—surrounded by daggermen—walked rapidly through the palace doors, up the aisle and sat down on his throne atop the dais. His heavily embroidered blue and purple robes were those of a statesman. Today he was a king, not a warrior. A broad, gold circlet shown above his black, square-cut bangs; the king did not travel with the tall, cylindrical crown of Babylon.

Nabo's translator followed him into the room and moved to stand behind him and to his left. The king's recorder took his seat on the top of the first step, at the feet of his master. The recorder unwrapped his writing kit, then he selected a stylus and took a wax tablet from his belt. He was ready.

The murmur of the crowd filled the audience hall as Egypt's fortunate few followed the Babylonians into their throne room. The fan-bearers positioned themselves around the room and stood their fans at attention at their sides.

Prince Necho, barefoot and clad in an immaculate white shift entered the room through the massive main doors. He wore a golden collar and royal cobra arm bands on his well-muscled upper arms. Straight and proud, he strode forward, and the crowd hurriedly parted to let their prince through. He did not turn aside at the sacred pool but waded right through, coming from the "Nile" to the steps of the throne of Egypt. The prince stopped directly before the top step where twin thrones had been set. Necho removed the kerchief of the First Prophet and laid it on the seat of the throne of pharaoh. He stood there with his bald head totally bare.

Entering at Necho's side was his brother, Chief of Protocol and Fan-Bearer to the Right Hand of the King, Prince Horiraa. Prince Horiraa wore no crown, just a short wig, but his sheer white top was covered with a royal golden collar only slightly less spectacular than Necho's own, and his white pointed skirt echoed that of his brother, the pharaoh-to-be. He held a golden shepherd's crook and a flail, much like the ones the pharaoh would take, but without blue stripes. To hold these tokens, Horiraa had put aside the gigantic fan of the fan-bearers. Dressed royally, the prince held only a small ostrich plume with which to symbolically fan the new pharaoh. His duty today was not to move the air but to direct these vital proceedings according to proper etiquette. The fan-bearer was an enormously important office, typically held by a prince, sometimes even the crown prince. Everything in the Egyptian palace must be done according to a strict code of behavior, and the fan-bearer was responsible for seeing that things ran according to plan.[5] Horiraa skirted the sacred pool and stopped on the second step from the top to the right of the pharaoh's throne.

Following Prince Horiraa came his second, the Cushite fan-bearer Nabopolassar had noticed earlier. Abdamelek, like the eight fan-bearing slaves now encircling the room, was bare to the waist; his black skin glistened slightly with sweat. He, unlike Horiraa, still bore one of the gigantic fans and he mounted the steps last, standing to the left of the Egyptian throne. That brought the total number of fan-bearers to the exact required number of ten. Abdamelek immediately took up his duty of fanning and at that cue, the eight slaves resumed their fanning as well.

Already surrounding the four pillars of the dais were Necho's family: his beautiful sister, Queen Nitocris of Thebes and his young daughter, his sister's heir, Princess Nitocris. There was also his wife, Chednitjerbone, who would soon be queen; and his son and heir, Prince Psammetik. In addition, filling the room, were Necho's other brothers and sisters, sons and daughters; an assortment of Egyptian nobility; and most notably, sixty of Nabopolassar's daggermen along with Rab Mag Nergalniari with several other of the Babylonian generals and their entourages.

The Scythians, disinterested and scornful of the Egyptians, declined to be present. Nabo was grateful for that! Who knew what kind of mischief they could cause at such an event? There would undoubtedly be mischief enough before all was finished here.

The emperor turned his attention to the young princess. There she was, standing on the floor directly in front of the dais, beside her stunningly beautiful adoptive mother. Petite and slim, Princess Nitocris did not appear to be nervous at all.

That was because she did not know.

Instead, she stared right back at him, looking him in the eye as if she were examining some exotic creature that was of no more importance than the immediate curiosity she felt.

Nabo was amused, but he also felt a small twinge of sympathy. Princess Nitocris had no idea that it was she who was about to become the exotic creature.

The Queen of Thebes must have noticed the Babylonian's interest in her ward, because anger suddenly flared up in the woman's light-brown eyes and she took a protective step forward, between the princess and the suzerain.

Nabo nodded to her. He could see why the Egyptians considered Necho's sister to be a goddess; she was flawless. Neither the girl nor the woman wore a wig on their smooth-shaven heads, and both were naked to the waist, a contrast of dark and light skin tones.

Queen Nitocris' lovely face was flushed and drawn tight with the tension of her emotion. The princess reached over and squeezed her aunt's hand. The queen looked down at the girl, and the hardness of her face eased. She smiled reassuringly and laid her hand briefly on her heir's bald head.

Nabopolassar frowned. The God's Wife was actually fond of the girl. Queen Nitocris was a powerful person, and the Emperor was not pleased to be making an enemy of her.

Horiraa, Fan-Bearer to the Right, raised his miniature ostrich feather and began fanning Necho. Horiraa pointed the golden crook of the Minister of Protocol at the musicians, and the ceremony began.

The musicians, a group of ten seated against the wall, began to play. A single note from a flute preceded a low tone, hummed by a single female singer. A small drum tapped twice and then was joined by a harp and two male singers. The remainder of the musicians, another female singer, another flute, a tambourine, a lyre and a lute came in. Flowery scented incense wafted across the area, the scent swirling in the fanners' vortices. The singers' sweet voices invited the presence of the gods as a witness and called down blessings upon the new king to be. All but the fanners and their enormous fans grew still, waiting for the song to end and the formal rituals to unfold.

Nabo knew that as far as Egyptian coronations went, this one was compressed in time and symbolism to the point of what the Egyptians considered sacrilege. Prince Necho had not spent the required month at his dead father's side. He had not descended to Osiris with him in the Duat ceremony. He had not spent the remainder of the months of the year reigning without being coronated. Necho had not killed the white bull with his bare hands, and he had not even performed the ceremony of the Smiting of the Enemy. It was, after all, Egypt which had been smitten. There had been no preliminary feast, and it was doubtful that there would be any celebration feasts in the coronal year to come. Nabo knew the Egyptians were insulted, but he didn't care. He had no time for all that. The Egyptians refused to eat with foreigners anyway. Besides, the Grand Procession *had* taken place. They should be satisfied with that!

At the first light of Ra's appearing, all Sais had become witness to the fact that Necho was taking the throne by the grace of Nabopolassar. Queen Nitocris and Princess Nitocris had stood waist-deep in the Sacred Lake and sang to Ra at his appearing. Then they strode out of the waters and headed towards the palace.

In the sight of all the people, the Wife of Amun-Ra and her daughter were followed, not by Necho, but by the King of Babylon in his immense chariot, surrounded by his guard, all in dress whites and reds. It was only then that Necho could follow, on foot and practically unescorted—save for the two fan-bearers. It all bore a distinct resemblance to a Babylonian triumphal victory pageant. The rest of the people fell in behind, and the procession had made its way from the lake to the palace gates, where the crowd had been dispersed, and only certain nobles were admitted. Nabopolassar had made sure that this travesty of a coronation was going forward with little ceremony and no delays.

The musicians concluded their musical prayers and the music dropped down to a respectful background strumming and humming.

Together, Nitocris, the Queen of Thebes and her heir, Princess Nitocris, stepped forward. The queen was draped in white, the girl in red. Their long, sheer skirts, reaching to their bare feet, hid nothing of their slender figures. They stopped before an ornate table which held five crowns.[6] There was also a linen cape, a gold and blue striped shepherd's crook—known as the Heka staff—and a gold and blue striped flail—known as the Nekhakha. Next to these were two slender, golden pitchers.

The woman and the girl lifted two of the crowns. Queen Nitocris bowed slightly and waited while Princess Nitocris reached up and set the Hedjet—the white crown of Upper Egypt, upon her head. The queen was now the incarnation of Nekhbet, the vulture goddess of Upper Egypt. In turn, the sister of Necho set the Deshret—the red crown of Lower Egypt—upon the head of the diminutive daughter of Necho. Princess Nitocris became Wadjet, the cobra goddess of Lower Egypt.

Together, the two goddesses each raised a golden pitcher from the table. They turned and waded into the sacred pool. Stooping down, they filled the pitchers with the water of the Nile. The water drenched their long skirts, making them cling to the short white underskirts of the incarnate deities. Slowly, sedately, they turned and walked back to the waiting prince, a trail of water left in their wake. They stopped directly in front of him.

From a side room, appeared the High Priest of Amun, Mentemhe. He was a direct descendant of the Priest-Kings who had been pharaohs of Upper and Lower Egypt before the Libyans. The Egyptian Priest-Kings had been conquered by the Libyan princes who in turn had given way to the Cushites. The Saites, Libyan princes themselves, had defeated the Cushites and regained power. But the priests of Amun, descendants of the Egyptian Priest-Kings, still ruled in Thebes, their ancient line unbroken. The priest addressed the gods and the prince.

Necho stood there, every hair shaved from his body. His head, chest, and feet were bare; and he stood with his back to the steps and the Babylonian—who sat on the top of the dais itself. The prince's golden cobra armbands and the pointed white and gold kilt proclaimed his royal status. This ceremony marked Necho's ascension to godhood. It was the last time that Necho could rightly be addressed directly, in the second person.

"By the sacred name of Amun-Ra, by the holy waters of the Nile," the priest chanted as the two goddesses came forward and poured their pitchers over Necho's head. Water pooled around their feet as Nabopolassar's translator whispered his translation in the suzerain's ear. "By the witness of Neith of Sais and the righteous judgment of Amut, the crocodile, you have been chosen from among the sons of the earth. You have been born of the waters of the Nile. You are the representative of the gods, the Living One, who is among us. What is your name?"

At the question, Necho trembled with rage but said nothing.

Smiling grimly, Nabopolassar rose from his throne, stood high above the crowd, and said in carefully enunciated Egyptian, "His name is Wahemibre."

The blood drained from the lovely face of the Queen of the Dead, and she looked askance at her brother. This was an insult to Egypt's autonomy. But Necho was not sovereign. He could not name himself; it was a father's right to name his son. Necho nodded, his eyes smoldering. "My name is Wahemibre—Ra's Will is Accomplished."[7]

The priest stood back, and the two goddesses set their pitchers back on the table while the graceful queen sent looks of intentioned murder towards the Babylonian suzerain. Nabo knew she was already his enemy and the worst was yet to come. The goddesses both took hold of the Pschent, the combined red and white crown of Upper and Lower Egypt. The crown held between them, they approached the prince, and the god's wife leaned forward and breathed on Necho's face. "Receive the ka, the divine breath of the gods," she intoned. "Pharaoh is Wahemibre Necho, the Son of Ra; the Son of Horus, the Son of Osiris—Pharaoh—He Who Lives, the God-King of Upper and Lower Egypt."[8] The queen and the princess raised the crown and held it over Necho's head.

Before they could lower it, Nabopolassar stepped down and took it from them as they held it there. He set it on the prince's head. "Marduk's will is accomplished," he said, inserting the Babylonian formula into the Egyptian cult. Then he switched back to Egyptian so all would understand. "I shall establish for you your crown on your head."

The music stopped. This was the standard Egyptian phrase from a new pharaoh to the wife he raised to be his queen. It said plainly that Necho's authority came from Nabopolassar alone. More than that, Necho was now pharaoh, but Nabopolassar had addressed him directly, not in the third person.

In the sudden, shocked silence, the god's wife drew in an inarticulate gasp and the princess, eyes wide, took a step backward. Then the girl crouched as if to jump and attack the suzerain, but the Queen of Thebes laid a denying hand on her shoulder and pulled her back. Twelve years old, the princess stood there, trembling with rage and, considering the red crown and skirt, looking for all the world like a miniature Neith, ready to do battle with the Emperor of Babylonia to protect her city. Nabo smiled with admiration at her courage.

A murmur went through the crowd, but after a moment, Prince Horiraa, motioned with his crook, resuming the interrupted ceremony and hurrying it on to its conclusion.

Unperturbed, Nabo stepped back up to the top of the dais and sat down on his throne again.

The priest, Mentemhe, looked to Necho, unsure of what to do.

Necho, his jaw tight with suppressed anger nodded at the table.

Mentemhe went to it and retrieved the linen cape, the shepherd's crook, and the flail. Prince Horiraa, the Fan-Bearer to the Right, gestured urgently, his feather and crook moving in insistent circles, to the musicians. Hesitatingly, the soft background music began again.

The priest approached and draped the garment over the damp back and chest of the new pharaoh, covering him with divinity. After the ceremony, the pharaoh would gift the cape to the temple of his choice—it would never be worn again. Necho crossed his arms over his chest, and Mentemhe put the striped crook in his right hand and the striped flail in his left. The crook symbolized the pharaoh's ownership of Egypt's sheep and cattle and the flail was the instrument of threshing for the grain.

Pharaoh owned all the wealth and bounty of the land. He owned all the land, except for the land belonging to the priests. Pharaoh was the people's shepherd and their supply.

The High Priest of Amun moved back to the table and lifted the fourth crown, the tall, flat-topped Modius. He approached the pharaoh once more and received the crook and flail back, trading them for the Modius crown. As the priest returned the two symbols of power to the table, Wahemibre Necho held out his free hand. His wife, Chednitjerbone, came forward and took it.

Chednitjerbone was not the most beautiful of Necho's consorts, her face was too broad, and her ears were too large; but her coal-black skin announced the obvious fact that she was a Cushite princess, a blood-link to the previous dynasty. Moreover, she was the mother of his heir, Prince Psammetik, as well as the mother of the heir of the god's wife, Princess Nitocris.

Necho moved her to his right side then set the Modius crown on her head. "I shall establish for you your crown on your head. It is to rule that you receive the crown," he told her and gently breathed on her face, raising her ka to godhood. Chednitjerbone sat on her throne. She was now the queen, the Great Royal Wife. In the circles to come, she would remain at the pharaoh's side and refresh the divinity of his ka with her own breath.[9] Necho mounted the first step of the dais to his new throne. He turned and faced the crowd.

Mentemhe lifted the last crown, the Chepresh, the blue war helmet of Egypt, from the table and set it in Necho's hands. "May the eye of Ra watch over pharaoh from the blue of heaven and give him dominion over the nations of Earth."

Necho tightened his jaw but said nothing. Instead, he stepped up the next two steps and laid the symbol of war at Nabopolassar's feet. "The war is over. May peace bloom forever between the Euphrates and the Nile." He backed back down to the first step.[10]

Nabopolassar stood and picked up the Chepresh. "May it indeed." He handed the surrendered war helmet to his rab mag. "One will excuse us, but we have other duties. If one would be so kind as to abide by the terms of our agreement?" The translator mimicked the mocking tone of the statement and question exactly.

Necho glared at him for a moment, then stepped forward and took his startled daughter's hand. Princess Nitocris had no idea what was happening until her father laid her hand in Nabopolassar's. She pulled back in horror, but the suzerain held her tight. "She is Babylon's, the guarantee of Egypt," the new pharaoh gritted.

Nabo smiled gently at the girl, despite her struggles and attempts to jerk herself free. "She is the wife of my son Nebuchadnezzar, our houses blended," he answered softly. Holding her hand with his left, he removed the red crown from her head with his right and held it out to the priest, Mentemhe. The priest, not knowing what else to do, took it.

Princess Nitocris did not understand the Babylonian's words, but she certainly understood the translator. She dropped to her knees, her hand still held fast in that of the Emperor. Ignoring protocol that forbade direct address to a pharaoh she screamed. "Father!" she cried, "Father, please!"

Nabo gave the girl's small hand to Arioch, Captain of the Daggermen. Arioch pulled her to her feet, covered her nakedness with his cloak, and began to drag her away, kicking and screaming. The Emperor averted his face, unwilling to watch.

Queen Chednitjerbone fell from her throne and shaking hard, shoved her fist in her mouth to keep from speaking. From before the dais, the God's Wife of Amun cried out and fell to her knees, choked with silent sobs.

As one, the daggermen drew their weapons and waited, daring any or all to act.

And they did. With a roar, the room erupted in chaos.

Yelling at the top of their lungs, a group of young Egyptian noblemen, led by Prince Psammetik, rushed the dais. Presumably, they meant to come to the aid of his sister, the princess. Since all were unarmed, the most they could do was attempt to break through the line of daggermen with their fists.

The Daggermen, Babylon's Imperial Guard, were the fighting elite. Skilled, experienced and deadly, they also knew how to enforce their will on their unarmed opponents. Easily ducking all but the best placed of the blows aimed at them, they lashed out with fists and feet. Almost effortlessly they brought their foes down—gasping, winded, and bruised—but not actually harmed. Some of the guards, following previous directions, moved to the new pharaoh, his queen, and the high priest, and herded them towards the side door opposite the one through which Nabopolassar had first entered.

Nabo saw High Priest Mentemhe resist. The man seemed confused, trying to see and understand what was happening. He pushed back against the guard who were in no mood for nonsense. One of them jerked the priest around and shoved him towards the main doors. Mentemhe dropped the red crown he had been carrying, and it rolled across the floor, but the guard did not allow the priest to stop to retrieve it.

Nabo shook his head and followed Arioch to the edge of the dais. The room around him swirled in confusion. Women ran screaming to the exits. Older, wiser noblemen, held their arms straight out from their sides, demonstrating that they were not resisting, and backed carefully towards the main entrance. The musicians, fanners, and other servants shrank against the walls, trying to protect their fans and instruments. The guard turned their attention to them, and the servants allowed themselves to be herded out of doors.

The Babylonian got a glimpse of Prince Horiraa shielding the bent and sobbing figure of his sister, Queen Nitocris, the God's Wife; she still wore the white crown. The determined daggermen forced them from the room. King Nabopolassar and Rab Mag Nergalniari stepped down the side steps of the dais to their side door. Nabo hesitated there, turning to watch the chaos of the audience chamber.

In the hall beyond, Captain Arioch gave up trying to drag the princess, and she found herself once more firmly flipped over a shoulder. Arioch carried her, screaming, kicking and biting toward the back entrance of the palace.

"Nitocris! Nitocris!" Prince Psammetik, yelling his sister's name, launched himself low at the daggermen directly in front of him. Hitting his opponent mid-waist with his shoulder, they both went down, but the Babylonian guard next to him brought the hilt of his dagger down on the prince's skull and at the same time landed a well-placed kick to his solar plexus.

Psammetik rolled onto his back, his mouth gaping with the attempt to breathe.

The Battle of the Coronation was over almost before it began. Two guardsmen scooped up Prince Psammetik, the new First Prophet of Amun, under his arms and dragged him to the main doors, tossing him out onto the growing pile of his fellows.

The throne room was cleared. The twin Egyptian thrones lay toppled at the bottom of the steps and signs of the struggle marked the walls, pillars, and floors, but no one had been killed, and very few wounded.

The red crown of Lower Egypt, fallen from the hand of High Priest Mentemhe, lay forlornly on its side on the floor. One lone officer of the court remained. Prince Horiraa's second-in-protocol scooped the crown up and sat it back on the table. Abdamelek shook his head in bewilderment and looked up at the Babylonian monarch who still stood at the door. "It is not possible," the eunuch said to him. "You are only a servant. How then can you impose your will on so many gods?"

Nabopolassar looked into the black man's face and felt for him. The poor man had just had his theology turned upside-down. The monarch searched for the words in Egyptian. "You are right; I am just a servant. So, it is not my will, but that of Enlil. He is the Most High, and all, even the gods, must bow to him."

Nabopolassar took one last look at the destroyed throne room and once more thanked Marduk that the Scythians had declined to attend. Then he turned and followed Arioch from the palace.

Outside, in the palace courtyard, Prince Psammetik lay in a tangled heap with the other young noblemen who had been so unceremoniously dumped on the brick-paved way.

With a whoop of intaken breath, Prince Psammetik sat up. He stared around him, wondering what had just happened. The battle had been a brief and only moderately violent interlude, but for the properly-minded Egyptians, it was unprecedented. The prince looked around wildly. Citizens hurried from the courtyard under the watchful eye of the Babylonian guard.

Princess Nitocris was gone.

Prince Psammetik had lost his wig, and a lump was swelling on his bald head. He wrapped his arms around his belly and doubled over, still gasping. The new First Prophet of Amun caught sight of his tutor, Prince Horiraa, Fan-Bearer to the Right, anxiously attending his aunt. He managed to stand and tottered over to them, accosting the God's Wife. "Great Queen!" In his distress, he dared lay his hand on her arm. "My sister! She is your heir! She is…." For a moment inarticulate, he struggled with the words. "She is the hope of Egypt!"

"She is certainly *your* hope, Prince Psammetik," she spat, looking like she wanted to claw someone's eyes out, though tears ran freely down her cheeks. "Without her, you have no claim to the throne!

"May the Euphrates turn to blood! May locusts consume the crops of Babylonia! May Amun-Ra devour Shamash so that their land be swallowed in darkness!" She stopped breathing hard and stared wildly at the prince. Then she slipped her arm over his shoulder and led him away from her brother, the Chief of Protocol. *"May Osiris reject his new son!"* she whispered hoarsely in her nephew's ear.

Shaken, Psammetik jumped back and stared at her. Necho was now Horus Necho, son of Osiris, but to be rejected by Osiris would mean no afterlife. He glanced quickly over at his uncle, but it was obvious that Prince Horiraa, Fan-Bearer to the Right and Psammetik's own tutor, had heard nothing. Psammetik swallowed hard and thought about it. How angry was he? How angry should he be? Did even a pharaoh have the right to do what his father had just done? "My little sister, the delight of my life!" he moaned. Then he nodded. "May my father's name be blotted out," he agreed softly, so only Queen Nitocris could hear.

"May it be so," she hissed at the young man, reminding him of a coiled royal cobra. "Then you will bring my daughter back to me, and Osiris will make of you a son worthy to own the Two Lands."

CHAPTER 3

Peace

Sais, Egypt

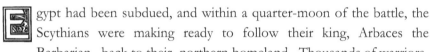

Egypt had been subdued, and within a quarter-moon of the battle, the Scythians were making ready to follow their king, Arbaces the Barbarian, back to their northern homeland. Thousands of warriors, men and women, mounted on colorfully clothed ponies took their places in the flooded fields, fetlock deep in the cooling waters of the Nile. Brightly painted covered wagons, filled with married women, children and the elderly, jostled for better positions on the road. It had all the feel of a feast-day festival, and the Scyths were in high spirits, yodeling, squabbling, and drinking. They were in total contrast to the civilized decorum of the serious-minded inhabitants of Egypt. The Scythians were a barbarian race and were proud of it.

King Arbaces, their leader, was a huge, middle-aged, jovial warrior who liked his beer as well as the next man and loved the spectacle that his nation brought to the world. Even more, he enjoyed the wild, nomadic life of his people and the freedom it gave him.

But the world was changing; civilization was encroaching on the most remote areas. If the Scythians couldn't make some accommodation for such changes, they would be left behind, perhaps even perish as a people—and Arbaces knew it. It was up to him to make such accommodations.

Standing on the road, the chieftain lifted his heavily tattooed arm. Holding the reins of his tall Assyrian stallion, he raised his new mug, made from the skull of an Egyptian commander, to Nabopolassar, King of Babylonia. "Not right we part with bad blood between us, so I forgive you," he announced and downed the contents—a honey beer from the breweries of Sais.

Quizzically, Nabopolassar leaned back against the huge nail-studded wheel of his war chariot and returned the salute with a mug of gold. "Forgive me? For what?"

"You not insist we come to crown giving. You not say it be so..." he paused, searching for the word, "entertaining." He laughed, showing a mouth full of cracked and yellowed teeth.

Despite himself, Nabopolassar laughed back. "It was that." He, too, drained his mug and handed it to his servant, Agga, who stood behind him. Agga took the cup and climbed up into the high chariot. The sleek white team of four abreast danced at the chariot's movement, champing at their bits and pulling on their reins against the iron grip of Nabo's driver.

The barbarian king turned to a dark-haired young man of about fourteen years standing before five other Scythian teens on the road, all holding the reins of their mounts. All had earned their first tattoos and scalps, most right here against Egypt. Arbaces thoughtfully regarded the clear-eyed young man, gave him a crooked smile, and embraced him. "Anacharsis, My Son," he said in his halting Aramaic, "you be good student. Obey King of Babylon and learn well. Bring learning to our people and make I proud."[1]

"Great King," the prince returned, also in Aramaic, but with scarcely an accent, "we will study hard and return with all that is needed." He pushed his shaggy black hair out of his bright green eyes and grinned, eager to finally attain his one desire. He was to become a scholar. He would learn to understand the world and the people in it, and he would bring his own people into the light of reasoned knowledge.

"We will take good care of them, Arbaces," Nabopolassar assured him. "Bit Mummi, the House of Knowledge, will make you proud of them."

The barbarian grinned and effortlessly swung up on his mount's high back. "I proud already!" He raised his short sword to the sky and yodeled a call that was echoed throughout what passed for the ranks. With enthusiastic yelps, yips and song, accompanied by the splashing of the ponies' feet and the groan of the wagons' wheels, the Scythians rode out at a trot, leaving Arbaces' second son and his company in the care of the Babylonians.

CHAPTER 4

A Marriage of Convenience

Babylon, Babylonia

"*You did what?!?"* Queen Ninnaramur exploded in exasperation.

Usually, Nebuchadnezzar would have tried to shrink away from his mother's wrath, but he was too busy staring, open-mouthed at his father. Nabopolassar, formally receiving his family in the cool, second story sitting room of his private chambers, had just informed his wife and sons that he had brought an Egyptian princess back to Babylon with him for Nebuchadnezzar to wed.

The queen slammed down her beer mug on a nearby table and stood, scattering her satin cushions and her meal of honey cakes and pork roast. She gestured at her eldest. "He already has a marriage contract with the daughter of Media, and you arranged that too! Do you intend to bring your sons back a wife every time you go out? If so, then you've been neglecting Shum!" She now motioned at their second son, a young boy, sitting to one side on his cushion.

Nebushumlishtar loved honey cakes and was pretending to be absorbed in the consumption of the sweet treat. At nine years old, he was still free of marital entanglements.

"What happened? Didn't she have a sister?"

Shum tried to sink deeper into his cushion.

The king's servant, Agga, dropped to his knees and unobtrusively began gathering up the queen's fallen plate and its contents.

Nabo grinned at Naram's sarcasm. "Actually, no she didn't, not a full-sister and certainly not one who was also adopted by the god's wife. You want me to go back out and look for someone suitable for him next time?"

Nebuchadnezzar, who was thirteen, recovered from the news of his betrothal and threw a wicked look at his little brother.[1] The queen was right; Shum should also be a party to their father's political maneuverings.

The king leaned forward, straightened Naram's cushions, and patted them, inviting her to sit back down again.

"Oh!" Naram swept a lion's head stone vase from its stand, and she stalked out of the throne room as it crashed to the floor. Red, pink and white roses flew everywhere, spattering water across the cushions, and the king's face.[2]

Agga ran for the bathroom and some towels.

Nabo turned to Shum, "You're excused."

The boy gained his feet in one fluid motion and fled, an assortment of honey cakes cradled protectively in his arms and a broad grin on his face as he threw his brother one last sly look.

Prince Nebuchadnezzar remained. Kadurri was growing tall and handsome with short straight bangs over a broad forehead. He had deep-set, highly intelligent eyes, and a nose like the king's, that came straight down from his brow to end above a mouth with small, thin lips. He had a charisma that had already captured the nation. The youth sat on his cushions before his father, pondering this unexpected development. An Egyptian princess? He held his plate, forgotten, in one hand.

"Don't you have anything to say?" the king asked him.

Agga returned, placed the roses back in their vase and began sopping up the floor.

Nabo took a white linen towel from the servant and wiped off his face.

"I will apologize for my mother," the young teen answered carefully. "She is a woman and is likely to ignore the larger aspects of a situation for the impact that it may have closer to her home."

"True," Nabopolassar gave him a broad smile, "but the queen is capable of apologizing for herself, and that isn't what I meant. What do you think about this marriage contract?"

"I…" the prince hesitated. "The king is aware of all political necessities. If the girl brings Egypt with her, what else could be done? But what will the Medes think? They could construe this as an insult against their princess." Nebuchadnezzar was already betrothed to the First Princess of Media.

"Which is why you cannot actually marry her until after Uvakshatra's daughter arrives. The Medes never considered that Amyhia would be your only wife, just your first and your queen." Nabo chuckled, "Kadurri, I should have known that your first concern would be for Babylonia, but I want to know how you feel about this personally."

The prince thought about it, chewing on his lip. Finally, he set the plate down on the floor, looked his father in the eyes and shrugged. "I'm not sure. Do Egyptian women make good wives?"

"I doubt it." The king laughed outright at the thought. "Probably not this one anyway. She has an attitude problem. She thinks she should be worshiped."

That didn't sound good. "But I still have to take her?"

Nabo popped a last slice of meat in his mouth and set his plate aside on the immaculate purple and white tiled floor too. "I'm afraid so. At least, she's pretty."

"Could I see her?" Kadurri had never seen an Egyptian before, and this one would hold particular significance for him. He was curious and more than a little anxious. Would he like her? Would she like him?

The king stood and held out his hand to his first-born. "Come with me. You can look, just don't touch."

"Wait a moment," Kadurri rose and walked over to Agga and spoke quietly in his ear. The servant bowed quickly and left to do the prince's bidding. Then the prince took the king's hand, and they left the room.

The king and his son made their way down the hall to the staircase. Descending two flights, they crossed a courtyard to a large, carved door opposite. Up two more flights of steps and they came to the harem. In a private suite decorated in soft blues, they found Nitocris, daughter of Pharaoh Necho. She had been seated on her narrow, reed-stuffed bed in the airy, second-floor room, but she stood up when they entered. Cautiously, she moved back against the wall. The Heir of the God's Wife was about twelve years old, more than a year younger than Nebuchadnezzar, and she had in her room, at her disposal, a Chaldean interpreter as well as a serving girl. Both stood against the far wall and bowed low and snapped their fingers before them as the king and his son entered.

The prince surveyed the princess critically.

Though she now stood, she pointedly ignored him. She held her defiant chin high, as she imperiously stared out the large window at the Euphrates. Small and petite, her mother's Cushite blood showed in her exotic brown-hued skin and huge black eyes. Her features were delicate, with a heart-shaped face and high cheekbones. Her teeth were small and very white. Her face was heavily painted in the Egyptian style, making her already large eyes seem enormous, and her lips were stained a brilliant red. She wore bright gold earrings and bracelets and had a slim golden cornet decorated with colored glass flowers and a protective cobra inlaid with lapis lazuli. Her sheer ivory shift showed off her budding figure and left little to the imagination. Her wig—blacker than her eyes—hung to her waist in a thousand tiny braids. Slim and petite, to Nebuchadnezzar she was more than pretty, she was stunningly beautiful—or she would be in a few years.

"It's a pretty circlet," Kadurri murmured softly to his father.

"I'm told it's called a Seshed," the king replied. "It's the crown for the dead."[3]

Nebuchadnezzar shot his father a sharp look.

"She is not in a very good mood," Nabo explained, apologizing. "She feels that by removing her from Egypt we have robbed her of her divinity and doomed her to return to clay rather than to have her body preserved for eternity while her spirit enjoys the company of the gods."

"I could see where that would be upsetting," Kadurri murmured. Looking at her all alone like that he felt sorry for her. "At least, she's not crying. Does she understand us?"

"Not a word."

"I shall order a tutor for her, then," he said, relieved to find something he could do to make her feel better. "And some more suitable clothes… and a more appropriate tiara, too." He cautiously approached her, trying not to alarm her. The interpreter stepped forward, ready to do his duty. She looked away, studying a bird which sang from its gilded cage, suspended nearby from a bronze stand.

Kadurri frowned. The bird was pretty, but a lute player would have been better. He decided to check if there was one available among the eunuchs.

The prince bowed low despite her obvious disdain for him. "Princess, I am Nebuchadnezzar, son of Nabopolassar, Prince of Babylonia. My father tells me we are to be wed. I am pleased to make your acquaintance and to welcome you to your new home. Anything that you require, just see that I am informed." He paused, waiting for the Chaldean eunuch to catch up. There was not even the flicker of acknowledgment in the girl's painted eyes.

Just then, Agga arrived, trotting quickly. Behind Nabo's manservant came one of the palace domestics with a small wicker basket and lid. Kadurri smiled and reached out. The servant placed the basket in his hands. "I am told your people like cats," the prince continued, addressing the princess. "We have none of the breeds you're accustomed to, I'm afraid, but we have a lot of trade with the northern countries. They have some unique varieties. I have brought you a kitten." He lifted the lid and gently pulled the creature out. The kitten was pure white with blue eyes and long, soft hair. Where the cats of Egypt were slender and elegant, it was round and short-eared. Kadurri handed the basket back to the servant and offered the kitten to Nitocris. It batted playfully at her with over-large paws.

The girl still made no move either to take it or to acknowledge his presence.

After an awkward moment, the prince set the cat on the floor at her feet.

Nabopolassar slipped his arm around his son's shoulder and led him from the room.

"Farewell, Princess," Kadurri called back to her. "I will visit you again tomorrow."

In the hall, Nebuchadnezzar paused and leaned back to look in the open door. Inside the room, he saw Nitocris snatch up the purring kitten and cuddle it close. He grinned, and let his father pull him away.[4]

PART 2: 609 BC

The Year Peace Died

The LORD*'s anointed, our very lives' breath, was snared by their traps. We had thought that we could shelter our lives forever in his shadow and the nations could not touch us.*

—Lamentations 4:20.

CHAPTER 5

Betrayal

Sais, Egypt

Necho, Pharaoh of the Province of Egypt sat on the Throne of the Living One and "shone" as he waited there with impatience. The throne room, lit with sweet-smelling torches was decked out with myriad wreaths of flowers, their heavy scent mixing with that of the brands and filling the air. The throne itself sat on a dais covered with rich carpeting, but it was merely a seat. Its embroidered canvas seat and back were comfortable and cool, and they folded, collapsing easily where the gold-gilt wooden legs pivoted upon their center wooden dowel. The throne was easily moved. Likewise, the matching embroidered cushion detached from its footstool, pretty, yet very functional. It was the canopy with its uraeus snakes on a sky-blue background that shouted the royal status of the man seated beneath it. The richly carved and painted wooden pillars of the canopy rested on the floor at the four corners of the dais with its row upon row of painted royal griffins.

Like his father before him, the current pharaoh wore the blue Chepresh. He had surrendered his father's war helmet to Babylon, but he had secretly had another made for this meeting. The war helmet reflected the good god's mood. Necho gripped the symbols of his office, the striped flail and the shepherd's crook scepter in his left hand, tapping them irritably against his leg. His bare feet rested on the cushions of the footstool—a god had no need for sandals, at least not in audience. The traditional attire did nothing to appease Necho's mood. His fake beard itched. His golden collar sat heavily on his sheer linen shift, which did nothing to ease the chafing of the jewelry. His stiff overskirt, its fashionable pointed front stating his prowess in no uncertain terms, refused to fold itself correctly to a seated posture. It interfered with the movements of his right arm, and its ridiculous lion's tail was not proving to be comfortable to sit on in what would probably be a long, drawn-out meeting. All this bode ill for the health of the chief bleacher. It was not easy being a god.

Necho calmed himself. Though it was not easy being a god, he had waited for all of his life for this, and he was not young. Psammetik had been in his seventies when he was killed, and Necho had had to wait until his middle forties for his father's death. But now the Two Lands were his at last.

The queen's throne, still on the first step down from the dais, was empty, and there was no recorder. The only officials present were the two Fan-Bearers to the Right and Left.

Prince Horiraa, with his face entirely neutral, began fanning his brother the pharaoh, with his ostrich feather and Abdamelek took up the great fan and began to move it. Horiraa pointed his golden crook to the guards at the large entrance door. They swung the doors open and the ceremony, which would escort the emissaries of Lydia into the presence of divinity, began.

Necho had arranged a clandestine meeting, with no written record, held in the dead of night against the chance of the Babylonian overseers, of the Great Royal Wife Chednitjerbone, or of Crown Prince Psammetik hearing of it! Necho's sister, Nitocris, Consort of the God, had traveled back to Thebes and by the time she learned of this night's work, it would be too late. The deed would be done. Necho understood that to betray Babylon meant the death of his daughter, but he was a realist. The girl was already lost, she was not coming back.

What would be worse was the possibility of Nitocris' continued survival in Babylon. Necho's daughter would marry Prince Nebuchadnezzar. Nebuchadnezzar would then usurp Prince Psammetik's place as heir to the Egyptian throne—unless the princess was no longer the heir of Thebes! But the Queen of Thebes adamantly refused to repudiate the princess' adoption and accept one of Necho's other daughters. She insisted she would hold her office until she died, refusing to step down in the absence of her heir. And once Queen Nitocris died, Princess Nitocris would automatically become the God's Wife of

Amun, whether she was in Babylon or not! Nebuchadnezzar, as her husband on earth, would then stand in Amun-Ra's place! Only Nebuchadnezzar or his sons could become the legitimate King of Egypt! Necho was a realist, he understood—the princess had to die. After tonight, Nabopolassar would take care of that for him.

The pharaoh intended to end ongoing hostilities and establish an official alliance with Alyattes of Lydia. Alyattes was in his late twenties and had been leading the army of Lydia since he was sixteen, waiting for over twelve circles to come to the Throne of Tantalus. Less than a circle had passed since King Sadyattes was laid in his grave. The new king, Alyattes, was an unknown factor.[1] Nevertheless, Egypt and Lydia had two things in common: a healthy respect for the nations of the Coalition and an overwhelming need to see them destroyed. Media had long been Lydia's enemy, and Scythia and Babylonia were Egypt's. It was only natural that Egypt and Lydia should be in an alliance and Alyattes seemed willing to explore that possibility where the late Sadyattes had not been.

Though Lydia was a small country, in essence, Alyattes ruled all the coastal countries of Asia Minor—all of them except Miletus. He could command the entire region, and all would obey. Therefore, the boundaries of Ionia were the boundaries of Lydia. An alliance with Alyattes brought the resources of all of Ionia—Phocaea, Aeolia, Caria, Lycia and the islands—all of Ionia except Miletus.

Which was another reason for keeping the meeting secret. Miletus had been Egypt's ally since Psammetik I had granted them a city on the Canopic branch of the Nile Delta, just where it opened onto the Mediterranean. They were the only Greeks to settle on pharaoh's land. They were the only foreigners to maintain a fortress in Egypt. The Fortress of the Milesians was of incalculable value. It was the port at the entrance of the Nile which led to Sais itself. Egypt's traditional hostility towards Lydia was the basis of Miletus' friendship and had resulted in the gifting of the use of the fortress to them.

King Thrasybulus of Miletus, alone out of all the kings in Ionia, had refused to follow Sadyattes' lead. The Milesians suffered for it. Lydia raided Miletus yearly for its crops, and the new king, Alyattes, intended to follow his father's tradition. King Thrasybulus of Miletus would not be pleased if he found out that Necho, supposedly his ally, was dealing with his worst enemy.

But Egypt's friendship with Miletus had been brokered by those who now wandered the fields of Aaru with Osiris. It was Necho who was pharaoh now! Necho the realist. If things went well tonight, the Babylonian occupation forces would be deported from the Two Lands or under arrest within a ten-day.[2]

A Lydian functionary came forward to stand between the painted pillars and whispered in Prince Horiraa's ear. "Forty thousand uten of Judean copper," the fan-bearer announced. The gifts the Lydians had brought began to arrive and to be displayed before the pharaoh. Two Judean slaves, bowing low and kissing the tiled floor of the throne room, set a sample of ten copper ingots before the throne. Copper was rare in Egypt, and this gift was highly valued. Necho nodded, and the slaves scooped up the treasure to follow Abdamelek, Horiraa's second, from the room. The Cushite would show the slaves where to put all that copper, but these duties temporarily left the throne room without an actual working fan. Luckily, the night breeze was cool.

"Thirty Grecian urns filled with olive oil." Four Greek slaves brought two of the vases before the pharaoh. These were large and exquisitely covered in heroic black designs, but it was the oil within them that held the value. The pharaoh waved them on without more than a cursory glance. They followed the copper bearers.

"Fifteen hundred cubic cubits of Lebanese cedar." A Lebanese slave laid a finely worked board at the foot of the dais by way of example. This was a lavish gift indeed. Egypt had very little wood and none at all of quality. Every pharaoh declared his worth by his building projects, and this would allow Necho to adorn his new buildings in breathtaking wealth. Lydia had saved the best until last and pharaoh was very pleased.[3]

Gifts received, the pharaoh gently touched his brother's arm with the shepherd's crook, and Horiraa motioned to the guards at the entrance granting audience to those without.

The Lydian courtier again whispered in the Fan-Bearer's ear. It was to Horiraa's credit as the picture of correctness that he didn't even bat an eye. "The

Emissaries of Alyattes, King of Lydia and the Ambassador of Ashurubalit, Emperor of Assyria," he announced.

The pharaoh's eyes widened in surprise. As the fan-bearer had introduced them, the emissaries entered and there among them was an Assyrian with his formal long tasseled robe of royal turquoise. It was not needful that high officials actually kiss the earth in the pharaoh's presence, so these, holding their arms stiffly by their side they bowed low, as was the fashion.

Horiraa took a step forward and began: "His Majesty Horus, the Good God, Beloved of Isis, the Goddess of Truth, Pharaoh of Upper and Lower Egypt, Great Chieftain of the West, Lord of the Diadem of the Vulture and of the Snake, the Son of Ra, the Living One, Wahemibre Necho son of Osiris Psammet…"

Necho abruptly cut him off by poking him with the striped flail and crook. "What is this?" he demanded of the Lydians. "Why have you brought this Ninevite?"

The entourage—still bowed over waiting for the end of the Fan-Bearer's spew—glanced confusedly at one another and slowly straightened. The spokesman of the group came forward. "The pharaoh is like Ra in all that he does and all that happens occurs according to the desires of his heart. Never have the Two Lands seen such wondrous works and prosperity as have been their good fortune since his crowning…"

"Yes, of course," Necho snapped, waving the striped crook in the spokesman's direction. Etiquette required that any and all supplicants supply a hymn or poem of praise before they began, but etiquette could take a long time. "Inscribe it on a scroll and get to the point. Answer the question."

"The good god is gracious to recognize his servants with such rapidity," the spokesman said uncertainly. "May Ra smile upon the reign of his son and make it prosper. I bring greetings from Alyattes, King of Lydia, Monarch of the Seas. My liege bids me give One his good wishes as One dons the red and whi.." the spokesman hesitated, confused. The pharaoh was definitely not wearing the double Pschent crown. The emissary hastily amended his speech, "Ah, the blue Chepresh Crown of War to begin One's reign. As tokens of his esteem, he has sent the gifts already brought before One and dispatched his humble nephew to discuss arrangements which may be of advantage to both Lydia and the Two

Lands. I am Gadah, Prince of Lydia, nephew of King Alyattes and One's humble servant." Gadah gave another little bow and a deprecating smile before he continued.

"The most worthy Ambassador of Assyria, Mesharapli, has traveled with us from Sardis at the bidding of his illustrious lord, the Great King Ashurubalit, to express his condolences on pharaoh's father, Osiris Psammetik, who has taken his place among the gods, and to assure One of his continuing dedication to the Egyptian cause."[4]

"Why?"

The question caught the emissary off guard so that he inadvertently broke decorum and addressed Necho directly, "Great Pharaoh?"

"Why is this Ninevite here?" Necho demanded, his eyes blazing. He handed the crook and flail to Horiraa and leaned forward on his throne, pointing a finger at the Assyrian ambassador. "Assyria has fallen and thanks largely to Ashurubalit, Egypt lost a great deal of her strength at Harran. We were pursued by the Babylonians all the way back here to Sais itself! It is for this reason that we are talking about an alliance with Lydia. The Two Lands are not interested in further dealings with a defunct nation that has already cost them so much." The pharaoh sat back in his chair and glared at the Lydian prince.

The diplomat studied the immaculately tiled floor and chose his words carefully. "One must know that Ashurubalit is only a man, he cannot read the future; and in recent events, his seers admittedly failed him. It was never his intention to cause harm to Egypt, only to obtain the help of Lydia. This he has done…"

"Enough!" snapped Necho. He leaned over and spoke softly to his brother, the Fan-Bearer. "This is absurd! The Lydians have always counted the Assyrians as their enemies! Why should Alyattes suddenly decide to welcome Ashurubalit with open arms?"

Prince Horiraa pursed his lips and whispered back, "Why not? The past is the past. Alyattes obviously has nothing further to fear from Assyria. But one knows, both Lydia and Assyria have a common enemy in the Babylonian Coalition."

"But do I recognize Ashurubalit's emissary? Would it insult Alyattes if I rejected Assyria by tossing him out instead?"

"He has come with Alyattes' ambassador. They are one unit. And one has already accepted their gifts."

Necho snorted derisively. "So, I have been tricked. I can't just throw the dog out."

"Pharaoh could gracefully accept their greetings and condolences and then cut the meeting short without offending. But another such opportunity with Lydia would then be unlikely to present itself," the fan-bearer warned neutrally.

Necho sighed. "And we need Lydia." Necho's frown deepened. "Brother," he said, "you see what is happening here? Lydia doesn't want Egypt to become too strong. If our new Alliance retakes Assyrian lands, Ashurubalit holds the first claim to them and that is the point."

"One is correct," Horiraa nodded, still speaking in the pharaoh's ear. "This move will effectively keep Egypt from expansion beyond Syria. Lydia prefers a weak and easily controlled reborn Assyria to a world-dominating Egyptian Empire."

The realist thought about it. "But even so, we would break free of Babylon and all our former glory would be restored. We would still be as big as before, and if we take Syria, we would be much bigger.

"Alyattes should beware, though. We will not forget Lydia's trickery." With ill-grace, the pharaoh nodded acknowledgment to the Assyrian ambassador and scowled as he noted the relief evident on the face of the Lydian, Gadah.

"Very well. Now about those ships?"

"The Glory of Lydia remains cautious about any permanent alliance so early in his sovereignty, but he can easily provide Egypt ten trireme warships in the Great Sea along with a fair contingent of sailors and military personnel. These we already have in stock, but ready-made ships are, of course, more expensive than waiting on construction. King Alyattes can also order additional vessels be assembled as pharaoh deems fit, but the good god's need for haste in such a matter will determine the price there as well. As to pharaoh's inquiry about ten expeditionary vessels to be transported to the Red Sea: these can be constructed and delivered to Gaza, but the costs of disassembly, overland transportation and reassembly on the Red Sea, even using slave labor, is prohibitive."

Necho frowned, then leaned over and spoke in Horiraa's ear.

The fan-bearer pursed his lips as he listened, then he answered the emissary, "Begin the construction and have them delivered to Gaza. We will take them from there."

"Mother, may I enter?" Prince Psammetik pounded on the thin copper covering Queen Chednitjerbone's massive wood door. He heard the sweet tones of a harp, abruptly cut off and the murmur of the queen's low voice from within her chambers.

The decorative double door opened a crack, revealing the figure of one of Chednitjerbone's ladies. The servant stepped aside and allowed the prince entrance to the living area of the queen's chambers.

Chednitjerbone was standing over an elegant table carved of ivory. The Great Royal Wife wore a richly embroidered, but opaque outer shift; her figure was not what it once was. She pulled a short wig from its stand on the table and set it in place. It was an advantage Egypt's women had above those of foreign places. Her "hair" would never show gray. The queen smiled at her son and beckoned him closer.

"I must speak with you," he took a step nearer and looked pointedly at the harpist in the corner and then at the other serving women, "alone." The serious expression on Psammetik's face must have made an impression, for the queen's smile died, and she clapped her hands. The harpist stood, and leaving her harp she accompanied the other ladies into the queen's bed chambers and shut the reed mat door behind them.

Psammetik embraced his mother. The son of Necho, grandson of Psammetik, Heir of Horus, First Prophet of Amun, was tall and handsome with the hawk nose of his paternal grandfather. Where Chednitjerbone's skin was almost as black as the kohl paint on her eyes, Psammetik's was a darkened bronze.[5] Chednitjerbone's handsome son now wore the kerchief and gold braid of the crown prince, next-in-line for the throne. He politely slipped a huge saffron crocus behind her ear. He always brought her a flower and even now, in these circumstances, he observed the custom.

"You are out early, my son," she said uneasily and motioned him to sit on a long low couch beneath her window. It had been a favorite place for them over countless conversations as the prince grew.

It was right there that he had sat and bounced his little sister on his knee when she was only a baby. He choked.

The fresh breeze off the Nile came in the second story window. Invitingly cool, it beckoned to the prince to accept his mother's invitation, but he did not sit. "I have come at the bidding of the Good God," he stated flatly.

Puzzled, Chednitjerbone raised one eyebrow but said nothing. She poured water from a baked clay flask into a brass cup and offered it to him, but he didn't take it.

"My sister…" the young man faltered. Princess Nitocris was Psammetik's favorite sister, his only full-sister. Nitocris was to have been the one who would have raised Psammetik's ka to divine status when he took the throne. Now, she was gone, promised to a despised foreigner.

The queen nodded. "We will work something out. We are at peace with Babylon; we would be welcomed at their court. One day soon, we will travel there to visit and see her. Would you like that?"

The prince stared at his mother in shock. She had no idea of the distances involved, nor was she aware of what he now had to tell her. He composed himself and nodded briefly. "Mother, pharaoh commands you to remain sequestered and pray for your daughter's well-being."

The queen paled under her dark skin. "What has happened?"

"The good god has donned the Chepresh war helm and renewed the alliance with Assyria. Moreover, he is negotiating a possible alliance with Lydia since Lydia is at war with Media of the Coalition."

Chednitjerbone sat down hard on the couch, her eyes wide. "But our daughter! Is He Who Lives mad? What will the Babylonians do?"

Psammetik looked away. He held no illusions. Pharaoh had already dismissed the girl from his concerns. She held no further place in his calculations. "Mother, I am sorry. And I don't know what the Babylonians will do to her. I will offer sacrifices for her. Perhaps… Perhaps with Assyria and

Lydia's help, we will overrun those dirty, bug-infested red-faced cowards and win her back."[6]

"Perhaps?" the panic was evident in her voice. "Perhaps the Babylonians will kill her!"

"Mother, if they do, they do." He threw up his arms in frustration. "It is already too late."

"But…"

"It has been decided. Even now, the Babylonian overseers are being rounded up and arrested. We can do nothing." His voice grew hard. "If the Babylonians harm her, we will avenge her."

"But she will be dead in a foreign land, and her ka will be lost forever!" The queen ended the sentence in a high-pitched wail. She rose to her feet, breathing heavily and tears began to roll down her cheeks.

"That will be her fate sooner or later regardless," the prince gritted his teeth, thinking of the small girl he had watched grow until she was almost old enough to assume her duties in Thebes. He took a step forward and laid his hand on his mother's shoulder.

"Thanks to your father!" She shook him off. Quivering with outrage and fear, she moved to the window and leaned out over the sill.

The Nile, seemingly unaffected by the circumstances, sparkled in the early morning sun.

"Mother!" Psammetik was stunned, no one criticized the pharaoh. He felt the same, but the Great Royal Wife, with her timid and mild nature, must have been moved almost beyond belief to react so. And she wasn't done.

"He has done this to her! Never forget it, Prince of Egypt! Perhaps we cannot help her, but at least, we can know. I must know what becomes of her. Send me someone who can find out."

"Someone?"

"Someone with contacts in Babylon. Someone who can act as a spy…" she stopped then blinked slowly and wiped the tears from her face. "Send me the merchant Ramose, son of your cousin Kaptah," she sniffed.

The prince hesitated. "A merchant?"

"He is your distant cousin, a Saite; but his father was also half Milesian, and that allows Ramose Milesian citizenship. He is an Ionian merchant. His hair is as gold as your braid, his eyes the color of Ra's heaven. No one would ever know him for anything but Milesian. And he's only sixteen. The picture of innocence. But his mother is the sister of the last sheik of the Chaldean House of Amukanni! Ramose carries the blood of the old Babylonian kings as well as that of the Great Chieftains of the West. You can recruit him by pointing out that if you were pharaoh and Babylon were to fall, his blood would make him a very suitable sub-king there."

"Mother! This is treason! I don't…"

"Is that worse than betraying Amun-Ra by sending his betrothed to Babylon to be killed? Ra is with us. So, go fetch Ramose. His mother works in the palace in Babylon, and he travels there with his wares. It has always been her dream to see her son on the throne. She will cooperate. Ramose will make the perfect spy, going back and forth. Send him to me."

Psammetik stared at the queen with new respect. He knew nothing of Ramose or his mother. How did she? The prince had had no idea that the Great Royal Wife had political savvy. She hid it well. This plan of hers, though, was dangerous. His father would not be pleased if he were to find out, but then the prince thought of his sister, and he nodded shortly. "Madam, as you will." He bowed and backed from the room.

That same morning, he sent a message down the Nile to the Fortress of the Milesians on the Great Sea. The merchant was required by the Great Royal Wife.

And that afternoon, the First Prophet of Amun sailed upstream to Thebes in his private bark.[7] Unlike his mother, Psammetik could not rely only on the return of his sister. He had to have another plan. He would handle this in his own way.

CHAPTER 6

The God's Wife

Thebes, Egypt

The City of Amun, Niwtimn, known the world over as Thebes, did not even remotely resemble the Greek city of the same name. Thebes was really two cities. On the east bank, there was Taopet, the City of the Living, which included the Southern Sanctuary. On the west was the City of the Dead with its tombs, monuments, shrines, and temples. There lay the tombs of countless pharaohs and other Egyptian royalty.

Sailing south, the rowers rowed hard against the current. The trip in the luxurious wooden yacht had taken Prince Psammetik four and a half days.[1] Sailing the Nile was cool and pleasant, but Ra was almost overhead in the sky as the bark docked at Taopet, the Living City, the vast Temple Complex of Amun. Crown Prince Psammetik had no interest in the City of the Dead, across the Nile.

The prince, grateful to stretch his legs, disembarked and walked straight ahead, down the quay, to the Avenue of the Rams. The avenue was lined on both sides by twenty peculiar, ram-headed sphinxes—forty of them in all. All down the long length of the Avenue, the large sphinxes alternated with smaller statues of Ramesses the Great, shielding the ancient pharaoh's images in their shadows.

Thebes was a war-damaged city. Fifty-four years before, Ashurbanipal of Assyria had invaded the Two Lands. He had advanced as far as Thebes, the Capital of Upper Egypt. The Assyrian had plundered and destroyed much of it, chasing the Cushite pharaohs forever from the Two Lands. This had been good news for the Saites, but fifty-four years were not sufficient time to erase the scars. Psammetik walked beside walls covered in plaster patches, bearing repaired paintings, and accented by cheap, colored glass "jewels." Though the prince had heard of Taopet's original splendor, he had never known the city to look any different.

Walking briskly, the First Prophet of Amun tied his kerchief behind his head and the pilgrims, catching sight of its golden plait, quietly dropped to their knees and bowed their heads between their outstretched arms as their prophet passed.

Thebes was not a city of commerce, or even families and residences. It was a city of priests. The holiness lent a hush that filtered everywhere and everyone—priest and pilgrim alike—kept a respectful silence; everyone but the Crown Prince. The hard, hafa-grass soles of Psammetik's sandals clicked on the pavement as he crossed the intersection of the Avenue and the Great Royal Road.[2] *Click, click, click*—the staccato sound resonated in the eerie silence of the Living City. It echoed off the representations of Ra as the prince approached the main entrance to the complex.

Psammetik reached the gate. Eight feet tall, the cast bronze portal was set in a wall painted all around with thirty-foot-tall representations of ancient pharaohs and their deeds.

Passing the outer wall and gates, Psammetik entered the holy city.[3] The gates were recent—built by the foster-uncle of the God's Wife. The guards of Taopet snapped to attention as the prince passed and a messenger discretely fled to announce his arrival, either to the high priest or the God's Wife or both, Psammetik wasn't sure.

Amun's city stretched all around him now; the City of One Hundred Gates. The square Court of Entrance was completely enclosed by temples, monuments to the gods and pharaohs of the past. Prince Psammetik had been here before. He was not intimidated. He strode right down the middle of the court. Directly ahead of him was his destination, the Great Hall.

The determined prince came to the main doors. They were cast bronze, but Psammetik knew that not so long ago, they had been pure, worked gold. Ashurbanipal had ripped the original doors from their hinges and carted them off back to Nineveh. It was of no consequence. Any metal was rare and valuable in Egypt. The towering bronze doors were still a wonder.

Two guards stood outside the entrance, but Psammetik was the First Prophet of Amun, this was *his* city. He was also the favored of the Queen of Thebes. The guards immediately pushed open the doors for him. Psammetik entered his realm and that of his aunt, Nitocris, the God's Wife of Amun.

Like most of the other constructions of the holy city, the Great Hall was made of red sandstone, patched here and there with plaster, and covered with bright paintings. It was here the god's wife held court. Around 650 years old, the immensity of the structure reminded worshippers of just how small they were. Rows of gigantic columns supported the roof, and the central nave, with its stone grid windows, was over eighty feet tall. The walls and columns were painted and decorated in raised relief, portraying Pharaoh Seti I in his deeds, wars, religious rites and political triumphs.

A flood of humanity, citizens who had traveled to Thebes for an audience with the God's Wife, pushed their way out past the prince as he walked in. Psammetik had obviously been announced, and the hall was being cleared.

The son of pharaoh strode forward between the first eight of the central nave's massive pillars to come to a stop before the last four. There—under a royal canopy of blue, and set with the golden disks of Amun—was the dais and throne of the God's Wife of Amun. The eastern antechamber, her royal apartment, was directly behind it.

The Queen of Thebes sat her throne with authority. She had held her office since she had been a tiny baby. Her father, Psammetik I, had given her to be adopted by the former god's wife, Shepenopet, sister of the defeated Cushite pharaoh, Taharka. Nitocris' adoption legitimatized Psammetik I's reign over Upper Egypt and united the two kingdoms. The Saite dynasty ruled all Egypt.

Nitocris sat on the embroidered cushions of the gilded throne; the tall white crown of Upper Egypt sat on her head. The God's Wife was in her mid-forties, but no one could have guessed it. She was as lovely as her brother the pharaoh was handsome. Her high cheekbones and huge, light-brown eyes—highlighted in green and thick black kohl—dominated her sculptured, rectangular face. Her red lips were large and full. Her nose was straight and narrow, as was her graceful, perfect figure—purposely shown off under the sheer linen gown she wore. The high, white, Hedjet crown was decorated with a golden royal cobra which perched above the smooth skin of her flawless brow. Around her neck, she wore a papyrus collar, sewn with blue lotus, cornflowers, and fragrant red berries. The nails on her bare feet and her delicate hands were dyed dark red as befitting her royal status. Queen Nitocris was as beautiful as Isis and most of the Taopet Guard, posted at the sanctuary's doors, were secretly jealous of the god, Amun-Ra.

The queen's graceful hand rested on the head of an enormous black ram, the sacred animal of Taopet. Its impressively long, loosely spiraled horns were painted gold, matching the golden collar and chain that kept the animal in place. Where the priests of Faiyum allowed crocodiles to roam freely through the degenerate Temple of Sobek, Nitocris preferred order and kept her "pet" on a leash.

Nitocris was attended by two fan-bearers and by Ibe, her chief steward. Ibe was old now. He had served the queen since she was a baby.

The ram was served by a slave with a brush, a scoop, and a woven basket.

Nitocris' beautiful eyes sparkled with pleasure at the sight of her nephew. The queen beamed with happiness as Psammetik mounted the steps.

The ram bleated at him, demanding his due. The prince patted its coarse, wooly head and fed it a handful of clover dipped in honey.

Straightening up, Psammetik slipped a purple papyrus flower, the national flower of Upper Egypt, behind the queen's ear. It perfectly set off the blue lotus collar she wore.

Nitocris rose and kissed him on the cheek before she settled back on her gilt embroidered throne.

Thebes was the heart of Egypt and Taopet was the heart of Thebes—protocol here was strict. Psammetik addressed his aunt with a poem he had composed on the barge.

"Great Lady,
Royal Wife of Amun-Ra,
Beauty of the Nile incarnate
With the impossible grace of Isis made visible to our eyes.

Long has your reign prospered Upper Egypt;
Longer still Lower Egypt has basked in its good fortune.
Daughter and sister of kings,
Mother of us all,
Grant this poor petitioner,
Your humble nephew,
Admission into your divine light.
Grant him audience,
Witness to your majesty, beauty, and wisdom.
Let him find favor in your eyes."

Queen Nitocris was delighted. She was always glad to receive her nephew, and any news he carried was always welcome. "My nephew! Scion of the gods, First Prophet and Favored of Amun-Ra. The city rejoices in the presence of its prophet. How kind of you to visit and to bring tidings from Sais in person." Then she must have seen his face, for she was suddenly filled with alarm. "Psammetik, what has happened?"

"Great Queen," he said slowly, carefully choosing his words, "Amun-Ra shines brightly on your throne, and the kingdoms are…"

"What has happened?" She demanded.

"The Good God has… he has…" he had not known that this would be harder than his audience with his own mother. Queen Nitocris had more at stake here than any—save him. "Pharaoh has sent for ambassadors from Lydia and Assyria. He has made a new treaty with Assyria, and things look favorable for an eventual treaty with Lydia. My sister…"

The God's Wife forgot about protocol. She jumped up from her throne. "He… *What?"* she sputtered. "No! He cannot do this! My daughter! Your sister!" Nitocris had held her position her entire life, and it *was* her entire life. She had only one love, her heir, her adoptive daughter, the one to whom she would give everything, her title, her lands, her wealth, *everything.*

"Great Queen," Psammetik said sadly, standing before her dais, "it is already done. She is lost to us."

"Never! NEVER!!! We have agreed! You have agreed. Necho's name will be blotted out! We are going to win her back! We will…"

"How?!?" Psammetik exploded, rudely interrupting her. "I have no power; you have no army."

"Horus Necho will die for this! I swear it!" From anyone else, that would have been blasphemy, but she was a goddess, so she could say whatever she wished.

"Perhaps. Perhaps Nabopolassar will indeed do this deed for us, but it won't matter, not to us. My sister will be dead. You will have no heir, and I will not inherit my father's throne either—unless you help me now."

She slowly settled back down on her throne and nodded. "You have a plan. What do you want to do?"

"You must adopt a daughter of mine."

She caught her breath. "Are you mad? No! Nitocris is my daughter. She is my only heir. I will have no other. You already know this. What is your real plan?"

Psammetik did know this; he had just hoped. "That is it." He shrugged.

"But…"

"Listen to me," he leaned forward, urgently pressing his case. "The Great Royal Wife, my mother, trusts in intrigue, she is sending a spy to Babylon. He is distantly related to us, and he also has an obscure, but real, claim to the Babylonian throne. He will find what has happened to my sister and bring us news. If Ra's protection extends to her in that foreign land and she still lives, it will now be very difficult to win her back. We are at war! It will take a long time, but I must be pharaoh to accomplish this. To become pharaoh, I must have my ka raised to divine status. You are my aunt—not my daughter, not my sister. You cannot do this for me! My mother has no other daughters, so I have no other sister that is acceptable. You must adopt my daughter. Then…" he hesitated, not able to acknowledge out loud the treason they were planning. "Then, I can become pharaoh and win Nitocris back. Then you will, at least, have her with you, even if she is no longer your heir."

"If Nabopolassar hasn't killed her first!" Nitocris stood up again and stepped down from the dais, standing directly before her nephew, shaking with anger. "And even so, by this plan of yours, another shall already be god's wife in her place! No!" She poked him in the chest to emphasize her denial. "Besides, you say you have no other sister who is acceptable. You have no daughter that is acceptable either. They are all illegitimate, and their mothers are common."

Psammetik took no offense. Instead, he slipped his arm soothingly around her shoulder. "But *I* carry the blood of Sais, Napata, and Meroe and I am promised Takhuita, the daughter of Mentemhe, the High Priest of Amun. She would bring the blood of the Priest-Kings, and she holds the rights to the family's lands around Athribis. Those would be added to the lands of the god's wife."[4]

Nitocris knew Mentemhe well. He administered the rule of the City of the Dead under her authority, and he was also governor of the Living City. His lineage was without peer. It was a persuasive argument, and Psammetik knew it.

"Even *if* you were to marry Takhuita, I would not adopt her! And even if I did, you would be her husband, not her brother or father. Amun-Ra would have to share her with you. That would make your reign barely legitimate and definitely scandalous."[5] She shook off his arm and took a step back, glaring challengingly at him.

"I don't want you to adopt Takhuita!" He threw up his hands in exasperation. "But she is old enough for me to marry her now! And if I were to have a daughter by her, the child would carry my blood as well as that of Thebes—the girl would be four ways royal![6] Takhuita's daughter..."

"I want MY daughter!" There were tears of frustration in her eyes.

"And to have any chance of getting her, I must be pharaoh first!" He glared at her.

"This plan will take years! My daughter will be dead!"

Psammetik wrapped his arms around her as she began to sob into his shoulder. "Either she is soon dead already, or she is likely to survive anything," he reasoned. "A few more years will make no difference."

She raised her head and said brokenly, "Except that if she lives, Nitocris will soon be a woman and Nebuchadnezzar will wed her!"

"Then we will make sure that she returns to us a widow."

She was suddenly angry again, and she pushed him away. "And what if she bears him children?" she demanded hoarsely. "They will have a better claim to your throne than you!"

"Not if you disinherit her in favor of my daughter." It was enough. He had said what he had come to say. "If you have a better plan, I would like to hear it."

The Queen of the Dead was silent for a long time. Finally, she swallowed and nodded. "This plan will take some time, but if Princess Nitocris survives your father's betrayal… I am the God's Wife! I hold the ka of divinity. If I were to declare that it could be passed *temporarily* through such a daughter to raise your ka to the heavens, it would be so. Marry Takhuita. Bring me her baby girl. Then may Annubis judge my brother's wicked heart and you will be pharaoh." She turned to Ibe, her chief steward. The old man was always near. "Go quickly; fetch the priest and his daughter."

Ibe bowed deeply before his divine mistress, turned, and hobbled out of the room as fast as he could.

CHAPTER 7

War on the Horizon

Jerusalem, Judah

It was the religious calendar's tenth moon, the civil calendar's fourth, and spring was merging into summer.[1] The land was covered with a brilliant verdant green, laughing at even the suggestion of the coming summer's heat. The Feast of Weeks had concluded, like everything else these days, without incident. The pilgrims were now, for the most part, somewhere between Jerusalem and their home villages. Fields needed tending.

The breeze was fresh and new. It swept into the throne room in Jerusalem and wafted through the high windows to spread the scent of fresh cedar shavings throughout the room. The carved walls of the Palace of the Cedars of Lebanon were 350 years old and had long since ceased to smell, but the brass bowls on the walls were renewed with fresh shavings every day.

The row of bas-relief cedar lions behind the throne, prancing, fighting, and snarling seemed to sink back sedately into the walls, tamed by the gentle sunlight streaming from above. The twelve steps up to the dais with their twenty-four full-size golden lion statues shown regally, calmly aloof from the centuries of crises to which they had stood witness.

And it seemed there was a crisis brewing now.

King Josiah sat on his throne high on the dais of the twelve steps and studied the small group far below him. His broad face was clouded over with dark and brooding thoughts as he listened to the officials.

Josiah was thirty-nine years old and had been crowned when he was only eight. During his reign, he had tossed out the rampant paganism of his father and grandfather and served the Lord only. With a ruddy complexion and reddish hair and beard, many compared him to David, his forefather, as a man after God's own heart.

But being king, even one favored of the Lord, wasn't easy.

Secretary Shaphan, Josiah's Prime Minister and erstwhile regent, stood next to General Kareah ben Nathan on the first step of the dais, facing the king. Behind the two, about a reed back from the stairs stood a captain of the army and three of his scouts. Kareah had brought them here directly upon learning their news and had dismissed everyone else from the throne room. So, now, King Josiah sat in a practically empty throne room, pondering the tidings the officials brought.

"The forces of Egypt are marching north. They will encamp outside Gaza," one of the scouts was informing the king.

Gaza was still owned by Egypt, and Pharaoh Necho had every right to be there, but not with an army.

"What are they doing there?" General Kareah put in. It was a valid question.

The scout shifted uncomfortably. "We bribed an Egyptian officer. He said they go to meet delivery of ten Lydian triremes, crewed by Lydian mercenaries. The Lydians have no alliance with Egypt, but they have built the ships anyway and are sending troops aboard them too. It appears that they will reinforce Egypt's forces once they arrive."

Kareah nodded thoughtfully. "Lydian troops cannot go to Sais directly because the Fortress of the Milesians oversees the Canopic branch of the Nile. The Milesians are at war with the Lydians and would deny them entrance," the grizzled old soldier reminded the king. "So, Lydian mercenaries would have to make port at Gaza."

"Lord King," the scout broke in, "the ships are already there, in the harbor, awaiting the pharaoh, who will arrive on the morrow."[2]

Josiah shook his russet-colored hair. "He wouldn't need an army to take delivery of some ships, and he wouldn't need to come himself, either. He is marching to war! The crocodile compounds his treachery! First, Necho arrests his Babylonian overseers, and now he forms an army and has ordered a navy and mercenaries! That man has no intention of stopping at Gaza; *this* is an act of war!" Josiah was shaking in anger. He slammed his fist down on the armrest of the throne. "Does he think we're just going to let him march across our lands to make war on our friends?" The king firmly believed in honor. Judah was independent, but Josiah was Nabopolassar's friend, he had taken his hand, forming a sacred trust.

"My King," the Prime Minister sought to take control of the situation, "listen to me. Those are not our lands; they are Philistine. The developments are disturbing, yes, but Nabopolassar does not expect us to fight for him. Judah and Babylonia are not allies, only friends."

"They will cross the mountains at Megiddo Pass and take the Valley of Jezreel through to Syria!" Josiah pointed out.

"The Pass and Valley of Jezreel belong to Samaria. It is still not our land."

"We had this discussion once before, that time regarding purging Samaria from her idolatry. My answer today is the same as then: Israel is Israel. All Israel belongs to the Lord. Since Samaria no longer has a king, we are responsible for it." Josiah glared at the secretary.

He loved the old man dearly. Josiah's mother, Jedaiah, had died when he was a baby, but the daughter of Adaiah of Boscath had been King Amon's favorite wife, and so he named the tiny baby his heir. Eight years later, Josiah had become king over the heads of his disappointed, older half-brothers.

Acting as regent, Shaphan had taken the young king in and raised him, protecting him against any and all plots; teaching him the ways of the Lord. Josiah owed Shaphan everything, but he was no longer a child, and Shaphan was no longer his regent. Josiah, as Shaphan had pointed out, was king.

"It is right to be angry, My Father. I am king and justice is in my hand. This very room is called the Hall of Justice!"

He lifted his voice in an ancient tune; his deep bass rumbled through his stocky body and seemed to vibrate up through the floor:

You have upheld my rights and my cause,
Sitting enthroned as the righteous judge.

You have rebuked the nations and destroyed the wicked;
You have blotted out their names forever.
The enemy is finished, in endless ruins;
The cities you uprooted will be remembered no more.
But the Lord reigns forever,
Executing judgment from His throne,
He judges the world with justice
And rules the nations with fairness.[3]

"Don't you see how David is speaking of our enemies? It applied to Assyria, and Assyria is gone, but it also applies to Egypt. Tanis is disappearing beneath the desert sands as we speak. Necho's name will be blotted out, removed from all records! You wait and see; it *will* happen! The Lord is righteous, so how could it be otherwise?"

"Then let Him take care of it! Majesty, you are a man of peace and Judah's security hinges on you! *Judah,* not Samaria! By the promise of the Lord, through the prophetess Huldah, the long-awaited disaster has not befallen Jerusalem and it will not while you live! For the sake of your country, for Judah, you must jealously guard your own life!"

Josiah sighed, the anger draining out of him. "My Father, you were afraid to throw the idols out of Judah and out of Israel because you feared Assyria's wrath; but it was the right thing to do, and it pleased the Lord. Where is Assyria now? I know you remember this. So, do not be afraid of Egypt! You are right; the Lord has promised I will go to my grave in peace. I will not see this coming disaster; so, while I live, Judah is safe. But the Lord also expects me to reign in righteousness and to see that His will is done. Necho's actions are insufferable. I will not give leave to that traitor to set foot in Israel." He turned to Kareah ben Nathan. "Gather the troops."

Stiffly, with military posture and grace born from a lifetime of service, the old general bowed and turned to go.

Shaphan interjected, "My King, at least send for the prophet."

Josiah's mind was made up. "Jeremiah expects us to live by the Word of the Lord, to know it and to obey it; so, I don't need the prophet. It is the

Chief Priest I need." He turned to an aide. "Have Azariah ready himself to bless the army."[4]

The air in the small side room of the Temple was still and heavy, almost as if the building itself held its breath, waiting, jumpy as a skittish colt. Jeremiah, sitting on a plush cushion in the cedar-lined office, seemed unaware of the tension that permeated his surroundings. He was struggling with a passage in a text, and he rarely paid attention to the world around him at such times. The prophet was a young man of thirty years, born the year after the child, Josiah, was named king.[5] Tall and thin, his scruffy brown hair hung over his dark eyes as he bent above the scroll he was studying.

Gemariah rocked back and forth on his own cushion and watched him. Jeremiah sat very still, listening to a Voice that others didn't hear. Consequently, the prophet seemed unaware that something was wrong. Gemariah felt it, though, and he looked about uneasily. Shaphan's youngest son was in his middle thirties, just older than the prophet, but he was definitely the servant here. Gemariah was a quiet and unassuming man, well-suited to his current occupation as Jeremiah's scribe. His steadfast nature had kept the prophet grounded, calming the emotional tempests that could burst from the Man of God at the slightest provocation.

Only now, it was Gemariah who was disturbed and Jeremiah oblivious. The prophet, a slight frown wrinkling his brow, continued to concentrate on the scriptures. The scribe had seen the prophet do this many times. This was Jeremiah, the Prophet of the Lord. He would know if something were wrong! The scribe forced his attention back to his own copy of the scroll they studied. "So, Asaph is speaking about the Council of Seventy?" Gemariah murmured, "About how under Solomon they ruled unjustly? That's what he means when he says, 'gods?' He's referring to how they view themselves?"

Jeremiah heard his friend's soft voice, but he listened to the Voice that spoke within him, that spoke through him. "Yes. He means they think their power is unlimited, that they can do whatever they want and answer to no one. The fate of the weak is in their hands, and all the while, unknowing, their fate is in the hands of the Lord. They walk in darkness, but ultimately, justice will be served."[6]

Gemariah scribbled some notes on his wax tablet, but the unease was still there, and it was growing. As a son of Shaphan, he was a member of the Great Council himself. This morning, the two studied together for a brief devotional Gemariah meant to give at the next council meeting. "Which of my fellows consider themselves their own gods, I wonder?"

"That is a very relevant question."

There was a disturbance in the palace court. It was a noise that had not been heard in the kingdom for decades. Gemariah laid down his wax tablet and looked questioningly at the prophet. "Nabi?" he ventured. "Something is happening at the palace."

Jeremiah finally looked up, cocked his head, and then shrugged. The palace court was full of activity, but heaven, through the vessel of the prophet, was silent. Jeremiah turned his attention back to his scroll.

Resigned, Gemariah picked up his tablet again. Whatever was happening, Jeremiah wasn't concerned. They both went back to work; unaware of Judah's forces assembling beyond the northern walls of the city.

CHAPTER 8

A Messenger

The Philistine Coast

The blue haze in the air and the crystal clarity of the azure waters of the Great Sea cast an aura of mystery about the environs. Gaza's origins were lost in the mists of time. Ruled a millennium before by Egypt, it was as ancient as any city on Earth. Rising and falling, only to be rebuilt anew, Gaza had been ruled by many different people, but for almost the past 100 years, it had become Egyptian territory once more—a gift from the Assyrians.[1]

Ra had not yet reached his zenith as the people of Gaza threw the city gates open wide and spread flowers and palm branches to welcome their new pharaoh. "Wahemibre! Horus Necho, son of Osiris Psammetik! Son of Ra! Living One! Beloved Son of Isis!" Hundreds—yelling and screaming—strained to push their way through to catch a glimpse of the most recent god to be added to Egypt's pantheon. A woman, shrieking in excitement, pushed her way past the soldiers and touched the sleek Egyptian chariot, then she sank to the ground sobbing, overcome with emotion. The pharaoh's perfectly formed face glowed with pleasure. Necho looked—every bit of him—to be a god incarnate to the adoring citizens of Gaza.

The pharaoh laughed, reveling in the crowd's worship as they showered him with flowers and petals in true Egyptian fashion. The people of Gaza knew Egyptian customs as well as they knew their own. The son of Ra found it very refreshing. "They sing from the heart," he yelled into the ear of his chariot driver.

The charioteer looked askance at him.

Necho knew the man well and understood the unspoken question. "No, we cannot stay to enjoy their homage. The men are tired, but one pigeon can fly farther and faster than the best horse can run and King Josiah almost certainly keeps Babylonian pigeons. He will already know of our arrival here, and very soon Babylon will know too. We cannot delay. The ships are already in the harbor, waiting for our arrival. We will restock and push on at Ra's awakening tomorrow. We must take Carchemish before Babylon can send reinforcements."

The ten ships anchored in the harbor held two hundred men each; two thousand Lydian, Greek and Philistine mercenaries, all under the command of Admiral Kaelus of Gaza. They would follow along until they reached the coast north of Mount Carmel, where they would disembark to march with the army through the Valley of Jezreel to Meggido and beyond.

A few small boats ferried back and forth, provisioning the ships.

One hundred huge Lydian war dogs patrolled the decks. They strained at their leashes, pulling their handlers forward as they barked and snapped viciously at each other and anyone else who came too close. Their snarls and growls competed with the music and shouts of the crowds.

The cacophony grew when the citizens of the city recognized Admiral Kaelus, their favored son, as he stepped out of one of the dinghies and they welcomed him home. The admiral waved, grinned, and trotted forward to meet the pharaoh.

Necho meant what he said. The Egyptians stayed only a day—just enough time to restock the army. As the chariot of Ra appeared in the east, the army assembled outside the city and made ready to march. The people of Gaza stood in the streets and wailed that their new god-king was leaving them so soon.

Necho shook his bald head as he hopped up into the flower-bedecked chariot. He gave his driver a lopsided grin. "I do believe their disappointment is real." He set the Chepresh war helm in place and braced himself. The driver flicked the reins, and the sleek black team jumped forward, then settled into their paces.

"Did the good god doubt it? The heavens smile down upon Isis's favorite, and so they smile down on all who surround him. Of course, they want that one to stay."

The chariot moved out of Gaza's main gate, and the pharaoh held his spear horizontally high above his head in a salute to the faithful of Gaza. A rolling, thunderous shout rose from thousands of Philistine throats and rocked the ground in answer. Necho laughed, shifted his grip on the spear and pointed its tip north. The blacks extended their stride to a canter, and the units and divisions of the army of the Two Lands settled in place behind the newest Son of Ra with strict order and discipline that was so in contrast to the chaos of the city the day previous.

Two days hard march up the coast brought the army of Egypt to the small strip of land north of Mount Carmel which divided Samaria from northern Philistia on the west and Philistia from Syria on the east. There was no way inland from the coast without passing through the Valley of Jezreel and over the Megiddo Pass. This didn't matter because the Samaritans were leaderless. The City of Jezreel was a shadow of its former glory, and the town of Megiddo wasn't even walled. They would cause no trouble.

The breeze off the Great Sea swirled dust around the pharaoh as the troops halted and started to prepare to camp. The ships came to anchor in the blue-green waters and began to disembark.

Necho hopped down out of his chariot and surveyed the road before them. His driver also got down and took the heads of the team. Then he froze, staring down the road. Necho followed his gaze.

There, in the middle of the road that led to the Megiddo Pass, stood a solitary figure, dressed in brown horsehair with a leather belt and sandals. No one had seen him an instant before. Where had he come from?

The army ceased their activity and grew still, stirring uneasily.

"A strange border guard to meet the good god," The driver's voice shook.

Necho felt an inexplicable chill run up his spine. His driver was right. There was something about this peasant that was not quite… well, natural. All the host felt it.

The King of Egypt took a deep breath and hardened himself to turn around and ignore the stranger.

He couldn't do it.

Angrily, he shook his head at his own indecision. It was ridiculous. What was he afraid of? One unarmed man in the middle of nowhere? He was a king at the head of his army!

He was a man quaking in his sandals.

The figure stared at him, and the pharaoh had the impression of large, dark, unblinking eyes under sandy-brown hair. It was uncanny. Necho had heard of the strange God of this place and of His messengers, holy men, dressed in hairy garments, who performed great miracles. Egypt's histories were full of the stories, who hadn't heard them? His nervousness grew. Just looking at the silent figure before him, pharaoh was certain that this was one of their prophets. What was that to him? He was a god! Why should he care about a lowly prophet? He had only to give the word, and the man would be pinned to the ground by a hundred spears.

Instead, by some compulsion, he found himself walking forward to meet the apparition. His officers and troops watched in consternation, but would not think of gainsaying their god. The pharaoh stopped before the holy man and stood there nervously. He opened his mouth, but it was so dry, he found he was unable to speak.

Surprisingly, the man nodded and gave him a half-smile. "You are right to come to the Lord in humility. It is He who has given you your office, and it is His right to do with all as He wishes, even with pharaoh."

Necho stared. This Samaritan spoke High Egyptian like he had been born in Sais itself, but he observed none of the etiquette necessary in addressing a pharaoh. He neither kissed the earth, nor addressed him in the third person, and his only hint of praise was an acknowledgment of Necho's humility of all things!

The messenger never paused. "The God of heaven and earth has decreed that you should march at this time. He commands you to make no delay, but to hurry on to the task appointed you. If any should stand in your way, this is the warning that you must give them, that God is with you and they must not oppose you or they will be opposing Him."

The air shimmered as if in a heat wave and the figure of the prophet undulated, then slipped into the wave and vanished as if it were the most natural thing in the world. Necho, Pharaoh of the Two Lands, stood in open-mouthed astonishment. One moment, the man had stood right there in front of him, the next, he was gone. Somewhere in the back of his mind, it registered that the coastal breeze was too cool for heat waves.

It was a credit to the discipline of the Egyptian army that they didn't bolt on the spot. It had been a long day, but despite their weariness, their training held.

Necho and his driver jumped back into the chariot. Tired or no, they continued on their way as quickly as possible, for it was certain that no man would camp in *that* place.

CHAPTER 9

The Death of Peace

The Megiddo Pass, Samaria

he King of Judah sat on his portable throne. Behind him, the army of Judah blocked the entrance to the Megiddo Pass. Josiah was flanked by his two oldest sons, Johanan, son of Hamutel and Eliakim, son of Zebidah. Both had the short, stocky build and coloring of their father.[1] Behind them stood Josiah's interpreter, his recorder, the two generals of Judah and a royal guard of seven.

The Kishon River flowed from the hills behind them. Calm and serene, it rolled past the army of Judah, past the king and his party, sparkling in the sun as it streamed on past the invading Egyptian host on its way to the Great Sea. It didn't care that the way it carved through the mountains was soon to be the route traveled by unwelcome foreign idolaters.

The two young princes were both twenty-five, not quite fifteen years younger than the king himself, and they had never before ridden with an army.

Neither had Josiah. Though the son of Amon was identified with David, David had been a man of war and Josiah knew that he was supposed to be a man of peace, like David's son, Solomon. Yet here he was now, with his sons, facing the road from the coast at the head of the host of Judah.

The faith the young men placed in their father seemed unwavering. Proudly arrayed in plate armor, they stood next to their father's throne and watched with great interest—rather than fear—as a small band of Egyptian chariots mounted the road at a rapid trot. Behind and below these, far broader than the narrow entrance to the pass, the entire Egyptian host was arrayed by its divisions and units.

The contingent, three sleek teams, arrived and pulled to a stop.

Josiah motioned for the Egyptians to come forward.

Two men stepped down from their chariots, leaving their drivers. The spearman of the third chariot remained, his hand on his weapon. The two emissaries came forward and prostrated themselves before the throne.

"Rise and speak," Josiah allowed them, his translator quickly interpreting.

Both men were courtiers, and they gracefully rose to their feet. One stood forward. "We bring greetings to our fellow sovereign, the great King Josiah, Ruler in righteousness, Shepherd of Judah, from Necho, Son of the Nile, Pharaoh of Upper Egypt and Pharaoh of Lower Egypt, Great Chieftain of the West, mighty in battle."

Josiah tapped his foot impatiently, but he did notice that the messenger was careful not to use any of Necho's more offensive claims to divinity. He nodded for the messenger to proceed.

"What quarrel is there between you and me, King of Judah? It is not against you that I have come. I march against Babylon. A messenger of the Lord, who is your God, stood before me in front of my entire army and bade me hurry on my way. Do not oppose me, son of Amon, or you will be opposing your God, Who is with me. He will destroy you."[2] The messenger glanced nervously at the king, and he and his fellow prostrated themselves once more, waiting for the reply.

It was too much. Josiah went into a rage. "Does a heathen dare presume to declare the will of the Most High?" he exploded. "If the King of Heaven had something to say, wouldn't He have said it to me and not pharaoh? The King of Egypt is worse than any other idolater on earth because he makes himself out to be a god. Why should I listen to *him?* You go tell that treacherous jackal that he shall not lay a single Egyptian sandal on land that is consecrated to the Lord.[3] Nor will I allow him access to this pass to betray Nabopolassar, who is Necho's liege lord and emperor. Heaven itself is witness that pharaoh has signed a treaty with Babylon." He turned to his guard. "Throw these traitorous dogs out of our presence!"

Josiah's sons aided the guards in scooping up the messengers and roughly returning them to their chariots. With a slap on the rumps of the teams of horses, they were sent speeding down the road, back the way they had come.

Josiah stood and stalked back and forth in front of the throne, struggling to regain his composure. Johanan and Eliakim exchanged glances. Josiah didn't believe the emissary, but suddenly, the princes didn't seem so sure. The king was disappointed in them.

Josiah abruptly stopped pacing. "Call the troops to order," he commanded General Kareah. "Pharaoh will arrive very soon now."

"Pharaoh will be out for your head after such an affront, My King," the general cautioned.

Josiah looked at the man and shook his head, denying the suggestion. "He goes against the Lord. He should be looking after his own head."

Kareah shifted his weight, uneasily. "Majesty, please. Don't give him an easy target. Let others..."

Josiah sank back down on the throne. "No! I will not stay behind while my sons lead my men in battle."

Kareah nodded wearily. "As you will. But don't go dressed like that. Don't wear your crown. Shed your plate armor for scale. Wear no cloak. Don't take your own chariot or raise your banner."

The king frowned, irritated. "You want me to go disguised? The men need to see their king!"

"But pharaoh does not. And all of the men of Judah would know their king even if he were dressed in beggar's rags. Please," Kareah begged him. "If you must go, please do this, My King."

Josiah thought about it. Ben Nathan was a soldier. He followed orders. He had never asked him for anything before yet he was pleading now. "Did Shaphan ask you to do this?"

The general's eyes fell, avoiding the sovereign's searching gaze. "Yes, Majesty."

Unexpectedly, Josiah chuckled. Warmth of affection for the secretary came over him. "Well, it doesn't pay to irritate my prime minister. We might as well humor him. Go ahead. Send for the uniform and chariot."

"They have been made ready, and they wait, just behind the crest of the pass, My King."

"Then you had better make sure that my sons are similarly disguised." Despite his acquiescence—as he stripped off his gilded chest plate and replaced it with a captain's helm and scaled mail—Josiah viewed his own disguise with derision.

From the distance, from just over the summit of the pass, came the rumbling thunder of an army on the march.

Josiah watched his driver furl his banner and lay it carefully beside the throne, out of the way.

The sound of shouted orders in a foreign tongue drifted down the slopes.

The army of Judah came to order. Nervous snorts and grunts mixed with the champing of bits and stamping of hooves. Uneasy shifting of feet mixed with the dull metallic sounds of swords, spears, and shields being readied.

Josiah finally admitted it to himself. If he had been sure that his actions were in accordance with his Lord's will, he would never have allowed even Shaphan to talk him into disguising himself this way. It was shameful, cowardly. Hardening himself, he put such thoughts aside. Mounting the chariot of an officer, the king spread his troops out to stand against pharaoh.

The troops of Egypt trotted up the first hill of the Megiddo Pass.

The army of Judah waited for them on the narrow road and spread out on the slopes of both sides.

The chariots of Egypt accelerated to a gallop.

The sound of the oncoming forces was now loud enough that Judah's officers, holding the eastern mouth of the pass, had to raise their voices to be heard.

Prince Eliakim took up his position on the northern slope beside his brother, Johanan. He was not happy at being relegated to an ordinary captain's chariot, but there, across the narrow valley was his father, the king himself, also in a lowly captain's chariot. He noticed his brother was also watching the king in his undistinguished disguise. "It's shameful," Eliakim leaned over the side of his chariot wall and addressed Johanan. "A king is a king. He should act like one. War is no time for cowardice."

Johanan was scandalized. "How can you say that? The king is following the advice of the generals and the prime minister. Egypt greatly outnumbers us. This is merely prudence."

"Well, look there," Eliakim pointed at the head of the approaching army. The heroic figure of the handsome pharaoh stood tall and proud in this brightly colored-chariot, leading his troops with flowers and petals flying off everywhere. "Necho will be first into battle. He makes himself a target, and shows his troops what courage is!"

Necho was crowned in warrior blue and wore an enormous golden collar which gleamed in the morning sun across his bare chest. His coal-black prancing horses were covered in blue sheets embroidered with golden sun disks. Huge blue and gold dyed ostrich plumes waved over the tops of their arched necks. The horses, the chariot, and even the quivers and spear sheaths strapped to its side were covered with wreaths of flowers.

"Have you ever seen anything quite that splendid? Look at him. That is a king! No wonder his people think he's a god."

"That is our enemy!" Johanan was incensed.

"He doesn't want to be. That was our father's decision."

"He is a traitor!"

"Not to us." Eliakim shook his head.

"He is a traitor in the sight of the Lord of Hosts!"

"Has the Lord asked us to enforce His will on the nations? Necho's quarrel is with Nabopolassar. We should have stayed out of it."

Johanan glared at his brother, then spoke in his driver's ear. A moment later, his chariot wheeled away to a point further down the line.

Eliakim clucked his disapproval as he watched his brother go. Then he reached down, pulled a spear from its sheath on the side of his chariot, tested it for balance and nodded to his driver that he was ready.

The trumpets of Egypt blew the charge, and the teams of Egypt's horses flattened out in a dead run. The hands of the captains of the Two Lands fell in unison, and the arrows of the archers of Egypt flew high. The volley outstripped the surging chariot core, overshadowing the road. It flew up the two slopes of the pass as well. Deadly, beautiful and swift they hung suspended for what seemed an eternity against the brilliant blue of the sky—silent lightning above the thundering onslaught that bore down on Judah's defenders.

Kareah's archers, positioned before the Judean forces, dropped to one knee and fired low, straight at the chests of the oncoming charge and many of the Egyptian teams dropped, bedlam breaking out everywhere, but Necho and his officers kept coming.

Then the Egyptian missiles fell, slamming into hundreds of Judean shields. Some found their mark and many more men and horses went down, wounded or dead.

Eliakim screamed a war cry as his driver released his team to plunge down the slope, past the Judean archers and straight at the oncoming forces.

The war dogs of Lydia, terrifying in their agile swiftness, launched themselves at the Judeans.[4] Dozens of men fell under their snarling attack. Some of the dogs went down too, with sharp bronze knives between their ribs. Eliakim speared one of them. King Josiah regularly held wild boar hunts to rid the country of the unclean animals. This wasn't that different. The dogs were filthy too, but they were taller and faster.

Shields over their heads, knives and short swords in hand, the Judean foot soldiers surged forward and the two armies collided.

The prince jabbed at an Egyptian chariot driver, and the man fell backward out of the vehicle. Eliakim's driver wielded his shield, turning the spear of the opposing chariot's warrior as the team plunged past, directionless.

Screams of men and animals filled the air, mixing with wild war cries, it was the auditory equivalent of the choking dust being churned up by feet, hooves, and paws. Eliakim noticed a big brindle dog standing—splay-legged and panting—in the midst of the fray. It looked around, confused at just who was to be its target in all the chaos. It located its handler and bounded back to him. The handler, riding astride, had outraced the core of the Egyptian army. He searched the fray for a new target, and dispatched the animal towards the rear of a chariot of a Judean captain… Johanan's chariot! It was behind him; Johanan would not notice it!

Eliakim dispatched the dog's handler with his spear, but the animal only had eyes for its new objective. Well-trained, the war dog obviously knew that a chariot's weakest point was the hind-legs of the team that pulled it. The dog raced past the chariot and before Johanan could react to its presence, it latched onto the horse on the right, hamstringing it. The horse fouled its traces and went down, dragging its teammate around sideways.

Eliakim's driver had seen the gigantic dog launch itself at Johanan's chariot and he pulled his team's heads around and headed straight towards the encounter. Eliakim watched in horror as Johanan's left horse caught his feet in his teammate's tangled traces and somersaulted. The light-weight chariot flipped over the horses' backs to land upside down, pinning the crown prince and his driver, underneath.

Just then, another captain's chariot came racing up. It was the king. Josiah had apparently seen Johanan's predicament. The king's team swung violently to the left to avoid a collision with the inverted chariot, and his own vehicle careened wildly on one wheel. Josiah's driver was tossed out, and the team of blacks raced on. "Johanan! Johanan!" Josiah cried out in panic, leaning over the leather-padded rail of his unguided chariot. The king scrambled to grab the team's reins and turn them around.

Eliakim's driver pulled up beside Johanan's mangled chariot. Eliakim and the driver jumped out. The driver ran to cut the traces, releasing the struggling team, one of which ran off, while the other tried to regain its feet. It could only straighten its front legs; its rear legs were useless. The driver slit its throat.

Eliakim, with a massive effort, pushed the chariot up off its occupants, and then just stared. Johanan's driver struggled to sit up, but Johanan was beyond mortal help. Eliakim's driver shook his head and wrapped his arms around his master, trying to pull the prince back to his own chariot.

Eliakim struggled against him. "No! I'm not leaving him! Johanan, wake up!"

Kareah's chariot suddenly appeared, and the general jumped down. He grabbed the prince and together with Eliakim's driver, they manhandled him into his chariot. "I'll take care of your brother," Kareah shouted at him. "Get back in your chariot and head for the rear of the lines. We need to protect you now!"

"Are you crazy?" Eliakim was wild with grief and tried to jump back to the ground, but already his driver had launched the team forward, and he found himself gripping the side rail instead. "Johanan needs help! Stop! Go back!"

But the driver ignored him.

Eliakim almost jumped out even though the chariot was racing at breakneck speed. But to be alone, on the ground, in this madness? A dog flew through the air and brought a footsoldier down by the throat. No, the ground was no place to be.

Egypt's archers just had time for a second volley before their own chariots would be compromised.

Eliakim, facing backward in his chariot as he yearned to jump out, saw his father. Josiah's team was plunging head-on underneath the rain of deadly missiles. The arrows arrived just as Josiah got control of his team. With no driver, the king had no shield, and suddenly, he was struck. Eliakim stared in disbelief, then screamed, "NO! THE KING!" He turned on his driver. "Go back! The King is wounded!" How could this be happening?

Eliakim's driver turned a shocked face to the prince and began to pull the team up.

Panicking, Eliakim turned back to the impossible scene he was being forced to witness.

A Judean charioteer launched himself from his vehicle as it raced by, grabbed the reins of the king's team, and hanging around one of the team's necks, pulled them to a halt.

Josiah fell backward out of the chariot to the ground. The battle swirled around them as the Egyptian chariots arrived and the scene was lost to view.

Eliakim's chariot finally made it back to the site of the disaster. Josiah was trying to sit up, but medics had already arrived, and they pushed the king back down to the ground and began to work on him, gently removing his armor.

Eliakim jumped out of his chariot. He stood still, wide-eyed and disbelieving at the sight of his father lying in the mud gasping, with two arrows still protruding from his chest. The guard was forming a perimeter around them, keeping the battle at bay. Eliakim looked wildly around. Through the fray, he spotted General Kareah cradling Johanan's limp body in despair. It was a total catastrophe! The prince gave an inarticulate cry and spun around. This had to stop! It had to stop, now!

His royal training kicked in, and he got hold of himself. He looked around again, this time to decide a course of action.

There! There was the pharaoh!

Eliakim's driver had dismounted and was looking to see if he could be of any help to the king, but Eliakim did not wait for him to come back. He grabbed a soldier's long, oblong shield, jumped up in the chariot and sent the team careening wildly in the direction of the pharaoh, yelling like a madman to gain the attention of the Son of Ra. He actually managed to get close enough to be noticed.

"Pharaoh! Pharaoh!" he yelled. Then he held the shield above his head and threw it to the ground in surrender. He pulled the team to a stop.

Necho, who had been about to loose an arrow in his direction, lowered his bow and stared at him. Then he tapped his driver on the shoulder, and his team slid to a stop. Necho frowned as he stared at what he took to be a Judean captain. Then his frown deepened as he looked around the battlefield. The pharaoh was clearly wondering where King Josiah was and whether this wild-eyed officer, in his king's absence, could really have the authority to surrender.

Eliakim steadied his nervous team and yelled back at the captains and generals of the Judeans. "Stop! Stop!" Then he jumped out of his chariot and prostrated himself before the pharaoh as the trumpets of Judah sounded.[5]

Obeying the order of their prince, the Judeans stopped fighting and began to lay down their weapons.

Eliakim, prostrate on the ground, looked back and caught sight of Josiah's royal chariot. They led it from outside the battlegrounds, and now they were gently laying the Judean king on its bed. He was alive, but hardly moving.

The pharaoh saw it too and seemed to understand. Necho nodded at the prince, then he grabbed a spear and his driver's shield and clashed the two together above his head. The horns of Egypt echoed the Judeans' silver trumpets, and the Egyptians stood down.

The battle was over.

Necho signaled toward the prostrate figure before him, and immediately two soldiers pulled the Judean "captain" to his feet and stood him before the pharaoh.

"Who are you?" Necho demanded in Hebrew. Necho had studied many languages. He could even speak some Greek and was fluent in Assyrian Aramaic.

"Eliakim ben Josiah, Prince of Judah," Eliakim answered.

"Your father has been wounded. Are you his heir?"

"No, but…." the prince looked behind him. The gesture was desperate. "My brother… I…"

Necho followed Eliakim's gaze to another destroyed chariot and the entourage of officers around it. He shook his head. "Then you are in charge. Get your men out of my way," he said harshly, angry at the waste. "I have an appointment at Carchemish."

He was in charge? Eliakim wrestled with the concept. "Great Pharaoh?"

"I'll see you when I get back—Lord Prince Eliakim." He spoke to his driver, who whirled his fist briefly above his head. The entire host of Egypt fell back in line and began to follow their king as the driver wheeled his chariot around and continued on its way. The army left their few dead but sent their wounded back down the Jezreel Valley toward the ships Eliakim knew waited for them.

The medics of Judah tended their dead and dying as the army of the Two Lands marched by.

Eliakim wanted to sink to the ground and tear his hair and beard, but he didn't dare. The army was watching, and *he* was in charge.

CHAPTER 10

Royal Prophet No More

Jerusalem, Judah

It was the worst day of his life, so far. Jeremiah ben Hilkiah stood just inside the door to Hall of Justice and tried to breathe, but the weight on his chest seemed too great. His gasping caused him physical pain. The prophet had been denying it for two days, ever since word had come by pigeon. How could this be true? It couldn't. It was impossible. He was having a bad dream.

But the pallid face of his beloved king could not be denied. Josiah, quiet and still, was laid on a bier. The bier was set on the dais where the throne normally stood. The slightly smaller bier of Johanan, Josiah's first born and heir, stood on the bottom step.

The room swirled, and Jeremiah staggered sideways a few steps, the result of his hyperventilating. He bumped into an official, who steadied him.

The audience chamber was packed with people. Josiah's family was there. His wife, Hamutel, had lost both her husband and her eldest son. The formidable lady of the court was broken. Distraught, she had collapsed over her son's body. Her face hidden in her hands, she wailed her distress. Her remaining son, Shallum, stood beside her. He tried to console her, while Eliakim and Mattaniah stood by their father's bier. Eliakim was angry, but Mattaniah was numb, staring at nothing.

Nearby were Josiah's adoptive father Shaphan and Shaphan's four sons: Ahikam, Elasah, Gemariah, and Jaazaniah. Besides these, the room was crowded with nobles and common folk too. All were Josiah's legacy, his sheep. But now the shepherd was dead.

Josiah was dead.

Josiah was dead? A wave of anger swept over Jeremiah and banished his despair. The prophet realized the low moaning he heard mingling with the bitter wailing and keening was his own.

A gentle hand was laid on his shoulder. Jeremiah looked up to see Gemariah standing there. The scribe had noted the prophet's distress and detached himself from the rest of his family. He had pushed his way through the crowd and made it to Jeremiah's side. The scribe tightened his grip and led the prophet out of the crowded audience hall into the equally crowded side hallway.

Jeremiah looked down at the shorter man as he followed him out of the throne room. Gemariah was only a few years older than he was and was his close friend and colleague. Gemariah's face was unimaginably sad but controlled. His eyes shimmered with tears, but they did not fall. He was sorrowful, but not despairing, not panicked, not angry.

Not like Jeremiah. The prophet didn't understand.

"Are you going to be all right?" Gemariah asked softly.

Jeremiah could barely hear him above the keening. He shook his head. "No! Of course, I'm not all right, and of course, I'm not going to be all right! None of us are." He was so angry, he spat the words out. He almost couldn't feel the sorrow, now. "The king has gone to his fathers in peace—in peace*time*. He will not see what is to come, but WE WILL! Huldah might have been clearer to say that he would go to his fathers *with* peace!"

Jeremiah shook with the conflicting emotions of anger, sorrow, and fear. "How dare he? He is dead, and now peace is going to die too! Don't you understand? How. *Dare.* He! He was a man of peace! He was responsible for the people, and he was their security! How could he march to war? How could the Lord allow someone like Necho defeat him?" It suddenly occurred to Jeremiah that he was actually more furious with his God than with the dead king, desperately furious.

A single tear finally escaped from Gemariah's eyes and ran down his cheek. "I do understand. Jeremiah, I do. Really. But Josiah was just a man, just like you or I. He could make mistakes, and he paid for this one with his life."

Jeremiah turned and pounded the wall with his fist. "Not like you or I! Not just a man! He was king! He was our security! He paid for his mistake with *our* lives! You don't know," he moaned. "You can't see."

"I know what you have taught me. It's in the Lord's hands. What's done is done." Once more, Gemariah laid his hand on Jeremiah's arm, this time, to stop the outburst. The people passing in the hall gave them a wide berth. "Nabi, Josiah was not our security, the Lord is. The Lord is our deliverance. Josiah was a man. He was bound to die, but the Lord is eternal, and He cares more than you do, Jeremiah."

The prophet glared at the scribe, then he dropped his eyes, ashamed at Gemariah's rebuke. He could see that it was true. Gemariah did understand, but what was important to him at the moment was Jeremiah's distress. "I'm totally selfish, Gemariah. I'm sorry. He was your foster-brother. How do you do it? How are you so… so composed?" The prophet drew a shaky breath that ended in a choked off a sob.

Gemariah smiled quietly, and shrugged, turning his hands upward in a gesture that said plainly: *What can you do?* "My big brother. He always kept Ahikam and Elasah from picking on me while we were growing up." He laughed softly, "They couldn't very well hit the king! Josiah used to come home from the Council with a thousand lessons they'd assigned him, and he'd teach them to me.

"Nabi, I'm composed because Josiah may not be here, but the Lord is. He only asks one thing of me, to be there for you. So, I'm composed because you need me to be. Anything else is too big for me, so I'll let Him take care of it. And Josiah may not be here, but I know where he is, and that's all right too.

"They will choose a new king, and we will continue the work and wait and see."

Jeremiah bit his lip and rubbed his cheek. It was sore from him pulling out his beard by its roots. Gemariah's simple faith shamed him, and he reached out with his spirit. Gemariah was right about one thing, the Lord was still there, and He was concerned for His prophet. His love remained. It always would.

And that will be enough for you.

That was the Voice that made everything all right, it numbed the pain and created a still quiet space inside where he could hide and find solace. Anger was replaced by resignation. "No, My Friend," he answered the scribe, "they will choose a new king, but things will be different now. Gemariah, you have aided me with the Holy Scriptures, but we were both paid by Josiah. It was his work. Mine begins now." He paused. "I'm thirty-years-old. Full ministry begins at thirty. It is time I step into my true calling." Jeremiah snorted, then hugged Gemariah. "Go back to your family. Take up your place in the Council." He released him and turned to push his way into the crowded hallway.

"Nabi, where are you going?"

"To my rooms. To take off these court robes and to pack."

Gemariah frowned. "And then, where are you going?"

"I'm not sure. Maybe Anathoth. Maybe I'll find a room somewhere here in Jerusalem." He raised his arm in farewell and turned to leave.

"Nabi, my father would like to see you," Gemariah called after him. "Could you meet him in the king's offices?"

Jeremiah stopped. "What does Shaphan want? Any questions have already been answered. He knows what is coming."

"Yes, Nabi. You're right. He does know that. He wants to ask you to compose Josiah's laments and to sing them while we lay him to rest."

Jeremiah swallowed. He tried, but he couldn't manage to speak. Instead, he just choked.

Gentle Gemariah stepped forward and wrapped his arms around the prophet.

Jeremiah broke and began to sob into his shoulder.

The scribe just held him and let him cry.

People pushed past in the hall, but many of them were crying too, and few paid the two any attention.

After a few moments, Jeremiah disentangled himself from his friend's arms, wiped the tears from his face and sniffed as he nodded. "Of course, I'll do it. I'll write his laments, and I'll sing them, too. Of course, I will. But Gemariah, it is the last act I will do as the royal prophet. After this, I'm through."

CHAPTER 11

Jehoahaz

Jerusalem, Judah

Zebidah, King Josiah's second wife, held no power--yet. But her son, Eliakim, was Josiah's eldest remaining son. Josiah's named heir was dead. Eliakim was eligible to inherit. He *should* inherit. And then Zebidah would be queen mother and her rival, Queen Hamutel, would be nothing.

"Mother, we should still be by our father's bier," Eliakim objected. "Why have you called us here?" He looked around her living area in exasperation.

Mattaniah, always the more sensitive of the two, poured her a cup of wine from a large alabaster jar on her desk. "Mother, I'm sorry. You must be exhausted. You should rest."

Zebidah took the cup and sipped it delicately. Why couldn't Mattaniah have been the elder? No matter. "Eliakim, you cannot be wasting time playing the good son attending his father. The Seventy will not wait. The times are uncertain and they will want a new king immediately. You are Josiah's eldest remaining son. You must go to them and press your claim. Now! Mattaniah, go with him."

"Mother," Mattaniah began, "it is very dangerous to be king right now. Nabopolassar..."

"Pharaoh Necho is stronger than that Babylonian upstart and he says Eliakim is the rightful heir."

Eliakim laid his hand on Mattaniah's shoulder. "She's right. This is our chance. We must take it. Come on."

Eliakim strode towards the door when it opened before him.

One of the pages of the Seventy stood there. "Prince Eliakim, Prince Mattaniah, you are summoned to the Temple Court to bear witness to the crowning of your brother, Prince Shallum.

"No..." Zebidah whispered and she dropped the cup of wine.

The flames of the great altar curled around Shallum's burnt offering, and the blood of the young bull dripped from the altar's base into the trough surrounding it and down a drain hidden in the tall platform on which it sat. The mouthwatering smell of the burning meat spread to the furthest corners of the Temple Court, and Eliakim's stomach growled. He stood in the crowd and watched, but no one would eat of it, it was a burnt offering and would be completely consumed by the flames. The prince had had nothing to eat since the evening before. This ceremony had better not last too much longer.

"Choose then what name you will take as you become the Servant of the Lord to shepherd his people." Chief Priest Azariah intoned the words as he shook incense from the burner. The smoke curled upward. It was the exact color of the gray streaking through his beard. Azariah was in his fifties and had come out of retirement to become Chief Priest two years previous when his father died. He took his job seriously, and Eliakim had to admit, he was very good at it. This was his first crowning, and the Chief Priest was managing to make it pretty impressive.

Mattaniah, Eliakim's brother, stood by his side. Mattaniah had brought a retinue of palace servants, two bulls and several baskets of bread, both leavened and unleavened. One of the bulls was already gone; only the delicious smell remained.

The Chief Priest, the giant altar with its smoking offering high above and behind him, stood over the prostrate form of Josiah's youngest son, Shallum. But Eliakim, standing in the crowd with his brother, knew the injustice of it all. He knew that he, himself, should have been the one lying there!

A priest took the horn of oil from Azariah and set it back in its stand on a small table which had been moved next to the altar. Eliakim recognized the middle-aged priest as Buzi, the second priest's assistant.

Prince Shallum, lying face-down before the horns of the giant altar, still seemed bewildered at the turn of events and hesitated in answering Azariah's question.

"Say something," Mattaniah hissed under his breath, even though Shallum was too far away to hear. "Do you want them to think you're an idiot?"

"He *is* an idiot!" Eliakim growled. "He's the youngest, so he never had enough imagination to envision the Council choosing him. He's totally unprepared!"

The hastily assembled crowd rustled restlessly at Prince Shallum's hesitation.

"That's not true. He's Hamutel's son. He must have suspected that if something ever happened to Johanan... Besides, it's only been about two hours since the Council called him. He's still..."

"In shock? Yes, I can see that. If you could get to him, you could yank him to his feet and give him a good shake until he comes up with an answer."

"Eliakim! That's our new king!"

"Who doesn't have a name because he isn't ready. How about, Atamukhan?" The Hebrew phrase meant, "Are you ready, yet?" Mattaniah shoved him, but Eliakim barked a short, bitter laugh. "I like the sound of that—King Atamukhan. It sounds like an Egyptian pharaoh!"

"Stop it!" Mattaniah warned.

"Countless petitioners, standing in line forever, waiting for King Are-You-Ready-Yet!"

"Your name?" Azariah repeated the question.

The olive oil from his anointing dripped from Shallum's hair and sparse beard to the pavement, forming little glistening pools. Shallum turned his head slightly and looked at Mattaniah. Mattaniah nodded encouragingly at him.

Shallum turned his attention back to the paving stone. "Jehoahaz," he mumbled.

Mattaniah heaved a sigh of relief, and the crowd cheered.

Eliakim considered the name his brother had given. It meant "God has chosen." But had He? Undoubtedly, the priests had cast lots, and so Shallum was there, in *his* spot. Did the Lord actually have anything to do with it? No. It was pure chance![1] But perhaps he should have seen this coming. The Council had also chosen his father and Josiah had been Amon's youngest son. .And Shallum was outspokenly pro-Babylonian…

Chief Priest Azariah nodded in satisfaction and began the traditional blessing, the prayer of David and Solomon for the coronation. The singers on the Temple Steps played softly as the son of Hilkiah swung an incense burner over Shallum's head, giving the crowd a visual representation of the song he raised on behalf of the new king:

Endow the king with Your justice O God,
the royal son with Your righteousness.

Buzi and a young priest-in-training that Eliakim recognized as Buzi's fourteen-year-old son, Ezekiel, stepped to either side of the Chief Priest and sang the response in a minor harmony:

May he judge Your people in righteousness,
Your afflicted ones with justice.

Azariah took up the next line in his smooth, even baritone and they continued like that, to the end of the psalm.

May the mountains bring prosperity to the people,
The hills the fruit of righteousness.
May he defend the afflicted among the people
And save the children of the needy;
May he crush the oppressor.

Back and forth went the song. Azariah's declaration followed by the lesser priests' affirmation. Eliakim had to admit he was a little intrigued. He had never seen a king-making before. But if it were his crowning, he would hold it in the palace court, on the porch of the chair, above the crowds. More people would be able to see that way.

May he endure for as long as the sun,
As long as the moon, through all generations.
May he be like rain falling on a mown field,
Like showers watering the earth.
In his days, may the righteous flourish and prosperity abound
Until the moon is no more.
May he rule from sea to sea
And from the River to the ends of the earth.
May the desert tribes bow before him
And his enemies lick the dust.
May the Kings of Tarshish and of distant shores bring tribute to him.
May the Kings of Sheba and Seba bring him gifts.
May the kings of all the nations bow down to him and serve him.

Eliakim thought of Pharaoh Necho and laughed to himself. Necho would never bow before King Jehoahaz! But Jehoahaz would certainly bow before him! What would pharaoh think about this development? Hadn't he already recognized Eliakim as the legitimate heir?

For he will deliver the needy who cry out,
The afflicted who have no one to help.
He will take pity on the weak and the needy
And save the needy from death.
He will rescue them from oppression and violence,
For precious is their blood in his sight.
Long may he live!
May gold from Sheba be given him.
May people ever pray for him
And bless him all day long.

Pharaoh Necho was not likely to be pleased, Eliakim convinced himself. But he *should* be informed. He looked over at Mattaniah somberly serious face and felt a twinge of guilt. But whatever happened now, it wouldn't be Eliakim's his fault, the Council and the priests had caused this.

May grain abound throughout the land;
On the tops of the hills may it sway.
May the crops flourish like Lebanon
And thrive like the grass of the field.
May his name endure forever;
May it continue as long as the sun.

No, the name of Jehoahaz was not likely to survive the year, Eliakim thought.

Then all the nations will be blessed through him
for they will call him blessed.
Praise be to the Lord God, the God of Israel,
Who alone does marvelous deeds.
Praise be to His glorious name forever;
may the whole earth be filled with His glory.
Amen!
And Amen![12]

The people shouted "Amen!" and the priest gave the incense burner to the youth, Ezekiel, and raised the new king to his feet.

"Jehoahaz, you are chosen by God to wear the crown." This was the royal crown that David had captured from the Ammonites. It was rich with gems and pearls and set in pure gold. It was hardly ever used except for the most ceremonial of purposes because it weighed an entire kikkar! The heavy crown required a stout back and both of Buzi's strong arms to lift it. Buzi deposited the crown in the Chief Priest's grasp. Shallum planted his feet, and Azariah set it on Shallum's oily brown locks as gently as he could.

The people cheered and clapped their hands, but Azariah held out his arms to quiet them, he was not done. The priest turned back to the king, "Jehoahaz, receive the testimony, the Word of God. By it, you will shepherd Israel, the people of the Lord." A long line of priests, holding the holy scrolls filed before the king. Jehoahaz laid his hands on them one after another.

Azariah nodded in approval and turned to the people. "Children of Israel! I give you your king: Jehoahaz, Anointed of the Lord!"

The silver trumpets sounded, and the people took up the shout: "Long live King Jehoahaz! Long live King Jehoahaz!"

Mattaniah signaled his retinue, and they made their way forward with the second bull and the offerings. In front of the altar, he bobbed his head to his half-brother in and stepped out of the way.

King Jehoahaz laid his right hand on the bull's curly head.

Some of the lesser sacerdotal priests took the baskets of bread. The king took one of each of the loaves and held them high over his head to his God. The priests took the two loaves and mounted the ramps to lay them on top of the burnt offering, to be totally consumed. Jehoahaz gave two other loaves to a priest, who broke them and shared them with his fellows.

Chief Priest Azariah quickly slit the bull's throat. Second Priest Jehoiada and Third Priest Buzi caught the blood in a bronze bucket as the bull gasped and sank to its knees. While the priests ascended the ramp and sprinkled the blood over the entire altar, Azariah and several others of the sons of Aaron butchered the animal, washing the parts in the basins at the foot of the bulls of the Bronze Sea. Quickly, they took the Lord's portion—the fat, kidneys, and a lobe of the liver—to lay atop the loaves to be burned. Then they set aside the priests' portions and laid them on one side of the altar and the people's portions they laid on the other. It was King Jehoahaz's peace offering, and all the people would get a taste of the meat and bread. But that would still take some time, and Eliakim was hungry *now*.

Besides, it was a waste, the prince decided, a total waste of two good bulls, a huge amount of bread, and an entire day. The prince wasn't as well versed in the Law as he should have been, he admitted this to himself, but even he knew that there were no laws prescribing offerings at a king's crowning. Historically, many kings had offered a burnt offering, others a peace offering, and some both, but many had offered nothing at all. If it was *his* crowning, Eliakim assured himself, he would have saved all the time and money involved. God didn't really eat, and the people should go home to fill their own bellies.

Finally, it was over, and that was good. The hour was late, and the new king needed to take his throne before the setting sun declared a new day! The Palace and Temple Guard cleared a path back from the Temple Court, through the New Gate and to the palace and throne room.[3] There, Jehoahaz climbed the twelve lions' steps and took the throne at the very end of the tenth day of the tenth month.[4]

The Levite singers on the Temple Steps lifted their instruments and took up a hymn of praise and thanksgiving. They seemed glad it was over, too.

Prince Eliakim sourly followed his brother, Prince Mattaniah, as they and the crowd filed out of the Temple Court. He stopped short of mounting the palace steps and entering the audience hall, however. Mattaniah didn't seem to notice and continued on, swallowed by the shadows beyond the cavernous doors to the cedar-lined Hall of Justice.

His stomach was now full, and it was time to act, Eliakim decided. The prince glanced around at the Palace Guard standing on the porch and found who he was looking for, Elnathan ben Achbor. Elnathan was his father-in-law, the father of Nehushta, one of Eliakim's wives. More importantly, Elnathan was the grandfather of Eliakim's oldest son, Jeconiah. The prince walked up to the guard and greeted him by laying his right hand on his shoulder. "Shalom, My Father."

Elnathan smiled and laid his hand on Eliakim's shoulder, "Shalom, My Son. It was a good crowning, don't you think?"

Eliakim glowered at him and pointed at the sun as it dipped behind the western wall. "It took too long. And for a moment, I thought Shallum was going to ruin the whole thing."

"When the new king couldn't come up with a suitable name?" Elnathan chuckled. "You would have been nervous, too."

"No, I would have been prepared. I *was* prepared."

Elnathan grew sober. "Except it didn't turn out that way."

"It should have!" Eliakim glanced around to make sure they were not overheard, but no one was paying any attention to them. The guards were hustling about, lighting the evening lamps. The people were hurrying to get home in the fading light. As long as they stayed away from the doors, they were practically inaudible in the bustle of the crowd. "It should have," he repeated. "My Father, even pharaoh recognized that I was the natural choice for the next king. But now, I must take my wives and children and leave the palace. I am no longer the king's son, only his brother."

Elnathan didn't miss the oblique reference to future hardships for his daughter and grandson. He shook his head. "Be careful what you say next, My Son."

"Do I have to say it? You are thinking it, as well. Judah is beholden to Egypt and pharaoh will not be pleased. He should be told."

Elnathan stared hard at Eliakim. "I will have no part in betraying the Lord's Anointed."

"Betrayal? Of course not! He's my brother! But we have surrendered to Egypt. We *are* subject to pharaoh. It is right that we send him a letter detailing these events.

"Besides, a courier does not break the seal of the missive he carries, nor is he responsible for its contents. It is perfectly normal that he would be completely ignorant."

Elnathan shook his head. "The scribe who records the missive would not be ignorant and could bear witness."

Eliakim smiled. "I will draft the letter, myself. I don't need a scribe."[5]

CHAPTER 12

Troops and Mercenaries

North Syria

"*Mólis dýo!*—Only two!"

Pharaoh Necho watched Captain Padisemataui, son of General Raemmaakheru, yelling in Greek, gesturing wildly and holding up two fingers at Admiral Kaelus' men standing on the golden sand of the beach, just north of Mount Carmel. Behind them, Egypt's fleet of ten new trireme battleships, their sails furled, waited at anchor on a calm, blue-green sea.

A slave fastened the royal breastplate across the splendidly muscled chest of the Son of Ra.

Admiral Kaelus, who had come with General Raemmaakheru to have their argument settled, watched the captain and scowled. Necho knew the Admiral didn't like the General or his ambitious young son either, and the sparks that flew when they interacted provided an ongoing source of amusement for the pharaoh.

Necho actually did like Captain Padisemataui. He disagreed with Kaelus in that. Though young, the captain's figure had already begun to spread, and his round face emphasized his bulk. He was an excellent wrestler, and Necho loved Greek wrestling. Besides, the Greeks adored the Captain for both his physique and for his fluency in their tongue. Padisemataui was useful.

"Mólis prin apó dýo tágmata!" Padisemataui bellowed at the mariners.

General Raemmaakheru held land for pharaoh that bordered the small delta town of Pharbaetus, near the Fortress of the Milesians. The Milesians' mother tongue, unlike that of the other nations of Anatolia, was Greek. Padisemataui had grown up surrounded by them and was as fluent in their language as he was in his native Demotic. It was the Milesians that had Hellenized their captain's name to "Potasimto."

"May you and your son wind up on understaffed ships in the middle of a cyclone!" Admiral Kaelus swore at General Raemmaakheru.

Kaelus' sailors were not Milesians, but they were Ionians and Anatolians. They spoke Greek almost as well as their mother tongues, so they understood the young captain's orders quite well. They did understand, the same as they understood their admiral to have ordered half of them back aboard their ships. They also understood that there was a battle being waged between their admiral and the pharaoh's top general regarding this conflict of orders. So, they stood on the shore and milled around in confusion.

"I have already given you half my men!" Kaelus turned to the pharaoh and insisted urgently, "The Good God must know that there are a minimum number of men…"

"Two battalions are adequate," the general interrupted, his tone completely reasonable.

"I am charged with protecting the harbor and the City of Gaza as well as the pharaoh's new fleet. Two battalions barely leave me enough to staff the oars, let alone fight!"

Necho, looking forward to leaving this place and the fiasco with the Judeans, watched the admiral's anger, the general's implacability, and the captain's antics and laughed quietly. "Only two? Only two battalions? General, why are you leaving him with any at all? The ships are at anchor. They have fulfilled their immediate purpose in transporting the Lydian mercenaries here. There will be no navy battles in the immediate future so the triremes can just remain where they are."

The admiral gasped and looked like a cat whose trusted owner had suddenly thrown it in a bath. "General Raemmaakheru honors Neith, Goddess of War, but he slights Wadjwer, who rules the sea!"

"It is natural for the general to favor Neith; her temple is near his land holdings north of Sais. We are Saites, we also honor our goddess.

"But, really Admiral, don't you think you're over cautious? There will be no trouble in Gaza." Necho shot a sideways look at General Raemmaakheru as the pharaoh submitted to his aide's ministrations, standing, legs wide, while the slave laced his intricate sandals up over his perfectly formed calves.

Kaelus shot a stricken look at the pharaoh. The one god had spoken, and he had lost the argument.

The General was magnanimous in his victory. "The army will not miss two battalions. The Admiral must have crews for his ships," he explained, 'because the ships *would* be better protected from storms in Gaza's port than here."

Necho shrugged. "As you will."

The funeral pyres were dying down. The smell permeated the air. At a nod from the General, Captain Potasimto ordered the sailors to begin loading the injured aboard the ships. The companies of the army were forming up. Miscellaneous cargo was stored, and the mules were harnessed. A groom trotted up, pharaoh's coal-black team in hand, and he began hitching them to Necho's golden chariot. Their beautiful blue and gold ostrich plumes danced on their heads, and the two stallions snorted and pawed the ground, eager to be gone.

"The God of this place is with me," Necho pointed out to the admiral. He warily eyed the very spot the mysterious stranger had appeared to him. "You know this. There will be no trouble for Gaza, so two battalions are sufficient. You are dismissed."

Kaelus, First Admiral of Egypt, the first admiral Egypt had ever had, bowed his head submissively and retreated.

The slave gently set the blue war helmet on the pharaoh's head.

Raemmaakheru also bowed low, and the pharaoh turned and stepped up into his chariot beside his driver. The team broke into a canter, and the chariot wheeled away. The pharaoh chuckled and called back over his shoulder at the back of the admiral, *"Mólis dýo!* Only two!"

For three days, the columns marched north, following the Typhon River Valley. The Typhon was not the Nile, and most of the men had never seen its like. The local people called the river Asi—Rebel—because it flowed south to north. Besides, it was a rebel. The Typhon was a rebellious, untamable vixen, playfully teasing, then jumping away, ever moving, dangerous. Its music was a constant soothing background or a roaring, thunderous battlefield, depending on its random moods. The Typhon was a white-water, rushing torrent—unnavigable and useless for irrigation—but its valley provided the only real road through which to move an army.

On the second day, the Egyptians passed right by the narrow road that branched off to their right and wound through the constricted, steep-sided pass to the great city of Damascus. They had no interest in Damascus. Instead, they loyally followed the path the river set for them. The raging Typhon crashed against rocks sending spectacular sprays skywards and drenching the unsuspecting soldiers when they were occasionally forced too close by the enclosing cliffs. The march was invigorating and refreshing, punctuated by shouts of surprise and laughter at the unpredictable river's antics. Down, down, down they descended, accompanying the roaring torrent. The scenic march was easy and beautiful, and the troops' spirits were high.

On the third day since the departure from the Valley of Jezreel, Pharaoh Necho, and his army, made it to northern Syria, to the plain which spread out before the city of Hamath. The Typhon settled down here, like an unruly stallion, unexpectedly curbed and harnessed, bouncing and prancing enthusiastically against the rocks in its bed while waiting impatiently to be released to run wild once more.

The weather was hot and clear, and the sun shone brightly down, but it was not as hot as in Egypt. The army hardly noticed. *Necho* hardly noticed. He stepped down from his chariot and stretched, arching his admirably proportioned torso, his hands clasped high above his regal head.

The pharaoh surveyed the activity as his men set up base camp. A prettier site really couldn't be found. The Typhon Valley was wide and green here. There was plenty of room, and plenty of water, the perfect place to camp and the constant rushing, trickling noise of the river was soothing to the soul. A pleasant, moist breeze from the river blew coolly over his skin, keeping insects at bay. The pharaoh's portable camp-throne magically appeared, and he sank gratefully into it, removing the Chepresh from his shaven pallet. A side table materialized next to his armrest, and he set the crown on it, relishing the fresh air that evaporated the sweat from his head.

On a knoll to the south was a small village, the picturesque but pathetic remnant of all that was left of the once mighty city of Kadesh. The fortress that had defied Pharaoh Rameses II and ended Egypt's war with the Hittites had vanished completely, but Necho knew his history. The Sea People had destroyed it almost six hundred years ago. It was a shame that they had left so little. Necho would have loved to have the opportunity to finish what Rameses the Great couldn't.[1] The village that stood there now didn't even have a wall.

A detachment of soldiers trotted up the hill and began raiding nearby farms for animals and searching the huts for supplies. Most of the inhabitants were noticeably absent.

Necho settled back in his comfortable camp stool. Lazily, he held up a hand. Instantly, his manservant was there. "I'm in the mood for beef," he told him. "And bread and fresh vegetables. And beer!" The pharaoh was well aware that a palm-wood cask had been pulled along in the river all day, keeping it cool.[2] The eunuch bowed and trotted off. The pharaoh sighed. There was nothing to do now but wait for the signal from Ashurubalit, the King Without a Country.

The very next sunrise, the dawning of the first day of the second ten-day of the fifth moon, the signal came.[3] It came in the form of a messenger, a Ninevite scout. Interestingly enough, there was also a Judean captain. But the Ninevite was expected, and he took preference.

The scout, disguised with brush and dirt, took the time to bath in the cool river and don full Ninevite court-dress before he presented himself to the pharaoh. Necho approved. As the Ionians and Egyptians mingled uneasily in the background, the Assyrian messenger prostrated himself before the pharaoh and before General Raemmaakheru, and he delivered his message. "Great Pharaoh, Protector of the Nile, Mighty in battle, I bring greetings to the Good God, Beloved of Hathor-Isis from Ashurubalit, Provider of Ashur, King of the Universe, Servant and Beloved of Sin.

"The situation has changed somewhat since we first laid our plans. The majority of the Scythians have not returned to their homeland. Uvakshatra, King of Media, has granted the barbarians land for a garrison just outside of

Harran. They are encamped there now in large numbers, only three days march from Carchemish for a normal army.

"The mounted Scythians move much faster.

"This action then will have to be as choreographed as a finely tuned dance. We must be fast and overwhelming, or we will fail utterly."

Necho's tan-colored face paled slightly. He wanted to shout at the messenger to stop so that he could ask questions, but no one, not even a pharaoh, interrupted a messenger in the course of his memorized dispatch. Instead, he looked to General Raemmaakheru, who stood at his side.

The general was very still, listening intently.

The pharaoh turned his attention back to the messenger.

"My king wishes to put pharaoh's mind at ease, his plan is well-laid and has had all winter to be set in place. It will move quickly enough. The Assyrian army has skirted Harran with its hated barbarian traitors and by now is just one day's march east and north of Carchemish. The Egyptian army is a day and a half from the target and, therefore, must move first. Today. Carchemish must have men in the surrounding countryside; which by now will realize we are coming. We estimate that pigeons will be dispatched to Harran today. Therefore, if we don't take this formidable fortress within two days, we will be caught outside the walls facing the first onslaught from the Coalition. Our mission will fail.

"Pharaoh must advance then, with all speed to lead his troops east and hold the crossing of the River for the arrival of the Assyrians from the west. The king requests one join him and together we will reclaim the Black Fortress of the River's Cliffs from the Babylonians.

"This will give us a base, and from there, we will also take Harran, the city of King Ashurubalit's god, by dislodging the Medes and the Scythian traitors.

"King Ashurubalit awaits pharaoh's pleasure."

Necho shook his head in dismay at the lack of details. "We are to move today?"

"Immediately, Great Pharaoh," the messenger kept his eyes on the Egyptian's feet as he nodded vigorously.

Necho turned to the general. "But he gives us no plan of action. This fortress has stood six hundred fifty years and never been taken except by surrender usually only following a prolonged siege!"

General Raemmaakheru chewed on his lower lip. "More information could not be sent by messenger. That would be too dangerous. Time constraints dictate that we trust the Assyrian and act as he requests."

"Trust the man who lost the Assyrian Empire?"

"That was his brother," the general corrected cautiously. "This is the former turtan of Assyria, the greatest military tactician of our time. We do as he asks, or we might as well turn around and go home."

Necho drew a deep breath and made up his mind. "Order the troops then." He dismissed the scout with a wave of his hand and turned to the Judean. "And who might you be and just what is your business?" He deliberately spoke Egyptian and let the recorder translate to Hebrew.

The captain nervously bowed to the pharaoh and held out a small papyrus scroll to Necho's recorder. "Pharaoh is wise, and his eyes see all far and wide, but his servant, Eliakim ben Josiah has thought it prudent to send this captain, his father-in-law, to call one's attention to matters as they are unfolding in Egypt's new territory of Judah.

"I am Elnathan ben Achbor, father-in-law and trusted advisor of Prince Eliakim. The message I bring is of great importance and was written by Eliakim's own hand."

Necho held up a hand to stop his scribe from breaking the seal of the letter. He raised an eyebrow and frowned, displeased. "Your master saw fit to prostrate himself before me. Is your status higher than his? Or mine?"

He was well aware that Judeans felt this was idolatry, but he was making a point.

As that was translated, Elnathan reluctantly sank to his knees and prostrated himself before the pharaoh.

For some reason, this made Necho feel magnanimous. He deliberately dismissed all thought about the lapse in etiquette. He said, "You may rise." The Judean, in obvious relief, stood. Pharaoh tilted his head and asked quizzically, "I thought you Judeans crowned your new kings faster than this. Why is Eliakim still only a prince?"

"The prince has explained all in the letter. One's servant is a courier, nothing more, and has no knowledge of the contents of the letter."

Necho waved his hand at the recorder, who broke the seal and began to read.

> *"To Wahemibre, Horus Necho, son of Osiris Psammetik, Pharaoh of the Two Lands, mighty in battle and generous in victory;*
> *From Eliakim, eldest living son of King Josiah, Prince of Judah and designated heir of that land by the word of the favored of Isis."*

The missive was written in Hebrew in a scholarly voice. The pharaoh recalled that his previous encounter with the prince had also been in Hebrew. Eliakim spoke no High Egyptian or Demotic, and he had obviously not wished to trust a translator with this letter's contents. He had written it himself. Necho was beginning to like this princeling more and more.

> *"I am certain that my lord, the pharaoh, has many things to attend to and I am hesitant to mention the distraction of recent events in Jerusalem. Were these minor annoyances or if they merely affected me, I would not. But these actions are contrary to pharaoh's expressed wishes and threaten his very honor. Since my father neglected to designate a second heir, the Great Council of Seventy has taken it upon themselves to choose my brother, Prince Shallum, and anoint him King Jehoahaz. As one knows, Judah now belongs to Egypt by right of conquest, and accordingly, pharaoh has already chosen its new king.*
>
> *"By itself, this is serious enough, but there is another matter of which I must speak. King Jehoahaz does not recognize Egyptian sovereignty. He is thoroughly pro-Babylonian and encourages the people in anti-Egyptian sentiment saying that the Nile is responsible for my father's death and must be held accountable. I have tried to speak with him to point out that it was our father who attacked Ra's chosen, and that the Glory of the Nile actually warned him ahead of time. Moreover, for Judah to continue the war with Egypt would be foolish*

in the extreme. However, I have been passed over by the Council, and to this point, my brother has found no time to speak with me in my disgrace.

"I am greatly concerned for the honor and reputation of pharaoh among his new people, the Judeans, as well as apprehensive for their safety should one return and deal harshly with them. I write today to plead for pharaoh's leniency and his speedy return to set these affairs in order according to his wishes.

"May Ra shine upon his son in all that he does and bring him rapid success in his endeavors so that pharaoh may soon grace us with his presence. May it come to pass that I am allowed the opportunity to show the Lord of Two Lands all the hospitality that Jerusalem has to offer.

"Anxiously awaiting your return, I remain your humble servant, Prince Eliakim."

Necho was silent for a moment, then he looked Elnathan in the eye. "Tell your master we won't be long."

CHAPTER 13

Preparations

Carchemish, North Syria

High up, on its reddish-tan limestone cliffs, the mighty black fortress of Carchemish overlooked breathtaking vistas in all directions. The Citadel had commanded this view for over 650 years. Its ancient road branched off from the Good Crossing Road and wound 300 feet up the southeast side of the mountain to the South Gate. It was still traveled by the same crowds of merchants, farmers, and soldiers that had toiled up it for centuries.

It was the Fortress at the Crossroads of the World.

Carchemish was the undisputed commercial hub which controlled all trade east, west and south. To the north lay only impassable mountains.

The dark and brooding stronghold marked the beginning of the tamed Euphrates. Upstream, the River's two tributaries rushed and tumbled madly through their mountainous routes; but here, the narrow valleys opened. The two torrents combined, slowed, and broadened as they became the River of the Good Crossing.[1] Completely navigable, the Euphrates was the primary commerce route traveling southeast all the way from Carchemish, past Babylon, and on to the Erythaean Sea.

East of the River, the Citadel safeguarded the road which wound through the tortuous foothills of the north. Finally, it came to the great City of Harran. Traveling on, it led straight through the heart of the former Assyrian Empire to Nimrud, capital of the new Babylonian Subkingdom of Assyria.

The stronghold overlooked the Typhon River Valley to the south. The main road, the Good Crossing Road, followed the valley and gave access through Syria to Damascus, Philistia, and Judah. It led all the way to Egypt.

Finally, the fortress also defended the road west, which branched off the main road. It was the only overland route to Ionia—including Lydia—and the Great Sea.

Any army from any nation in the known world, if it marched far enough, marched by Carchemish.

King Nabopolassar of Babylonia described the city as indispensable to the security of the empire and refused to entrust it anyone other than his faithful cupbearer, Belnasir. Belnasir, formerly Rab Shaq of Babylonia, still carried the rank of general, but he was now Commander of Carchemish. At the moment, it was not a position to be envied.

Because an army was marching. *Two* armies were marching. Egypt and Assyria were both defeated, yet they were coming.

Standing at the door to his office in the ancient Hittite palace, the dashing young general dismissed the bevy of scouts and watched them file out as his five captains filed in. Though only in his mid-thirties, Belnasir had been a soldier since his youth and was a master tactician. As such, he was worried. Very worried. He turned to his aide, stationed, as always, next to the door. “Light the signal fires. He handed a wax tablet to him. “Send the pigeons with this message.”

The sun was setting, and the signal fires would soon be quite visible. They would cover the distance to Harran, Nimrud, and Babylon itself with astounding speed. The signal fires meant they were under attack, but they would carry no other information. The pigeons carried the details and would fly until night as the armies were being gathered and equipped. In the morning, the pigeons would continue on but not arrive until the following evening in their respective cities. The armies answering their summons could not possibly march until the day after tomorrow.

Nervously, the officers stepped into the office, and the general firmly closed the door. He turned to face them. Belnasir’s orders and his furrowed brow informed his captains of the gravity of the situation.

Belnasir studied them all for a moment—Dadani, Labashisin, Nuranu, Ibilsin, and Sarili—all were young but tried and true. And they were all he had.

"Commander?" Nuranu pressed. It was still morning, and they had been summoned from their regular daily duties. "Is it Ashurubalit?"

Ashurubalit, last Emperor of the defunct Empire of Assyria, had wintered with the remnants of his army northeast of ruined Nineveh in the Hill Country of the Urartu. Apparently, he had refreshed his ranks enough to march. At least, he had enough men to march with Egypt's support.

Belnasir drew a breath, trying to think of the right answer to that. "It is, but as I'm sure you're aware we've been ready for possible trouble from that quarter since last season. It is not that dethroned pauper that concerns us. It is his friends."

He motioned them all over to the map table and lit the lamp illuminating it. The huge cedar table held a miniaturization in clay depicting Carchemish and the surrounding area in startling detail. "Ashurubalit and the remnants of the old Assyrian army have resurfaced from the Hill Country skirting north of Harran and are headed this way. They have kept to the byways so that they could pass unnoticed and they are barely a day's march east of the River." He pointed at the blue-painted thread of the Euphrates. "But his army is so depleted and under-supplied that it is hardly worth noticing."

"His friends?" Nuranu prompted.

Belnasir nodded and pointed to the south, to Hamath. "The Egyptian army encamped outside Hamath, yesterday afternoon. They are led by the pharaoh himself and will be marching on Carchemish by now. They will arrive at our west by Shamash's setting tomorrow night. Lydian mercenaries move with them. The scout bringing us this information crippled two horses to get here with one day's warning."

Belnasir watched the blood drain from the captains' faces until they were as pale as he suspected he was.

"But, but…" Dedani stuttered, "But… Necho has betrayed us? It's been only a few moons since he swore allegiance to Nabopolassar. Nabopolassar holds his daughter! What kind of man would abandon his own child?"

"Gods do it all the time," Belnasir shot a satirical look at the captain. "What about the Lydians? You say their mercenaries have joined with Egypt." Ibilsin interrupted. "Is Alyattes joining the Allies?"

"No, Commander, this can't be!" Dedani looked ready to panic. "Lydia hates Egypt!"

Belnasir gave him a grim smile. "King Gyages, his father, Ardys, and his grandfather, Sadyattes, all hated Egypt. But those kings are dead, and now it is Alyattes who reigns. We do not know him or what he's likely to do. We cannot forget that Lydia is still at war with our ally, Media. But these are only mercenaries, not the Lydian army. My guess is the Lydians still hate Egypt, and Alyattes' reign is too new to risk an unpopular alliance. Yet. So, Alyattes has agreed to Lydian and Carian mercenaries, and they are coming from the south, under Egyptian command. The road to the Great Sea remains clear. But these mercenaries may be a prelude to an alliance to come that would close that road."

Sarili spoke up at last. "Sir, this is Carchemish. We have nothing to fear, this fortress is impregnable, and the Scythians of Harran can be here almost as soon as our enemies."

"You are correct," Belnasir pointed at the tiny encampment of wagons and horses around the little clay model of Harran. "We have lit the fires, and the Scythians will arrive in four days, maybe three. Which is why this makes no sense. We don't know something. What? Because whatever it is, we have very little time to find out and counteract it!"

"The Egyptians are here," he pointed to the southeast. "The Assyrians, here," across the tiny blue-painted Euphrates. "Harran is here. The Scythians will arrive in four days. Commander Mitatti of Harran will also bring major forces, but…"

"The entire army of Harran could make it in five days sir," Sarili pointed out.

"Five days forced march, yes, but they would arrive in no shape to fight. Counting preparations, then, Commander Mitatti cannot possibly arrive with the forces of Harran before six days. The Allies' plan means they think they can take this fortress before four days or they will be caught in the open by the Scythians. How can this be possible? Any ideas?"

"Perhaps their timetable is not so swift," Naranu frowned. "If they are counting on superior numbers to both besiege us and to handle the Scythians and the Medes of Harran by holding them across the Euphrates, then…"

"No, Naranu," Dedani cut him off. "Arbaces, the Glory of Assyria, is in Nimrud, he could be here in a half-moon. Babylon would arrive shortly after. At that point, the Allies will be vastly outnumbered and caught without a base on the open plain. Not only could they never manage a siege under such conditions, but they are also without a viable supply line."

"Which brings us back to the commander's original premise," Sarili observed. He looked Belnasir in the eyes. "You really think they are planning to take Carchemish within four days?

Belnasir studied the tiny city on its tiny mountain. "I think that they are certain they can do it. Their actions make no sense otherwise. So, what are they planning?"

Silence. No one knew.

Belnasir looked out the window. His office was in the old royal palace, and its northern face was part of the city wall. Far, far below the Euphrates flowed past the red cliffs. "Those cliffs are vertical, three hundred feet tall and unscaleable. One or two men might make it, but an army? Carchemish has but two gates," he pointed them out on the clay model then looked up at his captains, "stop me if you see a flaw in our defenses. The Southern Gate on the southwest is our primary entrance. It can be reached only by this narrow winding road that scurries up the hillside directly under the fortress' walls." His finger followed the road, up, up, up it climbed, "Three hundred feet high, a quarter-beru long, and only two wagons wide—at most. It is said that only two children, one with a bow, one with a pot of boiling oil, can defend it from above."

"Commander," Labashisin broke in, speaking for the first time. "It's not there. No one could hope to march an army up that road and have it survive. And it's not at the West Gate either." The captain set his finger on the narrow, convoluted path that zigzagged up the cliffs to run the last eighth of a beru under the city wall itself, a heart-stopping cliff dropping off into nothingness on the other side. "Only one or two persons at a time can approach from this direction. If they mean to do this, then it must be the Water Gate."

Belnasir walked to the east side of the table and peered at the wall that rose from the Euphrates itself. Labashisin was right. The only other potential entrance was the Watergate. It was not a gate for people; it was a gate for the Euphrates.

Next to the Palace of the Citadel was the Temple of Enlil. Once the temple had belonged to Teshub, the Hittites' storm god. A pure white door opened out of the imposing black walls of the temple's north side onto a terraced path. This led down to the pool, the city's water source. The only way to the Citadel from the pool led up a torturous path, wide enough for two people to pass each other, right through the easily defended temple. The bronze bars of the Watergate were welded to a crossbar buried in the mud of the Euphrates' riverbed. The gate was easily defended from the walkways around the pool as well as the wall above. "An assault on the wall or the gate would have to come from the River," he pointed out. "The wall is too tall, and they cannot mount a battering ram on a boat." He thought about it. "To attempt to dig under the bars… It's over twenty feet deep! A very good swimmer could do it, though, and if they were going to try it, now would be the time. It's mid-summer. The water is at its warmest."

"It's still ice-cold," Sarili pointed out. "It's always ice-cold. It's snowmelt."

"No one could stay down there long," Belnasir agreed and shivered at the thought of it. "But if the rewards were great enough, some might attempt it. But it can't be there! Only two men at a time could make it up that path, to be met by a fully staffed battalion in the temple?"

"General," Labashisin cautioned him. "You are, of course, right. It's impossible. But since we don't know what *is* possible…"

"All right. Labashisin, have oil amphorae moved down to the waterside and barricades erected on all the terraces down to the water pool. If anyone should surface inside the Watergate, they'll do it to a wall of flame floating on the water. And post a full battalion at the temple."

Ibilsin straightened up. "Commander, may Marduk grant that you are giving them too much credit and they are fools. In that case, they will all be destroyed once and for all. But we should be cautious and evacuate the civilians. Obviously, we cannot send our people west to Lydia, and it seems that all other evacuation routes but the Euphrates are already cut off. In one day's time, we will be besieged. After that, the Euphrates will be inaccessible as well. If you are correct, and the Allies have some remarkable plan which will let them take this city… Commander, you served with the Assyrians, you know! They are the most ruthless warriors to have ever lived. They'll make an example out of our people. All our families may be dead within a quarter-moon if we don't act now."

Belnasir nodded, horrified at the thought. Carchemish was not just a fortress, it was a city, full of women, children and civilians. "It seems I've been a military officer too long," he swallowed hard. "I too have a wife to think about."

As Commander of Carchemish, Belnasir had finally had some stability come into his life. This posting had let him settle down and marry a young refugee girl from Anatho. His marriage had dashed the hopes of the daughters of all five Chaldean noble houses though many of those still dreamed of accepting a position as his second wife. Belnasir was not interested. Shadushushan was only seventeen, but she was infinitely dear to him.

The emergency session of Belnasir's captains yielded little else but plans for civilian evacuation and was soon dismissed.

Belnasir hurried to the storeroom of the palace. Even now, in the midst of summer, the plain stone bricks kept the large room as dark and cool as underground storage. Palace servants moved in and out, carrying meats and fruits. Some were restacking various commodities. Everyone stopped and stared at the unexpected sight of the commander at the door.

The general looked around, his eyes searching for something appropriate. He found it. A large side niche, full of shelves, was burdened down with wineskins and wooden beer barrels.

Ishtar loved wine.

"I need…" he stopped and thought about it. This would be the most important offering of his life, to this point. "Fifteen." Fifteen was Ishtar's sacred number. "She's the goddess of love, why couldn't her number have been two? That would make more sense," he mumbled to himself. He raised his voice again, "Fifteen! I need fifteen strong men, you and you… and you and you…"

But then several of the servants came forward of their own accord. He had his fifteen men.

"Good. Each of you, take a wineskin and follow me."

None of them said anything, and they all moved to obey, but their looks from one to another clearly asked if the commander had lost his senses. These wineskins were huge, the full body skins of half-grown steers. Fifteen wineskins all but emptied the shelves of the year's supply of wine. Nonetheless, they shouldered their burdens and turned back to Belnasir.[2]

"Well done. Follow me," he said and strode rapidly out of the room and out of the palace doors. Belnasir was their lord. They obeyed.

As Shamash dipped low in the sky, they passed directly under the shadow of the storm god's porch and its massive frieze depicting Teshub. The god wielded lightning while he stood in his chariot, which was pulled by fierce lions. The group didn't slow to admire the artwork. They passed under the triumphal arch and citadel wall into the central part of the city. Unable to stop himself, Belnasir broke into a trot, and the servants, burdened down as they were, followed.

They continued down the broad steps between Kubaba's stone lions and descended the corridor between the fortress wall on their left and the city wall on their right. The corridor's walls were lined with victorious reliefs in black basalt of the long-vanished Hittites. It was an unusual sight, admired by all visitors to the city; but Belnasir had no time for it. Astounded citizens stepped aside to avoid collisions with the general and his band of wine porters. The stone parade of ancient warriors and their conquered trekked up the steps of the basalt frieze as Belnasir, and his entourage hurried down them.

Hittite faces from bygone days, frozen in stone, seemed to mock the former rab shaq as he passed. They knew his mission and laughed at his naiveté. They had seen it before. This city still stood, but the artists who carved them had vanished. Over and over again, the "unconquerable" city had changed hands. Most recently, it had fallen to the Babylonians, but that was only through a non-violent surrender on the part of the Assyrian occupants. To take Carchemish militarily without a prolonged siege was something else entirely. As far as the commander knew, it had never been done. What could the Allies be thinking? Belnasir ignored the mocking images. He was going to do the only thing he could think of. He was going to pray.

By the time the Commander of Carchemish made his way to the lower city, he was running. The panting servants were still in tow. Abruptly, the handsome young general stopped. In front of him was the gleaming marble of what had once been the secondary temple of the city. It was now the very symbol of Carchemish. This temple was smaller than Teshub's. Originally, it had been the abode of the storm god's wife, the goddess Kubaba. Now, thanks to the Assyrians, it belonged to Ishtar.

Belnasir mounted the dark gray basalt steps. They were worn and grooved by thousands of feet and centuries of use. A priestess stood on the platform near the top. She was easily identifiable by her heavily painted face and her sheer and deliberately provocative dress. The priestess oversaw several young women who looked up hopefully as Belnasir approached. These were looking to fulfill their service before they could be married, but their faces fell as they eyed the porters. The commander had not come for one of them!

Before the doors of the sanctuary stood a Chaldean priest. This one was not a servant of the goddess, but rather of Esagila, the holy city located within Babylon. He stayed to make sure that the Chaldeans received their share of the offerings. His embroidered robes depicted the constellations and star charts of his religion. His peculiar, round, flat, hat was only worn by ranking members of the priesthood.[3] This was a trusted emissary from the clergy of Esagila to those of the black fortress, and he beamed at the commander as he spied the fifteen gigantic wineskins.

The palace servants struggled up the steps and gratefully deposited their burdens at the priest's feet. The greedy Chaldean accepted the extravagant offering readily, and stood aside, allowing the commander entrance into the sanctuary and the goddess' presence. The servants shook their heads in bemused wonder at the eccentricities of their general and headed back up to the palace in the citadel.

Ishtar's main audience hall was sheltered in shadows and gave access to a half dozen rooms on each side. Some of them were undoubtedly occupied by young women who were more successful in their endeavors than those still outside on the steps. Belnasir had eyes only for the goddess herself. She stood, tall on the dais, bathed in the pure light of her upraised oil torch. One of Kubaba's lions curled at her feet. Made of dazzlingly white marble, she gleamed in the darkened hall behind her altar. The top of the altar was hidden under piles of offerings, overflowing with precious gifts and her preferred fruit, pomegranates. Ishtar was the patron of Carchemish. The Assyrians had replaced the original basalt statue of the vain goddess Kubaba with her magic mirror and rededicated the temple to Ishtar, giving the city to her. Eight feet tall, the "new" statue was just over a hundred years old. Even without a magic mirror, she still seemed quite proud of herself and was recognizable as both Kubaba and Ishtar. Belnasir would never get used to the old Hittite gods, but Ishtar he understood; mighty goddess of love and war, holy Inanna, the beautiful earth mother. Like the priestess outside, Ishtar's voluptuous figure was thinly veiled in sheer violet linen. Her intricate crown, made of pure gold, was fashioned as a tiny replica of the fortress of Carchemish.[4]

Belnasir crossed the room and prostrated himself on the gleaming marble tiles before the altar.

The priest and the priestess entered the room. The priestess approached and poured out an amphora of myrrh over the goddess' bare feet on Belnasir's behalf. It was a lavish gift, but he had more than paid for it. The priest picked up a lyre from under the altar and sang a brief hymn.

Hear your servant and listen to his prayer.
Look how he sighs, full of sorrow.
In deepest distress and weeping he waits for you!
Show him mercy, My Lady,
Show him pity and be appeased.
Answer him, "You have suffered enough,"
And grant his prayer.[5]

The priest and priestess bowed to the goddess and respectfully backed from the audience hall, leaving the commander to his private supplications.

Who would Ishtar favor, the Babylonian interlopers or the Assyrians who had first given her the city? Did she really care as long as the offerings kept coming? Belnasir spent an entire precious beru in prayer in the hope that the goddess would see fit to preserve her adopted city.

The previous Assyrian commander had doubtless done the same. It hadn't helped him, he fell on his own sword, but though he had deported them, Nabopolassar *had* spared the people. Belnasir knew the Assyrians. He couldn't believe Ashurubalit would be so benevolent.

Night had fallen, and Sin was low in the east when Belnasir rose and went home to his wife for what he suspected was the last time.

It was a nightmare disguised as a perfect morning. Shamash's radiance streamed across the fortress to bathe the sparkling silver river in golden light streaked with red and violet. The breeze was moist, fresh and playful.

And it was happening again.

Shadushushan couldn't believe it, she refused. She hadn't awakened yet and was still dreaming. But no dream was so vivid, so detailed. Every flaw in the basalt wall far above her was enhanced, the sound of every splash and trickle from the river were crystal clear. The waves sprayed as they washed up against dozens of craft, already loaded and floating down the river with the current. The frightened faces of the occupants of the boats etched themselves on her memory forever.

"Shadu!" Xiamara, the girl's mother, took her daughter by the shoulders and shook her. "Shadu! The boat is waiting!"

A round, ox-skin coracle bobbed against the dock, just south of the river crossing. It was a merchant's boat, typically used for shipping goods from Carchemish down the Euphrates to Babylon. Its frame was made of a light-weight wood and was collapsible to allow it to be hauled back upriver on a donkey. Carchemish had held a vast number of such craft. Now, all were pressed into service, and the cargo they held was the city's most valuable assets—its citizens. This boat held its owner, a merchant who was acting as the tillerman; the merchant's donkey, lying curled up on a makeshift pallet by the side of the craft, contentedly eating hay; and five teenaged youths, these were Shadu's brothers and sisters.

Kneeling by the coracle's side, steadying it, was Shadu's father, Binyamin. Binyamin was a colleague of the tillerman. His oxen's wagonloads had been given almost exclusively to the boat's owner to continue their journey down the Euphrates. Now the vessel held Binyamin's family, but his oxen and wagon had to be left behind. The tillerman's family already lived in Babylon itself.

"Shadu, there's no more time" Binyamin yelled at his frantic daughter. "We must go!"

"No! Mother!" The girl wailed, appealing to her other parent. "Where is he?"

"Shadu," Xia coaxed her, "it's time."

"No! This is a dream, a bad dream. Isn't it, Mama? It's a dream, a nightmare. This can't be happening. Not again."

Once before the family had been evacuated, deserting their home in Anatho before the Assyrians arrived. Then the handsome Rab Shaq of Babylonia had appeared and miraculously whisked them away to Babylon into what had been a fairy tale existence for the girl. So, where was he now? "It's a dream, so why can't I wake up?"

"Shadushushan! You're awake! Let's go!"

"WHERE IS HE?"

And then he was there. How he had gotten there without her seeing him didn't matter. She flung her arms around his neck and clung there, sobbing. "Don't. Don't make me go."

He unwrapped her arms and stood back, taking her tear-streaked face in his hands. "Shadu, you must. How can I…" he searched for the words "how can I concentrate on my duties if all I can do is wonder if you are safe?"

"How can I live if you are not with me?"

She broke his heart. She could see it. His eyes shimmered with tears he angrily tried to blink away. She had made the former Second General of All Babylonia cry.

"Shadu, little one," Belnasir said and pulled her close to him again, "I am the commander of this fortress. How can you expect me to put my mind to defending it unless I know you are safe?"

"You would defend it all the harder if I were inside it!"

"And how would your mother and father feel about leaving you behind?" He turned to Xia, "Go, get in the coracle." Her mother nodded and hurried down to the dock where Shadu's siblings waited. Shadu's father, Binyamin, was a veteran and was missing one arm, but with the other, he helped Xia into the rocking vessel.

"Take this," Belnasir said. He detached his royal dagger from his belt. The red ruby eyes in the gilded dragon's head hilt said plainly that this was the dagger of one of the Great Ones, a gift beyond price. It would open the gates of the palace of Babylon, itself. "Keep it safe. It is the symbol of the office my house is founded on, the dagger of a rab shaq. You are my house."

"I don't want it!" Shadu pushed it back at him. "I want you!" She denied her parents, her family waiting by the boat. Her place was with her husband.

"Well, you must!" Belnasir stepped back, took her by the forearms and forced her to look in his face. "You must because I love you!" He shook her, trying to make her understand. "That is why you've got to go."

"Because you don't think the fortress will hold," she said, understanding very well.

He kissed her, softly, tenderly. "I don't know that it will or it won't. Not being sure, this is all I can do." He slipped the dagger beneath her belt.

"And if it doesn't, you won't have to go on without me, but I *will* have to go on without you!" She kissed him back, wildly, desperately. Then she buried her head in his chest, and he cradled her there against him for a long time, not quite willing to let her go. Not yet.

"You're brave. You'll do what has to be done. That's what made me notice you in the first place." He stroked her long, tightly curled hair.

She spoke into his shoulder, breathing in the smell of him. "We met as you evacuated Anatho, and now we say goodbye as you evacuate Carchemish."

He choked on his reply, "I have asked Ishtar that when we greet one another again, there will never be another goodbye. You must go, Shadu."

"I can't."

He must have believed her because he picked her up and carried her over to the boat. She started kicking and screaming as he set her in it.

"No!" She struggled to get out, rocking the boat dangerously. "No! No! NO!"

But her father held her down. "Stop it! Is this the way you want him to remember you? Like a spoiled child who doesn't get her way? He has made you a lady of the Bar Manuti, act like it! Smile for him. Let your courage be your gift, for he will count that smile beyond price and it will make him brave too! This is the way it is, with soldiers. They fight because of their women."

Shadu looked up, stunned. Then she actually saw her father, heard what he was saying and realized he was right. She owed it to Belnasir to be brave, to be the woman he had married.

The boat's master pushed it out into the current, surrounded by dozens of others, just like it, carrying the civilian population of Carchemish to safety.

Shadushushan sniffed and wiped the tears from her cheeks. Then she turned back towards the shore and smiled. "Belnasir!" she called out to husband and lifted her hand towards him. "I'll see you in Babylon!"

"Good-bye, little one! Give my greetings to the queen," he yelled back as the boat gained speed, then he turned and walked back to the fortress. He would not watch her leave him.

The seventeen-year-old girl sank weeping to the floor of the vessel and watched him go until a bend in the river carried him from her sight.[6]

CHAPTER 14

A Betrothal

Bethlehem, Judah

It was hot. The sweltering air withered the suffering olive groves that lined the way. The brilliant summer sun baked the Bethlehem Road until it was as hard and scorching as a pot fresh from the kiln. Daniel's sandals soaked up the heat and transferred it to the soles of his singed feet. He didn't care.

A month had passed since Josiah's death and the period of mourning was over.

Today, Daniel, son of Abda ben Sabaan, was thirteen years old. Today, Daniel was a man. Today, Daniel and his father were journeying outside of Jerusalem to visit their relatives in Bethlehem. It was time to make arrangements for Daniel's future. Despite his suffering feet, the youth strode forward through the stony hills with an eager stride. He was excited at the prospect of seeing his cousins again.

Daniel, Hananiah, Mishael, and Azariah were all close in age. All were descendants of King Hezekiah, with the same dark, reddish-brown hair, but unlike the other three, Daniel was growing tall and lean. All had been tutored at the palace together, though. But that tutoring had ended the year before; and Daniel lived in Jerusalem, not Bethlehem. He rarely saw them now, except on market days, and he was glad for this time to visit.

But it was Mishael's sister, Miriam, who Daniel really longed to see. Miriam was only twelve, but she had been promised to him from the time of her birth. This journey, if all went well, if Miriam were amenable to the arrangement, this journey would see his engagement sealed. Daniel planned to spend the next three years building his own house and working to establish himself financially so that when Miriam turned fifteen, they could be wed. Already, he had a shepherd working for him, over 200 head of sheep, two dogs, and a large lot in a stylish part of the New City.

Bethlehem was not far from Jerusalem, but they still had an hour's walk to cover when Daniel and Abda spotted the hill. It was high, and steep, and covered with scrub grass, but no trees. Several men stood on the hill's level top, laboring to erect a small structure whose use Daniel could only guess at. The men were easily identifiable by the white and black stripes woven into the red fabric of their tunics. All were of the tribe of Levi. These men were priests.

"The Lord forbid," Abda breathed. "So soon?"

"Soon?" Daniel was apprehensive. "Father, what do you mean?"

"They are *showbeb*, apostates!" He wiped the sweat from his receding hairline and shook his head. "The hills have flattened tops because the Canaanites excavated them for Asherah or Baal worship. When our people came, the Levites replaced many of those abominations with their own shrines, but the people largely still used them for pagan worship. King Josiah demanded the people worship at the Temple and removed the sites. They have been bare for many years, but now they are erecting a shrine here again. So soon after Josiah? They dare!"

Daniel was confused. "They're less than an hour from Jerusalem and the Temple. Why would they do this?"

Abda pursed his lips. "My Son, these are not sacerdotal priests, they are Levites, but not the children of Aaron. You have been taught how Joshua spread their cities out among the tribes so all could worship the Highest. The ancestors of these men *never* ministered at the Temple. Then, after centuries, they were ordered by Josiah to come in and serve at the Temple. Perhaps most of them obeyed, but in the Temple hierarchy, they are only lesser priests, tasked with ministering the most menial jobs. In their own shrines, they are in charge; they make the offerings, give the blessings, and keep the gifts! They guide the minds and hearts of the people who come to them. With Josiah gone, they are moving to restore what they have lost. But they will not submit to the Chief

Priest or his guidance. Many may never even have studied the scriptures. These Levites tend to be syncretistic, blending local pagan beliefs with the teachings of the Lord which they have retained. At times, their shrines seem more like those of the Canaanites then holy places to the One True God. *Showbeb!*" He spat on the ground and turned away.

A chill ran up Daniel's spine. If the people would tolerate having their worship so divided, what else would they put up with, perhaps even welcome with open arms? "Why does King Jehoahaz tolerate it?" he asked.

"Let's leave this place," Abda avoided the question. He laid his hands on his tall son's shoulders and turned him back to the south. Daniel and his father hurried past the place as quickly as possible.

About an hour later, they approached the small town of Bethlehem and found Mishael waiting for them by the gate. Mishael was shorter than Daniel, but his laughing, dark brown, almond-shaped eyes were identical. "Peace, cousin!" he shouted and scooped him up in his embrace. "Happy Birthday!" He turned to Abda, laid his hand on Abda's shoulder and said with only slightly more decorum, "Peace, Cousin Abda!"

Mishael skipped ahead of the two visitors, enthusiastically motioning them on. "Hurry up! My mother has made fig cakes and won't let me have one until you have been served first!"

There was another shrine erected inside the village gate, an open-faced shed, white-washed and painted with mysterious symbols. Mishael lowered his head and hurried by, but Daniel stared in horrified fascination at the Levite spiritist seated within.

"A shekel, a shekel for your horoscope!" The priest called out to them. This bore very little resemblance to the worship of the Most High as Daniel knew it.

"Come on!" Mishael hissed, casting a furtive glance at the priest. He pulled on Daniel's robes and urged him on.

"What's a horoscope?" Daniel asked his father looking back over his shoulder as the priest disappeared around a corner.

"Idolatry and witchcraft!" Abda grated. "The Sumerians invented it. They have taken the constellations and movements of the stars and used them for divination."

As Mishael pulled him along, Daniel continued to stare at them, even though he could no longer see the shrine. He had never seen any kind of divination before, but he knew what it was, the art of trying to discern the future without the benefit of asking the Creator of that future. It was a method of attempting to circumvent the Most High, to deny His sovereignty as well as His loving concern for His own people. It suggested that the people would have an easier time looking for advice elsewhere— that the Most High didn't care. That made it a form of idolatry, a terrible abomination, a sin whose penalty under the law was death.

"Surely the king is aware of this?" Daniel asked Mishael.

"He knows," his cousin answered.

They arrived at Mishael's house, larger and more ornate than most the houses in Bethlehem, it was white-washed and had real red tiles for a roof. Mishael's father, who greeted them at the carved wooden door, was very prosperous. "Peace, My Brother—and peace to you too, Young Adon," Shammua said, amiably opening his door wide to allow them to pass.

Shammua was the son of Abda's uncle. That made him a first cousin of Daniel's father, his "brother." Shammua was also the father of Mishael, Miriam, their younger brother Asa, as well as three other girls. Miriam was Daniel's second cousin, which made her a very suitable match.

"Peace to you and to all who dwell here," Abda responded.

"Peace," Daniel echoed.

"Father, they're reading horoscopes in the new shrine," Mishael reported as he shut the door.

"Something must be done and soon," Shammua scowled. "I knew that shrine would be trouble. Judah forgets how jealous her God is, and King Jehoahaz is too new and too green. He has not yet found enough backbone to stand up for what he knows is right." He motioned his guests to be seated on two padded benches.

Abda settled down on one of the benches while Daniel took the other. "The king is weak," Abda observed ruefully. "The people suffer from a lack of teaching. They follow whoever is willing to lead and that does not appear to be the king! Jehoahaz is well aware of the requirements of the faith. If he wishes guidance, he should send for the prophet."

"Jeremiah has resigned his place as the royal prophet." Shammua walked over to a low table which held a wineskin and several beautiful glazed cups. "The new king is still working on establishing his cabinet, and he is young and inexperienced. Once he has had time…"

"Time? Must the Lord take second place to earthly matters? But Jehoahaz is showing himself to be for anything that is Babylonian and against anything that is Egyptian. The people are still angry over Josiah's death and are eager to follow their new king in the only direction that they think will give them revenge. Jehoahaz is exploring any avenue to endear himself to Nabopolassar: even astrology and divination."

Shammua nodded. "You are right. He had better learn fast, or it may go hard with him. But enough politics. Let's speak of more pleasant things. He took the wineskin and poured, passing the cups around. "I believe this is not merely a social call? Who is this tall young man you've brought with you, My Brother?"

Daniel flushed as he accepted a cup and Abda laughed. "What? Don't you recognize my eldest? Then we have been away too long. We must visit more… before my Daniel forgets what your Miriam looks like, eh?"

Daniel's flush turned into a full-fledged blush, but just then he caught sight of a round face framed by long dark hair peeking at him from the opening in the loft just above the ladder. The girl, realizing she had been seen, vanished into the darkness above.

"Miriam! Daniel, I thought you wished to visit Mishael! Sometimes an old man is quite dense. But you are thirteen today, am I right?"

Daniel nodded and grinned.

"Well, *b'hatzlacha!* I am a stupid ostrich, proudly flapping my ridiculously useless wings while forgetting all about my eggs in the earth![1] I not only didn't recognize you for how large you've grown, but I also seem to have forgotten that my own egg has hatched and is growing up too. So, you're thirteen now, eh? Abda, have you come to make an official request?"

Daniel's father chuckled and drained his cup. "I think some things are best kept within the family, don't you?"

Shammua held up a cautioning hand. "Perhaps, perhaps not. The girl is a great help to her mother and doesn't eat overmuch. She would be a serious loss to my household. It could be difficult to recompense. Well, Mishael, go get your sister." The host refilled Abda's cup, then sat down next to him, still holding the wineskin.

Abda snorted, set his cup down on the floor, leaned forward and wagged his finger in Shammua's face. "You old fox. You have four daughters, and you won't actually lose this one for another three years."

Mishael had barely disappeared up the ladder when Miriam descended in his place.

Despite Shammua's claim to be ignorant of the purpose of the visit, the girl was dressed in her finest robe—the royal wine color of Judah—and had evidently been waiting for them. Daniel could see several new gold bracelets, a significant increase in her dowry. Miriam smiled demurely at him and sat down on his bench to his right. She didn't say a word and kept her eyelids lowered, but Daniel could see her dark eyes watching him from beneath her thick lashes.

"There, you see?" Abda observed. "Very grown up."

"Yes, and well behaved too. A treasure." Shammua raised his eyebrows expectantly.

"Well, let's say five ewes." Abda drawled. Daniel's family was royal. They were wealthy. Though neither Abda nor Daniel had ever worked as shepherds, they employed them and owned many flocks of their own. Abda preserved tradition by bartering in sheep.

"Five! F-f-five?" the Bethlehemite sputtered. "For such a flower? She's a jewel without equal, and you know it!" The "jewel" smiled modestly and kept her eyes on her feet. "Eleven. And a ram." He raised his tone on that last and waggled his finger right back in Abda's face in emphasis. Twelve sheep were recognized as a year's wages for the common laborer. It was an outrageous demand, but Hezekiah's descendants were well off.

"This for a girl you didn't even realize was growing up until she came and sat under your nose! Seven and no ram."

"You would rip out a father's heart for a measly seven ewes? Eight and a ram."

"A silly ostrich who didn't even remember he had eggs! Eight and no ram."

"Seven and a ram… and I get to choose the ram."

"Done." Abda smiled broadly and slapped Shammua's hand. He had several fine rams. He didn't care if Shammua chose his best, which he surely would.

Shammua nodded and handed the wineskin to Daniel.

Daniel had not expected the haggling to be settled so abruptly. He looked suspiciously at his father as he took the skin. Had they already come to an agreement on the price and were only observing formalities for appearances? It was a very high price, but knowing his father, probably so. That he had agreed to such a bargain was a great compliment to Miriam, but Abda had always favored the girl.

The whole thing was over so quickly that Daniel still wasn't quite ready. Now that it came down to it, he hesitated. Their families were in agreement, but what if Miriam wasn't? If he offered her the cup and she wouldn't drink, he would never have another chance. But if he didn't, he wouldn't have another chance either. Daniel reached into his pouch and brought out a new cup. It was bronze with a gold lip and had cost more than he could really afford. He had had to sell two ewes to buy it.

He poured the wine into the cup and offered it to Miriam. "Miriam, daughter of Shammua, I... I offer you this cup," he said. She looked up, turned those beautiful eyes on him, and took it. But instead of drinking, she held it and studied his face.

Daniel did not blame her for this. With the cup, he offered her his life and his love; to be her provider, the one she looked to from now on. He was asking her to marry him. If she drank, she accepted his proposal. It was a decision that would shape the rest of her life and Miriam was trying to determine his sincerity. His anxiety must have been evident, for abruptly she grinned impishly at him and drained the vessel.

"Done!" Shammua shouted in triumph and slapped Abda's hand in return. He turned to Miriam. "Now go fetch those fig cakes."

CHAPTER 15

The Fall of Carchemish

Carchemish, North Syria

he Assyrians set camp on the east bank of the Good River Crossing. Belnasir stood on the citadel wall and looked down across the River. Far below, he could make out King Ashurubalit in his chariot wheeling back and forth, urging his troops, commanding his officers, undoubtedly promising them all rewards beyond any they had ever known in Nineveh. Belnasir smiled. This stirring speech should have been made by a general, but Ashurubalit was short on generals. The Assyrians made no move to launch boats as an assault on the River Gate, nor did they attempt to ford the crossing. They just made camp and prepared their supper. Apparently, they were unperturbed by the fact that if they were still there in two days, the Scythians would inevitably crush them. Belnasir walked back down the steps into his palace to attend to his own supper.

That night, inside the impregnable fortress, no one slept. But no one realized that the attack had already begun, either. With the shadows of night obscuring their identities, thirty "soldiers" came together before the Temple of Ishtar and trotted up the stairs together to the eastern wall. No one stopped them. One soldier would have been challenged, but thirty? These men were obviously on official business.

And so they were.

The garrison at Carchemish was primarily made up of Greek and Ionian mercenaries. When Nabopolassar had gifted Carchemish to his former rab shaq, he had left him very few troops; he had needed them for his march on Sais. Belnasir had recruited mercenaries to fill his ranks. The Greeks did their duty and otherwise kept to themselves. They did not mix with the Babylonian officers or troops, for the language barrier was too great. They remained separate, strangers to one another.

Before the evacuation, the marketplace of Carchemish had been full of new merchants—Babylonians, Syrians, Judeans, Philistines, even Medes, and Persians. All were eager to trade at the gateway to the world; all were strangers to each other.

The houses of Carchemish had been full of new citizens, settled by the directive of Babylon and still barely familiar with their own neighbors.

In short, no one, not the military, not the merchants, not the citizens, *no one* in Carchemish really knew anyone else.

In the upheaval of the sudden evacuation, no one noticed anyone else's comings and goings. Thirty merchants, not known to associate with one another, just disappeared. They hadn't been evacuated, and they weren't missed.

The following morning the Egyptians arrived and surrounded the cliffs from the north to the west to the south. Carchemish was besieged. The Allies did not offer surrender terms. They were not predisposed to mercy. Instead, the Assyrians launched boats for an attack on the Water Gate. As most of Belnasir's men rushed up the steps to defend the Citadel, thirty grim defenders on the black eastern wall held their post and stared down the reddish-brown cliffs at the multitude arrayed against them.

Then they simply opened the gate.

One hundred huge Lydian war dogs flew up the road, their mounted handlers right behind them. There were no arrows and no boiling oil to stop them.[1] Well-trained, the dogs neither barked nor growled, but the moment they passed the open gate, they launched themselves at the defenders still in the lower city. This unexpected close combat ruled out spears and arrows. The dogs were skilled in disarming men with swords. Even so, many of the animals died immediately, but there were many more. Climbing over the fallen bodies of their fellows, the dogs created instant chaos and the screams of the wounded filled the square.

From the terraces above the water pool, Belnasir stared across the frigid waters, through the bronze bars of the Watergate and across the broad Euphrates to the boats and rafts of the Assyrian amassed on the other side of the bronze bars. These were anchored just beyond bowshot. From them, swimmers had begun diving under the water only to resurface and then sun themselves on the rafts in the warm sunshine of midsummer.

The oil was ready to be spread across the surface of the pool, should an Assyrian head break the surface on their side of the barrier.

The sudden screams and the clash of arms from the lower city told the commander that he was at the wrong end of the fortress. "This is a ruse!" he yelled to the soldiers around him. "It's the gates! The gates are down!"

Already, through the bronze bars of the Watergate, they could see the Assyrians abandoning the pretense of an assault by way of the river. The boats and rafts were being pulled back to the far shore. With yells of triumph, the Assyrians picked up and ran to ford the shallow river crossing to join with the Egyptians.

At the head of his main force of men, Belnasir rushed down the stairs from the citadel. The marble goddess stood distant and proud, visible through the open doors of her temple. Ishtar was unmoved. Belnasir drew his short sword and gave a wild yell as he attacked a dog handler, hacking him from the back of his horse. Enraged, the dog turned on him, and he skewered it.

Egyptian chariots were already entering the lower city. Desperate defenders, in an effort to regain the gates, were engaged in hand-to-hand combat, swords clanging, shields thudding. The commander looked at the walls and saw the men stationed there had thrown off their helms and were just watching the attackers rush up the road they were supposed to be defending. He recognized none of them. Not one cauldron of boiling oil had been spilled on enemy heads, not one arrow loosed at their onslaught. High up on the wall, Belnasir knew that every one of the real soldiers of the watch lay dead and piled in one of the guard houses.

Badly outnumbered, the defenders were being slaughtered where they stood. Panting heavily, Belnasir looked for some hope, some solution to the situation. There was none.

Though he understood the Assyrians were merciless, at least, they could live a bit longer. "Enough!" he yelled. "Stop!" He held his shield above his head and threw it to the ground in the midst of the mêlée. A group of Assyrians rushed forward and tackled the commander to the ground. His face smashed into the pavement. They snapped chains around his wrists and ankles and pulled him to his feet. The fighting gradually, reluctantly, stopped.

The fortress had fallen, and it was not yet mid-day.

Ashurubalit, last emperor of Assyria, laughed to himself as he hopped down from his massive war chariot in front of the Temple of Ishtar. He was a man in his late forties, but he was as strong as he had ever been, and his men—what was left of them—knew it. More than that, they knew that he was the most brilliant tactician Assyria had ever birthed, and today's battle had once again proved it. Never before, in all of its centuries, had Carchemish fallen without a surrender or a prolonged siege. Even the Egyptians would respect him now.

The garrison's survivors had already been rounded up and were gathered in the courtyard before the temple steps. Only about two hundred remained alive. His men were beginning to pile Coalition dead by the city gate, but Allied dead were laid out respectfully.

"Sharu lu dar! O King, live forever!" A captain approached. Two of his men manhandled a struggling captive between them. Captain Akhiramu, Ashurubalit came up with the name of the officer. Captain Akhiramu was an ambitious man who bore watching, but over and over he was proving himself more than capable for whatever task was put to him. Akhiramu's cousin, Lieutenant Samgunu, pushed the prisoner forward and down on his knees at the king's feet. "The Commander of Carchemish, Great King," Akhiramu explained.

The commander was in his mid-thirties and would have been handsome, were it not for his swollen nose or his two black eyes. The man glared at the king, with only a hint of fear hidden behind his bravado.

"Well, Commander, you should thank me," Ashurubalit said. "You will not live to report this to Nabopolassar." The King of Assyria turned to the captain. "Well done, Captain Akhiramu. Bring him."

The gratified captain followed the king as he strode off toward the Temple of Ishtar. Samgunu drug the unfortunate Babylonian behind. The commander's chains rattled and caught on outcroppings in the ancient rock of the steps as he pulled him up into the temple and he cried out in pain.

From across the courtyard, Pharaoh Necho had observed this interaction. He stepped down out of the spindly little cart that passed for a chariot and followed, a spearman on either side.

King Ashurubalit drew to a halt before Ishtar's marble altar and waited for his Egyptian co-sovereign. Akhiramu and Samgunu threw their struggling captive down upon the stone structure, scattering pomegranates in every direction. Assyrian priests were securing the temple's treasure, but fifteen huge wineskins still lay stacked behind the violet-clad statue of the goddess. Ashurubalit eyed the wineskins. An extravagant gift! He turned back to the commander, guessing that it was he who had made it. Well, Ishtar hadn't listened. The flecked and speckled altar had been designed for love, but Ishtar was also the goddess of war, and the victory offering had to be made. As the King of Assyria, Ashurubalit was Assyria's First Priest. He needed to make the offering himself. He pulled his short sword from its scabbard.

The Babylonian officer continued to try and free himself, but he was unable to wriggle loose. "You may kill me," he gasped, "but in the end, you will fail!" He looked around Ashurubalit to the pharaoh, who had just entered. "Necho, you traitor! Don't you know what will happen to your daughter? Nabopolassar will…"

Ashurubalit thrust his blade down into the man's chest with all his force. Though the Assyrians were known for their cruelty, it was a merciful blow, and the commander died instantly. The king was a military man, and he had always honored bravery. Besides, cruelty was a tool to inspire terror and capitulation; it would have served no purpose here. He pulled his sword free and wiped it on the commander's robes.

The pharaoh walked forward and looked down at the body which sprawled across the altar. Above, the cold stone eyes of the goddess stared sightlessly ahead and the flickering torch she carried grotesquely lit the scene. "Nabopolassar will do what he must, as will we all, Belnasir," Necho answered the corpse. "As will we all."

"Does pharaoh know him?" Ashurubalit asked, surprised. He couldn't imagine how the pharaoh would have been acquainted with the Babylonian Commander of Carchemish.

"Not really," Necho shook his head. "I never actually met him. But when Nabopolassar came to Sais, he did so with a new cupbearer because he had posted his old one to be commander here. That's him. Belnasir, Nabopolassar's former rab shaq."

For an instant, the king just gaped at the pharaoh. Then, outraged, he burst out, "He would have been more valuable alive than dead, then! Why didn't the good god say anything?"

Pharaoh laughed at him. "Well, My Brother, would the goddess have been pleased if you had offered her the second-in-command rather than the commander? Besides, I have been committed to our course since I entertained your ambassador and the emissaries of Alyattes of Lydia. From that point, Nabopolassar was obliged to count me a traitor. You, however, could have backed out on me anytime that the Babylonians took it into their heads to make an agreeable treaty with you. Nabopolassar is known for his preference to negotiate, but he won't be offering any more terms or agreements with anyone after today. Now it's personal, so you may no longer surrender or be tempted to plan any treachery against me. Now, I can trust you. Now, you and your men are as committed as Egypt is. Besides, Belnasir is fitting revenge for my daughter, whom Nabopolassar will certainly kill."

Ashurubalit glared at him and wondered about the consequences if he ran this trusting pharaoh through with the same blade he had just used to kill Belnasir. He gritted his teeth and calmed himself. The emperor was an intelligent and practical man. He had been the greatest general in the world, and he hadn't gotten that post by acting in anger or on impulse! What was done was done, and he needed Egypt. He consoled himself with plans for the day that that would no longer be true and then he turned to Akhiramu. "We will make the most of a bad situation, then. Captain, send the head to Babylon with my compliments, and throw the rest of that mixed-breed Babylonian and Ionian rabble from the wall." The black walls stood on a cliff and towered 300 feet above the river.

Captain Akhiramu turned to his lieutenant, "Get a basket and send that," he gestured, "to Babylon." Then the captain turned and ran to oversee the rest of his king's commands before some other officer could usurp his place.

"What now?" Necho casually asked the King of the Universe. He turned his back on Belnasir's body and walked out to the landing above the steps of the temple. Already, prisoners were being dragged up the broad stairs to the Citadel wall. Ashurubalit followed and stood beside him. "This is a solid city," the pharaoh observed. "She will be a jewel in my crowns. But Harran waits.

"Unless you wish to change your mind? Things change. Since we last made plans, the Scythians have taken up position outside of Harran and will be coming here. They will arrive on the morrow to besiege us unless we march on Harran immediately and cause them to fall back to defend it."

The first of the prisoners was thrown flailing and screaming from the wall. There was a brief pause then a splash. The prisoners still in the courtyard cried out and tried to get up off their knees, but they were quickly beaten back down. The second prisoner turned and twisted on his captors as they attempted to flip him far out. The following thud said he didn't quite make the water. The prisoners in the courtyard began to wail and shout prayers and supplications to the heavens.

"With the Scythians to aid them," Necho continued after a brief pause, "Harran will not be as easily defeated as we had hoped. And Arbaces the Mede will come from Nimrud. Now he will probably stop his march at Harran as well. We will no longer have the superiority of numbers there. It may be some time before we are able to take it. Are you sure that you must have Harran? Carchemish is already ours. It would not be a bad place to establish your new capital."

The King of Assyria was still angry, but there wasn't much he could do about it. He shook his head. "Break their arms and legs before you throw them over!" he yelled at his men. "Then they won't be able to resist!" The command made him feel better. He turned back to the pharaoh. "Carchemish, like Nineveh that was, is Ishtar's. She is the Queen of Heaven and reigned peacefully by the side of Ashur in Nineveh, but Ashur has bowed to Marduk and Assyria must have a king, not a queen, as its patron."

"Carchemish also belongs to Enlil." As Kubaba's temple had been given to Ishtar by the Assyrians, so Teshub's temple had been given to the mightiest of the gods.

"The Most High has Teshub's temple, but he is not the patron of Carchemish. Enlil is no one's patron! He refuses! But my family has deep roots in Harran. I have already established it as a true capital of Assyria. Sin is ancient and mighty. More so than Ishtar, for he is her father. He is also the father of Shamash, and that makes him the head of the Triad of the Sky. King Ashuretililani secretly believed that Sin is greatest—save for Enlil, who is aloof—and that Sin should have been Assyria's god all along! Ashuretililani was my father, and I believed him. Now he has been proven right!"

The prisoners were being thrown over five to six at a time now, and the soldiers were beginning to develop a rhythm to their work.

"No," the king rejected the pharaoh's suggestion, "it cannot be Carchemish! This fortress is not even in Assyria! We must have Harran. So, Carchemish will go to Egypt and belong to the good god, as we have already agreed and we will march on Harran.

"But one should beware. As one has noted, Nabopolassar will take what happened here this day personally. More, pharaoh now blocks the Babylonian's access to the Great Sea. Do not underestimate him. It is necessary that the Son of Ra holds the city well."

Far into the evening of the twentieth day of Ab, the soldiers of the Alliance continued their grisly work. Not one of the defenders of Carchemish lived to tell their story. All were thrown from the height of Carchemish's black basalt-lined walls into the clear waters of the Good River Crossing.[2]

CHAPTER 16

The Priestess of Sin

Harran, Media

"Bel Pihati!" A muscular man in his mid-forties pushed his way through the curtains of the palace library. His dusky blond-colored hair was cropped short to accommodate a battle helm, and his silvery gray eyes were sharp and intelligent. Commander Mitatti curtly dipped his head before the library's sole occupant—the governor of his city. The commander's visit was a courtesy. He did not actually answer to the governors Mitatti was a Mede, and he commanded the military forces of Harran. The commander answered directly to Uvakshatra, King of Media, and no other. But Mitatti was a wise man. He understood that the civilian governor needed to be informed of all military actions that affected his city.

Nabubalatsuikibi, Governor of Harran, was a short, rather stout man in his early fifties. Sitting at a desk with several large tablets, he blinked near-sightedly set down a piece of jewelry he had been contemplating and looked up. He was still pleased when he was addressed as Bel Pihati, for it was a title given to him by Nabopolassar himself. But Suiki was Governor of Harran under Media, not Babylonia. Commander Mitatti's presence was proof of that. "What is it?" he asked.

"Great Lord, Carchemish has fallen."

Suiki blinked again and then pushed aside the tablets and stood. "How is that possible?"

Mitatti shook his head. "I don't know, but the Scythians have turned back and rejoined with my troops. I have ordered them all back to Harran. Carchemish is fallen and there is no more reason to march. The fate of that city is now in higher hands than yours or mine. Accordingly, I have deemed it prudent to concentrate our strength here instead."

"Here?" The news of Carchemish was bad enough, but Mitatti's last statement had terrifying implications. The governor was becoming increasingly alarmed.

"The Egyptians and Assyrians are sure to march this way," Mitatti pointed out patiently, "once they have adequately established their rule over Carchemish."

"How long will that take?"

The commander dropped his eyes for a moment, then he looked hard into the governor's face. "If the city no longer holds any but allied troops, then…"

"Then they will have immediate and complete control."

"Yes."

"So, they will have killed everyone in the city."

"It only makes sense, yes."

"So, they are coming already." Suiki walked to the third-story window of the library and looked out over his city. The peculiar and very distinctive round-domed mud huts were symbolic of the city, the home he had come to love so much. "Carchemish may have fallen, but Harran will stand!" he turned back to the soldier. "Ashurubalit will want this city at any cost. He ruled Assyria from here once, and he intends to do so again. He will be very determined."

"As are we," the commander assured him. "We are King Uvakshatra's westernmost outpost. He means to expand even further west to the Great Sea for the shipping lanes there. We are point for that expansion. Don't worry. This battle has always been inevitable; we are ready for them."

Suiki was worried, anyway. "How long before I must call the workers in from the fields?"

"A quarter-moon, perhaps less."

Reluctantly, the governor nodded. "Then we must harvest all that we can immediately." Luckily, it was late in the Moon of Ululu. Many crops were already ripe for the harvest. But a quarter-moon would only see a fraction of the crops in. He began formulating plans for epitomizing work schedules. "I must make preparations," he murmured, absently. "Thank you for informing me, Commander."

Mitatti briefly squeezed the governor's hand, a symbol of respect and friendship. "Burn what you cannot harvest." He turned and left without another word.

The Bel Pihati of Harran gave his beloved library one last longing look, but there was no more time for reading. He retrieved the piece of jewelry, a necklace, and pushed aside the curtains of the doorway. He trotted down the pink granite steps that never failed to remind him of his old home in Nisibis.

Outside the palace, he followed the boulevard to Ehulhul, the House of Joy. Last year, the Temple of Sin had been sacked by the Scythians. It was still in a state of disrepair, but at least, the doors had been rehung in their places. The pillars propping up the overhang to the porch had been replaced, and Suiki thought they looked sturdy enough, so he walked under the overhang and entered.

Inside, the temple was still stripped. The gold was gone from the damaged under walls, the bronze lamps had been replaced by cheap wooden torches. They smoked. The altar was crudely plastered back together. Its two stone uprights balanced precariously under the cracked and slanting tabletop. A chipped jasper pitcher, filled with wine, perched on one side of the altar and seemed in danger of upending and pouring itself out before the empty dais.

The image of Sin was not there. The emaciated stone god of the crescent moon had been moved to his temple in Ur. From there, he awaited the rebuilding of his home in Harran and not even his throne remained.

But *she* was there.

The votaress, the high priestess of Sin, Addaguppi, half-sister of King Ashurubalit. Tall and beautiful, daughter and sister of kings, she was ageless. Adda defied current fashion and let her long black hair fall uncurled, straight down her back. Her cream-colored robe was elegant in its simplicity, and her large dark eyes stared coldly at Suiki as he entered.

"What does the governor require?" she asked in a severely disapproving tone. She folded her arms across her chest as if she dared him to come one step further into Ehulhul.

Suiki looked down at his own robes; though dyed in vibrant blues and purples, they were slightly crumpled and not exactly clean. He brushed off some crumbs from his breakfast of raisin cakes and then held out the filigreed gold necklace he had brought with him.

The priestess eyed it, noting the dozens of small sapphires worked into the theme. Haughtily, Adda looked back at the governor's face again, ignoring the gift.

The bel pihati walked gingerly forward, skirting the priestess' stiff figure, and carefully laid it out on the altar. "I had it made especially for you, for an offering to the god, for his priestess." He backed up, returning to the appropriate place for a supplicant.

She said nothing.

"I have a petition."

She shrugged and turned away. "Sin is not here. He is in Ur."

"But surely, he hears his priestess, no matter where the stone image of his presence may be! Otherwise, this city is without his protection!"

"Perhaps it is," she acknowledged.

"Then you are no priestess, and that I cannot accept."

Annoyed at the challenge, she pursed her lips and bit back an acidic reply. "Ask," she said finally, half-turning to the altar and tentatively poking at the intricate necklace with one long, delicate finger while still keeping a close, distrusting eye on Suiki.

"Your brother comes and Egypt with him. I entreat the great god Sin for victory in the upcoming battle and ask for blessings on our troops, and for a speedy harvest." He hesitated, unsure how to phrase the rest of his request. "And I must give him thanks for the aid of the Scythians and ask for blessings on them as they fight for us as well," he blurted out.

She gasped and stared at him, dumbfounded.

Suiki understood. She could tolerate prayers against her conceited brother—he was pretty sure she didn't like him. She could endure petitions made for the Mede warriors who now held her city—she had an understanding with King Uvakshatra of Media. But it was no secret that Addaguppi, votaress of the god Sin, hated the Scythians. Not only was she the half-sister of Ashurubalit, who claimed he was the rightful King of Assyria, but she was also the niece and foster-daughter of Harran's last high priest. It was the Scythians who had slaughtered him before his altar when the Coalition took the city. It was the Scythians who, beyond the unspoken norms of civilized society, had defaced Ehulhul, Adda's beloved temple. It was the Scythians who had repeatedly raped her. Only King Nabopolassar's interference had saved the priestess and preserved what was left of Sin's house. Suiki knew she wouldn't be pleased with this request.

"GET OUT!!!" the priestess screamed at the portly little man. He took no offense. It was pretty much the reaction he had expected. But she wasn't finished. "Get out of this house! You defile it further with your outrageous entreaty! May all the gods be praised that Sin is not here to hear it!"

"I am the governor," he replied in his most reasonable tone. "It is my place to ask this, and…" again he didn't know how to say it, so he just said it, "it is your place, Votaress, to offer this prayer."

"Fool!" she cried. "Do you actually think that Sin will be pleased? That he will listen?"

"Lady," he returned, "whether or not he listens is the prerogative of the god. I am merely doing my duty and asking that you do yours."

For a moment, he thought that she was going to strike him. Then, angrily, she scooped up the necklace and poured a bit of wine from the jasper pitcher on the altar. She slammed it back down in its place, and it rocked precariously on its sloped incline, spilling a bit more of its contents and adding to the offering. The priestess turned to the dais, quickly bowed her knee and head before the empty space, then she stood and turned back, glaring at him. "Sin has heard your prayer. May he grant your petition."

"Thank you, Lady," Suiki said gently. "You are very brave and worthy to have been chosen for your office." He smiled at her, turned and left without another word.

In far less than a quarter-moon, word came that the Allies approached. They had arrived in just five days. It was an astonishingly short period of time. The armies approached under smoky skies which obscured the stars and choked the people—almost all the harvest had been burned.

The Scythians sent their wagons north, into the hills.

In the pre-dawn darkness, Commander Mitatti called a strategy meeting with the Scythians, in his tent outside the city. Nabubalatsuikibi wished to just go back to bed and hide there, but he had a servant call for his chariot, instead. Suiki had less experience than he would like in military strategy, he was, and always had been, a civilian. Luckily, Uvakshatra's choice in a military commander was everything he could have wished in that area. Feeling useless, the governor mounted his chariot and went to the meeting.

In the fluttering leather tent, Commander Mitatti was completely at home. Suiki sat on a plush cushion on the ground. In the past few years, he had taken to sitting exclusively on benches, and he wondered how he was going to gracefully rise without asking for help. Mitatti could undoubtedly sit on the ground forever without a hint of stiffness. He was a veteran of many battles, and he was highly respected by everyone. But the commander was standing, at the moment. The flickering oil lamps on the floor cast light upward made the commander appear tall and courageous. His wavering shadow towered above them on the skins of the tent's ceiling. Mitatti walked back and forth in front of the governor, the garrison's officers and the nobility of barbarians as he earnestly set forth his campaign plans. Efficiently, he ordered the troops. Then he tried to talk the Scythians into agreeing to an organized and coordinated defense. The Scythians seemed to be perplexed as to the very notion of defense.

"We are many and much faster than Allies," one of the three chieftains present objected. "If warriors must wait for orders, we not fight as fast. Not as good."

"You are defending a city, not attacking some caravan to just vanish back into the hills. You must hold your lines."

Another of the chieftains shook his head stubbornly. "Warriors not listen. They charge. They fight."

"Only when and where they are told!" Mittati interrupted, slamming his fist into his open palm. "Are you chieftains or not? Are your men warriors or wild asses, charging about where they will?"

The three chieftains rose to their feet, their hands on their battle axes. "Follow Mittati's lead and all the stallions captured are yours," Suiki interposed. The blood of the sleek leggy Assyrian chargers and the unparalleled beauty of the Egyptian steeds were becoming greatly prized by the Scythians for improving the quality of their own mounts. "Promise each of your men a foal on their best mare—but only if they follow commands."

After a brief hesitation, the chieftains sank back on their cushions and grinned.

Commander Mitatti gave Suiki a grim smile of thanks. "Very well, then. You will look to your aids in interpreting my commands so there will be no confusion.

"In conclusion, the Egyptians have left a small occupying force at Carchemish and are leading this campaign with almost their full strength. They are augmented by the Assyrians and by Lydian and Carian mercenaries. King Arbaces of Nimrud will soon arrive for our support. How the battle goes will largely depend on the numbers that each side brings to it. If we haven't enough, we will be besieged.

"The Allies have refreshed themselves at Carchemish's expense and can count on that city for a supply line, but everything considered, this still seems to be a foolish move on the part of our enemies. Even if we are besieged, Harran is quite capable of withstanding this assault until Babylon's armies arrive," the commander finished.

"My Lord," Mitatti addressed the governor, "you had best be heading back into the city now. The enemy forces will be here within a half-beru."

Suiki frowned. He was a civilian, not a soldier. But now that it came down to it… He saw the contempt in the Scythians' eyes and understood it. To them, a man was a warrior, or he was less than a man. To his chagrin, it suddenly dawned on him that they were right. If he followed Mitatti's plan of action, he would not even respect himself.

"As Sin reigns in Harran, no!" the bel pihati exploded. "I will not!"

The outburst was so unlike the calm, rational politician they knew that the Median officers simply stared at him and said nothing.

"But… My Lord," a flabbergasted Mitatti objected, "you cannot stay here, the danger is too great."

"I have no intention of staying here. My chariot is outside, and it is a war chariot. This armor," he tapped his gleaming breastplate, "may be decorative, but it is also functional. Give me a spear. I should be able to handle that, it appears simple enough."

The tent was dead silent. The Scythians looked on with interest at this new development.

Then the commander spoke again, his voice quiet with suppressed outrage. "Governor! That is the Pharaoh of Egypt out there! This is not a sport. By the command of our king, you are a civilian governor. What am I to answer when both the Emperors Uvakshatra and Nabopolassar ask me to explain how it is that you came to die in battle?" Mitatti had a point. The commander's life would likely be forfeit.

Nevertheless, he had seen the approval in the eyes of the Scythian chieftains at his pronouncement. If he was going to continue to govern with these barbarians on his doorstep, he needed their respect, and this had finally obtained it. "It is my city. I am responsible for it, civilian or no. I will write a missive in my own hand and send it back into the city, explaining that I overrode your objections and that you are not to be held accountable for my actions. But I *will* ride to the defense of my people."

A half-beru later, he stood, shielded by his driver, his spear in hand, and accelerating faster than he had ever known a chariot to travel before. The thunderous charge of the enemy chariot corps bore down on him, and Suiki reflected that this was perhaps not the most intelligent decision he had made in his life.

Then there was no more time for reflecting on anything.

The two armies crashed into one another at breakneck speed.

The wild bouncing caused the governor to grip the side of his vehicle, and in so doing, he lowered the point of his spear. Suiki reeled back from the impact as his spear got caught in the wheel of an Egyptian chariot and broke in two.

The spear took out two of the Egyptian's spokes, and it careened into a second Egyptian chariot. That, in turn, collided with the bel pihati's massive war machine and splintered to pieces. Suiki was already off-balance from the sudden release of pressure on his spear, and the jolt threw him headlong into the air.

The battle was barely a segment old when Harran's governor was trampled under the hooves of yet a third Egyptian chariot, and he lost consciousness…

Black faded to gray, and the world fuzzily swam in front of his blurry eyes. As things gradually came into focus, Suiki realized that there was a wet compress being applied to his forehead and his side… and the wavering image of the person so attending him was Addaguppi, Votaress of Sin. "What happened? Where am I?" he asked her.

"You are at Ehulhul."

His vision began to clear, and he looked around. He recognized a side room of the temple. He was lying on a mat on the floor with the priestess kneeling beside him. Beyond the curtain door were the sounds of rapid, purposeful footsteps and the groaning of the wounded. Sin's temple had become a hospital.

"I've called you a fool before, and I shall undoubtedly do so again," she continued, but her tone was gentle, taking the sting from her words. She took the linen compress, rinsed it in a bowl of water, and applied it again—first to his forehead, then to his side.

At that moment, the physical pain became a reality. He gasped and tried to sit up, but the votaress pressed him back. "You took a spear in your side. Of course, that was only after you were run over by one of pharaoh's finest. Considering the magnitude of your folly, it can only be that you have found such disfavor with the gods that they have refused to have you. We're still stuck with you."

"Pharaoh's chariots and his horses are considerably smaller and lighter than our own," he pointed out. "Getting run over by one of them shouldn't cause too much damage."

"Nevertheless, Sin has shown you grace in allowing you to occupy his floor. Whatever made you think you should play soldier?" She emphasized her displeasure by pushing the compress down harder.

"Ach!" He jumped and gave her a reproachful look. "I suppose it goes back to my boyhood. I thrashed many a tree with my stick sword from the advantage of my hay wagon."

Adda smiled despite herself. "My foster-brother, Shadu, used to play a similar game." She paused. "Shadu was the general posted at Dur-Sharuken. He died there. It's strange. This is the first time I've been able to think of him since then without feeling…"

"There are so many dead since then."

"Yes. Well, Tasmit has decreed that our bel pihati will remain Governor of Harran for a while longer at least."

"I'm going to live, then?"

"Yes, but I've no idea why." She dropped the rag into the bowl and began bandaging his side. "I heard you thrashed a few Egyptians today."

"Is that what they're saying? I…" He saw the admiration on her face and decided not to disillusion her. "I… don't quite remember. Is the battle over? Are we victorious?" He winced as she pressed down hard and tightened the bandage.

"It's over. Arbaces, the Glory of the Province of Assyria, and the forces of Nimrud answered the signal and arrived in the middle of the fray. The Egyptians are gone, and my brother has seen sense in retiring back to the Hill Country again. It is still not entirely clear to the people of this city if that constitutes a victory or a defeat. Mitatti and Arbaces decided that pursuit seemed ill-advised, but the ignorant barbarians have gone to follow both groups. Perhaps the Allies will yet be avenged by slaughtering them."

Suiki snorted. The snort turned into a fit of coughing, and he curled up in pain.

"Here, drink this," she lifted his head and held a cup to his lips. It will dull the pain."

He drank and tasted the bitter herbs she had mixed with the hot wine. He eyed her curiously. "Don't you have better things to do than nurse soldiers back to health?"

She smiled. "I am not nursing soldiers—unless you count yourself as one. But I am the priestess of Sin, and you are his governor. If anything happens to you and I have not done my best to prevent it, how can I remain fit for my office?"

"I see," he said and wondered if that were the real reason. He found himself hoping it wasn't. His hope grew as she finished her nursing and stayed anyway, sitting down next to his pallet and pouring herself a cup of the doctored wine. They stayed there like that for a while. Then he felt a twinge of conscience, so he suggested, "I seem to be doing well, what about the other patients?"

"I told you, I'm not a nurse. I'm a priestess. Most of the other wounded are Medes—who only believe in their fire-god and so have no need of me—and Scythians—whose blood can only help cleanse this house that they have desecrated."

"So, I have the pleasure of your company by default. Tasmit is kind. You said the people are unclear as to whether they have a victory or a defeat. What do you think?" he asked her.

She actually laughed. It was a quiet, low, throaty sound and very attractive. "You mean, do I think of you as a friend or an enemy?" She thought about it. "Actually, I think you were very brave, and that you do not mean to be my enemy. While you were laying there dreaming of glory, it occurred to me that you have never done anything against me or probably anyone else—outside of a few alleged Egyptians today."

"Alleged?"

"You didn't really thrash anyone, did you?" she asked.

"No," he admitted sheepishly.

She laughed again. "I'm glad."

At the next new moon festival, they were married.[1]

CHAPTER 17

Princess of Babylon

Babylon, Babylonia

he first light of Shamash slanting through the linen curtains of the second-story bedroom did what the uproar in the palace couldn't, it woke the fourteen-year-old Crown Prince of Babylonia from a deep sleep. He pulled the light linen blanket over his head and tried to nestle back down into the down-filled mattress which lay atop the woven reed supports of the low bed. It was to no avail. The noise now lodged itself in Nebuchadnezzar's sleep-fogged brain, and he groggily opened his eyes. From somewhere, people were wailing and keening—bemoaning something with great distress. From down the hall? From the courtyard to the north? From the south, the great religious complex of Esagila? From the east, where the official buildings and the throne room overlooked the Aiibursbabu, the great boulevard of the procession? Yes, from all of them. The whole city seemed to have turned out.

Suddenly wide awake, Kadurri slipped out of his bed and wrapped himself in a fresh loincloth. He quickly bobbed his head and snapped his fingers to the east, towards the rising sun that he couldn't actually see from his rooms. Barely pausing in the enactment of this mandatory religious duty, he threw on a tunic and over robe and began lacing up his sandals. Something serious was happening, and he wasn't waiting for a servant to arrive to help him dress.

But it wasn't a servant who arrived. Nebuzaradan, the prince's best friend, and self-appointed bodyguard, abruptly charged into the room. The youth was breathing heavily from his exertions, and his mussed brown-black hair hung down over his eyes. "Kadurri!" he exclaimed urgently, as he brushed his bangs aside. "Hurry up and get dressed!"

The prince gave him an exasperated look and gestured to the clothes he already had on. He bent again to his sandals. "You're supposed to knock. What's going on?" He finished the sandals and moved out onto the balcony outside his quarters. The balcony ran around the entire second story of the south wing and overlooked an interior courtyard. The courtyard was filled with servants and what appeared to be refugees. Most were women and children. There was a good deal of wailing mixed with a general hubbub that was completely foreign to the quiet private quarters of the royal family. "What is going on?" Kadurri demanded again. "Who are all those people?"

"It just started," Seri said. He swallowed. "They're refugees. From Carchemish."

"Carchemish!" Kadurri stared at him. "Carchemish was evacuated? What has happened to the troops of the garrison?"

"We don't know for sure. There were some outriders who said… I heard they're all dead."

Kadurri shot him a horrified look and ran out through his quarters to the hallway. Two daggermen were on guard there, but Seri was an adequate guard, so they remained at their posts as the prince rushed past them. Kadurri reached the steps and ran head-long down to the first floor. The atrium was also filled with distressed citizens, sitting hunched along the walls or accosting servants to fill their needs. A crying baby nestled in the corner in its mother's lap. The baby refused to be hushed or distracted by a shiny bracelet of electrum his mother was waving over its face.[1]

Above them, a huge mural painted directly on the wall depicted the beautiful youth, Tammuz. Tammuz was joyfully planting some kind of seed while Ishtar, watching enraptured from a cloud, gazed lustfully upon him.[2] Kadurri thought the idyllic painting was jarringly out of place with the current circumstances.

Just then a small army of cooks and bakers arrived in the court, burdened down with foodstuffs and drink. Kadurri was swept up with the mob pushing its way out of the atrium to the court and the solace of substance. Miraculously, Seri had remained at his side, and the young daggerman cleared his way through the masses to the south side of the court. His path brought him to the back entrance of the throne room where he found his way blocked by more daggermen.

"Let me enter!" he demanded. There was no question in his mind that he would find his father within. The presence of the daggermen confirmed this. "I am sorry, Prince Nebuchadnezzar," the ranking guard responded. "We are under orders that no one enters." The golden doors, etched with royal dragons with entwining necks, remained firmly shut.

"Including me?" Kadurri had never been denied access to his father before.

"No exceptions were specified," the guard answered carefully. The young prince was known to be far more subject to outbursts of temper than his royal father.

"Then find out!" Kadurri's exasperation confirmed the guard's need for caution.

"I'm sorry My Prince," he answered, bowing his head in apologetic deference. "We are not allowed entrance either."

That stymied the prince. "But…" He stopped. This was obviously going to get him nowhere. "Very well. You must have some idea why. Who is within?"

"The king and queen, the rab mag, the rab shaq and the rab sharish."[3] The guard was relieved to actually have some information to offer.

"Well, of course, they are!" Kadurri snapped with a bit of sarcasm. "But that doesn't explain why they are there. Who else is in there?"

"The wife of the Commander of Carchemish, Great Prince. Plus ten of the daggermen and our captain, young Nebuzaradan's father, Arioch." He nodded an acknowledgment at the prince's companion.

Kadurri froze. The information told him more than he wanted to know. "Then Carchemish has really fallen? How? Who was it? The Assyrians? Could they have…?"

"Yes, Lord Prince, in alliance with Egypt."

He shook his head in disbelief. "Egypt? That's not possible."

The guard nodded firmly. "Egypt, Great Prince."

"But… But… No! We have a treaty! Necho broke it? He wouldn't dare! His daughter, the princess…" For a moment, he couldn't breathe. "Nitocris!" he gasped finally. He turned to Seri in alarm. "The king will…" He stared at his friend, willing him to contradict him.

"The princess will be the king's first target," Seri confirmed in a hushed, frightened tone.

Nebuchadnezzar abruptly abandoned the closed, gilded doors of the audience hall and ran, pushing and shoving, through the court to the hall of the main court, to the northern wing. He flew up the stairs to the harem.[4]

The eunuchs guarding the second-story floor gave Nebuchadnezzar's daggerman sullen looks, but they stood aside and allowed the prince and his friend to enter the harem. Seri took up guard just inside the door of Princess Nitocris' suite.

Nitocris sat on a bench under the window in her sitting room, stroking the white long-haired kitten in her lap. Before she could stop it, the half-grown cat leapt from Nitocris' lap and attacked the fringe on Kadurri's robe. He ignored it.

Nitocris stood up and stared at him with a confused look on her heart-shaped face. Her short wig was braided in blues and whites and woven intricately tight, forming a basket weave skullcap. Her robe, also blue and white, was embroidered with tiny golden lotus flowers and her heavily painted eyes were huge and frightened. Like a gazelle. Like Anuket, the girl/gazelle goddess of the cataracts of the Nile.

The resemblance was definitely not a good thing.

Nitocris' lady was still seated on the bench. The woman had not stood when the prince entered, but Kadurri was focused on the princess, not the servant's lapse. Besides, the nagir ekalli, the palace superintendent, had vouched for this woman as a hard worker and by some quirk, she spoke Demotic. She could communicate in the language of Nitocris' heart, the language the princess had learned at her Cushite mother's knee. Since that was likely to be a comfort to the daughter of the Nile, Kadurri had not objected to the appointment, and this former maid had become Nitocris' lady-in-waiting, despite her lack of manners. He wasn't about to address the issue at the moment.

Evidently, the woman had already explained the situation to the girl for there was no doubt Nitocris understood what was happening and the implications for her. Almost, she looked glad to see the prince when he arrived.

"Get water and towels," he ordered the servant woman shortly. "Get that paint off her face. Now!"

The lady tardily stood and snapped her fingers to the prince, then she fled to the princess' washroom. He ignored her and turned his attention back to Nitocris.

She looked so small and vulnerable, but she was a traitor's daughter. A traitor was given to the fire, he and all his family.

He reached down and scooped up the cat. It rolled over in his hands and batted at his nose. He held it out to her.

"Prince Nebuchadnezzar," she pleaded and took the animal. She shivered involuntarily and seemed ready to startle and run at any instant. Instinctively, she seemed to realize that he was her only hope.

"Princess," he answered, not quite sure what to do.

What could he do? The law was the law.

Wordlessly, she dropped the cat and slipped into his arms, hiding her face against his chest. It was the first time she had ever willingly touched him. Holding her like that, he knew that she was the only thing that mattered. She belonged to him, and he would protect her.

Even against the law.

Even against his father.

The lady-in-waiting arrived with a basin of water, and he stepped back, allowing her to scrub the princess' face clean. "That robe won't do either," Kadurri stated. "Her clothing must have a Babylonian theme. Go find something else. Quickly."

"She only has one," the lady objected. "And she hates it."

"Get it!"

She delved into a chest and emerged with a blue and purple over robe. It was embroidered in scarlet and white with royal Babylonian dragons. Perfect.

The princess backed away shaking her head furiously, arguing in Egyptian about the choice but Kadurri caught her by the shoulders and forced her to look him in the face. "Yes! Today, you are Babylonian royalty! You *will* wear it! You must." With one finger, he lifted her chin and kissed her. "I won't let them hurt you, little kitten. I won't."

Nitocris had not accepted tutoring well. Haughtily Egyptian, she clung stubbornly to her own languages. After six moons in Babylon, she still understood virtually no Aramaic, but she understood Kadurri's tone if nothing else, and burst into tears, allowing the maid to remove the lotus robe and replace it with the dragon-themed one.

Meanwhile, the prince was rummaging through a multitude of wigs on her dressing table. He held up one, different from the others. It was real human hair, not black wool, and it was long and curled, not braided. He had ordered it made for her, but she had never worn it. Today, she would! He removed her braided cap himself and set the sleek hairpiece on her bald head. Then he picked up a sapphire and diamond tiara and set it in place.

Despairingly, Nitocris picked up an electrum mirror and looked at herself. She said something he couldn't understand and then slapped her arm and poked her cheek. She said it again.

"She says no amount of disguise will change her skin color," the lady interpreted.

"Get out," was his only reply. Then he took Nitocris in his arms and let her cry on his shoulder while he tried to make her understand that he would protect her. The lady backed into the washroom, but she stood, hovering near the doorway.

Mere segments later, the Nabopolassar's guard appeared to find them like that. The lady-in-waiting was peeking around a corner from the washroom.

"Lord Prince!" the elder of the guard stammered. "We… we did not expect to find you here. We have orders from the king…"

"I will take her," he said calmly and guiding her around them he gently escorted her out of the harem, across the courts and back to the throne room. A grim-faced Nebuzaradan followed a half-step back.

Kadurri arrived once more at the back entrance to the throne room, and this time, the daggermen let him and the princess pass. They let Nebuzaradan enter as well, but they stopped the princess' lady who had been following at a discreet distance.

Nabopolassar's audience chamber was modest by Mesopotamian standards. Compared to the grandiose palaces of Assyria, it offered little in the way of sculpture, carvings, rare gems or valuable metals. The colorfully painted frescos of the banquet hall held no place in the somber hall of judgment. Its plastered walls were painted in a dull blue. A parade of alternating golden lions and white dragons encircled the walls at knee height and again, just above the heads of the tallest men. The row of high narrow windows and the doors were accented with gold leaf and a bright red banner with two white dragons, necks entwined hung behind the dais. That was the extent of the decor.[5]

Near the closed front entrance of the room, a eunuch sat with his back against the wall. He was strumming quiet, soothing chords on a lyre. His beardless cheeks were stained by tracks of tears.

The king and queen were seated upon their golden, high-backed thrones. The thrones were set, side by side, on a dais at the back of the room. The dais was carpeted in a dark brownish maroon color that matched the tiles of the floor and was approached by six steps from the front. Babylonia's first general, Rab Mag Nergalniari stood to the right. Behind the thrones and to the king's left was the new rab shaq, Belshumishkun. Behind the queen, his hand on her shoulder, stood an old man, the wise and wily Rab Sharish Mesharumishamash, Babylonia's prime minister. The queen shared the wide seat of her throne with a sobbing woman, whom she cradled against her shoulder. Kadurri took her to be Belnasir's widow though he had never seen her before. The woman looked not much older than he was. At her feet was a small wicker basket, its bottom was stained a rusty brown color.

Two steps in front of the dais stood Seri's father, Captain Arioch of the daggermen. He blocked all approach to the throne, but he stepped aside for the prince and princess as they skirted the dais and approached it from the front. The dark maroon tiles clicked under their sandaled feet and echoed off the walls as they walked. It was a cheerless, hollow, staccato sound.

Nabopolassar looked up as the heir to his throne guided the daughter of pharaoh to stand before him. The anger in his eyes turned briefly to surprise.

"Lord," Kadurri addressed the king as an intimate companion. He humbly bowed his head and snapped his fingers and signaled to Nitocris to do the same. She did. "I have brought the princess, my wife, as you commanded."

"Stand away from her, My Son," The king's face was like thunder, but deathly pale. He leaned forward from his throne and actually hissed the words at him, like a snake. "She is tainted. Her father is a traitor."

Nebuchadnezzar met his father's eyes, they were red from weeping. The prince had never seen his father cry before, but if Belnasir was really dead, he understood. The commander had been like a little brother to the king. He answered carefully. "Then, I am tainted as well. She is my wife." He slipped his arm over her shoulder, protectively.

The eunuch stopped playing, and the room held its breath. Nabopolassar opened his mouth to bellow a reply, then he stopped.

For a moment which seemed to drag out longer than a year, he just glared at his son.

Nebuchadnezzar didn't move. Neither did he stand away from the girl. The king was extremely upset, but he was, after all, the king and Kadurri knew him intimately. He did not let his personal feelings cloud his judgment or dull his perceptions.

Kadurri was more frightened then he had ever known he could be, but he was a prince, born and raised. He was not going to back down, Nitocris depended on him. And he knew Nabopolassar loved him.

Apparently, the king remembered this. Still shaking with anger, he dropped his gaze and shook his head. Then he turned to his advisors and raised a questioning eyebrow.

"My Lord," Mesharumishamash said hesitantly, eyeing the girl and noting her deliberately Babylonian regalia. "Prince Nebuchadnezzar has hit upon a delicate point." When the king did not explode, the rab sharish continued, "The princess is, in fact, his wife. More, she became his wife before her father became a traitor."

"Then he can divorce her," Queen Ninnaramur interjected sharply.

Stricken, Kadurri stared at his mother.

"Naram," the king growled at her. "The rab sharish is not finished."

"Lady," Mesharu continued, using the personal form of address only allowed to an intimate friend, "you are, of course, correct. She is his wife in name only. If he were to divorce her, she would revert back to the family of pharaoh. But at present, she is a member of the royal family of Babylon, not that of Sais."

"Mother," the prince appealed to her, "please. What has she done?"

"You do not count a cobra innocent simply because it has not yet bitten you!" Naram spat. "This girl is Egyptian! Her father has just sent us his regards in the form of Belnasir's head!" She gestured at the basket.

Kadurri looked at it. His head? The rusty brown stain spoke volumes. Feeling sick, the prince looked up at the distraught woman next to the queen. Belnasir's widow let out a wail and began sobbing again. "The princess has innumerable ties to home," Naram continued. "You will never be able to trust her, and since, by this act, her own father has turned his back on her, she has no value at all!"

"That is enough," the king said firmly.

The queen flashed a look of pure venom at the unfortunate princess and rose to her feet. Laying her arm around the shaking shoulders of the grieving widow, she guided her from the room.

Nebuchadnezzar stood still, face ashen but determined, before his father and his king.

Nabopolassar carefully studied the girl, and she trembled beneath Kadurri's sheltering arm. "Are you willing to divorce the daughter of Necho?" Nabo asked, already knowing the answer.

"Never." The prince glanced again at the basket and shuddered.

"Then I will not force you. But the queen has a point, My Son. Nitocris is yours, but do not trust her. You say you will never divorce her. Very well, but be careful you never fall in love with her either. Take her back to her rooms, she is safe from me."

Almost overwhelmed with relief, Kadurri bowed to the king and snapped his fingers once more. He made Nitocris do the same. Then he took her hand and led her towards the back door of the throne room. The son of Arioch promptly fell in behind. The girl, suddenly realizing her reprieve, gave the king a look of gratitude, her eyes large and liquid as twin pools at midnight.

Kadurri saw it but hid his smile. That was a look that would have brought the monster Kingu crawling to surrender the Tablet of Destiny by laying it at her feet. No, Nabopolassar hadn't stood a chance. The prince led the princess back through the courtyard and the north wing's atrium. He dropped her hand and slipped his arm around her shoulders again to shield her from the harsh, hateful stares of the crowd.

The survivors of Carchemish certainly had reason to hate her, but none of them dared say anything in the presence of the heir. Nebuchadnezzar barely noticed Nitocris' lady-in-waiting as he passed. He did not see the glint of her dagger when Marrat slipped it from her sleeve back into her bodice. He did not know how close he had come to becoming the victim of the Queen of Egypt's revenge, or that when he had saved the princess, he saved himself as well.[6]

CHAPTER 18

Jehoahaz's Sin

Jerusalem, Judah

Autumn arrived, and the weather couldn't have been better. It was just before sunrise on the day after Yom Teruah, the last day of the year, the Feast of Trumpets. Today was the New Year, the Day of Reckoning.[1] It was the first of ten days set aside for self-examination and repentance before the Day of Atonement.

The shophars of the Feast had stilled, but the people refused to subside into the required quiet introspection. In the palace court, a raucous party, now in its second day, rampaged in and out of the open palace doors. Despite the early hour, drunken crowds shouldered their way past each other, laughing uproariously, spilling wine all over themselves or throwing the occasional punch at someone's nose. The new king, Jehoahaz, had reigned three full months, and still, he had not begun to transcribe his own copy of Moses' Law,[2] but now it was the New Year—the official beginning of the first year of his reign. Jehoahaz celebrated this, his first regnal year, with a lavish feast and with the unveiling of the first monuments to his sovereignty: two brand new bronze lamasu, ten feet tall, to guard the King's Gate of the Temple.[3] Lamasu were Mesopotamian spirits, portrayed either as winged bulls or winged lions. They sported human heads and guarded gates and palaces throughout Assyria. Lions, even though standing up, would have been far too reminiscent of Egyptian sphinxes, so Jehoahaz had used bulls.

Jeremiah ben Hilkiah stood at the New Gate and stared, aghast, at the monstrosities. Then he turned on the guard of the gate, his eyes flashing.

Maaseiah ben Shallum had just taken up his post, and he flinched and drew back as he saw his hair-clad cousin coming at him. Tall, like all the priests of Anathoth, Maaseiah had a bigger frame and was better muscled than Jeremiah. As a guard, he was a daunting figure, but Jeremiah took him by the shoulder and jerked him around to face the eastern gate, known as the King's Gate. He pointed at the lamassu and a rollicking group of party-goers who had abandoned the palace court to stand on Temple grounds, between the lamassu. "How did they get in there?" Jeremiah raged. "Maaseiah, it's your job! How could you let those drunken celebrants into the Temple Court?"

"But…"

"But nothing! Just kick them out, then shut and lock the gate! How hard could it be?"

"Cousin, I have just come on duty…"

"It's the time of self-examination, but all Jerusalem has gone mad! And you just let…"

"Jeremiah, stop!" the priest-guard protested. "I just got here, I let no one in. But look at them! That's Prince Mattaniah! What do you expect me to do?"

Jeremiah glared at him. Maaseiah was the eldest son of his youngest uncle. At twenty-one years old, the guard was almost ten years younger than Jeremiah; and Jeremiah had always been very fond of him. Reluctantly, the prophet turned away and looked across the Temple Court.

The priests were just standing about, not sure of what to do. No one was asking for their services anyway. The Temple Guard, lined up on the Temple Steps under the portico, was making no effort to contain the situation. And the singers just stood there, their instruments hanging at their sides, staring at the desecration.

On the east side of the Grand Altar, the priest Buzi was firmly holding both shoulders of his eldest son, restraining him so that he stayed in place. Young Ezekiel looked like he wanted to tear across the court and confront the party goers. Jeremiah was well-acquainted with the fiery temper of the youth. Ezekiel often sat in his sodh and was never too shy to offer his opinions. Of all the priests on duty, the only one willing to stand up for his office was a fourteen-year-old boy.

Inside the King's Gate, between the two monstrosities, the group of celebrants was standing, heads tilted back, admiring the new king's handiwork. Mattaniah, the king's half-brother, staggered from the off-balance position of looking straight up, and in his condition, he almost fell, emptying his goblet of wine all over himself. His companions roared with laughter.

"Fine. I'll take care of this," Jeremiah gritted, and he strode rapidly away over the paved cobblestone of the court.

The sun broke over the eastern wall, and the Levite singers took up their ministry of praise.

"Mattaniah!" Jeremiah confronted the prince and pointed towards the New Gate. "Take your friends and leave this courtyard immediately! This is a holy time, and you are standing on holy ground, even though your brother has seen fit to defile it! Get out!"

Startled, the jocular prince turned to face the prophet and waved his empty goblet at him. "Oh! Jeremiah! It's good to see you!" He paused. "I thought maybe you had left town, because… Well, sunset marked the first day of the king's inaugural year, and you weren't at the celebration. Poor Shallum, he had to call on the House of Prophets to forecast his reign."

"I am no longer the royal prophet, as you well know. Or you would know if you cleared the fog of wine from your head! Now take your friends and get off Temple grounds before young Ezekiel over there does something his father will regret."

"The prophets said he would reign long and prosperously," the prince continued, oblivious to Jeremiah's words. "His great-great-grandson will be a mighty king." Then Jeremiah's statements finally filtered through his wine-fogged awareness. "Defile? What's that supposed to mean?"

Jeremiah said nothing. He just pointed up at the lamassu.

"That's crazy!" One of the party-goers put in. "Look at them! They're magnificent!" He gestured unsteadily at the base of the nearest statue. "See that? It says 'King Jehoahaz, installed on the occasion of the first day of his regnal year.'" he leaned conspiratorially in towards the prophet, stumbled a step and pointed at the prince. "That's his brother, you know."

Jeremiah pushed him away. Just then, Pashur ben Immer, Captain of the Temple Guard, arrived. "Jeremiah, they're not hurting anything. Just let them be."

Jeremiah turned angry eyes on the captain. "Well, Pashur! Finally, you show up! Where were you when they were installing these abominations?"

Pashur pursed his lips. "I'm trying to be reasonable here. Jeremiah, those are not abominations, they're..."

"Assyrian lamassu. I know what they are!"

"Assyrian!" objected Pashur. "That's an insult! These are Babylonian, not Assyrian! Well, I mean they're neither, they are Judean! Look at the heads! That's Abraham and Moses!"

Startled, Jeremiah peered upwards. "Is that who they're supposed to be?" He blinked and then turned on Pashur again pointing a finger right at his nose. "Moses couldn't stand the golden calf of Egypt, so King Jehoahaz mounts the image of our teacher's head on that of an Assyrian winged bull? Abraham left Ur to reject its idolatry only to end up as an idol himself in the land promised to him?"

Clearly, this hadn't occurred to Pashur, and he groped for a response. "That golden calf was an idol! These aren't! And Abraham..." he sputtered, pushing Jeremiah's finger away, but he could find nothing to say about Abraham. Finally, he continued, "Jeremiah, the lamassu are merely symbolic. They represent angels, guardian spirits protecting the entrance to the court of the Lord, like the Cherubim. Lamassu are not and have never been gods! No one worships them! But by putting them there, King Jehoahaz lets Babylon know of our continued support and friendship."

Jeremiah snorted. "The Babylonians have never built statues to the lamassu, Pashur. The Sumerians did, and the Assyrians did, but not the Babylonians. The Sumerians are gone and the time of the Assyrians is all but over. Shallum should have checked his facts concerning which idols have dominion where. I doubt King Nabopolassar will be impressed."[2]

The captain's jaw dropped. He had not been aware that the lamassu could be construed as an insult to Babylon. "But... but..."

"Syncretism with Babylonia is not pleasing to the Lord!" Ezekiel broke away from his father and sprinted up, yelling over the noise of the party next door in the palace court.

"This would be syncretism with Assyria," Jeremiah drawled.

Ezekiel never paused. "And those are not angels, they're demons!"

Pashur put out a hand and stopped the headlong rush of the youth. "Go back to your duties, Ezekiel."

"What duties?" he replied hotly, whirling around and gesturing at the all but empty court. "No one is here! It's a time of prayer and fasting, but everyone is in the city throwing a wild party!"

Buzi came up to reclaim his son.

"That's enough!" Prince Mattaniah stated, planting his feet and mustering all the royal dignity he was capable of in his inebriated state. He swayed a little before he steadied himself. "You're all lucky that we're having a feast and the King is in a good mood, or he'd have you all hauled away for treason!" He slapped the dully gleaming haunch of one of the winged bulls. "These are a magnificent monument to the beginning of a long and prosperous reign." He turned to one of his friends and whispered conspiratorially, "That's what the prophets said you know."

"I know," his friend nodded vigorously as he assured him.

"We've seen them now, anyway," Mattaniah muttered. He pulled at one of his companion's sleeves. "Let's go back to the palace where we're wanted."

Jeremiah swallowed hard, a wave of sadness suddenly overshadowed him. "Mattaniah?"

"What?" The prince stopped and peered blurrily at the prophet.

"Pharaoh reported that the Lord had said that He was with him. He told no one to oppose him because he was to hurry on his way. That means pharaoh was on a divine timetable. He was to be somewhere at a precise time. Was it the Lord's will that your father die at Megiddo? Was it the Lord's will that pharaoh attack Carchemish? Truly, the Lord knows everything, He knew these things would come to pass, but that doesn't mean He sent pharaoh to do them!

"So, what is it that the Lord has sent Necho to do? Where is the pharaoh to be, that requires such strict timing? Who was it that the Lord was warning when He used pharaoh as His messenger? Was it Josiah, or was it, perhaps, Jehoahaz?"

This was too difficult for the prince, and he looked forlornly at his empty cup. Then he looked back up at the prophet. "What?"

Jeremiah glanced back up at the monolithic statues above them, then he sadly turned back to the prince; all his anger had drained away. "Egypt comes," he said, "right on time." The prophet turned and made his way back to his Temple office, the three priests, Buzi, Ezekiel, and Pashur, staring after him.

Prince Mattaniah shook his head in confusion, threw his arms around the shoulders of two of his friends and the group staggered off towards Gatekeeper Maaseiah and the New Gate.

Jeremiah was right. He was always right. Sometimes, he wished he could be wrong. But the Lord's words could never fail, and Jeremiah was His mouthpiece.

That afternoon, a large contingent of the army of Egypt arrived outside the city. The partying ground to an abrupt and confused halt. Pharaoh Necho was at Riblah, and he had sent for Jehoahaz.

Jeremiah was not surprised when King Jehoahaz summoned him. Jehoahaz was young, but he was no fool. Despite his posturing and bragging, the king had to know that Judah was no match for Egypt, at least not in the natural. Jehoahaz realized that his only hope was in divine intervention. So he determined not to make the same mistake his father had. When it came to Egypt, King Josiah had not sent for Jeremiah. King Jehoahaz did, and so, Jeremiah came.

Jehoahaz sat on the lion throne of Judah, surrounded by the scent of cedar. The tall, lean, hair-clad figure of Jeremiah stood directly in front of him on the top step of the dais.

The king leaned forward eagerly to hear the word of the Prophet of God.

"Well?"

"Surrender." Jeremiah showed no emotion. He gave no sign that he even saw the king before him. It was his duty to speak, so he did. The prophet just stood there and said it.

The king was speechless in shock. Finally, he demanded, "What did you say?"

"Surrender."

Rage and frustration replaced disbelief. The king sat back in his chair. "That's it? The advice of the Oracle of God? I could get better from a child on the street! I guess I'm glad I had the prophets of the House prophesy at my feast and not you!" He slammed a fist down on the armrest of the throne. "No wonder my father didn't think to consult you under such circumstances!"

That hurt. Jeremiah finally looked at the king. He regarded the young man before him with deep regret in his eyes. "Your father's situation was different than yours. All he needed to do was stay out of it. Thanks to your own actions, you do not have that option." Jeremiah pointed a finger at the king, "The Lord has chosen to make a swift example of you. Surrender, and perhaps we can stave off disaster for a while longer. Perhaps the people will take note and repent. The Day of Atonement is just over a week away, perhaps they can yet be saved. But only if *you* surrender."

"But the Lord!" Jehoahaz protested. "He can work this out! Prophet, I'm asking. Tell me what I must do."

The prophet's eyes flashed with brief anger, and he stamped his foot. "Enough!" For three months, this man had done what was right in his own eyes and never once thought to consult the Almighty. Never once had he sought to constrain the idolatry that was enveloping the land. Indeed, he had encouraged it! "This is the word of the Lord to you, Jehoahaz, King of Judah. The Lord is not with you for you have not been with Him! You have encouraged the people to stray. Surrender and you will be taken away alive in chains. This is the only mercy the Lord of Recompense has for you. Resist, and you will certainly die and bring disaster on all Judah."

The prophet paused then he added softly, "I'm sorry, but now you must be a king. Think of your people."

Without another word, the son of Hilkiah turned and left the presence of the king. He had not been dismissed.[4]

CHAPTER 19

Jehoiakim

Jerusalem, Judah

rince Eliakim stood on the palace steps and watched guiltily as his brother was led away in chains. The Egyptians were taking Jehoahaz to Riblah, the old Hittite fortress at the headwaters of the Typhon River in central Syria. All alone, the King of Judah would face Necho's judgment there. If only Shallum had refused the crown. This was definitely his fault.

Egyptian soldiers and officials occupied Jerusalem and were overseeing every bit of its administration. They were wasting no time. From the palace steps, Eliakim surreptitiously sent a nervous glance around at his entourage—all of them, save one, were Egyptians. That one was a palace guard, Elnathan ben Achbor, his father-in-law. The prince swallowed and leaned close enough to speak in the older man's ear. "No matter what happens, don't leave me."

"They won't harm you, My Son. Not under pain of death. They are under orders from their pharaoh." He studied the prince. "This is what you wanted. It is your time."

"I know. Shallum was a fool. He announced his hatred of the Egyptians to the winds."

"And you informed pharaoh of it."

"No! That's not the way it was. Pharaoh Necho had already chosen me. Of course, I had to report to him." He turned a hard look at the guard. "And you delivered that message! But this is what you wanted!" he accused. "And now you think it is your time. Well, just remember, your daughter is not my only wife, and Jeconiah is not my only son!"

Elnathan nodded. "But now you will be king, and they will be royal. Kings know that silence has a price, My Son."

Eliakim snorted derisively. "You can prove nothing, and I will not be extorted."

Elnathan shrugged. "My daughter can find her own way, but Coniah *is* your eldest son."

"He is only six years old. I have two other sons, and for health reasons, I think I will take my time in choosing between them. However, it would be fitting to send a palace guard to pharaoh with my brother. Perhaps someone who has already established a contact there."

There was a pause. "Appearances are important, especially at the beginning of a king's reign. It would show respect to send someone of rank to accompany King Jehoahaz, someone like the Captain of the Palace Guard." Elnathan suggested.

The prince laughed out loud. "And not you. But that would leave the position of captain vacant. My father is ambitious."

"Some things, like some secrets, are best kept within the family, My Son."

"Yes, where they can be more closely watched."

Eliakim looked out over the people. Most of the women of the court were wailing and carrying on, some of the younger men were on their knees pounding the ground, their robes were torn and cheeks bleeding from where they had pulled parts of their beards out by the roots. The procession taking King Jehoahaz captive filed through the Horse Gate and made its way towards the hills surrounding Jerusalem. He saw his brother, Mattaniah, standing by the gate with his arm around their mother, Zebidah's shoulders. She had a very satisfied look on her face. The prince understood. Pharaoh had been right, there was really only one suitable choice for King of Judah.

The Egyptians swung the gate shut with a thud. King Jehoahaz was gone.

Almost immediately, a large black official appeared from the palace porch and signaled the prince's Egyptian guard. The Egyptians took Eliakim by the arms and propelled him bodily forward towards the Temple grounds. Eliakim did not resist.

They reached the New Gate and Maaseiah the gatekeeper stood aside and let them pass. In the Temple Court, before the Grand Altar, the Chief Priest and his immediate staff already stood there waiting. The singers on the Temple Steps were silent, watching.

Two men came running with the heavy crown and pushed past the prince to lay it on the table before the altar. Under the Egyptians' watchful eyes, and a minimum of ceremony, Chief Priest Azariah poured oil over Eliakim's head. "Oh Lord," he called to the sky, "look down from heaven and anoint your son. Bless his reign and teach him to follow you." With an effort, Azariah picked up David's heavy crown and set it on Eliakim's head. The prince hadn't even had time to prostrate himself. "Remember how your ancestors angered the Lord, but how your father pleased Him. Rule with righteousness and faith, ever guided by the light the Lord provides.

"What is your name?" the priest intoned.

"Jehoiakim," the new king answered, the anointing oil dripping from his beard and robes. It meant "the Lord has raised him." It was the name he had long ago promised himself if he should ever gain the crown, and Pharaoh Necho had agreed.

But Jehoiakim was enraged by the insult of this quickly orchestrated crowning. Most of the people were still out by the Horse Gate mourning Shallum! They didn't even know they had a new king! Azariah had not bothered to sing the coronal hymn for him! He glared at the priest. "My ancestors didn't begin to know how to anger God!" he retorted. "But I have friends in pharaoh's court. Together, we will dig the gold of Solomon's mines in Egypt and become great enough to provide our own light!

"My name is Jehoiakim. Remember it. It is a name that will live forever!"

It was a name that would live forever in infamy.[1]

That afternoon, Jehoiakim sat in the king's chair on the palace porch, the black Egyptian eunuch by his side, carefully watching his every move. The sounds from the Temple Court told the new king that the priests were busy tearing down Shallum's monumental bulls.

That evening, Jehoiakim's first official act was to lay a burdensome tax upon the people. The tax was necessary, for the eunuch demanded one hundred talents of silver and one talent of gold to seal the treaty that gave up Judah's rights as an independent state.[2] The amount was a heavy debt, but Jehoiakim was eager to please his new masters and set out to pay it almost immediately. It won him no points with the people. The citizens of Judah had been free from tribute since they had thrown off the Assyrians. To begin paying again was a bitter herb. No longer were they free. Within a week, it became apparent that many could not pay the tax. Those who failed were thrown into debtor's prison to await their fates. Jehoiakim had just begun his reign, and he was already one of the most unpopular kings Judah had ever had.

CHAPTER 20

The Median/Persian Empire

Ecbatana, Media

In Ecbatana, in the royal palace of Media, a new life had begun.[1] Though it was the middle of the night, the royal family gathered in the sitting room of a pine-paneled suite of the harem. None assembled there waiting could know it, but the birth of this one child would change everything. Due to this small baby, backward and despised Persia would one day rule Media and the world.

The oil wall-lamps flickered, gleaming on the golden stained walls, as the oak door to the inner chamber opened just far enough to allow a woman, the royal midwife, to squeeze through. Her arms were wrapped around a squalling, struggling bundle. King Uvakshatra and Queen Mandane leaned forward eagerly to catch sight of the firstborn of their eldest, nineteen-year-old Crown Prince Ishtumegu. The prince moved forward to accept the child from the woman.

"Great Prince," the midwife bowed low before him and the rest of the royal assemblage in the waiting chambers and held out the screaming and kicking newborn, "I regret to inform you that you have a daughter." She deposited the baby in Ishtu's arms. Her duty discharged, the midwife fled.

Prince Ishtumegu, mighty warrior, and heir of King Uvakshatra was left there awkwardly holding the squirming, caterwauling infant. He looked helplessly out from under his unruly chestnut bangs, wordlessly pleading help from his mother. Mandane, Queen of Media, beamed at him with a smile that lit up the room. She held out her arms for her first grandchild.

Ishtu gratefully gave up his burden.

"Oh, she's beautiful," the queen cooed in the new princess' face. The baby, sensing a sympathetic touch, settled and looked up wonderingly into her grandmother's lovely visage.

Prince Ahasuerus, upon learning he had a niece instead of a nephew, shrugged his sympathy at his brother. Losing interest, the youth headed for the hall. He scooped up the seven-year-old Persian hostage, Kambuzya— who was listening at the door—and carried him off, kicking and squealing. "You are supposed to be in bed!"

"But I want to see!" Prince Kambuzya wailed, his voice fading as Ahasuerus carted him off down the hall.

Back in the room, Princess Amyhia giggled, pushing in under the king's arm to get a peek. The princess was nearly twelve and growing too tall for that particular trick, but she did it anyway. "She looks like you, Mama," Amyhia pointed out, touching the newborn's cheek.

"She looks just like you did," the queen told her. "Except you are the sunset and she will be midday." Amy's coloring was a mixture of both the king and queen. The baby hiccupped, and Mandane and Amyhia both laughed.

Uvakshatra sighed and turned to his heir. "Women! If babies looked like lizards, they'd be just as delighted."

The king was a large and powerfully built man with just a touch of gray in his copper beard. He had brought Media to be the power it was today, and his dynastic hopes included Babylon through young Amyhia's marriage to Prince Nebuchadnezzar. That marriage was the treaty that had created the Coalition. Prince Ishtu, meanwhile, had married a Persian princess to appease the wild Persians and cement Media's rule among them. "But don't be disappointed, Ishtu," the sovereign continued. "She is beautiful, and there will be other children. You will give me many grandsons—just not today."

He laid his hand on Amyhia's head and agreed with her generously. "You're right, My Heart, the baby does look like your mother. See how dark blue her eyes are? They will turn brown, just like Ishtu's and just like your mother's. Do you see that fuzz on her head? Her hair will be bright as sunshine, just like her mother and just like the queen."

The princess and the queen both beamed.

Ishtumegu leaned in close and saw it was true; the girl-child was the image of his mother. "Then her name is Mandane," he said. The queen rewarded him with an elated smile. Ishtu shrugged and gave a lopsided grin to his father. "A daughter is still a wondrous gift!" He ran his finger across the soft downy head and cooed at her too.

That night, the crown prince retired to his bed alone. A strange exhaustion had come over him, and he wished only to rest. Ishtu chased his servants from his chambers and fell onto the soft down-fill cushion covering his bronze couch. Almost immediately, he was asleep.

Somewhere, from deep within and from infinitely far away at the same time, he became aware of a light glowing, growing in the blackness of his subconscious. Struggling to focus and comprehend, the prince discovered that the light emanated from a figure that walked out of the darkness. The man, unearthly tall and dressed all in white, stopped before him and looked down, as from a great height, into his face. The visitor invoked such overwhelming fear that in his dream the prince cried out and fell down flat, although he uttered no sound and was lying sound asleep in his bed the entire time.

"Do not be afraid," the man said to him. "I come to announce great events which are about to unfold. You are told ahead of time so that when they come to pass, you will know that there is One in heaven who knows the future from eternity past. You are being given the opportunity to honor Him and give Him glory."

The prince dared to look up then and found that the intruder was holding his baby, the light from his face reflecting off hers. "Look," he said, "you have a new daughter. Rejoice in her, Prince of Media. Don't seek for a son to follow. It is decreed that this child shall bear your heir. Her son will be glorious and has been set apart from before the world to accomplish great things. Through him will come the instrument through which the King of Heaven will deliver His people."

In terror, Ishtumegu raised his eyes to gaze at the apparition, barely comprehending what he was being told. The Medes believed in the One God of Heaven, the God of Fire, who not even the mountains could contain, but they never expected to hear from Him.

"This has been ordered from on high," the glowing man continued. "Do not fight against it, Prince of Media, and you will prosper. If you seek to thwart the plans of the only true God, however, be assured that you will lose your throne and your kingdom and another shall be established in its place. Do you understand these things?"

Realizing that a response was required, the prince swallowed and nodded… and sat up in his own bed wide-awake. He looked around wildly, searching for some trace of the intruder but saw only the wood paneling of his royal chambers, dimly lit by the brazier.[2]

Persia

Late that fall, the campaigns of Media resulted in Uvakshatra's defeat of Araramnes son of Teispes, King of the Persian half-tribe of Parsa. The majority of the other still unconquered Persian tribes almost immediately succumbed, ostensibly bringing all of Persia under the rule of their cousins, the Medes. However, the land was rugged. Many of the Persians did not recognize their tribes' new allegiance and took to the hills. Ishtumegu's half-Persian child, if she had been a boy, would have provided some legitimacy to the Mede's Persian rule, but the baby was, after all, just a girl. With no reason for the Persians to recognize Median rulership, the unrest was likely to continue for years and require a great deal of effort to subdue. Meanwhile, the Assyro-Egyptian Alliance had been reborn. Babylonia desperately needed Media back, hopefully by the following spring. Uvak's forces would have to be split.

CHAPTER 21

The Fan-Bearer to the Left

Jerusalem, Judah

bdamelek shivered a little. From the palace portico, he watched the light of Amun-Ra growing behind the eastern hills. The early morning would still be growing colder until the god actually appeared, however. It was the best time of the year in Egypt, but the coolness there meant cold here. Abdamelek hoped he could get used to it because he doubted he would ever see Egypt again. He knew that Jerusalem was his new home.

When the chariot of Amun-Ra appeared over the hills, so Pharaoh Necho would appear as well, but Abdamelek had already seen that all was ready. On route home from Riblah, the pharaoh was stopping by Jerusalem to receive the tax Abdamelek had demanded and that Jehoiakim had already collected. Jehoiakim had forced the tribute from the people in a mere three months. That was the mark of a good king.

Pharaoh had sent the captive King Jehoahaz on ahead of him to Egypt. Jehoahaz would be housed in the new prison Necho had ordered, a prison dubbed "The Fortress of the Babylonians," for it was being built to house Babylonians, prisoners of the war yet to come.

The population of the city had been awakened and forced out to face the palace's eastern gate—the Horse Gate—to await the spectacle to unfold before them. King Jehoiakim, dressed in heavily embroidered royal robes and flanked by his three wives and seven children, emerged from the House of

Cedar. The king took his place on the porch throne. A contingent of Palace Guard formed a semi-circle around them. All was ready.

The silver trumpets on the walls sounded. Jerusalem's city guard came out of their tower and swung the interior wooden gate back. They marched through the court between the walls and pushed the massive bronze exterior gate wide, just as the sun appeared. There, before the Horse Gate, was pharaoh. His kohl-outlined eyes were huge in his impossibly handsome face. His oiled skin, stretched taut over his perfect physique, shone as brightly as his gold collar. The bright blue Chepesh battle helm was covered in shining sun disks, and his biceps wore armbands of coiled golden cobras. Necho's chariot was adorned with crocus and saffron blooms. He stood in it, his legs heroically braced apart, with purple and white flower petals up to his knees. His team of blacks—draped in blue and gold sheets—danced sideways in protest of the driver's firm grip. Their blue plumed heads on their arched necks bobbed, and their gold-painted hooves flashed as they pulled the good god along the base of the Horse Tower and the stables towards the palace. Ten chariots, carrying Necho's advisors and officials paraded through the gate. Their occupants' faces had been carefully painted, and they wore gold and silver armbands and collars with bright kerchiefs on their heads. Two battalions of honor guard, wearing only bleached loincloths and white headscarves, followed. Their bare feet slapped on the cobblestones. Some blew straight brass horns in a staccato military march while the others smacked their spears in time against their multi-patterned and speckled cowhide shields. The metal helms of the officers gleamed in the early morning light—until they passed beneath the shadow of the tower.

The people simply stood there, sullen and disapproving, like horses whose spirit had been broken.

Abdamelek watched the Judeans in amazement. They obviously were not appreciative of the honor given them to actually see a god ride through their midst. The fan-bearer glanced over at Jehoiakim, but the king had eyes only for the pharaoh. Necho himself looked neither right nor left. He was seemingly unaware of the people and their lack of enthusiasm. And of course, he was right. Necho was a god, and public opinion was beneath his notice.

The pharaoh pulled up to the portico. The Favored of Isis grinned and raised a hand towards Jerusalem's royal family as he hopped down and jauntily mounted the steps to greet them. With a final beat, the army divisions came to a halt. Silence fell as the pharaoh stopped on the porch of the palace of Jerusalem.

The Fan-Bearer to the Left prostrated himself. Jehoiakim stood and motioned to his family. Obediently, they dropped to their knees. Then Jehoiakim knelt and lay flat. His family did the same, followed by the entire group surrounding the throne. Abdamelek had been nervous about this. The Judeans were reluctant to recognize any god but their own. Jehoiakim, however, had been entirely amenable to Abdamelek's instructions. In this, as in everything else, Judah's new king was eager to please. The Judeans in the courtyard, however, remained standing and an ominous muttering hovered around them.

Pharaoh nudged the Cushite with his toe, and Abdamelek hastily stood and addressed the royals in flawless Hebrew. "The Son of Ra has recognized his servants. You may rise." They did so, and at Necho's encouraging nod, Jehoiakim once more took his throne. Abdamelek continued, "His Majesty Horus, the Good God, Beloved of Isis, the Goddess of Truth, Pharaoh of Upper and Lower Egypt, Great Chieftain of the West, Lord of the Diadem of the Vulture and of the Snake, the Son of Ra, the Living One, Wahemibre Necho, son of Osiris Psammetik has come to shine upon the reign of his new son, Jehoiakim, son of Josiah of the House of David, Anointed of his God and beloved of his people. May your reign be long and prosperous, royal scion of the line of Abraham." Abdamelek then fell to his knees and bowed his face to the porch tiles. He was not quite prostrate, but Jehoiakim was not a god.

Necho, smiling broadly, side-stepped the huge Cushite, and laid his right hand on Jehoiakim's shoulder. He too spoke in Hebrew. "At last, we speak face to face, and in far more joyous circumstances than when we last met. I have yet to express my condolences on your father and brothers," his grin faded and he stared somberly in the face of the intimidated Judean. "None of this is how I would have had it." He gave him a lop-sided smile, "except for you now being on the throne, of course."

"Of course," Jehoiakim stammered. "Once again, pharaoh shames me with his fluency in my language, when I must confess, I still have none in his."

"None of which is your fault, My Son," Necho said, affectionately slapping him on the cheek. "We both know that your father's kingdom, in which you were raised, was not a good neighbor to the Two Lands." Jehoiakim paled, but Necho laughed. "Don't worry. We know that his opinions are not yours. Besides, I trust Abdamelek more than makes up for what you see as your lack of language and protocol skills." The pharaoh gestured to the bowed-down form of the Cushite eunuch. "I assume he has told you that he was the Fan-Bearer to the Left, the second officer of protocol under my own brother, Prince Horiraa. As such, he was also responsible for much of the schooling of the royal princes and, of course, helping to make sure that everything at court was done properly. He was a very highly valued official of my court."

Jehoiakim nodded. "He has made himself indispensable already, but I have trouble with his name. Whenever I'm not concentrating, it comes out 'Ebedmelech.'"

Pharaoh shrugged. "It's not a name, it's a title. I'm giving him to you permanently. Call him whatever you wish."

Abdamelek didn't care, he didn't need a name. "Abdamelek" meant "servant of the king," and he had been that!

"Ebedmelech, then," Jehoiakim smiled. "But one is overly generous to his loyal son," Jehoiakim said, and he rose. "If one would deign to accompany me, my servants are waiting to refresh one from his journey, and a banquet is even now being set on the table in the main hall. My family and I will dine in the adjoining rooms." Jehoiakim was fully aware that Egyptians never ate with foreigners. "Then we will assemble in the audience chamber for the presenting of the taxes." The king looked down at his new protocol officer, absurdly pleased that the official who had been his keeper was now his to command. "Come along, Ebed."

A new life, a new "name." The big black man jumped to his feet and trotted after the group as King Jehoiakim entered the palace and showed the pharaoh to a side room to freshen up before the banquet and the presenting of the taxes. Slaves poured hot water over the pharaoh and the minister of protocol and gave them rich, heavily embroidered, Judean-style robes to wear. Ebed finally felt warm.

It was the fourth month of the Judean civil calendar—Meshir by the Egyptians'[1] The breeze that wafted through the windows of the planning room was chill, but the windows were left open to the fresh air anyway because the room was over-crowded with the king and his attendants. Ebedmelech was not surprised that almost all these officials were from the same family, former Secretary Shaphan's sons and grandsons. This was entirely proper, as was their relationship to the king. Jehoiakim's father had been Shaphan's foster-son. These relationships would be totally understood in Egypt. What he couldn't grasp was the almost openly hostile aura emanating from the group.

Nekhtu-Ra, Jerusalem's new master builder, refused to give up Egyptian dress and he shivered in the cold.[2] Ignoring the chill, he spread his scroll open before the king on the over-sized stone table of the planning room. "It will be magnificent, Majesty, think of it! The area of the Temple Court west of the Temple is just an empty space and has been ever since your father demolished the old Assyrian shrine. We have housed the Egyptian pantheon in the north Temple annex, but other nations must be made welcome in Jerusalem as well. They need a temple of their own."

The king seemed troubled in spirit. He glanced at his advisors and actually trembled at their outraged expressions. "The people fear Egypt. Your military is everywhere, and your officials oversee everything. Even so, my people murmur about your gods in our Temple. You have already taken the entire Northside rooms—all three floors!"

"It is not just the gods who must have housing, Lord King." Nekhtu-Ra reasoned. "Each god has his own court. There are many priests here already, and more are coming."

"But our priests are angry, and the people listen to them! And now you are proposing a whole new temple for gods from other nations, too? The people respect Egypt, but they don't fear the Philistines or the other nations. If we attempt to raise a building for the sole purpose of worshipping their gods, there will be riots in the streets!"

"My Lord King," Ebedmelech interjected, puzzled by the king and his antagonistic cabinet. "The great pharaoh faced a similar problem. The Egyptians hate foreigners and their gods, but Horus Wahemibre is a visionary, he understands that all the world must come together, welcomed under his outstretched wings. Our great Temple of Neith at Sais now houses many foreign gods. Who would dare gainsay the Son of Ra? His rule, and so his policies, extend here to Jerusalem as well. Lord Nekhtu-Ra is correct. This new temple must be built. Besides Great King, you have no monuments. A great king leaves his mark on history. You must build. This will be your first project. Your name will be inscribed on the cornerstone right under Wahemibre Necho's."[3]

Jehoiakim paced two nervous steps away, found himself face to face with Former Secretary Shaphan's angry brood and then abruptly turned back. "This is all splendid in theory!" He exploded, shaking his finger in the protocol officer's face. "But this builder is planning without taking into consideration that all workers are currently deployed, and all taxes are already spent. I *have* been building! What about the new pillars for the Temple! What about the portico outside Ra's door! My new throne room and the renovations on the upper floors of the palace…"

"Lord King, these are merely remodelings. You must build!" Nekhtu-Ra said.

Jehoiakim turned on the builder and pounded his fist on the scroll. "No, Master Builder! We can have no new projects for years."

Nekhtu-Ra gave the king a sly smile. "Lord King, look around you. This city is flooded with workers. Merchants from the coasts must cross your lands to get to their markets in Edom and Moab. Many foreigners might find an unexpected import-tax difficult to pay. Also, many of the locals seem to have more than enough money for offerings. Perhaps there are other things that should be taxed that you have neglected? Thus, you have both money and workers by continuing to enslave those who do not pay."[4]

Ebed frowned. In Egypt, everyone was already pharaoh's slaves, but it was reasoning like this that had first made him a eunuch. The king's advisors began murmuring heatedly amongst each other. The Cushite understood their protest. Judeans were a free people, and they should not treat that freedom lightly. Yet many had already been enslaved for the taxes Jehoiakim had already levied. More taxes and enslavements would cause increased unrest.

The meeting was interrupted by a disturbance outside. Abruptly, the doorway curtain parted, and a tall, thin man with wild eyes came striding into the room, brushing right past the palace guards posted there. None dared stop him.

Ebedmelech stared at the intruder. He was dressed in rough weave and wore a mantle of leather cowhide, hair-side out. His shoulder-length hair was hanging in curled strands, much of it across a face passionate with emotion, where it blended into his tangled beard. The power that emanated from this apparition was astonishing. It was as if the messenger of Set, the desert storm god, had suddenly materialized among them. Lightning and thunder seemed to roll from his person. Ebed couldn't help but think of the unearthly figure from the desert that had suddenly appeared and confronted Pharaoh Necho. It was as if that phantom had manifested itself here in Jerusalem. The enormous black man, his eyes wide, fell back from the stone table and realized that the builder and king had done the same.

"Jeremiah," Jehoiakim whispered fearfully.

The prophet? Ebedmelech had heard of him but had never seen him before.

Jeremiah shook with anger. "That!" he panted, holding back the curtain that led from the planning room to the remodeled throne room, "That! What is all of *that* supposed to be? Jehoiakim, where is the lion's throne of Judah? *That* throne is the throne of a jackal!"

Ebed stared in astonishment. The prophet had addressed the king directly and by name, without a single title. He demanded an explanation as if the king were required to answer to him!

"What are those paintings and that writing on the walls and pillars?" Alternating cedar panels of the throne room had been plastered over and painted in Egyptian mythological style, causing the room to be enveloped in series of colorful murals accented by rich red wood. Ebed considered them inspired. The artwork had been completed earlier that morning.

King Jehoiakim said nothing, he just looked at Ebedmelech, his minister of protocol.

It was Ebed's place to restore order and quell discord, so the eunuch stepped forward one step. He towered over Jeremiah, but he had never felt such power from anyone before, not even pharaoh. This was not a man he could intimidate. The Egyptian swallowed hard and politely answered the madman,

"Nabi, those illustrations are scenes from the Book of the Dead. The king has had them painted in the Hall of Audience to honor his father, King Josiah and his brother, Prince Johanan." He pointed to the two figures, shown over and over again in various poses walking with the Egyptian gods in the fields of Arahu.

Jeremiah stared, flabbergasted. "Isn't that the goddess, Isis? That shows Josiah walking hand-in-hand with her!" He shook his scruffy head, drug his eyes away, and went back to yelling at the king. "And what about the Temple? That is what brought me here! The sound of workmen's tools defiles the Holy Place to further desecrate it by housing Egypt's gods! Is it your intention to bring us a pantheon of new kings so that our only true King may have neighbors to share His glory? And you're building everything on the blood and sweat of the people of Jerusalem! Jehoiakim, how can you so soon have forgotten your roots? It is less than a month since you entertained pharaoh, and already the holy hill is beginning to resemble the City of Thebes! You impoverish the people by forcing them to pay for this travesty. Those who are already destitute and can't pay, you enslave and make them labor for free instead!"

King Jehoiakim spoke at last, "Prophet, I did not call for you, and you have overstepped your boundaries! I'd tell you to get out, but you are the Lord's prophet, so I will answer you. The people must pay their taxes. If they can't pay, they must work to pay off their debt. It has always been this way, and you are well aware of it. Now, you can get out."

Jeremiah bent over the table to look at the plans laid out there.

The builder nervously grabbed up the scroll and huddled protectively over it as he rapidly rolled it tight. Jeremiah glared at Nekhtu, who had backed off and was trying to shrink into the wall, his precious plans with him.

For the first time in years, Ebed wasn't sure what to do. It had never occurred to him that anyone could come into the presence of the king so abruptly and without his permission. It was absurd, but now this wild holy man ignored the king's dismissal as if he hadn't even heard it. The protocol minister glanced over at the advisors' faces. Ahikam, Gemariah, and Gedaliah were smiling grimly; their eyes blazed fiercely. They were not outraged, they approved. The entire population of this land must be as insane as their prophet!

Jeremiah, still breathing heavily, slowly raised an arm and pointed at Jehoiakim's face. "Listen to the word of the Lord, King of Judah. You sit on David's throne, so listen! You, your officials and your people who come through the gates of the city!" Ebed understood the implications of that statement. Jeremiah was saying Jerusalem was David's city and those who lived there were responsible for remembering that, as was their king. Changing the throne's appearance did nothing to change the source of its authority.

The prophet's clear voice shifted to the sing-song chant of his profession:

"The Lord says:
Do what is just and right!
Save victims from their oppressors!
Give equal justice to the aliens as to the citizens,
To the weak, the orphans and the widows
as you would to the important!
Stop shedding the blood of the innocent!"

Ebedmelech couldn't believe his ears. He had never heard anyone stand up for foreigners or peasants before as if they had rights. "Justice?" he stammered, trying to halt the prophet's rant, "for foreign filth and commoners? They are assets to be used. It is their only honor to serve!"

But Jeremiah was not interested in Egyptian protocol. He ignored the Cushite intermediary and still spoke directly to the king, his voice was deep and measured, as if it echoed from beyond the ceiling.

"If you are careful to reign with justice,
Then there will continue to be kings
who will sit on David's throne.
Your descendants will ride through the palace gates
in royal splendor,
They will ride in chariots or on horses.
Their officials will be for them,
And their people will support them."

Ebedmelech glanced again at the king's officials. These men feared their king, but they did not respect their king. It was possible that they actually represented a threat to his person. These secretaries were all scribes. Scribes carried the instruments of a writing kit on their belts, and so did this cabinet. One of those instruments of the kit was a sharp, little, dagger-like knife, used to scrape wax tablets clean. Ahikam's hand rested on the hilt of his scrapper.

The prophet's song took on a menacing tone.

"But if you don't, the Lord says:
I swear by Myself that this "renovated" palace
will become a ruin!"

The man of God stamped his foot, and the tiles beneath their feet actually seemed to shake. Ebedmelech was not sure that he had imagined it. Still, the Fan-Bearer could not understand. The Palace Guard stood just outside the doorway, with only a curtain for a barrier, but they did nothing. This man should be dead already, except who would dare accost the messenger of Set, the desert storm god? The eunuch wouldn't have wanted to be the one to have to attempt to lay a hand on the intruder either.

But Jeremiah's attitude was intolerable! He leaned over and whispered in the king's ear. "Lord King, the guard is right beyond that doorway…" The curtain was still partially pulled aside, but the guards outside were pretending to be oblivious to the events within the planning room.

"No!" Jehoiakim hissed back at the fan-bearer, his eyes on the rest of his officials. "The people are already at the point of rioting in the streets. The arrest and murder of a prophet—at this point—is not a good idea!"

Jeremiah may not have been able to hear the exchange, but he easily read the king's expression. It wasn't the first time people had murdered him in their thoughts. He smiled grimly and continued:

"This is what the Lord says concerning this palace:
You are strong as Gilead,
And lofty as the summit of Lebanon.

Even so, I will utterly destroy this place
until it is as barren as the desert,
And empty as an abandoned town."

The palace was ancient, built of the massive cedars of Lebanon centuries before. The thought of it being laid waste—especially with the plans for its renovation tucked against the master builder's chest—was unthinkable. That didn't stop Jeremiah. He continued,

"At My command, heavily armed ravagers will come
And they will chop up your precious cedar beams
And throw them into the fire of the city's destruction.
Then, when people from all the world pass by here, they will ask:
'Why did the Lord do such a thing to this great city?'
And others will answer:
'Because they gave up following the covenant
of the Lord their God
And went and worshipped and served other gods instead.'"

The officials nodded in satisfaction and whispered to one another. Jeremiah looked at them—Ahikam, Elasah, Jaazaniah, Gemariah and Ahikam's young son, Gedaliah. The prophet's expression softened, and the thunder died from the room. "Don't weep for King Josiah's death," Jeremiah told Shaphan's brood, his voice gentle, the structured chant vanishing. "He's gone. Instead, weep bitterly for King Jehoahaz, who is exiled. He will never return to see his native land again. This is what the Lord says about Shallum ben Josiah: 'He's not coming back. He will die a captive in Egypt. He will never see this land again.'"

Ebedmelech really scrutinized the group for the first time and realized that these weren't King Jehoiakim's men: they were King Josiah's, and they were hoping for Jehoahaz' return to depose the man who currently sat on the throne!

Ahikam, Shaphan's eldest, turned accusing eyes on the prophet. Ebedmelech had heard the story of how it had been Jeremiah who had counseled the young king to surrender to Egypt. He had thought the prophet must be a sensible man. He didn't think so anymore. Jeremiah seemed to be out to alienate even his supporters.

The son of Hilkiah took a deep breath and turned back to the current king, once again taking up his song:

"Woe will come to him who builds his palace by evil deeds,
Who constructs his living quarter by injustice.
He forces his countrymen to labor for free,
He pays them nothing for their work!
He imagines: 'I am going to build myself a magnificent palace
With large and airy rooms upstairs.'
So he makes huge windows
And uses costly cedar paneling
And decorates it using the best red dyes.

He stopped singing and asked the king, "Are you more of a king than your father, just because you've got more cedar? Your father had everything he needed, didn't he? And he got it by doing what was right and just! He stood up for the poor and needy, and all went well with him. So, now the Lord asks you: 'Isn't that what it really means to know Me?'

Jehoiakim glared at the prophet.

Ebed saw Jehoiakim clearly for the first time. The new king was not cunning and shrewd, he was cruel and shallow. He apparently didn't care about knowing his God better, but yes, he did want more cedar. This was how all kings acted, but they weren't supposed to! The thought was revolutionary. The words of the prophet cut the fan-bearer to the heart. Ebed stared in astonishment at the ideas the prophet threw at the king, ideas that had never occurred to him.

In Egypt, the people had a duty to the pharaoh, and the pharaoh, in turn, had a duty to the gods and their temples. A good ruler kept the gods happy, who in turn blessed the ruler and things went well with the people. But never, never was the pharaoh answerable to the people! Nor would the gods expect such a thing! "What kind of religion is this?" he whispered to Jerusalem's Master Builder.

Nekhtu-Ra just continued to cradle his scrolls close. He was too angry to answer.

Jeremiah shook his finger at the king, and his voice grew and echoed from the room like Set's thunderstorms. "BUT YOU! Your eyes and heart are fixed on profits, no matter how you obtain them; even by spilling innocent blood or by oppression and extortion! That being the case, this is what the Lord says about *you,* King Jehoiakim ben Josiah of Judah:

The people won't cry for you!
They will not go to their brothers or sisters for comfort.
They will not mourn for you!
No one will say: 'Oh, my poor master! His splendor is no more!'"
You will have the burial they accord a donkey;
You will be drug away
And thrown outside the gates of Jerusalem on the rubbish heap!"

Finally, Jehoiakim's anger overrode his fear. He choked, then acted on Ebedmelech's suggestion. "Guards!" he sputtered. But though the guards were now peeking through the doorway, they looked not to the king, but to Shaphan's sons. Ahikam's face was grim. His grip on his scrapper tightened, and he gave a barely perceptible shake of his head, denying them.

The guards turned back to their posts and studiously ignored the planning room once more. Jehoiakim gaped at them. Ebedmelech had never seen such disobedience before, and for the first time, a hint of doubt and fear appeared on Builder Nekhtu's face. What if these men decided to assassinate their new king, right here and now? Ebed wondered what he had gotten into.

Jeremiah snorted derisively, calling the king's attention back to him. The prophet wasn't finished.

> "You don't believe this will happen, do you? Fine. Go up to Lebanon and see for yourself! Let your cry of anguish ring out in Bashan and Abarim, because you will see your enemies coming and your allies crushed! I have warned you now when you still feel secure when you still have time. But I see your heart.

You are saying: 'I won't listen!' You have been headstrong like this since you were a child. You have always refused to obey Me."

The fan-bearer saw Ahikam nodding in agreement. He remembered that all these men had known Jehoiakim since he was born and Shaphan and his sons had chosen to crown another as king. Shaphan's sons may have been Jehoiakim's advisors, but they were not loyal. They agreed with the prophet and a stirring in his soul made Ebed see the world from their point of view.

This God of theirs was overwhelming and ruled everything. He was everywhere! And King Jehoiakim was a pathetic excuse of a man who dared call himself king and rule this, God's people, all the while ignoring Him. Ebed blinked at the realization. Jeremiah was not mad—Jehoiakim was a fool!

Jeremiah was fearless, a champion of justice standing up against a foe that should have swept him away like chaff. Instead, he prevailed. He was an epic figure who outshone any of Egypt's heroes of old.

Jeremiah was unaware of the effect he was having on the Egyptian minister of protocol. Instead, he turned to Ahikam and his relatives and sang to them.

"As for Israel,
All your shepherds will be blown away in the wind;
And your allies will be captured and taken into exile.
Then you will be ashamed and disgraced by your own
wickedness.
Inhabitants of 'Lebanon' nestled in your homes
built with Lebanese cedar!
How you will groan when pangs come upon you,
Pain like that of a woman in labor!"[5]

The prophet turned on his heel and left as abruptly as he had come.

Silent tears were running down Gemariah's cheeks, and Ahikam put his arm around his brother's shoulders.

King Jehoiakim abruptly lifted a small oil lamp and threw it at the guards outside in the hall. "Worthless! You're both worthless! Where's your captain? Go! Fetch Elnathan! Now!" Both the guards fled.

Ebedmelech shook his head in confusion, but he was certain of one thing: Jeremiah the Prophet had made the king into an enemy for life.

PART 3: 608 BC

Idols and Desecrations

WHY is My love doing this?
—Jeremiah 11:15

CHAPTER 22

Anathoth

A prophet is not without honor except in his own town,
Among his relatives and in his own home.
—Mark 6:4

Jerusalem, Judah

he fourteenth day of the seventh month came, and with it came the day of the slaughter of the lambs. The Feast of Passover would begin on the new day—when the first three stars came out in the evening.[1]

The afternoon was clear and breezy, inviting thousands of pilgrims to come fill the narrow streets of Jerusalem and make their annual sacrifice. The blessing of the Lord awaited them. The murmur of their voices filled the air mixed with the bleating of lambs. All the inns and every spare room in the city were filled.

Three priests, twenty years between each, stood by the New Gate of the Temple. The young man, thirty-year-old Zephaniah ben Maaseiah, was tall and lean, the seventy-year-old second priest Jehoiada was thin and bent, and the strong fifty-year-old Third Priest Buzi supported the older man by the elbow. The trio surveyed the scene before them. They had paused to observe the ancient ritual. The smell of blood and smoke from the sacrifices filled the air and the courtyard echoed with the instruments, bells, and songs of the Levite .singers. The sacred sounds competed with the crowd's yells and exclamations, and the bleating of sheep and goats—and construction's sounds of foul corruption.

Crowds of pilgrims carried struggling lambs, all in their first year, over their shoulders. The people forced their way past the three priests into the clogged Temple Court. The trio was just south of the gate, in the palace court, looking through it to the crowded Temple area.

In the past months, the Levites had been ousted from their quarters in the rooms on the north side of the Temple and housed elsewhere; the New Gate now held the homes and offices of many of the sacerdotal priests. Looking through the gate from the palace side, the steps of the Temple and the ramps of the altar itself were almost directly in front the three priests. Across the congested Temple Court, the shameful presence of the Egyptian shrine was entirely hidden from their view. It was one of the reasons the priests had grudgingly agreed to be housed here.

But now… Zephaniah glanced left, to the west. The priest couldn't see the Egyptian shrine on the north of the Temple, but he *could* see the almost completed building, the new Wood House, right behind the Temple. This new version of the abomination had an opening to the east, like the original, to the back side of the Temple. But its new, grandiose main entrance now faced the West Gate; and the West Gate was the main entrance to the Temple grounds from the New City.[2] Most of the pilgrims walked around it, but the three priests couldn't help but see that many walked right through it. These worshippers, wriggling and thrashing lambs still held tightly around their necks, stopped to do service to the pagan gods as they passed them.

Over the noise filling the courtyard, Zephaniah could not hear any verbal exchanges, but he and his companions could see them.

A man paused, arguing with his wife, who shook her head violently and turned, depositing a copper bracelet in a box on the east steps of the Wood House. A priest of Baal cried out a prayer while he poured a few drops of oil on the lamb's head, consecrating it. The man glared at his wife, then made his way back into the crowd to take the lamb to the priests of the altar. They had made the same lamb serve as two very different offerings and saved money in the process.

"Disgusting," Zephaniah said. "We should be taking down their names."

"To what purpose?" the second priest asked. "We are powerless to act. But the Lord has noted their names, Zephaniah. Be sure of it. In the end, justice will prevail."

"Except we won't live to see it."

"I hope not."

The pounding of hammers and the shouts of overseers continued and could be heard even above the bleating of lambs and the noise of the crowds.

Jehoiada followed his gaze and snorted. "They don't even stop the desecration of their perverted construction for the Passover." Tools for construction were never to be used on Temple grounds.

The Third Priest gave them both a wicked grin. "They're lucky it is the Passover. My Ezekiel is too busy helping his assigned families with their sacrifices to carry out his plans of arson. He says that with just a touch of oil that big black Baal of theirs would make a splendid torch."

Zephaniah raised his eyebrows at the idea, then cocked his head as he considered the possibility. "The Ashtareth and the Dagon they brought in last week are made of wood too," he mused. "But you'd better keep him in line, Buzi. The king wouldn't stand for it."

Jehoiada shrugged. "If it makes you feel any better, the priests of Amun-Ra have been complaining to me. It seems that sacrificing sheep is an abomination to them. So, is roasting and eating them. I told them it is this way every year, so they have temporarily fled the city." He sighed. "I supposed they'll be back after the feast ends. But as for the Passover, it's going to be a good turnout. You've done exceptional work, Zephaniah, making sure that all remember their responsibility and come."

Zephaniah shrugged. "Passover attendance is mandatory."

"But expensive. With Josiah gone, there is no way to enforce their attendance. With the new taxes, this feast is a heavy burden. If the people discovered that, under our new king, they would be excused from their religious duties, then by next year there would be no Passover! We would find ourselves back in the days of Manasseh and Amon. Instead, despite the times, your visits have reminded the people that they are obliged to serve the Lord."

"Despite the times and despite the king. But I wasn't the only one making visitations…" Zephaniah began modestly. He was secretly pleased, glad to be included in the company of the second and Third Priests.

"You organized the program, though," Buzi told him.

"I know," the second priest affirmed. "Thanks to you, Zephaniah, the Temple treasury, though not fat, is acceptable. You are to be commended. But it is the Passover and Buzi's Ezekiel is not the only one who has a heavy schedule. We must be going."

As the three pushed their way through the gate and the crowd towards the altar, Zephaniah smiled to himself. He was an ambitious man, and Jehoiada's notice could only further his career. He had already made himself invaluable in Chief Priest Azariah's service by organizing and coordinating all the various ministries performed on the Temple grounds. He took a few steps up the altar's massive ramp and looked far above his head to the top. He was determined to mount to as high a post as he could in the priesthood. Zephaniah was a descendant of Abiathar, not Zadok, but that wasn't going to stop him! Abiathar's line was elder, and King Josiah had effectively negated the stigma that King Solomon had placed upon it. It was time for the priesthood to recognize the preeminence of Abiathar's line once more.

As Second Priest Jehoiada struggled up the steep altar ramp with Buzi's help, a disturbance caught Zephaniah's attention. Something was going on behind the Temple, near the Wood House, the pagan shrine. He hesitated, and then let curiosity take him. He strode back down to the pavement and pushed his way through the throng on the south side of the Temple. Shouts and yells made him move faster, and many in the crowd were moving with him now, pressing in and eager to see what was happening. The priest reached the rear of the Temple. The people crowded around watching. In a cleared area before the pagan shrine's half-finished main entrance a tall, lean figure stood, holding a lash meant for a recalcitrant ox. The figure looked enough like Zephaniah to have been mistaken for him at first glance, except for his hairy overcoat. It wasn't Zephaniah's brother, it was his cousin, the prophet. Jeremiah was yelling at the people, cracking the long-handled whip in a circle above his head.

"The Lord, the God of Israel, your God, has a message for you," Jeremiah spoke, his clear voice carrying easily above the noise of the Passover crowd.

"He says this:

> I gave you commands in the form of a covenant to your ancestors when I brought them out of Egypt. I told them to obey Me and do everything I commanded, and I would be their God, and they would belong to Me. I promised to fulfill the oath I swore to them, to give them this land flowing with milk and honey. This is the land you possess today. But be sure of this, the man who does not obey this covenant is cursed!"

A small group of mediums and Moabite priests of Baal were selling incense and charms and telling fortunes for the tourists outside the shrine. The acrid smell of their incense censors wafted over the heads of the people.

Wielding the lash, the prophet rushed to the front of the shrine and brought it down on the heads and backs of the enemies of his Lord. "Evildoers!" *Crack* went the whip. "Lawbreakers!" *Crack, crack, crack!* "You dare? Right in the Temple Court at the time of the feast?"

The occultists broke and fled in the face of what they could only assume was a madman. They didn't resent him, though. Some of them actually laughed—those who hadn't been stung by the whip's leather lash! To the heathen, all holy men were, at least, a little mad and were to be indulged in their antics. The workmen stopped their labors, though, to come watch the spectacle unfolding outside the door of their architectural endeavors.

Panting, Jeremiah threw the whip after the retreating pagan priests and turned once more to the citizens who packed the courtyard. A large part of them encircled the prophet, more interested in this new development than their sacrifices.

Jeremiah shouted in a voice that carried over the cacophony and echoed off the back of the Temple.

> "These are the terms of the covenant. Listen and obey!
>
> Ever since I brought your ancestors out of Egypt, I have warned them over and over again to obey! But they paid no attention; they stubbornly followed their own evil inclinations. So, all the curses of the covenant they were commanded to keep, but didn't, fell on them. The people of Judah and the inhabitants of Jerusalem have not learned from this. They are conspiring together to go back to the sins of their ancestors, who wouldn't listen to Me either."

He gestured behind him, to the construction in progress.

> "They turn to serve other gods. Judah, like Israel before her, has broken My covenant. Her people will not escape the disaster that I will bring on them. Then they will turn to Me and cry out, but I won't listen! So, Judah and Jerusalem will go to their idols and plead and burn incense. But even though the gods of Judah are as numerous as its towns and villages and its altars to the shameful god Baal number like the streets of Jerusalem, when disaster strikes, idols cannot help at all."

The prophet directed his attention through the doors of the rebuilt shrine of the Wood House. The gods of the Canaanites and Philistines stood within, and the crowd peered into the gloom to see the objects of the prophet's attention.

"WHY is My love doing this?"

The cry in his voice was so heartbreaking that Zephaniah felt his heart constrict and his eyes tear. Angrily, he brushed the tears aside. Jeremiah was very good at what he did, and Zephaniah agreed with him, but Jeremiah had no sense!

The prophet would not have cared what his cousin thought though and abruptly he turned to the east and pointed at Temple's backside, at the rear of the north annex. The back door was open to welcome the crowds of worshippers for the Passover. The pantheon of Egypt, painted and carved into the walls, stared at the crowd from out of the shadows within.

> "In My very Temple, she works evil schemes with many different gods!"

Clouds of incense floated within, partially obscuring the bizarre frescos of snakes, creeping creatures and misshapen animals from the Egyptian "Book of the Dead." Dark miniature figures of the host of the Nile gleamed on shelves throughout the shadows of the shrine. The smell of the smoke mingled with that of the sacrifices and roasting lamb.

> "Do you really think that meat consecrated to idols will divert your punishment?" the prophet addressed the crowd. "You rejoice in your evil deeds! The Lord saw you as a beautiful olive tree, full of fruit, but in a furious storm, He will strike you with lightning and set you afire. Your branches will be blown down. It was the Lord Almighty Who planted you, but neither Israel nor Judah would recognize this, and they have burned incense to Baal instead, provoking the Lord to anger, so now it's too late; it's over. Now He has decreed your destruction!"[3]

Too Late? Zephaniah pondered this. Was there actually an end to the Lord's patience? If so, would Jeremiah be privy to it? Did he believe Jeremiah? His father certainly did. Did he? He didn't want to. Zephaniah looked at the Temple. It was as strong and beautiful as ever. All he wanted was to serve in its courts and rise high enough in the ranks of the priesthood that he wouldn't have to retire at the mandatory fifty-years-old. Chief, second, or Third Priest, that was his dream. He had twenty years to get there. Too late?

The astounded crowd moved aside as the son of Hilkiah strode right through them, heading now for the West Gate. This crowd was angry. If he had waited much longer, they might have turned their anger on him. It seemed

Jeremiah knew this and took advantage of their indecision. He simply left, as shouts and jeers were pelted at his back.

"Jeremiah! Wait!" Zephaniah rushed to catch up with his cousin. The prophet turned, already in the West Gate, and waited.

"Brother!" Zephaniah said urgently and put his arm around his cousin's shoulders, ushering him out of the gate, off Temple grounds. He leaned close and spoke low, "You know you're my favorite cousin. We grew up together. I only want what is best for you. The priests, we all share your frustration, all of us. But it's the Passover! Things are chaotic enough around here without you stirring things up more. Please, Jeremiah. Not now."

Jeremiah allowed himself to be led aside, out of the way of the crowds and into a nearby narrow street, but his eyes were still flashing. "My frustration? Those were not my words, Zephaniah. I'm only a messenger."

"A prophet, I know. But the prophets of the House don't act like this.[4] Couldn't you try to be a little more like Zedekiah? He stands by Huldah's Gate with the rest of the prophets and serves when he is asked. You can be sure he doesn't like the idols any more than we do, but he's not causing any trouble. Do you want to get arrested?"

Jeremiah snorted derisively. "Cousin," he answered more calmly, "your brother serves the House of Prophets well, but those prophets do not prophesy! They merely expound on the Law and apply it to people's lives, and they only do that when they're asked. They perform a necessary function, but they wouldn't recognize the Word of the Lord if Balaam's donkey stood in front of them and delivered it.

"But I think you do, don't you?" Jeremiah gave him a lopsided smile, and Zephaniah felt ashamed. He hung his head. "I thought so. Cousin, when the Lord speaks, I can't help it, I have to bring His message, or I'll explode. It is precisely because it is the Passover that He speaks now. He wants all the people to be here to hear."

Zephaniah had no answer. He shook his head angrily and stalked back towards the altar, swinging the palm of his hand behind him dismissively.

Jeremiah's tiny quarters on the roof of the widow woman's home had an olive-wood door, a high narrow window in one white-washed mud wall, a reed mat that served as a bed, and a small wooden table and bench. A large wood and leather chest held his belongings, and a few copper and brass pots and vessels were scattered about. He had rented the room when he had left Josiah's palace and abandoned his royal clothes on the palace bed. Now he had a hairy mantle and a room with a mat. He needed nothing else. Troubled in spirit, Jeremiah prostrated himself on the mat and called out to his God. He protested and continued a previous conversation, one he had interrupted to deliver the Lord's message. Now he continued, trying to still the unrest in his soul.

"I delivered Your message, but how can You tell me not to pray for them? How can You refuse to listen and be merciful?" His God was the God of Peace, but Jeremiah's unrest only grew.

Watch. It is because of this. This is how they all feel, of what they are all guilty.

And then Jeremiah was in the Temple Court once more. He was bound and laying across the shoulders of his cousin, House Prophet Zedekiah. Jeremiah realized he was a paschal lamb, destined for sacrifice, and he began to struggle wildly. He yelled at his cousin and the people in the court, but they didn't seem to hear him. Zedekiah's determination gave him great strength, and he ignored Jeremiah's struggles as he mounted the ramp of the great altar under stormy skies.

A voice cried out, "Kill him!" The voice was Pediah's—a neighbor of his father from Anathoth.

"Kill him," the cry echoed from a dozen throats.

Jeremiah looked down, the altar's ramp was crowded with men from Anathoth—men he had known since he was a small child.

Back in his room, the afternoon sun streaming through his window, the prophet sat up abruptly, his eyes wide. "Anathoth?" he asked out loud. "The people of my own village want to kill me? But why?"

And he stood in a barren meadow with a beautiful fruit tree in its center. From every direction, many dying people came crawling through the dried grass and thorns to pick the fruit and eat it. The fruit restored them to life.

Suddenly, the tree was surrounded by the same men from the altar ramp, all wielding axes. "Cut it down," they raged. "Destroy him! Get rid of the fruit so that his name will be remembered no more!"

Zedekiah took a mighty swing with his ax. It bit deep into the wood.

Jeremiah gasped in pain and was in his room again. He held his stomach as he sat up, but there was no wound. "They wish to kill me to destroy the words You put in my mouth!" He exclaimed and shuddered. He looked askance at the ceiling and repeated his question. "Why?"

The man of God stood and walked to a nearby shelf. He took a pitcher of water and poured himself a cup. *"Do not be afraid of them for I am with you and will rescue you,"* he quoted softly. "I was twelve years old when You told me that. Well, I'm not afraid of them, I'm angry!" he slammed the empty cup back down on the shelf. "They think that by silencing me, they can silence You? This is blasphemy! Your words are everything! My cause is Yours. I follow You! You are the Lord Almighty, Who judges righteously and sees all men's hearts and minds. You know mine, and You know theirs. So, I'm asking for You to judge between us. They seek to destroy me because what they really want is to get rid of You! Besides, I have Your promise. So, let me see Your revenge fall on their heads!"

There was a shout at the wood door. The angry voices of several men clamored for him to come out.

"Already?" Jeremiah asked the heavens. Then he turned and went to the door and lifted its latch.

A group of men from Anathoth stood on the steps leading up to his quarters just as the prophet had seen these same men standing on the altar ramp. They held an assortment of clubs, knives, and rocks.

Despite himself, the prophet chuckled. "What? No axes?" he asked the ceiling.

They were led by one wearing a mantle of camel-hair, his cousin, Zedekiah ben Maaseiah of the House of Prophets. The son of Hilkiah was not surprised by this development. "Zedekiah! My Lord and I were just speaking about you. I was talking to your brother about you earlier, too."

"I heard," his cousin answered. "Zephaniah told us when he came and found us having a meeting about you. He said I'd better accompany our brethren here to keep them from…"

"That's him!" shouted one of the other men.

"Stone him!" shouted another, and he threw a stone, but his aim was off, and it bounced off the wall, leaving a black mark on the white-washed surface.

"Why were you having a meeting about me?" Jeremiah asked Zedekiah, seemingly unconcerned about his personal safety.

The first man pushed Zedekiah out of the way and walked right up face to face, nose to nose, with the prophet. "Jeremiah, you are of Anathoth, just as we are! You are a descendant of Abiathar, the same as we. Our ancestor was the rightful Chief Priest. Yet thanks to Solomon, it is the descendants of Zadok who hold that office. But up until you, we, the descendants of Abiathar have continued to minister as we always have, in our village shrine.

"You, on the other hand, incited King Josiah to have the Ark removed and that shrine torn down!"

"What? I did no such thing!" Jeremiah objected, stunned at the accusation.

"You did!"

"Pediah," the prophet reasoned with the man, "You live next to my father. You watched me grow up. When King Josiah made that decision, you know that I was only a teenager. I had no influence on the king; I had barely met him, except for those times when I was hauled into court before him…"

"You did it!" Pediah insisted. "And now, without the shrine, the pilgrims stay away. We're obliged to bring trinkets to the Temple to sell and after today… Jeremiah, are you bent on destroying what's left of our businesses? People shy away from anything from Anathoth on your account. It's Passover, and we've had to close our booths in the Temple Court because the people have been threatening to tear them down. But even worse, travelers skirt our town. They hurry by, looking the other way. We are being ostracized from Judah, and we are afraid of Egypt's wrath because of your prophesying."

Zedekiah pushed Pediah back, moving both his palms up and down placatingly before him. The townsman nodded and let Zedekiah speak.

"Jeremiah ben Hilkiah, listen to us," Zedekiah announced in what was obviously a practiced speech.

Jeremiah had never noticed before how pompous his kinsman was becoming. He leaned against his doorframe and listened.

"We are your kin and neighbors. As you say, you have known us all of your life. Jeremiah, we care about you. Our intentions are only to straighten you out for your own good. If you do not stop preaching in the streets and Temple Court, soon you will not be able to come home! But you won't be able to stay in Jerusalem either because they'll stone you! You prophesy against your own people! We are allied with Egypt, and you prophesy against them, all the while upholding our enemies. You have placed the people in an uproar at a time when they should be engaged in worship."

The group nodded and murmured to each other over the wisdom of this speech.

"Kinsman," Zedekiah continued, "the time of Josiah is over. The Lord did not save him. He gave the victory to Egypt! The Egyptians have placed our present king on his throne, yet you cry out against their gods. The Moabites are our brothers, but you denounce their belief in Baal. You object to any kind of trade with them and act as though they were unclean! There is nothing wrong with Egyptian, Moabite or Greek goods. And now you are bothering the pilgrims who come to worship the Lord!"

Jeremiah stood straight again and fixed Zedekiah with a stare that made him glance away furtively. "Zedekiah, you are not here to keep these men from harming me, you are here as their spokesman. If your brother were here, he would not be a party to such reasoning, and it is unbecoming to a member of the House of Prophets. But since you do not seem to understand that, I will tell you that it is not foreign goods that I object to. It is the fact that their foods have been dedicated to their gods. Their gods decorate all their pottery, and their gods are becoming commonplace additions to the dwellings of our people! It is Passover, but how can the people celebrate freedom from Egypt, when the gods of Egypt rule over them once more? Along with the paschal lamb, they eat meat consecrated to idols!"

Zedekiah's eyes narrowed. "The Egyptians are no longer our enemies. The truth is that many of our people consider Baal to be just another aspect of the Lord. There is a growing consensus among the priests and at the House of Prophets that this could very well be so. Even your friends the Babylonians recognize that Baal is just a form of their god Bel.

"The Almighty appears to different people in different ways; argue about it with Him, not us. To put it bluntly, Jeremiah, stop prophesying in the name of the Lord or your prophecies are going to fall flat, and by the Law, we will have no choice but to end up stoning you."

Jeremiah shook his head. "You follow the Law where it suits you and break it where it does not. I have known all of you for all of my life. I know you now. The Lord tells me that you have been plotting against me and you seek my life. But I have committed my cause to the King of Heaven. It is His justice that I seek and..." Jeremiah turned eyes suddenly heavy with sorrow on his townsmen, "this is His answer:

> 'I will punish them. Their young men will be slain by the sword and their children by famine. Anathoth will be completely destroyed, and none of them will remain because I will destroy the people of Anathoth on the Day of Judgment.'"[5]

With that, the man of God slammed the door in their faces.

CHAPTER 23

Military Training

The Hill Country, Mesopotamia[1]

The evening breeze rose with Shamash's descent. It rustled the leaves on bushes and whistled through the branches of trees. The tall grass of the hillsides yielded before it, rippling northward in undulating waves. The armies of Babylonia and Media shivered under it, for the weather was chill. The troops set up camp slowly. The exhaustion of the day's march left a lethargy that not even the thought of their evening rations could lift. Prince Nebuchadnezzar was one of the first in line to the food wagons. Rank had its privileges. He gulped down the hot stew, then dropped exhausted onto his bedroll. It was cold, he left his tunic on.

Nebuzaradan took Kadurri's bowl and set it aside. Then, he sat down on a nearby rock and sparked a flint on some tinder. He was trying to build a fire from some wood he had carried over, and he managed to get the tinder lit on his third try. The daggerman was probably just as tired as the prince, but he never seemed to show it.

At fourteen, Kadurri had dreamed of glory and conquest. He could hardly wait to get out into the field and revenge Belnasir and the men of Carchemish. Now he was fifteen and actually in the field. His first season of marching with the troops showed him a reality that his tutors had somehow forgotten to mention. Soldiering was hard work, and mostly, it was just plain boring.

Two moons had passed since he had first ridden proudly out of Babylon in his own brand-new chariot. He had a shield bearer and driver all his own. Nebuzaradan rode a prancing gray protectively to his right. Under the command of Rab Mag Nergalniari, the army had left Babylon early in the morning, and the weather had been chill. For two moons, Nergalniari and King Uvakshatra of Media had led the Coalition forces on, and on, and on. Seri's gray no longer pranced.

The campaign had seen several minor skirmishes, but nothing major. Nergalniari seemed glad for this. The rab mag suffered from an ongoing condition, fever, dysentery, stomach aches, joint and muscle pain and headaches. None of the physicians could cure him; none of the priests could obtain the gods' favor. Campaigning was like torture for him, but the grizzled old general continued. Niari was determined to carry on his duty as long as he was able. He had served only twenty years of his thirty-year term, and he was not ready to quit yet![2]

The armies had been tied up chasing guerilla groups. The Kingdom of Urartu was in decline and its ruler, Sarduri son of Rusa, was only nine years old. He had begun his reign as a toddler, installed with the permission of Assyria's King Sinsharushkin. Of all his father's sons, the Assyrian monarch had left only him and his younger brother alive.

Now, Urartu was independent once more. It covered a vast area beginning north of Harran and moving east to the Median border. Assyria had claimed the territory, and the Alliance had been the Hill People's security against Scythian and Median incursions. The Assyrian Empire was gone, but the Urartu still counted themselves as members of the Alliance and so refused to recognize the Coalition's rule over Assyria or them. In fanatic worship of their warrior god, highwaymen ambushed traders on the road, disrupting commerce and supplies. A growing Urartu army raided villages just over their border. The Hill People had to be subdued.

For now, the continued harassment by the fiendish Urartu kept the Coalition forces from actually moving on Carchemish. The Coalition armies were stalled only a quarter-moon west of Harran. Here, on the open road just south of the hills, the troops stopped, defeated in their campaign by the terrain to the north. The infantry could march in pursuit, but all their officers rode in chariots, and the Hill Country was no place for chariots.

The rugged hills to the north grew dark and foreboding; their twisted trees cast ominous shadows in Shamash's fading light. The wind finally chilled the prince, and he rolled himself in his bedroll as darkness fell, but before sleep could take him, he heard footsteps approaching.

The Babylonian prince looked up to find Prince Ishtumegu of Media standing over him. The flames of the fire danced in the wind and lit menacing shadows and lights on Ishtu's face. Unlike Kadurri, the Median heir had already spent several years with the troops. He was a married man and had a child of his own awaiting him at home. He was considerably older than Kadurri, and this was the first time he had ever stopped by his tent—they were not friends.

"I was curious," Ishtu began in perfect Aramaic, but with no polite formalities at all, "how does the prince of Babylon find the accommodations in the field? Does it suit my brother, or would you rather return to your down-stuffed bed in your big city?" The Medes scorned cities and viewed their inhabitants as pathetically soft and weak-willed.

Kadurri snorted. Unfortunately, Ishtu literally *was* "his brother." Ishtu's sister, Amyhia, was to be his bride. "My father, the king, requires my service where he will. My father is the delight of my life, and his slightest wish my highest command," he rudely rolled over and closed his eyes.

After a moment, Ishtu chuckled. "My father has sent me to summon you, young one. The 'delight of your life' has arrived, however belatedly, and our presence is required in the tent of strategy."

Kadurri scrambled to his feet and briefly considered tackling the older prince. King Nabopolassar was not late! He was obliged to remain in Babylon for the New Year Festival, and Ishtumegu certainly knew this. But his father was here! …And he wouldn't be pleased to find that his son had been brawling. Kadurri kept his tongue and his temper.

Ishtu eyed Kadurri's grimy red tunic. Then sniffed and wrinkled his nose. "Maybe you had better have your man there find you a fresh tunic, first." This was another insult. Seri wasn't Kadurri's man; he was a nobleman, a daggerman of high rank, responsible for the crown prince himself.

The Prince of Media sauntered off.

"I see he's changed his own tunic," Seri growled, digging through Kadurri's pack. "His driver told me that one of his team soiled its tail today and then smacked him with it right in the chest!"

Kadurri laughed. Seri could always make him laugh. It was unlikely that the story was accurate, but Ishtumegu was a bully. That was the best word for it. It was undoubtedly true that his driver wished him ill. The prince abused his men and his horses with words and whips. Such a man was not to be trusted, and it worried Kadurri that one day he and the Median prince would undoubtedly find themselves in an alliance based on their fathers' friendship and his marriage to Ishtu's sister.

The daggerman tossed the prince a fresh tunic, and he quickly changed. "I hate Bar Manuti like that, the ones who think they're better than everyone else." Ishtu was Mede, so he wasn't actually Bar Manuti, but Seri couldn't be expected to know the Median term for a nobleman.

"Let's just hope Princess Amyhia is nothing like him," Kadurri agreed.

"Well, they say she is very pretty. He's definitely not."

Kadurri laughed again. "She's too young to be pretty, Seri. She's only a little girl, just twelve years old—the same age as Shum." Looking over his shoulder at the departing back of Ishtumegu, he couldn't help but think about her, though. He shuddered. "But please Ishtar, don't let her grow up to be like him," he added quietly.

He would soon find out. At the end of the year's campaign, Nebuchadnezzar would accompany his father north and east. They were going to visit Ecbatana. "I'm ready, let's go."

He took two steps in the direction of the strategy tent when out of the shadows stepped Seri's father Arioch, and next to the captain of the daggermen came King Nabopolassar, himself. Seri quickly bowed his head, crossed his arms and snapped his fingers.

"Father!" Kadurri began, "I was just coming…"

"No need. Uvak sent Ishtu to get you, but I really only needed a brief update. Niari gave me all the details I need for the moment. There will be no more meetings tonight. Tomorrow will be soon enough for that." Nabopolassar gave his son that disarming grin, he was so famous for.

There was a fallen log lying nearby, and the great Provider of Marduk plopped himself down on it. He patted the log beside him. Kadurri tardily bobbed his head and snapped his fingers, then he walked over and sat next to his father on the log.

The two daggermen stood by and began to chat quietly as the king and crown prince greeted each other.

Nabo took Kadurri's hand, a Babylonian sign of intimate friendship.

"You're looking well," the king observed. "You've been out for two moons, seen a lot of marching and you have a handful of dead Urartu to show for it," Nabo shook his head with a wry grin. "So now that you've gotten a taste for campaigning, what do you think?"

Kadurri laughed quietly. "I'm on my third pair of sandals, Lord."

"Then you should stay in your chariot more."

"The chariots are seeing no action, father! It's only the infantry that can penetrate into those hills."

"And they can't go far without officers. And the officers won't march."

"Yes. King Uvakshatra's cavalry can go there, though. They're carrying almost all the fighting. The Medes are right, you know. We need to get our own cavalry units."

The Assyrians had employed a large cavalry for almost two hundred years. They had maintained the mounted units for the same reason Babylon was now seeing the need. The Elamites and the Urartu, traditional enemies of Assyria, fought from horseback and lived in a mountainous country with few roads.

The Babylonians had never faced such a foe and so had always viewed cavalry with disdain. The Bar Manuti, the nobility, refused to ride. The Babylonians had always had some mounted riders, but these were basically used only as guards to the king's chariot or as mobile small-bow divisions.

The wind briefly switched direction, and the smoke from the fire blew into their faces. They coughed, and the emperor dropped his son's hand so he could cover his mouth. Arioch quickly grabbed a cloth and fanned it away. The wind switched back again, and after rubbing their eyes, they resumed their discussion.

"So Uvak says, and I have been working on it. We've got the horses and even men to ride them, but we still lack officers," the emperor pointed out. "The Bar Manuti won't march, but they won't ride astride, either. They feel they might as well become Scythian! I'm very proud of you, though: that you've been marching into those hills showing the officers that they can march with their troops when necessary. It's a good example."

Kadurri shook his head and frowned. He was not going to let a little praise shift him from the subject. "Father, we need that cavalry and the cavalry needs officers, so the Bar Manuti will have to change their minds! We'll have to convince them that rank in the cavalry is civilized and an honor."

"You feel strongly about this, don't you? Well, Uvak and I do agree with you. So, what would you think about setting another example? You're young and agile. You should be able to keep up with these mounted Medes! If my heir doesn't feel it is beneath him to sit astride a horse, thus saving his sandals, then who can look down on a cavalry posting? Maybe you can even make it popular, at least among the younger nobility. As a plus, you wouldn't even be wearing out sandals anymore. You'd have to get boots."

Kadurri shifted uncomfortably. "You want me to ride? So, I get to blister my rear rather than my feet?" When it came down to it, he found that he had the same prejudice against riding that the other Bar Manuti exhibited.

It was Nabo's turn to laugh. "They say it takes about a moon before you can walk right again, but Arioch and Nebuzaradan there would know more about that than I." The two daggermen were bodyguards. Despite the stigma against it, they rode because of the greater mobility this gave them. "What do you say, Kadurri? Are you going to let Seri show you up?"

"You're asking? I'm flattered. But you know, the desire of my father is my command."

"I know," the king grinned again and slapped his son on the back. "Next year, you'll bring our new cavalry out here and see what it can do."

"Next year!" Kadurri looked out at the rugged hills, black against the black night sky. "We'll still be at this next year?"

"With the way this is going so far, I'm afraid so. But two moons experience stalled here is probably enough for you at the moment. I have something else in mind."

"Marduk be praised!"

Nabopolassar laughed again. "I thought maybe you'd like something else to do. I've just heard back from King Arbaces of Nimrud, and his news made me think of you." King Arbaces was a Mede, a cousin to Uvakshatra of Media. He ruled conquered Assyria as a Babylonian province. "This unrest is spreading," Nabo pointed out. "You know the mountains north of what used to be Nineveh?" He picked up a piece of wood from Seri's pile and used it to stir the dying fire. Then he tossed it in. It crackled and hissed, spitting little sparks into the night. The fire flared up higher.

Nebuchadnezzar grinned. "You mean what used to be Dur Sharuken?" Both cities were former capitals of Assyria, and both were utterly destroyed.

"Right!" the king affirmed. "Well, with the Assyrians gone, the Urartu have claimed independence, and that includes both those around Van and those of this area. Up around Van, they're holding several forts on whatever old roads they have up there."

"I know. It's driving the Medes crazy. We think Ashurubalit is hiding among them, possibly even at Van itself. He is making the situation worse by promising King Sardini and his people everything the old Assyrian Empire allowed them."

"Then Ashurubalit's an idiot" Nabo observed, "because Sardini's not going to bow down to Assyrian rule again. Besides the Hill Country should be Media's and Harran should be their governmental seat. King Arbaces of Nimrud agrees, those mountains should never have been Assyrian lands, and he lays no claim to them. He just wants the area secured.

"Rab Mag Nergalniari reports you've done very well under difficult conditions here. You have learned much about warfare with the Urartu. You've gotten out of your chariot and actually marched with the troops. You've earned their respect. They are saying you take the time to understand their lives and you care about them."

"They are?" Kadurri was surprised, the men never talked to him.

"They are. They trust you. And the officers say you carry out every command without complaint and to the best of your ability. You never mention that you're my son to get favoritism. They like you."

"They do?"

"They do. And Rab Mag Nergalniari and King Uvakshatra say that every time they have asked for your input, your strategy has been flawless. Niari says I should be proud of you, and I am. Uvak says I'm wasting resources because you're ready for more. How would you like your own command with some actual fortresses as targets? These Urartu are actually occupying land that should belong to Assyria. They have some roads there. Chariots are in order. You would be seconded to King Arbaces, but he has promised half the booty."

Kadurri threw an eager glance at Nebuzaradan, who grinned back at him. "My father is generous beyond measure."

"Good. Let's pray that the Eastern Urartu turn out to be generous, too."

So, for the next three moons, Nebuchadnezzar rode with Arbaces of Nimrud, taking a third of Babylon's chariotry and infantry forces and mixing them with Assyria's. The Coalition decimated the Hill People all the way to Media's borders. They left the mountain fortresses in smoking ruins. The plunder was very, very good.

At the end of the warring season, three and a quarter-moons later, the prince, flushed with success, wheeled his chariot back into Babylon.

Babylon, Babylonia

The mounted maneuvers were going very well. King Arbaces of Nimrud had sent horse masters from Assyria's old army to advise and conduct drills.

Nebuchadnezzar recruited, wooing the younger sons of the Bar Manuti for his cavalry. Following the example of their fifteen-year-old prince, more and more of the lesser noblemen joined. Younger sons had no hope of higher command in the regular forces, but on horseback, they were promoted rapidly.

They drilled to the staccato rhythms and commands of the balag drums, held on the left shoulders of their drummers. The mounted battalions, under the horse masters' watchful eyes, moved together as well-coordinated as a dance troupe. Sporting banners and weaving in, out and around one another, some of their movements were going to look magnificent in the next New Year's parade, better than the dancers of Sarpenitum's maidens.

Nebushumlishtar, Nebuchadnezzar's little brother, though he was too young to actually ride to war, had insisted on joining one of the units and he was doing spectacularly well. Kadurri was glad. The crown prince was not a younger son. Eventually, he wanted to get back to the chariot core, and he was happy to see that he had a likely replacement as Commander coming up.

The year was growing late for campaigning, but the king had not yet returned from the field. Nabopolassar had sent word that although Uvakshatra had returned to Media, he was northeast of Harran, on the upper Euphrates. He had taken the fortified village of Samsat from the Elamites. Its proximity to Carchemish made it the perfect launch point for a campaign against that city and the king meant to see his men well-established there before he returned.

"The rab sharish wishes to see me?" Nebuchadnezzar peeked around the door of the Prime Minister of Babylonia's office. It was on the first floor of the House, the Marvel of Mankind, the Shining Residence, the Dwelling of Majesty. Its windows opened onto a garden, and the midday sun entered as the sharp scent of cinnamon trees filled the autumn air.

The wizened figure of an old man was seated on a bench at a cedar desk, pouring over still slightly damp clay tablets full of numbers. They hadn't even been baked yet. They were the most recent records of income and expenses of the royal treasury. Rab Sharish Mesharumishamash looked up, then waved the prince into his office. "Yes, yes. Come in, My Prince. Come in."

Kadurri stopped in front of the desk and eyed his father's prime minister, third of the trio of the "great" royal postings. Mesharu was close friends with Queen Ninnaramur, and in the king's absence, ran the government with her. He had never asked to see the fifteen-year-old prince before. "Is something wrong?"

"No, not really. But there is something that I need to discuss with you, Highness."

Kadurri raised a questioning eyebrow.

"These are the final reports of the finances for the past moon." He pointed to a total. "This is… Well, this is an unprecedented level of income from Esagila, and I'm not finding even a comparable level of gifts back to them."

"Father said that when I returned to Babylon, I was to work on financing for the war," Kadurri explained.

"Which is why I'm asking you," Mesharu nodded. "What did you do?"

"I asked nicely." Kadurri gave him an impish grin.

"The Gate Keepers have always insisted that the royal treasury—that your father—is indebted to them. The king is the Provider of Marduk; they are not the provider of the crown."

"Which is why I didn't ask them. I asked Sajaha."

"The priestess?" Mesharumishamash was dumbfounded. "How? When?" Sajaha was the First Priestess of all Esagila. She was the priestess of Sarpenitum. Chosen out of all the young girls of the empire, she was the highest-ranking member of the clergy. She lived in seclusion in the golden sarahu atop the ziggurat and rarely left it. But as the servant of Marduk's wife, she didn't have many duties. She certainly had nothing to do with the finances of the Chaldeans.

"I've gone to see her almost every evening since I've been back. I climb the ziggurat, and we sit on the top step outside the sarahu and watch the stars come out. She hardly ever gets any visitors up there you know."

"Of course not! Who would dare approach the Sarahu of Marduk's Couch without a good reason?"

"She's lonely," Kadurri stated flatly. "She needs a friend. Also, she knows some amazing things about the stars."

"So I've heard. She's a seer without equal, but what does she have to do with Esagila's finances?"

"Obviously, whatever she wants. She's the First Priestess."

The rab sharish pursed his lips and stared at the prince with narrowed eyes. Sajaha was five years older than Kadurri, a fully developed woman of twenty years, and she was very attractive. Her looks and her abilities were what had gained her her post. "That young lady belongs to Marduk. She is not available, My Prince."

Kadurri laughed. "She's the servant of Marduk's wife and at Marduk's disposal. Don't worry. I know that. So does she. We're just friends."

"All of these gifts she is giving won't earn you any friendship with the Keepers of the Gate." The keepers were a trio of high ranking priests who ruled Esagila—the High Priest, the Priest of Ekua and the High Chanter. They commanded their due, and King Nabopolassar paid.

"She outranks them," Kadurri shrugged. "I'm more concerned with pleasing my father." He came around the desk and pointed at the summary of figures. "The Treasury is getting fat and the war next year will be well-funded."

"At Esagila's expense. Something the king has never managed to do." Mesharu nodded, thoughtfully. "You have done very well, My Prince, but be careful here. One day, you will be king, and you do not wish to make enemies of the priesthood. The Keepers are dangerous. We have no proof, but there are rumors."

"That somewhere there is a connection there with the uprising of Bit Amukanni? I agree. It is almost certainly so. That is another reason I would rather deal with Sajaha."

The rab sharish gasped. "Highness, be careful to whom you say such things. How do you know this?"

Kadurri grinned. "About the connection with the Keepers and Amukanni? I reasoned it out, but you just confirmed it. My father's prime minister does not need to worry. I will not speculate in public."

"That is well, My Prince."

"Mesharu?" he looked down in the old man's eyes, suddenly very serious, and his voice had the edge of sharpened bronze. "You are right. One day I will be king. Marduk grant that day is long in coming. Nevertheless, I mean to be ready. So, from now on, you will keep me up to date on any further developments from Esagila or the keepers." It was unmistakably a command. Somehow the rab sharish, one of the three great ones, had become Kadurri's subordinate and he found himself just nodding and agreeing to this astonishing young man.[3]

Finally, as winter began to set in, Nabopolassar returned to Babylon. His triumphant entrance to the city masked the fact from the populace that the war seemed to be stalled. Strategy called for the establishment of a bridgehead above Carchemish from which they could retake the fortress. At least, they had managed to do that with the fortress of Samsat, but the Assyro-Egyptian Alliance continued to harass Harran. The trio of King Arbaces of Scythia, Commander Mitatti of Harran, and Bel Pihati Nabubalatsuikibi also of Harran continued to hold them off. The Orontids in the Hill Country—though they had lost most of their villages and all of their fortresses—likewise continued to harass travelers and merchants on the important east-west trade routes. And so it went, more and more of the same.

But for this year, it was over, and there were promises to be kept. This year, Nabopolassar would ride to Ecbatana, the capital of Media. And for the first time, Nebuchadnezzar would ride with him to meet the girl who would one day be his queen.

CHAPTER 24

The City of the Seven Walls

Ecbatana, Media

Ecbatana, the mountain capital of Media, was distinctly beautiful. It wasn't given to ostentatious temples and statues like the cities of Babylonia, Assyria, and Egypt; in fact, there were no temples or statues anywhere in all of Media. The Medes did not build such monuments, what would be the point? They couldn't hope to compete with the splendor of their surroundings, so they didn't even try. They were far more interested in the breathtaking vistas that encircled them. They treated nature and their gardens with a reverence that bordered on worship. What little they built, they built to enhance the scenery and never did they lay an ax to a living tree.

The City of Seven Walls was the only city in all Media, and its construction reflected the views of the Medes. It was an exquisite jewel, snuggled and protected—almost hidden— between two jutting foothills of a towering snow-capped mountain. Though it was only the sixth moon, the jagged crags and sharp pinnacles high above were mantled in blinding white against the pale blue afternoon sky.[1]

To reach Ecbatana, Prince Nebuchadnezzar and the rest of the Babylonian party had followed the Forest Road east. The trail began its climb at its intersection with the Foothill Road, on the banks of the Tigris River. From there, it wound through the stunning Zagros Mountains to Ecbatana. If the party had continued on, the road would have led them to the high, inland plateau of central Asia.

As the two chariots, two wagons and ten outriders came out from beneath the shade of the forest, Nabopolassar's chariot driver pulled up, allowing his passengers the full view of the spectacle that unfolded before them. Kadurri, riding beside his father in that chariot, was awed. The prince had grown up on the flat Plain of Shinar. Trees there were scarce and short, and nothing obscured the view to the horizon in every direction. Up to this point, the Hill Country of the Urartu was the most rugged land the youth had ever seen. Here, the forest thinned and opened on an expansive meadow—the meeting place of the Medes. The mountains surrounded them on every side in an uninterrupted view of grandeur. Kadurri had had no idea that nature itself could be so magnificent. "If the gods can do this," he asked himself aloud, "why do they need men for their servants?" The mountains of Ecbatana dwarfed Etenamenaki, the tower of Marduk, into relative insignificance. Surely a god would prefer such a habitation. Why then had Marduk chosen the flat plain of Shinar?

Nabopolassar smiled. "Like it?" he asked.

"It's incredible."

"It is good for a man, especially one who will be a king, to be reminded of how small and unworthy he really is."

The prince grinned at his father. "If Princess Amyhia has any sense, she isn't going to want to leave this."

"Then I guess it will be up to you to convince her."

The group started forward again. Crossing the meadow, they came around a bend in the foothills and there, directly before them, stood the first gates, glistening white, of the City of the Medes. Nestled against the shoulders of the peaks as if it had sprung out of them, Ecbatana's battlements rose, spiraling up a cone-shaped hill. The city was not large, but Kadurri knew it did not need to be. No commoner lived inside those walls save the servants of the royal family. Nevertheless, it was an impressive site. The seven concentric stone walls mounted higher and higher, the colored battlements marked each successive parapet: white, black, red, blue, orange, and silver… until the last. The seventh wall had towers trimmed with plates of pure gold, and it encircled the citadel of the palace itself on the very crown of the hill. The palace was built of hardwoods and rough limestone masonry.

An eagle circled high overhead in the pale blue sky.

Amyhia's home almost seemed a natural part of the forests and mountains around them. Nebuchadnezzar studied it somberly while he thought about the girl he would soon meet. Babylonian intelligence had reported that the girl was less than thrilled with her marital prospects. Influenced perhaps by her mother, the princess seemed to feel that she was being sold out to foreigners to be married to a prince with a one-generation pedigree.

"Convince her? Father, that's going to be hard to do. We won't be here more than a half-moon. I know she doesn't have much choice, but it does concern me. They say she loves these mountains, is attached to her mother and…"

The chariot creaked and gave a lurch as it bumped over a large stone in the road, cutting off the prince as he grabbed the side of the vehicle for support.

"And that Queen Mandane thinks Amyhia's too good for us?" Nabo guessed. "Well, your mother thinks you're too good for Amyhia. I guess women want to protect their babies even when they're all grown up."

The massive white-painted oak gates swung open, and the party trotted through. A few curious servants and several troops stared, but the cobbled street was otherwise quiet.

"But she's not grown up, and I do want the princess to be happy, Father." They began their climb to the next gate.

"In that case, you couldn't have chosen a better gift to bring her. Starting to prepare her now will make it easier for her then. I'm very proud of you for having thought of it." The king coughed. This year, he had returned to Babylon with a fever, and he still hadn't quite shaken the illness.

Kadurri watched him, worried. "Are you sure you're all right? Maybe we shouldn't have come. This could have waited until next year."

Nabo grinned. "I'm fine. And this couldn't wait any longer.[2] Next spring we must head back to Syria. We won't have time for Ecbatana." He laid his arm across his son's shoulders. Kadurri was taller than his father already. "Listen, son. If you can't make her happy, no man could. In that case, she wouldn't deserve you, and you shouldn't waste your time worrying about it. There are plenty of other women out there."

The prince pursed his lips doubtfully. “But this one will be my queen.”

“I know, and I have petitioned Ishtar that you should have what your mother and I share. Don’t worry. If you can’t make her happy, I will. I’ve always wanted a daughter. I plan on spoiling her rotten.”

Kadurri was watching the buildings as they passed. They were all alike, not homes but housing for the troops during their postings in the city. “You don’t feel like spoiling Necho’s daughter?”

Nabo gave his son a crooked smile. “Very funny.”

“I wasn’t trying to be funny. Nitocris is my wife, too. Father, she’s really very nice.”

“Kadurri, I appreciate it that just because I have a dispute with Nitocris’ father, you don’t take it out on her. But don’t trust her either. She may be disenchanted with her father, but one day it will be her brother, not her father, who is pharaoh. They were very close. She was to have been the link that made him pharaoh. Remember that.”

Kadurri glanced sharply at his father. “What then of Amyhia?”

Nabo was puzzled. “What about her?”

“What is her relationship with her brother?”

Nabo was taken aback. It was obvious this had never occurred to him. “You don’t trust Ishtumegu?”

Kadurri hesitated. This was something he had never discussed with his father. Nabopolassar loved Uvakshatra, but Ishtumegu was not Uvakshatra. The sovereign of Babylon had a right to know of his son’s concerns, so the prince answered. “Only as long as Uvakshatra remains king. Ishtu’s a bully. He’s likely to become a tyrant. Haven’t you noticed?”

The suzerain hadn’t. “He worries you.”

“Father, he should worry *you.* When I marry Amyhia, he will have a blood-tie to the throne of Babylon. So, have you heard? How is his relationship with the princess?”

They reached the next gate, the black one. It was already open, and they trotted through without a pause.

Nabo was amazed at his son. “You think like Mesharumishamash,” he finally replied. “Ishtu’s relationship with Amy? I haven’t heard. But the Medes are unaware that women have any value at all. Ishtumegu may not even have noticed that he has a sister."

Nebuchadnezzar frowned. Could he trust either of his wives?

The banquet was rich, but not exactly as it would have been in Babylon. Ecbatana's Great Hall wasn't that large because the Kings of Media never entertained many guests at a time. This repast was for five men: King Uvakshatra, Prince Ishtumegu, Prince Ahasuerus, Nabopolassar, and Prince Nebuchadnezzar. With the kings' two cupbearers and ten musicians, seventeen men in total were present. There were no guards, though Nabopolassar's cupbearer, Rab Shaq Belshumishkun, was as good as any daggerman. The five diners were seated on plush, velvety and extremely comfortable cushions, and they were served by women from Uvak's harem. It was more of a family dinner than a feast.

Kadurri hadn't seen many other banquet halls, and none of them had looked like this. The walls were only about twelve feet tall, but they were paneled in multi-colored walnut. The windows, which did not open, ran down the length of both sides of the hall. They were narrow, ten feet tall, and had panes of transparent, sliced-glass sheets. They kept out the cold, admitted the sunlight, and showed slightly distorted scenes of jagged, white, mountain tops. Heavy blue drapes could be fastened by golden tasseled cords against the chill of winter.

The only portrait of anything in the entire hall was the rug on which their cushions sat. In the middle of the gleaming oak floor, the thick woven carpet portrayed a leafless tree in a mountain meadow. The rug's white peaks were set off by albino deer that pranced through the stylized design of blues and greens surrounding the tree. The fringe on the rug was of the same gold as the drapes' cords and tassels.

The walls and doors on either end of the hall were hidden by wood screen dividers. These were carved partitions of polished walnut. Their patterns were intricate as any woven lace and held as many tiny holes. Anyone hidden behind them could observe everything, yet never be seen. Those partitions could hide a squadron of guards and Kadurri decided they probably did.

All in all, Media's banquet hall was elegant with understated grace. The meats were served on golden dishes and were mainly wild game and fish. Media's growing season was short, but they had arrived at the end of the harvest, and there was an abundance of vegetables and some thick bread made from an unfamiliar grain. All this was served, along with dark ale, by a group of young women who stood near their charges to answer their every need.

Other than the girls, the only women present were the dancers.

Although he'd been warned, Kadurri was still surprised at what the dancers were doing. The women beckoned suggestively to the guests and left pieces of their clothing everywhere.

The music was heavy and dramatic. A section of drums of all sizes, beaten with sticks and hands, boomed its responses to a group of strings, deep and compelling. The guests had to shout at one another to be heard over it. The style was entirely opposed to the light bells and lutes of Babylon, and Kadurri couldn't decide if he liked it or not. It was certainly designed to stir the blood and give the dancers a chance to loosen the inhibitions of the guests.

The serving girls kept their clothes on, but they didn't act like any servants Kadurri had ever known. Temple prostitutes in Babylon stayed at their temples! But then, the women of Babylon were guests at the feasts and would likely have voiced their opinions of such goings-on. Kadurri grinned as he thought of what his mother, Queen Ninnaramur, would do to his father if she found out about this. These women were not prostitutes; they were all from Uvakshatra's harem. They belonged to the king and were kept for just such occasions, to share with his guests. The serving girls draped themselves around their charges' necks, giggling as they served and removed food and drink. The women of Media and those of their cousins, the Persians, had made love into an art form. Coached and pampered by the eunuchs and older women, these girls existed for the purpose of pleasure alone and no one in the world knew more about the business of love than they.

Kadurri shrank back from the voluptuous brunette that plopped herself down on his lap and began to nibble on his right ear. That didn't stop her, though. She just moved with him, her heavy, brass necklace jangling. The prince looked helplessly at his father. The King of Babylon wrinkled his nose, gave his son a wry smile and waved his blond, blue-eyed companion away. She went willingly but was immediately replaced with another. This one had flaming red hair and huge green eyes and was dressed in sheer, red-violet linen. Nabo shrugged at Kadurri and gave up.

"I thought we were here to meet the princess," the prince yelled over the music at his father. The brunette poured ale down his throat, and he sputtered. She giggled and did it again.

"Different people have different ways," Nabo shouted back. "Media is changing. Uvak is seeing to that, but many things are staying the same as well. I think this," he gestured at the dancers and serving girls, "will probably never change. Except, of course, at this banquet, we are honored by the presence of the king!" He raised a cup in salute to Uvak, who sat nearby.

Uvakshatra, King of Media, had already had a great deal of ale, and he roared with laughter.

Kadurri had spent much time studying the Medes and knew the King of Media was not supposed to attend banquets with anyone other than his family. He also knew Uvakshatra was a king who did as he wished. "Because tradition says he shouldn't be here?" the prince asked rhetorically, his eyes on his father-in-law's face.[3] The Kings of Media were unapproachable by all but members of their own royal family. Anyone who had business with the king was obliged to deal with his family as intermediaries. Uvakshatra should have been represented at this feast by one of his relatives, probably his heir. Uvak's heir and his second son were both here, but Ishtumegu and Ahasuerus were completely absorbed in the pretty wenches snuggled up to them. They ignored everyone else and allowed Uvak to represent himself.

"Nonsense," the King of Media laughed. "You are my daughter's husband. You're my son! Your father is my brother by rank and by your marriage. I can feast and celebrate with you two anytime I wish without offending my fathers. We are all family here, except for Belshumishkun, of course. But your father has to have his cupbearer."

Kadurri looked around. It was true, he realized. The women and girls were from the harem. The musicians were eunuchs and as servants were, by extension, also part of Uvak's family. There was no one else, not even Nabo's bodyguard, the daggermen. It was a bit bizarre.

The prince wriggled out of the brunette's grasp. "But what about your daughter, Lord?" he yelled to the King of Media.

"Patience!" the king roared good-naturedly, waving him off and stuffing venison into his own mouth.

Kadurri sighed. On arrival, they'd been whisked off to this feast. He hadn't even met Queen Mandane yet, and it was unlikely that he would meet the girl before her mother. He tore into a portion of wild boar and ignored the attentions of the young serving girl. She seemed to take his indifference as a personal challenge and began wrapping a lock of his hair around one of her fingers. She tugged at it, trying to get his attention.

"We have brought Amyhia a present," he heard his father yell in Uvakshatra's ear. "A new servant. She is extremely highly valued and dear to our hearts. Her name is Shadushushan, and she was the wife of Belnasir." The music ended abruptly and the dancers, winded, fell to the floor in artistic poses to await the next piece. One of the serving girls unobtrusively gathered up their discarded garments and returned them to their owners. In the sudden quiet, Uvak raised a quizzical eyebrow. "Your old rab shaq? You're giving my daughter the wife of the Commander of Carchemish? It must be difficult for you to part with her. That is a treasured gift indeed.

My daughter will be deeply honored." The King of Media noticed his son-in-law's irritation with the brunette and waved her away. A platinum blonde, covered in silvery sequins, took her place and began massaging Kadurri's shoulders.

"It is Nebuchadnezzar's gift," Nabo said. "My son means it to express how highly he esteems the daughter of my closest friend. He hopes that Lady Shadushushan will become both mentor and friend to the princess. For the past year, she has been one of my queen's ladies. She is intimately familiar with the Babylonian court."

"And just about all of Babylonia itself as well, poor thing." Uvakshatra was well aware that the lady had been displaced from Anatho as well as Carchemish. "A very suitable gift." He turned to Kadurri. "Thank you, My Son."

The prince inclined his head with a pleased smile stealing upon his lips. "My father should also be made aware that the lady brings her baby son with her."

Uvakshatra gave Kadurri and surprised and delighted look. "Well, well. Belnasir has an heir then? That is good news. We'll do what we can to revenge Carchemish for him. What's the lad's name?"

"Ugbaru."

The drummers suddenly took up their beat, and the dancers sprang to their feet once more.

CHAPTER 25

Amyhia

Ecbatana Media

he Lady Shadushushan of Carchemish; her son, Lord Ugbaru bar Belnasir; and her secretary, the Chaldean, Ashpenaz," the queen's annunciator announced formerly.

Princess Amyhia squirmed nervously as she stood by her mother's chair in the queen's sitting room. She had never had the chance to be introduced to any foreigners before and these were the emissaries of her future husband! Neither the princess nor the queen was veiled. Here in the harem, it was unnecessary; the only men who ever came here were eunuchs. The lack of veils allowed the princess to read the disapproval on her mother's face and she quickly masked her enthusiasm with royal disdain.

A woman, followed by a eunuch carrying a sleeping baby, brushed past the servant and the open door and entered the light and breezy chambers of the Queen of Media. Her complexion was as dark as a peasant who spent all day laboring under the sun. Despite that, her skin was flawless, and her hands had no calluses, she was a lady. The eunuch was as dark as she, but the baby had golden overtones in his light brown hair and his skin was barely darker than Amy's own. The lady dropped to her knees before Queen Mandane and demurely bowed her head as she crossed her arms over her chest and snapped her fingers. It was the most graceful bow Amy had ever seen.

The eunuch dropped to his knees behind his lady, but hampered by the sleeping child, he did not snap his fingers. Even so, Amyhia wondered if this was a break in Babylonian protocol. She had no way of knowing.

Queen Mandane gestured for the lady to rise and she did so effortlessly. The servant behind her, cradling the infant with great care, struggled to his feet as well.

Amyhia studied the contrast between the two women with interest. Shadushushan was—at the most—twenty, while Mandane was approaching forty. But aging gracefully, Amyhia hastily amended. The lady's hair was thick and black, worn down and curled. The queen's fine blond hair was piled high on her head. Shadushushan wore a light green gown of fine linen; the queen wore a dark violet robe of the heaviest velvet. The queen's jewelry was crowded with sapphires and rubies while the lady wore a single pendant of smoky quartz, carved with the figure of an eagle. The queen sat, the lady stood.

Amyhia wasn't sure which of the two appeared more royal.

The baby whimpered, and the secretary shushed it, but not before it drew the princess' attention. The eunuch had his face bent low over the infant, but his eyes were watching her! Impertinence! She tossed her head and deliberately snubbed him, turning her attention back to his mistress. The queen's annunciator, one of the eunuchs of the harem, continued reading the introduction from a wax tablet. "The lady is a gift as lady-in-waiting from His Most Royal Highness, Nebuchadnezzar of Babylon to his wife-to-be, Princess Amyhia of Media. The prince expresses his wish that the gift of the lady conveys to the princess how deeply he holds her in his esteem.

"The Lady Shadushushan is widow to Belnasir, the late commander of Carchemish and former cupbearer to the great king Nabopolassar.

"The lady and her son are both inexpressibly dear to the royal family of Babylon. The prince feels that only such a gift could properly represent how profoundly he honors the princess. He hopes that the lady will become a valued friend and confidant of her Royal Highness, for there is no greater gift that he could give her than one of friendship."

Having finished the missive, the clerk laid the tablet in front of the princess' silken slippers, bowed, and backed unobtrusively to the wall.

Queen Mandane frowned and looked at her daughter. The queen did not look pleased by the gift. Her eyes fell on the necklace and bracelets Shadu wore. An expression of dimpled amusement briefly crossed her face as she read her mother's thoughts: Couldn't Babylon afford something better? Where were the jewels? The fabrics?

The girl, however, was delighted. She knew that as Nebuchadnezzar's first wife, she would have no lack of gold and jewels, but friends were not a thing to be taken lightly. This gift had indeed cost Babylon dearly, much more than gold or jewels ever could and the princess recognized it where the queen had not. From the corner of her eye, Amyhia caught the eunuch nodding his approval. Of her, or that baby? He prodded the child with a finger, and it giggled, but the lady smiled warmly at her. Amyhia smiled back.

The queen extended her hand, and the lady and her servant came close. Shadu took the queen's hand and bent over it. Mandane nodded politely to her daughter and to the lady. "We are very pleased to have you with us, Lady," Mandane said, and the annunciator translated. "I hope that you will feel at home. It was very kind of the prince to send such a thoughtful gift. Now, if you will excuse me, we have more preparations to make."

"Of course, Great Queen," Shadushushan murmured.

The queen nodded once more and barely waiting for her annunciator to finish his translation, she rose from her chair and retired, disappointed, back into the depths of her suite.

The annunciator dipped his head to the princess and withdrew from the queen's quarters.

The princess was left standing there with her new attendant and her secretary. Amyhia eyed the lady curiously. She had had nurses and slaves but never an actual lady-in-waiting before. "I heard about Carchemish. I am very sorry about your husband," she said, stepping forward to take the lady's hands. She hoped the lady would understand her tone of voice if nothing else.

To her surprise, the secretary spoke, translating her words. Shadushushan smiled at the girl and spoke in Aramaic. Again the Chaldean interpreted, this time into Median. "My lady thanks you for your kindness, Princess. She also apologizes; she is unfamiliar with the language of Media but wishes to assure the princess of my fluency with many tongues. She asks leave of Your Highness to have me interpret for her until she is able to manage on her own."

Amyhia laughed. "That is wonderful!" she responded. "Until you learn to speak properly, then."

Shadushushan nodded to the eunuch, and he stepped back behind her. "My Princess, I shall, of course, endeavor to learn your language. And I am certain you understand that it is your husband's wish that you learn his. We will be happy to help you with this and with other skills you may need in the Babylonian court." The eunuch continued to translate her unintelligible babble into proper words.

"I am already fully trained here," Amy responded, a little insulted. "But I suppose it *will* be necessary that I learn Aramaic. I hadn't thought of that. Very well, we shall schedule time for lessons.

"I see that you had time to freshen up before you were brought here, but have you already taken lodgings for tonight? It is not too late to have your things brought here to the harem."

"That is very kind of you, but you needn't bother. Tomorrow will be soon enough to…"

"Oh, nonsense!" the princess quipped. "It's no trouble at all. We have plenty of room. You will need to have access to my room," she paused, embarrassed. "*Um,* I only have one room. I won't have a suite until I turn thirteen, but…"

"What?" the Babylonian lady was shocked and outraged. "You are the intended of my prince! His first wife! You are not some daughter of a… a… of a concubine! This is not to be borne! Ashpenaz, call the head eunuch at once!"

"Yes, Lady," the secretary finished his translation, bowed and backed from the audience chamber.

"No, wait!" Amy laid her hand on Shadushushan's arm. "It's all right. This is how it is here, I'm only twelve." But her words were useless as her interpreter had left the room. Shadushushan just smiled and patted the girl's hand saying something soothing.

In a very short while, Ashpenaz was back with the head eunuch. He continued his translating immediately for upon sighting them, Shadushushan erupted.

"What is the meaning of this?" she exploded. "Her Royal Highness informs me that she is being lodged in a lowly room entirely unsuited to her status as the wife of the heir to the Babylonian throne."

The slave stared at her dumbfounded as Ashpenaz translated the outburst. Amy stared as well. Women in Media, especially women of the court, behaved with decorum. They did what they were told, how and when they were told to do it. All the ladies understood this, but apparently, Shadushushan did not.

"Lady," the servant objected, "the princess is in no way being insulted by her quarters. She has her own room! No other child here can say that.

If it were not for her engagement, she would be sleeping in the main dorm with the other children."

"She is the jewel that seals the treaty between Media and Babylonia!" Shadu expounded passionately upon hearing Ashpenaz' interpretation of the head eunuch's explanation. "If my king should hear how little this treaty is valued…"

The eunuch's eyes went wide as it suddenly became apparent to both him and Amy that this woman could have him gutted with just one little word. "My Lady, you are correct." His outstretched palms held placating before his lowered head needed little translation. "It is inconceivable to me how such a detail could have been overlooked. It will be corrected immediately."

That night, Amyhia found herself in the suite that had once belonged to the long-deceased queen mother. The Lady Shadushushan had an adjoining sub-suite with rooms for her, her secretary, her baby, and his nurse. The princess laughed as she lay on her new down-filled bed—and it *was* a bed, not a cot—and decided that the Lady Shadushushan was worth more than a mountain of gold and jewels. She wondered about the prince who had come up with such a brilliant idea. Perhaps he was not quite the clod Ishtumegu had described to her.

The morning sun shone brightly as it cleared the mountains and illuminated the white and gold furnishings of the queen mother's huge suite. Amy stood very still as Shadushushan selected and rejected garments and jewels for her and Ashpenaz sat in a corner interpreting as always.

"No. No, that won't do at all," Shadu laid a heavily embroidered purple gown back across the massive bed. It was the fourth of that shade the lady had rejected. "I'm sorry princess, but with that hair and complexion, purple is just not your color." She stepped back and regarded her charge critically. "I know that royal purple is called for today, but… White with purple trim won't work either." She tugged on the princess' white shift. "Your skin is too pale for white. You should be dressed in emerald green and gold."

Amyhia was getting used to Ashpenaz's echo and by this time, almost didn't notice that there was an intermediary in their conversation. The princess shook her head. "Not today. It must be purple or red. Today it is my rank that matters, not my looks."

Shadushushan laughed. "Not with your husband, I'll wager. You are young, princess, but you are old enough to know better than that! Still, even if we were to dress you in sackcloth, I think you would pass on that score. But red? With that rose-gold hair? *Ach!* Well… All right, let's try this." She scooped up a pale violet gauze with silver trim from the arms of a slave and held it up against the princess' cheek. "That does do lovely things for those gray eyes. Perhaps with some violet eyeshadow, but there's still that hair… Is there a tailor at hand?"

The slave nodded. "The queen's own."

"Well, fetch him. And bring gold trim!" She eyed the princess critically. "Make it red gold. All of this silver must be replaced immediately."

Ashpenaz emphasized the lady's words with a shooing motion and the servant scurried from the room.

Nebuchadnezzar waited impatiently in Uvakshatra's audience hall. The throne room was, like the other "public" areas of the palace, very small. Uvak did not hold court for the masses. Kadurri was surprised to find that he was nervous. Over meeting a twelve-year-old girl? He glanced at his father and the Mede. Someone had brought a chair and sat it next to Uvak's throne, and the two sat there, relaxed and chatting as if they were two old soldiers in a tavern. The daggermen stood around, as did Uvak's cupbearer and Kadurri faced the dais. He uneasily shifted his weight from one foot to the other.

The prince had received Ashpenaz's report on the princess last night. Uvak was undoubtedly aware that the lady and eunuch would conduct minor espionage and be sending regular reports back to Babylon, but he apparently didn't care. This first report said the princess was pleased with his gift and she seemed to be very suitable, pretty and intelligent. Not much to go on, but Kadurri didn't have long to wait now. He would be able to make his own assessment very soon.

Too soon.

A clerk entered and bowed low. Nabopolassar glanced at his son and chuckled. "It's too late to run now, Kadurri."

"Her Royal Highness, the princess Amyhia," the clerk announced shortly in Mede. Apparently, that was all the introduction he felt was necessary.

Kadurri turned to watch, and she entered through the main doors. The prince found that he had been holding his breath and he deliberately let it out. She is only a twelve-year-old girl, he reminded himself angrily.

The princess stepped up to the dais and curtsied low. She was a veiled, ephemeral creature clothed in lilac gauze. Tall for her age, she was slender and graceful with no figure at all.

The Mede smiled and held his hand out to his daughter. She rose and took it, her slender hand dwarfed by her father's massive paw. "Nabo, Kadurri, this is my daughter, Amyhia. We call her Amy. Amy, this is Nabopolassar, King of Babylonia, and his son, Nebuchadnezzar, your betrothed."

"Princess," Kadurri responded.

"Hello Amy," Nabo said pleasantly.

The girl said nothing, and it occurred to Kadurri for the first time that she was probably more nervous than he was.

Uvak smiled and put his daughter's hand in Kadurri's. Her fingers were long, but very small-boned and held no rings. Her long dark-pinkish-gold nails contrasted with Kadurri's short ones which were painted a traditional kohl-black. "She's your daughter now, Nabo, but we'll take care of her for a while yet. I believe the Magi are waiting for the formal betrothal. Shall we go?"

The ceremony was long and drawn out and made no sense at all as far as Nebuchadnezzar was concerned. They didn't even go to a temple. There were no temples in Ecbatana. Instead, they walked right out of the city, through the seven concentric walls. Counting them backward now, the prince noted the painted battlements as they passed, gold, silver, orange, blue, red, black, and finally, outermost, white. They were at the bottom of a slight valley, and they turned and mounted the nearest slope. All the while, the girl walked beside him, her hand warm in his, and she said nothing. From time to time, though, she turned an amused gaze upon him. Her eyes were an amazing color of gray-blue.

It was a long trek up the mountainside until they reached the snow line. Someone had built a fire pit there, and a blaze crackled and spit as it consumed the pine that fed it. The Magi, the priestly tribe of the Medes, bowed down before the fire, then each of them threw a branch into it and began their rituals.

The priests of the Fire God could have given the Chaldeans lessons in vague innuendoes. Nebuchadnezzar understood very little, but he knelt when they told him to, prostrated himself at the appropriate times, stood when prompted, repeated arcane formulas and otherwise kept his attention on the princess, wondering what she looked like under all those veils. The breeze, cold and wet off the snowy slopes caused the gauzy cloth of her arraignment to billow and ripple but still managed to reveal absolutely nothing.

The girl's voice during her responses was soft and cool, a child's voice, but pleasing, not squeaky. It was the first time he ever heard her speak. And that was the extent of Nebuchadnezzar's impressions.

Then it was over, they were back down the mountain, and Shadushushan whisked the princess away. The banquet was about to begin. Kadurri, the center of attention, walked between the two kings, his two fathers, to the main hall.

"Well, what are you thinking?" Nabo asked the prince as the entered the small wood-paneled hall.

The music—this time surprisingly light and quiet—made Kadurri look twice to see that yes, it was the same musicians. It was also the same guest list. As he seated himself, now between the kings, he answered, "I still don't know her, but now I'm committed."

"You were committed before," Nabo said reasonably. "You've been committed for over six years."

"By the treaty, yes. But now, I'm the one who has agreed to it." He thought of the diminutive Nitocris, with her large, dark eyes and brilliant smile, who waited for him back in Babylon.

Uvak laughed and clapped his hands. A servant, the eunuch Ashpenaz, entered and laid a cushion before the prince. Then the princess herself entered, followed by her new lady, and she seated herself facing her new husband. Shadu took her place just behind, to serve her mistress.

Uvak reached over and gave Kadurri's shoulder a playful tug, chuckling all the while.

Kadurri closed his mouth and swallowed hard. He suddenly realized that not only was the music subdued, but there was no entertainment. They were being served by eunuchs, not harem girls. The setting was meant for the princess to be there all along.

Kadurri lost his appetite and simply watched her. Amyhia apparently wasn't used to being invited to banquets and ate heartily. The prince was disappointed to discover that she was perfectly capable of eating without lifting her veils. He gave up. It had been a frustrating and trying day all the way around. Well, if he couldn't see her, he could, at least, talk with her now.

"How do you like Lady Shadushushan?" he finally ventured.

She looked up, startled. She obviously hadn't expected him to deign to talk to her, let alone be able to speak her language. "You speak Mede?"

He laughed silently. "If I didn't, I'd have the sorest knuckles in Esagila. For six years, ever since the Coalition was formed, it's been one of my most stressed subjects."

"They wouldn't dare touch you."

"Well, not anymore maybe. But even your lady's secretary, Ashpenaz, has taken his share of turns at laying a stick to my backside."

She dropped a morsel of cold meats she had just taken and looked at him, those blue-gray eyes horrified. Then she glared at the unfortunate eunuch. "I'll have his head!"

"What?" This was supposed to be a twelve-year-old girl from an ancient house. Dioka's blood, as chieftain of the Busae, traced far back beyond all records. But then, it was tribal blood, perhaps she was not quite as civilized as he had thought. "*Umm,* I don't think that would be a very good idea, Princess. Besides, he was just doing his job. I must admit that there were times when it took some pretty strong coaxing for me to keep my mind on my studies. If I hadn't learned, my father would have been the one who had his head."

"Oh," she turned her attention back to the prince and settled back down on her cushion. After a moment, she asked, "You have sent me your personal tutor? That was very sweet of you, but you know, but as I explained to them last night, I don't need a tutor. I have finished my schooling."

"Princess, I did not think to presume to do any such thing. Ashpenaz is Shadushushan's secretary. He is here to help her to learn Mede. His specialty is languages. When he has accomplished this task to her and your satisfaction, he will be reassigned.

"And he wasn't my personal tutor. I've had many teachers, and he has had many students. Originally, he tutored me on Sumerian. After the treaty was signed, he also worked with me on your language. Perhaps you would find him useful to brush up on your Aramaic and Akkadian before you come to Babylon."

"Yes, we did discuss that briefly. His specialty is languages? How many does he speak?"

"I've no idea. You will have to ask him. Princess, I really don't wish to spend our dinner conversation discussing a eunuch. I asked how you liked the lady?"

"I am sorry, Prince," she was mortified that she had been so rude. "I was side-tracked. I am very pleased with your gift. The Lady Shadushushan is a rare treasure—a very unusual gift. I adore her. I don't think the queen was quite so impressed, however," she added candidly.

Nebuchadnezzar blinked. "Oh?" What had she meant by that? And wherever had such a child learned to speak as though she was twice her age? Had he detected a hint of mischief in her tone? No. One shouldn't look for hidden depths in a child. But… she was the daughter of a fox, and she was as old as Shum. He shouldn't underestimate her either. Ashpenaz said she was intelligent. He tried to remember what it had been like to be twelve. That was three years ago. Too long.

"Well, the gift wasn't meant for the queen," he pointed out. "But perhaps your mother will be more impressed by this?" He pulled a small carved wooden box from under his robes and handed it to her. On a word from Shadushushan, he had picked it from among all that he had brought.

The girl opened the box and gasped. "How? But… How?" Nestled in black velvet, she found a large necklace in red gold filigree heavy with dark purple amethysts. On either side were matching drop earrings. They were the perfect complement to her lilac dress. Had she been wearing the expected dark violet, they would have been plain, but with this shade…

"Pearls are traditional, I know. But you probably have chests full of them.[1] Until your father decides I can be trusted to have a look at your face, it's difficult to know what to choose…"

"This is perfect! At least for today." She held them up, and Shadu hurried forward to fasten them on her.

"There," Uvakshatra interrupted. "You seem to have made a good impression on the young lady anyway."

Kadurri smiled. "That was the idea."

After the dinner, Nebuchadnezzar was escorted by his father into a small garden. Nabo left his son seated on a bench and disappeared, leaving him only with the new rab shaq, Belshumishkun, as a companion. It was evident that the king trusted in the Mede's security absolutely. Not even the daggermen, usually standing quietly somewhere in the shadows, could be seen. Not even Nebuzaradan. Of course, Kadurri reflected, if the daggermen had been around, it would have been an insult to their host. As guests in his house, Uvakshatra would see to their safety before that of his own or his family. Still, it felt strange not to see them anywhere.

Many of the fall flowers in the garden, carefully covered with straw every evening, were still in bloom. Their scent mingled with that of the cool, crisp snow, drifting down from the heights. The garden was on the north side of the Citadel, and here, the knoll of the hill actually was high enough to look over the golden parapets of the seventh wall to the still-green slopes of the majestic mountain whose white-capped peaks towered far overhead. Fall was heavy in the air, and the leaves of the forests surrounding the area were turning the most amazing shades of red, orange, and gold. It was as if the trees had become flowers themselves. Nebuchadnezzar had heard of this phenomenon but had never seen it. He had only seen the deciduous trees of the Hill Country in the spring and mid-summer. Mesopotamia's trees consisted mainly of palms, and in Babylon's alluvial plain, even these were rare and carefully cultivated.

The innermost palace wall, which completely enclosed the area, was covered with vines and was almost invisible. Interestingly enough, from here, the six outer walls were downhill and so not only was the golden inner wall mostly concealed, but you couldn't see the outer walls either. It gave the illusion that the garden opened on a dense forest leading back into the mountains. The downplaying of architecture to emphasize the splendor of nature was a novel idea to the prince, and he found the garden to be an altogether amazing place.

At that moment, Uvakshatra entered, his daughter following behind. Kadurri rose to meet them. He was surprised to see Shadushushan and her secretary were acting as the princess' chaperones. He had expected a Median lady. The monarch smiled and once again placed his daughter's hand in Kadurri's.

Saying no word, Uvak simply turned and left, his young daughter surrounded by no one but Babylonians whose first loyalty was to the prince, not the princess. Kadurri could have done whatever he wished with her, and no word of it would ever have gotten back to the Mede. In his trust, Uvakshatra could have paid his new son-in-law no greater compliment.

The girl stood quietly, passive and waiting, as she'd been taught. She didn't even remove her hand from his. It was humiliating. From Kadurri's Babylonian perceptions, holding Amy's hand implied an intimate and close relationship that was in no way warranted between two almost complete strangers. He didn't even know what she looked like! He may have been less embarrassed if he could have thought of her as a little girl, but hidden behind her veils, even her youth was difficult to detect. He released her hand and spoke. "Princess."

"Prince." Nothing else. It was awkward.

"Uh… I see you are still wearing the amethysts."

"Yes, thank you."

She stood there, perfectly composed, slender as a willow and remote as the cedars of Lebanon. The silence grew. He shoved a twig from the flagstones with his toe. This was ridiculous. He had been schooled in court decorum since he could barely walk. He knew the right response to any question or situation. He knew the correct way to open any conversation with anyone about any subject.

He shot a glance at Ashpenaz, who had been one of his instructors in the art. The Chaldean was studiously looking elsewhere. He was probably reflecting on what a miserable job he'd done in tutoring his prince. The secretary's face was totally deadpan, a telltale sign of a servant trying very hard not to laugh.

How could anybody expect him to carry on a conversation with a walking handkerchief? "Bel take it all, anyway!" he breathed. Then he frowned. Now that was a great attitude to reflect in front of a lady. He counted to twelve, calming himself as he'd been taught. "*Um*… Princess?"

"Yes?"

"Would you do me a favor?"

"Prince?"

"Would you get rid of those blasted veils?"

Amyhia giggled. His suggestion was terribly improper, and she should have been incensed. Instead, she looked at Shadushushan, who gave her a nod and a secret smile.

Shadu removed the tiny silver circlet from Amy's head—in Media, no one but the king could wear a gold crown. The princess pulled off the wispy veils and handed them to her lady. "You'd better not tell my father." She grinned impishly at him while Shadushushan discreetly restored the small tiara.

She was definitely a child, and Ashpenaz had reported her as pretty, yet he was still taken completely by surprise. She was not pretty, she was breathtakingly beautiful. Though he had grown used to many of the northern peoples in Babylon, it suddenly occurred to him that, other than Uvak's shameless harem girls, he had rarely met any of their women.

Tall for her age, slender and stately, she was exotic in the extreme. The slight blush of her cheeks was a true pink against her pale skin. Her red-gold hair was the color of the autumn leaves in the oak tree behind her. Her eyes, thanks to Shadushushan's ministrations, looked enormous and almost violet beneath the lilac eyeshadow. A delicate, pert little nose, not at all like her father's, punctuated her oval face and her lips were painted a light pink to match her cheeks.

There was no mistaking that she was a vixen, the daughter of the fox. Her eyes were laughing at him and his embarrassment. She, on the other hand, was not at all self-conscious.

"Princess," he answered her solemnly; "I have no need to tell your father. When he left you here with only Babylonians as companions, he expected nothing less and so gave his tacit permission."

"Oh." Her face fell, disappointed at having done something daring only to find that it was allowed.

"But I still wouldn't say anything to the court, if I were you," he added conspiratorially and grinned at her.

"Or my mother." She grinned back. "Do you like my garden?" It was the first thing she had said to him that was not a response to some word or action on his part.

"Very much. It's like you."

"How do you mean?" she was puzzled.

"This tree," he walked to the gigantic oak, and she followed. Plucking a leaf as broad and long as his hand he held it to her hair. It was ablaze with autumn, and the color was identical. "The trees of my land do not have such leaves, nor are they so majestic. This tree needs do nothing but stand here to inspire the proper respect. But you are more slender and graceful—perhaps a willow, then."

She looked at him in wonder. "Prince, are you aware how we feel about the trees?"

"Well, I couldn't help but see the carpet in the Great Hall." The huge white woven tree was obviously a national icon.

She smiled. "Yes." She plucked an acorn. "The garden is the focus of the palace—of our lives, really—but the trees are the focus of the garden. They give shade and food. They provide wood for shelter and heat. They are the gift of the god. Our gardens hold flowers, but it is the trees that are important."[2]

"With trees like this," he murmured, bending back to admire its incredible height, "it's understandable. But you are like the entire garden, princess. It's not just the tree, it's all of it. The breeze here is cool and fresh, young and playful. This flower," he picked a purple trumpet-like flower, the same color as her gown and gave it to her, "is pale and delicate and, at the same time, strong to weather the winter here. And the mountains… they are beyond description. The land surrounding Babylon is flat to the horizon in every direction. And there is nothing…" he stopped short.

"Nothing? Nothing what?"

The prince hesitated, then took her hand and kissed it. "Nothing remotely resembling you there, My Princess. I shall never see another garden without thinking of you."

She flushed, with her pale skin, it was enchanting. "I… I'm called Amy."

He smiled. "I know. They call me Kadurri. It means a border stone."

"It should mean a poet. Are you always so well spoken?"

"Usually. Until I have to find something to say to a girl I've never met before but that I'm supposed to marry."

"For being tongue-tied, you're doing very well."

"Thank you." He glanced over at the eunuch. Ashpenaz and Shadushushan were engaged in conversation and studiously ignoring the two. "Ashpenaz over there should be glad to hear it. I fear he had his doubts. It's another subject he took pains to beat into me."

A genuine smile lit her face then, and she said demurely, "Then your knuckles should escape unbruised today. I'm glad. It would totally ruin the occasion to have to end it with the execution of an old and faithful servant."

Kadurri laughed, pleased at her cleverness. He realized that he had just made a friend.

CHAPTER 26

Uriah

Jerusalem, Judah

riah ben Shemaiah of the House of Prophets wandered slowly to his assigned place before the House. He gazed sadly at his sandaled feet as he went, refusing to look at the rampant idolatry of the Temple court. He was ashamed. Uriah was a good and honest man, at least, he had always thought of himself as such.

Five years previous, he had moved from his father's home in Kirath Jerim, just north of the city, to wear the Mantle of the Prophets. He was a Levite, not a son of Aaron, he was not required to serve in the Temple, but he had seen it as a way to serve his Lord and do good towards his people. Weighed down with disillusionment from five years of such service, he was no longer the young, eager idealist from Kirath Jerim.

Now, he was thin and bent, almost like an old man, his face was drawn with care. The House of Prophets was more a political than a spiritual force in Judah, but Uriah had tried to strive for reform from within. He had very little influence on the institution, however, and now, for the entire year and a half since King Josiah's death, the forces of decadence had been intensifying and escalating. More and more of the prophets were listening to and spreading the lies emanating from the palace. Uriah was succumbing to hopelessness.

Still, he doggedly went on. For fifteen months, ever since Jeremiah had denounced the king, the officials, the priests and the people, Uriah had prostrated himself before the Grand Altar and prayed. Even though people walked around or stepped over him, he continued. He prayed for his king, he prayed for the priests and prophets, he prayed for his people until he thought his heart would break. The Prophets of the House berated him for leaving them to do all the work of prophesying for the people.

Except now. Now, the Day of Atonement approached. The crowds filled the Temple Court, and the Prophets of the House forced Uriah to stand his watch. So, he sat in front of Huldah's Gate and answered the people's questions from the Holy Scriptures. He sang their choice of Psalms. He prayed for them and tried to encourage them while he dolefully considered informing his clients that they probably wanted someone else. The Most High wasn't listening to his prayers. The house of idols behind the Temple was almost complete, and the gods of Egypt owned the Temple's north annex. The people came to Jerusalem for the sacrifices, but despite Jeremiah's admonition, they used the opportunity to give honor to the seduction of demons. And Uriah said nothing. No, the Most High wasn't listening to *his* prayers.

Uriah was ashamed of his silence. He tried to appease his conscience with his service. During the past nine days, ever since the Feast of Trumpets, he obediently held his post at the northern gate. Today was no different. The prophet studiously ignored the pagan activity of the court and laid his offering box at his feet. He was ready to carry out his duty.

A petitioner, a farmer, came to enquire. The first of the day. "There is a field," the grizzled man announced. "I want to buy it. All of my friends, except one, say I should. That one says I need to enquire of the Lord. So, what does the Lord say?"

Uriah could see that the farmer was only humoring his friend with this token deference to religion. He wanted to yell at the man, "What difference does a field make at this point? Judgment is coming!" But the farmer would not have listened. He would not have understood, and he would probably have been offended and complained to the House. Uriah ignored his impulse and picked an answer from his morning devotions. *"A man of many companions may come to ruin,"* he quoted, *"but there is a friend who sticks closer than a brother."*[1]

The petitioner looked confused. Then he shrugged, dropped a copper weight into the box and walked away to do as he wished, satisfied with the cryptic answer. Uriah wanted to kick the box over. It went on like this every day! To the people's enquiries, he quoted the prescribed scriptures and did nothing for their actual need.

Judgment is coming! The people are being enslaved for Egypt's glory! The king is an idol worshipper! He wanted to shout the words from the Temple steps!

Uriah did nothing. His songs of praise sounded flat to his own ears, and his unceasing prayers for mercy had stalled against heaven's unyielding cloud of disapproval. The Lord was not pleased with him, and so, there was no answer. There could be no reply. Uriah knew what to do, his heart burned within him to act, but he was afraid. Disgusted, he branded himself a coward.

A scream cut through his revelries and pulled his focus from his own misery to witness a scene all too common these days. Behind the Temple, the finishing touches were being added to the Wood House's back entrance. The half-finished brick porch was easily visible from the north court.

An Egyptian builder was applying a whip to the back of a young woman. As a slave, she had not celebrated Passover or been given the chance to confess her sins. She was working. Today, she made the mistake of falling and dropping her load of bricks and now her back was being cut to pieces. The woman's dark hair hung in strands over her face, as she dropped to all fours beneath the lash.[2]

Uriah couldn't see her face, but he knew her. It was Sarah, the daughter of an old friend. Her father and her husband had both been killed at Megiddo when they stood with King Josiah against Pharaoh Necho. Consequently, the entire family had then been enslaved when they had failed to pay the taxes King Jehoiakim's building projects had forced upon them.

This time, Uriah didn't think to be afraid. Outrage fed the flames within him until they roared like a bonfire out of control. In the time it would take to count to five, the prophet sprinted the distance, reached the foreigner's side, and snatched the whip from his hands. With all his might, he turned the crop on the startled Egyptian and struck him across the face with it. "Go on! Get out of here!" he shouted at the girl.

Pilgrims screamed and shouted, milling around in confusion. The slave girl looked up at her deliverer with wide, terrified eyes.

"Go!" he yelled. Sarah scrambled to her feet and darted off, lost in the milling crowd of pilgrims in a matter of seconds.

Dazed, the son of Shemaiah looked at the stained whip that trailed on the ground, its long handle still in his hand. What had he done?

The Egyptian curled up on the paving stones moaning, with his arms covering his face.

It was just a matter of moments until the Temple Guard would appear in response to the disturbance. Well, let them come. It was too late to turn back now. He had begun, and now he must finish it. He must fulfill his purpose and whatever happened would happen.

He decided.

Grasping the whip handle firmly in his hand, he turned and ran for the palace. The crowd scattered to let him pass.

His mad dash across the cobblestone court seemed unreal to him. Disembodied faces loomed out of nowhere, and vanished as he dodged around them. Past the Grand Altar, through the New Gate and suddenly he was there—the courtyard under the terrace of Jehoiakim's chambers. The palace court was full to overflowing with pilgrims seeking entrance to the Temple grounds.

Uriah stood there panting more from excitement than the short run across the Temple Court. Finally, he was free of his fears! It was exhilarating! Now, at last, he could do what he had always known he must. The consequences were no longer of any import. He knew the Lord was pleased with him at last. He was so filled with joy that the anger was almost buried beneath it. Almost.

Uriah, you will die for this, a voice told him inside. But the voice was the source of joy, and it was a simple statement, not a warning.

"Yes, and in dying enter paradise!" Uriah laughed in answer. He flung his arms open wide and with the whip trailing, he spun around in a circle for pure joy, his face to the heavens.

It was still early morning, and the king was relaxing in his chambers before beginning his daily routine. The breeze from the open window was fresh and crisp, and Jehoiakim was seated by his fire pot enjoying the soft music of a harpist, and the company of one of his wives.

Abruptly, a projectile sailed through his window right past his face. Jehoiakim leapt to his feet as the brutally cruel whip of a slave-master clattered to the floor before him.

Nehushta, the lovely, graceful daughter of the Captain of the Palace Guard, had been sitting on Jehoiakim's lap and now she picked herself up off the floor with as much dignity as she could manage and huffily wrapped her beautifully embroidered robe tighter around her.

"King of Judah," a voice called from below the king's window, "I brought this back to you, I believe it's yours."

Jehoiakim stared at the whip then picked it up and strode out on his balcony. An almost skeletal figure, a house prophet by the camel-hair mantle he wore, stood below, in the crowded palace court. Jehoiakim had never seen the man before in all his life. "What is the meaning of this? Who are you? What do you want?"

The Levite grinned up at him while the crowd gathered around, watching the encounter. "My name is Uriah ben Shemaiah, of the House of Prophets, Lord. What I want is to finally ply my trade in honesty. As to the meaning of this, I have already told you. The whip is yours. Its blood has stained your floor, which is where it belongs. Listen to the word of the Lord, King of Judah. It is unlawful to keep the people enslaved, to oppress the weak.

"Moreover, you have been called to lead this nation, and you lead them straight back to Egypt! All of Judah, ever faithless, has been enslaved to the Nile once more and they welcome their imprisonment. So, they will be taken captive in truth. Jerusalem will fall, and the people will be led away.

"Listen well, Jehoiakim! The blood of this people is on your head, and you will answer for it. The stain on your floor will become an ocean, and you will drown in it!"

Uriah turned and walked back through the crowd. They stood back and let him pass, staring, dumbfounded, at the man in the dress of a house prophet who had actually taken it upon himself to prophesy!

Jehoiakim was beside himself with rage. "Let him be cursed with all the curses of the Law!" the king spat, addressing the air. "Who is this Uriah, that he dares such a thing? I did nothing to Jeremiah, so now every fool in the city thinks he can approach and berate the king? It is enough! I will tolerate no more! You!" he yelled down at the two palace guards on the palace steps below. "What are you waiting for? Go get him! Bring him to me!"

The guards stared up at their king in consternation. They had served all their careers under King Josiah. That king had honored the prophets and allowed them to do as they liked. This short time under King Jehoiakim hadn't quite managed to undermine the guards' priorities. One of them leaned over and spoke in the ear of the other, who just shook his head. They continued to stand where they were, looking nervously up at the king.

"What is the matter with you?" he yelled, flinging the whip at them.

They dodged out of the way.

"Are there no men in Judah, to stand up against a lunatic in the streets?" the king raged at the crowds. "Who will bring this insurrectionist to me?"

The people stirred and muttered amongst themselves, but none moved to hurry after the departing prophet.

"No one?" Jehoiakim couldn't believe it.

There was a brief pause, then Nehushta stepped out onto the balcony, laid her hand on his arm and said calmly, "I will."

It stopped Jehoiakim cold. Nehushta was a beautiful woman. All three of his wives were beautiful. And they all fought like cats, for he gave preference to none of them. It was safer that way. As a consequence, they continually sought ways to buy his favor and obtain status over one another. The king was tired of the whole thing.

"Very well," he growled, looking slyly at her out of the corners of his eyes. He laid his hand Nehushta's shoulder and directed her back into his chambers. "Since there are no men with courage, we will let a woman try. If you can do this, well and good. It will please me very much."

"How much?" she asked and caressed his chest. "Enough to make me your first wife?"

"Yes, that much. In fact, if you do this, I will make you queen and your son my heir. But Woman, beware! If you do not, then I will have your head, and my other wives will hear of it and bother me no more. Do you accept this bargain?" Either way, it would cool the bickering.

Nehushta stepped back from him and her normally flawless brow furrowed attractively as she thought about it.

Jehoiakim laughed. "Are you afraid?"

Her expressive eyes flared as she looked up at him. "No, Lord. I accept," she said in a low breathless voice. "And I will not fail you."

"Humph!" Jehoiakim snorted derisively. "We shall see." Gathering his robes, he strode from the room.

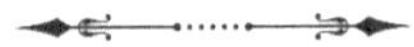

Elnathan ben Achbor was holding a meeting with his six lieutenants in his office. The guardhouse of the Palace Guard was located in the Horse Gate Tower, just inside the Horse Gate on the east side of the palace court. So, far, the guards' offices had escaped being redecorated in Egyptian moyen, and the captain was grateful for that, at least. The white stonework was solid and comforting, strong and timeless.

But today, more signs of growing unrest had surfaced, and the solidity of the walls surrounding them didn't seem quite so strong. The seven men stood around a large stone table, cups of wine before each of them, and listened to the captain's summary of the events of the past two days.

"During the feast time?" Lieutenant Azrael exclaimed. "Trumpets has just concluded and the days of confession are nearly at an end. Sunset marks the beginning of the Day of Atonement! The people should be deep in prayer and meditation; it is supposed to be a time of quiet. I don't understand. Why are there prophets popping up all over to stir up trouble?"

Elnathan held up one hand to bring order. The officers fell silent and looked expectantly at their superior. Elnathan was Captain of the Palace Guard and commanded the respect of his men, but he was all too aware that he had never had a chance to prove his worthiness. He owed his position to his daughter's marriage. The lovely Nehushta was the apple of the captain's eye and Jeconiah, his seven-year-old grandson was his pride and joy. Nevertheless, he was surprised to see at that very moment, his daughter and grandson at the door. They had been stopped by the two guards on duty there. The offices of the Palace Guard were not a suitable place for a wife and child of the king.

"Peace, Daughter. What is it?" he asked.

She looked pale. "Peace, Father. I'm afraid I've been too bold. I need your help."

"You know you always have that. But what could you need that the king cannot give you so that you come to me?"

She shook her head and looked meaningfully at the other men in the room.

"We're in a meeting," the captain explained. "If you need to see me alone, come back later."

"Now," she insisted. "Please, Father."

The officers were insulted, and Elnathan hesitated, but the girl turned huge, haunted eyes on him. She was terrified of something. The captain took a deep breath, then nodded and dismissed his lieutenants. They glared at the king's wife as they pushed past her to go and resume their other duties. Several of them snatched up their cups and brought them with them.

"Very well," the captain said, once they were gone. "What is it that is so urgent?"

"I need you to arrest a prophet. My lord seeks his life."

Elnathan gaped at her, and she hurried on. "My lord will make me queen and Coniah his heir if I can bring Uriah ben Shemaiah. But if I do not, he has promised to have my head."

Elnathan was speechless. He stared at the girl for a long time then he drained his cup.

She smiled a little. "I did the same thing. Father, I cannot do this by myself. So, I have come to you."

The drink helped Elnathan find his voice. *"What have you done?"* he gasped. "Woman, you are speaking of a prophet! The people will stone me!"

"Not if you are the father of the queen. Think! This is our chance, Coniah will be king!"

It was Elnathan's dream. He would do anything to make the boy heir, or he had thought he would. He poured another cup and downed it too.

The child's expectant eyes were fastened on his grandfather. They were the same large, expressive eyes as his mother, and his grandmother, Elnathan's wife. If he refused, the child wouldn't have a mother. How could he do that to him?

"If Jeconiah is heir, you will have real power," she tried again. "You will be the grandfather of the next King of Judah. Father, you can use your position to exert genuine influence on the throne itself." She turned to the boy and stroked his silky hair. "Coniah, you will always listen to your grandfather, won't you?" The boy's gaze had never wavered from the captain's face. He nodded solemnly.

"Father, these House Prophets are unhappy with my lord, the king. But by the very death of this prophet, they will be promised what they want, a good king on the throne. Jeconiah will be a good king. He will reign in righteousness because you will help see to that. Isn't that what the prophets want? Isn't this the will of the Lord of Heaven?"

The Lord of Heaven wanted his prophet executed? It seemed unlikely. Elnathan continued to stare at the boy. How badly did he want him to become king?

"Father, if you do not do this, the king will kill me."

Slowly, the captain raised his eyes to his daughter's lovely, frightened face. He loved her, what could he do? "May God forgive me," he whispered.

Nehushta rushed forward and hugged him, pulling the boy into the embrace. Not one of the three noticed the guards outside the tower whispering to the other, and then one of them deserted his post and slipped quietly into the crowded palace court.

Uriah wandered back to his quarters in Huldah's Gate. Huldah was dead, and her girls' school now provided chambers for the House of Prophets and for the Temple Guard. Once more, the structure was becoming known as the Benjamin Gate, as the people forgot their prophetess. For five years, Uriah had lived here with the other house prophets inside the gate. His quarters were small and quiet. No outsiders ever came there.

He was surprised to find this was no longer true.

There, sitting bent over in a corner, he found the slave girl, Sarah, waiting for him. She was crying. "Sarah!" he exclaimed in surprise. "What are you doing here?"

She looked up with red and puffy eyes. "I didn't know where else to go. I have no home or family, and the slave master will punish me more if I go back. Besides, I… I don't think I can."

He saw then that she had a bowl of water and some cloths and had been trying to wash the wounds on her back. The lash had shredded her tunic and done a terrible work on her flesh. Uriah realized that if he hadn't stopped him, the Egyptian might have killed her. Now the gashes were stiffening, and she could hardly move. He went to her and helped her up and to his cot. Then he began to carefully bath her back.

"Peace, child. It's all right. But how ever did you get here without being seen?" The Temple Court was crowded. The Day of Atonement would begin with the setting sun. There were pilgrims everywhere.

"I… I'm not sure. I may have been seen. But everyone seemed to be heading towards the palace. There was some disturbance there, I guess."

"Oh." He paused and set down the bowl and wet rags. He wondered how much he should tell her. Well, it was her life that was now in danger as well as his. She should know what was going on so she could make her own decisions as to what to do. "That was me. At the palace, I mean. I went there and threw the task master's whip through King Jehoiakim's window."

She gasped. "Why?"

"I had a message to deliver from the Lord." That sounded insufferably pretentious. "I *am* a prophet, you know," he added defensively. He pulled a cotton cloth out of a cubby and tore it into strips.

"Yes, but the prophets don't… Well, Jeremiah does, but…"

He chuckled, stood and located a small jar of balm on a high shelf. He glanced back at her over his shoulder as he took it down. "But not the prophets of the House.

"Well, generally you're right, but remember, Elijah and Elisha were Prophets of the House in Samaria, and Joel ben Pethuel was a prophet from this very house, and he prophesied too." Uriah sat next to the girl and began to apply the balm to her back. The scent of the balsam was sharp.

Sarah flinched from the potent balm, but she wasn't distracted from the conversation. She knew her history. "Joel prophesied 250 years ago."

"That's right," Uriah beamed at her, the teacher in him pleased at her answer. "So it can happen, but I've never had a message before. I guess if you only have one, it might as well be for someone important. So, I told the king that Jerusalem was doomed and the blood of the people was on his head. I suppose soon it will be my blood he will have to account for as well."

"He wouldn't dare!"

He began winding the strips of cloth around her. "Wouldn't he? You had to pass through the Temple Court to get here, Sarah. Egypt has claimed the north annex of the Temple and the king is rebuilding a house for the idols of this land as well. Which is worse, the desecration of the Temple or the murder of a messenger?"

"You are a prophet!"

"A pretty poor prophet whose entire life's ministry is bound up with a message that didn't even last ninety parts! I didn't even take the time to properly compose and sing it." He tied the bandage off and went to a small trunk where he found a new tunic. "Sarah, you can't stay here. It's too dangerous. I told Jehoiakim who I was." He tossed her the tunic. Sarah was a widow, she should cover her hair. Uriah found another cloth and tossed it too.

"Why?"

"I don't know. He asked. It seemed like a good idea at the time." The prophet turned his back while she changed.

"Well, it wasn't!" she scolded. "And I can't leave. I don't have anywhere else to go. That's why I came here."

"I know. That's what you said. I'll have to find you someplace then. There must be someone we can trust. And someone not too far away. You're not going far in that shape, but if I can get help, we can move you." He thought about it. "I do know someone. There's one of the scribes. He has no sympathy for Egypt or the king. His house is just outside the West Gate, we only have to make it across the Temple Court."

"With all the people out there?" She finished changing and sat down heavily on the cot. "The Palace Guard must be looking for us both by now."

"And if we stay here, they are sure to find us. Don't worry. We've both made it across that court unobserved at least once today. We can do it again. The crowds are a good thing.

"And Baruch can be trusted. He's a good friend. Wait here, I'll get him."

It was unnecessary to tell her to wait; she could hardly do anything else. Sarah was watching him anxiously as he closed the door.

Baruch ben Neriah was home. Most whose work was tied to the Temple made their homes on the approach to the holy hill or even in the walls surrounding the Temple itself. Baruch had his tiny home on the highest terrace, just outside the West Gate where the populace had to pass right by his door to get to the busiest of the Temple Court entrances. He was quite proud of that door, it was of cedar with a scroll carved into it to advertise his craft.

During the feast time, Baruch normally had more work than he could handle. Today, however, few people wanted to send letters. Most were milling around telling stories about a certain Temple prophet who had suddenly gone mad and attacked the king and city. The scribe was not quite sure what to make of it all. It certainly didn't sound like the Uriah he knew.

There came a knock on the door, and the young man gathered his writing materials in anticipation of the need. It wasn't a customer; it was the subject of the scribe's speculation. "Nabi!" Baruch exclaimed. "What is going on? The city is in an uproar!"

"Peace to you, too" the prophet responded dryly. "Baruch, I need your help."

The scribe hastily ushered the prophet through his door. He looked up and down the street nervously, and yes, people were watching them. He quickly closed the door and set his writing kit back on its table. Facing the house prophet, he asked, "I've heard a hundred rumors. What actually happened?"

Uriah shrugged. "I told the king that this city will fall, the people will be enslaved, and their blood will be on his head. I don't think he liked it," he added with a wry smile. Then he said thoughtfully, "Jeremiah told him the same thing at the beginning of his reign, but I suppose another witness was needed. If Jeremiah's word stood alone…

"Anyway, I need your help."

"Of course, anything." He poured a cup of water from an earthen jug and handed it to his friend.

"Not for me," Uriah took the cup and held it. "There's a young woman, her name is Sarah. She's a widow, and her father is also dead. She and all her father's family have been enslaved for unpaid renovation taxes. An Egyptian was beating her, so I stopped him and told her to get out of there." He paused. "That's what started all this," he explained. "Anyway, she ran, but she ran to my quarters, and that's where she is right now. If they catch her, she will be severely beaten at the very least, and they're sure to find her if she stays where she is. Also, she needs some doctoring. Could you take her in for a while and see that she's cared for?"

Baruch shook his head in amazement. "You've had a busy morning, Nabi. What are you planning for this afternoon? I could use some forewarning."

"Please. Could you take her? I'll need some help getting her here. She can't walk very well, and there's the crowd to consider."

Baruch couldn't refuse. Uriah was a good friend and besides, the thought of Abraham's children once more enslaved and answering to Egypt's whips had nearly driven him crazy himself. "Yes, of course. We'd best hurry, then. But you had better get out of that coat. They'll be looking for a Temple prophet. Here," he threw him one of his own robes. "A scribe is safer dress for you these days. Keep your face down and your head covered."

Uriah slipped off the brown camel-hair mantle and donned Baruch's light gray and green robe. The two hurried back to the House of Prophets. Pilgrims crowded around the northern gate, looking for answers from Heaven, two more were not noticed. They crept unobtrusively through the crowd and hurried to Uriah's door. Sarah was waiting for them, seated on the cot in the prophet's sparse quarters.

"This is Baruch," Uriah bent over her. "He'll help you. You are going to stay with him for a while."

She gave the scribe a shy, half-smile.

Baruch regarded her critically. Her grimy face, bruised and covered with cuts, peaked out from beneath her head shawl. It was still obvious that she was young, not yet thirty. She might even be pretty if she was cleaned up. "All right," he said. He helped her to stand and then he pulled the blanket off the cot. "Wrap this around you and keep your head covered and your face down." She moved stiffly, like an old woman. He nodded, satisfied.

A quick knock on the door made all three jump.

"Don't answer it," Baruch whispered.

The knock came again. Three sharp raps, followed by a low, urgent voice, "Nabi, open the door. Quickly! Please!"

Baruch couldn't believe it. The voice was that of his brother, Seraiah. "Seraiah, is that you?" he called out.

"Baruch?" came the surprised answer.

"It's my brother," Baruch said to the prophet.

Uriah raised an eyebrow.

Baruch understood. Uriah trusted him, but the prophet wasn't sure he could extend that trust to the scribe's brother. Seraiah ben Neriah was a member of Jehoiakim's Palace Guard.

"Please, Nabi," Seraiah pleaded. "Open the door! I've got to talk to you."

At Baruch's urging, Uriah did, reluctantly. "Peace to you, Seraiah," he said, and the guard pushed past him into the room. The prophet shut the door again.

"And to all in this place," the palace guard responded with impatience. Seraiah looked nothing like his younger brother. Baruch was small with dark eyes and an eager, intelligent face, like an overgrown boy. Seraiah was tall and athletic, a handsome man in his prime with a short, military cut that was growing thin in front. He carried a traveler's bag. Seraiah frowned at his brother. "Baruch, *what* are you doing here?"

"I asked him to come," Uriah explained. "I need his help."

"Nabi, you are going to need a lot of help," Seraiah told him earnestly. "You're in deep trouble. My captain, a man named Elnathan ben Achbor, is coming here to arrest you! His daughter is one of Jehoiakim's wives, and she will be named queen if she can bring you to the king so that he can take your head."

Baruch stared at his brother, aghast.

Uriah narrowed his eyes. "It sounds like she would make a fitting queen for our king."

"Who's she?" Seraiah demanded, giving Sarah a hard look.

"My new house guest," Baruch offered.

Seraiah looked confused. "What? Oh, never mind. Nabi, you have got to get out of here, now!" Seraiah tossed the prophet the bag he had been carrying. "There's food and wine. Also, I just got paid, and I opted for metal instead of goods, so there's a pouch with some silver and copper weights in it." The guard began throwing some of Uriah's clothes into a cloth. He bundled them up and tossed it to the prophet as well.

After a brief hesitation, Baruch moved to help him.

"Wait a moment…" Uriah began.

"I don't know that you can afford to waste a moment." Seraiah snapped. "It's well you're already in disguise. There's a caravan leaving the city this forenoon. They're holding a place for you, so hurry."

"And just where am I going to?"

"Where do all caravans go these days? Egypt."

"What!"

"It's the best I could do. Hurry up."

Baruch stared at his brother as Uriah meekly shouldered the sack.

PART 4: 607 BC

Prophets and Politics

Jerusalem, Jerusalem,
You who kill the prophets
And stone those sent to you,
How often I have longed to gather your children together,
As a hen gathers her chicks under her wings,
And you were not willing.
Look, your House is left to you desolate.
—Matthew 23:37-38.

CHAPTER 27

The Last Emperor of Assyria

The Hill Country, Mesopotamia

Nebuchadnezzar rode astride out through the tall gates of the proud city of Harran. The prince had been riding at the head of Babylon's new cavalry for a half a year now, and it was finally time to test them. The Hill Country of the Urartu was utterly unsuited to chariots, and Kadurri was eager to finally use the men he had trained so carefully.

To his surprise, the prince, like his men, had found cavalry to his liking. Kadurri delighted in riding and the freedom it gave him. Chariots had drivers, and the warrior was only a passenger, but on a horse, he was totally in control, and he and his men could change directions and tactics in the blink of an eye. There was no contact with the team in a chariot, but in riding, the horse became his partner, and an undeniable bond of trust was formed. Kadurri was certain that his mount would race into a wall of spears for him.

Not that he would ask that. A wall of spears was work for the chariot core.

No, the cavalry was designed to hunt the Hill Country, to destroy the Urartu and any lingering trace of the old Assyrian Empire that they might find hiding out there.

Today, Kadurri rode his favorite charger, a striking black war stallion. It had four long socks and a wide blaze, its markings being one of the things that had caught his eye to begin with. The animal was agile as a Scythian war pony and fast as a messenger horse.

Nebuzaradan, riding a gray mare, trotted along next to the sixteen-year-old prince, just like always. Kadurri had adopted the Assyrian tactic of riding in pairs. He could handle his own horse if he used the lance, but if he used the bow, Seri would take his mount's reins. The style was in opposition to the Medes and Scythians who yielded their mounts to no one, but Kadurri had drilled in Nimrud, under Assyrian horse masters.

So, he rode out paired with Nebuzaradan, and behind them came five hundred horse, also in pairs. The younger sons of the Bar Manuti, eager for glory of their own, were flooding the recruitment offices for the chance to ride under the command of the charismatic prince.

And outside the gates, with whoops and yodels, a horde of Scythian warriors enthusiastically fell in behind their barbarian king. Their numbers were obscured by the dust raised by their galloping ponies' hooves.

Harran was Media's. Kadurri's father had given it to King Uvakshatra because the plan had always been that this city would rule over the Hill Country, once the Urartu were subdued. The Hill Country was a natural extension of the borders of Media.

But Media's cavalry would not be coming to help. They had gone with Crown Prince Ishtumegu into the east to continue the war with the Persians. King Uvakshatra himself could only arrive at Harran after the snows subsided enough to allow him to move his forces. Media's cavalry could move through the snowy peaks, its chariots and foot soldiers could not, and chariots were of no use in most of the Hill Country anyway.

But the Scythians' camp was right outside Harran's walls. Arbaces, the Chieftain of the Royal Scythians, looked forward to testing the Babylonian prince on this mission. It was the Scythian's duty to keep Harran safe, and that meant clearing the Hill Country of vermin.

Besides, it was time for the prince to learn how to use horses in this kind of terrain to his best advantage. Arbaces, son of Medyas, was the perfect teacher for the lesson. Ambush and melt back into the landscape—it was the Scythian way.

So when Harran's Commander Mitatti reported that Ashurubalit, the dethroned King of Assyria, had been spotted by his scouts, Arbaces had called his men to order. The king without a country had left King Sardini of Urartu's capital of Van and was moving west through the hills, presumably towards Carchemish. Arbaces saw an opportunity to gain himself a new skull mug.

To the east, Captain Akhiramu wove his mount through the trees, his cousin and lieutenant Samgunu rode beside him as dappled sunlight filtered down through the small bright yellow-green leaves of spring. The Hill Country north of Harran was densely wooded. All around, the vastly depleted forces of Ashurubalit, the debatable King of Assyria, marched forward with them. The Scythians had devastated Ashurubalit's army. This was all that was left. But it was time. With or without sufficient forces, Ashurubalit needed to be in Carchemish soon to meet the pharaoh as he returned from Egypt.

A branch slapped the captain in the face. "Ashur take this gods forsaken country!" he exclaimed. "The road is less than a beru to the south!"

Samgunu eyed his cousin warily. "You want to take the road right through the Scythian encampment around Harran?"

"Right! Where we will be unable to fight because we have no chariotry! But that's no problem; we'll just outrun their ponies on foot." He threw a satirical look at the "army," trudging wearily through the underbrush.

"At least, we have enough horses for the officers to ride," Samgunu pointed out.

"But no archers. So, now you're going to tell me that slings are better because arrows must be made, but rocks are just lying about on the ground!"

Samgunu shrugged and lay against his mare's neck to avoid another low hanging branch. "The king says, 'March,' so we march. We have enough infantry to hold up our end in this season's fighting and Egypt will supply the rest."

"If we make it to Carchemish, we shouldn't have to fight at all," Akhiramu said.

"If?"

Ahead, a flock of birds took to flight, chirruping in alarm at their coming.

The captain was silent for a moment, then he fixed his cousin with a serious look. "Samgunu, we have almost lost as many men to desertion as to attrition. Arbaces the Mede—that pretender in Nimrud—welcomes them home and gives them back their families! Meanwhile, Ashurubalit has no throne or city, and we live on scraps. Our families—yours and mine—are captive in Nimrud." He paused, letting this sink in while he skirted a bush. Then he added, "And the Mede is always looking for seasoned officers."

"Cousin, that's dangerous talk."

"Your wife was pregnant, and you don't even know what happened to her. Is she well? Do you have a son, or maybe a daughter?"

The trees thinned, and they rode out into a clearing on the top of a hillside. Down below, was a small, sparkling stream. Three riders were there, their horses—a bay, a black and a gray—had their heads lowered to drink. The bay looked very familiar to Akhiramu. The rider was also familiar. That horse used to be his, and the rider was Arbaces, Chief of the Royal Scythians. The other two riders were Babylonian—one of them a prince from his helmet.

"Captain!" Samgunu hissed.

"I see them." The army of Assyria began emerging from the woods around them, and Akhiramu frantically motioned them back.

The barbarian chieftain pulled his mount's head up, patted its proudly arched neck, and looked up the hill, straight at the two Assyrian officers. Arbaces of Scythia grinned. "Captain Akhiramu!" he bellowed, his voice carrying clearly to them. "You come see how I train you old horse? He much better now!"

"Nergal take him," Akhiramu swore.

King Ashurubalit rode up beside the captain. "Isn't that Arbaces the Barbarian?"

The Scythian threw his head back and yodeled. The bay stallion screamed a challenge and reared, pawing the air with hooves painted bright gold. Then Arbaces charged right at them, the horse bounding up the hill with his ears laid flat against his head.

From all around came answering yodels, whoops, and yips.

The Babylonian prince raised his fist above his head, then gestured sharply forward, pointing at the enemy.

The drums of the Babylonian cavalry sounded, and the younger sons of the Bar Manuti answered with an enthusiastic roar.

The prince and his second sent their chargers racing up the hill after Arbaces's glossy bay.

"That it is, Great King," the captain answered his king grimly. "And *that* is Nabopolassar's son."

He had waited too long to desert. He was never going to see his family again.

The Assyrians were hopelessly outnumbered, and on foot, they had nowhere to go. The nearest friendly fortress was Carchemish, and it was impossibly far. As shaggy Scythian ponies and sleek Babylonian chargers thundered down on them from all sides, the captain of Assyria readied his lance and commended his spirit to Nergal and Sin.

Out of the dust of battle, Arbaces materialized right in front of them, riding his retrained Assyrian stallion. With a whoop of glee, he swung his short sword at Ashurubalit's neck.

Then the prince of Babylon was there, and the flash of the sun on the bronze tip of his pike temporarily blinded the captain, masking the blow. It was Tasmit, fate; the captain didn't even attempt to block it. He was just grateful that it wouldn't be his skull that was going to wind up covered in gold and full of ale.[1]

CHAPTER 28

Rab Mag

Harran, Media

The governor's palace of Harran was the center of a celebration that threatened to engulf the fortress city. Ashurubalit, the last Emperor of Assyria, was dead! Uvakshatra had arrived at last and honored by the presence of the three kings of the Coalition, Bel Pihati Nabubalatsuikibi had all he could do to see that the preparations were adequate to the occasion. The Assyrian Empire was no more! She would never rise again!

Nabopolassar, King of Babylon, was seated on a velvet cushion near the head of the over-crowded pink marble feast hall. His son and heir sat between him and the King of Media. Nabo toyed with his food but ate next to nothing.

Rab Shaq Belshumishkun stood behind his sovereign, ready to serve, but he had little to do. So, he held Nabo's cup, just as Dioka held Uvak's, and did nothing.

The other guests, of course, didn't have cupbearers and instead were seated around huge, four-man beer steins, which needed constant refilling.

Kadurri held his own cup, but Shum kept it filled for him.

Nabo was not enjoying himself. The guests were, and they were making so much noise that Nabo couldn't even hear the musicians, tucked in a far corner of the room.

"What is it, My Brother?" the Glory of Media, King Uvakshatra clapped one arm around the Babylonian's shoulder, while he held a huge shank of mutton in the other. "This is a time of great joy, and from the look on your face, I'd say someone had died." He paused and glanced across the room at the grotesque skull mug in the hands of the Scythian chieftain, Arbaces.

"Other than Ashurubalit, I mean." Uvak was only a guest, but even so, as King of Media, he shouldn't have been there, appearing in public. True to his quixotic temperament, he was. Uvak followed Median tradition when it suited him and ignored it when it did not. "You are shaming our host," he gave a quick nod to Bel Pihati Nabubalatsuikibi, who sat at the head of the room.

The governor unhappily looked back at them.

Nabo waved at Suiki and gave him a half-smile that did nothing to encourage him. "It's probably just my sour stomach," he replied to Uvak. "How can a man celebrate if he can't eat or drink half of what is put before him?" Nabopolassar still had not recovered from the sickness that had struck him the year previous. At times, he was better, but the condition was beginning to take its toll. He was starting to feel old.

"Ah, My Friend, haven't the physicians been able to help with that yet? You have been too long at war, drank from too many strange streams and lain too many nights on cold, wet, foreign ground. Now, you must rest, for a while at least. After the celebration, go home to your queen."

Nabo broke into a fit of coughing. Recovering, he chuckled. "She is better looking than you. But there is still Egypt, and Carchemish is impregnable. How can we rest with Necho grinning at us from the cliffs of the black fortress? You know as well as I do that as long as it's held against us the trade routes to the Great Sea are shut off. Babylon has very little resources of her own. She is built on trade. If we ignore Egypt, pharaoh will sit there and slowly choke us to death."

"Nabo, of course, we won't ignore Egypt. Arbaces there would never stand for it." He gestured at the Chief of the Royal Scythians and the barbarian, close enough to have overheard, grinned in acknowledgment. He lifted his macabre mug in salute. "We will retake Carchemish," Uvak continued. "You need it to block Egypt. Besides, since it is on the way to Lydia, I need it in friendly hands. But don't worry, we can handle things. Go home. Rest up. Come back next year when you're feeling better.

"Leave Kadurri here with us. He can represent your interests. It would be a good experience for him, and I can get to know him better before I turn my daughter over to him. I think he would like to spend a bit more time with my governor there anyway." Suiki knew they were talking about him and looked puzzled. Uvak continued to Nabo, "We'll send Kadurri back to you soon enough."

The prince glanced at his father, and the king considered. He had seen the eagerness in his son's eyes, rapidly suppressed though it was.

Nabo chuckled. "You are right, My Brother, and that brings us to the other reason for this feast!" He stood, and the guests immediately fell still. "Nergal has blessed us all!" he called out. Then he took his cup from Shum and lifted it to the heavens. "To Nergal!" The emperor drank deeply to the god of war, pretending he liked the brew.

"To Nergal!" The men surrounding them roared and they bent over their straws and did their best to drain the huge steins.

"Assyria is in good hands, and her old, bloodthirsty regime is gone forever!" He lifted his cup and drank again, as did the men. "So for now," he turned to Rab Mag Nergalniari, who was seated in a grouping of generals to his left and held out his hand.

The grizzled old soldier took it and rose to stand, hand in hand with the king, facing the officers of three armies, most of whom were deep in their cups.

The king raised Niari's hand into the air. "This is my right hand! The triumph of Babylon!" The air reverberated with the men's approval. "For twenty years, he has served as my rab mag!" Again, there were cheers mixed with comments, appropriate and otherwise. "This year, he has seen his vision fulfilled. Assyria is conquered. Babylon will no longer look to the north in apprehension. This is Nergalniari's legacy to us! But even the great grow old and tired. He has conquered Assyria, what more is there for him? The rab mag has requested that I release him."

The hall went silent with surprise and consternation. The "rab" postings were for thirty years. As rab mag, Nergalniari had ten to go. No one had expected this.

"Return to your wives and family, My Friend," the king released the general's hand and patted him on the shoulder. "Babylon is now and forever in your debt." Then Nabo hugged the general, and the confused crowd snapped their fingers in respect.

Niari sat back down on his cushion and bent over the straw of the gigantic beer stein that he shared with the other generals. All four of the generals drank together, and the men yelled their approval and drank as well. Servants moved everywhere, refilling steins with a dark ale.

Nabopolassar still stood there. "This leaves me with an open post. Nergal has seen fit to provide a worthy replacement who, this past season, has proven his ability and worth. Prince Nebuchadnezzar, stand!

Flabbergasted, Kadurri looked up at his father.

"Stand!" Nabo repeated.

Hastily, the prince got to his feet. The king held out his hand, and the prince hesitatingly took it. Nabo raised his son's hand into the air for the men to see. "This is my rab mag, my right hand! This is Nebuchadnezzar, First General of Babylonia. Obey him as you would me!"

The men jumped to their feet and went wild.

Two days later, Rab Mag Nebuchadnezzar, resplendent in the red of the chariot core, with the plumed and flowing turban of an officer, stood quietly listening to his father's final instructions. The suzerain was returning to Babylon and leaving his forces under the command of his son. It was Marduk's will. It was time for the "cornerstone" of the empire to begin to receive the glory.

At sixteen years old, Kadurri had only a little over a year's experience at command, but he had studied tactics until he would lie in bed at night mumbling them in his sleep.[1] Nabopolassar looked at his tall, athletic son and nodded, satisfied. The prince was no hotheaded young fool. He recognized his own inexperience and would listen to his advisors, just as he was genuinely listening to his king now. To a stranger's eye, the young man appeared calm and confident; ready to do his duty but equally ready to defer to more experienced advisors should the situation demand. The father could see the excitement and nervousness in his son's eyes, but no stranger would have realized it. As the new Rab Mag of Babylonia, Kadurri was responsible for all the men in the entire army, not just the cavalry. But Nabo knew his son better than anyone. Kadurri would do well.

He would have been certain of it even if the Chaldean priests hadn't concurred. They had. Two beru before Suiki's celebratory feast, the astrologers had declared the king's plan was agreeable as the moon had not been covered by a cloud on its first day and it had been surrounded by a halo! Apparently, Sin spoke favorably, the land would be happy, and one arose with great strength. It was nice to have the priests' approval, but that hadn't actually mattered to the king. Nabo listened to the Chaldeans less and less these days, and he only enquired of them because they expected it. So, he memorized his son's face and prayed silently to whatever god would listen that Kadurri would learn to do the same.

Then the emperor hugged his heir close and mounted his chariot, to stand next to his friend, the old general Nergalniari. Together, they left Harran and their military responsibilities behind them.

CHAPTER 29

The Murder of a Prophet

Sais, Egypt

riah ben Shemaiah had been in Egypt for half a year. The haunted look had left his eyes, replaced by inner peace and joy. He had actually put on weight. But he vowed to himself that he would never come here again. The trip was long, hot, and dusty and on arrival, he had nowhere to stay. Thinking that it would be better to lose himself in the crowds, he had stayed with the caravan all the way to the capital of Sais. He had been wrong. There was no way he could lose himself amongst the Egyptians.

Struggling through a mass of light brown, scantily clad, bald people on his way to draw water from the Nile, Uriah reflected on his foreignness. He didn't look like the Egyptians, dress like the Egyptians, or speak like the Egyptians, even though after a half a year, he actually could communicate somewhat. The prophet couldn't even eat most Egyptian food because it had been offered first to idols and was unclean.

The people he passed moved aside, pulling in their shoulders and arms to avoid touching him. They shunned him, viewing his hair, beard, and clothes with suspicion; as if these coverings hid a host of vermin ready to leap out and attack the unwary. Uriah wondered how they would have reacted if he had still had his hairy prophet's mantle.

He had been in Egypt half a year, and yet he knew no one. No one wanted to know him. He admitted it to himself, he didn't want to know them either. Despite local opinion, it was not he who was unclean, it was everyone else. The Egyptians were all as *tä·mā* as their food. Idol worshipers, every one of them, and they were spreading their sin throughout Judah.

He drew his water and made his way back to the mud-brick inn where he was staying. It was comfortable. Its whitewashed plaster walls and woven reed floors were spotlessly clean, and there was even a scribe in the lobby who spoke a little Hebrew if he felt the need to talk to anyone. Sais could be very cosmopolitan if it were so inclined. He found his room and sat down hard on the cot. "Lord," he complained, "why am I here? It would have been better to have stayed in Jerusalem."

You would have died in Jerusalem.

It was strange how clear that soft, inner-voice was, now that he knew how to listen.

"True," he answered. "And by now that city probably looks as Egyptian as this one. But it's still home, and that's better than to die in Egypt." His humor returned. It always did when he spoke to his Lord. Joy bubbled up from deep inside him that destroyed all depression. "I know You made the Egyptians too, but they don't seem to be aware of the fact." The presence of his God surrounded him more thoroughly than the air itself, and yet it was unobtrusive, waiting on him. "I want to go home," he said.

He was not in the least surprised when the next morning Captain Elnathan of Jerusalem's Palace Guard and five of his subordinates broke into his room. "You could have knocked," he said, and they snapped shackles on his wrists.

Jerusalem, Judah

Baruch ben Neriah was in the Temple Court, busily writing a letter for a client when a white-faced Sarah came to him with the news. Uriah ben Shemaiah had been taken alive in Egypt and was at this very moment facing King Jehoiakim in his judgment hall. Baruch quickly returned his fee to his startled customer and ran to the palace.

"You can't go in," Seraiah told him. Baruch's brother was on duty outside the palace porch, and his drawn expression was not encouraging. "It's a closed court."

The crowd in the courtyard mingled and milled around, but they spoke in hushed voices.

Resigned, Baruch sat down on the step at his brother's feet. Together they waited.

A half-hour later Elnathan ben Achbor emerged, carrying the head of the prophet. Baruch jumped to his feet in shock. "No! Seraiah, this can't be."

"It is," Seraiah put a restraining arm around his shoulders.

In dead silence, the people of the court parted, leaving an empty path for the Captain of the Palace Guard and his gory burden. Elnathan walked through them and was followed by several of his men carrying Uriah's body. They marched towards the Horse Gate.

"Let me go," the scribe shook off his brother's arm. "Seraiah, I have to see…"

"Don't. They will fasten his head on the gate and throw his body to the crows."

"Then I have to recover it and bury it. He has no kinsman here."

"No," the shaken palace guard forbid it. "The Levites are his kinsmen, and the Prophets of the House will be responsible. But King Jehoiakim will post a guard and arrest anyone who interferes. When there is nothing left but bones, the prophets will be allowed to bury him in the common place.

"Go home, Baruch. It's over."

"Go home? How? What will I tell Sarah?"

"That the Lord is a God of justice."[1]

CHAPTER 30

Topheth

Jerusalem, Judah

he day was dark as the early afternoon sun was covered in threatening clouds—clouds that reflected their Creator's mood. A group of men made their way through Jerusalem's Lower City to the Potsherd Gate.

The servant of that Creator—the tall, thin figure walking in their midst—felt the weight of his Master's mood. Jeremiah was himself the picture of distress. He wore his cow-hair prophet's mantle over rough sackcloth, which he had torn and covered in ashes. He had shaved his uncovered head bare. His eyes were bloodshot orbs within hollow, dark-blue circles. He hadn't been getting much sleep. Jeremiah had taken to struggling all night, every night, in prayer. He was emaciated from extended fasting. At thirty-three years old, he was bent over as if he were eighty.

Sharp shards of pottery lay everywhere cast on the ground, desolate before the city's garbage dump. The prophet's feet were bare, and the pitiless shards ravaged them so that Jeremiah's uneven steps left a small red trail behind him. The prophet's eyes were haunted with the knowledge of the future.

"Ah, Lord God," Jeremiah breathed. "It is even worse than You have said. How can this be?" Despite his protests, he had already known what he would find there, he just couldn't believe it. The approaching storm whistled over the city wall and through the gate, whipping the mantle around Jeremiah's wasted figure as the scene of oncoming doom loomed before him.

Jeremiah looked thoughtfully at the men he had summoned; the men who had followed him here. Some he counted as friends, most he did not. The priest, Captain Pashur ben Immer of the Temple Guard, led the way as if this had been his idea. Jeremiah's cousin Zephaniah, the priest, had come to stand beside his brother, Zedekiah, the prophet; they were among a small group of priests which included Second Priest Jehoiada and Third Priest Buzi as well as Buzi's young son, Ezekiel. The Captain of the Palace Guard, Elnathan ben Achbor, was amid the advisors of the king, which included the four sons of Shaphan.

Jeremiah knew that if he never said another word to these men, this message, at least, would not be forgotten. He turned and stepped into and through the gate.

Topheth, the place of burning, that was what they called the fiery altars of the Baals, and the unquenchable flames of the garbage heap of Jerusalem had appropriated the name. It was the picture of eternal damnation to the people of Judah.

Tongues of fire flickered before the prophet's face, casting eerie lights across his visage in the shadows of the city wall. The flames burned, attempting to devour the rubbish of the city which fed them. The rejected and outcast broken remnants of society were consumed here forever amidst the swarms of flies and the scavenging creatures which tried to gorge themselves on their share of the refuse before the flames could claim it.

Jeremiah faced hell and knew it could be avoided no longer. Here, just outside the gates of Jerusalem, paganism reigned.

King Josiah had defiled the site with the garbage heap and named it Gehenna, the picture of an ever-burning hell. But with Josiah gone, the Chemarim, Molech's priesthood, had just piled the garbage up high and covered a spot on one edge of the mound with new dirt.

And now, the abomination was back. Molech, the destroyer of babes, was suddenly illuminated by a flash of lightning. Heaps of refuse spread out from the gigantic idol's feet as if it were the source of everything unclean. On the artificial high-place, with the noxious fumes of the burning garbage pit rising around it, the Chemarim served their demon god.

No one did anything to put a halt to it. Most chose to simply take a different route. If someone was decadent enough to choose to follow Baal-Molech, it was his decision. It was his children, after all. No one stopped him. There was no Josiah to defend the innocent. King Jehoiakim allowed the people to follow their non-existent consciences and did not interfere.

This Molech was the old Molech's big brother. Unlike Jerusalem's original, which had come from Tyre, this Molech had been made in Rabboth Ammon itself, the birthplace of the cult. It sat on a throne, yet despite that, it was a full reed tall.[1] It wore a short skirt over its loins, but from the waist up, this idol had the physique of a Greek wrestler. The one King Josiah had destroyed had been fat with a burning pot belly.

Instead of the Tyrian's grotesque laughing head, this Molech had the enormous head of a bull. Massive horns, wider and higher than any man, stretched out on either side, overshadowing the altar. The bull's nostrils flared to catch the scent of the burning sacrifices, but its eyes were vacant, aloof.

The flames were not found in this Molech's belly, but rather in a huge pit in the middle of the altar. His mechanical arms were outstretched over the fire. The deceived now laid their children on those arms to prove the sincerity of their worship. The arms would drop, allowing their precious burden to fall into the ferocious flames while the priests and parents watched.

This Molech, this Ammonite Molech, was somehow more ancient and primal than the former Tyrian pot-bellied god. It was unabashedly evil. The Chemarim wished to inspire terror, not worship. Tyre had ofttimes been an ally of the House of David, but Ammon always had been an enemy. While Jeremiah watched, a child, the innocent victim of his parents' misplaced piety, was laid lovingly in the monster's arms by a Chemar.

There was a pause, then the mechanical arms dropped the squalling child into the altar's roaring fire.

The infant's father sobbed out loud. The mother just stood there in shock. The heavens rumbled, and the wind fanned the newly fed flames as the child's screams were cut off.

Jeremiah and most of his group cried out. The prophet fell to his knees amongst the broken potsherds. Supporting himself on all fours, he vomited. The shards sliced into his knees and the palms of his hands.

The mother suddenly came to herself and screamed, forcing her husband to grab her around the waist to prevent her from leaping into the holocaust after her baby. He dragged his thrashing and kicking wife back, away from the altar.

Jeremiah sat back and struggled to get his stomach under control as another couple, cradling another little one, made its way up to the pagan priest.

"That is enough!" Secretary Ahikam, Shaphan's eldest son, charged the Chemarim and they scattered.

Gemariah, one of the sons of Shaphan, helped the prophet to his feet and handed him the clay jar Jeremiah had earlier entrusted to him. "Nabi?"

Jeremiah clutched the pot to his chest and nodded at his friend. "I'm all right, Gemariah. But our people are not!"

Ahikam glared at the contemptible couple. Then, not wishing to touch them and defile himself, he stalked back to Jeremiah's group.

Besides the worshippers of Molech, a surprising amount of people stood around the garbage heap. The people came many times a week to dispose of their refuse. Jeremiah looked them over, then lifted up his voice: "Hear the word of the Lord, you rulers of Judah and people of Jerusalem!

> The Lord Almighty, the God of Israel, says:
>
> Listen! I am going to bring such a disaster on this place that the ears of whoever hears of it will ring! They have abandoned Me and made this a place of pagan gods; they have burned incense here to idols that neither they nor their ancestors ever knew, and they have filled this place with the blood of the innocent! They have built up high places to burn their children in the fire as offerings to Baal-Molech—I didn't command this, I never mentioned it in passing, it never even entered My mind!"

The woman, whose child had just been consumed, looked at the smoking altar in horror at what she had just done and continued screaming. Her husband tried to console her, but she turned her distress on him and started beating on his chest. "You did this! You! You! You!"

"Beware!" Jeremiah thundered.

"The Lord declares:

The days are coming when you people will no longer call this place Topheth or the Valley of Ben Hinnom, but the Valley of Slaughter. Right here, I will ruin the plans of Judah and Jerusalem. Right here, I will make them fall by the sword before their enemies who want them dead, and right here I will give their carcasses as food to the birds and wild animals, and there will be no one to frighten them away. I will bring an end to the sounds of joy and gladness and to the voices of bride and bridegroom in the towns of Judah and the streets of Jerusalem, for the land will become desolate. I will devastate this city and make it an object of horror and scorn. Anyone who comes by here and sees this will be both appalled and will laugh derisively because of its mutilated defilement."

The woman sank sobbing to the garbage-strewn ground. Her husband just stood there, hollow-eyed in shock and guilt. The altar continued to smoke, and its flames cast flickering light up under the bovine chin of the god, making its demonic face seem to gloat. The people stood so still around the flames of the garbage that they, themselves, appeared to be a host of idols carved of wood and stone.

Jeremiah cast a desperate glance at Gemariah. His old friend and former scribe was still there, giving him the strength to go on. He swallowed hard, then continued, showing no mercy to the guilty couple or anyone else who could hear.

"I will make them eat the flesh of their sons and daughters!"

"Well, they're already cooking them," Ahikam growled, his fury barely contained.

"And they will eat one another's flesh too,"

Jeremiah told him, his face gaunt and pale at what only he could see,

> "because their enemies' siege will be so terrible. And it will continue until it has destroyed them."

The man of God raised the clay pot high above his head and threw it at the city wall. It shattered into a thousand pieces, and its sherds joined those already scattered about on the ground.

A startled gasp drifted through the crowd, and they involuntarily moved back, but they stayed. They seemed to be held there by invisible chains, wanting to run, but needing to hear.

The prophet continued,

> "The Lord Almighty says:
>
> 'I am going to smash this city and nation just like that jar so that it cannot be repaired. You will throw your dead on the Topheth until there is no more room! This whole city will be a Topheth! All the houses and even the king's palace will be as defiled as this place, a Topheth because they burned incense on their roofs to the stars and poured out drink for foreign gods."

Jeremiah stopped suddenly and listened to the voice only he could hear.

Go. Stand in the courtyard of the Lord's House and speak to all the pilgrims of Judah who are coming to worship. Tell them everything I command you, every word. Do not omit anything.

Incredulous, the prophet looked up at the threatening sky. "You wish me to tell them *everything* You have said? You even want me to tell them that You commanded me: *'Don't come to Me anymore to ask anything for this people?'"*

"Nabi?" Gemariah peered into the prophet's face, but Jeremiah didn't see him.

"Lord, the people!" the prophet protested, ignoring the statement he had just made about not praying for them. "They cannot continue this way.

They may yet repent. Sunset marks the start of the Feast of Weeks! Your Law will be read. They will hear! They will surely see…"

It is possible, they may yet repent. If they do, then I will relent and not bring the disaster upon them that I have planned because of their evil. Go!

The shrieks and sobs of the devastated mother haunted the prophet as he staggered back through the Potsherd Gate, his hollow cheeks wet with tears.

His entourage followed.[2]

CHAPTER 31

The Feast of Weeks

Jerusalem, Judah

The appearance of the first three stars of the evening was to have marked the start of Shavuot, but the dark and threatening sky was going to make the sign impossible to see. It would soon be the Feast of weeks, seven weeks after the Passover. It commemorated the day the traitorous Prince Moses gave two stone tablets to some freed slaves, and the strange religion of the Hebrews had been born. Ebedmelech stood inside the New Gate and watched pilgrims fill the temple court. He hesitated to follow them.

Ebed was an Egyptian of Cushite heritage. He had no desire to take place in a celebration that was obviously so prejudiced against his former nation, but he had made it his duty to give a daily offering to the priests of Ra and to do this, he had to push past this unyielding crowd.[1]

The late afternoon was ominously dark, and thunder rumbled overhead. Temple servants appeared and began lighting the lamps on their stands and hooks.

The Prophet Jeremiah staggered unsteadily, unseeing, through the gate and stopped, right beside Jehoiakim's protocol minister. Ebed took a step backward, distancing himself from Jerusalem's infamous crazy prophet. As a highly-placed member of Jehoiakim's court, he knew all about Jeremiah. This was the holy madman of Judea, and his power was real. Ebed had felt it before, and he felt it now. As the prophet stood there, swaying slightly, Ebed could feel the power emanating from the son of Hilkiah, stronger than the sun struggling to shine through the thick storm clouds. The efforts of the sun were cloaked with clouds, but Jeremiah cloaked the presence of a Divinity of devastating power. A chill ran up the big man's spine, and his black skin prickled all over.

The prophet definitely looked the part of a madman. Egyptian priests shaved their heads, but it was almost unheard of for a Judean one to do so. It indicated extreme duress and mourning. Even Ebed knew that. Jeremiah's tunic was torn and in tatters and his cow-hair mantle was covered in ashes. His feet were bare and left a trail of bloody prints back across the palace court and down to the palace's western gate.

Suddenly the prophet's eyes cleared, and they flashed fire. He stood up straight, his feet planted slightly apart. "Hear the words of the Lord!" he yelled, his clear piercing voice cutting above the murmur of the crowd. "All you people who come through these gates to worship Him!"

Jeremiah lifted his hands towards heaven and lightning arced across the sky as a thunderclap shook the Temple Court. When the thunder died away, the Levite singers and the masses in the Temple Court also fell silent and turned in trepidation to face the odd-looking spectacle of the Man of God.

Ebed had moved out of the gate and into the crowded Temple Court. He didn't want to be too close. Still, Jeremiah, or something in him, pulled on the official and awoke a longing he couldn't explain. The big Cushite eunuch stood surrounded by a sea of shorter light-colored faces, making him an easily seen spectacle himself, but all eyes were on the prophet, and no one was watching him.

Ebed glanced nervously upward at the roiling clouds. Trouble was brewing, there was no question. The minister of protocol decided to make his way to the north annex and present his offering so that he could leave as soon as possible.

Jeremiah seemed bent on inciting trouble. He called out,

> "This is what the Lord says:
>
> Look! I am preparing a disaster for you and devising a plan against you. So, turn from your evil ways, each one of you, and reform your ways and your actions and I will let you keep

living in this place. You have been listening to deceptive words which are telling you that this is the Temple of the Lord!'

The prophet lifted an arm encased in the hairy sleeve of his coat and gestured at Temple's porch with its four columns, two legitimate, two pagan.

"You say: 'the Temple of the Lord is the Temple of the Lord, nothing can happen to it!' So, you feel that by living in its shadow you are safe!" He dropped his arm and shook his head. "That is not what the Lord has said." The prophet walked towards the Temple, his voice echoing throughout the courtyard.

"But if you truly change your direction and reform your actions, deal honestly with each other,"

he stopped before a merchant. The rich man dropped his eyes and backed into the people surrounding him. They all backed away, creating a path forward for the prophet.

Jeremiah took it, moving forward until he stopped in front of Ebedmelech, who had gotten as far as the Temple Steps. The prophet placed his hand directly on the eunuch's shoulder. Ebed shrank from the touch.

"If you deal fairly with foreigners,"

Jeremiah cried out, and to Ebed's relief, he walked on.

The prophet stooped and picked up a small child. He handed the child back to his mother and at the same time gave her a couple of copper weights.

"If you have compassion on the fatherless and the widow,"

Jeremiah turned and pointed to the Horse Tower, visible above the Temple wall—the tower where Uriah's head was still on display to all who entered the city.

"And do not shed innocent blood here…"

Many of the crowd shrank back at this, but others were getting angry. They were no longer silent.

"You can't blame us for that!"

"*We* didn't do it!"

Jeremiah glared at them. Then he pointed to the southeast, to Ben Hinnom and the Molech. "What about the innocent children you burn?"

The prophet from Anathoth kept walking. Ebed saw now that he was surrounded by a kind of honor guard of royal officers and priests. The group marched right past the Temple portico with its singers and came to the entrance of the Temple's northern annex.

Ebed didn't know what to do. Jeremiah had taken his show exactly where the big Egyptian had been heading. He had thought that if he could only reach the annex, he could slip inside and escape whatever mischief this wild prophet had planned. Now, however, his destination was the center of the crowd's interest!

Jeremiah mounted the annex's steps, but his entourage stopped before them, refusing to touch the desecration. It didn't bother Jeremiah though, and he only stopped when he was directly in front of two small black sphinxes which flanked the doors.

"AND…"

Jeremiah's voice and the sky thundered together in anger.

> "If you do not follow other gods to your own harm, then I will let you live in this place, in the land I gave your ancestors forever and ever."

Ebed looked down at the four silver-weights in his hand. Would Osiris mind if he offered them tomorrow instead of today?

> "Tonight, you will listen to the words of the Law: *'You shall not murder. You shall not commit adultery. You shall not steal. You*

> *shall not give false testimony against your neighbor.'* Yet you are doing all of these! And why bother to keep them anyway, when you break the very first two Commandments? Tonight, you will hear:
>
> *"I am the Lord your God, who brought you out of Egypt, out of the land of slavery. You shall have no other gods before Me. You shall not make for yourself an image in the form of anything in heaven above or on the earth beneath or in the waters below. You shall not bow down to them or worship them.'*[2]
>
> "Don't you know that if you break these commandments, you have already broken all the others? Have you forgotten that the Lord is jealous? Or do you just not care?"

Jeremiah turned and reached through the open door to the annex. He grabbed one of the green-basalt arms of the seated idol known as Osiris and without pausing, he whipped around backward and sideways, and the idol's throne toppled, breaking the ostrich-plumed crown from the overturned god's head.

Ebed gasped. He had never heard of anyone treating the gods in such a manner, especially not Osiris. Osiris was the god of the underworld, the god of death and rebirth. His status could be seen in the fact that he was one of only two full-sized idols in all the annex. The other was the Bull of Amentet that the Hebrews knew as the golden calf, Apis. It held particular relevance to them for some reason. All other idols were only small figurines on shelves or sunken relief paintings on the walls, insignificant in comparison despite there being dozens of them.

Jeremiah grabbed a golden disk of Ra from its perch and threw it at the worshippers inside the shrine. The unfortunate Egyptians scattered and ran for the back door. The disk clattered on the floor.

> "You burn incense to Baal and follow other gods you have not known, and then you dare come and stand before Me in this House, which bears My Name and say: 'We are safe because nothing can touch the Lord's House.' Do you really believe you are safe when you do all these detestable things?"

Another peal of thunder rolled across the Temple grounds, and many of the people actually crouched down. There was a deafening silence for a brief moment, and then the huge crowd erupted. Most were shaking their fists and shouting back at the prophet.

"Heretic!"

"This is the Temple of the Lord!"

"The City of David is forever!"

And it wasn't just the crowd either. The prophets of the House had come out of their offices in the north gate, and they too were shouting.

Zedekiah ben Maaseiah stood forward and shouted "Jeremiah! Be silent! It is a feast time! What are you trying to do? Start a riot?"

Lightning flashed and struck somewhere just outside the city walls. Jeremiah yelled back at his cousin, "It is you who should be silent, Zedekiah! You stand before the House of the Lord and take the people's money in exchange for telling them lies!

> The Lord has a word for all of you:
>
> 'Have you made this House, which bears My Name, into a den of robbers? I have been watching!'"

"This is the Lord's house!" A priest, Ebed saw it was Chief Priest Azariah ben Hilkiah, made his way through the crowd to stand at the foot of the steps of the annex. He was surrounded by several others of the sacerdotal priests. They wouldn't go further. The Egyptian remembered that they considered the area unclean. "And this is a feast time!" Azariah shouted. "Jeremiah, go away and come back later and we will discuss this with you. But do not blaspheme. The Lord's House is indeed the *Lord's* House! We may no longer have King Josiah for our guarantee, but we still have the Temple, we have the sacrifices, we have the Lord's forgiveness, and so we are indeed safe, even if we do sin."

"If that is what you think, Azariah," Jeremiah shouted, still standing in the annex of Egypt, "go to the place in Shiloh where Joshua pitched My tent, and I made a dwelling for My Name. See what I did to it because of the wickedness of my people Israel!"

Azariah opened his mouth again and then shut it.

Ebed understood the priest's consternation, for he had learned much since he had become protocol minister for Jehoiakim. Shiloh, in the hill country of Ephraim, had indeed housed the Name of the Lord, off and on, for over three hundred years before Solomon had built the Temple. Despite this glorious history, it was in ruins, forgotten. Solomon's Temple was now just over three hundred years old. Even Ephraim, the symbol of Israel, was now gone. The comparison was chilling.

Even more chilling, in Ebed's opinion, was the change of person. Jeremiah was no longer speaking at all, Azariah was being addressed directly by an angry God, and the prophet was merely a mouthpiece.

The God of Heaven was not done. Jeremiah stepped back out of the annex and addressed the people. "The entire time that you have been doing all these terrible things, I have been calling you over and over and over again, but you won't listen. You won't answer. If you do not listen to Me, if you will not follow My Law, which I have set before you," it was not only a reminder of the feast day reading of the Law, but the phrasing was also a deliberate reference to the last words of Moses, warning the people to follow the Law, "if you will not heed the words of My servants, the prophets, then what I did to Shiloh, I will now do to the House that bears My Name, the Temple that you trust in, the place I gave to you and your ancestors. I will thrust you away from My Presence, just as I did all your fellow Israelites, the people of Ephraim, and all the nations of the earth will count this city as cursed."

Lightning flashed once more, and this time, it struck the Horse Tower. Broken bricks flew in all directions, and Uriah's head vanished in smoke and flame. The deafening report reverberated throughout the Temple Court.[3]

The people stared in shock as flames shot through the offending tower's windows. Then many of them broke and fled. The storm abruptly burst forth all around them. Rain and hail pelted the priests and prophets as they ducked down and shrank back, causing them to look like comical caricatures of the conspirators that they were. From the shelter of the Benjamin Gate, they consulted amongst themselves, and then they hurried off through the gale in several different directions.

Ebedmelech pushed past the prophet and under the eaves of the north annex where he stood and shivered. He had to step over the fallen Osiris to do so. Ebed knew that Jeremiah's time was short now. His enemies had gone to fetch the Temple Guard and the Great Council.

Jeremiah knew it too, but that only spurred him on to make one last appeal to the people. The rain paused as he stepped out from under the eaves onto the steps between the sphinxes and pleaded with the people who remained, panting with his passion. "The Lord told me not to pray for you anymore! He said that He wouldn't listen! He has shown me what you do in the streets of this city and in all the towns of Judah. Your children get the wood that your fathers set afire so your mothers can make cakes to offer to Ashtareth, the Queen of Heaven, wife of Molech![4] You pour out your drink offerings to other gods! This does not harm the Lord, it only harms you. You are an embarrassment!

> "So, the Sovereign Lord says:
>
> My anger and My wrath will be poured out on this place— on man and beast, on the trees of the field and on the crops of your land—and it will burn and not be quenched."

With the pause in the rain, the crowd was beginning to regather and regain their courage. They jeered and tried to shout him down.

"The Temple is forever, Jeremiah!"

"It is your shrine at Anathoth that is torn down!"

"*You* are the embarrassment. You embarrass us before the foreigners who have come here specifically for the feast!"

"Why are you the only prophet who feels this way?"

"Why do the other priests sacrifice, but you just run around speaking nonsense? Even if you do not respect them or their work enough to join them, have you no respect for the Chief Priest? Tonight, he will read the Law. He would tell us if what you are saying was true."

"And have *you* no respect for that Law?" Jeremiah shot back. "Go ahead, then. Add your burnt offerings to your other sacrifices and eat the meat yourselves! Tonight, you will hear once more how the Lord brought your ancestors out of Egypt and how he spoke to them. Have you forgotten that He did not just give them commands about burnt offerings and sacrifices? He said:

Obey me, and I will be your God, and you will be My people.
Walk in obedience to all I command you that it may go well with you."

The crowd's jeers were deafening.

"The Lord told me that you would not listen!" Jeremiah bellowed back at them. He was shaking with anger, but there were tears running freely down his face. "He told me that you would not respond!"

Impossibly, the jeering got louder.

Jeremiah raised his arms and face towards heaven. "Lord, You are correct. This is the nation that has not obeyed the Lord its God or responded to correction. Truth has perished; it has vanished from their lips." He lowered his arms and yelled at them. "Look at yourselves then! This is the nation that has not obeyed the Lord its God or responded to correction. The Lord has rejected and abandoned this generation. *Your* generation! *You* are under His wrath!"

The wind came up again. Cold gusts blew sheets of spray across the courtyard, whistling around the bulls of the Sea and the huge ramp of the altar. Jeremiah's mantle wrapped itself around his gaunt figure and whipped out behind him. He took one step towards the crowd, one step out from between the sphinxes, one step down to the middle step. From Ebed's perspective behind him, the prophet was outlined by flashing lightning against an oppressive, angry sky of boiling clouds.

Jeremiah's time had run out, for the Temple Guard arrived. Their captain, Pashur ben Immer was at their head. At a nod from Pashur, the Temple Guard rushed up to the bottom of the unclean steps and pulled Jeremiah down off of them.

Jeremiah did not try to defend himself. He said nothing. The voice of the people in the court was an indignant roar so even if he had tried to speak, he could no longer be heard. Though the Temple Guard surrounded the prophet, the people pelted them with their fists or whatever they had at hand, trying to break through their circle and to get at Jeremiah.

"Get out of the way!"

"Give him to us!"

"Blasphemy! Even the Chief Priest said so!"

"He must die!"

Captain Pashur held up his hands and they quieted enough for him to yell back at them, "I agree! Jeremiah has prophesied against this Temple and this city. You have all heard this with your own ears. These are crimes against his own people and blasphemy against our God. He should die, but that is for the Council to determine. Let us through!"

The brooding storm suddenly burst forth again in a downpour that hit the pavement with such force that it bounced back upwards into the people's faces, making it hard to breathe. It pelted them all anew with hail.

In awe filled with fear that sent chills through his entire body, Ebed stepped back off the annex portico into the shelter of the shrine to the gods of Egypt. A few others, all Egyptians, pushed their way inside too. Ebedmelech looked at the brightly painted walls and the bizarre little statues with animal heads, and for the first time in his life, they struck him as figurines merely fashioned from wood, stone, and metal. They did not see, and they certainly did not speak, but the God of Judah did!

A storm raged beyond the door that not one of Egypt's host could have summoned. This was the Temple of the God of Israel, and He was jealous. He would not tolerate Egypt's gods here. The prophet said they defiled the Temple by their presence. The Egyptians around the big eunuch were whispering and shaking their heads, but they didn't seem to understand.

Ebed did.

This God did not compromise; He cared nothing for protocol or politics. He demanded perfect loyalty and obedience. With Him, it was all or nothing.

What kind of a God was not willing to settle for what He could get? If He destroyed His own people, where would be His heritage?

Ebedmelech stared after the figure of the prophet as Jeremiah was roughly drug away by the Temple Guard. What would it be like to serve such an intolerant God? He looked over at the inferno enveloping the Horse Tower and then down at the toppled Osiris. He put the silver for his offering back in his bag.[5]

CHAPTER 32

The Great Council

Jerusalem, Judah

Despite the howling wind and the torrent of rain and pelting hail, some people still tried to attack the circle of guards around Jeremiah the Prophet. Others ran for shelter. The Temple Guard pushed and pulled and managed to get their prisoner intact as far as the New Gate, between the Temple and palace courts. They shut and barred the gateway complex from both sides. And from both sides, the people shouted and assailed it, shaking the bars. There were no stones available for them to throw; the Temple and palace courts were paved with sand-set cobblestones.

The area inside the gateway was roofed over and provided some protection from the fury of the storm. Benches, stacked along the walls, were taken down and set in place. A chair was set against one of the walls, and the benches were aligned in a semicircle on either side of it. To the right side of the chair, the seventy members of the Council moved forward and sat. To the left, the priests and prophets took their seats. The mob stood outside in the tempest, rattling the bars and looking in. Captain Pashur ushered Jeremiah directly in front of the chair as Chief Priest Azariah gathered his robes and sat down on it.

This was the Great Council. It rarely convened, but when it did, it met in the New Gate, which joined the political and religious worlds of Judah into one.[1]

The cloudburst began to subside and the heaving clouds rolled by leaving a sullen and still threatening sky.

Pashur positioned Jeremiah to stand before a hostile court filled with over a hundred men.

The prophet peered around. No, not all present were hostile. All of those he had called to the Topheth were still here with him, including Jeremiah's favorite cousin, Zephaniah ben Maaseiah. Zephaniah was seated among the priests and looked desperate to the point of panicking. Third Priest Buzi and his son Ezekiel were there too. Buzi was busy trying to keep Ezekiel from starting a fist fight with some of the other priests and prophets around them. The keeper of the New Gate, another of Jeremiah's cousins, Maaseiah ben Shallum, moved up to stand protectively by the prophet's side, his spear ready. And there, on the civil government's side were several members left from Josiah's court, including his close friend and former scribe, Gemariah ben Shaphan.

But the Chief Priest was angry. Azariah stood and raised his hands and waited until the crowd quieted. Then, he looked to heaven, praying an invocation for guidance. "O Lord our God, Almighty and Just Judge, guide our thoughts, words, and hands this day. When Jehoshaphat assembled the Council, he commanded them:

'Consider carefully what you do, because you are not judging for mere mortals but for the Lord, Who is with you whenever you give a verdict. Now let the fear of the Lord be with you, judge carefully, for with the Lord our God there is no injustice or partiality or bribery.'

So, let us look beyond our feelings and judge with impartiality, knowing You are watching."

He gathered his robes and sat in the central chair. Silence, filled with tangible expectation, followed. "Jeremiah, *what have you done?"* Azariah suddenly leaned forward and cried out. "You have put me in an impossible position! All of Judah has heard your words. They are saying it is blasphemy…"

"It *is* blasphemy!" House Prophet Zedekiah, spat, rising from his bench among the prophets. "Jeremiah! Why do you prophesy, claiming it is in the Lord's Name? You say that the Temple will be razed to the ground like Shiloh and that this city will be torn down and deserted! That is blasphemy, and the penalty is death! You must die!"

Zephaniah jumped over his bench and shoved his brother back down onto his seat. "What are you saying? That's our cousin!"

The court erupted, the priests and prophets pushing at each other.

"Leave him alone!"

"He's a prophet!"

"Let Jeremiah speak!"

"If he's a prophet, where are the miracles, then?"

"Has anyone ever seen Jeremiah perform a miracle?"

"Be quiet!"

"Zedekiah's an official prophet, let him speak!"

"Zedekiah's right, it is blasphemy!"

"Jeremiah must die, or this sedition will spread throughout the land!"

"He's no cousin of mine!" Zedekiah regained his feet and yelled in his brother's face. He turned towards the Chief Priest, pointing at Jeremiah, "You must sentence this man to death because he prophesied against this city! You heard him with your own ears!"

"Peace!" Azariah bellowed, standing up himself. "Sit down!" The tumult quieted, and after the others had reluctantly sat back down, he took his seat again himself.

Azariah shot a warning glare at the priests and prophets, then turned a scowl on the civil component of the Council for good measure. When no one offered any further disorder, he got hold of himself and sighed. "Very well, Jeremiah. What have you to say for yourself?"

Jeremiah was totally unrepentant. "For myself?" he asked in his clear, penetrating voice. "Nothing. It was the Lord who sent me to prophesy against this Temple and city and to say all the things that you heard me say. Take it up with Him. You don't like the idea of this happening? Then reform your ways and actions and obey the Lord your God. Then He will relent and not bring the disaster that He has pronounced upon you."

The court exploded once more. On their feet again, some of the members of the priesthood moved to physically attack the prophet, but Gate

Keeper Maaseiah jumped in front of the prophet and stood in their way, his spear held ready.

"Sit down!" the Chief Priest roared again and rushed forward to stand beside Maaseiah. Together, the Chief Priest and the Temple Guard faced the Council down. Order slowly returned. Azariah laid his hand on Maaseiah's shoulder, and the gatekeeper moved back to Jeremiah's side and placed his spear at rest. The Chief Priest resumed his seat. "If there are any further disturbances, the perpetrators will be arrested." The statement was met with angry murmurs, but no outright defiance, so Azariah continued, "Jeremiah, it is not the Lord Who is on trial here today."

"No," the prophet replied sadly, "it is all of you. As for me, I am in your hands; do with me whatever you think is good and right. Be assured, however, that if you do put me to death, you will bring the guilt of innocent blood on yourselves and on this city and on those who live in it, because the Lord was the One Who sent me to you with this message, and that *is* the truth."

The Council was conferring amongst themselves. The sons and grandsons of King Josiah's secretary, Shaphan, stood as a group. Ahikam ben Shaphan was their elder, and he stepped forward and addressed the Chief Priest. "May I speak?"

"You are recognized," Azariah acknowledged him.

Ahikam nodded and gathered his thoughts. He faced the priestly section of the room across from the civil court. "You are the priests and prophets of the Lord," he called out. "Have you no fear of Him? This man should not be sentenced to death. He has spoken to us in the Name of the Lord our God.

"The sun will soon set. It was on this day that Moses spoke to us from the mountain in the Name of the Lord, and our nation was born! Is it so hard to believe that the Lord would again choose this day to deliver His message?

"In the days of King Hezekiah of Judah, a man named Micah of Moresheth prophesied that one day Zion will be plowed like a field. He said Jerusalem will become a heap of rubble; the Temple hill will be a mound overgrown with thickets. That is pretty much the same as what Jeremiah has just said. And the Prophets of the House at that time sought Micah's life also. Yet did King Hezekiah or anyone else put him to death? No! Hezekiah feared the Lord and turned to Him to look for His mercy! What happened then? The Lord relented! He did not bring the disaster He pronounced against them. But here we are, about to do the exact opposite and bring a terrible catastrophe upon ourselves!"

The Chief Priest was silent for a few moments, thinking, then he nodded. "Unfortunately, we have no Hezekiah. Our king is not afraid to spill the blood of a prophet, but that doesn't mean we have to mimic his actions."

Jeremiah saw Azariah glance in the direction of the smoke and flames from the Horse Gate and shiver.

"Ahikam is correct. Jeremiah, you are free to go."

"You're going to take his part?" House Prophet Zedekiah stood and shouted in disbelief. He was surrounded by cries of:

"No!"

"Impossible!"

"Blasphemy must not be tolerated!"

"Azariah, I thought you were one of us!"

There was an uproar from the people outside the gate as well.

"Quiet!" Azariah bellowed. Gradually, the tumult died. The Chief Priest turned once more to the prophet. "But understand this, Nabi, you are a trouble maker and these days are troubled enough. I will have no more riots in the Temple Courtyard. From now on, you are banned from the Temple grounds! Captain Pashur, see him back to his house."

There were gasps from Jeremiah's friends and murmurs of reluctant affirmation from his enemies. Jeremiah had been banished from the presence of the Lord. He would never more have the benefit of sacrifice to cover his sins, the privilege of prayer before the altar, or even the solace of the fellowship and enlightenment of the sodh. If he were separated from the Lord, surely he could prophesy no more.

Jeremiah was unmoved. He gave the Chief Priest a bland look. Then, marshaling his dignity, he turned and walked out of the gate, which Maaseiah opened for him. The crowd parted, allowing the prophet and his unwilling escort of the Temple Guard, to leave by way of the palace court.[2]

CHAPTER 33

Progressivism

Jerusalem, Judah

The people of Judah did not heed the words Jeremiah had spoken. That evening, the Ten Commandments were read, and the people swore to follow them. The fire of the Horse Tower was extinguished. The idol of Osiris was patched up and set back in his place in the shrine.

And life went on. If Jehoiakim could worship the gods of Egypt, then the common people felt they could recognize the spirits of the earth, the trees, and the air. Following the lead of their king, the high places multiplied in the countryside. There had always been opponents to Josiah's reform. Businesses had been hurt and freedoms curtailed by the strict observances the king had ordered. Now new voices rang out among the people. Modern thinkers were brazenly outspoken. Current logic said Deuteronic theology was clearly and patently untrue. Had following the Law forestalled disaster for Josiah? No! The king lay in his grave. King Jehoiakim had not even deigned to attend the Feast of Weeks with its scripture readings, and he had never, not even under his father, attended the Festival of Tabernacles in the Sabbath year when the complete books of Moses were read. Yet he prospered. To say that the Lord alone was God was narrow-minded and bigoted and it offended those who held a different opinion.

Daniel ben Abda was on his way to Bethlehem to check on his family's flocks and holdings. At sixteen years old, he was quite grown, and he made the trip every week. He was glad to have the excuse. Daniel's betrothed, Miriam, lived in Bethlehem and he was falling deeper and deeper in love with her.

This week, the youth had barely left Jerusalem, when he stopped dead and stared at the top of the small hill. A chill run up his spine. Last week, the rocky hill had been empty. It wasn't empty now.

It was almost two and a half years since King Josiah's death. It was now the beginning of Jehoiakim's third year, and this was the result. On the top of the hill stood wooden poles that were decorated with strange symbols and strings of feathers and beads whose purpose Daniel could only guess at. There wasn't even a pretense that this was meant to honor the Lord. It was pure paganism. The poles had not been raised in such a way as to be the start of some kind of construction; rather they seemed to be an end in themselves.

A Levite sat on the dusty ground with a row of colorful pottery vessels in front of him. They appeared to be full of wine and oil. Daniel had heard of such things from his father. The poles were in honor of Asherah, wife of Baal. The oil and wine were to be poured out to her to claim her patronage as a fertility goddess. The priest was there to collect money from those who wished to make an offering. Undoubtedly, this Levite had decided that being self-employed paid better than his duties under the priests at the Temple.

But the Levite's rejection of the Temple was more likely due to his politics than his avarice. On the ground at the feet of the poles stood a tiny stone statue, a two-sided statue of a woman with multiple breasts. On one side, she had a complicated hairstyle and held a bundle of wheat on the other she wore a war helmet and carried a shield which bore the symbol of a star within a circle. She stood on a crescent moon laid on its side. This was no Asherah. It was the Babylonian goddess, Ishtar.

Long ago, the Sea People had brought their goddess Asherah to Sumer. Inanna of Sumer mixed with Asherah of Canaan, and the result was Ishtar of Babylonia. Now Ishtar was returning to her Canaanite roots. The Levite favored the old king Josiah's support of Babylon, even if he didn't hold his views on idolatry. He was pro-Babylonian, so he was promoting Babylon's gods and refused to serve in a Temple Court that was rife with Egyptian politics.

The people were divided. Daniel had heard the arguments in the city and the sodh. Now he saw the results. To declare their political affiliations, some honored the Babylonians by erecting their gods on the high places outside Jerusalem and some in the city acknowledged Egypt by worshipping their idols in the Temple itself! The only thing the people seemed to agree upon was that it was not necessary to follow the Lord. Judah was as idolatrous as Israel had ever been and Jeremiah had said she would share her sister's fate.[1] Daniel shivered, for he knew she deserved it.

He hurried on his way. Miriam was waiting.

PART 5: 606 BC

The Signs of the Times

But look, you are trusting in deceptive words that are worthless. Will you steal and murder, commit adultery and perjury, burn incense to Baal and follow other gods you have not known, and then come and stand before Me in this House, which bears My Name, and say "We are safe"—safe to do all these detestable things?

—Jeremiah 7:8-10

CHAPTER 34

Domestic Bliss

Harran, Media

"My Lord Governor," the midwife was all smiles, holding a tiny squirming bundle in her arms, "I have the best of news. You have a son." She deposited the child in the arms of the Bel Pihati of Harran. "The votaress is doing very well, despite her age. Forty is old to be bearing a first child, but she has the favor of the moon god. This is a day of great joy for the whole city!"

The sun shone through the holes in the design of the decorative bricks of the second story of the palace in Harran and reflected brightly against the white-washed walls. Nabubalatsuikibi looked down on the red and wrinkled face of his only child and marveled. He had long ago given up any thought of becoming a father. "Look Kadurri, a boy! He has his mother's eyes."

The Rab Mag of Babylonia, still in the city, stood in the hall outside the birthing room with the governor. He bent over the baby and peered down at the minuscule visage. When Uvakshatra had departed for the field two weeks earlier, Kadurri had remained. He had waited in Harran for this. "No offense, Lord Governor, but how can you tell? He squints like his mother's god in the light of Shamash."

Suiki grinned. The moon god Sin hated the light of the sun. "All babies squint so, Great One." The baby gurgled.

"Will you name him for Sin?"

It would have been appropriate. His mother was Sin's votaress.[1] But the child had seen fit to arrive in the morning on the day of the dark of the moon. "Sin will not visit us this day. The god will be surprised upon his return to find his servant has become a mother." Suiki grinned. "Since he is not here to welcome the little one, I think that we are free to name him as we see fit. I greatly honor the god of writing and learning, all the more so since your sire is also named for him. He shall be called Nabonaid."

The prince straightened up and peered searchingly at the governor. People often named babies in honor of the dead. Nabopolassar had declined to take to the field so far this year, and Suiki was well aware of the gravity of his illness. "My father only remains in Babylon for the Akitu, Suiki. His illness is minor. He will recover, and take to the field soon."

Suiki's grin died. "Of course, Rab Mag."

Nebuchadnezzar looked back down at the child and touched the tiny cheek. "It *is* a good name, though. My father will rejoice to hear it. He will be here within the moon to see his little namesake for himself."

"I await his visit eagerly."

"Yes. But now I have seen that for which I have waited."

Suiki blinked. "You're leaving so soon?"

The rab mag looked up at the new father. "I have delayed too long already, My Friend. Our enemies wait for no one, not even little Nabonaid. I must go to join the first of my fathers-in-law to fight against the second."

The Bel Pihati of Harran nodded sadly. "My king is waiting for you, I know. But I feel like I have just gained one son to see another leave. Be careful Kadurri, and listen to my king. Uvakshatra is wise."

Kadurri grinned. "I will listen, but some battles cannot be won if one is over careful. Don't worry, My Friend. I will be back. I want to see if this little one as he grows really does have the eyes of his mother."

Jerusalem, Judah

The small house of Baruch the scribe may have been more crowded than formerly, but it was a good problem to have. Baruch was happy to have Sarah there. It was pleasant to have someone to talk to, even when, like now, she pushed him to resolve problems which had no solutions.

"The people forget too quickly," the former slave-girl complained while leaning over a pot suspended above the hearth. She stirred the simmering pot of lentil and vegetable stew for their supper. The wooden spoon dripped on the fire in the hearth, and it sizzled.[2] The mixed smell of baking bread and savory stew was amazing. "They are swayed this way one day and that way the next," she continued. "They have heard Uriah and Jeremiah, and they believe when they hear, but…" Sarah checked the bread, browning on its stone. Then she straightened up and frowned.

"No, they don't. They don't believe," Baruch said.

"Some of them believe."

"Maybe."

"No, they do, but it doesn't last."

The scribe sighed. "They live day to day. Under the burden of all their daily cares, a message heard a year or two ago doesn't seem all that urgent," Baruch answered from his seat on the ground before the low table in their tiny kitchen. "I know."

Sarah grinned, happy to have made her point. She lived with Baruch permanently. He had used his earnings to pay her family's taxes and then he had married her. It had seemed the only logical way to get a return out of his investment. Or so he had told her. She had laughed and said that she would be glad to be obligated for the rest of her life. Baruch had no problem with that. They may have been destitute, but for the most part, they were happy, and Sarah was a much better cook than he was. Baruch was slowly working his way back on his feet financially, and things were getting better, but Sarah still mourned Uriah and brought the subject up at least once a week. She couldn't stand to think that his death had been for nothing. Baruch didn't know what to say to her because he felt the same way.

"Uriah was very brave, but most of the people don't even know who he was anymore," she returned to her original argument. "Baruch, if you could record his words, they could read them. You're a scribe. You could make copies and send them to the villages…"

"Sarah, Sarah…" Baruch chided her. He sniffed the delicious smell as it wafted from the pot. "That would be very dangerous."

"I don't care, do you? If the king finds out, well!" She snapped her fingers defiantly, "That for him! Your brother Seraiah has managed to buy a small piece of land outside the city. It has a little hut on it. We could hide out there."

She had badgered him this way for months. Finally, he lost his temper. "For what purpose?" He snapped at her and slammed his fist down on the little table. One of the legs cracked.

Sarah jumped back, from the pot, startled. She spilled some of the contents of the ladle on the fire, and it flared and sputtered.

Baruch ignored it and continued, "You want me to give the people a short, ninety-part of an hour missive we both know would be inaccurate? I didn't even hear it myself. No one seems to have, except King Jehoiakim! What do you want me to do? Go ask the king what Uriah said?"

She stared at him, taken aback.

"I'm sorry." He heaved a sigh. He was quiet for a moment, then he unfolded his legs from beneath him and stood up in disgust. "You're right, I feel we should do something, too. But for it to be effective, we would really need something longer; and for it to be accurate, we would want Uriah himself to dictate…"

"All right!" she interrupted him, frustrated. "I know you're right, but so am I. I've been thinking about it. Baruch, it is possible! Not for Uriah, but for the stand he took and the message he died for! There's Jeremiah! The man is in his mid-thirties, and he's been preaching since he was twelve. Uriah said his message was very similar to the things Jeremiah has said about the king. And Jeremiah's a major prophet—his standing has got to be as great as Isaiah himself.[3] Think about it, Gemariah no longer scribes for him, he has no secretary! Baruch, it's unconscionable."

Baruch laughed, both at the idea and at her delivery of it. "Unconscionable." He rubbed her shoulder. "That's a big word for a slave girl."

"Not for a slave girl married to a scribe." She swung the pot away from the fire to let it cool. "Baruch, I think you should do it." She slipped her hand over his and turned around, face to face. "No, I think you must do it. He needs you."

This was typical of Sarah. Her moral indignation over the situation overrode her innate good sense. It was one of the reasons he loved her. The scribe chuckled at the thought. "Jeremiah has said a lot. That's a lot of work. I wouldn't have time for much else." He caressed her cheek and then slipped his arms around her waist. "What would we live on? You agree that asking the king is a bad idea, so now you want me to go to Jeremiah and say, 'Nabi, I want to record your work, and I think you should pay me for the privilege?'"

It was Sarah's turn to laugh.

There came a knock at the door. Baruch released his wife to go answer it and found Jeremiah himself standing there, a tall, dark shadow against the bright day outside. "Peace to you, Baruch ben Neriah. The Lord says I have need of a scribe," the prophet stated.

Astonished, Baruch stared at him. "But… Oh! And peace to you, Jeremiah ben Hilkiah. But... You wish to write a letter?" Jeremiah was totally literate. He could write his own letters.

"Not really a scribe, more of a secretary. Would you be interested?"

The floor itself seemed to tilt beneath Baruch's feet. He steadied himself on the doorpost. "But… But Gemariah?" he sputtered.

"Gemariah was never *my* scribe, not really. King Josiah paid him, and besides, he is now engaged in other work. You, on the other hand, have never been associated with Josiah. The people need to understand that this is not the same work as I was doing before. This is new, so I must have someone else, preferably someone not associated with the royal secretaries." He gave the scribe a quizzical look. "I thought you would be expecting me. You weren't?"

A very strange chill ran up Baruch's back as he stood back to let the prophet enter. "Actually, I think my wife Sarah was.

"And she's just made dinner."

CHAPTER 35

Setbacks

North Syria

Nabopolassar coughed. It turned into a sneeze. Despite the heat, the King of Babylon felt the chill off the Euphrates and shivered. If he had been able to direct the campaign from Samsat, the little fortress that he had captured the year previous, he would probably have shaken off the illness already. But Samsat was lost.

Samsat was just south and on the same side of the Euphrates as the reddish-brown cliffs of Carchemish. The little town would have been the perfect base to direct operations against the black fortress on the top of its mountain. But a moon earlier, just before King Uvakshatra and Rab Mag Nebuchadnezzar had arrived, Egyptian and Lydian reinforcements *had* arrived in Carchemish. They were led by Necho himself. Samsat had fallen and was in ruins.

By the time Nabopolassar had arrived with the remainder of Babylon's army, the King of Media and Rab Mag of Babylon had set up field operations from the town of Quaramati. Quaramati was farther from Carchemish then Samsat had been, and it was on the wrong side of the river, as well. Using it as a base meant assailing Carchemish by way of the Good River Crossing. So, now, Nabo stood shivering in his chariot, contemplating how wet that freezing river was going to be. Behind him, the horses of the Enlil Chariot Corps, draped in royal red and trimmed in white and gold, stood impatiently champing on their bits.

"The king should stay on the east bank," Nebuchadnezzar's light tenor voice came from the right. The king turned to see his tall son coming trotting up in his own chariot. Kadurri had come to love riding at the head of the cavalry, but as rab mag, it was beneath his dignity. The First General of Babylonia had to ride a chariot into battle. Kadurri's driver pulled in the team, but nervous for action, one of them reached over and took a quick nip at the gray nose of one of the king's team. The white mare squealed and struck at Kadurri's offending teammate. "The River is a natural barrier which will protect your position, and you can see the entire field from the east bank of the crossing," the prince continued. "You can actually direct operations better from here."

"I will not stay back when the men responsible for Belnasir's death are brought to account!" Nabo snapped. His voice was hoarse. It was always hoarse, now. "Uvak is crossing, is he not?" Both the prince and the king had been present at the meeting in the tent where the battle had been planned. Nabo *knew* Uvak was crossing. A sudden spasm of coughing made him grip the rail of the chariot.

Kadurri watched his father with a concern that irritated the king. His word was law, and Kadurri should respect that. After a moment, the prince nodded curtly and had his driver wheel his chariot away to the front of his chariot core, the Rab Mag's core, the Nergal Chariot Core, with its bright blue display of colors overlaying the Babylonian red and white.

Nebuzaradan was there too, on his gray mare, holding the rab mag's banner: the god Nergal thrusting a mighty spear like lighting across a deep blue sky. Nabo glanced across his chariot at Captain Arioch of the Daggermen. Seated on his leggy chestnut, next to the king, the captain held the royal banner: two white dragons, their necks intertwined on a field of blood red.

It was time. Nabo nodded at his son and the Rab Mag of Babylonia raised his fist above his head. Seri shoved the blue standard forward. As one, the entire chariot core rushed forward into the Euphrates and the icy water sprayed high in the air.

To the left, Nabo saw Prince Ishtumegu leading the Median First Cavalry, their green and gold colors flying. They leaped into the water sending a shimmering spray high into the air.

The roar of the Babylonians and Medes was answered with a defying shout from the fortress and the army stationed on the other side of the river.

And Pharaoh Necho stood high on Carchemish's walls and laughed at them.

The battle that day saw heavy losses against the Coalition. The Egyptians, aided by Lydian and Carian mercenaries fell back under the umbrella of their archers from high above. Mostly untouched, the Egyptians retreated back up the steep, narrow road to the gates, to shortly regroup and charge again.

Two more days of the same wore down the Coalition's resolve and exhausted, they fell back to their headquarters at Quaramati.

The Egyptians halted just out of bowshot of the city while the Coalition pressed into its walls. Here, the pursuing Egyptians no longer had the cover of a hail of arrows from above but Quaramati's walls were not remotely tall enough, and the Egyptian forces were fresh and mostly untouched.

"Well?" Nabopolassar sat shivering, wrapped in a blanket by the fire in his small white-washed hut in Quaramati. Rab Mag Nebuchadnezzar and Rab Shaq Belshumishkun stood before him. It was evening, but the rab mag and rab shaq and ordered the troops to remain ready to march.

"We have netted a dozen of the Lydian war-dogs," Kadurri reported, skirting the issue. "The Lydians have made plans for this contingency. All the dogs are neutered males—useless for breeding purposes."

Belshumishkun spoke up. "I haven't much experience in dogs, Lord, but I have bred horses all my life. To breed our own animals into such as these will take decades. We can probably retrain the captured beasts for our own use, but what difference would a paltry dozen make?

"We have come to you on a far more pressing matter. The generals agree. Lord, it's time to return to Babylon."

"In defeat?" Nabo exploded and managed to stand up in outrage. "We still outnumber them!"

The rab shaq looked to the rab mag. Kadurri nodded and spoke. "Quaramati can stand no longer. Tomorrow will see this fortress besieged and all escape cut off, so we must fall back. King Uvakshatra will be retreating within a half-beru. We may outnumber the Egyptians, but by tomorrow, we will have no base of operations."

"It's my health, isn't it?" the king asked shrewdly. "I saw the doctors reporting to you."

Kadurri studied his toes. "You have pneumonia, sire. You need to return to Babylon. By next year…"

"Necho will have all of Syria!" Nabo coughed and held a cloth to his mouth. He sank back onto his seat."

"And both you and our army will have recovered, and we will have had time to plan a new campaign," the prince returned.

The iron in his son's voice caught Nabopolassar off guard. No one talked to him this way. "*I* am the king!"

"And I am your rab mag, you should listen to me. Father, Belshumishkun had to take you from the field early today. You didn't see. Our troops still fought, but all the while, they were looking for you. They are hurting and only fight on because they love you. If they realize how sick you are…"

Nabo looked at Belshumishkun. His cupbearer looked as determined as his son. "You are in agreement on this?"

The rab shaq looked the king in the eyes. "I am your rab shaq. Your safety is my foremost concern, and in that, you cannot override me. Lord, you know this. I have had your chariot made ready. You *are* going to Babylon. Now."

On the morrow, Pharaoh Necho captured a deserted Quaramati. He now owned all of Syria.[1]

CHAPTER 36

To Save Harran

Harran, Media

The polished marble and granite of the official areas of the palace of Harran gave way to the softer, warmer tones of the gleaming wood and tapestries in the ruling couple's private quarters. Nabubalatsuikibi stood beside the desk where his guest sat. In a corner, his wife, Addaguppi, cuddled and cooed at their baby son. The chill of the coming winter was banished by the brightly burning hearth, and the luxurious carpets and fabrics soaked up all sound, so that little Nabonaid's squeals and giggles didn't echo, but rather added to the intimate feeling. The surroundings were warm and comforting, but Nebuchadnezzar, the figure seated at the desk, sat with his head in his hands.

"You have been rab mag for almost two years, Kadurri," the governor pointed out. "It's a heavy burden for a seventeen-year-old. I may not be a military man, but I know that no one can fault your tactics. They praise you for being absolutely brilliant. None of this is your fault."

"Brilliant? So, why does Necho now hold all of Syria?" Kadurri looked up at the governor. "Suiki, Harran still stands, but for how much longer? If we don't stop him, Necho will be here next year. You need to think of your people."

"Evacuation?" Suiki glanced at his wife and shook his head. "It cannot be."

"Don't worry so, Great Prince," the Priestess of Sin murmured as she continued to bounce her son. Little Nabo laughed out loud. "Things will work out," she told him. "Sin will not abandon his city to the Egyptians. This I know. They do not recognize him."

Nebuchadnezzar had seen such certainty a thousand times over from those who now lay in the dust, along with their gods. They had also been certain their gods would not fail them. Kadurri did worry, but he stood, reached over, and briefly laid his hand on hers. He smiled for her, then he turned back to her husband, leaning over the desk. "I can't help you. Suiki, I have been rab mag for two years, and I've tried everything I know. I've listened to all the advisors my father and King Uvakshatra have to offer, and the pharaoh is still entrenched as deeply as ever. He controls Syria.[1] Harran is all we have left guarding the Syrian border from our side and Necho will be here in force next year. So, even though Belshumishkun took my father home, I've come here to see you. You know your city is crucial to both Media and Babylonia.

"Suiki, you know what Necho will do to you if he takes this city and he *will* take it unless we can retake Carchemish. But we can't even get close to it. I don't want to see Nabonaid grow up without his father. King Uvakshatra wouldn't agree, but as your friend, I need to ask you again. You need to consider evacuation. I would make sure that your people are well resettled."

"No!" Addaguppi said sharply, her eyes flashing.

The Governor of Harran held up his hand, hushing her protest, and he smiled gently. "My Prince, I do not think this suggestion would earn you points with your father-in-law, my king. You are right. King Uvakshatra has no intention of abandoning this city. Harran is vital, and even more so to Babylonia than to Media! What would you do if the Egyptians pour into your empire because we no longer stand in their way? In any case, I don't think that we could persuade my lady."

Kadurri frowned and straightened up. "I apologize to the priestess." He bowed politely to her then turned back to the governor. "And you're right, Harran is vital. But I don't see how we can save it. At least this way, we save the people."

"For how long? I'm no military strategist, but if you just give Harran away, Egypt, and most likely Lydia too, will come streaming into the main part of your father's empire. Besides, I don't think many of my citizens would leave, Rab Mag. Not unless I were to order it, and I won't do that. Uvak is my king, and he would count it as treason. Commander Mitatti would likely have my head because even if the people left, I wouldn't. Kadurri, I want to save my people, but how can I order them to do something I won't do?"

"I could put you someplace where neither Uvakshatra nor Mitatti would ever find you."

Suiki laughed. "You want to hide me? Kadurri, you are not listening. I won't leave. Adda is Votaress of Sin. She is the symbol of Harran. She cannot leave, so I will not. But Harran is not lost. We still have the Scythians." He gestured at the window, towards the Scythians encamped outside Harran's walls. "With their help, we have stood this far." It was true. The barbarians had stood firm and their savagery in battle as they defended their settlement had protected the city up to this point.

Kadurri looked at them in frustration. He could not order an evacuation. Harran belonged to Media. Nabubalatsuikibi was not his father's subject. "There has to be a way. I can't just let you die here."

"If it is so fated, so it will be. You know that."

"Then send Nabonaid to Babylon. Make it a visit to my father, he thinks of the boy as a grandson. I think it would make his heart glad."

Adda pursed her lips stubbornly but said nothing. It was the governor who shook his head. "Nabonaid is our only child. What would the people say if we were to send him away now, under such circumstances? If Sin is willing, the boy will make the journey one day, and your father will jump for joy to see him. But for now, he will stay here with us."

The governor came around the desk and took the prince's hand. "Kadurri, you are young yet. You may think you know everything, but you don't. And when you consider all of history, it just may be that your generals and advisors are all too young as well. Many battles have been fought over these grounds in the past, some against odds as great as these, and yet they were won! I know, I have read about them. They are recorded back in Babylon. Those records can serve as examples. I am a scholar, Highness, not a soldier. I do not know how to profit from what I have read there, but you, you're a warrior; a great tactician they say. You are going back to Babylon. Make use of your library,

Rab Mag. The wisdom of the ages is recorded there. If Marduk wills, perhaps there will be something that you will find of use."

Nebuchadnezzar frowned. Apply history to battle strategy? It was a crazy idea, but he was open to anything at this point, so why not? "Thank you, My Friend," he said, discouraged. He squeezed the governor's hand and released it. "I guess I've done everything else. I'll try it."

CHAPTER 37

Taking the Reins of Power

Babylon, Babylonia

The windows were shuttered against the breeze of outside air, and the room was dim and stifling hot from the brass brazier. A tall incense burner in the corner enveloped the room in a thick cloud of vaporized medicinal herbs.

"Sire?"

The man on the bed pried open his eyes and willed them to focus on the shadowy figure that had entered his room. The king recognized his son standing just inside the half-closed door. He managed a smile and pushed aside a heavy comforter and two stoppered bladders full of hot water. He propped himself upright in his huge down-filled bed. "So. You have returned." Nabo's breathing was ragged, his words, wheezing. Salty sweat ran down his face. The king's bare chest was plastered with a mustard paste that smelled strongly of garlic and peppermint. He looked terrible.

"Yes, Lord," Nebuchadnezzar answered. "Just now. I wished to report to you first thing, but if this is an inconvenient time…"

"No, this is a good time," Nabopolassar paused, "and there are more bad times than good lately. You'd best report now."

Kadurri's brow wrinkled as he eyed his father with concern. "Perhaps I should call the physicians instead."

"They've been already, they'll be back at midday, again as Shamash leaves us, and again at the second watch," Nabo replied irritably. "I'm just starting to shake off whatever it is that they keep putting in my drink, so if you want me coherent, you'd best report now." He broke into a fit of coughing, covering his face with a towel.

Kadurri's concern turned to dismay. He finished closing the door behind him, crossed to the bed and laid his hand on his father's shoulder.

Nabo waved him away as the coughing subsided. The suzerain lowered the towel and quickly folded it to try to hide the blood stains, but Kadurri saw them. The prince missed almost nothing.

"Stop worrying," the king grumbled and lifted a cup from the table beside the bed. He took a long draught. "It's been well over two moons." Nabo cleared his throat and sounded some better. "I'm actually recovering. They tell me pneumonia, when it kills, usually does so within seven days. If they'd stop drugging me, I'd be up. I don't need their drugs; this boiled wine is quite sufficient." He took another long sip, then set the cup back on the table. "But I'm glad you're here." He pulled his signet ring from his thumb and held it out to his son. "You'd better take this for a while."

"Sire!" Kadurri protested.

"Take it. There are several tablets containing public issues that need signing. The ring will make your thumbnail print my official representative."

"But…"

"Mesharu said they can't wait. Just… take care of it."

Kadurri swallowed hard, then took the ring and slipped it on. It fit. "Now, report!"

"Lord!" Kadurri snapped to attention and transformed into the rab mag. "My lord knows that the Egyptians hold all of Syria and that we are, so far, at a loss as to how to dislodge them," he paused, allowing for his father's comments. There were none.

Kadurri launched into a recitation of the events of the year's campaigns, recalling for his father the troop movements and strengths, he detailed topography and battlefields. He projected expected provisions and enemy forces in the year to come.

All the while, he became increasingly aware that his father only half-heard him and offered no thoughts or suggestions. He only coughed and choked, occasionally turning his eyes on the rab mag's face as he struggled to listen. Kadurri's stomach tied itself into a knot that was threatening to make him sick. He loved his father, he had admired him above the gods themselves his entire life long. It had never occurred to him that he would find him so helpless. It frightened him more than anything he could ever remember. It was a gnawing fear, growing inside.

The prince showed no sign of his feelings to his father, however. He was Rab Mag, First General of all Babylonia. Nebuchadnezzar faced his fear, his feelings, and understood himself. He did feel like a small boy afraid of losing his father, yes of course, he did; but that wasn't it. His father was not just any man. If he were to lose his father, the nation would lose its sire. And he, Nebuchadnezzar, would no longer be rab mag, he would be king, ultimately responsible for… everything. Kadurri knew he was not ready for that!

The general continued to outline strategies to the man who had now lain back on his bed and closed his eyes, oblivious to his son's voice. Nabo began to snore. Kadurri paused and drew a deep breath. He had better *get* ready. He twisted the ring, then settled it back in place. It seemed the responsibility was already his by default. "Suiki," he whispered, "may your wisdom become my light. I will seek my guidance from the records of the ages; there is no guidance for me here any longer."

Quietly the prince backed from the royal bedchamber. Nebuzaradan, standing just outside in the hall, closed the massive carved wood doors behind the prince and fell into step behind him.

Nebuchadnezzar, accompanied by his guard, escaped the palace and went straight through the southern gate to Ekua, Marduk's temple. There, at the prince's bidding, High Chanter Amelanu offered a bull and sang a petition for the health of the king. The offering and ceremony took the rest of the day. Kadurri, now acting as crown prince, spent that evening and the next day with Prime Minister Mesharumishamash, going over affairs of the state that the rab sharish was running in the absence of the king and queen. The prince found no fault with any of his decisions and, using the signet ring with his own thumbnail print, ratified them all in the name of his father. They were his first official documents. Kadurri knew it was good that he had someone he could trust who could run the empire's civil affairs.

CHAPTER 38

The Procession Bark of Bel

Babylon, Babylonia

Two days had passed since Nebuchadnezzar's return to Babylon. The congestion of traffic leading to the docks was worse than usual. Angry merchants shouted to be heard over one another as they raised their hands to attempt to gain the attention of the dock officials. The milling crowd of businessmen couldn't get to their boats and barges. Most of those same boats and barges dropped anchor in the middle of the river, the docks were already full. The vessels which had successfully moored there waited in vain to be unloaded. Their crews added loud and colorful opinions of the situation to the cacophony, and the dock officials threw up their hands in exasperation.

Princess Nitocris sat on the massive concrete docks outside the market area and dangled her feet in the water. The Euphrates was not the Nile, but it was the best she could do. The princess' lady, Marrat, stood behind. The nearby daggermen held open a circular area around the princess and her lady.

"The boatmen and customs officers are displeased," Marrat spoke quietly in Demotic. "We should be going soon."[1]

"It's hot, and the water cools my feet," Nitocris answered in the same language, irritated. "The boatmen and customs officers are peasants and should have more respect." The milling crowd, though not allowed close, was still loud enough that her head buzzed with their dissidence. "In Egypt, I had my own bathing area by the river where no one but my ladies and the eunuchs could come. I could swim there all day if I wished."

"My Lady, you know you cannot swim here. The river is too deep, and with all the boats, it's too dangerous. Also, your robes would weigh you down."

Nitocris laughed, suddenly mischievous. "I don't wear robes when I swim."

Marrat didn't think that was funny. "This is not Egypt! And it is not private! The daggermen are not eunuchs, lady. Neither are the dockworkers."

"And they would think me a harlot," she sniffed. "I know, the Babylonians are embarrassed by the natural beauty of their own bodies. And they *should* be! They smell! I smell too because all the water I get for bathing comes from the bucket you pour over my head. It's been four years, Marrat! I want to swim!" She stood up and began to undo the ribbons which served as ties on her outer robes.

"Princess!" Marrat hissed at her.

The daggermen came suddenly to attention.

Princess Nitocris dropped the ribbon and looked over Marrat's shoulder to see what was had caused this to happen. She saw her husband and his brother striding towards her. A contingent of daggermen, commanded by Nebuzaradan, walked before, beside and behind. Nitocris curtsied low, her arms stretched out before her lowered face as she snapped her fingers. The Babylonian gesture came naturally to her now.

"Princess," Nebuchadnezzar stopped in front of her, took one of her hands, and raised her upright.

"Husband," Nitocris responded. "I heard you had returned to us."

Kadurri opened his mouth and shut it again, momentarily unsure of himself. He had returned two days before and was only now coming to find her, so he definitely deserved that. "My brother informed me you were here. He says that you often come here."

"My lord is kind to inquire as to my whereabouts," she piled on more guilt.

He winced. "Your lord is negligent not to have taken the time to notice that you have a need." Kadurri cocked his head and looked at her quizzically. "Your vocabulary and accent have improved a lot."

She smiled and looked down at her feet, suddenly shy and absurdly please at the compliment. "I have worked hard while you were away."

"You have. Princess, I apologize for not coming to see you sooner. I'd like to make it up to you. Would you take a ride with me?"

"Lord?"

"In the bark," he nodded at the royal vessel moored nearby.

"The Procession Bark of Bel?" Nitocris was astounded. "It belongs to Marduk! Are we allowed?"

Kadurri laughed. "It is the royal bark. Marduk has lent it to my father. The god only uses it once a year. Otherwise, it's at my family's disposal." He took her hand and led her down the quay towards the waiting vessel.

Marduk's bark was not one of the round, skin-covered boats that were so favored by the Babylonians. Constructed of wood planks and beams, it was firmer and larger even than the *Star of Two Lands,* the royal barge she knew on the Nile. It had to be, it was designed to carry the massive Babylonian god without sinking.

At home in its slip, *The Procession* was a familiar sight on the quay, and the princess had become so accustomed to seeing the *Star's* Babylonian counterpart that Nitocris had grown to ignore its presence. The brightly painted bark bobbed as its gold trim sparkled in the sunlight and reflected off the waves which lapped gently at its flower-bedecked stern. Four men in red, royal livery emerged from the cabin and bowed low before their prince. The crew's only duty was to be available should they be called upon. Kadurri tried to escort Nitocris aboard, but she hesitated; this was the vessel of the King of Babylon's god. To use it this way, was it sacrilege?

Was her husband teasing her?

The prince grinned at her and tugged on her hand again. "We could get out of the way of the customs officials and go enjoy the gardens at Bit Akitu. In the process, we could lose most of this escort of ours as well."

He was serious! So, using the bark for recreation must be allowed… Nitocris' face lit up. Boating was another pass-time she dearly missed. She hopped lightly aboard. There were a few cheers from some of the dockworkers that were quickly stifled as Lieutenant Nebuzaradan glared their way.

Kadurri stepped up onto the deck, followed immediately by Nebuzaradan. "Seri," the prince addressed his friend and bodyguard, "tell the crew to standby. Shum…"

The younger prince still stood on the great quay. He grinned slyly back at his brother. At thirteen years old, he was starting to take an interest in girls, himself. "I'll take the rest of the daggermen back to the palace," he volunteered. "I'm not really interested in flowers." He rounded up all but four of the bodyguard and bowing to his brother, he ushered them back to shore with him.

Kadurri looked expectantly at Marrat, now standing by herself on the dock. Nitocris saw that her lady was displeased. Marrat knew a dismissal when she saw one, and she could hardly slip uninvited onto the royal ship. She curtsied low to the couple as she snapped her fingers then she turned and headed back to the palace. Kadurri leaned against Nitocris and spoke low in her ear, "Princess, I know you are fond of that one, but…"

Nitocris stared uncomfortably at her sandals on the gently moving deck. "Lord, she is like the mothers I have left behind."

"Mothers?" It was Kadurri's turn to be astounded. "You have more than one?"

"I have two: The Great Royal Wife, my birth mother; and The Queen of Thebes, my adoptive mother."

"Oh." He frowned. "Princess, I do not see that these great ladies are honored by comparing a serving woman to them."

The remaining the daggermen mounted the boat. The royal crew pushed off as the dock men and customs officials finally resumed their work on the quays. Unfurled sails filled with the breeze as the bark tacked effortlessly upstream to the island of the Bit Akitu.

"Nitocris," the prince studied her face and paused, he seemed to be searching for the right words. "Your lady, she's not exactly the kind of person we'd usually choose as a companion for someone of your station. She's a cleaning woman."

"No, she *was* a cleaning woman, now she's my lady. Husband," she said added gravely, "whom would you choose? With Marrat, I may speak in my own tongue. It gives my head a rest. And she accepts me as I am."

"Meaning?"

She didn't answer but reached down and plucked a flower from the multitudes of blooms hung in the netting strung across the boat's sides. She dropped it in the water and watched it bob away in the bark's wake.

"So. There is something else of which I have been ignorant. The women of the Bar Manuti mistreat you because you are Egyptian?"

It was a delicate subject, and she answered carefully. It was easier now that her Aramaic had improved so much. "Not directly, Lord. I am your wife. They would not dare. But neither does anyone…" She trailed off.

"You're lonely."

For an instant, Nitocris thought she might cry. It had been so long since anyone but Marrat had given her a sympathetic ear. She blinked the tears away angrily. "Not even the Rab Mag of Babylon can command the hearts of the women of the court."

At a loss, Kadurri watched her. "I'm sorry, princess," he murmured.

"That's twice you've apologized now." It pleased Nitocris that she could make the Crown Prince of Babylon grovel, and she smiled at him; her small, perfect teeth strikingly white compared to her dark skin. "Anyone would think you considered yourself guilty of causing all the wrongs of the world." She tossed her head to clear a braid from her face. Where Babylonian ladies wore their hair long and curled, Nitocris' hair was coarser and not suited to such a style. So, even though she had adopted Babylonian dress and no longer wore Egyptian style face paint, she still shaved her head and wore an Egyptian style wig. This one hung to her shoulders in a thousand tiny braids. Her deliberate movement caused the myriad golden beads caught in her tresses to chime like bells heard from far off. She knew she had the prince mesmerized both by her beauty and by her plight. He was completely at her mercy, and this new-found power delighted her. She sat down on the observation bench and patted the seat next to her.

Kadurri sat. "Well, I suppose I am guilty of most of them where you're concerned anyway," he confessed with remorse. Do you know how beautiful you are?"

Of course, she did, but she answered demurely, "It is the river." One dark, delicate hand motioned over the water, mimicking its movement and gentle waves. "The Euphrates is the sister of the Nile. I am her niece. Though she runs backward, she is still beautiful and she, at least, is kind enough to lend me some of her beauty." She only told the truth. At sixteen, she was slender and graceful, petite like a water sprite summoned from the depths to grant him the honor of sitting by his side. "Besides, I do not think you are guilty, My Lord," she added, relenting just a bit. "It was not you who brought me here."

That was a mistake. Nabopolassar was a sensitive subject. There was a spark of anger, quickly suppressed, behind Nebuchadnezzar's intelligent eyes as he said, "No, that was my father, and he is still king, besides being ill. You should watch how you speak of him."

"I meant no disrespect, Lord," she soothed him and gently caressed his hand. "It's only that I never think of you as my captor. But I do try not to think of him that way either."

"Thank you," Kadurri was mollified. "I don't want to talk about the king right now. I've spent the last two days worrying about him. That's why I was late in coming to you. But this is *your* time, Princess. Being here with you, it makes me feel like everything's going to be all right.

"And I may not be able to solve the world's problems, but at least, I can handle yours." He leaned forward to kiss her gently, and his soft, warm lips sent a thrill through her that she had never felt before. "You are far more beautiful than the river, Nitocris; and you are mine. You should always come to me with your concerns. You are right, I cannot change the hearts of the women, but maybe I can do something to make things easier for you." They arrived at the island, and the crew pulled the bark to its mooring.

Kadurri stood and pulled her to her feet, too. They stood there, just a moment, facing each other, holding hands, and her heart beat like a small bird trying to escape her chest.

"Lord?" He made her feel safe and protected. Suddenly, she was not so sure that it was she who was in control, and just maybe she really didn't want to be. "I don't understand."

"Just wait a little." Nebuchadnezzar hopped down on the dock and caught her around the waist, setting her on her feet next to him. Then he took her hand and led her off down a path surrounded by masses of flowers that bloomed in a spectacular array of colors despite the lateness of the year.

The priests arrived. After they accepted a token gift, a small gold weight, from the prince, they discretely disappeared again. That left the princess and the prince alone, save for the ever-present Nebuzaradan.

Kadurri picked a delicate purple lily and held it for her to smell its spicy sweetness. She looked up, startled that he knew of the Egyptian custom and he smiled at her. "Bit Akitu is guarded by the river," he told her, and tossed the bloom into the water, mimicking her earlier actions. "That makes it not only one of the most beautiful spots in all of Babylon, but also one of the most private, at least at this time of the year. During and just after the New Year it's amazing any of the flowers survive the trampling." He led her down a path beneath the tall trees, which were so uncommon in the city itself.

Nitocris was almost overwhelmed by the place. In Egypt, the Nile Valley was an oasis in the desert and the people carefully cultivated plants and flowers, guarding them as rare and wonderful treasures. To her, the island of the Bit Akitu represented wealth more striking than all the gold of Esagila. "It is… beautiful. No, that's not right, but I don't know the right word. Do you know, in all the time I've been here, this is the first time I have visited the island?"

He still held her hand as they walked. "I suppose I knew it, I just didn't think about it. I should have brought you before. And that's my fault too!" He was teasing her now, and she grinned at him. He picked another flower, a huge white rose. He dethorned it and slid it behind her ear, where the contrast with her black hair was stunning.

This too was an Egyptian custom, and she laughed. "I think that you know very much more than one would guess. Very well. You're guilty as charged. What shall your sentence be?"

"What if I were to make sure that you could come every day if you wanted?"

"I should become a pest to the crew of the bark," she tossed her head.

"I suppose. But I was thinking of the canal that passes by your quarters. I could give you a private garden there with a pool all your own. We could even put in a small boat and build a little island with its own garden. No one will bother you there, and you can go all by yourself for the entire day if you would like."

She stared at him. Then she let out a squeal and kissed him with a passion that was entirely unsuited to their pre-nuptial status.

CHAPTER 39

The Tablet House

Babylon, Babylonia

Prince Nebushumlishtar took his daggerman and returned to the religious complex of Esagila. He walked down the temple-lined lane, through the huge marketplace and back to the corner of the scholars, to Bit Mummi the House of Knowledge. There, right in the center was a massive, multistoried building, the library. The double hung doors were swung wide, and the prince mounted the steps and entered the vast front room. The click-click-click of his sandals echoed as he crossed the expanse towards one of the hundreds of large, thick shelves. The wisdom of millennia of civilization was archived here, and though there were scores of scholars present, their voices were hushed with reverence and they did not disturb the peace of history laid to rest.

The Chaldeans were hard at work, just as Shum's brother had ordered. Find a way to save Harran. Find a way to retake Carchemish. The prince looked around him and sighed. There were hundreds and thousands of clay documents stored here—pile upon pile upon pile, and they were not organized with these tasks in mind. Shum made his way to the records of the wars, found a spot where no one was reading, and pulled down the first tablet of a series.

Shum's daggerman, Marshipar, merely stood by and watched. He was on duty and would not let his attention be diverted by reading. "What do you think?" Shum asked him. Marshipar was almost twenty and had been Shum's daggerman for five years. Since Marshipar was his constant companion, the young prince often asked him for his opinion. "You always liked history. Is there anything buried here that will save Harran?"

"I'm a daggerman, not a scholar, My Prince," Marshipar answered, "but the rab mag is wise beyond his years. Trust him."

"And get to work." Shum nodded. He plopped the tablet down on a convenient lectern and began to carefully scan it. "It would help if I knew what I was looking for while the wise rab mag is preoccupied at the Isle of the New Year."

Marshipar grinned. "Finding time to spend with that one *is* wise."

Shum laughed. "If any woman could take a man's mind off his troubles, it's Princess Nitocris," he agreed, "and it's certainly better than picking through infantry enrollments and menus of… Oh look, King Ninurtaaplax requested and was served elephant at the New Year's Festival; let's see, 184 years ago. It was his last year. So, what have we learned from this? *Don't eat elephant.*

"That's not really relevant to either Harran or Carchemish. I can understand why Kadurri prefers being on the island with Nitocris, but they should just let him marry her. Then he could get his mind back on business."

Marshipar shrugged. "Princess Amyhia comes first, everyone knows this. But matters of state are beyond a simple daggerman, My Prince."

Shum punched him in the arm. "Do you know something, Marshipar? I'm very glad I'm me and not my brother."

"Great Prince?"

"If Harran falls, I won't have to feel personally responsible. When the army suffers a defeat, it's not my strategy that's to blame. If the king… He could die, Marshipar."

The daggerman knew better than to acknowledge any such thing. He said nothing but waited on the prince.

"If he does, I won't be the one who has to take Marduk's hand. And Marduk asks a lot."

"Marduk is the hero of the gods, Highness. Much is expected of him. Is it wrong that he expects much of his servant in return?"

"But Kadurri is not yet his servant, and he still expects it! Isn't it wrong for Kadurri to be required to leave the princess sitting all alone in the harem just because there's some other girl, he barely knows, in Media, who has a treaty that says she takes precedence? It doesn't seem fair."

"Ah, it's thoughts of romance that have brought this on." The daggerman grinned. "The Egyptian girl *is* pretty, and you're thirteen. I suppose it's normal for you to have noticed."

The prince was shocked. "She belongs to Nebuchadnezzar!" Then he saw the grin. "There, you see? If I were my brother, you wouldn't even think of teasing me. But I'll tell you one thing: when I find a girl I want to marry I'm just going to go ahead and do it without having to worry about the international political implications!"

"Yes, My Prince," Marshipar smiled to himself.

Then he returned the tablet to the shelf. He pulled down the next tablet. A quick scan showed it to contain records of the same war, against a long-vanished tribe of the Qedar and their Assyrian overlords. "'And Mardukbelzer succeeded him.' So, let's see, similarities between a bunch of traveling skirmishes against a tiny nomadic tribe to a siege of an impregnable fortress on a high cliff or an Egyptian siege of Harran? None. *All* these tablets are useless. Let's go around the corner."

They did, and Shum stopped dead. There, before the shelf he had targeted, were six familiar, but very strange, students. The six were all around twenty years old and covered in colorful tattoos. They wore their bright gold, red and brown hair in long braids. These were Scythians. They had been in Bit Mummi a long time now, though—five or maybe six years? They were now elder brothers and well on their way to becoming instructors in their own right. Shum had never gotten used to their presence.

Marshipar pulled his dagger and began to nonchalantly twirl it around, the tip balanced in his palm.

"I've told you, they're not a threat," Shum hissed at him.

"And I've told you, that you can't possibly know that," Marshipar nodded agreeably. "They may convince themselves that they've become Chaldeans, but we know they're really barbarians whose allegiance is to a barbarian king. Choose another shelf, Lord Prince."

Too late. Their leader, Prince Anacharsis, had already seen him. "Prince Nebushumlishtar," he grinned, "thinking of avoiding us?"

Since that was exactly what his daggerman had been thinking, Shum flushed slightly. Anacharsis was simply too perceptive to be a Scythian. "Uh, I was just wondering where I could be of most use," he said lamely.

Anacharsis cocked his dark head—of the six foreigners, he was the only one with brown hair. "Check with Melzar, he's keeping track." The Scyth's Aramaic was immaculate, as were his Greek and Mede. His teachers said he was an excellent student, far better than Shum, the young prince knew that.

But it only made sense. These six were the pick of the entire Scythian nation and who knew what their people would do to them if they did not succeed in their studies and so embarrassed their king.

"Thanks," Shum said awkwardly. "I'll do that." He turned away to search for the eunuch, Melzar.

Three aisles away, a familiar voice said, "Good day, Your Highness."

Shum spun around to find Melzar waving him over as he searched some shelves over to the right. Dwarfed by his surroundings, the prince had, at first, not even seen the chubby Chaldean, though he was looking for him.

"Good day, Teacher Melzar," Shum answered politely as he walked over to him. "It's good to see you. Prince Anacharsis said you could tell me where to start?"

"Have you come to help too, My Prince?" He seemed delighted at the possibility.

"The rab mag is elsewhere and does not require me, so I might as well."

"The more, the better." The Chaldean waved to the countless stacks of clay tablets piled high on the hundreds of massive shelves. They were surrounded and hemmed in like colossal cliffs around a narrow chasm. "Here, Highness." The eunuch showed him a shelf. "These tablets contain the military records of various conflicts during the last Assyrian occupation. We have gotten this far."

The prince pulled off the first tablet of the next series from a shelf and laid it on a lectern.

"The rab mag is well, I hope?" The Chaldean enquired.

"He's well. Just…" the prince stopped. It was not proper to discuss his concerns with a servant. But the old eunuch was a friend as well. He had been one of Shum's teachers and ofttimes confidant. "He went to Bit Akitu today with Princess Nitocris."

Melzar blinked. "If the queen hears…" He stopped midsentence. "Forgive me; it's not my place, Great Prince."

"She *is* his wife," Shum said defensively.

"Yes, Great Prince. Please excuse me; I was going to check over on the west wall next." The scholar hurried away, and Marshipar laughed silently.

Shum punched the daggerman in the arm again. Turning his attention to the tablet, the prince found that his record held nothing at all of interest, only some lists of rations distributed to the forces during King Esarhaddon's occupation. He returned the document to its place and pulled another.

CHAPTER 40

Growing Up

Ecbatana, Media

"A messenger brought this up at midnight for your birthday," Shadushushan announced as Princess Amyhia poked her head out of her bedchamber. The lady held out an intricately carved box of shining wood. *"From Babylon."*[1]

Amyhia squealed with delight and bounced into the sitting room of her suite. "From Kadurri? He remembered!" She grabbed the box and greedily pried off the lid. "Oh," she breathed, "Oh Shadu, look!" She plucked a polished silver mirror, set in red-gold and studded with amethysts from the box. Then she held out a matching comb and brush set. "He remembered my birthday!"

Shadu smiled demurely at the young princess who stood there in her white linen shift. It was far more likely that he had, years ago, sent a number of presents with instructions on when they were to be delivered. "He has remembered every birthday, Princess."

"No one else has." There was a brief pout on Amy's flawless features. "Today, I'm thirteen. I'm all grown up. Old enough to marry." She laid the box and the mirror set on a tall side table. Then she plopped down on her soft cushioned bench by the window. "There was no message?"

"Happy birthday, Princess of Media, Treasure of Babylon and my heart. May you have 1,000 years and may each year have 5,000 days. But I will pray those days to be shortened until I see you again," Shadu recited.

The princess absorbed that and sighed. "But he must know that I am thirteen. *Somebody* must know that I'm thirteen! I'm no longer a child!"

"*I* know, princess."

The girl jumped up and ran the brush through her long, red-gold hair. "You do, but no one else. I could probably stay up here for days, and no one would ask about me."

"You've only just gotten up and the day is brand new. Give them a chance." Shadu held out a gown for her. "This should make them notice! And it arrived at midnight, too."

"Oh! It's beautiful!" Amy held up the bright green fabric against herself and studied her image in the new mirror.

"It's from your father and mother. You see? You are not forgotten. It's lovely, Amy."

"It is, but does it matter what I wear?" She dropped it to the rich blue carpet and stalked, barefooted, to her window and threw the shutters open wide. The view displayed the garden below where she had once walked with the prince. From the height of her window, the seven concentric walls of the city were clearly visible. Behind them, the peaks of the mountains were capped with white. The cool, wintery breeze tickled Amy's bare skin, and she shivered.

Shadu retrieved the dress and frowned. Amyhia was not typically given to moodiness. "What's the matter, My Princess?"

"What isn't? You say the dress is lovely. Well, it is. So, now I'm to put it on, and you'll set my hair up, and here I am, all dressed up for another day of embroidering. I really don't think the needles and yarn care how I look, and I don't feel like spending my birthday that way anyway!"

The lady walked over to her charge and laid her hand on the girl's creamy white shoulder. Amyhia was almost as tall as she was now. She was going to be a good deal taller. "You shouldn't be standing at your window dressed only in your shift, Highness."

"Why not?" She tossed her head defiantly, and her shining red-gold tresses fell over her face. Impatiently, she brushed them away. "Who cares? There's no one out there. And even if there were, they couldn't see me anyway. And even if they could, they all think I'm still a little girl!" She stamped her perfectly pedicured foot, very much like a little girl throwing a temper tantrum.

"Maybe if I were to walk around the palace dressed like this they'd get a good look at me and realize that I've grown up!"

Shadu giggled. "Your mother would have an attack."

"It would do her good. Shadu, you and Ashpenaz have spent a lot of time making sure that I can do all sorts of things. Now Ashpenaz wishes to return to Babylon. He says that I have learned all he has to teach me!"

"Yes, and you did it in less than the three required years too. You are to be commended, Princess. And I will dismiss Ashpenaz when the opportunity arises for him to travel back safely. Meanwhile, I still need practice with my Mede, even if you are fluent in Aramaic."

"You are changing the subject, Shadu, but dismiss the eunuch if you wish. I no longer need him. I am 'educated.'" She spoke the word with distaste. "Due to my position, I have the standard harem education and all the pampering that goes with it. I know how to take care of my hair and skin and all about how to treat a man, but thanks to you two, I suspect I know more about politics than most of my father's advisors! I am schooled in court protocol for both Media and Babylonia. If asked, I could name all the lords and ladies of the high court at Babylon along with their pedigrees and political affiliations. I can speak, read, and write three languages and I can add, subtract, multiply and divide as well as any bookkeeper. I know the positions of the stars in the sky and can construct a clay map of the entire world, marking all the capital cities. These are things that probably no other woman in all my father's empire can do. Only I can't do them either because no one will let me! I have finished my education, but it seems I am still just a little girl. So, what am I to do now?"

Shadu pulled her back into the room and slipped the gown over her head. "It is not your education or your age, Your Highness. Even though you are grown up, most people will not consider you an adult until you are actually married, because you are a woman."

"And when you are married you are *still* not a real person, just your husband's wife!" Amy knew that her attitude was considered shameful in Media, but today she was an adult and legally, she was a princess of Babylonia, not Media!

"Many women would love to be nothing else in the world than to be considered your husband's wife, My Princess. But you will be more than that. One day Nebuchadnezzar will be king in Babylon, and you will be queen. That is what we have trained you for."

"But *when?* Nebuchadnezzar sends presents, but he doesn't send for me! I am old enough, and he's seventeen! But he 'counts the days!'" She mocked the message he had sent with the mirror and brush set.

"The rab mag is very pressed right now Amy, you know that. He is trying to run the empire and salvage the war at the same time. Seventeen may sound old to you, but it is still very young for so much responsibility. If he were to send for you, he would have to take a year out to properly honor your marriage. A year ignoring the Egyptians? What would happen to Harran?

"You say you understand politics, then think like the queen you will be. What would become of the empire you will inherit? It would be overrun, and Princess Nitocris would likely become its queen in your stead." The lady pushed her charge down on the window bench and began to plait the girl's silky hair.

Amy sighed. "But Shadu, the war has already gone on forever. People do get married in spite of it. Life goes on. Nebuchadnezzar is not king, he is only rab mag. He could find someone else to take responsibility for a while or, if he is not willing to do that, he could shorten the time that he takes off. If he had sent for me instead of just sending presents, we would still have had four moons after I arrived before the New Year and before he had to march back out of Babylon again. It wouldn't be exactly proper, but I would not yet be queen so it wouldn't be so bad and I wouldn't care. After all, there *is* a war on."

"Princess," Shadu said gently, "Nebuchadnezzar is king in all but name. Ashpenaz and I keep close contact with the Babylonian court. Prince Nebushumlishtar tells us that his father has not been competent for some time. We have talked about this…"

"Yes, but…"

"But," the lady said firmly. "Amy, you are a princess. You can't just think of yourself. Perhaps if you were fifteen or sixteen, you would have a legitimate complaint, but you are barely thirteen." She piled the braids high on the girl's head, adult style, and fixed them there with pearl combs and a silver tiara. "I waited for Belnasir from the time I was thirteen until I was sixteen and I did not complain."

"The rab shaq hadn't spoken for you, though. You didn't have anything to complain about."

"I waited just the same, and it was hard. He sent me to Bit Mummi. That is where I learned what I've passed on to you. He paid for it. No, he had not spoken for me, but what was I to think? I loved him, Amy. You barely know the rab mag. Your complaint is not being separated from him; it is being cooped up here and treated like a little girl. That is hardly a reason for rushing into marriage."

Amy blinked. Shadushushan was never harsh with her, not even when she sloughed off her lessons. "I'm sorry Shadu," she said. "I know you loved Belnasir. I didn't mean to make it sound like that," she trailed off lamely.

"No, I know. But if you are going to act like a little girl, you shouldn't be angry when you are treated like one. Think, Your Highness. When Nebuchadnezzar does call for you, you will have to leave here. You may never see Ecbatana or your mother again. Do you really want to rush that?"

"I will visit."

Shadu's light laughter flitted by like a bird. "Maybe. Do you know how far it is from Babylon to Ecbatana? I do. I've traveled far more than most women ever have and I will be very grateful to settle down and not be obliged to move anymore. If you plan to watch your husband march off to war every summer than run back up here to enjoy the mountain breezes, you can count on traveling without me!

"Amy, you should be happy for the time you have left here. You are grown and a daughter of the king. No one can tell you what to do anymore, and you still have no real responsibilities. That won't be true in Babylon. You may find that you wish you were back here again where people would leave you alone and you have no decisions to make."

The princess, grown-up and regal in her gown and tiara, held up the mirror and looked at herself again, considering. Finally, she nodded. "All right Shadu, you win. I'll start acting my age… tomorrow." She pulled off the tiara and shook down her hair. She grinned. "I think I'll wear my blue smock instead. I've decided to take a picnic up in the meadow, and this is a little overdressed."

Shadu opened her mouth to object. Then she laughed. "It's your birthday, Highness."

CHAPTER 41

The Tumilat Canal

Gesem, Egypt

Pharaoh Necho sat on his stool on the deck of the *Star of Two Lands* and gazed about him with satisfaction, as his brother, Prince Horiraa, stood by and fanned him. He was actually here, Gesem, the land that slaves had once named Goshen. He had *sailed* all the way here! *The Star* had launched from Sais on the Canonic branch, traveled south, up the Nile, to the first branching, then turned north again to the Tanic branch and from there across the new canal to the Bitter Lakes. The Tumilat Canal was open all this way as it had not been for over six hundred years, not since the days of Rameses the Great. But for the moment, they could go no further. Though the day was still young, the last lake was still not connected all the way through to the Red Sea.

"Is that it?" he inquired, pointing to a distant patch of blue. "That's not a mirage, is it?"

"That is it," Prince Horiraa confirmed, gently moving his giant ostrich fan over the king. "That is the Red Sea. The Good God has the sharp eyes of Horus the Hawk… and an even sharper sense of economics," the Fan-Bearer to the Right added shrewdly.

"It won't be long now, will it Brother? They are making good progress?"

"The engineers say it is just a matter of months," Prince Horiraa assured the handsome god seated beneath the canopy.

"Then you and I will be the first since the great Ramses to sail all the way from the Great Sea to the Red Sea.[1] Perhaps we will take *The Star* and lead our armada all the way to the coasts of Persia!"

Horiraa laughed. "Cambyses would have a heart attack."

"He would, but I jest. Persia has no harbors worth the name. We could not land, and they have no navy to come out to play. No, you are right, as always, this is an economic, not a military endeavor. The merchants of the world will come crawling to us. None will dare displease us and so lose their shipping rights."

"Dangling this treat before them has made Lydia, Tyre and all of Greece as eager as dogs at a kill," the fan-bearer acknowledged.[2]

"They understand the tariffs, brother? You have made certain?"

"Pharaoh's prices are steep, but using the canal will move freight much faster, and it is still considerably cheaper than overland freight and the tariffs Judah charges. They understand. What they don't understand is that pharaoh is also correct. Our economic partners are unwittingly instrumental in helping to make the Two Lands into a naval power such as the world has never seen. The good god will lead an armada greater even than Tyre's! One that will command both the Great Sea and the Gulf of Persia."

"Well, brother, politics and economics are often one and the same, but what I really want is the capitulation of the rest of the world."

"You mean Babylonia and Media."

"Yes, and the lands still beyond our knowledge."

He gazed across the expanse of land yet to be excavated to the waters of the Red Sea. By the Tumilat Canal, Pharaoh Necho would control the east/west commerce of the world. But was there another way? Rumor had it that if you went far enough south along the coast, you would eventually come around and head back north again. Once the last strip of land was removed, the ten expeditionary ships would sail. Eventually, the explorers would confirm or deny the rumor. If successful, the mariners would discover if sailing around the Land of Punt was profitable. Of course, if it were not successful, Egypt would never see them again. They could only return through the Pillars of Hercules and the Great Sea. The crew would almost certainly be Greeks and Lydians, but they would not disobey the orders of a god. They would succeed or never return. Either way, pharaoh would be buying no more expeditionary ships. War and cargo, those were the only types of vessels he would purchase from now on.

"My Brother?"

"Great Pharaoh?"

"The ships of the expedition are finished and at harbor in Sais. When we return with the army from this march on Harran, I want you to oversee the final recruiting of their officers and crews. Stock those ships. The canal should be finished by then."

"How much in supplies?"

"A year, and seed so that if necessary, they can farm and restock."

Horiraa looked surprised. "More than a year?"

Necho shrugged. "If it were less, someone would have done it by now."[3] He nodded to himself and rose, going back to his cabin.

The workers on the shore, prostrate in the presence of the pharaoh, got up and went back to work.

CHAPTER 42

The Wisdom of the Ages

Babylon, Babylonia

t had been a full moon since the Chaldeans had taken up their search of the archives. A full moon! Kadurri stepped through the door of the Tablet House and sourly eyed the activity within. For the past quarter-moon, the rab mag had taken to passing by the house every evening to personally assess the progress.

The eunuch, Melzar, nervously noted the newcomer's presence and hurried to greet him, bowing low and snapping his fingers before his prince. "Welcome, Great One! Welcome!"

"Any progress?"

The eunuch cautiously stood up straight. "We have finished three more sections, Rab Mag…"

"Melzar, you know that I am not interested in the number of records you've dusted off today. I want to know their content! Anything that will help with the dislodging of the Egyptians from Carchemish. Anything that will defend Harran! Anything," he finished bleakly. He was running out of time. One more moon and he would be forced to ready his troops to march again. How could he march out without offering a feasible plan to his father that had some chance of succeeding? How could he save Harran's governor and his family? How could he save the empire?

"Great One," Melzar admitted sadly, "we came across only one mention of Carchemish today and none at all of Harran or the Egyptians."

Kadurri sighed. "All right, what was it, a list of provisions? A description of the statues there?"

"No, General," Melzar replied. "It concerned a battle, but it was with the Hittites. King Sharuken found that he could not dislodge them from Carchemish either, so the tablets are of little help in the task you have set for us."

Kadurri nodded, resigned. "The answer is here somewhere, though. It has to be." He started to turn away, and then he stopped. "Wait. King Sharuken could not breach Carchemish? Then these tablets show that the *Hittites* won? But, didn't Sharuken defeat the Hittites?"

"Oh, most assuredly, Rab Mag. Surely the Hittites fell, but it was not by the taking of Carchemish."

Nebuchadnezzar stared at him. "What do you mean?"

"The Hittites were not behind their walls when King Sharuken took them, Great One. The king lured them out and defeated them."

"He… He lured them…? What?" Kadurri was shaken. "What would make the Hittites so foolish as to abandon the impregnable safety of Carchemish?!? Show me those tablets. NOW!!!"

The five tablets containing the records of King Sharuken and his conquest of the Hittites were brought and laid before the prince. With Melzar standing by nervously, he deciphered them himself. And as he did, a growing sense of excitement filled him.

He had been going at it backward.

But this was a plan he could bring to his father. He could prove his father's faith in him was not misplaced. Bel Pihati Nabubalatsuikibi was right. History held the answer. Nebuchadnezzar had a plan, and it would succeed.

PART 6: 605 BC

Nebuchadnezzar Comes

And some of your descendants,
Your own flesh and blood who will be born to you,
Will be taken away,
And they will become eunuchs in the palace of the
King of Babylon."
—II Kings 20:18 c.702 BC

CHAPTER 43

Seventy Years and the Cup of the Nations

Jerusalem, Judah

The reconstructed Wood House, the infamous shrine of the world's idols, faced the West Gate of the Temple Court. The entrance was grand with pillars, porticos, and steps gilded in gold, all paid for by King Jehoiakim's tax levies. Many of the priests, colorful as butterflies in their "sacred" robes, stood on the porch, competing with each other for the attentions of the crowds.

It would soon be Passover, and the Wood House priests were doing a booming business. The majority of the pilgrims entered the Temple Court from the West Gate and so came first of all to the house of idolatry. When they finished there, the people moved on to skirt the massive stone structure that came next, finally arriving directly in front of it, Solomon's Temple, the House of God Almighty. Levite singers lifted their voices from the shelter of the Temple portico. Levite workers moved in and out of the crowd, selling lambs and doves, incense and blessings. The sons of Aaron, who had reached the requisite age of thirty, conducted sacrifices. Here, if not for the reminder of the two pagan pillars, the people could almost ignore the sacrilege throughout the rest of the Temple grounds.

Daniel led Miriam up the steep road through the New City to the Temple Mount, to the West Gate. Though they were technically still members of their fathers' houses and would celebrate the Passover with their respective families, Daniel wanted to buy a dove. He and Miriam had determined that they would paint the threshold of the foundations of their new house with its blood and each of the households would serve half the dove with their lamb at the paschal supper to proclaim their families' unity.

The crowd ground to a confused halt and moved restlessly around.

Blocking their way into the gate was a tall, gaunt figure in a roughspun tunic and a speckled brown cow-hair coat.

"Jeremiah," Daniel breathed in Miriam's ear. "It's the prophet." Miriam had never seen him, but she was short. At Daniel's announcement, she jumped up and down, trying to see over the heads of those surrounding them.

It was the prophet. For two years, Jeremiah had been banned from the Temple grounds, banned from the Passover, banned from the Day of Atonement. None of that had stopped him from preaching outside the Temple walls, just as he was doing now.

The citizens of Jerusalem backed away from Judah's most infamous celebrity. Finally, he stood alone in a cleared area in front of a house with a scribe's insignia carved on the door, just outside the West Gate.

In the ominous silence, the clear, penetrating voice of the prophet suddenly rang out, and Daniel jumped. Miriam pushed up against him for reassurance. Her dark brown eyes were filled with the apprehension Daniel also felt.

"I have spoken to you over and over again for twenty-three years," Jeremiah called to them. "From King Josiah ben Amon's thirteenth year until today I have spoken, and you haven't listened. Nor was it just me. Before I came, the Lord sent you other prophets over and over again, and they also told you to repent of your wickedness and not to worship other gods. They said that if you complied, the Lord would let you stay in your land forever. But you didn't listen to what the Lord said through them either.

> So, now the Lord says to you:
>
> 'You did not listen to Me. You made your gods by your own hands in order to make Me angry and in so doing you have harmed yourselves.'"

The crowd in the street erupted.

"Jeremiah!" A well-dressed man, probably a wealthy merchant, shook his fist toward the prophet. "You've been banned from the Temple; do you want to be banned from Jerusalem as well?"

Involuntarily, Daniel found himself glancing through the gate at the gleaming façade of the Wood House. He saw Miriam look that way too. "But that's not fair," she objected. "We didn't put the idols there, the foreigners did. We didn't give the Egyptians the northern annex of the Temple for their gods either, the king did."

"Leave him alone," A young woman, leaning on the scribe's door, yelled at the crowd. "Let's listen to what he has to say."

Daniel shook his head. "And we didn't rebuild the shrine of the foreign gods behind the Temple? Miriam, of course, we did, the builders were Judean, overseen by foreigners, but Judean just the same and they were paid by Judean taxes." He stroked her hair then set her shawl over it. Though they were not actually married, it was a gesture of possession and protection. Single women typically did not cover their heads. "Maybe not you or I, but as a people, we're guilty. The soulless and uncircumcised crowd through the West Gate into the Temple Court, desecrating holy ground, and we do nothing. Worse, many who offer doves at the altar stop first to burn incense to the Bull of Amentet. They say Egypt is our heritage."

She tried to object, "No! They wouldn't say that."

Daniel interrupted her, "Miriam, I've heard them! Ra, Horus, Nut, and Isis, the long-forgotten gods have reappeared, and our people have welcomed them to please the king."

"Jeremiah's a heretic, denounced by the Chief Priest!" The well-dressed merchant was still on his tirade.

"No, he wasn't denounced, just banned because he caused a riot." A citizen yelled back.

"He's still causing one!" The merchant ranted.

"Because the king knows worshipping Egyptian gods is an economically shrewd move," Miriam answered Daniel. Her face was screwed up, thinking hard to make sense of politics. "And so, the people, sheep following their shepherd, have turned back to their apostasy once again."

"That's right," Daniel agreed.

"Be silent! Everybody just keep quiet!" The scribe himself appeared from out of his front door to stand next to the woman who was probably his wife. The young man closed the door behind him and waved a medium sized wineskin and a wooden cup around his head, directing the crowd's attention at him, rather than the prophet.

Daniel thought this distraction probably forestalled the people from rushing forward and attacking their prophet.

"Do you want to bring the city guard down on us all?" the scribe bellowed at them. "Everyone just hold your tongues and let the prophet speak!"

Two Temple Guards emerged from their stations in the West Gate and stood to watch, spears ready, but their authority ended at the gate, and Jeremiah was still in the city. The guards could go no further.

Jeremiah unslung his lute from his back, and his clear voice sliced through Daniel's thoughts and the crowd's turmoil, suddenly switching to an eerily beautiful melody:

"Therefore, the Lord Almighty says:
Because you won't listen to My words,
I will summon My servant,
King Nebuchadnezzar of Babylon,
And all the northern peoples,
And bring them against you here,
And against all your neighboring nations.
And you and they will be completely destroyed,
Scorned by the nations
Who will look at your land with horror
And see only a complete ruin.
There will be no more joy and laughter
ringing out from wedding celebrations,
No more will grain be harvested or ground,
And no more lamps will shine cozily
from windows at night.
This place will be deserted."

"No more weddings? Not before our wedding!" Miriam protested hotly.

Daniel held her close against his side and gave her a little shake. "No, not before our wedding. Miriam, Nebuchadnezzar is not the King of Babylon, Nabopolassar is. He's talking about the future."

"Nebuchadnezzar is no servant of the Lord Almighty, Jeremiah," a heckler from the crowd yelled out.

Jeremiah just looked at them and continued to strum his instrument.

"If you're a prophet, explain yourself! This doesn't make any sense! Are you trying to make us stone you?"

"But not long in the future," Daniel continued, looking anxiously into her beautiful eyes. "Nebuchadnezzar is alive right now. He's already rab mag, and he is Nabopolassar's heir. He holds real power. Even if he isn't yet king, he soon could be."

"Not before our wedding!" she vowed again.

Jeremiah whirled around in a circle, pointing the neck of the lute at the horizon in every direction as he continued to play and sing:

> "This entire country will become a desolate desert,
> And it and its neighbors will serve the King of Babylon
> for seventy years."

The music continued, though the crowd was shocked to sudden silence, finally obeying the woman in front of the scribe's house.

Daniel's jaw dropped. *"Seventy years?"*

"Seventy years!" Shock finally turned Miriam's attention away from thoughts of weddings. "But… But… Is he saying that we're all going into exile in Babylon and we'll die there? That can't be. He must be wrong."

"Jeremiah is never wrong," Daniel breathed. He fought down panic. "Not before our wedding, though. We'll be together. We'll be together, even in Babylon, Miriam."

> "After seventy years,"

The prophet sang as if seventy years was nothing,

"I will punish the King of Babylon
and all the Babylonians for their guilt,
And Babylon will be desolate forever.
Everything I have spoken against it I will do
And the Babylonians themselves
will become slaves of many great nations and kings.
I will revenge myself on them according to what they have done."

"The Lord will make the Babylonians slaves because they will make our children slaves?" Miriam began to cry.

Jeremiah strummed a last chord, slung the lute behind his back, and beckoned across to the scribe. The young man came to stand beside the prophet, and Jeremiah took the cup from his hand. He held it out, and the scribe filled it from the wineskin. Holding it high above his head, Jeremiah addressed the people.

"This is what the Lord, the God of Israel, said to me:

'Take from My Hand this cup filled with the wine of My wrath and make all the nations to whom I send you drink it. When they do, they will stagger and go mad because of the sword I will send among them.'

"People of Jerusalem!"

Jeremiah's words echoed down the street.

"People of the towns of Judah! King Jehoiakim! Priests and officials! This cup is cursed with horror and scorn. Drink of it!"

The people pressed backward, trying to put more distance between this madman and his words.

Daniel found himself and Miriam pushed up against the scribe's wife, at the door of his house.

She smiled sadly and laid her hand on Miriam's shoulder. "It is awful, but the Lord will bring good, even from this."

Miriam shrank away from the woman as if she were a leper.

No one came forward to take the prophet's cup.

After a moment, Jeremiah said:

> "You *will* drink it, whether you agree to it, or not. Here it is."

He poured the cup on the ground, a wet reddish stain on the pavement.

Behind the prophet, on the gilded Wood House porch, all of the pagan priests had come out from their booths to watch. Even the priests of Thebes, once pharaohs in their own right, had left the north annex and joined their fellow pagan priests to stand between the Wood House's intricately carved pillars. It looked to Daniel as if they alone here approved of the man of God. But Daniel understood them. Jeremiah was known to be a holy man. To the pagans, it was appropriate for Jeremiah to be causing a disturbance. To them, holy men were usually mad, possessed by spirits.

The prophet must have felt their eyes on his back because he turned to face them.

"What is he going to do now?" Daniel wondered aloud.

"He is sent to them," the scribe's wife answered. "Those are the representatives of the kingdoms of the world. Anything they hear is relayed back to the courts of their kings and officials. Jeremiah has a message for their masters. Israel will not listen, so the Lord speaks to foreigners. It will soon be their time."

Astonished, Daniel looked at the woman, "What? He's sent to *them?* I… You mean the pagan priests are spies? How can you know any of this?"

"Well, of course, they're spies," she said with just a hint of derision at his thickness. "And how can you *not* know? Jeremiah is the Prophet to the Nations. He is sent to them. My husband, Baruch, explains these things to me.

He knows. He is the prophet's scribe," there was a touch of pride in that last statement.

Back in front of the gate, at a nod from his master, Baruch obediently refilled the cup. Jeremiah spoke directly to the pagan priests, addressing first the great enemy of Israel's soul.

> "Egypt!"

He summoned the Priest of Osiris forward.

> "Pharaoh, King of Egypt! His attendants, officials! All his people, all the foreigners there subject to him! Drink!"

He held out the cup.

The priest, a son of the Governor of Thebes, shook his bald head and backed all the way into the Wood House's golden wall, his painted eyes looked enormous with sudden fear.

Jeremiah snorted in derision at the cowardice of Osiris' servant, and he poured the cup out, letting its contents drain slowly into the growing pool at his feet. Baruch refilled the cup.

> "All the Kings of Uz! All the Kings of the Southern Philistines, including Ashkelon, Ekron, Gaza and... what's left of Ashdod!"

Jeremiah emphasized this poetically by repeating the names of the countries immediately surrounding Judah.

> "Uz, including Edom, Moab, and Amon! The Northern Philistines, including all the Kings of Tyre and Sidon!"[1]

The priests and priestesses of Derketo/Aphrodite, Dagon, Beelzebub, Melqart, Baal, and Ashtareth, suddenly anxious for anonymity, pressed close together, their petty feuds and competitions forgotten.

Jeremiah held a fresh cup out towards them, but most were studying their feet. The prophet poured it out. Wine stains splattered the hem of his long, hairy coat.

Baruch refilled the cup.

Daniel marveled that Jeremiah was still speaking and no one had accosted him or the scribe. None of the priests, none of the Judeans, now that they had settled down, not even the Temple Guard protested. Not yet, anyway. Miriam watched, spellbound.

Jeremiah's eyes flashed with anger at the cowardice of the nations. He tried again, once more holding out the cup.

"The kings of the coastlands across the sea!"

The Priest of Zeus and the Priestess of Hera, in their flowing white linen, made no more response than their fellows and once more the wine was poured out.

> "Dedan! Tema! Buz! You Sheiks of Arabia and chieftains of the tribes of the wilderness!"

Surprisingly, yes, there were even two desert magicians present to offer potential clients protection from the desert djinn. These superstitious shamans had none of the condescension of the more organized religions. At Jeremiah's words, the Qedar fled; ducking back into the Wood House for shelter. Jeremiah did not laugh; he just poured out the cup and held it out for Baruch, who refilled it.

"All the Kings of Zimri, Elam, and Media!"

The Medes and Persians did not have temples or use idols. They were not present, but a priestess of the Elamite goddess, Manzat, was. Many of the

Elamites still held towns and fortress in the Hill Country north of Harran, and they were scattered throughout Media and Persia, noble women keeping their shrines to their rainbow goddess. This priestess, her multi-hued robes covered in brilliant sequins, was suspicious, but not afraid. She stepped forward, down onto the first step of the house.

Jeremiah held out the cup to her, but she came no closer, turning her nose up and away in disdain. Disappointed, Jeremiah poured it out.

> "All the kings of the north, near and far, one after the other—all the kingdoms on the face of the earth,"

Jeremiah summed it up. He had poured out wrath on them all, except for one. Jeremiah turned his face to the northeast, and Baruch filled the cup one last time.

> "And after all of them, the King of Sheshak will drink it too."

Of course, there were no Chaldeans present. The Egyptians would have had them arrested on the spot. But Jeremiah called out to them anyway, and then he threw the newly refilled cup through the air toward Babylon. The pagan priests ducked as it flew over their heads and splattered its contents over any of them close enough. It crashed into the Wood House wall.[2] The prophet sighed and pushed back into the crowd of Judeans outside the gate. He reached Baruch's door, gave Daniel and Miriam a lopsided smile, filled with grief, and went inside. Baruch and his wife followed.

The crowd, with access to the gate restored, dispersed and Daniel put his arm around Miriam's shoulders and guided her through the gate to the Temple grounds.

CHAPTER 44

Last Chance

Jerusalem, Judah

haraoh Necho was a guest once again in Jehoiakim's palace. The forces of Egypt were encamped once again outside Jerusalem's walls. And when pharaoh led his troops north once again, it would begin.

The narrow streets of Jerusalem's Lower City seemed claustrophobic. It had been a week since Jeremiah had condemned the nations and Ebedmelech told the Son of Ra everything he had said. Passover had come and gone, and the crowds of the Passover were thinning because the Feast of the Unleavened Bread could be concluded in their own homes. Some still lingered, though, enough that Jeremiah found their presence in the city stifling. Jeremiah had become infamous. He could no longer walk the streets openly without causing an incident simply by being there. So, now, he wore a shawl over his head and kept his face lowered, his prophet's coat he had folded and tucked under his arm. The prophet made his way down from the market. He headed south and east to the Potsherd Gate.

Baruch, ever faithful with his wax tablet in hand, followed his employer. "But you've already told them," the young scribe was confused.

"I know. I don't want to go before the people again. But it's time. Pharaoh has come, and it begins. So, the Lord is giving us one last chance. His patience is astounding."

The prophet made his way to the open courtyard just inside the Potsherd Gate. It was a beautiful day, and people were out and about their business, passing in every direction while they enjoyed the late afternoon sunshine. Prosperous looking houses lined the square. A giggling group of small children was playing with a puppy while their mothers watched indulgently nearby. A man led a loaded camel through the square and headed for the marketplace. Two members of the watch stood near the gate, observing all who came or went.

Jeremiah stopped right in the middle of the square and let the scarf slide down off his head to his shoulders. His head was once again shaved bald, and once again, his beard had been pulled out by the handfuls. Despite his appalling appearance, the people recognized who it was that stood in their midst, and they began to back away, their voices hushed to a stunned whisper. The prophet was used to this reaction. Determined, he slipped his arms into the leather cow-hair coat as he lifted his voice. "Stop right there!" he commanded, and the crowd froze.

"The Lord says:
'Pay attention! The disaster I have planned is ready.
So, repent, all of you! Think and do what is right!'"

The people recovered from their consternation and became angry. They started to heckle him. "Look, it's the madman again!"

A woman gathered up her little girl and hurried away.

"Jeremiah, *you're* the disaster!" It was one of the two city guards at the gate.

"If we promise to reform," a citizen yelled, "will you promise to go away once and for all?" The people laughed derisively.

"Close your mouths and listen!" Baruch was angry. "You are all fools. Don't you understand? This is your last chance!"

The prophet gritted his teeth, and laid his hand on the scribe's shoulder, silencing him.

"Since that is your attitude, the Lord has something else to say to you:
Go ask the foreigners,"

he pointed up the hill towards the desecrated Temple grounds. It was crowded with heathen people and their gods.

> "Have they ever heard of any among them wanting to trade their gods for new ones? Israel has done something horrible. Can't you see I haven't changed? I still maintain the snow on the peaks of Lebanon and its cool spring waters still flow. No, I haven't changed, but My people have forgotten Me and turned to useless idols to burn incense. The ancient gods lead them on the old, dark, twisting paths where they can't see, and they stumble and fall in their evil ways. They won't follow Me, to walk on My straight and even roads. So, their land will be laid waste. Forever after, those who see it will be aghast and will shake their heads scornfully. Like a sirocco wind, I will blow them away in front of their enemies. The day of their disaster is coming, and when it does, they will look for Me, and I will turn My back on them."

A man stepped forward to confront the prophet. "Jeremiah, you're crazy! The teaching of the Law by the priests and the words of the prophets cannot be lost! They have been established by the Lord, and they are everlasting! This is blasphemy! Think of what you are saying."

The crowd murmured and nodded their agreement. Since they were just a gate away from the garbage pit, various pieces of refuge that hadn't quite made it to the pit lay scattered about on the ground. Someone found a rotting piece of fruit and threw it at the prophet. It splattered across his chest to the jeers of the throng.

Something in Jeremiah broke. The supreme strain, the knowledge of the immediate looming disaster reached a plateau, and then it shattered, taking all his composure and self-control with it. Jeremiah wiped the rancid mess off with a shaking hand and held it up to heaven as he called out, "Lord, listen to me! Listen to what they are accusing me of! I am trying to help them, and this is how they treat me! Is this right? They are digging pits to trap me. Remember that I stood right in front of You, blocking Your path to plead with You on their behalf so that You would not bring Your anger down on them and this is my thanks!" He threw the putrid matter to the ground with a splat and wiped his hands on his robe. "It's too much.

"Fine! Give their children over to famine, then! Hand them over to the power of the sword. Let their wives be made childless and widows. Let their men be put to death and their young men slain by the sword in battle. Let them wail in their homes when suddenly You bring invaders against them. They won't accept what I have tried to do for them so I won't stand in Your way anymore. They have dug a pit for me to fall in and have hidden snares to catch my feet. But Lord, You know all about their plots to kill me, so don't forgive their crimes! Let them just try to stand before You in all of their sin. They will be flattened by Your presence. Treat them as they deserve. Deal with them in Your anger!"[1]

Baruch stared at him, open-mouthed.

The mob was scandalized into silence. It was true; Jeremiah had always been their advocate, defending them before their God. Never had they heard Jeremiah rant so against them. Always he had come to them with pleading and saved his curses for the king, the priests, and the officials.

"He really *is* mad!" a voice called out. Jeremiah recognized his cousin, Zedekiah ben Maaseiah of the House of Prophets. "Jeremiah, are you going to call down fire from heaven?" The heckler's companions tried to hush him, but he shook them off and continued, "Who is trying to kill you? Not even King Jehoiakim, though you've certainly given him cause enough. I haven't seen anyone lay any pits or snares; you're free to come and go as you please! But maybe someone should! Something should be done to take you off the streets and keep you from frightening women and children as they go about their business!"

The crowd began to murmur their agreement though they shifted and stirred; peering upward as though trying to see if fire would indeed fall. Apparently, they hadn't quite forgotten the lightning that struck the Horse Tower.

Captain Pashur of the Temple Guard emerged from the audience and stamped his foot in frustration. He could not legally touch the prophet, not here. But that didn't stop him from rebuttal. "You people, listen to me! Jeremiah says that Jerusalem shall be besieged! I tell you that the Lord has promised grace!

It is written that he who lives in the shelter of the Most High rests in the shadow of the Almighty. He is your refuge and your fortress! His Word says you will not fear the terror of the night or the arrow's flight by day. It says even though ten thousand fall beside you, it will not come near you![2] How can Jeremiah prophesy such things when the Word of the Lord so clearly contradicts him?"

"I am not speaking from myself!" Jeremiah yelled at him. "This 'fortress' will be besieged, and this 'refuge' will be surrounded by 'terror!'"

"You think that coat makes you a prophet?" Pashur spat out the words in an anger he could hardly control. Shaking in rage, he stalked right up to his adversary and leaned forward, face to face as he yelled "Then where are the miracles? I'm not the only one who has asked you that question, but you have never answered it. Where are the miracles, Jeremiah? No one here has ever seen you do even one!"

"Prophets do not do miracles, Pashur," Jeremiah countered hotly. "The Lord God does. You are a priest, even you know that! And what has this people done that He should grant them a miracle?" Jeremiah's shaking was growing worse. It was all too much. He just wanted to go back to his rooms and curl up in a corner. Let what was coming happen without him.

"That is enough!" House Prophet Zedekiah ben Maaseiah, could contain himself no longer. "Jerusalem is the City of God! The ground sanctified by the Temple of the Almighty shall never be made unclean! You blaspheme, so all the world hears it and is witness!"

"Apparently, all the world is blind," Jeremiah gritted through his teeth, and he gestured with a sweeping motion to the evidence of the grotesque idol just outside the gate. Tiny burned bones of children were scattered near it. The bones were from children killed that very day, for at the end of the day the priests of Molech would gather up the bones and put them in little urns, interring them in the city wall, a monument to Baal Molech's greatness. Already, so many had died that day. Their plight gave the prophet new resolve. Furious, Jeremiah turned away from the slaughter. "You need more evidence? Come with me!"

The prophet walked deliberately through the midst of the mass of people. They parted to let him pass and closed in behind to follow him up to the Temple Mount.

"Nabi," Baruch was troubled. He alternately walked and trotted to keep up with the long, determined stride of his tall employer. "Nabi, they're fools, but they have a point. The people would believe if there were miracles."

Jeremiah shot him a look of mingled surprise and madness. "The Sovereign Lord will not even allow me to pray for them. Do you really think He will grant them miracles?" He sighed. "Baruch, think. The Almighty can grant me no miracles. The purpose of miracles is to encourage belief, to turn the people to the Lord and strengthen their faith, but these people won't listen, they refuse to be turned, and they have no faith to be strengthened, so the Lord wastes no miracles on them. They wouldn't recognize a miracle if it landed on their noses."

Baruch thought about that. "They won't listen, but you're going to preach to them anyway? By your own argument, it's a useless gesture, but you're going to do it, and you really think the best place to do it is in the Temple Court?"

The prophet never paused. "You're right. It's insanity. The whole world has gone mad, so, why can't I? But look, Baruch. They're following. They may not listen, but they will not be able to say that they didn't hear. That will not be my fault."

"But the Temple court? Nabi, you are forbidden. Preach in the marketplace, they can plug their ears all they want there, and still, no one will harm you. Just stay out of the Temple Court. Or even better, let's just go home. You've already warned them all. Isn't it enough?" He tugged on Jeremiah's sleeve.

"No. It's not enough; I think maybe it never will be. He always asks more because there is always more that needs doing. But My Friend, Dearest of Friends, don't you see? We're all doomed. What happens to me now doesn't matter. It has started. Judgment comes."

"Because pharaoh is here and tomorrow he continues north."

"Yes. Pharaoh will see judgment first. But judgment on us, and on all the nations, will follow him home. The world is about to erupt in war, and we are caught in the middle. That is why I am called to go to the Temple, even though that's crazy. They will be sure to notice me there, if nothing else, news of it will spread throughout the city. We must make sure they hear, and this will do it. Besides, it is the Lord's House, not Azariah's. The Chief Priest doesn't have the right to decide who is and who is not welcome there." He stepped forward, again, turning a corner. They continued north, entered the broadway that went past Baruch's small house and led to the Temple's West Gate.

Baruch tagged after. "Then the Lord will protect you?"

"Do not be afraid of them, for I am with you and will rescue you.' He has promised me my life, Baruch, not that I won't suffer."[3] Jeremiah stopped and looked at the scribe, troubled. "We are all going to suffer, but I just don't care anymore. It's all useless." He hurried forward before the crowd behind could catch up and accost him before he reached his destination.

"It's not too late, the people could still repent!" They passed Baruch's house. Sarah sat outside scrubbing laundry. She waved to them, and Baruch lifted his hand in reply. Her anxious eyes followed the prophet.

Jeremiah watched her as he passed by, then he looked at Baruch, pity in his eyes. "Israel repented, and the Lord spared them. Then they turned back to their old ways, and Assyria carried them away. They are gone. Jonah preached, and Assyria repented so that the Lord spared them, too. Then they forgot their vows, and now they are gone. Under King Josiah, we followed the Law, but now? Josiah is gone, and Judah follows Jehoiakim and will not listen. You were there, at the garbage pit. Did that sound like repentance to you? Child sacrifice, and even the priests don't object."

"They're about to object to you," Baruch grumbled.

They reached the West Gate, and a guard stepped out of the guard house, directly in their way.

"Move," Jeremiah commanded him shortly.

"You are forbidden," the priest-guard said, but the prophet's wild appearance seemed to unsettle him. Uncertainly, he picked up his spear.

"That cannot be because the Lord of this House commands it."

The guard shuffled his feet nervously, and a second came out of the guardhouse to join him. "Jeremiah! What do you think you're doing?" the newcomer demanded.

"The Lord has sent me with a message," the prophet was not intimidated.

The new guard planted the tip of his spear at Jeremiah's feet. "Really? Ben Hilkiah, you've been preaching the downfall of Jerusalem and this Temple for years! But we are priests too. We know the Word and what you're saying is ludicrous! How could the Lord let His own land be destroyed? If we go into captivity, the Law will be lost; there will be no priests to preach it or Temple to offer sacrifices and celebrate the feasts! The Lord would become a God without worshippers. Haven't you thought of that?"

Of course, he had. It didn't matter. It was almost over now, and he didn't answer the charges. "Move," he repeated.

The first guard took courage from the second. "You are a priest, but you are also a madman, Jeremiah. Just look at you! You imagine you're a prophet, but you have no fellowship with those of the House of Prophets. Besides, your prophecies fall flat, the Temple cannot be destroyed and the Lord's people scattered. It's impossible. I don't know why the Chief Priest doesn't have you stoned. Look around you. The crowds shun you!"

It was true. Those who were passing were crowding the far side of the gate and avoiding any part of the conflict.

"So, go back home," the second guard put in, "before the Chief Priest has us arrest you."

"That's enough!" The authority behind the voice was unmistakable, the guards turned to see Buzi, the Third Priest, crossing the Temple Court and stomping towards them. Ezekiel was trotting at his side. "Believe or not as you will," Buzi growled at the guards, "but this man is of higher parentage than you! If not for Solomon, it is likely that he would be Chief Priest at this very moment, and you know it. Let him pass."

"But Azariah *is* the Chief Priest, and he has forbidden it!"

Ezekiel looked ready to take the guard's spear away from him. Buzi placed a restraining hand on the youth's shoulder and sighed. "I will talk to Azariah," he said. "Now let him pass."

The two guards did not have the authority to deny the Third Priest. "It's on your head, Buzi," the second guard warned him. Then he pulled his spear from the ground, and the two stood aside.

Jeremiah walked straight onto the Temple grounds and passing by the Wood House, he stopped in front of the northern annex. He stood there, facing the sanctuary of the gods of Egypt.

Even in his present state, Jeremiah had not forgotten he was restricted from access to the Temple grounds or that the Captain of the Temple Guard was not far behind him and would be arriving soon. He knew he had better be short.

The Levite singers under the portico saw him and fell silent in consternation.

Jeremiah mounted the three defiled stone steps and turned to face the crowd from between the black sphinxes. He planted his feet apart, and the wind suddenly came up and whipped his prophet's mantle around him, making him look like some kind of demented Moses looking down on the crowd from the mount as they celebrated their idolatry. "Pay attention to what the Lord Almighty, the God of Israel says!"

Chief Priest Azariah trotted down the ramp of the Grand Altar and stared dumbfounded at the prophet. Jeremiah saw him and called out: "It is time, Azariah! Listen, all of you! I am bringing every single calamity I declared against you because you are stubborn and will not obey My commands. It is time!"

And then Captain Pashur caught up to him, and two Temple Guards were with him. "Finally!" the captain gloated. "You have finally done something for which you can be called into account! By entering this courtyard, you have disobeyed a direct order from the Chief Priest. You are on Temple grounds and under Temple jurisdiction. The king may not wish to touch you, but you force us!" He gestured to the guards who grabbed the prophet. Jeremiah did not struggle. Pashur stripped Jeremiah of his cloak and threw it on the ground in disgust. "See if you can beat some sense into him, then let him spend the night in the stocks and think about it."

The guard drug Jeremiah off to their headquarters in the Benjamin Gate while Baruch ran to retrieve the prophet's cloak.

The Benjamin Gate housed the House of Prophets and the jail of the Temple Guard. The Guard itself occupied the Benjamin Tower. In his wake, the prophet saw Azariah turn dazed and questioning eyes on Baruch. But the young scribe just shook his head and shrugged. Then Buzi came up and began speaking earnestly to Azariah as the crowd returned to their various forms of worship and the Levites on the Temple Steps took up their songs.

CHAPTER 45

The Price of Obedience

Jerusalem, Judah

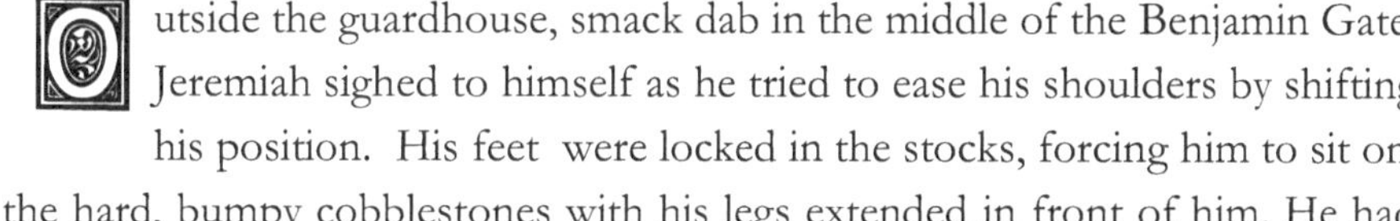

Outside the guardhouse, smack dab in the middle of the Benjamin Gate, Jeremiah sighed to himself as he tried to ease his shoulders by shifting his position. His feet were locked in the stocks, forcing him to sit on the hard, bumpy cobblestones with his legs extended in front of him. He had no backrest, and so he held his arms stiff at his sides to brace himself in this posture. The ground was cold and damp. He couldn't shift his weight much; the cruel wood and chains saw to that. He'd been here since mid-afternoon and could feel his vertebrae compressing.

He twisted his stiffening neck enough that he could look up at the brilliant stars overhead. "So, are You watching this?" he shouted at the heavens and groaned as the effort broke open the scabs of his thrashing on his back. His tunic hung in shreds from where they had ripped it off his torso. "Am I supposed to be grateful that Azariah made Pashur stop whipping me? That I only received twenty lashes? Yes, I deliberately disobeyed the Chief Priest. Yes, I provoked Captain Pashur. So, what? You told me to do it! Orders are orders. I had no choice!"

He stopped, it wasn't true. He always had a choice. Except that even if no one else obeyed, Jeremiah was loyal. He always had a choice, and his choice was to obey.

But it was too much, more than any mortal man could bear! Angrily, he screamed at the top of his lungs at the silent sky. Then he screamed again until his voice went hoarse. The stiffness of his spine had long ago given way to agony, and he couldn't feel his legs anymore. Screaming helped, but he was still locked in the stocks, so he gave that up too.

Time crawled by.

A group of Judeans came out of the Wood House and passed by, heading for the front of the Temple. They whispered to each other as they passed the prophet in the stocks. With a shock, Jeremiah recognized some of the elders of Jerusalem and Jaazaniah ben Shaphan was among them. Baruch's brother Seraiah had warned the prophet about Jaazaniah, but even so, Jeremiah had not thought he was an idolater.

Their words carried to him. "He's not going to get out of there until morning. I suppose now we'll see if it is Jeremiah who is surrounded by terror at night!" They stifled their laughter behind their hands like young girls giggling.

"Jaazaniah, is that you?" Jeremiah croaked at them through thick lips. He hadn't had anything to drink for hours, and the screaming had damaged his voice too. "Sneaking around to worship pagan idols under cover of darkness? Does your father know where you've just been? When I get out of here, would you like me to tell him?" He groaned. The effort of screaming had stretched muscles on his sides which now pulled on his back and sent dizzying pains throughout his body.

"You shut your mouth!" Shaphan's son snapped, a hint of panic in his voice.

Silenced, the group hurried on.

"Don't worry on my account. I won't tell him. Shaphan's an old man, and he loves the Lord. I wouldn't want to hurt him like that," Jeremiah muttered after their departing backs. Never had he suspected it was possible to feel so hopeless and dejected. It was all over anyway, so if only he could just keel over and die! But he couldn't, so he held his peace and shifted his weight, leaning on his right arm. Time crawled on and the stars wheeled around in their places overhead.

After a while, Jeremiah flexed his bruised neck and saw two of his cousins leaving the Temple to return to their lodgings.

Zedekiah nudged his brother, Zephaniah, with his elbow and said something too low for the wild prophet to hear, then he laughed outright.

Zephaniah scowled at his brother, “Go home,” he told him.

Zedekiah shrugged and skirted his felonious cousin as he headed for his quarters in the opposite wall of the Benjamin Gate. Zephaniah walked over to his cousin and scowled at him too. “He’s right, you know,” the priest said softly. “You got yourself into this mess, cousin. It’s disgraceful.”

Jeremiah disagreed with Zephaniah’s assessment. “I didn’t. I didn’t get myself into this mess. I only obeyed.”

“So, this is the Lord’s fault? This is obedience’s reward, and the idolaters just get to keep walking around free?”

“Sometimes, it seems like it,” Jeremiah tilted his head to look up at him and his head cleared. The overwhelming stress was still there, but it was pushed into the background, and he could think again. Zephaniah was there for a purpose, he needed to talk to him. “Zephaniah, appearances aren’t always what they seem. No one is walking around free. It’s time. When Necho returns, judgment begins.”

Zephaniah clucked his tongue in disapproval and bent over so he could better see Jeremiah’s bruised and swollen face. “The king is loyal to Necho. The pharaoh won’t hurt him. Would you like me to bring some ointment for your back, cousin?”

“No, but thank you. Just go home and make sure you’re ready.”

“For what?” The priest straightened back up. “You said King Nebuchadnezzar would come and I believe you. But Cousin, you do know that Nebuchadnezzar is not the King of Babylon yet, right?”

“By the time he gets here, he will be.”

The utter confidence of the statement left Zephaniah speechless. He opened and shut his mouth twice, but no words came out.

“He *is* coming, Zephaniah. Go home and get ready. Go and make sure our family in Anathoth is ready.”

“How?”

“Tell them to get out. Now. While they still can. Then pray.”

The priest briefly laid his hand on the prophet’s beaten and bloodied shoulder. “I can pray.”

“Good, because I can’t! The Lord has forbidden me. But tell our family to get out,” he insisted.

Zephaniah sighed. "I'll tell them you said so." Then he walked off, heading for his quarters amongst the sacerdotal priests in the New Gate.

Jeremiah was left alone with his agony.

Except he wasn't.

He was never alone, which was why Zephaniah was wrong, and he had *not* gotten himself into "this mess." That being the case, the prophet felt he had a legitimate complaint. Jeremiah had never been one to keep his feelings or his thoughts to himself. The Lord knew it all anyway. The stress was a burden too great to bear, he had to speak, to let it out.

"Ah, Lord," he murmured, glancing again at the marvelous beauty of the sky. Here, down on earth, he had cramps in the calves of both legs even though they were both numb. "When You first called me, You told me that I must go wherever You sent me and say whatever You told me to say. You said that I shouldn't be afraid of the people because You were with me and You would rescue me. So, You convinced me, and I was misled into believing that You would save me from the consequences of speaking for You.

"Besides, how could I refuse? You are stronger than I. So, You overpowered me and got Your way and now look where *I've* ended up! This was Your idea, but everyone walking by taunts and mocks *me,* Lord! The worst part is that it's sure to happen again. Whenever I speak, all I do is cry out violence and destruction, because You make me do it. Prophesying for You has done nothing but bring me insults and reproach all day long!"

A horsefly bit him on his forehead, and he slapped at it, but having temporarily lost the support of his hand, he fell over and skinned his elbow on the round unyielding stones. He pushed himself back upright, and the fly buzzed around and settled on his back.

"It's not my fault," he avowed, and he began to cry. He had never felt so utterly dejected. "I can't help it. I can't stop. I've tried. I've told myself: *'I won't speak in His name anymore.'* Then Your Word burns my heart like fire. It penetrates clear to the marrow of my very bones, and I get tired of trying to hold it in. I can't do it!"

The fly bit him again, but he couldn't reach it or shake it loose, so he tried to ignore it, but he couldn't help thinking that the fly couldn't have bitten him if he had been wearing his mantle.

"I hear the people whispering and mocking 'terror on every side!' Every time I speak for You I hear them. They say: 'Report him. Let's turn him in!' Even my so-called friends are just waiting for me to make a mistake. They hope that maybe I'll prophesy falsely then they'll be able to take revenge!"

The Lord said nothing. He was just there, listening, letting His prophet rant.

So, Jeremiah ranted. "Job was right," he yelled at the heavens, "I wish I were never born! Lord, I curse that day, it was not a joyous occasion. And the man that delivered me of my mother and brought the news to my father—well, curse him too! Let him be like all those towns You have overthrown without pity. Let him live through these times to wake up in the morning to the sound of wailing and to be witness to the cries of battle in the afternoon. That man should have killed me before I was born, but he didn't, so don't have pity for him!

"Why was I ever born, just to see trouble and sorrow and to wind up like this? To die in shame?"

Jeremiah surprised and offended himself. Was he really as bad off as Job? But it was Job's faithfulness that had caused his troubles, and so it was with Jeremiah. He doubled over, racked with sobs, unable to continue.

A cool, night breeze caressed his scabbed cheek. *Would you really rather never to have been born?* The amused, familiar voice sought to tease him into admitting the truth.

Jeremiah was having none of it, and he found his voice again. "Yes!" He hesitated and thought about it. "Well, at the moment, anyway." The tears had provided relief, and he felt empty but calmed. "Lord, maybe the people are right. Maybe I am mad. This compulsion to speak, is it a form of insanity? If it is, would I know it? Does an insane man know he is insane?"

The fly, finally discouraged by the breeze, flew away.

Jeremiah looked up to see Baruch sitting on the prophet's mantle as a pad. His back was resting against the tower wall. One of the Temple Guard there was watching him carefully so that he couldn't return the cow-hair cloak or bring Jeremiah water or food. The scribe wasn't even allowed to talk to his friend. Baruch was balancing his wax pad on his knees, his stylus was busy scratching. He was working, but he was also crying. Baruch noticed Jeremiah looking at him, and he angrily rubbed the tears from his eyes and his sparsely bearded, youthful cheeks.

Baruch doesn't think you're crazy, came the Voice.

Jeremiah laughed and spoke low, out of Baruch's hearing. "No, he doesn't. But he's sitting over there recording everything I say. And if anything survives the coming holocaust, You and I both know it will be Baruch's work. So, everyone else for all time will read it, and *they're* going to think I'm crazy! And even if they don't, they're going to remember me this way, humiliated for all eternity."

They will remember My brave and faithful Prophet to the Nations and think there was never one like you. Have you considered My servant, Job? There is no one on Earth like him. The teasing voice reminded Jeremiah that He could quote Job too.

"Maybe, but tomorrow I'll be released, and at that point, if I can still walk, I'll have some comments of my own to add to Baruch's notes!" His wry humor banished the temporary panic of doubt. Jeremiah resigned himself to the rest of a long and uncomfortable night. He meant to spend it complaining, but with Baruch there, he decided he was going to do it silently. So, all that night, Jeremiah leaned on his God. The comfort he found there was not the gentle, loving touch he knew so well, but a hardening of the will so that outside circumstances, including many more flies, could no longer touch him. When morning finally came, he was stronger and more unshakable than he had ever been. With the help of his God, he was going to make it through even what was coming.

With the dawn, Captain Pashur ben Immer came, and with a clunk, he opened the locks and released the prophet. Baruch was there instantly and supported Jeremiah while he got to his feet. The scribe slipped the leather coat around the prophet's torn shoulders.

Blood began to circulate in the abused limbs, and it was like thousands of tiny daggers getting one last twist of agony out of Jeremiah's tortured body. He cried out and would have fallen if Baruch hadn't had a firm grip around his waist. Jeremiah managed to get his legs braced and finally to support his own weight though he couldn't quite stand upright.

Baruch held a skin of water to his lips, and he drank greedily.

"I hope this has taught you to hold your tongue!" Captain Pashur spat.

Jeremiah, still bent over, looked up at him slowly, rage smoldering in his eyes. "Your hope is in vain. My tongue is not mine to hold. Nor are these grounds yours, or even Azariah's to say who may, or may not, gain entrance. This House is the Lord's." He managed to straighten up.

"Next time, if we have you before the Great Council again, Jeremiah, your punishment will not be the stocks, it will be stoning!"

"Well, maybe. If the Lord gives us a next time," Jeremiah shot back at him. "As for you seeing fit to go prophesy to the people under your own authority, the Lord has given you a new name. You are no longer Pashur; your new name is 'Surrounded by Terror.' He says:

> 'I will make you a terror to yourself and to all your friends. You will see them fall to their enemies' swords with your own eyes. I will give all of Judah to the King of Babylon, and he will exile them to Babylon or execute them with the sword. All the goods and valuables of Jerusalem and all the treasures of the king I will give to the Babylonians. They will plunder it all and take it back with them to their city. And you, Pashur, and all your family will be exiled to Babylon as well. You will die and be buried there, both you and all your friends to whom you have prophesied your lies.'"

Pashur was left gaping at the back of the departing prophet as he limped off, the faithful Baruch at his side, supporting him. Almost. The captain had almost believed.[1]

CHAPTER 46

Egypt's Defeat

North Syria

mmediately after the New Year, Rab Mag Nebuchadnezzar rode out of Babylon at the head of the chariot core divisions. Kadurri's brother, Prince Nebushumlishtar, was thirteen and was beginning his military career on the back of a flashy blood-bay charger. Shum was proud to serve in the cavalry under the newly appointed General Narambel.

Nebuchadnezzar stopped at Nimrud, Capital of Assyria, to collect King Arbaces the Mede and his army. They were, after all, marching on Carchemish, a territory Arbaces claimed belonged to him.

At Harran, Kadurri met up with his father-in-law, the Glory of Media, Uvakshatra. Prince Ishtumegu was continuing Media's advances in Persia, leaving Uvak free to tend to the demands of the Coalition. Uvak left the Scythians to protect his star city, and the three armies continued on together.

Now, it was the first of Simanu, the moon of the wheat harvest.[1] Now the Coalition was encamped on the Derezor Road, outside the pathetic walls of the town of Til-Barsip.

The Derezor Road made it possible for even chariots and infantry to pass through the desert in a single day and come to the vulnerable Syrian coast. The Road was the preferred route of travel because it crossed the desert at its narrowest point. There was only one other feasible crossing of that wilderness, and that was the Damascus Road. It ran from Hit to Damascus and required camel caravans to survive the passage of the desert.

Til-Barsip was located about twelve miles south of Carchemish in a bend of the Euphrates. The village thrived on three industries: the mining of the red stone breccia, the sale of boats, and the trade and industry based on its location at the Derezor crossing of the Euphrates. Ownership of the crossing meant control of the commerce which flowed down the road from Derezor near Palmyra, right by Til-Barsip with its ford, then across the desert to the Syrian coast.

But the village wasn't what it used to be. The glories of its past had ended over three centuries before, and now it was simply the city of the boat builders and stone harvesters. Til-Barsip had no armed forces. The city officials took one look at the forces arrayed against them and threw open their gates in submission.

Nebuchadnezzar parked his father's royal chariot next to King Uvakshatra's massive copper and green one and watched the gates swing open with a great deal of satisfaction.

"You were right," Uvakshatra grunted, contemplating the river crossing and the "conquered" city before them. "Necho hasn't even thought of stationing troops here."

Kadurri's smile was predatory. "The Assyrians might have seen this coming, but Necho doesn't have them to advise him anymore."

"You look just like your father when you smile like that," Uvak chuckled. "Like a lion ready to pounce. If this works, your glory will reflect his."

"And yours. It is your governor who is responsible for this plan."

"Yes, Suiki and his love of libraries." Uvak had long ago given up on trying to pronounce the governor's full name. "Don't worry. I will not forget him. If we succeed, the Bel Pihati of Harran is going to be a very wealthy man."

The records of the Tablet House had told the prince what he already knew, barring treachery, Carchemish couldn't be taken. Barring a miracle from the gods, no one could protect Harran from Egypt. The Coalition did not have the strength to push Egypt out of North Syria. Long ago, the Assyrian Emperor Sharuken had faced a similar situation and also found it couldn't be done, so he didn't try. He did something else entirely.

It was Sharuken who had simply ignored Carchemish and came here, to Til-Barsip instead. Sharuken was the first to commission the citizens of Til-

Barsip to provide him boats to transport his troops across the river. They had been building boats ever since and selling them up and down the river.

By that afternoon, the citizens were willingly building boats for Nebuchadnezzar. Egypt had claimed Syria, but the people of Til-Barsip had their roots in Assyria and were more sympathetic to the King of Nimrud than the pharaoh. All that was left of Assyria was now a province of Babylonia and Arbaces the Mede was its sub-king under Nabopolassar of Babylon. When they had found out who was outside their gates, they had switched their allegiance without a qualm.

The village's capitulation meant the Coalition was well on the way to controlling the Derezor Road all the way to the Syrian Coast. Carchemish's lines of supply, communication, and retreat back to Egypt were in danger of being cut off. North Syria itself would be cut off. The only route left back to Egypt would be west straight through Lydian territory. Necho had been wooing King Alyattes economically with orders of ships and the promise of the Tumilat Canal. The Anatolian king was leaning towards supporting the Two Lands, but at present, he remained friendly but undecided and uncommitted. If Egypt attempted to march across his lands, using Ionia as a route to the sea, Lydia would be likely to rise against her.

Pharaoh Necho, already in Carchemish, needed a supply route and a way home. He could not let the Coalition cut him off; he needed to protect the route south to the Philistine coast.

Nebuchadnezzar had engineered a confrontation in the field, away from the safety of the Fortress of Carchemish. The Babylonians and Medes held the advantage of a greater number of troops, and pharaoh had no choice, he had to respond.

Two days later, as the forces of the Coalition marched out of the desert, they found an ominous black line facing them, blocking their way to the coast. As they drew nearer, the line coalesced into the host of Egypt. The blue haze of the Great Sea permeated the air behind them, but the sunrise glinted on the Lydian chainmail given by Alyattes to the Egyptian nobility. Necho was a pragmatist. He knew the tradition of fighting virtually naked had serious drawbacks in chariot warfare. So, under *this* pharaoh, the officers were now wearing armor. Kadurri didn't care. It made it much easier to spot the army's commanders.

The rab mag signaled his driver to stop. Nebuzaradan rode his grey up beside the chariot and unfurled a double standard—the royal red with the white dragons above and the rab mag's blue with the god Nergal below. Kadurri surveyed the opposition. Egypt was formidable, but he had expected nothing less.

Uvakshatra and Uvak's cousin, King Arbaces of Nimrud pulled their chariots up next to him. Their standard bearers unfurled their colors as well, copper with gold and turquoise blue. At the sight, the tension in the air above the Coalition armies became tangible. Battle was imminent.

"Well, My Son," Uvak murmured, "now we come to it."

"I know," Kadurri answered. All-out war with Egypt—this day would change the world forever, one way or the other.

The impatient squealing of the warhorses behind him blended with the stamping of hooves and the chime-like clinking of bits and tack as the animals pulled eagerly at their reins. They waited for his signal. Otherwise, it was quiet. Even the birds had ceased their singing.

Uvak looked at him quizzically.

Kadurri frowned. The Mede had recognized his hesitation. "But here I am wondering about this strategy of Sharuken's? Well, I do have doubts. I'm risking your men as well as mine. What if something goes wrong? Our closest holding is Harran, and it's across the desert—far too far away…"

"It's too late for doubts, Kadurri. We're already committed. So… there's only one way to find out."

Kadurri looked at the King of Assyria. For the past two years, the Prince of Babylon had trained off and on under the former First General of Media. Arbaces was proud of him, but he merely grinned at his protégé and said nothing. Arbaces was a warrior, and like the chargers, he too was champing at the bit. The young rab mag set his jaw, then he raised his spear to the sky, and the trumpets and drums sounded the ready.

The morning was young, for the desert crossing had been done in the cool of night. The troops of the Coalition were tired from the long, forced march. Nevertheless, the Babylonians raised a mighty war cry in response to their charismatic young commander's order.

The chariot of the Kings of Media and Assyria whirled almost in place and then sped away to the front of their respective forces. Their banners flowed out in the wind behind their racing standard bearers, and the entire host shouted their defiance of Egypt.

Then, as another trumpet sounded, the chariots of the rab mag and the two kings charged. As one, the chariots of the rab shaq and the other generals leaped ahead, right on their heels. At a third blast, the cavalries charged, fanning out to the flanks of the host and then with a deafening roar, the infantry surged forward. Ignoring their fatigue, they ran as though they had just been roused from a good night's sleep after a moon of rest. The peace of the morning was irrevocably shattered.

The Egyptians did not shift their position. Letting the Coalition come on, their longbowmen stood forward and let fly. The cavalry and chariots took the full brunt of the well-prepared Egyptian archery. Screams added to the sound of the trumpets and war cries as many horses and men went down. The second volley was joined by stones hurled from hundreds of slings. The third volley was followed by an onslaught of Lydian war dogs. The dogs launched themselves at the throats of the horses, at their legs, at their riders and drivers. General Narambel's cavalry was decimated. Scores of the younger sons of the Bar Manuti went down; but the survivors—including the general, Prince Nebushumlishtar, and his daggerman, Marshipar—hurled themselves over the fallen as if they were barriers placed down in a horserace.

Despite the horrific slaughter, the Babylonian line never broke or slowed. They slammed into their enemies with a force that drove them deep into the midst of the fray.

Screaming wild and defiant shouts, Kadurri wielded his spear like Nergal himself.

Uvak, laughing like a Scythian, drove right through Egypt's leading forces and with a hand-picked few was wreaking havoc on the inadequately armored Egyptian infantry. A dog jumped into the Mede's chariot and he grabbed it by the scruff of the neck and threw it back at his enemies.

After the first clash, Arbaces of Nimrud pulled back from the battle. At the head of his forces, the King of Assyria led his men around and behind, aiming to cut off all retreat back toward Carchemish or the questionable shelter of Lydia.

Meanwhile, among the Egyptians, the chariot of General Raemmaakheru swung in front of the pharaoh's bringing Necho's driver to an abrupt stop.

"What is it?" pharaoh demanded angrily. He loved battle and was not pleased with being stopped like that.

"The Median pretender is moving to block the way back to Carchemish! If he succeeds, we will be caught out here with our closest base being Gaza."

His anger faded as Necho understood. He stood there in shock as his handsome face drained of color. "But… But… The Coalition's closest base is Harran!"

"Except that, even though it is far, they hold a clear road back to it!"

"Then we must turn and stop that Assyrian pretender now!"

"If we do that, we may be able to return to Carchemish, but we will be cut off from our own country. To prevent that is why we are here in the first place."

"So even if we win here, we have lost Carchemish?" Pharaoh couldn't believe it.

The general nodded. "And all of North Syria. But the Good God should observe that we are *not* winning here."

"How can that be? The rab mag is young and inexperienced."

"And brilliant, apparently. Besides, neither King Uvakshatra nor his former general is inexperienced."

"We need to send pigeons to Admiral Kaelus and the mercenaries at Gaza…"

"They are at least two to three days away, and their strength is in ships, not infantry. We must go to them, not have them come to us. And we must do it as quickly as we can."

Necho stared at him. "Retreat? You can't be serious. This battle is young. They have already lost hundreds whereas our losses are light. How could you possibly say that we are losing?"

"I am the First General of the Armies of Egypt. It is my place to know. The numbers they lost were in their first charge, but that charge is now over. We are outnumbered and outmaneuvered they are slaughtering us. If we stay here, we die. If we go north, we will be cut off from Gaza and Egypt, and we die. We must pull back to Gaza. Now."

"No matter what we do, we lose?"

"Yes."

Nebuchadnezzar had never before been in the midst of such a fierce battle, but it exhilarated him in a way that nothing else ever had. He slew all he faced. Each new foe became a fresh opportunity for revenge for all his people had suffered, a new chance to let the glory of Marduk resound. He killed all, yet none touched him. Kadurri inspired his men to fight all the harder. He was the son of Marduk's chosen, and it seemed as though the hero of the gods himself fought at his side.

"Heretic!" Suddenly there, almost on top of him, was the undersized but agile chariot of the Crown Prince of Egypt, Psammetik.

Kadurri recognized him by the golden braid fastened to his battle helmet and the gold trim on his gleaming chain mail. Besides the dark tone of his skin was identical to Nitocris'.

"Red face!" Psammetik shouted in Aramaic quite well, the heritage of his fathers' background in the Assyrian military. "Even the red of your helmet and chariot declare it! Heretic!"

Red was the color of the Deshret crown of Lower Egypt, but the Egyptians also considered the color to be symbolic of heresy and lined their walls with paintings of defeated heretics and undesirables with red faces.

Egyptians were inconsistent in their hate of the color, though, Kadurri was well aware that Princess Nitocris preferred her nails painted a bright scarlet.

"Ravisher of my sister! Desecrator of her office!" The First Prophet of Amun raged on and tried to run his brother-in-law through with his spear. Nebuzaradan knocked it aside as the Egyptian chariot rushed by at full gallop.

The Rab Mag of Babylon had a clear target at the naked back of the Egyptian prince's neck—but this was Nitocris' beloved brother. Besides, Egypt was probably going to need a new pharaoh soon. "Psammetik!" Kadurri yelled after him in passable High Egyptian. "Your sister, my wife, is well and flourishes in Babylon. Do not worry yourself for her sake! We need to talk, but this is not the place! I think our quarrel is not with each other, but with a mutual enemy, your father!"

Taken aback, the Egyptian prince had his driver pull up. They stood there for a moment, parked, as the whirlwind of the battle raged around them. Then the horns of Egypt announced the retreat. Egypt's strength was broken.

Still, the two remained, staring at each other.

Babylon's trumpets sounded the disengage and regroup; the crack troops of Babylon came to heel. Kadurri jerked his attention back to the battlefield. Someone had to call the troops to order, it was his responsibility, but Rab Shaq Belshumishkun had just done it. He touched his driver's shoulder, and they wheeled away, Kadurri's cheeks burning.

The stunned Egyptian prince was left behind them.

The Egyptian infantry, their rear, and flank guarded by the chariots, was quickly falling back to the south, to the coast.

Uvakshatra was too busy to notice. He was issuing commands and had already called his host to order.

Arbaces did not recall his men. They stayed on the field, refusing to relinquish the ground they guarded; denying Egypt a retreat northward.

Nebuchadnezzar ordered his driver to the side of Rab Shaq Belshumishkun. There he raised the double standard beside that of the rab shaq's yellow crescent moon on a blue-black field. Belshumishkun gave him a dark look that plainly said Nebuchadnezzar should have been the one to command the disengage. This time, no harm had come of it. There had better not be a next time.

Kadurri squirmed inside, determined not to disgrace himself or his father further. As though there had been no lapse, he signaled the trumpeters to sound assembly. In a remarkably short time, all troops had been recalled, and order had been restored.

Within a half-beru, the field was cleared, and King Uvakshatra joined the prince, King Arbaces, and Generals Belshumishkun and Narambel in a quick strategy session in the middle of the combat zone.[2] The Glory of Media had a ragged bandage tied around his upper left arm, but he was grinning broadly. He lightly jumped down from his chariot, barely missed tripping on a fallen Egyptian and came up to slap his son-in-law on the back. "It appears we did find out, eh?"[3]

Despite his earlier embarrassment at his momentary lapse, Kadurri laughed. It had been exactly the right thing to say. "I guess we did," he admitted. He shook his head in mock disbelief and reflected that he could see why his father loved the Mede so.

"And now?"

The rab mag shrugged. "Things are going so well, why make any changes? Egypt is my problem, Carchemish is Arbaces' and Lydia is yours—as we agreed."

"As we agreed, Great One." Uvak's grin died, and he searched the prince's face. "Kadurri, this victory must be absolute. You've got to finish this, and you've got to do it now."

Nebuchadnezzar knew what he meant. He had to make sure that Egypt would never recover. But he hesitated, thinking of Nitocris' brother, Psammetik. He had never given such an order before, and he didn't want to do it now.

"My Son," Uvak fixed the young man's face with his eyes. He spoke softly so that only he could hear, "Necho showed no mercy at Carchemish. If you do not respond in kind, Egypt will certainly rise again. Not only that, you will never again be able to lead your men in battle because both they and your enemies will view you as being weak. Your armies will not fight for you anymore, and your enemies will not fear you.

"So, cut down the troops of the jackal as they flee south with their tails between their legs. And send pharaoh's wicked heart to overbalance the scale of Maat."

Kadurri looked out at the battlefield. Doctors, priests, and anyone who could be spared were out seeing to the wounded. The groans, cries and occasional screams of the injured had replaced the thunderous crashing of mass slaughter.

There in the midst was the eunuch, Ashpenaz. He had just come off his assignment to the Lady Shadushushan. Instead of sending the eunuch back to Bit Mummi, Nebuchadnezzar brought him along and set him up as chief of supplies and logistics. Ashpenaz, with his usual efficiency, was carrying out his duties, ordering medics to travel here, supply wagons there.

Seeing him made the rab mag think of Lady Shadushushan and her child, Ugbaru. "Belnasir never saw his son," Kadurri growled to Uvak, watching the eunuch work. "He never spoke his name. He never even knew that he was to be a father." The thought angered the prince and stiffened his resolve. "The palace treasury pays a monthly stipend to the widows and fatherless children of Carchemish, thanks to those same Egyptians that Necho left still entrenched up there in what should be little Ugbaru's city. The survivors of the fortress deserve better. It's my duty to give them revenge."

Uvak nodded and Kadurri looked over at Arbaces. The sub-king was ready to do the rab mag's bidding, but his eyes kept glancing northward. Arbaces stood there with the generals of the Coalition but looked as though he could hardly keep his feet still. The King of Assyria wanted to move on the fortress he viewed as his by right.

"So, Carchemish first. King Arbaces," Kadurri addressed him, "the fort lies there before you. Since Necho emptied it of its troops, it has little more than a city guard to protect it. And since we now stand between it and Necho, it has no hope at all for supplies or reinforcements. It is at your mercy. Give those Egyptians one chance, if they don't surrender, exterminate them."

"I swear by the Fire God of my Median fathers, by Ashur, god of my Kingdom of Assyria, by Marduk, god of my emperor, and even by that same Ra those Egyptians worship, that within a moon it shall be so, Great One." He bowed his head and crossed his arms before his chest, snapping his fingers in submission to his emperor's son.

"Go, then."

The warrior king straightened, then turned smartly and marched off towards his army with a determined stride that said clearly that he had a mission to accomplish and he was going to do it right now.

"Generals," Kadurri addressed Belshumishkun and Narambel, "We will take Babylon's chariots and the rest of our forces south and eradicate the remnants of the opposition and any pockets of resistance.

"Uvak…"

The Mede's face was lit with a fierce joy; finally, *finally* he was going to get the chance he had been waiting for. "I will push Alyattes of Lydia into the sea. Did you hear? He lost the war with Miletus."

Kadurri looked at him questioningly. "What I heard was that Alyattes burned the Milesians' Temple of Athena to the ground by accident. Overcome by contrition, they say he is in the process of rebuilding it better than ever. Thrasybulus and Alyattes are, at present, the best of friends. Which, incidentally, happens to be very convenient for Alyattes because if he wants to use pharaoh's canal for passage through to the Red Sea, he has to pass right by the Fort of the Milesians down there at the mouth of the Coptic Nile."

"All right, maybe it was more of a political concession than a military loss," the Mede admitted, "but with the Milesians and the Lydians as friends, there are no more free crops there for Lydia. Anyway, the sooner we start, the sooner we finish it. Lydia is doomed."

Syria

For half a moon, Nebuchadnezzar led his men as they swept south through Syria, destroying their enemies as they went. The remnant of the Egyptian army finally took a stand in the District of Hamath, along the Typhon River. It was an area where many had settled their families and had homes. Hamath had once been the capital of the Hittites and sat on a hill above the river. The view from the city was undoubtedly beautiful, but its defenses were practically nonexistent. The wall was only partially standing. The people of the surrounding villages fled to the city, but they had little more hope there than if they had stayed in their homes in the countryside.

When he saw the Egyptian settlements and the desperate determination of the Egyptian army, Kadurri almost wavered in his resolve. These were not only men but also women and children. The Egyptians were fighting to defend their families. The rab mag wasn't interested in harming civilians, but the King of Media was right. The men had to be eliminated and the Egyptian settlements had to be uprooted.

He ordered the attack.

Though the Egyptians fought valiantly, they stood no chance. By evening, it was all over. The prince put their homes to the torch, took the women and children prisoners to be sold, and slaughtered the men. This time, the order came a little easier.

The next morning, the rab mag sent the crown's share of the booty and slaves back to Babylon. By midafternoon, they received a messenger telling them of the surrender of Carchemish. King Arbaces was holding the Egyptians in the fortress's prison until he should return to Nimrud with them where they would be sold as slaves. The King of Assyria had won back the homes of the widows of Carchemish. Now, it was Nebuchadnezzar's duty to complete their revenge. The prince laughed grimly, and despite their fatigue, he chased his quarry south.

The villages they passed were no problem. The local peoples, astonished by the strange sight of the mighty Egyptians in such a hurry to regain their country, were overawed by the Babylonian prince who pursued them. They quickly rushed to provide the army with whatever supplies they required, almost before they were asked. In this manner, the paysans declared their new allegiance. For Nebuchadnezzar, it was proof of the gods' favor. Not having to deal with the inhabitants, he was able to continue to press the Egyptians hard.

The Egyptians abandoned Riblah before the Babylonians ever arrived. The palace in which Necho had set up court stood empty. The Egyptians had left so precipitously, that they had not even taken the time to destroy the city behind them. The fortress stood at the headwaters of the Typhon River, on the east bank, and on the border between North Syria and Judah. With the loss of Riblah, Egypt had retreated out of Syria entirely.[4]

Riblah was very strong and Nebuchadnezzar approved of the outpost. It was abundantly watered by natural springs. The lands both east and west were fertile and green and Lebanon, with its prized cedar, so rare in Babylon, was nearby. It already had a very suitable palace and court, Necho had seen to that. Rather than burn the fortress, the rab mag took it as his own.

The next morning, he left a garrison behind and rode victoriously out of the fortress as he had already ridden out of so many, but with one difference.

"Are you sure about that thing?" Nebuzaradan's gray mount trotted beside Nebuchadnezzar's royal chariot. The daggerman nodded at the tall white linen hat stretched over delicate golden wires. Nebuchadnezzar had set it on his own head that morning, replacing his helmet with its red horsetail that was in such questionable taste according to the Egyptians.

"Yes. I don't want the Egyptians to identify me with red, even if it is the red of Babylon. Heretics are red."

Seri snorted. "So, you don the pharaoh's crown? I would think that would be even more heretical."

"It's called the Hedjet. It's the crown of Upper Egypt, the crown of Thebes. I am Nitocris' husband so it is mine by right," he answered stubbornly.

"Kadurri, *that* is the crown of a god. Marduk's servant…"

"Is my father. He can't claim to be a god, but nothing is stopping me."

For a second Seri was absolutely speechless. "Except, except… except that, you're his heir!" Seri finally sputtered. "What happens when you inherit?"

"Then my father would be dead and the people of Babylon will be concerned with a lot more than a crown of Egypt!"

Seri sighed, but Nebuchadnezzar grinned. He was telling anyone who wasn't blind that he was the rightful King of Upper Egypt. The rab mag led his army south, the Hedjet on his head.[5]

Unimpeded, the prince advanced through Judah. He was moving on Jerusalem—which was now recognized as the capital of an enemy state, and on Sais—where the traitor Necho reigned.

CHAPTER 47

The Faithful

Anathoth, Judah

Nebuchadnezzar was coming.

Anathoth, northeast of Jerusalem in the territory of Benjamin, stood high on a ridge of hills, which provided a spectacular view of the Jordan River. Hilkiah the Priest and his brothers Maaseiah the Elder and Shallum stood together outside the gate that opened onto the small plaza their houses shared. They looked out at the panoramic vista from over a large mound of upraised earth—the burial place of their shrine. Anathoth had belonged to their family for over 650 years, ever since it was allocated to them by Joshua ben Nun.

"Thirteen years until the Jubilee, and we'll be back," Shallum murmured.[1]

Maaseiah shook his grizzled head. "There are seventy years of judgment coming. Perhaps our families will return after that."

"It is hard to leave," Hilkiah acknowledged sadly.

Phineas ben Hilkiah was loading the last of their families' belongings into their carts. He set his wife on the top of the bundle, next to his mother, and put his baby son in her lap. Shallum's son, Hanamel took the headstall of the biggest of the donkeys and led it, with his mother, past the patriarchs, out the gate, and onto the road that led down the hill. Phineas ben Hilkiah followed Hanamel. Shallum ben Shallum, the youngest of the three patriarchs, took the last donkey and wagon, with his wife, and followed Phineas.

In two months, Phineas would be thirty years old. Hilkiah shuddered. He only had one son to carry on his name, because Jeremiah belonged to God. But if it had been two months later, the patriarch of the sons of Abiathar may have been left with only his baby grandson. At thirty, Phineas would have been ordained as a Temple priest and no longer able to freely leave. He would have been required to stay and so await the destruction to come. But Phineas was still only twenty-nine. Hilkiah's son and his younger cousin had left the Temple service under the direction of their cousin, Zephaniah, and had returned home. They were safe.

Hilkiah shut the gate. He felt old. He was fifty-three, he was three years too old to serve in the Temple any more. Maaseiah was fifty-two and Shallum had turned fifty only four months ago. All were dismissed from Temple obligations and they too were safe.

Hilkiah had lived a long life that had seen many changes. Once, he had been the Priest of the Ark. He had given himself to its service and that of the shrine, but King Josiah had put an end to that. The Ark was in the Temple. The Shrine of Anathoth lay buried under the mound and now, the former priest was even losing his home.

And not all of the children were younger than thirty. Not all were safe. "It is hard to leave," he repeated.

"It would be harder to stay," Maaseiah answered shouldering a blanket stuffed with personal articles. "It doesn't pay to doubt your Jeremiah. Anathoth is doomed. Nebuchadnezzar will be here soon, just as he said."

"He said Nebuchadnezzar was king, but Nebuchadnezzar is only rab mag." Even after all this time, it was hard for Hilkiah to picture his son as anything but the small boy he had taught to tend the shrine and the Ark. "I am still not convinced that we are not deserting Anathoth too early."

Maaseiah was surprised. "My Zephaniah said that your Jeremiah told us to get out. Do you doubt your own son?"

"No, I'm saying I believe him. That means there is nothing to worry about until Nebuchadnezzar actually inherits his throne."

"Zephaniah was pretty clear," Shallum broke in, stopping the donkey. "Jeremiah said to get out of Anathoth. Hilkiah, that boy of yours was chosen when he was very young. He has been a prophet almost his entire life and he knows things we don't. I don't know why he was set apart, I haven't a clue.

"Well, maybe I do, he has the courage of a lion. He is braver than the rest of us put together. You should be proud."

"Of course, I am, but because of him, here we are, heading down the road with everything we own."

"The new owners are moving in tomorrow," Shallum pointed out. "It's a little late to be vacillating."

"We have been warned and we're giving heed to the warning!" Maaseiah declared. He turned to Shallum, "The new owners are fools. They shouldn't be looking for bargain properties; they should be coming with us." He put his arm over his brother's shoulder. "Hilkiah, you say it's hard to leave, and it is. You are not the only one with doubts here. I have to keep reminding myself, you are leaving Jeremiah behind. But your Phineas? We are ensuring he and his family will be safe. Shallum, you are leaving your son, my namesake Maaseiah. But your youngest, Hanamel and his wife and daughter are safe.

"And then I think, what about my sons? How can I leave both of them? They are both priests in the Temple and they trust in it. They will not listen to their cousin though he is yelling in their ears! How can I leave my children?"

"If we were to stay in Anathoth, it would not help Zephaniah or Zedekiah, brother," Hilkiah said. "They are grown men. They must make their own decisions."

"They are in the Temple service and are not free to leave. But they are serving the Lord," Shallum put in. "He will protect them. Jeremiah is His mouthpiece. Maaseiah keeps His gate. Zedekiah interprets His word for the people and Azariah has just named Zephaniah the Fourth Priest after Jehoiada and Buzi. The Lord *is* blessing them. He will protect them all. We must have faith."

"Jeremiah has the Lord's promise. We know he will survive. But you see?" Maaseiah dropped his arm from his Hilkiah's shoulder and raised both his hands in an exaggerated shrug. "Both of you have stronger faith than I. Fourth Priest in the land, you say. A priest of Anathoth?" Maaseiah joked. "A descendant of Abiathar? *That* is proof of miracles!" He sobered, "But is serving the Lord supposed to be a guarantee? How many innocent priests died at the hands of Saul?"

Hilkiah gestured at the town. "The other children of Abiathar have their roots here too and they are not leaving. These are our people, the children of Aaron. Is the Lord going to protect them?"

"They've heard Jeremiah's words. Some of them were right there at his door when he said them," Shallum pointed out. "They should know as well as we do that Anathoth is doomed. *They're* the reason it is doomed. The wagons are loaded. It's time to leave."

"That's my pack," Hilkiah tried to pull it from his younger brother's back.

Shallum laughed. "You only get it back if you can take it!" He trotted down the hill pulling his reluctant donkey and wagon behind him.

"I'm not that old!" Hilkiah objected, and hurried after him.

Maaseiah bent down and kissed the mound of earth in front of their former homes. King Josiah buried the uncut stones of the shrine there; the shrine that had housed the Ark of the Covenant for three centuries. Maaseiah blinked back tears and then he turned his back on the view of the Jordan gorge. He hurried after the small tribe who had set their faces toward their kinsmen in the desert country of the Negev.

Jerusalem, Judah

Nebuchadnezzar was coming.

The flight of the Egyptians from Riblah passed through Judah. It alerted Pharaoh Necho's officials in Jerusalem, and they fled the city. Ebedmelech went with them.

The people panicked.

Abda ben Sabaan went to the Temple to meet with his sodh and pray in one of the side rooms of the south annex. It would have been his first objective even if there was something else he could have done, as it was, it was the only thing he could do. The wealthy Bethlehemite merchant arrived to find the entrances to the side rooms barred. The Temple Guard was busy ushering those within out into the courtyard, where they joined an ever-growing and increasingly agitated crowd. Though Abda struggled to stay abreast of the entrance, the crowd pushed him backward, along the sides of the structure. Still, he had caught a glimpse of what was happening there.

The Levite singers were nowhere to be seen. Instead, Chief Priest Azariah, dressed in the full authority of the high priesthood, was standing on the Temple Porch. His tall white linen turban towered above all—the thronging mob couldn't help but see him. The twelve jewels of the golden breastplate shimmered in the sun. The chime of the bells and tinkling of the pomegranates on his hem were inaudible in the uproar of the Temple Court. Three priests, Jehoiada, Buzi, and Zephaniah of Anathoth, stood directly to his left, to his right stood his son and heir, Seraiah.

The four attendants of the Chief Priest were attired as sons of Aaron, visually stating their authority by their priestly turbans and richly embroidered tunics. Their long blue sashes trailed behind. These men on the porch were God's authority on earth.

Below the five men on the steps were two other groups: to Azariah's right stood the rest of sacerdotal priests, to his left, the Temple Prophets. Before all these, forming a protective semi-circle on the pavement, was the full contingent of the Temple Guard, led by Captain Pashur. The priests and guard were shouting above the tumult, attempting to quiet the crowd, but the masses were growing more unruly by the moment.

"Go home!" Seraiah yelled, but his voice was drowned out by the crowd.

Abda, who was still being forced backward, heard, but most were not interested in listening, even when they could hear.

Second Priest Jehoiada, though a very old man, could still yell quite loudly. He added his voice to Seraiah's. "Go home! You are pulling the priests from their duties! If you are seeking the Lord's protection, then go away and leave us so that we can offer prayers and sacrifices!"

The crowd was an agitated blur of boiling color. "Jeremiah was right!" a voice from somewhere within the mass screamed back at the priests. "You so-called priests and prophets have lied to us, and now you think we want you to represent us to the Lord?"

The mob surged forward, plowing into the guard. The guard, their elbows locked together, held their place and the crowd bounced back. The sudden movement in the opposite direction and the consequent release of pressure caught Abda unawares, and the nobleman lost his balance. The crowd pushed forward again, and the Temple Guard rebuffed them. Those to the fore of the throng fell back against those still pushing forward. The crowd was like waves, crashing back and forth against the rocks of a stony coast. It pressed in against the Bethlehemite until Abda thought he was going to suffocate.

Then, somehow, he found himself in front of the abomination of the northern annex.

Abda had steadfastly avoided the north side of the courtyard, but now he was smashed up against the very doorpost of the house of Egypt's idols. Another surge of the crowd pushed him tumbling inside on a crest of humanity to land sprawling at the golden feet of the Bull of Amentet. The surreal paintings of Egypt's improbable imaginations loomed above him on the walls mocking and laughing at their unholy triumph.

"Azariah," he heard someone outside screaming. "Your father was Chief Priest under Josiah, and he oversaw the cleansing of this Temple from this very sort of thing!"

Abda managed to locate the speaker: he was waving a little golden idol with a falcon head, crowned with the red and white Pschent crown. Abda didn't have a clue what it was supposed to represent.

"How could you have let this happen again?" the man raged.

"Zephaniah, Zedekiah!" another shouted, "you are Jeremiah's cousins! Why didn't you believe? Why didn't you warn us?"

The roar was deafening now, and any answer by the priests or prophets was lost in the tumult.

The people, held back from the priests, poured right through the north annex and attacked the Wood House shrine to the rear. Someone was using a miniature Isis as a club to batter down an Ashtareth.

Abda was still in the annex, where the people were crushed up against the Bull of Amentet. It began to topple. Abda was struck in the head by its haunch and was knocked to the ground. He smacked his face flat against the tiles and broke his nose.

The people swarmed over him.

Abda couldn't breathe.

For an instant, all he could see was the red of blinding pain. He was going to die. Gasping, he realized he was going to die in a heathen shrine underneath Apis, Aaron's calf, the very symbol of Israel's idolatry. "No Lord!" he cried out to the floor, and he felt his ribs cracking under the feet of his people. "If I must die, let me do it with my family! Please!"

At least, he hadn't brought Daniel with him today. Daniel would not be harmed by this madness.

Someone grabbed him under the arms and pulled him out from under the idol and the deadly tread of his countrymen. He shook his head, and as his vision cleared, he saw that he was being pulled and pushed out the doorway of the shrine to the safety of the annex steps by a young man. "Thank you. May the Lord bless you."

The lad solicitously sat Abda down on the desecrated steps and wiped Abda's face with his own grubby tunic. "Will the Lord bless any of us?" he returned.

Abda knew him now, he was a young priest of the House of Zadok, destined to be one of the sacerdotal priests, the elite. "Kohen, should you be here?"

"I'm not Kohen, not yet. I'm only eighteen. I'm Ezekiel ben Buzi. Are you all right?"[2]

"I've seen you; you used to sit in Jeremiah's sodh when he taught."

"Sometimes. When I could. Are you all right?" Ezekiel asked him again.

"I… I think I will be. I'm Abda ben Sabaan."

"King Josiah's cousin. I know. That would not have been a good place to die," the young priest observed.

"That's what I was thinking. That and that you should not be setting foot in that abominable annex."

Ezekiel gestured to his dirty and very unpriestly garment. "I have already made myself unclean today. I was out collecting the bones around the Molech and burying them. Someone needed to, and I'm not yet Kohen, so I could. It will be a week before I can be made clean again but Jerusalem? How can she be made clean from *any* of this?

"The elders can't very well just break a heifer's neck and claim ignorance. *Everyone* knows about the Molech, so *everyone* is guilty, and no heifer could erase that! I have done what I could at the Topheth, but *this* abomination remains. So, the people started rioting, and I thought that since I am already unclean…"

"You have come here, and so the Lord has used even the unclean. It is by His grace that I am saved. Thank you and may the Lord bless you, Ezekiel."

Ezekiel gave him a crooked smile. "It will be His blessing if He yet grants us a week before the Babylonians come because by then I will be clean again." He added seriously, "I hope so because I don't want to die in this state." He wrinkled his nose distastefully and stood. Then he helped Abda up.

Abda managed to totter off the steps back to the front of the crowd. Out of the corner of his eye, he saw Ezekiel step back into the annex, saw him pulling down miniature idols from their shelves, and smashing the false deities on the floor.

The riot continued in the court.

At that moment, over the roar, Abda heard shouted orders and the clash of arms from behind the West and the New Gates. The Palace Guard had arrived to reinforce the Temple Guard. They began to clear the Temple Court. Unlike the Temple Guard, the Palace Guard were not priests. They had no compunction against entering the annex or the shrine. They did both and they forcibly restored order.

Abda saw two of them hauling the protesting son of Buzi away. He was waving one of the golden horns of the Egyptian bull in the air. Abda wondered how he had managed to break it off.

Captain Pashur was about to order the Temple Guard to join the guard from the palace, but at a word from Chief Priest Azariah the captain kept them where they were, guarding the steps to the Temple.

Captain Elnathan of the Palace Guard pushed his way through the throng to confront the Chief Priest. "Just what do you think you are doing? Are you just going to stand there and let the people tear the place down?"

Azariah ben Hilkiah looked down at the father of the queen from the height of the Temple Steps, his tall white hat caused him to tower even higher. "We are protecting the Lord's House. The house of the gods of Egypt has no right to the protection of the Temple Guard, nor does Baal's shrine. What the people do to them is not our concern."

Elnathan said something very unsuitable in the presence of a Chief Priest and turned back to the business at hand. The troublemakers were arrested, and the Palace Guard set the toppled idols back in their places while the Temple Guard merely watched.

Abda cradled his ribs and grinned at the destruction. Then he turned and made his way back to the southern annex for his appointment with his sodh. This time, he gained entrance.

CHAPTER 48

The Unrighteous

Jerusalem, Judah

Nebuchadnezzar arrived.[1]

It was the third week of the fifth month and King Jehoiakim couldn't wait, not any longer. The armies of Babylon were a sea washing up on the shores of the all too tiny isle of Jerusalem. The king had to take action. Except he had no idea what action he should take. Egypt's advisors had deserted him. His own advisors had no advice, only blame.

Anathoth was gone. Nebuchadnezzar's whirlwind arrival had taken the citizens of the town by surprise. Even though the sons of Abiathar had been alerted by the fleeing Egyptians that the rab mag was coming, there was no way they could have imagined him traveling so quickly. Common sense told them that the Babylonians would have been delayed by having to conquer the territory through which they marched. They could not have known that their countrymen had actually aided the Babylonians on their way. Having no time to flee to the safety of Jerusalem's walls, the men of Anathoth perversely refused to believe the warnings of Jeremiah.

They did not surrender, they attacked.

Nebuchadnezzar swatted them like a fly.

The Prince of Babylon made an example out of the priests of Anathoth. The Babylonians killed all of the young men. Then, under the rab mag's orders, they allowed the rest of the population to flee in terror to Jerusalem. The women, children and the elderly increased the mouths Jerusalem had to feed without adding anything to the city's defense. Anathoth's dead were piled in the town square, and Nebuchadnezzar ordered the city burnt to the ground. Now, a black cloud of smoke drifted over Jerusalem's wall. The wailing of the bereaved village folk was added to the screams and shouts of the people of Jerusalem. The already panicking citizens went mad, and the streets were raging with terror-stricken citizens.

As King, it was up to Jehoiakim to do something. Jehoiakim's Judean advisors with all seventy of the Council of Elders stood in the audience hall. They debated and argued before the king as he sat on his Egyptian-style stool and Nebuchadnezzar sat at his gates. The architecture of the remodeled throne room, its cedar walls plastered over and brightly painted with Egyptian gods, mocked him—the Egyptians themselves had fled.

"Who could have foreseen this? Why haven't plans been laid for this eventuality?" the king demanded. His words met with a sudden silence, and he saw the answer in the eyes of every one of the men before him.

Jeremiah *had* foreseen it. King Jehoiakim had chosen not to listen. The thought haunted him. Jeremiah couldn't be right. But he had certainly been right about Anathoth.

"No," he answered their unspoken accusation. "Jerusalem is not doomed!"

Ahikam ben Shaphan came forward. For four years, Ahikam had been spokesman for the Seventy. Shaphan, King Josiah's prime minister, had retired and for four years, Ahikam had used his position to try to influence the new prime minister, Elishama, and to steer the course of the wayward king's administration. For four years, Secretary Elishama had ignored the spokesman because the secretary was full of himself and listened to none but Jehoiakim.

Considering the circumstances, Ahikam now dealt directly with the king. "Majesty," he began, "the Babylonians pride themselves on their civilized behavior. They will listen to reason. We haven't actually done anything against them, at least not yet. We've broken no treaties; we never had one with them. We had every right to ally ourselves with Egypt.

"However, your father *did* take King Nabopolassar's hand. Even though the King of Babylon never called *you* friend, Rab Mag Nebuchadnezzar is understandably upset. If you were to open the gates to him and submit…"

"And agree to become a vassal state I suppose? Where is your real allegiance, Ahikam? Are you in Babylon's pay? You and your father, you couldn't get King Josiah to bow and scrape to Marduk, but you thought you'd have a chance with my brother, didn't you? How disappointed you must have been when Necho carried Jehoahaz off to Egypt and you were stuck with me in his place!" The king turned on his secretary, "And you are no better! Elishama, I expect you to keep the government running smoothly, that means keeping this council in line!"

The king's secretary pursed his lips but said nothing.

"My King," Captain Elnathan of the Palace Guard spoke up. The king was his son-in-law, so perhaps he would listen. "My King, I have friends and commercial contacts in Egypt, as you well know. Since that is so, you know that I am not now, or ever would be, in the pay of Babylon. But though it leaves a bitter taste in my mouth to say it, I agree with Ahikam ben Shaphan. He's right. If you do not wish to see Jeremiah's prophecies fulfilled right here and now, you *must* surrender. Repudiate your alliance with Egypt, and enter into a new treaty, one with the Babylonians.

"We are indeed the children of the Lord, but we are a small nation. We couldn't possibly pose a threat to Babylonia and Nebuchadnezzar will be happy not to have to bother with us when he still has to deal with Egypt."

"You!" Jehoiakim spat back. He leaned forward on his stool and glared. "You think I'm not on to you? You are looking for Nebuchadnezzar to take me away in chains so that your grandson will inherit! Do you remember where you hung Uriah's head on the Horse Tower?" He pointed in the direction. "That place is currently unoccupied."

It was an empty threat, no one could get to the outside of the wall to hang anything there, but Elnathan bowed his head and backed away from the madman on the throne.

General Kareah ben Nathan, the head of Judah's army was also there. After that last outburst, the general hesitated, then came forward anyway. He had led the forces of Judah since the days of Josiah and was known for his courage. He needed it to stand before the king in his present mood. "My King, if I may…"

"Are you against me as well? I am very aware that you stood with Ahikam here and rescued Jeremiah when the people would have stoned him. As I recall, Jeremiah was preaching some incredibly seditious ideas at the time. Are you pro-Babylonian too?"

"No, Majesty. I and all my men are for you, but…"

"But?"

"My King, I have no love whatsoever for the Babylonians. Like you, I would lose much, maybe even my freedom, if you agree to this surrender. But I would save my life and the lives of my family. We cannot win…"

"The Lord will not let His city fall!" Jehoiakim yelled.

The stunned silence told the king that his advisors were dumbfounded that he, the man who had disposed of a prophet, would resort to such an argument. *"Jeremiah is wrong!"* He howled at them.

The elders remained silent.

"You are all in this together against me," Jehoiakim whispered into the accusing silence. "You've been against me from the beginning. You chose my brother in secret over me, and when pharaoh corrected this injustice, you plotted against me to bring this day and my downfall. If I do not do this…"

"My King," General Kareah protested, "I am unaware of *any* plot against you! But if we surrender, we may yet live. The King of Babylon has a reputation for leniency, and the rab mag is his son. The Babylonians are bound by honor. They can be trusted to abide by their sworn word. Bargain before you open the gates, and it may be that you will even keep your crown.

"You are not a military man, and you do not think like one. But this is a military matter. We have the only thing that the rab mag values at this moment—time. He will likely agree to much to be free to continue on his way. Egypt flees before him, and he must be able to press his advantage as quickly as possible. He will jump at the excuse to pass us by. Go to the wall and bargain with him. If you make him a reasonable offer, he will accept."

The king had not thought of this. "But… We will certainly have to surrender our sovereignty to Babylon. We will be aligned against Egypt…" He shook his head.

"Majesty," Captain Elnathan dared to speak once more, "from the way things look, Egypt may not last much longer anyway. We are already a vassal state, we would just be switching masters but one way or the other, we are going to end up changing masters. It would be wise to do it on our terms."

Jehoiakim searched the faces of the men before him. "You are all agreed on this?"

The elders of the Council murmured their assent.

Jehoiakim rose from his throne and threw up his arms in exasperation. What could he do, if the Seventy were against him and both the Palace guard and the army supported them? If he didn't listen to them, what would they do?

He didn't want to find out.

Desperately, he tried another tact. "The Babylonians hate Egypt. Maybe if we just surrender the idols of the Temple Court to them, starting with those of Egypt… That will clean out both the north annex of the Temple and the Wood House. It should please the priests and the Lord!"

Most of the Council was watching him with strange expressions on their faces.

He explained, "Babylon will then see we have rejected Egypt because Egypt has abandoned us. They will see that we are no threat."

"My King," Captain Elnathan objected, "this will be viewed as a rejection of Egypt, certainly, but… we would only be giving them something that was not ours to begin with. It will hardly be viewed as a surrender. It will look more like a bribe; as if we are trying to buy them."

"We *are* trying to buy them!"

"Great King, we cannot possibly buy Babylon."

"Just what are you trying to say?"

"We must show them that we capitulate totally in a way that they can understand. We must open the gates to them and… Majesty, the Babylonians take a country's gods hostage when they subjugate them. Surrendering Egypt's gods does not qualify."

Jehoiakim laughed. "I hardly think that even Nebuchadnezzar can take the Lord of All the Earth captive."

"No, My King, but he is both young and a foreigner. He can't be expected to understand that. We have no idols to surrender, however…"

Jehoiakim cut him off. "The Ark? No! Never! It is the very heart of our country." Unexpectedly, he laughed. "Though it would be amusing to see all the men of Babylon hobbling along down to Egypt stricken with hemorrhoids and boils. But no. Not the Ark."

"No, Lord. Of course, not the Ark," Captain Elnathan denied the notion. "But there are the gold and silver accouterments in the House of the Lord…"

The sons of Shaphan turned to Prime Minister Elishama and began to urgently confer with him and amongst themselves. They were not happy with the suggestion, and King Jehoiakim knew it. Perversely, that made him feel more open to it. He sank back down on his royal stool and thought about it. "Will the rab mag find this to be acceptable?"

"Perhaps," Elnathan was not confident of this.

"My King," Prime Minister Elishama put in, "the people…"

"Wish to keep on living." Jehoiakim cut him off. "Do you?"

The secretary fell silent, and the king was too inexperienced to realize that even though Elishama was his cousin, he was making himself an enemy that he would do well to watch in the future.

"Very well," Jehoiakim continued after a pause. "We must cooperate in every conceivable way and give the Babylonians no excuse to move on us. General Kareah, if that is what it takes, then take what men you find necessary to deal with the priests and Temple Guard and go empty the Temple of its treasure."

The general hesitated, a worried look on his face, but he was first and foremost a soldier. He obeyed orders even when he didn't agree. Kareah bowed and left.

CHAPTER 49

A True Prophet

Jerusalem, Judah

Nebuchadnezzar did not enter Jerusalem. The rab mag had gone no further than the outer wall of the city and established himself in one of the cubicles of the northeast gate, the Horse Gate. Jehoiakim's advisors were correct: Nebuchadnezzar was not interested in entering the city itself, just in wrapping up business as quickly as possible and continuing on to Sais, the Capital of Egypt. Accordingly, he had required King Jehoiakim to come to him in the gate. It wasn't far, the Horse Gate opened on the palace court.

"The Lion of Judah, Anointed of the Lord, Jehoiakim son of Josiah, King of the Promised Land," Zedekiah ben Hananiah, Jehoiakim's new announcer, carried out his duties—first in Hebrew, then in Aramaic.

Jehoiakim, in full royal dress, but wearing only the small daily crown, entered the little office trembling. He was followed by Prime Minister Eliakim, the head of the army, General Kareah ben Nathan, and Captain Elnathan ben Achbor of the Palace Guard, the king's father-in-law.

No one announced Nebuchadnezzar, it was rightfully assumed that everyone knew who he was, and besides, he was only his father's representative. The rab mag was seated on a bench behind a little table. Kadurri was flanked by a half-dozen armed imperial guards, by Rab Shaq Belshumishkun, his personal daggerman, Nebuzaradan, his personal recorder, Nergalsharusar, his brother, Prince Nebushumlishtar with Marshipar, *his* daggerman, and the eunuch Ashpenaz.

As King Jehoiakim stood there, his fear began to be replaced by rage. He had been summoned like a palace servant and then humiliated by being forced to stand silent, waiting on the rab mag to speak.

Kadurri sized up Josiah's son then spoke. But he spoke no Hebrew and Jehoiakim spoke no Aramaic. "Is it your intention to surrender without reservation?"

Nergalsharusar interpreted.

"It is," Jehoiakim growled in Hebrew, but his eyes showed there was some lingering fear behind the bravado.

Once more, Shar translated.

"You don't speak Aramaic," Nebuchadnezzar observed through his translator. "How about Egyptian?"

"Not really, but I have been trying to learn," Jehoiakim answered defiantly.

Nebuchadnezzar smiled and shrugged. "Well, now you can be adding Aramaic to your linguistic skills." Shar continued to translate. "Are you going to cause me trouble?"

Jehoiakim thought about it for a second. "No, Great One. We are ready to acknowledge the terms of surrender."

The rab mag nodded and gestured to a seat on the other side of the table which served as a desk.

Jehoiakim sat and laid the heavy gold plate he had been carrying on the table before Kadurri. Prime Minister Elishama handed a scroll to Annunciator Nergalsharusar, and Shar began to read, translating into Aramaic. "These are the offerings to signify our surrender. In return for the privilege of the protection of the Empire of Babylonia and as a Babylonian province, Judah offers a tenth of the inventory of silver and gold vessels from the Temple…"

Nebuchadnezzar held up his hand, and the recorder stopped instantly.

The rab mag picked up the single golden plate that Jehoiakim had provided as an example, a tenth of the "entire inventory" would never have fit in the little office. The plate was solid gold and very heavy. The brim was engraved with the curious writing of the Hebrews. "Ashpenaz?" Kadurri prompted.

The eunuch stood close by, and he came forward to inspect the plate the prince offered him. "Holy to the Lord," he said simply.

The rab mag shrugged and dropped it carelessly on the desk. "Continue," he said to the recorder.

"In rejection of Egypt, Jerusalem offers the images of the gods of the Two Lands, currently housed in the northern annex of the Temple of the Lord." the recorder consulted his notes and named them one by one. "A full-sized Horus, made of green basalt, a half-size Isis, made of ivory, a full-sized Bull of Amentet, overlaid with gold, but damaged and missing one horn, ten golden disks of Ra…" the list was very long, but the recorder read it all.

"In recognition of the dominance of Babylonia over all surrounding lands, and in accordance with our priests' desires, Jerusalem adds the images of the gods from the shrine known as the Wood House—a full-sized carved ebony Baal, a matching full-sized Asherah, a Dagon of the style of Tyre…" again, the list went on and on.

"It's acceptable," Kadurri acknowledged. "Is that it?"

"For the initial surrender, yes Great One," the recorder said.

Nebuchadnezzar nodded though he noted that there was nothing at all from the palace treasury. He didn't care. Now was not the time for haggling. "Have it all sent to Ekua," he ordered. The storehouse of Marduk had vast treasure rooms. "Has the surrender been drawn up?"

"Yes, Great One," the recorder said and produced two clay tablets, still soft and encased in their wooden frames.

The rab mag pushed them across the table for Jehoiakim's inspection.

They were written in cuneiform and Hebrew.

The King of Judah did not even look at them.

"You have something else to say?" Kadurri was curious. "Now would be the time."

Jehoiakim suddenly gave a bitter laugh. "It is, but it isn't. It's what he said, and yet it's certainly *NOT* what he said. The first thing I do when I leave here is put that so-called prophet to death."

"What prophet?" Kadurri was even more curious now.

"Jeremiah. The one that the priests should have stoned. I'm going to behead him! He said you were coming and Egypt would be defeated."[1]

"Really? You have a prophet that said I was coming? Not my father? Did you have other information, other sources, announcing that I was coming?"

"Not until the Egyptians came through four days ago."

"Yet Jeremiah said I was coming, and not my father?" Kadurri insisted.

"He said Egypt was defeated, and you were coming, but he also said that we are going to go into exile! Is that true? It doesn't look like it to me!"

"Well some of you will be, but that will be up to the ambassador I leave behind."

This was news to Jehoiakim, and he looked wildly around at his men for advice, but they wouldn't meet his eyes.

"What else did Jeremiah say?" Kadurri was fascinated. The prophecies of the Akitu were pure fantasy and vague at that, but this was incredibly specific.

Jehoiakim shrugged. "It doesn't matter. It was inaccurate, and I'm going to behead him," he insisted sullenly.

"What did he say?"

Jehoiakim sighed and turned to his secretary. "Elishama? Tell the rab mag Jeremiah's latest."

The prime minister stepped forward, looking troubled. He too spoke in Hebrew, "I haven't seen it written Lord King, I only heard him."

"Then tell him what you told me!" Jehoiakim barked at him.

Secretary Elishama glared back at the king, then he nodded and dipped his head politely at the rab mag. "Briefly, he said of Pharaoh Necho that he would be defeated at Carchemish. That he should get his shields in order, harness up his horses, get his army ready and march out into battle."

Nebuchadnezzar abruptly stood up and leaned across the table and its tablets. He was angry and amazed at the same time. "He said Necho should ride out of Carchemish?"

"That's what I hear," Jehoiakim affirmed. He wanted to ask why this angered the rab mag, but he was in no position to be asking questions.

Nebuchadnezzar rounded on General Belshumishkun, "How is that possible?"

The rab shaq shook his head. "It's not. Lord, only the Kings of Media and Assyria, plus your generals knew that we planned to follow Sharuken's ancient strategy and draw him out of the fortress. There could have been no leak of this information."

"When did he say this?" Kadurri demanded of Josiah's son.

"Eight days ago, just after sunrise. He stood in the palace court and…"

"As it was happening?" the rab mag was dazed.

No one said anything.

After a few moments, Kadurri incredulously took his seat once more. "What else did he say? Tell me all of it.

Jehoiakim nodded at his secretary and Elishama continued. "He pretended he saw something far away to the north. He asked the sky what he was looking at, or maybe he asked *why* he was looking at it, I'm not sure what he meant, then he said that Egypt's army was terrified, retreating defeated. I believe he stated that there was 'terror on every side.'"

"That's a favorite phrase of the man, lately," Jehoiakim put in dryly.

"Yes, Lord King," Eliakim affirmed. "Then he said that warriors from Cush, Put and Lydia would go down in surging rivers of blood—or something like that—and that their warriors would stumble over each other in their haste to flee. Finally, he commanded that his words be relayed to Egypt, to tell them that you were coming and would lay waste to their land. The king's head of protocol was Egyptian. When he heard that, he packed up and left for Sais, presumably to relay Jeremiah's message."

Nebuchadnezzar drew a shaky breath. "And that is exactly what happened. So, how can you say Jeremiah is inaccurate?" he demanded of the Judean king.

"Because he didn't just say you were coming, he said, and I quote exactly: 'Nebuchadnezzar, *King* of Babylon and his officers!' Forgive me, Rab Mag, but he said you were king. He's made several prophecies lately saying the same thing. How could he get a detail like that wrong? He's crazy."[2]

Kadurri shifted uneasily on his bench. "One mistake. He's still unbelievably precise."

"An error is an error! If a prophet makes one mistake, *just one,* he is no messenger of the Lord! The Lord makes no mistakes. A man claiming to come from the Lord, who prophesies inaccurately, is a false prophet! The Lord has not sent him, and the priests are supposed to have him stoned! He said you were king. So, since the priests will not stone him, I will behead him. I'll do it myself!"

Despite himself, Kadurri snorted. "Do you kill all your prophets for one error? With those kinds of requirements, I could do away with all the prophets and priests in Esagila."

"He's not *my* prophet! He claims to be the Prophet of the Lord to the Nations. That grand sounding title makes him as much your prophet as ours."

Prime Minister Elishama cleared his throat.

"You have something to add?" Kadurri asked him.

"The prophet also said that when you came, the town of Anathoth would be destroyed. He said it months ago. Yesterday, it came true."

The rab mag exchanged a startled look with the rab shaq then he turned back to the prime minister. "You say he is a prophet. Your king says he's crazy. What do the people say?"

"They're divided, Great One."

"Fine." He turned back to Jehoiakim. "You're *not* going to kill him. You are not to touch one hair on Jeremiah's head. Understand?"

Jehoiakim shot a look of absolute fury at his secretary.

"Is that understood?" the menace in Nebuchadnezzar's tone was unmistakable.

Now was not the time to argue. "Understood."

"Then back to business," he nudged the tablets fractionally closer to the king. "These are the terms of the surrender, here before you." King Jehoiakim barely gave the tablets a cursory look. He just glared at his new overlord and pressed his nail to them both.

Nebuchadnezzar raised an eyebrow. He would have made sure he read them very carefully. But he could hardly take offense that this petty king took his word for the document. With a half-smile, he pressed his thumbnail beside Jehoiakim's, then added the authority of his father's signet ring. Recorder Nergalsharusar and Secretary Elishama witnessed it, and Judah became a province of the Empire of Babylonia.

Though Kadurri didn't like the King of Judah very much, the rab mag decided that he was behaving sensibly and he deemed him unlikely to cause any more trouble for the present. He dismissed the problem of Jehoiakim and his policies for a later time.

He had other things to attend to. The prince was simply relieved at Jerusalem's capitulation. The "siege" had started one day and ended the next—only two days' delay in the pursuit of the Egyptians. Allowing Jehoiakim to keep his throne was a small price to pay for such an unlooked-for advantage. He smiled to himself. He had the distinct impression that Jehoiakim had not agreed to any of this willingly. The tension between the king and his secretary seemed to hang in the very air. Kadurri decided that the King of Judah would be well advised to go to his Temple and thank his God that his advisors seemed to be wiser than he.

"Ashpenaz, you are appointed Temporary Ambassador and Overlord until my father should send someone to fill the post permanently." The Chaldean eunuch looked up, surprised.

The rab mag read the look. The Chaldean had expected Prince Nebushumlishtar to be assigned the position. "My brother will continue on to Sais with me. I'll need him there. Messengers have already been dispatched to Babylon. A permanent ambassador should be here within a moon and a half."

Ashpenaz grinned broadly at this unexpected honor.

"As my personal representative, you have the duty under my authority of bringing the Province of Judah into order, according to accepted policies and the terms of the surrender. I leave it to your discretion to decide what that means."

CHAPTER 50

Consequences

Jerusalem, Judah

hat afternoon, King Jehoiakim sat impatiently behind his desk in his office when his brother, Prince Mattaniah arrived.

"Finally!" the king snapped. "You took your time. I need you to stand in as an official. You're holding things up. The sooner we finish things here today, the sooner things can get back to normal."

"My house is all the way down by the market," Mattaniah pointed out. Then he came around the desk and stood behind the king. "Of course, I'll stand in," he said as if he had a choice, "but why me?"

"Ebedmelech has fled back to Egypt," Jehoiakim growled.

"Yes, because the Babylonians would have killed him. But what about Secretary Elishama?"

"Elishama is out of favor."

"But surely, one of the Council, Ahikam ben Shaphan, or…"

"Mattaniah! They are all plotting against me!"

"That can't be so…"

"They blame me for all of this. Why would I want them to be a part of anything? They're traitors. By the time they would be done with this meeting, they would have the Babylonians leading me away in chains! Is that what you want?" The king turned and eyed his brother suspiciously over his shoulder.

"Eliakim! How can you say that? Why would I want that? Jeconiah is too young to have to take the throne."

"He is eleven. That is older than our father was, and you would end up as his regent. So, I repeat, is that what you want?"

Mattaniah was aghast, "You know me! I'm too… *me.* I like my house down by the market. My wives love it too. I don't want to move back to the palace, and I don't want to be regent. I don't like politics. I want no part of any of it!"

Jehoiakim nodded and looked back at the door. "You're right. That's why I sent for you in the first place. You're afraid of power; you really *don't* want any part of it. I can trust you. Only you. *You're* not plotting against me. You're my brother." He stood up and hugged Mattaniah. Then he took his seat again and called out "Guard!"

One of the palace guards poked his head through the door. "Inform the ambassador that I am ready for him."

The guard bobbed his head and disappeared. A short time later, Ambassador Ashpenaz and two Chaldean scribes were announced and shown in.

"Lord King," the ambassador crossed his arms and snapped his fingers. "I am honored by your presence at this meeting and pray that your God shall guide our minds and hands to fairly make the decisions that need to be made."

Jehoiakim decided that he would have to get used to the Babylonian gesture, but he was amazed by the Chaldean eunuch's fluency in Hebrew. The ambassador's court manners were as polished as the highest born nobleman, and his power was real. The king reminded himself that Ashpenaz could yet remove him from his throne. "I have every intention of honoring the treaty we signed this morning. At the same time, I will only go so far in giving up my freedoms or those of my people."

Mattaniah leaned forward slightly to whisper in his brother's ear. "The ambassador is a civil servant and not a soldier, brother. That should be construed as a good sign."

Jehoiakim listened to him. Mattaniah always had been clever, just timid. His instincts were good, and his insights were to be trusted.

And Ashpenaz proved it. "Your office is safe, Lord King. If not, the rab mag would already have taken away your throne. And we will not presume to enact anything here today but the time-tested standard agreements already in place throughout the empire."

That sounded encouraging. Jehoiakim smiled agreeably.

The king and his brother worked late into the first watch with the Babylonian ambassador and his contingent. While crickets began to sing outside in the garden, and a servant entered and lit the evening lamps, the scribes scratched out each point on their wax tablets. When the details were agreed upon, they transferred them to clay, scrapped the wax clean, and moved on to the next point.

Dinner was just finishing as they discussed the annual taxes. The initial tribute Jehoiakim had paid was satisfactory, but future taxes had to be hammered out.

"It's too much," Jehoiakim insisted, pushing aside his empty plate. He felt like he was a maidservant bargaining in the marketplace. It was humiliating. Perversely, he was still pleased. The Chaldean would not budge further, but there had been no bargaining at all with Necho, and Babylon's requirement was to be far less than Egypt's had been. Not that Jehoiakim was going to mention that.

"The bitu is twenty percent. We recognize that Judah is very small and not that wealthy. We will ask no more on top of it, but you must pay the twenty percent. That is non-negotiable. Esagila itself pays that much.

"In summary then," Ashpenaz reiterated the terms as the scribes recorded. "Jehoiakim ben Josiah will remain and govern under the authority of Babylon. The yearly bitu will be set at twenty percent on all profits, to be paid annually at the New Year Festival in Babylon and subject to annual review by our auditors. The people will continue their everyday lives as usual, and Judah will provide from among their best for representatives at the Babylonian court."

Jehoiakim frowned. "We have not agreed on that last point."

Ashpenaz looked up, annoyed. "It is *always* this way. The rab mag told you, and I have also informed you. It is necessary."

"To the Babylonians, it may only be a passing matter, of no great importance, but to my people…"

The Chaldean sighed wearily. "King Jehoiakim, we have been over this, and it has been a long night already. We are all tired, and there is no agreement to be reached here. This is another non-negotiable point.

"The Babylonian Empire is built on many different ethnicities and cultures. It embraces them all. All must come to see themselves as members of a vast empire. They must begin to visualize themselves as part of that empire, extending over unimaginable distances, one huge brotherhood of man. You are not being singled out by this. As we speak, Syria, Philistia and the Qedar are obediently choosing their representatives, under Chaldean guidance. I will be picking up their recruits on my return.

"As one nation among many, Judah must also be incorporated into the brotherhood. Then the City of Peace will truly be at peace. We are only trying to help you with this. Your people must be represented in their capital by those who understand them. That means Judah must provide her own representatives to the Babylonian government.

"They must be young men, not yet fully grown. They must be of your most prominent families— royal blood is preferred. I know that this means that some are likely to be your close relatives, but you cannot object to it.

"It will be painful at first to them and their families, we know that, but to deny them the opportunity solely based on sentimentality would be a crime! We want your best, those who have shown the most promise. We will set them free to realize all their potential. They will travel to Babylon to be educated, and they will enter the ranks of the Chaldeans. Do not doubt it, those who are good enough will rise to power and influence and so your people will have a voice in their own government.

"They will be Chaldeans."

"Like you?" Jehoiakim pursued, knowing what he was asking.

"Exactly like me," Ashpenaz said looking him straight in the eye.

"No," Prince Mattaniah objected. "Eliakim, you can't. May I speak?"

"I recognize my brother," Jehoiakim responded.

"Thank you, Great King." He turned to the ambassador. "How can you expect my brother the king to order this?" he asked. "I mean no disrespect Ambassador, but you *cannot* do this to a son of Abraham! No eunuch can enter into the Assembly. It is the Law. What you propose will cause these young men to lose their families, their country, their people, and even their right to worship! They will no longer be part of us!"

Ashpenaz massaged his temples wearily. "That is the point. They will be a part of *us*. This is non-negotiable.

"King Jehoiakim, if you will not do agree to this treaty in its entirety, then we will have to find someone who will."

The king laughed bitterly. "What a time to find I have a conscience, after all, eh Mattaniah? Pharaoh Necho said something to me. He said a good king was a realist. Expediency must rule conscience. And he sold his own daughter."

Mattaniah looked down at the king sadly. *"And some of your descendants, your own flesh and blood who will be born to you will be taken away, and they will become eunuchs in the palace of the King of Babylon."*[1]

"What?" Startled, Jehoiakim questioned his brother.

"Isaiah told that to King Hezekiah, a hundred years ago."

"Really?" Jehoiakim poured himself a cup of strong wine and drained it while he thought. He had never paid much attention to Scripture, but Mattaniah was good at it. "Well there, you see?" he asked his brother and slammed the cup down on the table. "It's foreordained. It's not my fault, and it's not yours. Isaiah was a true prophet, not like Jeremiah." Then he nodded, and the scribes transferred the point to the clay.

At dawn, on the palace steps before all the people, King Jehoiakim pressed his thumbnail next to that of Ashpenaz in the treaty that sealed the fate of the nation and the fate of a yet undetermined number of undesignated youth who would never fully become men.

The abrupt knock at the door interrupted Abda ben Sabaan and his family as they sat on their cushions before their low table and took their evening meal. Abda rose and went to see who was there. Daniel followed. To their surprise, they found five armed soldiers. The soldiers were Judean, not Babylonian, but they did not appear friendly. Daniel looked at his father in confusion. He had thought that it was over, that they were safe…

"What is it?" Abda asked. "What has happened?"

"You are Abda ben Sabaan?"

"Yes. Am I under arrest? What have I done?"

"Nothing. You are not under arrest. We are looking for your eldest son, Daniel."

Involuntarily, Daniel moved half a step behind his father.

Daniel's younger brother, Joash, came up next to him. He looked frightened.

"Why?" Abda asked. "What has he done?"

"Nothing. But there has been a decree. Those young men known to be of good families and possessing an active mind are to be taken to the palace. Your son is among those who must appear. He is to be tested."

"For what?"

The soldier appeared uncomfortable. "I am only a soldier. I must do as I am ordered. Your son's name appears on a list, so I have to bring him. I don't know why. I'm sorry." He reached around Abda and pulled Daniel out the door.

"Father!" The young man struggled in the soldier's iron grasp, and Abda launched himself at the king's man.

One of the other soldiers smashed him to the ground with the butt of a spear.

Joash tackled one of the soldiers and took him down, but another kicked him in the jaw and knocked him back into his mother.

She caught her son and cried out, reaching for Daniel.

"Leave my sons alone!" Abda picked himself up only to be struck by the spear in the face. His right eye, still purple-black from his broken nose at the Temple riot, took the brunt of the blow. He saw stars, and he was flattened again. This time, he rose only to his knees and shook his head dizzily. "Stop! Please!" he begged, but they were already dragging Daniel away.

"I'm sorry," the first soldier called back over his shoulder. Joash struggled back to his feet and tried to get around Abda, but his father held him back.

"Faaaather!" Daniel's panicked wail echoed in Abda's ears.

"What do you want with him?" he yelled, holding tight to the struggling Joash. Abda's wife sank down to the ground, sobbing and his other children stood in a tight group behind.

"Daanielll!" Joash yelled but was unable to free himself from his father's grip.

The soldiers looked back at them, but said nothing and kept going.

Daniel was roughly ushered through the streets of the Old City and into the courtyard of the palace. The courtyard was lit by torchlight and lamps. Guards stood at all the gates, their spears ready. The plaza thronged with many other youths. Daniel knew most of them, some well.

"What do you want with us?" He demanded of his escort. Four of the soldiers left without a word, but one stayed and explained briefly: "By order of the king, all young, unmarried youths between the ages of thirteen and eighteen of the prominent families of Jerusalem and the surrounding towns and villages must report to the palace. I'm sorry, lad." With that, he left him, fading into the indistinct shadows left by the torches.

In confusion, Daniel whirled clear around, his face to the sky, trying to make sense out of what was happening to him. "Why?" He cried out to the heavens, then, because he wasn't watching his feet, he stumbled and almost fell. As Daniel steadied himself, he suddenly spied a familiar figure. "Hananiah!" The young Jew was somehow relieved and reassured to see his cousin standing there among the others.

Hananiah ben Boaz looked up at his name and recognized Daniel. With a cry, he ran forward. The cousins met halfway and, like children, they hugged and clung to each other.

"Daniel, what is happening?" Hananiah looked as frightened as Daniel felt. "What do they want with us? They've been taking us out one by one to the guardhouse by the New Gate. Then they start asking the strangest questions…"

"Who?"

"The Babylonians."

"The Babylonians! Why? What do they want?"

"They… I don't know. They want to know what we think. Like what we feel the political repercussions could be if the Greeks were to side with Lydia and what would King Alyattes then be likely to do next? Things like that."

"That's what they asked you?"

"Yes."

Desperately, Daniel grabbed the front of his cousin's tunic. "Hananiah, what did you tell them?"

Hananiah looked at him like he was crazy. He took Daniel's hand, removed it from his clothes, and smoothed the fabric. "I told them what I thought. That Nebuchadnezzar is going to take Egypt, and obviously, he has left Lydia to the attention of the Medes. But King Alyattes isn't likely to just give up just because the Medes are at his border; he has already committed himself this year at Carchemish. And even if Egypt is defeated, if Alyattes can get the Greeks to stop squabbling long enough to join with him, then Lydia will be a major force to be reckoned with, even without Egypt. And the Greeks just might agree to join him because they don't want their Milesian brothers to gain an even greater advantage than they already have. Since we are now a Babylonian province, all this could conceivably result in the Coalition recruiting forces from Judah to march against Lydia and the Greeks, maybe even by next year.

"But Daniel, that's not the kind of a question that's meant to weed out potential troublemakers among us. What are they looking for?"

Daniel's mind raced.

"Daniel?"

Daniel snapped out of it and looked at his cousin. "You said that? Oh, Hananiah…"

"That's bad?"

"Very bad."

"Why?"

"Because you're right. You should have said something stupid like: 'Lydia's a long ways away so why should I care? And who is Alyattes anyway?'"

Daniel jumped at a bark of laughter right behind him. He turned to see one of the Chaldeans standing there. Evidently, the Babylonian understood Hebrew, and he had heard every word. "But it's a little too late for you to act stupid, isn't it?" the foreigner asked. "Let's see, you're Hananiah, and you're Daniel, right?"

Daniel and Hananiah looked at each other.

"Well, Daniel. I suspect you have a very good mind, but you're a pretty poor liar. That last bit about Alyattes would have given you away. You two had better come with me."

"Why?" Hananiah breathed the question to his cousin.

"Daniel knows why, don't you Daniel?" the Chaldean asked.

Horrified, it took Daniel several seconds before he could nod. He leaned against Hananiah and said hoarsely, "Because I do know why, and he doesn't want us spreading it around. Not yet. Not until they're done asking their questions anyway."

"But…"

"The Babylonian army hasn't started looking for recruits yet, but the eunuchs of Bit Mummi have, and we've just passed the test."

Hananiah felt his world come crashing down around him as the Babylonian took them by the shoulders and propelled them away from the others. "Ah, Lord God," he gasped.

The eunuch took them up the palace steps and handed them over to a small group of Babylonian guards stationed there. "I know how you feel," he told them. "I've been through it too. But it's really all right. It's a good thing.

"Besides, this is only the first screening. Most that make it this far still end up being rejected, but if you are chosen, it will be the greatest honor of your life. Someday, you'll understand that." He turned and left them, going back to the others that were still being questioned.

Daniel and Hananiah sank to the stone tiles of the palace porch.

There, they leaned against each other and wept in terror and despair.

All the candidates were identified. Some tried to flee or hide, but since they were all of prominent families, they were well known, and all were eventually brought into the palace grounds, even those from the outlying communities. As the night wore on, all were interviewed.

Finally, a few were separated from the others and joined Daniel and Hananiah. The rest were let go.

For once, Daniel was not pleased to see his cousins from Bethlehem, Mishael, and Azariah. They were included in those selected.

The youths were brought food and wine, the best of the palace, but no one felt much like eating.

Dawn was breaking in the east and friends, relatives and acquaintances of those still detained came to the New Gate, clamoring to be let onto the palace grounds or for their sons to be released.

"What do you want with that lazy son of mine?" Daniel looked up as he recognized his father's voice. Abda had pushed his way to the front of the crowd only to be stopped by the Palace Guard. A Chaldean stood in the palace court facing him. "Seriously, he can't even watch the sheep properly. Last week, two lambs were carried away by a wolf, ask anyone!"

"The lad is no good," the crowd roared in agreement.

"None of them are! What kind of officials are you? You have the dregs from the bottom of the wineskins there!"

In spite of himself, Daniel laughed. He very rarely had to watch the sheep but did he have a big hairy friend named Benjamin that everyone called Zeeb—Wolf. Zeeb had indeed carried off two lambs and paid Daniel a very good price for them too.

"If he is chosen," the Chaldean answered agreeably, "we will make sure he is not entrusted with any sheep."

"Chosen? Who would choose him?"

"Father!" Daniel called, and Abda turned his disfigured face towards the palace porch to catch sight of his son. "Tell Mother that I'll be all right! Tell Miriam I'll be back soon!"

The Chaldean shook his head. "Don't make promises you may not be able to keep, My Son."

"That's enough," a captain of the Temple Guard marched out of the palace and pointed his finger at the Priest of the Gate. "Close that gate on the Temple side. We've no more time for this."

Gatekeeper Maaseiah pushed the people back from the gate's meeting square into the Temple Court and sadly shut the gate on the Temple side.

The day wore on and one way or the other, the Chaldeans examined their candidates and got the facts they were looking for. The majority of the young men remaining on the palace porch were released.

Daniel and his cousins were among those who remained. Their tears had dried, but they sat together in black despair and said nothing.

By evening, the questioning was over. The Chaldeans cast lots among those who remained. The will of the gods had to be taken into account. The number of eligible youth dwindled to a dozen. Daniel, Hananiah, Azariah, and Mishael were all in that unfortunate few.

Night fell once more, but the familiar night sounds were drowned out by the persisting cries of those families at the gates demanding back their sons. On occasion, Daniel thought he could still hear his father's voice among them, but it did no good to answer, so he sat where he was.

In a daze, Daniel was barely aware when he was pulled to his feet and taken to a private courtyard nearby. Where was Miriam right now? What was she thinking with her betrothed and her brother both snatched from her? He couldn't quite grasp the concept that he was never going to see her again. He was almost certain the whole thing was a bad dream, and when he woke up, he would find that none of it was real.

In shock, he didn't even try to resist when they pushed him to the ground and pinned him down, spread-eagled. But when they pulled his robes up around his waist, he suddenly realized what they were going to do and he began to struggle and scream. It was too late. A knife flashed, and Daniel fainted.

CHAPTER 51

Chaldean Recruits

Jerusalem, Judah

aniel opened his eyes. The room spun crazily around him. He closed them again. Room? He wasn't in the courtyard anymore. He was in a bed. The pain in his groin was excruciating. Involuntarily, he groaned.

"Daniel?"

He opened his eyes again to find Mishael kneeling next to him. His cousin's face was streaked with the tracks of tears, and his eyes were red and puffy. "Mishael? Where…?" Daniel sat up and propped himself, on one hand, to keep from falling over again.

"We're in the palace. Azariah asked them to put us together, and they did." The room was filled with cots and a dozen young men. It was spacious and airy, but it was obviously a prison. Palace guards stood by the windows and door. The night sky outside was beginning to fade to gray. The lamps in the room were turned down low.

Daniel looked over to see his other two cousins sitting together whispering on another bed nearby. "Did they…?"

"Yes. To all of us. They left us wine. They said it would help some." He handed a decanter and cup to Daniel.

Daniel's hand shook, and he splashed some on the bed as he poured. He drained the vessel in one gulp and blinked back tears of his own. "How could this happen? How could the God of Israel allow this?"

"Daniel, I… I don't know. Azariah says just because God is sovereign doesn't mean He is responsible when men sin. The innocent do suffer, but the Lord hasn't caused it. That doesn't answer the question: where is justice? We have done nothing to deserve this, and He could have protected us, so, why didn't He?"

"It would have been better if they had just killed us."

"I know."

"Your sister… How will she stand this?"

Mishael wrapped his arms around him, and they clung to each other and wept until they had no more tears.

Just before sunrise, the Babylonian ambassador, a eunuch himself, came to see them. Though they tried to stand when he entered, not all managed it. The Chaldean shook his head and motioned them back down on their beds. "It's all right. Don't stand. Not yet. I certainly don't expect it. Though these beds are a lot better than I had when I was in your condition. You'll recover soon enough. I expect the pain is already better today."

They said nothing.

"You four, you're cousins, all from the House of Hezekiah." Ashpenaz looked them over, and when his eyes fell on Daniel, he stopped. "You're the one, aren't you?"

Daniel looked puzzled.

"You're Daniel, right? The one they had to separate early. You never got a chance to actually answer the first set of questions."

Daniel frowned and looked down. The memory made him angry. He should have seen that Chaldean standing there. He should have been more careful as to what he had said. He had got himself into this mess.

"Yes, I thought so. Disgusted with yourself, are you? You shouldn't be. Even if they had tested you, you'd still have ended up here. This way, I've been notified to keep an eye on you."

"You came just to see me?" Daniel was so confused by that he forgot that he wasn't going to say anything.

"Well… I came to see you all. Eventually, I need to talk to everyone. I just came to see you a little sooner than most, that's all."

"Why?"

Ashpenaz grinned. "I'm responsible for you. Didn't you know that? I have to answer to King Nabopolassar on anything and everything that Jerusalem gives to Babylon by this surrender. That includes you. You have the potential to be very valuable to the Empire, much more so than mere gold or silver. So, I have to keep an eye on you to find out just what it is that we've got."

"This is the way you treat valuable property?"

"Oh Lad, you're not property. You're family, one of our sons. You're a child of Bit Mummi."

"Hardly a 'son.'"

"A son. Daniel, your people use circumcision to initiate you into your nation. In a way, this is what we have done. You are full and legal members of the Chaldean nation. We can count you thus through your adoption because now you will never have children to whom you may pass on a foreign lineage."

"You make it sound like an honor."

"It *is* an honor. You will be immersed in the Babylonian culture and learn our ways. You are a part of us. You will learn to blend in." He looked them all over again. "You are Babylonians. This is your new identity.

"Babylonians have Babylonian names. To keep your present names would greatly handicap you in society. It would forever mark you as outsiders, of foreign origin, and you are not foreign! I am privileged to be the one who names you and gives you your new identities. This is the task of a father, and I am your father. You are my children. You are under my care, and you are going to be staying under my care. My assignment here in Jerusalem is only temporary. You will learn to trust me, and I already know that I am going to take great pride in you." Ashpenaz looked at them kindly.

"Daniel, your name means that God is your judge. You actually could keep your name because we have the same name. Our Daniel was a hero who…"

"No! I do not want people associating me with some Babylonian mythical hero!"

The outburst surprised the Chaldean, but then he grinned. "There's some spirit in you yet, I see. Very well, I'll call you…Belteshazzar. It means

'Favored of the Lord.' It's actually a contraction of Belbalatshusur which means 'the Lord guards your life.'"

Daniel looked away. He spoke only Hebrew, but he knew to the Babylonians "Bel" meant "Lord," and by it, Ashpenaz meant Marduk, not the God of Israel. He did not care to have some false god as his guardian, but despair made him feel it was useless to object further. He swallowed and looked away to the window. A bird on a tree branch began to sing, announcing the dawn. How could birds still sing?

Ashpenaz put his hand on Mishael's shoulder. Mishael flinched at the touch. "Your name asks 'Who is like God?' It's a good name. We have a similar one. You will be called Meshach."

"And you, Hananiah," the ambassador continued, placing his hand on the youth's shoulder in his turn, "your name means 'Mercy of God.' To us, this is an enigma. We believe that the gods can be merciful, but who can tell what mercy means to a god? Aku alone could read such a thing. So, I will call you Shadrach. It means 'Under the Command of Aku.' Aku is the Sumerian equivalent of the god, Sin. He reads the future and the dark destinies of all men. Aku would understand what mercy is.

"Azariah, your name means 'Helped by God,'" Ashpenaz looked genuinely sad, and he shook his perfectly coiffed head. "I'm sorry, lad, but you absolutely cannot use this name or tell people what it means if they were to ask. I'm warning you ahead of time. In Babylon, it would be viewed as blasphemy. The superstitious would take it as a bad omen that you ever had such a name and you would be shunned. We serve our gods. They do not serve us. You will learn that the reason the gods made us was to have someone to serve them. This is fundamental to our religion." He let that sink in, but Azariah's eyes were glazed over, and he showed no interest at all. Ashpenaz continued. "They tell me that you wished to be a merchant, so we will call you Abednego, it means 'Servant of Nebo.' He is the god of fire and trade, the brother of Marduk. It is a good name, and the Chaldeans need merchants, we run the largest marketplace in the world. There we will show you things about commerce that you never suspected."

Neither Hananiah nor Azariah reacted to the surprising news that a moon god and a divine merchant had become their patrons.

By now, many birds were singing. Daniel sat looking stubbornly out the window the entire time Ashpenaz spoke to them. But as he did so, his confusion grew. The Babylonian was like no other government official Daniel had ever known, though admittedly, he was young and had actually known very few. Still, at present, Ashpenaz was the most important man in all Judah, yet here he was, sitting around chatting with a bunch of invalids as though he were indeed a father talking to his sick children. It had to be a cleverly designed ploy to win them over, and Daniel was determined he was not going to fall for it.

Eventually, Ashpenaz moved on to the other recruits.

CHAPTER 52

The Choice of the Negev

The Negev Desert, Judah

Nebuchadnezzar marched south. All the land of ancient Mitanni was now his.[1] The Chaldeans recorded it. What they didn't record is how he felt about it. Having taken Carchemish, the Egyptians, and all their allies, fled before him. North and South Syria, including Philistia and Judah, fell like the leaves on Princess Amyhia's trees. It had been too easy—almost effortless. But if he failed to take Egypt, holding the new territories would be another story. Their populations were not being deported and replaced—there was no time. So, Nebuchadnezzar left them in place. Unless Egypt was conquered, it would beckon and woo unfaithful governors with the promise that Babylon could yet be withstood. If another power still existed to which they could appeal, they would certainly rebel. Although the moon of Elul was already half over and by rights, the rab mag should have been leading his armies back to Babylon, he could not stop.[2] This campaign was everything.

The green mountains of Jerusalem gave way to a dry, rocky valley through which the lonely wind whistled its melancholy song. The Valley of Beersheba marked the beginning of the desert lands to the south. The vast, wide-open sky blazed with a relentless sun as the rab mag led his army on.

That afternoon they passed over a small mountain range to emerge by evening in a rolling rocky land. They encamped at the foot of a huge cliff, and as Shamash woke, they were on their way once again.

It was a desert country similar in some ways to that of Qedar but without the sand or the dunes.[3] The ground here was hard, and so were the people. Most of the population was nomadic, and the few towns they passed were virtually empty. Salt flats and barren ridges passed beru after scorching beru. The most abundant signs of life were the many grazing flocks under the watchful eyes of their shepherds. What even sheep and goats could find to eat there was a mystery.

The army did make an impression on the wildlife, however. The marching feet and beat of hooves stirred up dust and collected a following of mice and rats, desperate for whatever scraps the host might leave behind them. The rodents, emboldened by their lack of resources, moved among the infantry, from time to time taking nips at unwary feet and eliciting random surprised yelps from the feet's owners.

The rab mag had been unsure as to how the Judeans of the desert would react to the passage of his army, but, for the most part, if any people were around, they ignored him. Since there seemed no threat in the area, Nebushumlishtar was allowed out of his cavalry unit to ride beside his brother's chariot. The two daggermen, Seri, and Marshipar, also rode, flanking Kadurri's chariot with three horsemen.

Not only were the inhabitants peaceful, but to Kadurri's surprise, some even came out of their way to greet him and bring him gifts. A boy, about twelve years old—with a medium-sized black and white spotted dog and a dozen tan and white short-haired sheep—appeared. The boy came over a ridge and headed down into the dust of the passing army. The dog nipped and herded the sheep before him.

Kadurri touched his driver's shoulder, and his chariot wheeled out of place to stop directly in front of the boy. The First General of Babylon hopped down out of his vehicle and walked up to the lad. The boy's clothes were clean. The green-striped material showed signs of wear and had been stitched up in several places, but they were the only part of him that wasn't dirty. Apparently, he had been quickly dressed in his finest and hurriedly sent out to meet up with the army. Kadurri looked the lad up and down. The boy, realizing just who it was that was before him, stood there, his eyes wide, his hand on the dog's back, his disturbed sheep milling around. Prince Nebushumlishtar came cantering up and looked the sheep over.

"It's the third time in as many days."

"I'm aware," Kadurri nodded.

"We'll eat well tonight."

"Except we don't need the supplies, we're only four days out of Jerusalem. We haven't asked these people for anything. I need a translator, go get my recorder."

But just then, Recorder Nergalsharusar arrived in the chariot of the rab shaq. The recorder hopped down from his chariot too and snapped his fingers to his master.

"Ask him," Kadurri commanded. "Why has he been sent with this gift?"

A brief flurried exchange took place in which the boy animatedly described his task, his arms emphasizing his words.

"Rab Mag?" Rab Shaq Belshumishkun gave the prince a quick half-bow and salute by the snap of his fingers as his chariot rolled to a stop beside the Nebushumlishtar's flashy bay.

Standing by the studded wheel of the royal chariot, Nebuchadnezzar watched the troops continue to march past the youth and his sheep. The rab mag frowned. "Belshumishkun, you know the Qedar better than any man here. These people are similar. What are they trying to accomplish by these gifts?"

The rab shaq was from Ur, a son of Bit Yakin. For all practical purposes, the Yakin lived surrounded by the Arameans. In many of the smaller villages of Bit Yakin, it was difficult to tell the Babylonians from the Arabs. The cupbearer may have understood the Qedar, but these people had him at a loss. "My Prince, I can't begin to imagine."

"Well, let's find out." He addressed the recorder, "Shar?"

"Great One! He says his people are greatly honored and merely wish to express that honor in some small way."

"Is that so?" Kadurri smiled at the boy who treated him with a smile that lit up his dirt-smudged face. "Shar, tell the lad that I wish to meet with the head of the family that so honors me."

The recorder delivered the message, and the boy grinned, bowed low, and disappeared over a ridge in a bare-footed run.

"Why?" Prince Nebushumlishtar asked from the back of his tall bay as they waited for the man to be brought to them.

"Why what?" Kadurri asked his brother.

"Why do you want to see him? What is there to understand? What's so strange about some peasant giving you presents so you'll hurry on and leave them alone?"

The rab mag shook his head then smiled. Nebushumlishtar was young and inexperienced, and he did not really hold much promise as a soldier anyway. "You haven't been looking around you, Shum. What do you see?"

"A lot of rocks and hills."

Kadurri laughed. "How about you, Rab Shaq?"

Belshumishkun glanced briefly at the barren landscape, the hot, dry sun, the rocks, the low, contorted ridges, the withered plants, and trees. There were no buildings or even watering holes in sight. "A lot of hiding places and nothing that needs or is worth defending."

"Right! Shum, why are these people bringing me presents when all they need to do is herd their sheep over the next rise? I'm not going waste my time trying to chase down a bunch of tent dwellers in that maze, and they can't possibly be so stupid as to think I would. So, they aren't trying to bribe me, but what are they trying to do?"

"I don't know," the young prince said.

"Neither do I. But I think I ought to find out."

After only the briefest of intervals, a group appeared over the top of the tortured ridge.

"They were hiding right on the other side?" Shum asked incredulously.

"Evidently," Kadurri answered, amused. "They probably have hiding caves everywhere."

The patriarch of the clan was an elderly man wrapped in gray and green Bedouin robes. His hair was a grizzled gray, and his skin was darkened and wrinkled from the sun and wind of the desert, but he was spry as a man in his forties. He trotted down the hill with five other men, probably his sons, in tow. They promptly dropped armloads of melons and spices at the rab mag's feet.

Motioning at the small flock of about twenty sheep which had accumulated over the past few days and were now under the care of the rab mag's kitchen staff, they all began to cry out at the same time.

Kadurri looked at Shar, who was listening intently. "Great One," the recorder said, "It is difficult to say with so many talking all at once but…"

Nebuchadnezzar held up his hand, and the group fell instantly silent, but they continued to beam at him with mouths filled with broken teeth. "These people came as quickly as they could when they heard you would pass near. They wished to see the 'Servant of the Lord.' They say that they will not be misled like the people of the cities; they will stick to their own religion and will not have foreign gods. But they are extremely honored to have you here."

Kadurri was puzzled. "I don't understand. You," he gestured to the old man who looked immensely pleased with having been so noticed. "My sire is the Servant of Marduk, not me. I am not King. What do you mean?"

The old man listened to the translation than nodded quickly. "You are not the Servant of Marduk; you are the Servant of the Lord. The Prophet Jeremiah has said so. We have prayed and prayed for you to come, and now you are here. You have even removed the gods of the idolaters from the Temple in Jerusalem! The Priests of Arad have ordered us by the word of the prophet to help in any way we can. The people of the Negev are not idolaters. We obey the Lord!"

"Jeremiah again?" Kadurri looked at Rab Shaq Belshumishkun, who shrugged.

"Who can say, Your Highness? Sometimes superstitions are enough to move people like this, but they seem to mean what they say."

The rab mag frowned, looking one more time at the empty loneliness of the land. Now that he thought about it, he hadn't actually noticed any shrines to any gods since he had entered the region. It was a barren place, but there were springs and other areas which would have been suitable for the placement of shrines. He thought back. What was it his father had said? In Josiah's day, all of Judah had been like that, no shrines, no high places. Strange. "But what does that matter to them? Why do they care what Jeremiah has said? How do they even know about it?"

The old man grinned even wider, and the interpreter echoed his words. "Jeremiah's family is here, in Arad. We know."

"Jeremiah's family is here?"

"Yes, yes. They are from Anathoth, but Jeremiah warned that you would destroy that town, so they came here. Arad belongs to the sons of Aaron, to their tribe."

Visions of the flame and smoke of Anathoth flitted before Kadurri's eyes. He swallowed hard as he realized that he had come so close to destroying this extraordinary man's family. "Jeremiah's family ordered you to give us gifts?"

"Yes, but we do it willingly. You are the Servant of the Lord. You have emptied Jerusalem of her idols."

Nebuchadnezzar wrinkled his brow as if he were trying to get an unfamiliar concept to make sense. "This Jeremiah has got to be the greatest prophet the world has ever seen," he said to Shum. He turned back to the old man. "I didn't just go there and take the gods of the other peoples," he said. "Your king gave them to me."

The patriarch shrugged. "Whether or not you demanded the idols or Jehoiakim gave them up willingly doesn't matter. They are gone just the same, and you are responsible. We are grateful and will help however we can."

In spite of himself, Kadurri grinned back, and pointedly pushed the white Egyptian Hedjet crown back, exposing his forehead and calling attention to the fact that he wore it. "You're not fond of Egypt's gods?"

The old man turned and spat on the ground. The small wet spot vanished almost instantly into the dry sand. "Or its kings," the old man answered. "The white crown of Upper Egypt looks much better on your brow than Necho's."

The rab mag laughed. "Well, I agree with you there. So, you wish to serve your God by serving me. Being so close to Egypt's border has nothing to do with it, I'm sure."

"You are the Servant of the Lord," the old man insisted. "You will free us from the tyranny of Egypt!"

Nebuchadnezzar laughed and slapped the old man on the back. "I think we understand each other, Father. I will do what I am able. Babylon thanks you for your generosity. The Negev will not be forgotten. Nor will Jeremiah or his family."[4]

The old man and his sons all began to babble at the same time as the rab mag mounted his chariot and waved to them. The chariots moved out to take their place before the infantry.

CHAPTER 53

Sharu-lu-Dar

Pelusium, Egypt

Five days later, Nebuchadnezzar crossed the Wadi of Egypt and pushed his men on to Pelusium on the Egyptian border, and there he set camp as Shamash sank into the west. Pelusium was the easternmost city of Egypt. Here, Necho diverted the Nile to the south. The Tumilat canal joined the Bitter Lakes, to allow passage from the Great Sea to the Red Sea. It traveled through a pervasive marsh that made the area all but uninhabitable. Pelusium's name even meant "City of Ooze." Bugs swarmed in the humid heat, and the men smelled of yarrow liniment.

"A sphinx is a lion with a man's face, probably a king's," Seri was explaining to Shum and Marshipar as they came up to share Kadurri's camp in the growing darkness. It was far too hot for a fire, so he had a central torch thrust into the ground for light, instead. It was too hot for a tent too, but the bugs made it a necessity. Kadurri sat on a large rock in front of his tent and watched the sunset as his best friend, his brother and his brother's daggerman came up. Shum plopped himself down on the rock next to Kadurri, but Seri and Marshipar stood behind, assuming their usual, watchful positions.

"They are kind of like the Assyrians' lamassu, guardian spirits, only they're never bulls. The Greeks have them too, though theirs are generally female," Kadurri expounded on Seri's comment to Shum. An aide who had been laying out his bedroll appeared from inside the tent. Kadurri pulled off the Hedjet, handed it to the man and wiped the sweat from his brow.

"I know that," Shum snapped. He was tired of being treated like he was ignorant. The mosquitos were terrible, and his temper was running short.

But Pelusium's sphinxes were strange. Kadurri had never heard of anything like them. Neither Egyptian, Assyrian, nor Greek, they were their own interpretation of the monster. Where Egyptian sphinxes lay down and Greek sphinxes sat, these, like the lamassu, stood. Where Greek sphinxes were feminine, and the Egyptian and Assyrian versions were male, these heads were not even human. Their crudely made faces *were* of men, presumably kings, but they were set in lion's heads and topped by lion's ears and covered by lion's manes. Like the Greek and Assyrian, but unlike the Egyptian, they had wings. And here any resemblance to any other protective spirit ended.

Pelusium's spirit guardians were malevolent. There was no other word for it. Their wings were curled but outstretched, threatening to fly and pounce at any moment. They glowed down on Nebuchadnezzar's army with malicious intent, like an evil omen, like harbingers of some doom the rab mag could not fathom. The coarse brick statues were a testament to an ancient tribe who had once ruled here in defiance of their titan neighbor, Egypt. Kadurri sat and looked at them for a while, then he shuddered and swatted at a mosquito and rubbed his face and arms with a yarrow salve he pulled from a side pouch.

The aide from the tent, having put the Hedjet away in its place, had disappeared briefly. Now, he reappeared with four bowls of mutton stew and a large melon. The meal attracted marsh flies which joined the circling mosquitos in a growing swarm. Kadurri waved them away from his bowl and his face.

Suddenly, Seri looked up. "There's a messenger."

Kadurri stood up and followed his friend's gaze. Now that Seri had brought his attention to it, he heard the arguing of the guards. Then a distant pounding of hooves as a figure on horseback separated itself from the group and galloped in their direction. Several of the guards had broken off and followed the messenger at a run.

The man approached quickly, pulled his mount to a sliding stop and swung off. Sweat ran in rivulets down his filthy face as he hastily prostrated himself, trembling, before his prince.

The horse, its reddish coat white with foam and sweat, stood splay-legged. It lowered its head to the ground as it quivered in exhaustion. Froth fell from its mouth and nose as it gulped in air and blew it out again. At the very least, the animal had been foundered, and the whistling sound of its breath said that the animal's wind was broke from running too far.

The rider looked in little better shape.

Kadurri knew the message was important, for a good horse was not ruined lightly. "Speak," he commanded him shortly.

"Great One! May Marduk choose you! Your mother, the queen, sent this message by night, unobserved by the city. Your father, the king… May the name of Nabopolassar live forever, Great One, but he has gone to his destiny and your mother bids you return in all haste to secure your throne lest the Chaldeans arrange for Marduk to take the hand of another more to their liking."

The horse's knees buckled, and it collapsed.

For a second, Kadurri thought his knees were likely to give out too. "The king is dead?" He couldn't have heard that right. Then, another thought intruded. "He said I was king."

"Kadurri?" Shum's voice was a hoarse whisper.

Kadurri looked at him. "Jeremiah knew. He said I was king. He said it before we ever got to Jerusalem. He knew."

The boy stood there in shock, eyes as round as chariot wheels. He appeared to be carved from stone, he was so still. Kadurri laid an unsteady hand on his brother's shoulder.

Then Belshumishkun was there. "Lord," the rab shaq took Kadurri by both shoulders and shook him almost imperceptibly. "Lord?"

Kadurri drew a deep breath. "It's all right, Rab Shaq. I'm all right."

Belshumishkun took a step back then shouted with a voice that probably carried all the way to Sais, "The king is dead! Sharu-lu-dar!"[1]

Every man in sight fell to the ground and prostrated themselves shouting the chant, "Sharu-lu-dar! Sharu-lu-dar! Sharu-lu-dar!"

The rab shaq turned to the prostrate messenger, "Your mission is fulfilled, go rest." He helped the man to his feet, and the prostrated host stood up too. The messenger stumbled away towards the mess wagons. The growing crowd opened respectfully for him and let him pass.

"Go to your tent," Belshumishkun said to Kadurri in a low voice. "Take your brother with you."

Numbly, Kadurri turned to obey, then he stopped. "Wait."

"Great King," the rab shaq protested.

"No! The men need to know they still have a king, and they need to know it tonight, right now." He looked around at the murky forms of his men just out of the circle of the torchlight. "Where is Narambel?"

"Here, Great King," a black shadow coalesced into the general as he strode forward. Narambel bowed very low with his arms crossed before his chest as he snapped his fingers. "Sharu-lu-dar!"

Kadurri reached out and took both Belshumishkun and Narambel's hands, putting them on his right and left. He lifted their hands high over his head and called out in a clear voice, "The Rab Mag and Rab Shaq of Babylonia! Obey them as you would me!"

The roar of affirmation from the host told Kadurri that by accepting his right to appoint the generals to those offices, they now accepted his authority without question.

"Well done," Belshumishkun said under his breath.

An involuntary tear rolled down Kadurri's cheek, and he angrily brushed it away. "*Now* I can go to my tent. You are in charge, Rab Mag."

"So I see. Don't worry; I'll take care of this. Get your mourning done tonight, Lord. Before Shamash awakens, we ride."

Kadurri pushed Shum ahead of him and ducked under the tent flap. Behind him, he heard Belshumishkun order, "You! Put this horse down and bury him with honors. Dye the tail-hair red and have it affixed to my helmet by midnight."

Narambel was adding his instructions to the hubbub as well. "Marshipar! I want twenty daggermen encircling this tent at five paces. Now!"

Belshumishkun continued, "You! Call the captains of the cavalry to the planning tent! You! Send the lieutenant of supplies to me at the planning tent as well…" his voice faded as he strode away.

"But what about Egypt?" Shum looked dazedly at his brother from the other side of the tent.

The Hedjet lay on a cushion by the tent wall. Kadurri picked the white crown up and threw it on the ground. He stamped on it, crushing the delicate golden wires that held its form. "Egypt can wait!"

Then the tears came.

The traditional route from the Wadi of Egypt to Babylon was close to 170 beru. It had taken a string of messengers and horses only eight days.[2] But the army could not move at the speed of the messengers and speed was necessary.

Nebuchadnezzar had left the planning to his generals. Belshumishkun had overridden all objections and chosen the desert route and only the Nisroch Cavalry Division would ride it.

It was still dark when they sent for him. Kadurri found Rab Shaq Narambel holding the reins of his own mount and those of Kadurri's sleek black charger. Kadurri swung up on the stallion's tall back, and the rab shaq gave him a skin of beer and a bag holding a small collection of cold meats and bread. Nebuzaradan was already there on his gray mare, finishing his breakfast.

Kadurri looked across at an area illuminated by torchlight. The Nisrochs were there, mounted and ready with the rab mag at their head.

"No," Kadurri objected. "Belshumishkun must stay with the army. Besides, you're in charge of the cavalry."

"Not anymore," the rab shaq answered. "Now, I'm in charge of you. Besides, we need the rab mag. We're crossing the desert. He says it can be done because the Qedar do it. Well, Sin knows, that one is practically Qedar, himself. He knows the desert, and we need a guide. So, the rab mag leads us."

"The desert?"

"Yes, Majesty. The rab mag says it's fastest." He turned to Seri. "You stay on his left, I'll stay on his right." Seri nodded and moved into place. Narambel swung up on his fiery chestnut.

Prince Nebushumlishtar groggily poked his head out of the tent. "Stay with the army, Shum," Kadurri commanded him. "I'll see you in Babylon!" The three cantered over to the waiting cavalry unit. The young prince was left standing forlornly outside the tent as the horses thundered away into the darkness of predawn.

Morning after morning and evening after evening they rode, hiding in the afternoons from Shamash's relentless gaze. Sometimes trotting, sometimes cantering, they steadily ate up the distance. The brutal scorching heat of day gave no clue that summer was drawing to a close. The cold of night showed no trace that summer had ever come at all. Sand dunes followed sand dunes, often without any plant or animal life in sight.

It was a grueling trek across a barren wilderness, but it was almost a third shorter than the traditional route. It was a journey meant only for camel caravans, but even if he had had camels, Belshumishkun would not have used them now. Horses were faster, and speed was essential. Rab Mag Belshumishkun, wise in the ways of the desert, knew all the oases and wells. He led the men on. And Rab Shaq Narambel stuck as close to the new king's side as Daggerman Nebuzaradan did.

Kadurri had no idea of what would await them when they arrived in Babylon. There was every likelihood that they would have to attack their own city, and one cavalry unit was not going to be enough.

Kadurri mourned his father, but he did it in private. The arduous desert trek was no time to make a public show of his feelings. His men needed him. They suffered the brutal ride through the wilderness because they believed in him. Though they numbered only two hundred strong, they were willing to follow him against Babylon itself if need be. He needed them to believe in him, so the exterior he presented to his men was the efficient and determined leader they had come to know.

Babylon, Babylonia

By the time Nebuchadnezzar crossed the Euphrates at Sippar and reached the plain of Shinar, Nabopolassar had been dead for a moon and a quarter. What had the Chaldeans been planning in that time? The current regime was not popular with the priests and the house cleaning of Bit Amukanni sympathizers after Meskalumdug's uprising, eight years before, was known to be incomplete.

Racing across the plain at the head of his men, Nebuchadnezzar had never seen so little activity. The canals of the flat land flowed full, but no one opened them to the fields. This was not so very strange because the growing season was all but over. However, the crops were ripe, ready for harvest, and no one worked the fields. Occasionally, the division passed a shepherd or oxherd attending their livestock, but that was all.

A dozen times they pulled up at a village to inquire about the political state of the land, only to be told that all was well. The people wept and jostled each other for a view of their new king, then they hurried back into their houses.

"But if there *is* treachery, would they know?" Kadurri asked the rab mag as they galloped on, leaving the last hamlet in their dust.

The gigantic walls and towers of Babylon obscured the skyline and loomed ever larger.

"No," the old warrior replied. "Not if a trap has been laid for us. They only know what they've been told, and that is of course only that they are to stay inside."

"Then we're only going to find out by trying to spring that hypothetical trap. So, let's get at it!" Kadurri slapped his stallion on the rump, urging it to a faster pace.

Babylon lay straight ahead.

They had made the crossing from Pelusium to Babylon in an impossible twenty-six days.

The rab mag held his fist to the sky, and the cavalry pulled to a halt.

The city was quiet. No one moved in or out of the gates. They reached the city's famous broadway. No one traveled it.

But from somewhere within the walls, a horn sounded.

Belshumishkun circled his fist and pointed forward. The division started up again, with Belshumishkun at the fore. The rest of the cavalry moved into a wedge shape with Kadurri in their center.

Trotting up the Aiiburshabu, the leather-covered hooves of the cavalry thudded a muffled rhythm on the pavement. Over the dike they trotted, and straight on towards the unadorned mud bricks of the Ishtar Gate where the city guard stood watch. The most trafficked street in the world held no merchants, no travelers, and no citizens.

"It's martial law," Seri said, his mount trotting beside Kadurri's. "It's been this way for over a moon?"

"It means nothing," Narambel answered grimly, trotting protectively on Kadurri's other side. "If all is well, then the queen mother means to make sure it stays that way until the king arrives. If not, then the city has fallen, the traitors are making certain that we don't know about it, and we're riding into a trap." He pulled his bronze sword from its scabbard on his left hip and laid it across his horse's withers. Seri did the same. As if that were a cue, the air was filled with the swish of swords against their scabbards as all the cavalry followed suit.

Approaching Babylon unseen was impossible. The land stretched flat to the horizon in every direction, so the city was never caught unawares. This day was no exception. As they passed through the Ishtar Gate, a single chariot approached. It was not a war chariot. Drawn by only two horses, it would have been dwarfed by the huge conveyances of the chariotry. Low to the ground, this chariot was of the type used by lords and ladies of the Bar Manuti for travel, and it held only two people. The chariot rolled to a stop, and an old man gingerly stepped down.

Nebuzaradan gave an audible sigh of relief. It was Nabopolassar's prime minister, Rab Sharish Mesharumishamash.

Belshumishkun again held up his fist, and the host pulled to a halt.

Kadurri nimbly swung his right leg forward over his stallion's neck and hopped down onto the pavement. He ran forward and hugged the old man.

Mesharu hugged him back, then gently disentangled himself. "The king is dead," he announced in a raspy voice. "Sharu-lu-dar!"

"Sharu-lu-dar!" came the thunderous response from the host.

"Mesharu, what news?" Kadurri asked anxiously. "What is the situation?"

That the rab sharish was enormously relieved to see him was evident from his eyes, but he reached around into the chariot and pulled out the tall, hammered crown of Babylon and the scepter. "Lord," the Prime Minister said, with tears in his eyes "now that you are here, all is well."

And he set the crown on Nebuchadnezzar's head.[3] "Sharu-lu-dar!" he yelled as loud as he could.

The host went wild. In the uproar that followed, Kadurri took the scepter from the old man and held it up for them to see. Impossibly, they yelled louder.

"Your mother and I have followed your father's instructions, and the city is secure," the rab sharish shouted in his ear, "but it has been an unsettled time, and we have made many arrests. Unfortunately, anyone that could have led us to higher prey was found dead.

"Your mother and I are very glad to have you back with us. It has been a moon and a quarter and the people need to know that they still have a king.

"Once we have you safe and secure in the palace, we will recall the guard and rescind martial law. Tonight, the people will be free once more.

"Tonight, we will begin to celebrate your coronation."

"Thank you, Mesharu. I will not forget this, I promise."

It was not at all a traditional crowning, and the new king understood the ramifications. The Priest of Ekua, first of the three gatekeepers, should have set the crown on his head. The coronation should only have happened after a long and complicated ceremony involving all three of the Keepers and the High Priestess, Sajaha. The implications were clear. The rab sharish had denied the Chaldeans the honor of crowning him and thereby called into question their authority over the king.

So, they *had* tried to oppose this crowning. Mesharu had very good reason for declaring martial law.

As Kadurri led his mount into the city, still surrounded by his cavalry escort, he saw the Chaldean priests gathering in front of the gates of Esagila. The new king laughed to himself at their expressions as Rab Mag Belshumishkun brought the entire unit, two hundred strong, into the temple complex and escorted Nabopolassar's son past his enemies to the door of Marduk's house.

The enormous golden god, clothed in dark purple linen, sat on his throne on the porch outside Ekua, his temple. His left hand held his lightning scepter, but his right was empty and outstretched, waiting.

Flanking the deity stood Queen Mother Ninnaramur and the Lady Sajaha. Positioned behind the queen mother was Nebuchadnezzar's wife, Princess Nitocris.

The queen mother was also clothed in dark purple. The color was a variant of the black of mourning, but it declared royalty and so was suited for the occasion. Naram was veiled, but her veil was sheer and brilliant white. She mourned, but she also rejoiced, her son was home, and he was King.

Nitocris was draped in bright violet. Her huge dark eyes were shining. *She* did not mourn Nabopolassar. Her face was illuminated from within with joy as she watched her husband.

Kadurri gave the princess a tight smile, and handed the stallion's reins to Nebuzaradan. He jumped up the steps, and took his mother's hands. Then he kissed her veiled cheek. Her smile was her answer.

He turned from her and took the gleaming metal hand of the patron god of Babylon.

The Priestess of Sarpenitum wore a long gown of the deepest red, announcing the goddess' presence in the form of her servant. She took a long red cape from Marduk's lap and solemnly draped it over the shoulders of the one who had been her closest friend.

The cavalrymen finally backed their mounts away and allowed the Gatekeepers and other priests to approach. After all, Nebuchadnezzar already had the god's hand. It was too late to start a rebellion now—Nebuchadnezzar was already the Chosen of Marduk.

The Chaldeans picked up Marduk's servant and carried him into the temple. The gigantic god, however, sat on a wheeled pallet, allowing him to be pushed into place.[4]

The throne room of Ekua was of blue painted brick, but the floor was imported marble and so highly polished that it reflected the lamps even as the daylight filtered through the high windows. The altar before the dais was for incense, and the smoke drifted up to the idol's golden nose.

Nebuchadnezzar truly wished to serve his god, and by extension, his people. At that moment, he felt the weight of the responsibility he had been groomed all his life to meet. As king, he was responsible to his god for his people's behavior. If it were unacceptable, the god's disfavor would fall on him, not them. If misfortune did come to the people, it would be his fault.

The new king felt decidedly unworthy and unready as he handed the crown back to Shar and knelt. The High Priest, second of the gatekeeper trio, poured an amphora of scented olive oil over the king's head. The suzerain prostrated himself before the god to accept his commission. But did a statue made of pure gold really have ears to hear? That was irreverent. Especially on the occasion of his choosing and coronation! Having thought the thought, Kadurri couldn't erase it. He pushed himself to his knees again.

The Priest of Ekua stepped forward to the kneeling king and struck him across the cheek. The blow knocked Kadurri to the side, but it brought his attention away from blasphemy and back to the ceremony.

The High Priest came forward and struck him on the other cheek. This time, Nebuchadnezzar was braced for it and remained in place, but it split his lip.

The High Chanter then hit him over the head, and this blow had the desired effect, bringing tears, supposedly of repentance, to the king's eyes.

Satisfied, the High Chanter stepped back and took up a slow drum beat on a small drum he had brought. Surrounded by the Rab Trio, the queen mother, his wife, the three Keepers of the Gate and High Priestess Sajaha, Nebuchadnezzar stood and sang the ritual coronation prayer.

Without you, Lord, what would happen to the king you love,
That you've called by name?
You will decide how to bless his title
And you will guarantee him a straight path.
I am your obedient prince;
You created me with your own hands
And appointed me to rule your people.
Because of your mercy,
Which blankets your people,
Lord, overshadow your awesome power with your love
And make a reverence for your divinity grow in my heart.
Give as you think best.

But *did* Marduk love him? To even ask the question made him ashamed. He really did need reverence to spring up in his heart, because it didn't seem to be there at present. The tears had been a sham—the result of pain, not humility.

Where his father had doubted the priests, Kadurri suddenly discovered that he doubted his god. It was not an auspicious beginning for the new Provider of Marduk.[5]

EPILOGUE

Jerusalem, Judah

"Nabi?" the knock at the door of Jeremiah's small upstairs apartment sounded again. "I've brought you some mutton, bread, and wine."

There was no answer, but Baruch knew he was in there. "It's still warm." The scribe lifted the basket so that the enticing smell could filter through the window.

No answer.

"Jeremiah ben Hilkiah!" Baruch was angry. "You've been up here for a month! It's time to come out! No one blames you; it's the Lord's privilege to change His mind!" Of course, that last was untrue. Almost everyone blamed Jeremiah, but Baruch was afraid for the prophet's health. He needed to see him and was ready to say anything.

It worked. The prophet rose and opened the door. He stood there, breathing heavily, his eyes wild. "Change His mind? Change His mind! Are you insane?"

"Nabi," Baruch chastened him gently, "I think I'm the one who should be asking that question. And peace to you, too."

Jeremiah apparently had not bathed in some time. He was barefoot and skeletally thin. He smelled, his rough-spun tunic was stiff with grime. But short brown hair covered his head once more, his beard had grown back in, and the scabs on his face had healed.

The Prophet to the Nations reached out, grabbed the front of Baruch's robes, and pulled him inside, slamming the door behind him. For someone still suffering back problems from the stocks, he was amazingly strong.

Baruch deposited his small wicker basket on the little table.

Jeremiah eyed the basket for a second, sighed and knelt down on the rough-hewn floor next to the table. "Thank you." He grabbed a piece of mutton and held it up towards the ceiling. "And thanks be to the Lord, Whose loving-kindness endures to all generations." The prophet began to voraciously devour it. "But I can't wish you peace in turn. I don't believe in peace anymore."

"When was the last time you ate?" Baruch watched him with disapproval.

"Not sure, yesterday, maybe."

"That's not too bad," the scribe acknowledged. "Jeremiah, what do you think you're doing? Hiding? Why? It's all right. It's over. You were right as far as it went, everyone knows that. Nebuchadnezzar was even king when he came here. You should have seen the looks on the faces of the priests and prophets when they realized that! But the Lord has relented; He took care of it another way. The Babylonians took all the idols with them! The priests have cleansed the Temple grounds, and it's over. Nebuchadnezzar is probably back in Babylon by now."

Jeremiah took a long swig at the small wineskin and stoppered it again. "That's what they're saying? That He's relented?" He tore off a chunk of dark bread and stuffed it in his mouth. "Baruch," he said as he greedily chewed, "don't you understand what holiness is? The Lord is holy, and He cannot change. We cannot be his people and still be stained with sin; we'll be destroyed by His very Presence." He swallowed. "Not His fault.

"The idols are gone? Baruch, think! Remember King Josiah's question: if I murdered someone yesterday, but I let someone else live today, am I then holy today? Of course not! Yesterday's sin remains. That is why Joshua and Caleb were to drive everyone out of the land before them, to keep temptation away from the Lord's holy people. No, Baruch. Sin must be dealt with, or we will all face eternity without our God." He took another bite of mutton. "Because His holiness cannot begin to be compromised by the sin that permeates our souls."

"But the Lord forgives! If you murdered someone yesterday, He could forgive you today."

"And He would, if I repented and turned to Him for mercy. If in humility, I sought His face in the manner He has proscribed. Our people have not repented. They think they can come to Him in the manner they proscribe. That's not repentance, it's rebellion."

"But Nabi, it hasn't happened," Baruch reasoned. "It's just like with Josiah. Judgment has been delayed. Perhaps in the time of our grandchildren…"

Jeremiah choked on the bread. After he had got his breath back, he glared at his scribe. "Jehoiakim is not Josiah! And neither have the people repented. They didn't give up their idols; Nebuchadnezzar took them. Tell me, is the Molech gone?"

"Well, no, but in the Temple Court…"

"NO! And the people are still sacrificing their children there?"

Baruch hung his head, ashamed of his own people.

"Yes," Jeremiah answered for him. "And if the idols were still in the Temple Court, they would still be sacrificing to them too. New idols will be back there shortly."

"But no one has gone into captivity!" Baruch objected. "Well, no one except a few young men, to serve in Babylon's courts. That's not even close to what you were saying, Jeremiah."

"You mean what I prophesied, not what I said. And no, it's not even close. But now I know. It's going to be worse than I thought. It's going to drag on for years until finally all is fulfilled." He took one last bite of the mutton and stood up. "War, famine, disease—the horror has just begun, Baruch. You can't see it, but I can."

He patted his friend on the shoulder with one grimy hand. "You are right, however. I can't stay locked up here. I've been sitting here arguing with the Sovereign Lord to choose somebody else. He says no, He wants *me.*"

He pulled his folded cow-hair mantle from the shelf and slipped it on. With a decisive tug, he fastened the belt.

"We've got work to do."

ENDNOTES

Part 1: 610 BC

1. Jeremiah 46:24 is found in a prophecy describing the fall of Egypt to Babylon. It is dated much later than Princess Nitocris' kidnapping. Instead, it was probably given concurrently with the events in Carchemish it forth tells, but it uses her fate, well known to the people of the day, as a word picture foretelling the fate of Egypt.

Chapter 1

1. The Egyptians didn't actually use the title "queen." Instead, they relied on a woman's relationship, for example, "Great Royal Wife," or "God's Wife." In the case of the god's wife, she obviously rule, had her own palace and throne, etc. *Empire,* as almost all literary works referring to ancient Egypt, uses the title "queen" as it is easier for the modern reader to understand. In the same way, *Empire* refers to the Egyptian city of Niwtimn as Thebes, since this is more easily understood. Thebes Egypt was located where the City of Luxor is today. It was the Greeks who gave the city the name of Thebes, calling it after their own city by the same name due to a slight phonetic similarity to the name of its temple complex, Taopet. The city's Egyptian name, since 700 years before—the time of Amenhotep the Heretic—was Niwtimn, (Waset) the City of Amun. The Bible names it No-Amon, the City of Amon (Amun). Thebes was really two cities, the City of the Living—Taopet

and the Southern Sanctuary on the east bank; and the City of the Dead— with its tombs, monuments, shrines and temples on the west bank.

2. The first pharaoh of the Twenty-Sixth Dynasty, Psammetik I, forced the Cushite Adoratrix, Shepenupet II, to renounce her niece, Amenirdis, and adopt his daughter, Nitocris. The baby, despite her age, was then declared God's Wife of Amun and Psammetik I's rule, already in its ninth year over Lower Egypt, became legitimate in the eyes of both Upper and Lower Egypt. Psammetik I's son, Necho II, was this Nitocris' brother. Necho could rule by right of either Queen Nitocris, his sister, or Princess Nitocris, his daughter. To inherit, Necho's son, Psammetik II, needed a sister or daughter as god's wife, so Queen Nitocris adopted her niece, the Princess Nitocris. In all fairness, direct documentation of this adoption has not been found, but the facts should be allowed to speak for themselves:
   a) Princess Nitocris was the Queen of Thebes' namesake.
   b) Nabopolassar took the girl as an assurance of her father's cooperation and married her to his son, Nebuchadnezzar.
   c) From Lebanon, there exists a bas-relief façade of a youthful Nebuchadnezzar wearing what is obviously the white crown of Upper Egypt. The inference is that he believed he had a right to wear it. He could only have had that right if his wife was considered the legitimate god's wife and as her husband, he would be her closest male relative.
   d) Psammetik II was furious with his father over some "unnamed" transgression (Necho II not only agreed to give his daughter to Babylon, but his betrayal of Babylon should have assured Princess Nitocris' death) and when Psammetik became pharaoh, he blotted out Necho's name (from monuments, etc.).
   e) Queen Nitocris refused to name Psammetik II's daughter, Ankhnasneferibre, as her heir apparently because she wanted her true heir back. She only granted the princess status as Prophet of Amun, declaring it was enough for Psammetik to

inherit. This was an outrageous act since the office of Prophet of Amun was held by the crown prince. Psammetik II did not need the title anymore since he was then made pharaoh. However, Psammetik's chosen heir (Apries) was unable to hold the office of First Prophet, since Princess Ankhnasneferibre already had it. Presumably, Ankhnasneferibre herself could have become pharaoh since she was already granted the right to the divine ka by Nitocris' proclamation (so that Psammetik II could become pharaoh). It was only many decades later, when forced by Apries (Hophra), that Queen Nitocris ceded Princess Ankhnasneferibre the ultimate title of god's wife. This vacated the office of First Prophet of Amun and Apries, Ankhnasneferibre's brother, then was able to become the crown prince (first prophet), so that he could subsequently become pharaoh. This whole situation caused such chaos that Ankhnasneferibre was the last to ever hold the title God's Wife of Amun. The religion went through a major restructuring to prevent this from ever happening again.

3. Less than fifty miles downstream from Sais, on the Mediterranean Coast, was the Fortress of the Milesians. As a reward for their help in securing his throne, Psammetik I had granted the small city of Piemro to the Ionians of Miletus to house Milesian merchants and mercenaries there. Egyptians were xenophobic and objected to foreigners living freely among them. Piemro was then renamed the Fortress of the Milesians. Having their own city in Egypt gave the Milesians a great advantage over the other Greeks, as far as their trading status was concerned. Later, under Pharaoh Apries (Hophra), the fort became the Emporium of Naucratis and was divided into sections under many different Greek city-states. With so many Greek immigrants, the area expanded and eventually it was built up across the branch of the Nile. This section became known as Heracleon. Together, the sister cities became the foremost ports in this part of the world. They flourished from the Sixth to the Fourth Centuries BC. Heracleon continued on until about 300

AD when it finally sank beneath the waves of the Mediterranean, however Naucratis was slightly more inland and it remained.

Chapter 2

1. "Daggerman" was the Babylonian term for a member of the king's bodyguard. They were fanatically loyal and went everywhere with their king. In the Bible, daggerman is usually translated as "Imperial Guard."
2. Nabopolassar would never have known peace before. Growing up, supposedly in Ur (he was a lord of Bit Yakin) under the Assyrians, he was born during the war with Urartu. He eventually rose to the rank of general in the Assyrian forces and was dispatched back home to Babylonia to quell the uprising of the Sea People. He then took the throne in Babylon for himself, which put him at war with Assyria. Now, with only minor skirmishes to mop up, Assyria and even Egypt were conquered. Media and Scythia were Babylon's allies, and Judah, though small, was a friend.
3. In most cases, descriptions of the characters in *Empire* are accurate, based on surviving busts and carvings. Nabopolassar and Necho II were both extraordinarily handsome. Some have claimed that the sculptures fudged the details and made them better looking than they actually were, but the realistic-looking busts of other historical figures of this time don't bear out this theory. They are portrayed with all their irregularities and faults.
4. The Late Egyptian language would still have been used by the nobility of the Saites, but Demotic, introduced by the Cushites, was already the language of the people. From the time of the uniting of Upper and Lower Egypt under Psammetik I, Demotic spread from Upper Egypt to Lower Egypt. Under Pharaoh Amasis, Demotic became the official language of the court and all its documents. As it had an alphabetic writing system, it was a vast improvement over hieroglyphics.
5. The pharaoh had many crowns for many different purposes. The Chepresh, a blue battle helm with the golden sun disk of Ra, is thought to be the favored crown of Psammetik I, declaring himself to be a warlord. However, carvings of him wearing the double crown during religious ceremonies exist. The Deshret, the red crown of Lower (northern)

Egypt and the Hedjet, the white crown of Upper (southern) Egypt could be combined, symbolizing the unity of the Two Lands. It was then called the Pschent and seemed to be the most royal and formal of the crowns. There was also a more informal headdress called the Nemes, which was a striped kerchief with wings that came forward over the shoulders and hung down over the back of the neck. The Nemes was most often worn with the Uraeus, the golden rearing cobra which protected the royal family. There were a dozen more crowns and headdresses and diadems the pharaoh could don combining them to suit his need. There were several that the queen was allowed to wear as well. As to the royal braid: in past dynasties, the children of the pharaoh shaved their heads except for a braid on the right side identifying them as heirs of the youthful Horus. By the Twenty-Sixth dynasty, the actual braid had vanished, but the crown prince donned a kerchief with an attached golden braid, instead.

6. *Empire* assumes the office of Head of Protocol is synonymous with the Fan-Bearer to the Right Hand of the King. This is because the Head of Protocol would have to stand by the pharaoh at formal government functions and that is exactly where we find the Fan-Bearer, announcing, directing and overseeing these functions, acting as the Head of Protocol. Contemporary records have Prince Horiraa as Necho's Head of Protocol and the tutor of the next two pharaohs, Psammetik, and Apries. Traditionally, it was the Fan-Bearer who was the royal tutor. Both arguments say that Prince Horiraa, Head of Protocol, was, in fact, Fan-Bearer to the Right, though there does not seem to be any existing records actually giving him this title.

7. A pharaoh added four names at his coronation giving him five names total. However, Necho II's son, Psammetik II, attempted to blot out his father's name. Only Necho's birth name and prenomen appear to have survived. As to the coronation itself, the pharaoh's heir generally took the throne on the day after the pharaoh died, but he was not coronated until the beginning of the next season or year. Very little information exists on Egyptian coronation ceremonies, so *Empire* uses what is known of his badges of office and the transference of the divine "ka"

to fill in the blanks. Depictions of various coronations show either two gods or two goddesses crowning the pharaoh. *Empire* assumes that the gods or goddesses had actual stand-ins to accomplish this task. The "I shall establish" phrases were part of the ritual. A standard coronation would be much more complicated than this one, with the pharaoh being crowned various ways with various crowns over the course of several days. This was not a standard coronation.

8. The term "Pharaoh" means "Great House" or "Royal House" and originally was not the title of the King of Egypt at all. Since he was a god, however, it was necessary to refer to him indirectly, such as the embodiment of his family, the royal house. Over time, "Pharaoh" actually became his title, as we find it in the Bible and as is recognized in *Empire*.
9. Most Egyptians were monogamous, but the pharaoh could and often did have lesser wives and concubines. The great royal wife, though technically not a queen, was the first among his wives. Initially, historians thought that the royal line was inherited through her. Though she is depicted in some carvings as breathing the divine ka into the pharaoh, her husband, it is manifestly not true that the royal inheritance is passed through her. The "queen" does not have to belong to the royal line, nor is it necessarily her son who inherits the kingdom; it is the king's son. This realization caused a widespread refutation in the 1980's of the concept of matriarchal inheritance. However, this dismissal fails to recognize the place of the god's wife, not the great royal wife, in the succession, making the passing of the ka and the inheritance matriarchal after all. The modern rejection of Ancient Egypt as a matriarchy is probably based, in large part, by Islamic Egyptologists rewriting history in a clear attempt at downplaying the importance of women in the royal hierarchy and political structure. But Diodorus plainly wrote: "Among the Egyptians, the woman rules over the man." This is the very definition of a matriarchal society.
10. The Chepresh was given to the pharaoh upon his crowning.

Chapter 3

1. Herodotus and Diogenes Laertius say that Prince Anacharsis was the son of Gnurus. Lucian says that he was the son of Daucetas, who he supposes may have been Gnurus, but the French scholar Sainson wrote in 1723 that this is entirely unfounded. Indeed, these Greeks have inserted three kings in their lists after Medyas (in less than forty years), and the place they give to Gnurus is that of Arbaces, not mentioning Arbaces, King of Scythia, at all. But Diodorus Siculus identifies Arbaces as the son of Medyas, with no kings in-between. We know that Anacharsis was the brother of Saulius, who was the heir and probably the son of Arbaces. The Greeks tell us that Anacharsis claimed his mother was Greek and it was she who taught him the language. Did he also give them information on his father and his father's relatives and if so, did he tell them that his father was someone other than Arbaces? The Greeks knew that Anacharsis was Saulius' brother, but did he and Saulius have the same father? Because Anacharsis was the brother of a Scythian king, did the Greeks wrongly assume that these other names, supposedly Anacharsis' father (and grandfather?) were in the line of the Scythian kings? Gnurus and Daucetus are otherwise unknown to history.

Chapter 4

1. *Empire* assigns Nebuchadnezzar the age of thirteen at this point, despite the modern historians tendency to claim a birthdate of around 634 BC, which would make him around twenty-six. It should be noted that this older age is merely a guess on the part of the moderns; undoubtedly due to the astounding success the prince had commanding the army. However, a careful look at the facts shows that 634 is impossible.
    a) *Empire* agrees with the ancient historians. Both Josephus and Berosus claim that Nabopolassar made Nebuchadnezzar rab mag in 606 and sent him after Necho in 605 BC "while he was still a youth," i.e., eighteen or younger. Giving him the oldest possible age of seventeen in 606 would here make him thirteen to fourteen at the oldest, and he could well have been younger.

b) “Nebuchadnezzar” was the prince’s given name, not just his throne name. “Nebuchadnezzar” means “Nebo’s border stone” or “Nebo protects the borders,” but more precisely, it was a name which could only be given to a crown prince of Babylon as the inference is “the inheritance (of the ruling family) is established.” His very name meant that he was heir to the throne of Babylon. That means he could not have been born before Nabopolassar made himself king in 626 BC. If Nebuchadnezzar were born immediately upon Nabopolassar’s crowning, he would have been eighteen at this time. If we assume he was born a few years after Nabopolassar took the throne, we are back to him being thirteen to sixteen years old at this point in the narrative.

c) Princes typically took to the field of battle at about thirteen years old. We have no mention of Nebuchadnezzar in battle until two years after this point. If modern historians, who assign an older age for the prince (around twenty-eight at his first mention in battle), are right, why is there no mention of his military exploits over the previous decade? Instead, using *Empire’s* timetable, we have Nebuchadnezzar first entering battle as an older fourteen-year-old.

d) Nebuchadnezzar was still a child, i.e., ten or younger, when he hauled bricks for Etenamenaki, at his father, the king’s, command. Modern historians would have us believe he was already eleven when Nabopolassar was crowned king, and hence, he could never have been a brick hauler as a child in his father’s realm because, at twelve, he would have been a youth, not a child. Upon his crowning, Nabopolassar had to give his attention to securing his crown in a very uncertain political climate. This would have taken some time. It is noted that at the founding of the ziggurat’s remodeling project, (two to three years after he took the throne) Nabopolassar presented his heir and declared his name to be Nebuchadnezzar, (i.e., the crown prince). The implication is that the prince was a baby. That would make the prince thirteen or fourteen here. In defense of the older age, however, it seems that Nabopolassar gave Nebuchadnezzar a royal shovel at this event and a baby couldn't hold a shovel, but a waiting servant could.

e) A bas-relief from Lebanon made in 605 BC, when he traveled through there, depicts Nebuchadnezzar as a youth, not yet having grown a beard. Likewise, a medallion, depicting him as rab mag (an office he held for less than two years before becoming king) and likely commemorating his coronation in that same year, clearly pictures him as barely sprouting whiskers. The mature Nebuchadnezzar had a very thick beard. So, he was much more likely to have been nineteen (not thirty-one) at his coronation, as *Empire* asserts. That would again make him thirteen at this point in the narrative.

2. Roses were native to the area and very popular.
3. The Seshed Circlet, worn by members of the Egyptian royal family when they were buried, is the only crown actually recovered from ancient Egypt. The others are known from records, statues, and carvings.
4. In 610 BC, Nabopolassar pushed all the way to Egypt and Psammetik I was killed. The history of the conquest is fragmented, and details are obscure so that some later historians have questions as to the importance of the campaign! Their objections are probably based on the fact that Necho was allowed to ascend the throne, even though Berosus clearly states that Egypt became a province of Babylonia and that Nabopolassar appointed Necho as pharaoh in his father's place. Also, they must either ignore the implications that Necho's daughter, Nitocris, was taken hostage and betrothed to Nebuchadnezzar or perhaps they are actually unaware of the event.

Part 2: 609 BC

Chapter 5

1. A "circle" was an Egyptian year. Most records agree that Alyattes took the throne of Lydia in either 609 or 619 BC. Taking into account that his father reigned about 20 years and his grandfather reigned about 30 years, he was probably about 30 when he took the throne and would

have been born around 639 BC. However, there seems to be one historical inconsistency which has Alyattes as the king who defeated the Cimmerians in 637, 626 or 625 BC. Choosing 625 as the latest date, and guessing the youngest a king would be leading a battle would be at age sixteen, that would have him born at the latest around 641 (only two years earlier than the above estimate). It would have made him, at the youngest, around fifty-six at the Battle of the Eclipse on May 28, 585 BC, which is entirely possible. Of course, it is also possible that he was sixty-eight, but his actual participation in the battle would then be in doubt. Alyattes reigned until 560 BC, so (still choosing age sixteen at 625 BC) he would have been at least eighty-one. This makes the 637 birthdate (where he would have been at least ninety-three in 560 BC) possible but very improbable. *Empire* tries to make sense of this by assuming he did lead the battle of the Cimmerians in 625 as a sixteen-year-old "co-king" under Sadyattes rule, and then actually took the throne at 28 years old in 609.

2. Judah had a seven-day week, the Babylonia had a quarter-moon, and Egypt had a ten-day.
3. Although pharaoh gave many gifts of camels and other livestock and foodstuffs, these were the things of Egypt's wealth, in other words, gifts from Egypt. It was proper to give gifts that were of great value to the receiver. Gifts to pharaoh were typically of metals and wood. Copper was preferred. An uten was an Egyptian weight unit normally used for copper weights, just under fifteen hundred grams, or about three and a third pounds. A temple workman made five uten of copper a month, or sixty uten of copper a year, along with an allowance of grain. An ox was worth about eight uten, or almost two months' wages. Forty thousand uten would have been the equivalent of a year's work for six hundred sixty-seven workmen. The Lydian gold mina is thought to be based upon this Egyptian weight standard, and sixty utens of silver equals one gold mina, the wages of a Lydian soldier in a year. Values for the exchange between copper and silver vary widely with the country and the time period, anywhere from eight-to-one to one hundred twenty-to-one (in Greece). The scarcity of copper in Egypt

gives credence to the lower exchange, in this case, making a soldier in Lydia earning eight times that of a temple worker in Egypt. A cubic cubit was the unit of measure for raw wood. Fifteen hundred cubic cubits would be just short of one hundred thousand board feet or twenty cords of wood.

4. While he lived, a pharaoh was entitled to the title "Horus." When he died, he received the title "Osiris" before his name to denote his status as having ascended to the gods.
5. Necho II and his adult son, Psammetik II had Libyan features. As a child, however, Psammetik II definitely shared features with his mother, Chednitjerbone, such as a squarish face and overlarge ears. Psammetik's skin would have been darker than his father's due to Chednitjerbone's Cushite heritage.
6. This would have been a terrible insult. The Egyptians hated dirt and thought all foreigners were bug-infested. To be called a "coward" was a deadly, unthinkable affront, and red was a color associated with unholy desecrators. To be red-faced was to be a heretic. In comparison, the gods were commonly thought of as black-faced.
7. Before 3000 BC, woven reed boats were often used to sail the Nile and its canals. These boats could be easily guided with a paddle and float north with the current or were light enough that the north wind would blow them upstream, south, against the current. But after 3000 BC, Egypt transitioned to wooden boats to be able to carry heavier load. Nobility employed barks which typically took eight rowers and a captain—it is assumed that they would carry relief crews as well. These boats could still be made of reeds as well as those now made of wood and rose to a high, stylized bow and stern. Some had cabins and the pharaoh's bark, The Star of Two Lands, was large enough to host great parties.

Chapter 6

1. It is close to six hundred miles up the Nile from Sais to Thebes. The Nile's current averages about three and a half miles per hour. A team of eight rowers can reach speeds of fifteen miles per hour but could not keep it up for long. So, with relief crews changing off and averaging perhaps six miles per hour rowing against the current, it would take rowers

around one hundred hours or just over four days to make the trip. This is still quite a bit faster—and for the passengers, much more relaxing—than horseback or wagons struggling along the muddy banks.

2. This intersection was between the seventh and eighth sphinxes on either side from the gate. To make a hard sole for sandals, haffa grass was dried, then coiled and sewn together.
3. The first pylon, at the main entrance to the temple complex, was built by the Cushites in 656 BC and was only forty-seven years old at this point, undoubtedly the newest location in the city. The square was completely walled-in by temples. From the main gate to the left was the Grand Temple of Amun. To the right, an addition to one wall of the Great Temple, was a much smaller temple to Ramesses' son, Ramesses III. Out of sight, somewhere behind the smaller temple was the Temple of Ramesses the Great. Directly ahead was the Great Hall, the audience chamber of the god's wife. The Great Hall was about two hundred fifty by two hundred feet, equaling about fifty thousand square feet. To grant some idea of scale, the Cathedral of Notre Dame in Paris could have fit inside of it, though of course, Notre Dame is much taller. The hall was constructed to be supported by sixteen rows of pillars, one hundred thirty-four in all. The columns were thirty-three feet around, and their open papyrus flower capitals were eighteen feet in diameter. One hundred men would easily fit on each capital.
4. Most of the pillars were forty feet tall, but in the raised central hall, the center columns rose over seventy feet, holding up a roof over eighty feet tall. This nave was lined with fifteen-foot-high windows set as stone grills running the length of the room, east to west.
5. The Cushite pharaohs had no problem with this, but their culture was black African, and they were quite willing to have a wife who was also married to a god. The Saites, however, were Libyan. Their culture, before they became pharaohs had a more patriarchal outlook. Men didn't share their wives, even with a god. Or perhaps a god did not share his wife with a man.
6. The Great Chiefs of the West were the so-called Libyan tribes and were of middle-eastern background. They ruled northern Africa from the Nile

to Gibraltar as sheiks. After the Cushites, some their princes were in contention for the throne of Egypt until Assyria chose Psammetik I, son of the Chieftain of Sais Necho I, and made him pharaoh. This is the blood of Sais (Libyan). Necho I's wife, Psammetik I's mother, was an Ethiopian princess. This was from the time that Ethiopia counted their capital to be at Meroe. Ancient Ethiopia was east of Egypt and north of Cush, along the Gulf of Suez and not to be confused with the placement of the modern-day country of Ethiopia on the east coast of Africa. This princess brought the blood of Meroe (Ethiopia). Psammetik I's wife, Necho II's mother, was Mehtenweskhet, the daughter of Harsiese, one of the priests of Atun at On (Heliopolis). While this was not royal blood, it was definitely nobility. Necho II's wife was Chednitjerbone, a Cushite princess. Cush and ancient Ethiopia are often confused because many times they were synonymous. They were often both referred to as Cush, or as in the case of the Greeks, both were called Ethiopia. The Cushites and Ethiopians at this time, however, were separate and the Kingdom of Cush (that had so recently ruled Egypt) was now centered in Napata. Prince Psammetik and Princess Nitocris were both descendants of Cush through their mother, and this is the blood of Napata (Cush). Hence, Psammetik II was three times royal, a descendant of the Houses of Sais, Meroe, and Napata. Mentemhe was the high priest of Amun. The priests of Amun were no longer pharaohs—the Libyan chieftains had ousted them long before the Cushites had arrived—but they were the only priests who had ever also been pharaohs. They were still the only line from which Amun could draw his high priests and governors. In essence, they still ruled in Upper Egypt. Princess Ankhnasneferibre was therefore descended from the kings of four different kingdoms.

Chapter 7

1. Judah had not yet adopted the Babylonian names for the months (the new calendar names), and though they did actually have their own names (the old calendar names), most of these have not survived. In practice, their calendar simply numbered the months. It is generally agreed

because of other historical documents of these events that Josiah died in the tenth month.

2. Egypt's ships arriving at Gaza at this time is speculation. There are no historical texts to say it happened. But early in 609 BC, Pharaoh Necho ordered ships made "from the Greeks" for both in the Mediterranean and the Red Sea. These ships played a part in the battle in which King Josiah was killed. It seems reasonable that the ships were first delivered at this time. A few Lydian mercenaries also took part in this battle with their dogs; therefore, they probably came on those ships. Lydia was known for shipbuilding under Alyattes and under his son Croesus until Croesus was forced to concentrate on his army rather than his navy. Necho's attempts to woo Alyattes make it likely that he ordered his ships from Lydia, who many ancient historians dumped in the same class as "the Greeks." The ships could not have landed at Ashkelon because the Scythians had destroyed that city and there had not yet been time to rebuild it. If the Lydians built the ships and/or were on board, they could not have come down the Nile to Sais because they would have had to sail by their enemies at the Fortress of the Milesians. Again, this leaves only one possibility for delivery, Egyptian-owned Gaza. Disembarking there would have given time for the Judeans to report the happening to Jerusalem and so warn Josiah.
3. Psalms 9:4-8
4. According to the storyline in *Empire of Gold: Foundations,* in 610 BC, when Nabopolassar marched past Jerusalem on his way to conquering Egypt, Jeremiah advised Josiah that Nabopolassar came to Judah in peace. There are no historical records as to Josiah and Nabopolassar's meeting, but it would be very difficult to hold to the position that Nabopolassar just marched by, and they ignored one another. Circumstances show undeniably that by 609 BC, though Judah remained independent, King Josiah was pro-Babylonian. Likewise, there is no record that Josiah bothered to consult Jeremiah before he marched against Necho. It is inconceivable that Jeremiah would not have mentioned such a meeting so it can only be assumed that Josiah thought he knew the Lord's will and did not need to send for the

prophet. Considering the circumstances, it seems likely that this was the case. From the natural perspective, Josiah did the right thing.

5. No one knows when Jeremiah was actually born, but speculation would put him at anywhere from thirty-one to forty-nine at this point. *Empire* chooses the youngest age possible for three reasons:
   a) If the oldest age is selected, Jeremiah would have been well into his sixties when the Lord warned him not to marry, this is very unlikely.
   b) At this point in history, a priest or prophet could be fully invested and begin his ministry when he reached thirty years old but was to retire at fifty (except the Chief Priest and possibly his second or third which held the office for life). *Empire's* timetable puts Jeremiah's age just within these limits for his entire ministry as Prophet to the Nations.
   c) It seems fitting that the prophet would have been born soon after Josiah became king, and to begin the ministry he was called to when he came of age, around the time of Josiah's death.
6. Psalms 82

Chapter 8

1. Unfortunately, Gaza, despite her long history, has not been able to provide the wealth of archeological treasures that surely lie buried there. Ever a victim of political unrest, Gaza's archeological sites have been raided and destroyed almost as they were uncovered. Consequently, little is known of the layout of the city or its structures from this period. Lamentably, raiding and destroying all archeological sites in the Middle East has become endemic in recent years to the point where there may soon be no more such sites remaining.

Chapter 9

1. Of all Josiah's sons, his eldest, Johanan, is the only one of whom the Bible never mentions his exact age and we are told that he was eldest. Eliakim was twenty-five at this point, meaning that Josiah would only have been fourteen and a half or fifteen when Eliakim was born! It is hardly reasonable to think Josiah had children at an earlier age than that. I Chronicles 3:15 lists Johanan, the first-born, Jehoiakim (born Eliakim)

second, Zedekiah (born Mattaniah) third, and Jehoahaz (born Shallum) fourth. Josephus gives us this same order and tells us that Johanan and Shallum were the sons of Hamutel while Eliakim and Mattaniah were the sons of Josiah's second wife, Zebidah.

2. II Chronicles 35:21. There is a theological debate as to whether the Lord God actually said this or whether Pharaoh Necho was making it up. How could the Lord be with Egypt in the matter of the overthrow of Carchemish? At any rate, King Josiah apparently did not believe him. However, verse 22 plainly states that Necho spoke at God's command. So, what event would the pharaoh have missed if he was delayed? The most glaringly obvious answer is the prompt arrival of Egypt's army at Jerusalem just days after the New Year Festival to dethrone Jehoahaz, an already evil king.
3. To the Egyptians, a jackal was an honorable animal, the symbol of Anubis, god of mummification. To the Hebrews, it was despicable. In the Bible, a jackal symbolizes a cunning two-faced man, saying one thing, meaning another; walking in the darkness but hiding in the light. His motivations are evil and secret, looking to betray and pounce on the unwary at his first chance to do so.
4. Alyattes of Lydia is the first recorded user of war dogs. He employed a breed of dog that was larger and heavier built than the sleek Egyptian hounds. It had flopped-over ears and a short muzzle, much like a giant Pit Bull, and was only slightly shorter than a Great Dane, but much stouter. It was undoubtedly due in large part to these enormous and fierce war dogs that Alyattes owed his dominance over the kingdoms of Asia Minor. The dogs were probably ancestors of the breed the Greeks knew as Molossus.
5. The Israelites used hammered silver trumpets for most occasions and reserved shophars for Rosh Hashanah and Yom Kippur.

Chapter 10

Chapter 11

1. Literally, "God has grasped." Jehoahaz viewed his choosing by the lot as God having grabbed him and set him, the youngest, in the place of the king.

2. Psalms 72 appears to have been written by both David and Solomon, for Solomon's coronation.
3. The wall dividing the palace court and the Temple Court was added sometime after Solomon. The New Gate was the gate in the wall between the two courts. Presumably, there had been an "old" gate there previously, hence the title "New Gate." Speculation has Hezekiah as the one who installed the New Gate. This gate is not to be confused with the "New Gate" of the Herodian Temple in New Testament times, which was on the west side of the Old City walls.
4. We don't know the exact date Jehoahaz took his throne. Due to the timing of the battles listed in the Babylonian Chronicle, it would have been early in Du'uzu (Tammuz). Du'uzu is the Babylonian calendar's fourth month and the Judean religious calendar's tenth month (June of 609 BC). Solomon built a huge bronze platform in the court for purposes like coronations and addressing the crowds. Pharaoh Shishak undoubtedly took it away, and if it was later replaced, it is never mentioned again, so *Empire* assumes there was no longer any platform. However, if the Judeans hid David's crown from the pharaoh's pillaging, then it is probable that this was the crown still being used at this time for coronation purposes. The Bible does not mention pearls, only gems, but pearls were included in the meaning of the word commonly translated "gem," and they were precious, so it is almost certain that pearls were also found on the huge Davidic crown. This crown weighed about seventy-five pounds! There is no way to tell how old the crown actually was since David captured it from the Ammonites. The "testimony" Jehoahaz received is generally thought to mean the Law or the Scriptures. However, some take it to mean the royal insignia. For instance, David, upon being crowned, received Saul's bracelets and jewelry.
5. The hypothesis that Eliakim (Jehoiakim) plotted with Pharaoh Necho to overthrow his brother, King Jehoahaz, is based on Eliakim's temperament and the cruelty of his reign. It provides an explanation as to how this singular turn of events (Jehoahaz' rapid overthrow and arrest by Egypt and Eliakim's gaining the throne) came about. There is

no doubt that Necho looked favorably on Jehoiakim as a kind of protégé. He put him on the throne, lent him his master builder, along with many other high officials, and counseled him on how to run his country. In return, Jehoiakim tried his best to remake his palace and his city in the image of Egypt.

Chapter 12

1. According to Egyptian records, Ramses II bragged that he conquered the Hittites at this battle, but this was obviously propaganda. Instead, he was forced to sign the first known existing peace treaty, and Egypt's advance was finally stopped.
2. Palm-wood casks of wine and beer were invented by Babylon's famous breweries around the time of these histories. *Empire* assumes that such a useful container would have been noticed and copied, if not exported to Assyria. Egypt's association with Assyria makes it virtually certain that the Egyptians would have become familiar with casks as well, though no archeological evidence has been found to support this.
3. Sometime in late July 609 BC.

Chapter 13

1. "Euphrates" is actually the Greek name for the river, the people of the area called it "Prath Frot" meaning "good to cross over," or, like the Hebrews, simply "the River." The Tigris, on the other hand, comes from a Persian word, "Tigr" the equivalent of the local Aramaic name "Deqlath" meaning "the swift one." Mesopotamia, the area between the rivers, was "Bethnahrin," meaning "home of the rivers."
2. An average large wineskin would hold about thirty-five liters of wine and would weigh about one hundred pounds, including the skin.
3. The shash is an ancient hat still worn by the clergy of the Chaldean Coptic Church today.
4. The Statue of Liberty is a depiction of the Roman goddess Libertas, who was based on, and portrayed identically as one of the millennia-old guises of the goddess Ishtar, raised torch and all.
5. Excerpt from the Hymn to Ishtar.
6. The story of Belnasir and Shadushushan is total fiction, neither ever existed. However, the story of the fall of Carchemish must be told from the

viewpoint of someone who was there, and no information on any such person is available. Moreover, someone had to have been Nabopolassar's rab shaq, Nabopolassar had to have made someone Commander of Carchemish, Queen Amyhia would have had a lady-in-waiting, and Ugbaru had to have a mother. The invention of this ill-fated couple fills all these needs.

Chapter 14

1. B'hatzlacha means good luck or best wishes. The ostrich reference is from Job 39:13—17.

Chapter 15

1. The Lydians seemed to have had a huge number of these dogs. Friezes of battle scenes show a dog beside every horse. It is possible these horses were ridden by the dogs' handlers.
2. Early August, 609 BC. Details of how the Allies took this fortress are lacking. This is one possible scenario. Throwing the defeated Babylonian troops alive from the walls of Carchemish was one of the most infamous acts ever committed by Assyria. Of course, the Assyrian Empire didn't actually exist anymore, so most of the blame for the heinous deed seems to have been heaped onto Egypt.

Chapter 16

1. Addaguppi wound up married to Uvakshatra's governor, Nabubalatsuikibi. Their son, Nabonaid, eventually became Nebuchadnezzar's son-in-law.

Chapter 17

1. Electrum was a natural alloy of gold and silver (and sometimes copper) that gave a very high luster, did not tarnish, and was greatly prized.
2. In the myth of Tammuz, he was first seen as a beautiful youth who loved to farm. He became the god of agriculture who died annually and was resurrected by a love-struck Ishtar. In his death, he was known as the god of the underworld, Du'uzu.
3. Rab translates as "great." The rab postings were thirty-year terms given by the king himself. The rab mag, shaq, and sharish were the trio of highest ranking officers in Babylonia. The rab mag was the first general. The rab shaq was the cupbearer. In times of peace, he answered to the rab

sharish, and in times of war, he was the second general. The rab sharish was the prime minister of the empire.

4. Historical records show that harems unequivocally existed in Nineveh, Ecbatana, Susa, Jerusalem and all of Egypt's capitals as far back as the Old Kingdom. But regarding Babylon, only Herodotus mentions a harem and that only in passing. Talking about the palace grounds, he says "housing the palace and the harem." However, the lack of historical records for a harem at Babylon, does not, as some claim, mean that a harem did not exist there.
5. Nebuchadnezzar built over the old palace, including Nabopolassar's throne room. That makes it very difficult to know many details other than its location. Babylon's lack of wall carvings and statuary fit into its generally understated grandeur, and Nabopolassar followed this tradition. The House, the Marvel of Mankind, the Center of the Land, the Shining Residence, the Dwelling of Majesty, had a more impressive name than presence. Still, it is known that there were five courtyards, with many small rooms, the royal residences were in the second and third stories, and that the banquet hall was huge.
6. Why didn't Nabopolassar revenge himself on Princess Nitocris for her father's treason? She was, after all, a hostage against this very thing and any other royal house would have acted decisively. This is one of many instances in which the Dynasty of Bit Yakin showed incredible restraint and mercy to the families of royalty that betrayed them.

Chapter 18

1. The first month of the Judean civil year, Etanim was by Babylonian reckoning Tashritu, the seventh moon. It began on the first sliver of the new moon in the autumn.
2. A new king, upon his crowning, was required to transcribe his own copy of the Pentateuch and to read from it every day for the rest of his life. Deuteronomy 17: 18-19.
3. Lamassu were guardian spirits, not gods. Despite the similarities in culture and religion between Assyria and Babylonia, lamassu were never found in Babylonia. Later, however, lion lamassu were imported to Persia and have been found on Persian capstones or above Persian stone friezes.

Though the Assyrians seemed to prefer bulls, the Persians always identified with lions.

4. Under King Josiah, Judah followed the Law. What could his son, Jehoahaz, possibly have done in three short months to earn him the ominous condemnation "he did evil in the sight of the Lord," and cause him to be taken away to die in exile in Egypt? Jehoahaz's full third month commenced on the New Year, the day marking the beginning of his regnal year. It is logical to suppose that he threw a party during which he sinned greatly. In any case, divine retribution was swift. Egypt's army arrived within days.

Chapter 19

1. In addition to these supposed scandalous statements that Jehoiakim made upon his crowning, Jewish tradition also counts Jehoiakim guilty of many other sins. They list, among other things: burning the Books of Jeremiah and Lamentations, blatant idolatry, incest (with his father's wives, his mother and his daughter-in-law), adultery, murder, theft, blasphemy, tattooing himself with the name(s) of idol(s) and/or the Lord and wearing clothes of mixed wood and linen. These traditions must be taken with a grain of salt. It may be possible that he committed incest with some of Josiah's widows and/or his daughter-in-law, but his own mother was probably dead long before this. If he had various affairs with married women and then murdered their husbands and took their belongings, it does not seem to be recorded anywhere else. And though it is true that he cut up and burned Jeremiah's first scroll, we know that he could not have cut passages out of Lamentations and burned them, since he was dead before that book was written.
2. Three and three-quarters tons of silver and seventy-five pounds of gold. Interestingly enough, the gold was the same amount that was in the official crown. If that crown was still in existence, Jehoiakim could have given it up to satisfy at least that amount of the taxation. He did not, because the Bible expressly says that he "exacted the silver and gold from the people of the land" (II Kings 23:35).

Chapter 20

1. Descriptions of Uvakshatra's Ecbatana are according to Herodotus. Modern archeology has failed to come up with any ruins dating earlier than 248 BC, the Persian era. It may be that the Persian Ecbatana is not actually the site of the Median capital. Thanks to Nabonaid, we know that the entire area was known as Ecbatana, "the gathering place," and tradition holds that Uvakshatra's capital was on an entirely different mountain than that of the Persian Ecbatana. The Medes held such an aversion to living in cities or to any large-scale construction that we have yet to find any archeological remains. Sadly, the lack of Median archeological data includes any busts or friezes, so no one knows what Uvakshatra and his family actually looked like.
2. Ishtumegu's dreams regarding his daughter Mandane are literally the stuff of Persian legend, but behind legend, there is sometimes truth. His actions certainly indicated that he had some sort of advance knowledge so that he tried to make sure that this child would not bear his heir. Herodotus admits this story may or may not have been true. According to Herodotus' sources, though, Prince Ishtumegu had no (legitimate?) sons. Herodotus falsely assumes Ishtumegu was king by the time the princess was born. He says Ishtumegu was plagued by dreams regarding his first-born daughter, Mandane, some of the details of which are recorded in *Empire's* storyline. To thwart the future, Ishtumegu first married his daughter to the heir of an insignificant Persian half-tribe. Later, he attempted to kill Mandane's baby son, his grandson, Cyrus (the Great), with the aid of his steward, Harpagu. When it was discovered that Harpagu had failed to carry out his commission, the consequences were severe.

Chapter 21

1. The Hebrews named the month Tevet (December 609/January 608).
2. Nekhtu-Ra was Necho's chief builder. That he sent him to Jerusalem speaks volumes about how important the pharaoh viewed the city's renovation. Obviously, Jerusalem was to be a monument to the pharaoh. Jehoiakim's building programs under the direction of Nekhtu-Ra resulted in heavy taxation and enslavement of the people.

Though some details are known and used here, excavation on Temple Mount is forbidden, so exact architectural details of the old city including the Temple, palace, many official buildings, the city walls and their gates are difficult and must rely on existing written records and clues from the Bible. The Book of Nehemiah gives the position of many of the gates, but few were the same as in former days, and even when they were, the names tended to have changed. The position of the walls themselves differed. The site of the Temple grounds under Nehemiah was significantly reduced. For example, the Potsherd Gate became Nehemiah's Dung Gate. The Benjamin Gate (Huldah's Gate) became the Ephraim Gate, though this was no longer on Temple grounds. The Middle Gate became Nehemiah's Old Gate. The Horse Gate remained the Horse Gate.

3. The proliferation of foreign idols in the Temple of Neith was one of the things that in later years caused the Egyptian people to turn against Pharaoh Apries so that General Amasis was able to usurp his throne. Later, Cyrus II removed the foreign gods from Neith's temple and even though he was Persian, the Egyptians hailed him for it and welcomed him as their new pharaoh. In Jerusalem, the shrine known as the Wood House was probably demolished by Josiah. According to Ezekiel 43, many gods seemed to be settled in the side rooms of the Temple itself—probably in the north rooms as Jeremiah was known to have used a room in the south, both for addressing the people and for giving a banquet. *Empire* assumes that the first gods Jehoiakim installed would have been Egypt's and these were those that were settled in Jerusalem's Temple. However, the shrine west of the Temple (the Wood House) appears to have been rebuilt, probably because the Temple could only hold so many gods and their priests. Later, the northern gate, known as the Benjamin Gate, which faced the northern rooms of the Temple, was also used to house a pantheon of idols. Given the three locations, it seems likely that Jehoiakim was guilty of installing hundreds of idols on the Temple grounds.
4. Moab and Edom's primary complaint against Judah was the high taxes charged to transport goods overland across the country.

5. Jeremiah 22:1-30.

Part 3: 608 BC

Chapter 22

1. The sixth month of the civil, not the religious calendar. *Empire* tends to use the civil calendar since the series has a political, rather than religious, point of view. The fourteenth day of the seventh month would be Nisan 14 according to the new names of the months adopted during the exile. The Judean civil calendar was half a year off from Babylon's, but their religious calendar, adopted after the Exodus, was the same as Babylon's and had the New Year at Nisan 1. The lambs were to be sacrificed on the afternoon of the fourteenth, and the Feast of Passover actually began after sunset, so on the fifteenth.
2. Many of the names and exact positions of the gates of Jerusalem from the time of Solomon until Nehemiah are unknown. The positioning of the Temple gates, however, are surer. The northern gate, called the Benjamin Gate (or Huldah's Gate); the eastern gate, called the King's Gate; the southern gate, called the New Gate; and the western gate, whose name being unknown, is here dubbed the "West Gate."
3. Jeremiah 11:1-17. The Biblical text does not say that Jeremiah had a vision here, just that the Lord revealed this plot against him. Jeremiah's poetic language may be only a verbal, not an actual, picture.
4. The House of Prophets was an old and honored tradition. It dated back to the time of the Judges, over 400 years before this. The Prophets of the House were given to ecstatic utterances and, for a fee, personal forecasts. In general, they were a political tool, meddling in the civil aspects of the state of Judah, under the jurisdiction, direction, and authority of the priesthood. They did not lead, they took orders. The Temple prophets are not to be confused with the true messengers of the Lord, who, starting with Jonah, Amos, and Hosea almost 200 years before, had begun appearing on the streets proclaiming judgment and the "Day of the Lord." This is not to say that a true prophet could not be a member of the House of Prophets. Both Elijah and Elisha obviously were members of the Samaritan chapter of House of Prophets, and it appears Elijah may have been the head of that house.

5. Jeremiah 11:21-23.

Chapter 23

1. The Hill Country is a term used for various mountainous areas, in this case, the Kingdom of Urartu. It stretched from the north of Harran to the east, north of what had been Nineveh, to the foothills of the Ural Mountains and so, to Media. The unrest there marked the start of Nebuchadnezzar's military career. The Urartu had been subject to the Assyrians. *Empire* assumes that even at this point, they still counted themselves members of the Assyro-Egyptian Alliance and Ashurubalit may actually have stationed himself and his army at Sarduri IV's fortress at Van. Nebuchadnezzar campaigned in the Hill Country for three months, then he, himself, led his own troops on a three-month campaign in the mountains of Zamua (Lake Urmia, northeast of demolished Nineveh, supposedly against Urartu incursions in which he seized and burned forts and "gained much loot." As King Nabopolassar marched on Samsat (Kimuhu), (northwest of Harran on the Upper Euphrates, other records have it just south of Carchemish), his son, Nebuchadnezzar, returned to Babylon. There, the prince raised a surprising amount of monetary support from reluctant temple authorities for his father's war, something Nabopolassar had never managed to do.
2. The Nile, along with most freshwater in Africa, is infested with a parasitic worm that can be absorbed through the skin, resulting in schistosomiasis. The condition existed well over 3,000 years ago. Many of the Babylonians who invaded Egypt would have developed it. *Empire* uses this to explain what happened to Nabopolassar's rag mag, clearing the way for Nebuchadnezzar to assume the post.
3. Nabopolassar and Nebuchadnezzar's campaigns that year are well documented.

Chapter 24

1. The excavations of Ecbatana on the northern hill of the city of Hamadan in Iran (at the feet of Mount Alvand/Harvant) have so far yielded no artifacts earlier than from 248 BC. These artifacts are of the Persian Achaemenids, leaving doubt as to whether the city of the Medes was at

this site at all. Indeed, before the excavations were confirmed to be the Persian Ecbatana, the site of the Median Ecbatana was believed to have been at Mount Bikni. The name "Ecbatana" is a transliteration of "Hagmatana" which literally means "the gathering place." This indicates that the Medes did not consider the site to be a place to live, but rather to meet and conduct business. There is literally no mention of the city having a population (other than the palace with the king and his family). Accordingly, the Nabonidus Chronicle identifies the entire area, not just the fortress city, as Ecbatana. It is possible that the actual city of the Medes has yet to be discovered. Perhaps the original belief in Mount Bikni may be correct. The Medes' reluctance to raise monuments or to invest in architecture is a definite hindrance to any archeological finds. *Empire* mostly follows the description of the city walls given by Herodotus; however, it is probable that Herodotus, when he gave the city's total size, making it comparable to Athens, was exaggerating. Such a city would have had a large population, and the Medes' city had none at all, as far as we know. Other historians, notably Xenophon, have given other accounts, making the city much smaller—a very credible 300 x 300 meters—and even claiming it had no walls other than that around the citadel at the very top of the hill. As to this discrepancy, it may be that what Herodotus called walls (fortifications), were simply painted terraces, foundations for the road, spiraling up around the hill, and leading up to the palace, which was walled and accented in gold. If the area around the outside of the hill where the road began its rise is counted as part of the "city" its size would come much closer to Herodotus' claims. The Ecbatana Herodotus and Xenophon knew would have been that of the Summer Capital of the Persians, but it was still 200 years before the date of the site that is being currently excavated, so it may indeed have been the city of the Medes. Perhaps the Persians moved their summer capital some distance away from the original, about 400 years after the events recorded in *Empire.*

2. According to Berosus, Nebuchadnezzar married Amyhia a few years before he became king. All this means is the marriage contract was drawn up.

A marriage took place over a period of time, possibly years. First, the families agreed to the match. Next, the groom visited the bride's family and paid the bride price to the bride's father. A marriage contract would then be drawn up. Last, the bride would be delivered to the groom, and the bride's father would return the bride price to him in the form of a dowry. If he were to divorce his wife, the husband would then need to give her back her dowry to return to her father's house.

3. Herodotus says Dioka of Media (not Xerxes of Persia as some historians have it) was the one who first made the law that no one could come to him while he sat on his throne unless he was called for. If that is the case, then Uvakshatra—Dioka's grandson—would have followed this law. As to the feast, other than ancient written records, there is no physical, archeological information on Ecbatana at during this time period. Descriptions of the palace and fortress found in *Empire* are based on what is known of Median culture and those ancient records. The Medes had once been nomadic tribesmen. King Dioka had united five tribesof the tribes: Busae, Parataceni, Struchates, Arizanti, and Budii. A sixth tribe, the independent, priestly tribe of the Magi, served them all by serving the king. They were one nation, at last, with the exception of a small rebellious tribe known as the Mannai. Dioka then built the fortress of Ecbatana and began a tradition in which the kings were expected to separate themselves from their own people to perpetuate a kind of myth-like aura, convincing their own subjects that they were not mere men. They certainly didn't eat or fellowship with them. Uvakshatra, on the other hand, led his own men in battle and was often found among them, apparently breaking tradition whenever it suited him.

Chapter 25

1. No one had chests full of pearls. They were the rarest and most precious of jewels. Media, with no seacoast of its own, would have considered them that much dearer.
2. Trees and gardens were of the utmost importance to both the Medes and the Persians, and reverence for them was ingrained into every small child. When these people changed their religion to become Zoroastrians, the

eternal tree became an important religious symbol. There is a story where King Ahasuerus was leading his troops, and they were caught in a blizzard. He ordered them to make fires, but they disobeyed. The king then took an ax himself and laid it to the largest tree and so persuaded his men and saved their lives. This leads to the question of whether the Medes and perhaps the early Persians ever harvested live trees or merely relied on dead wood.

Chapter 26

1. Proverbs 18:24
2. Leather is perishable so that the earliest known long whips ever recovered are from ancient Greece and Rome. However, old Egyptian medallions depict men (slave owners?) wielding long-handled whips with even longer lashes, similar to the stock whips of today.

Part 4: 607 BC

Chapter 27

1. The real fate of Ashurubalit, last emperor of Assyria, remains a mystery. He disappears from all historical records at about this time. But at sixteen, Nebuchadnezzar took his new cavalry to the hill country north of Harran. Arbaces the Scythian probably joined him since he was encamped around Harran. The area was a likely spot for Ashurubalit to be stationed. At any rate, something or someone was stirring up the peoples (mostly Elamites, and Urartu) of the hill country and it very well could have been Ashurubalit.

Chapter 28

1. The ancient historians say Nebuchadnezzar was only sixteen when he became rab mag. He assumed total control of the forces of Babylonia because his father remained in Babylon from then on, due to illness. The rab mag posting was for thirty years, unless withdrawn. Since Nabopolassar had only ruled for twenty years at this point, his old rab mag could not have held the office longer than twenty years. Accordingly, either the posting was withdrawn in Nebuchadnezzar's favor, or the old rab mag died, or was disabled, perhaps of the same unknown illness which Nabopolassar contracted.

Chapter 29

1. Isaiah 30:18. The story of Uriah is found in Jeremiah 26:20-23, almost as an aside thrown in by the prophet or his scribe, Baruch. Either way, Baruch was at least well acquainted with Uriah's fate and may have known him personally. The story seems to be included in the scriptures as an example of how bad King Jehoiakim actually was, but other than this short passage, not much is known about this prophet. For example, it is not known if Uriah actually belonged to the House of Prophets, what it was that he prophesied, or for how long he continued. He could have started right from the beginning of Jehoiakim's reign.

Chapter 30

1. Almost ten feet.
2. Jeremiah 19, Jeremiah 7: 33b-34.

Chapter 31

1. It was an ancient custom for a subordinate nation to honor the gods of their masters by erecting them in their temple areas. Likewise, conquerors would take a defeated nations gods captive and hold them hostage in their own gods' temples. The references to the practice in the Jerusalem Temple are vague, and it's hard to know exactly how many times this happened, but it appears that after the Assyrian gods had been removed, the Egyptian gods were in place two different times.
2. The Feast of Tabernacles was the feast where the people would gather to hear the reading of the Pentateuch. However, it seems that the Feast of Tabernacles was not properly celebrated from the time of Joshua until the time of Nehemiah, over a hundred years after the events in Chapter 31 (Nehemiah 8). Perhaps they did read the Pentateuch at the Feast of Tabernacles, but it is reasonable that the Law, as in the Ten Commandments had a place in all the feasts.
3. The storm and the fate of the Horse Tower mentioned here is fiction.
4. The title "The Queen of Heaven" appears twice in the Bible, both times by Jeremiah about Asherah/Ashtareth, the wife of Baal. However, "Queen of Heaven" was actually the title of the goddess Ishtar. Since Ishtar was a Babylonian combination of Asherah and the Sumerian Inanna, the Judeans often made no distinction between Asherah and

Ishtar. The title "Queen of Heaven" came to be ported over to apply to Asherah as well. The reference "Queen of Heaven" comes from the myth of Ishtar's excursion to the netherworld. When Neti, the chief gatekeeper of the dead, inquired who knocked at his gates, the goddess answered: "I am the Queen of Heaven, the place where the sun rises."

5. Jeremiah 7, 26. The text of Jeremiah 26 reads: "As soon as Jeremiah had finished telling all the people" but it gives a very truncated version of what he must have said! Whatever it was, it must have been a whopper of an indictment to cause the problems that immediately followed. *Empire* here inserts the text from Jeremiah 7, as it fits very well. However, it appears that this was a parallel sermon, given sometime later, after he was banned from the Temple grounds as he is told to go "stand at the gate," not "stand in the Temple Court," like he was in Jeremiah 26.

Chapter 32

1. Since this trial took place in the New Gate and yet the people from the Temple Court were obviously witnesses of the event, it seems that the New Gate was made of two sets of metal bars or grills, which could be closed while still allowing the people to watch. The Great Council was the forerunner of what became known as the Sanhedrin. It was composed of the Council of Seventy (or Seventy-One) who were instituted by Moses, and the clergy, with the Chief Priest presiding. According to the Talmud, it had the authority to judge false prophets. If that is so—and it appears from this trial that it is—then Jehoiakim overstepped his bounds in judging and executing Uriah.

2. Leviticus 26: 3, 12; Jeremiah 26. The Book of Jeremiah doesn't say how it was that the prophet came to be restricted from entering the Temple grounds. Nevertheless, it had to have happened after he gave his Passover Sermon (Jeremiah 11) and before he and Baruch completed the scroll and Baruch was sent to read it since Jeremiah could not (Jeremiah 36:5). Logically, the riot he caused at this point—which seems to have been during the Feast of Weeks (Pentecost)—would appear to have been a good enough reason for the Chief Priest to declare such a restriction. To be barred from the Temple grounds was

tantamount to excommunication. The discussion groups (the "sodh") met on Temple grounds, so he could no longer teach. All sacrifices were conducted there. Jeremiah was being denied spiritual fellowship and forgiveness.

Chapter 33

1. The cult of the Baals became pronounced among the people of Israel 250 years before the events of *Empire* when King Ahab of Israel married a Philistine princess of Sidon, Jezebel. Their daughter, Athaliah, married King Jehoram of Judah, son of Jehoshaphat, and apparently turned his heart from the Lord, encouraging Baal worship in Judah as well as Israel.

Part 5: 606 BC

Chapter 34

1. The moon god, Sin, was the patron god of both Harran and Ur. His symbol was the crescent moon. Interestingly enough, Nebuchadnezzar's rab mag, Belshumishkun, was from Ur and was a Sin worshiper. Nebuchadnezzar granted his rab mag rule over the nomadic tribes of Arabs when he made him Lord of Sin Magyr. The Arab tribes gradually adopted Belshumishkun's god as the head of their pantheon, too; but they called him Allah.
2. Cooking at this time was done mostly indoors in a separate kitchen. The hearth had been introduced by the Philistines and its use continued even into the exile. cf. Ez. 43:15-16.
3. By word count, the Book of Jeremiah is the longest book of the Bible, larger even than Isaiah.

Chapter 35

1. *Empire* follows the basic facts of the campaign of 606 BC. Specific details are lacking.

Chapter 36

1. Judah, Philistia and Upper Syria.

Chapter 37

Chapter 38

1. The customs offices in Babylon were located just off the docks.

Chapter 39

Chapter 40

1. Since the Persians started their day at midnight, it is probable that the Medes did as well. Amyhia's birthday would have begun in the middle of the night.

Chapter 41

1. Ramses II had initially cut through the land, creating the Tumilat Canal, which flowed right by Tanis, greatly increasing that city's status. The channel brought the territory of Geshem (Goshen) a remarkable prosperity. After Ramses, the Tumilat quickly filled with sand and remained that way until Pharaoh Necho II.
2. Opening a port on the Great Sea was a problem. The deadly currents off the coast from Tanis and Mendes made such a port inadvisable but from Rosetta it was possible. The route was longer, but it necessitated passage by the capital of Sais, which was a significant advantage to the Saites. It also meant that the traffic generated had to pass by the Fort of the Milesians and was probably the major factor in the sudden growth of that town into a major Greek trade center with several city/states represented. If some doubt remains as to the importance of this canal, it should be observed that it was at this point that the Lydians suddenly reversed an eighteen-year-old policy and apologized to King Thrasybulus of Miletus, for their yearly burning and crop snatching raids. Since King Alyattes of Lydia went so far as to rebuild the temple in Miletus, Thrasybulus accepted his apology. This opened the way for Lydia to use the new canal because to do that they had to pass by Thrasybulus' fortress (the Fort of the Milesians) down on the Nile. Coincidence?
3. The expedition, led by a Philistine (Phoenician) named Kaelus, sailed from the Red Sea in Necho's third year and returned through the Straits of Gibraltar (the Pillars of Hercules) in his sixth, having stopped to plant and harvest twice. Interestingly enough, the historian Herodotus doubted the records and thought that this could not have happened. He could not lend credence to the testimonies of the crews that the sun and the heavens rotated incorrectly and that the seasons were reversed.

Chapter 42

Part 6: 605 BC

Chapter 43

1. In the Bible, the name "Uz" can refer to an unspecified land to the east, somewhere beyond the Euphrates. However, Jeremiah's use of it in Lamentations 4:21 shows that to him, Edom was located in "Uz." Here he inserts a Hebrew poetical repetition, a clarification that shows "Uz" also included Moab and Amon, at least in Jeremiah's eyes. Perhaps a translation for "Uz" should be "eastern lands." In an artistic twist, Jeremiah first mentions the southern Philistine city/states and then, in the repetition, he adds Tyre and Sidon, showing a recognition of the Greek designation as Phoenician for the northern cities, while still grouping them together with their southern counterparts. This part of the passage (Jer. 25:20b-22) is talking to all of Judah's immediate neighbors to the east and west. Jeremiah uses a complex and intricate weaving of themes, giving us meanings within meanings, worthy of the major prophet and master musician that he was.
2. Jeremiah 25. The note inserted by Baruch at the beginning of the chapter dates this occurrence Jehoiakim's fourth year. That is in Nebuchadnezzar's first year, even though he had not yet been crowned at the time.

Chapter 44

1. Jeremiah 18.
2. Psalms 91:1-2a, 5, 7.
3. Jeremiah 1:8.

Chapter 45

1. Jeremiah 19-20. Job 3.

Chapter 46

1. Simanu (Sivan) ran from sometime in May to sometime in June.
2. A half-beru was one modern hour.
3. This battle was horrific, and many men on both sides were lost. Jeremiah 46 records Jeremiah's all too accurate prophecy of the "battle of the north, by the Euphrates." Jeremiah 46:12 may suggest that many of Babylon's troops fell along with the Egyptians.

4. The records of these events vary. *Empire* follows the majority of historians and differs somewhat from Berosus, who wrote: "When Nabopolassar heard that the governor (Necho) whom he had set over the province of Egypt and over the parts of Coelesyria and Philistia had betrayed him, he could ignore this annoyance no longer. So, he gave part of his army to his son Nebuchadnezzar, who was still a youth, and sent him against the rebel. Nebuchadnezzar met Necho in battle and defeated him, bringing the land once again under his father's control." While Necho certainly dominated these territories until Nebuchadnezzar drove him out, other histories make it clear that the pharaoh conquered the areas. Nabopolassar most certainly did not give them to him to rule (except for Egypt itself). That the pharaoh took them was the very essence of Necho's rebellion. Also, Nebuchadnezzar was rab mag. He had not been given "part" of the army, he had it all.
5. A carved, bas-relief image in Lebanon portrays a youthful looking Nebuchadnezzar wearing the white crown on his way through to challenge Egypt. Why he would don the Hedjet must be subject to speculation. Certainly, this claimed both spiritual and political authority over Upper Egypt (the south), but without the red crown of Lower Egypt (the north) he was perhaps saying that he had no intention of physically staying (at Sais in Lower Egypt) and ruling from there. Why not the blue Chepresh battle helm? It could be that he was saying that as the rightful pharaoh, he didn't wish to declare war on his own people (Egypt), but that was almost certainly the outcome that he did intend since he marched on Egypt with the armies of Babylon behind him.

Chapter 47

1. Anathoth was destroyed, yet Jeremiah's cousin was back there, eighteen years later in 582, asking Jeremiah to redeem the land from him. Apparently, at least, some people from Anathoth, notably some from Jeremiah's family, heeded his warning and got out before it was too late. It would make sense that they sold their properties at Anathoth to those who didn't leave. Many Judeans from Jerusalem in this, the first deportation, did the same thing and used the capital to make a fresh start in Babylon. The land could not actually be sold, however. It was an irrevocable

family inheritance. A sale was more of a long-term lease with the property reverting back to the family on the Jubilee. It has been calculated that the Israelites entered the Promised Land in 1406 BC and that the first year of Jubilee took place fourteen years later in 1392. The Sabbatical Year took place every seven years, but it is uncertain if the year of Jubilee ran concurrently and with the seventh Sabbatical Year or was just after it, in the fiftieth year. Arguments for the fiftieth-year Jubilee include the fact that this would make it a kind of a Super-Pentecost, a year-long Feast of Weeks. Since the Feast of Weeks celebrates the birthday of Judaism, this would be like a super-birthday, every fifty years, reminiscent of our centennial and bi-centennial celebrations. It is a celebration of the harvest in which the land rests for an entire year. If these figures are correct, then the next Jubilee would have been in 592 BC, thirteen years after 605, and the events as recorded in the Bible fit perfectly in this timetable. So, in 592, the land would have reverted back to Jeremiah's family, even though they had "sold" it, leaving Hanamel free to ask Jeremiah to redeem it from him in 582. A lack of documentation, however, leads to skepticism as to whether Israel or Judah ever actually celebrated the Jubilee after that first time in 1392 BC. Leviticus 26 predicts that they wouldn't give the land the seventh-year rest either.

2. Ezekiel went to Babylonia as part of the second exile, but he wasn't fully vested as a priest until his thirtieth birthday, which occurred during the exile. Ezekiel went into exile in the second stage of deportees. It was only the skilled craftsmen, the men of war and the aristocracy who were taken at that time. Ezekiel could only have fallen into the third group, the aristocracy. Also, from his writings, it is evident that he was a man who was personally immersed in the traditions of the Temple worship and the people of his village recognized his authority as their priest. Therefore, he was almost certainly of the House of Zadok.

Chapter 48

1. Nebuchadnezzar took the throne on September 23, 605 BC. Leaving twenty-six days for his flight across the desert from Egypt to Babylon, and nine days from Jerusalem to the Egyptian border (one hundred seventy-five

miles at twenty miles a day) plus a day at Jerusalem, we can count back thirty-six days from Nebuchadnezzar's coronation to come up with the date of his arrival at Jerusalem as August 18, 605 BC—two days after the date of his father's death.

Chapter 49

1. It would be very hard to support any theory that suggests Nebuchadnezzar did not learn about Jeremiah when he arrived at Jerusalem. The city would have been buzzing about the prophet and his words concerning the arrival of the "King" of Babylon. Later, Nebuchadnezzar's orders concerning the care Nebuzaradan is to take for the prophet bear this out.
2. Jeremiah 46:1-12. Jeremiah's prophecy here is fascinating. In the form we have it from Jeremiah's second scroll it looks back to the time it was initially given, adding several editorial remarks as to the time and circumstances. At the time it first spoken, the details of the location, participants, actions and outcome seemed ludicrous, yet turned out to be entirely accurate. Alyattes of Lydia, looking to block Uvakshatra's path into Anatolia had for the first time, sent many troops, not just a few mercenaries, to Carchemish. The prophecy commands the army of Necho to put on their armor. The twenty-sixth dynasty was known for its traditional style of battle, no armor. Yet here, Jeremiah tells us that at least some of Egypt's troops, presumably the officers at the very least, were wearing armor. An explanation could be that Necho had finally recognized the foolishness of this non-battle dress code in the fast-moving chariot battles of the day. Egypt was metal poor and metal used for armor was metal not being used for spears and swords, but there was always leather armor as well as plate and chain. Also, he could have bought or been gifted armor, at least for his top officers, from Lydia, who is suddenly a very real presence in this conflict. The Scythians bought their armor from the Greeks, and much of Lydian culture is so close to Greek that for years it was mistaken as being the same thing. Moving on, Jeremiah's prophecy calls Necho out of Carchemish, an unassailable fortress, to battle. Jeremiah would not have known of Nebuchadnezzar's plan to follow Sharuken's strategy,

forcing the pharaoh from the safety of the city on the cliff. Many English translations give the impression that verse five is the Lord asking "What do I see?" or "Why am I seeing this?" but another way of looking at it is that Jeremiah is asking this of the Lord, "Why are you showing me this?" The Lord then answers him. Viewed in that light—along with the date given—the text suggests that Jeremiah saw the battle as it was happening and was giving a running account to an audience, making it a forth telling rather than a foretelling. Ezekiel did something similar as he kept the people of Nippur current on the events in Jerusalem leading up to its fall.

Chapter 50

1. II Kings 20:18; Isaiah 39:7. Egypt, Lydia, Assyria and Babylon were all known for the practice of taking of aristocratic youth to become educated eunuchs in the service of their kings, and so represent their respective countries. Centuries later, Josephus expounded on this (Antiquities of the Jews, Book X 10:1) concerning Daniel and his cousins. Although Josephus wrongly concludes that Zedekiah was king at the time, it is evident that the Jews understood the fulfillment of Isaiah's prophecy to mean Daniel and his cousins.

Chapter 51

Chapter 52

1. The Babylonian Chronicles tell us that Nebuchadnezzar conquered "the land of Hatti" i.e. Anatolia (Asia Minor). This was the area controlled by Lydia! While it is possible that Uvakshatra, and hence, Nebuchadnezzar, did indeed conquer Lydia at that time, it seems strange that more wasn't made of it. Nor does there appear to be a record of Lydia afterwards revolting and regaining their independence. Instead, as far as we can tell, it seems they were independent all along. This text, however, is in cuneiform and is probably the original, so there is no copy error involved. It is possible that the Babylonian scribes were merely bragging due to the Medes successfully holding the border against Lydia. If it had been honest, the tablet probably should have read, "the land of Mitanni," i.e. North Syria.

2. Nebuchadnezzar would have marched out of Jerusalem on August 19, 605 BC.
3. Kedar was a son of Ishmael. His tribe eventually gained such power that the other Arab tribes were also identified by the name, much like Ephraim came to mean all the northern tribes of Israel. The Aramean tribes Puqudu, Sutu, and Qutu, lived east of the Tigris and are thought to be the tribes technically meant by the designation "Qedar." These are also the tribes which are usually associated with the "Pekod, Shoa and Koa" of Ezekiel 23:23. The term "Qedar" itself is confusing. Sometimes it seems to incorporate Edom, Moab and Ammon even though they were not Arabs. They were, however, settled peoples who were greatly harassed and dominated by the Bedouins. It is logical to assume that "Qedar" could be used to mean the land where the influence of these tribes was felt. Therefore, it is entirely possible that when Belshumishkun became "Prince of Qedar," he actually was overlord not only of the Arabs but also of Edom, Moab and Ammon.
4. According to the Babylonian records, Nebuchadnezzar noted that the people of the Negev, (including Beersheba) and apparently its borders (including the city of Hebron which modern archeology has shown was also continuously occupied by Judeans during the time of the exile) were pro-Babylonian and that they remained faithful to him. Accordingly, he separated them from the Province of Judah and made them their own province, giving them their own government. He refused to punish them with the rest of the Judeans. They were not taken into exile.

Chapter 53

1. Literally, "O King, live forever!"
2. The Babylonians created posts and riders, just like the famed Pony Express of the Old West. The distance from Babylon to Pelusium, on the Egyptian border, was about 1,075 miles by the longer, traditional route. The desert route was only about 800 miles, but the messengers would have had to take the longer route to be able to change horses and riders when necessary. Nabopolassar died on August 16 and the message

presumably left Babylon at that time. It arrived at Pelusium on August 28, making the passage in twelve days or almost ninety miles a day!

3. The crown of Babylon was about a foot tall, with a small sphere attached to a dome on the top. Unlike the Assyrian crown, it was cylindrical, but not tiered. It was fashioned of gold, with designs, possibly of flowers, worked in the same metal and probably weighed about twenty-five pounds. It may not have had any jewels at all. The scepter of Babylon, if unchanged from Hammurabi, was an unadorned stick, presumably of gold, but it could have been bronze or iron, about eighteen inches long.
4. The figure of Marduk weighed over three tons. It required sixty priests to pull it up to the Sarahu on the ziggurat every night and to lower it back down in the morning. Both the chariot and the bark of the Akitu would have had to have been very hefty to support it.
5. The ceremony is based on what we know of Babylonian coronations and the song is the traditional prayer of the New Year and the taking of Marduk's hand to renew the friendship with the king. In historical reference, Berosus wrote: *At this time,* (i.e. when Nebuchadnezzar took Carchemish and chased Egypt south beyond their own borders) *his father Nabopolassar became sick and died in the city of Babylon after a reign of twenty-nine years* (Josephus corrects this to twenty-one years. Nabopolassar took the throne of Babylon in late 626 or early 625 BC and he died on August 16, 605 BC). *Not long after, Nebuchadnezzar heard of the death of his father, set the affairs of Egypt and of the other countries in order, and committed to his friends the prisoners he had taken from the Jews, the Philistines, and the other Syrians, as well as from the nations dominated by Egypt. These friends were charged to conduct the heavily armed troops with the rest of the baggage back to Babylonia while Nebuchadnezzar himself took a small escort and hurried through the desert to Babylon. On finding that affairs were being managed by the Chaldeans, and the kingship being maintained by the noblest one of these, he took charge of the whole of his father's realm. When the prisoners arrived, he ordered that dwelling places be assigned to them in the most favorable parts of Babylonia.* The tension between Esagila and both Nabopolassar and Nebuchadnezzar is well documented, although both kings are noted to

have been very religious. Nebuchadnezzar's frantic twenty-six-day flight across the desert from Pelusium to Babylon was motivated by the possibility of the Chaldeans using the opportunity to choose another king by simply allowing someone more to their liking to take Marduk's hand. As it turned out, there is no record that they actually attempted this and the crown passed from father to son on September 23, 605 BC, seemingly without incident. Berosus' words "(he) set the affairs of Egypt… in order…," do not seem to be justified. The Babylonian Chronicle has Nebuchadnezzar going no further than Pelusium on Egypt's border. There was no time at all in the recorded events to allow for an Egyptian reconquest. Nebuchadnezzar was preparing to invade the Two Lands, but word of Nabopolassar's death reached him and he had to turn his attention homeward instead.

Epilogue

APPENDICES

APPENDIX I

Who's Who in Prince of Babylon

Key:

(a) = actual historical character
(f) = fictional character
(s) = character is partially historical
or is supposition based upon facts.
(?) = character follows actions described by ancient historians,
but the true historicity is in doubt.

Any attempt at pronunciation of most of the names below would be approximate since all are transliterations into English and no native speakers of any of the languages or dialects in *Empire* from this time period exist today anyway. Accordingly, the author encourages the readers not to worry about it.

Abda ben Sabaan—(s) By Jewish tradition, the father of Daniel.

Achbor ben Micaiah—(a) A Judean army officer under Josiah, who strongly supported Josiah's reforms. He was the father of Elnathan, who stood against his son-in-law, King Jehoiakim when he burned Jeremiah's scroll, but he obeyed him and sought out the Prophet Uriah in Egypt to kill him.

Addaguppi—(a) Votaress, or high priestess of Sin at Harran. She was the mother of Nabonaid, the grandmother of Belshazzar, the wife of Nabubalatsuikibi, and successor and foster-daughter of Ashuretilsameirsitiuballitsu, high priest of Sin. She was also the daughter of King Ashurbanipal and sister or half-sister of King Ashurubalit. Her occasional identification as Esarhaddon's daughter should be taken in the sense of his descendant: she was born over thirty years after he died. She survived four reigning Assyrian monarchs (five if the short-lived reign of the eunuch, Sinshumulishtar, is counted) and the whole of the Neo-Babylonian Empire down to the year 547, the ninth year of the reign of her son, Nabonaid, when she died at the age of 102 or 104. She was buried with royal honors.

Agga—(f) Nabopolassar's personal servant.

Ahasuerus—(s) Father of Darius the Mede and possibly brother to Ishtumegu. It is known that he was of royal blood, but it is speculation as to who he actually was. It is possible that he was Ishtumegu himself, although this seems unlikely since some sources say that Ishtumegu had no male children, although this may only have meant legitimate sons. It is also possible that he was Arbaces the Mede, appointed sub-king over the Province of Assyria by Nabopolassar, King of Babylon.

Ahikam ben Shaphan—(a) He was Shaphan's eldest son. A royal scribe, he was the father of Gedaliah, who became governor of Judah under Nebuchadnezzar. In *Empire,* Ahikam is Josiah's first scribe.

Akhiramu—(f) An Assyrian captain. In Foundations, he earned his rank by successfully escorting the chieftains of the Scythians to a meeting with King Sinsharushkin.

Alyattes son of Sadyattes—(a) He was the King of Lydia, the great-grandson of Gyages and the older brother of Croesus. Alyattes stopped Uvakshatra's advance to the west.

Amelanu—(s) High Chanter. The Chanter was one of a trio of the highest priests of Babylon, known as the Gatekeepers. His real name is unknown. The other two gatekeepers were the High Priest—who was over all the priests and the 1,000 plus shrines of Babylon—and the Priest of Ekua, who served Marduk himself.

Amyhia—(a) Daughter of Uvakshatra. Some historians assume she was the granddaughter, not actually the daughter of Uvakshatra. This is probably because her brother, Ishtumegu, did have a daughter named Amyhia, but that princess married Cyrus II, not Nebuchadnezzar. Amyhia is better known historically by the Greek transliteration of her name, Amytis. She was Queen of Babylon and great-aunt of Cyrus II. Depending upon the identification of Ahasuerus, she may possibly have been the aunt of Darius the Mede. Amyhia married Nebuchadnezzar as part of the terms of the treaty alliance between Uvakshatra and Nabopolassar. It was for Amyhia that Nebuchadnezzar built the Hanging Gardens, one of the seven wonders of the ancient world, to break her depression and to remind her of her mountainous home country in Media.

Anacharsis—(a) The brother of the Scythian king, Saulius. He may or may not have been the son of Arbaces of Scythia though Herodotus and Diogenes Laertius say he was the son of Gnurus and Lucian says he was the son of Daucetas. He was known to the Greeks as the "wise barbarian," and was executed by his brother for attempting to introduce Greek worship into the cult of the Scythian goddess, Tabiti.

Araramnes son of Teispes—(a) Brother of Cyrus I. He was King of Medu, also known as Parsa, which was half of the Persian tribe of Pasargadae (the same name as the city later built there). He held out longer than his brother against Uvakshatra because of the remoteness of his kingdom and so became the dominant half of the tribe Pasargadae of Persia (known as House Parsa). He eventually lost his sovereignty to Uvakshatra and later he lost his dominant place among the Persian tribes when Kambuzya married Mandane of Media. One source incorrectly places Araramnes as the son of Cyrus I and grandson of Teispes. This is impossible because it would make Cyrus I King of Medu and Anshan, yet he clearly reigned only from Anshan, not the more prestigious Medu, and when Cyrus was defeated by Uvakshatra at Susa, Medu still remained free of Media under Araramnes for some time following.

Arbaces son of Medyas—(a) King of Scythia. Diodorus Siculus calls him "the son of Medyas," but he is not to be confused with Arbaces the Mede. Arbaces carried royal Assyrian blood, but he was no Mede, i.e. he was not "the son of Media" (*Empire,* however, *does* have his mother as being a Mede). "Medyas" is not a transliteration for Media. Medyas was an actual King of Scythia and as such appears in multiple lists of kings. Arbaces was probably the father of his heir and Scythia's next king, Saulius.

Arbaces the Mede—(a) First General of the Forces of Media under Uvakshatra. After the fall of Nineveh, he was crowned King of Assyria under Nabopolassar. As Nimrud was the only former capital of Assyria that was rebuilt after the flood, it appears he may have ruled the Province of Assyria from there. Based on clues from history, *Empire* supposes he may have been the maternal grandfather of Darius the Mede, but it is possible that he was the Biblical "Ahasuerus" and so would have been the father of Darius the Mede. It is equally possible that he held no relationship to Darius whatsoever.

Arioch—(a) Probably literally "Eriaku" i.e., "servant of the moon god." He was an officer of Nebuchadnezzar, who held the title Rab Thabahaya, roughly translated "Lord High Executioner," but was probably closer to "Chief of Police." In *Empire,* Arioch begins as Captain of the Daggermen and is the father of Nebuzaradan.

Asa ben Shammua—(f) Brother of Mishael and Miriam.

Ashpenaz—(a) Chief eunuch under Nebuchadnezzar. His real nationality is unknown. Speculation that the name "Ashpenaz" is a corruption of the Persian word "aspanj" meaning "guest" was never supposed to suggest that the eunuch actually was Persian. Instead, the point was to bolster the claim that the Book of Daniel was a fable, written under Persian influence so that it would be natural to pick a name for a character using a Persian word. Historically, it would have been very difficult for a Persian to find himself in the court of Babylon at the time of Daniel's arrival there. In all probability, "Ashpenaz" was a transliteration of some kind by the Jews of his Babylonian name, given to him when he joined the Chaldeans. As it is a transliteration, it is impossible to know what that name may have been.

Ashurubalit—(a) Last Assyrian Emperor. He had been Turtan (first general) of the Assyrian forces under King Sinsharushkin. Some scholars question his relationship with Sinsharushkin, speculating he was Sinsharushkin's son and crown prince, but he was probably his brother (and the son of Ashurbanipal) due to the ages of the men involved. Ashurubalit crowned himself the last Assyrian emperor when Nineveh fell and briefly made Harran his capital, but was defeated and forced to flee. He was last heard of in 609 BC when he and Pharaoh Necho tried to retake Harran, but he may have survived until 605. His true fate remains a mystery.

Azariah—(a) Government official under Nebuchadnezzar II and a cousin of the Prophet Daniel. He was also known as Abednego.

Azariah ben Hilkiah—(a) Chief Priest in Jerusalem. It is uncertain of the exact dates that he served, but it was between his father, Hilkiah—who discovered the Law in the Temple—and his son, Seraiah—who was executed when Jerusalem fell.

Baruch ben Neriah—(a) His name means "Praise." He was the scribe, servant, and friend of Jeremiah the Prophet. He was probably the brother of Seraiah ben Neriah, one of King Zedekiah's guards.

Belnasir—(f) Cupbearer (rab shaq) to Nabopolassar and later commander of Carchemish. There actually was a Belnasir, who was one of Esarhaddon's inner-council, perhaps also that king's cupbearer, in Assyria, 100 years before this.

Belshumishkun bar Nabuepirlai—(a) Lord of Sin-Magyr. He was made a prince/sub-king under Nebuchadnezzar II in 599 BC of the Arabs of Qedar and possibly Edom, Moab, and Ammon as well. He was the father of Nergalsharusar (Neriglissar), who usurped the throne of his brother-in-law, Amelmarduk. Nergalsharusar referred to his father as "King of Babylon" without any mention that Belshumishkun was actually only rab mag under Nebuchadnezzar. Thanks to Berosus, we know that Nergalsharusar was of one of the Chaldean tribes, but does not identify which. However, we have records from Ur where he paid taxes on his land in the territory of Uruk. He also paid tithes to the god Sin at Ur. Bit Yakin owned Ur and the territory around it. The inference is that Belshumishkun was a member of Bit Yakin. Bit Yakin was bordered by the Aramean tribes to the north and east, so it would then make perfect logic to appoint Belshumishkun Prince of the Qedar (the Arameans). It follows that Belshumishkun was probably a cousin of Nabopolassar. Consequently, *Empire* makes him the son of the Governess of Ur, who was also a real person, but her name is unknown.

Binyamin—(f) Shadushushan's father.

Boaz—(f) The father of Hananiah, cousin of Abda ben Sabaan, Daniel's father.

Buzi—(a) A priest, the father of Ezekiel. The name means "My Contempt." Almost nothing is known about him, other than a tradition that he is descended from Joshua and Rahab, bringing the blood of Ephraim into the tribe of Levi. This tradition, however, mistakenly identifies Jeremiah's father, Hilkiah, with Hilkiah, the Chief Priest, and so makes Jeremiah's mother out to be a daughter of Benjamin. A little study will show this to be false. The priests of Anathoth were descendants of Abiathar, not Zadok. Following this false tradition has caused some to speculate that Buzi may have been Jeremiah himself, literally making Ezekiel, the so-called "son of Jeremiah," into his actual son. This is absurd, as Jeremiah was not married, nor did he ever serve as a priest, but Buzi was most definitely a priest. However, the tradition does seem to relate Buzi very closely with Chief Priest Hilkiah (citing the same blood ties), suggesting Buzi may have been the Chief Priest's son. In *Empire,* Buzi serves as Azariah's Third Priest.

Chednitjerbone I (Khedebeneithirbenet I)—(a) Queen of Egypt, speculated to be the queen of Necho II, the mother of Psammetik II and the probable mother of Necho's daughter, Nitocris. It is known by her sarcophagus that she was a queen of the Twenty-Sixth Dynasty and a wife and mother to pharaohs, but nothing else is known of her. Necho's queen and Psammetik's mother are not named in the records but since the other queens of the dynasty are known, Necho's queen must, by default, have been this woman. On top of this admittedly negative argument, a surviving statue of Psammetik II as a child shows striking similarities in the shape of his face and overlarge ears to the image on Chednitjerbone's sarcophagus (though as he grew older, Psammetik changed to more resemble his father).

Dadani—(f) Officer under Belnasir at Carchemish.

Daniel ben Abda—(a) He was the author of the Book of Daniel, and a high government official under Nebuchadnezzar, Darius, and Cyrus. He was also known as Belteshazzar.

Dioka—(f) Cupbearer to Uvakshatra.

Dioka of Busae—(a) Grandfather of Uvakshatra. He united the six Median tribes (some sources say seven, but there is no name given to the seventh tribe) to form a kingdom over which he reigned from 727-675 BC. It was Dioka who built Ecbatana.

Ebedmelech—(a) An Egyptian courtier to Jerusalem's court. The title is a translation into Aramaic of his Egyptian title, Abdamelek, which means servant or counselor to the king. Accordingly, he was presumably an officer of protocol, in which case he would have been subordinate to Prince Horiraa in Egypt. A correct translation of the text shows that he was a Cushite, not an Ethiopian as some English editions have it—though translators in the Middle-ages could not have known that at this time there was a distinction. The Bible calls Ebedmelech a "eunuch." The literal translation of the word "sares" as "eunuch" is an example of a translation which could cause the reader to assume something which we do not know and is as likely to be untrue as it is to be true. Egypt did indeed have many eunuchs, but any servant of the king could be called a "sares." For example, Potiphar, a married man, is also called a "sares." The correct translation should read "court official," which we do know to be true. In Jerusalem, he rescued Jeremiah from the cistern and saw to it that he was installed in the Courtyard of the Guard instead.

Elasah ben Shaphan—(a) A royal scribe.

Elishama—(a) He replaced Shaphan as personal secretary/prime minister to the King of Judah. As Jehoiakim's secretary, he allowed Jeremiah and Baruch time to flee and hide before he presented the prophet's first scroll to the king. He was the grandfather of Ishmael ben Nethaniah, who was instrumental in the murder of Judah's first governor, Gedaliah. According to II Kings, Ishmael was of royal blood so Elishama may have been as well.

Elnathan ben Achbor—(a) Father of Queen Nehushta, grandfather of King Jehoiachin. He was a member of the Council of Seventy (later known as the Sanhedrin by the Hellenists starting in the first century BC) and witness to many of the events recorded in the Bible. He was Captain of the Palace Guard under Jehoiakim and Jehoiachin. He was in charge of the men sent to Egypt to kill the Prophet Uriah, but he stood against his son-in-law King Jehoiakim when he burned Jeremiah's scroll. Elnathan's father was Achbor ben Micaiah, who was a military officer who strongly supported King Josiah's reforms.

Ezekiel ben Buzi—(a) A prophet to the exiles, Ezekiel's ministry spanned more than 22 years. In the book of the Bible which bears his name, he never mentions Jeremiah. Likewise, Jeremiah never writes of him. Nevertheless, he has been called the "Son of Jeremiah," because he was obviously one of the prophet's students. Much of his work echoes that of the prophet of Jerusalem, but Ezekiel differed greatly from Jeremiah in temperament. Where Jeremiah was the "Weeping Prophet," Ezekiel never even shed a tear at his own wife's death. Though he was greatly moved by it, he kept his feelings to himself. Where the Temple was a side issue to Jeremiah, it was central to Ezekiel. Where Jeremiah looked to a spiritual reality beyond the physical, Ezekiel was concerned with the particulars of the re-establishment of the religious ceremonies in the new Temple to be built. He was largely responsible for the Jews turning away from idolatry once and for all and the establishment of the institution of the synagogues. He was called to be a prophet five years into his exile and was immediately overcome by his encounter with the Almighty. He remained mute, except for when he had a prophecy to deliver, for the next seven and a half years until news reached the exiles that Jerusalem and the Temple had fallen.

Gadah—(f) A prince of Lydia

Gedaliah ben Ahikam—(a) The grandson of Secretary Shaphan, he was appointed by Nebuchadnezzar's officials to be governor of Judah after

Jerusalem's fall. He was murdered by his own people, on the order of King Baalis of Ammon, after only two months in office.

Gemariah ben Shaphan—(a) He was a royal scribe, son of Josiah's personal secretary, brother of Ahikam and father of Micaiah, who brought Jeremiah's first scroll before the Council. In *Empire,* he is Jeremiah's the first scribe.

Hamutel—(a) Daughter of Jeremiah of Libnah, she was a wife of King Josiah and the queen mother to King Jehoahaz. Ezekiel 19 and Jeremiah 13:18 seem to indicate that she wielded great authority.

Hanamel ben Shallum—(a) A cousin of Jeremiah and brother of Maaseiah ben Shallum (who was the keeper of the New Gate); he sold his field and gave up hereditary rights to it to Jeremiah.

Hananiah—(a) Cousin of Daniel, he was a government official under Nebuchadnezzar and was also known as Shadrach. In *Empire,* he is the son of the fictional Boaz.

Hilkiah ben Shallum—(a) Of Anathoth. He was the father of the prophet, Jeremiah. He was of the priestly House of Abiathar, the eldest surviving line of Aaron.

Horiraa—(a) A prince of Egypt. He was probably Psammetik I's son making him Necho II and the God's Wife Nitocris' younger brother. Under Necho II, he was Chief of Protocol, a vital position in Egypt. *Empire* assumes Chief of Protocol is the same office as the Fan-Bearer to the Right Hand of the King because the fan-bearer was traditionally the tutor to the heir and Horiraa was the tutor of both Psammetik II and Wahemibre Haaibre (Hebrew-Hophra, Greek-Apries).

Ibe—(a) Chief Steward of Nitocris, the god's wife. He was her steward from the time she was a baby and adopted into her position.

Ibilsin—(f) An officer under Belnasir at Carchemish.

Ishtumegu son of Uvakshatra—(a) He was King of Media from 585 to 549 BC. He was also known by the Greek name of Astyages, which is not to be confused with Alyattes of Lydia, who was the father of one of his wives. Friction developed between Ishtumegu and Nebuchadnezzar, and Nebuchadnezzar's distrust of his brother-in-law caused him to build a wall along the edge of his domain to hinder a possible Median invasion of Babylonia. According to some sources, Ishtumegu was overthrown by his son-in-law Cyrus in 549 BC, according to others, Cyrus was his grandson and the legal heir of Media. The two versions are not necessarily in conflict with each other. Cyrus was not only Ishtumegu's grandson, but he also married his aunt, Ishtumegu's daughter, Amyhia, to cement his claim to the Median throne. Supposedly, Cyrus was Ishtumegu's only legal male heir, but Ishtumegu did not wish to leave his throne to a Persian, so Cyrus had to conquer Media to win it.

Jaazaniah ben Shaphan—(a) Most Biblical scholars assume Jaazaniah was the son of Shaphan, Josiah's secretary, but he could have been the son of some other Shaphan. Shaphan's three other sons, Ahikam, Elasah, and Gemariah, along with his foster-son, King Josiah, all followed the Lord. Only Jaazaniah was guilty of idol worship.

Jeconiah ben Jehoiakim—(a) He was eighteen when he took the throne and the throne name of Jehoiachin. He was only King of Judah for three months when Nebuchadnezzar invaded in 598. Jeremiah prophesied to him that he would be carried into captivity with his mother. In exile, he, his five sons, their tutor and his entourage received twenty times the issuance of grain, oils, and other rations than anyone else from Nebuchadnezzar. After a brief Judean uprising, which attempted to put Jehoiachin back on the throne in Judah, Nebuchadnezzar imprisoned him. He remained in prison until he was freed by Nebuchadnezzar's son, Amelmarduk. Jeconiah died in Babylon.

Jehoahaz ben Josiah—(a) Born Shallum, Jehoahaz was Josiah's fourth and youngest son. Though he was Josiah's youngest son, he was the only remaining son of Hamutel, daughter of Jeremiah of Libnah, so the people chose him to be King (II Kings 23:30). Jehoahaz reversed Josiah's practices against occultism and idolatry. Jeremiah prophesies to Jehoahaz to continue as Josiah had done or he would die in captivity. He had reigned for three months before he was deposed by Pharaoh Necho. He died, under arrest, in Egypt.

Jehoiada—(a) Second Priest in Jerusalem. He was taken to Babylonia in the second exile and replaced by Zephaniah. No one knows when Jehoiada gained the position of Second Priest, however, so *Empire* supposes that the Second Priest could, like the Chief Priest, hold the office for life. Accordingly, in *Empire,* Jehoiada holds the office of Second Priest under three different Chief Priests: Hilkiah ben Shallum of Jerusalem, Azariah ben Hilkiah, and Seraiah ben Azariah.

Jehoiakim ben Josiah—(a) Born Eliakim, he was placed on the throne of Judah by Pharaoh Necho II when he was twenty-five years old (cf, II Kings 23:31-37). He used Hebrew slaves to expand his palace in Egyptian style and probably installed more idols in the Temple than any other king. By Jewish writings and tradition, he was accused of committing murder, incest, rape, and theft. Jehoiakim was twenty-five years old when he took the throne, and he had at least two wives. Eventually, Nehushta, daughter of Elnathan ben Achbor manipulated her way into becoming his queen. Jehoiakim was the full-brother of the infamous King Zedekiah and their mother was Zebidah, daughter of Pediah of Rumah. Jehoiakim was the King who confiscated the scroll of Jeremiah's oracles from Baruch. He sat by the fire in his palace and ordered it read. As each section was finished, he cut the text columns off the scroll and burned them. At the beginning of the seige 598-597, Jehoiakim surrendered, and Nebuchadnezzar was about to take him prisoner back to Babylon when something happened. Jehoiakim was killed and left to rot on Jerusalem's garbage heap, fulfilling Jeremiah's prophecy and the seige continued.

Jeremiah ben Hilkiah—(a) Called to be the Prophet to the Nations, he was the prophet who predicted Jerusalem's fall, Babylon's call from God to chastise the Judeans, and the Judean seventy-year captivity.

Joash ben Abda—(f) He was Daniel's brother and the husband of Miriam.

Johanan ben Josiah—(a) King Josiah's oldest son and probable heir. He died before he could inherit, however, possibly in the same battle that claimed his father's life.

Josiah ben Amon—(a) His mother was Jedaiah, daughter of Adaiah of Boscath. Josiah was known as the good king. He led a reformation in Judah and discovered the books of the Law of Moses in the Temple. His first wife was Hamutel, daughter of Jeremiah of Libnah. His second wife was Zebidah, daughter of Pediah of Rumah.

Kaelus—(a) The Philistine mariner who, sponsored by Egypt, led the first expedition around the Cape of Good Hope. *Empire* assumes he was from Gaza, as this is the only Philistine city that was under Egyptian control at this time.

Kambuzya son of Cyrus—(a) King of Anshan. Known to the Greeks as Cambyses I, he was raised in Ecbatana as a hostage to secure Cyrus I's vassalage. He became the son-in-law of Ishtumegu of Media and the father of Cyrus the Great.

Kaptah—(f) husband of Marrat. He was killed in the uprising of Bit Amukanni in 613 BC.

Kareah ben Nathan—(a) He was an official under Josiah and an elder of Jerusalem, i.e., a member of the Council of Seventy. He defended Jeremiah against the people when they would have stoned him. He was very likely the Kareah who was the father of Johanan and Jonathan. In *Empire,* it is assumed that he was a military commander since Johanan and Jonathan were both military men.

Labashisin—(f) an officer under Belnasir at Carchemish.

Maaseiah ben Shallum—(a) He was one of three gatekeepers of the Temple in Jerusalem, and his post seemed to be the New Gate exclusively. The Temple wall had four gates, so it is a mystery why there were only three gatekeepers and also who the other two gatekeepers were. Maaseiah, though, was Jeremiah's cousin. Jeremiah's father was the eldest of three brothers (Hilkiah, Maaseiah, and Shallum). So, the other Maaseiah would have been this Maaseiah's uncle, and this Maaseiah would have been named after him (his uncle). Maaseiah was the brother of Hanamel ben Shallum and should have had the first right to redeem Hanamel's field. He evidently refused this right, and so it went to Jeremiah.

Maaseiah of Anathoth—(a) He was the father of Zephaniah the Second Priest and Zedekiah of the House of Prophets. He was also the brother of Jeremiah's father, Hilkiah, and the brother of Hanamel and Maaseiah's father, Shallum.

Mandane—(s) Queen of Media. The correct name of Uvakshatra's queen does not seem to be known, but since many women of the Median royal family carry this name, *Empire* supposes that they may have been named for her.

Mandane—(a) Daughter of Ishtumegu, wife of Kambuzya of Anshan. She was the mother of Cyrus the Great, and the niece of Amyhia, Queen of Babylon.

Marrat—(f) Personal servant of Nitocris, daughter of Necho. As a lady of Bit Amukanni, her Egyptian/Ionian husband, Kaptah, was killed in the uprising of 613. With her son, she was a contact between Nitocris, wife of Nebuchadnezzar and the throne of Egypt.

Marshipar—(f) Daggerman for Prince Nebushumlishtar

Mattaniah—(a) A middle son of King Josiah, later crowned as King Zedekiah.

Melzar—(a) A eunuch of Bit Mummi. "Melzar" is actually a title meaning "steward."

Mentemhe—(a) High priest of Amun, a descendant of the Priest-Kings, he was the grandfather of the famous Princess Ankhnasneferibre.

Mesharapli—(f) Ambassador of Ashurubalit of Assyria.

Mesharumishamash—(f) Rab sharish (prime minister) of Nabopolassar. He was in charge of internal affairs in the absence of the king.

Miriam—(f) Sister of Mishael and betrothed of Daniel.

Mishael—(a) Cousin of Daniel and government official under Nebuchadnezzar. He was also known as Meshach.

Mitatti—(f) Military commander of Harran under Nabubalatsuikibi.

Nabonaid bar Nabubalatsuikibi—(a) Son of Addaguppi. He was King of Babylon from 556 to 539 BC. He is also known by the Greek transliteration of his name, Nabonidus. He assassinated Labashmarduk, son of the usurper Nergalsharusar, and married Nebuchadnezzar's daughter, (Bauasitu) Nitocris, whom he loved with a passion. At her death, he went into seclusion. He was the father of Belshazzar.

Nabopolassar—(a) King of Babylon from 625 to 605 BC. Father of Nebuchadnezzar II. According to Diodorus Siculus, Nabopolassar was a Chaldean, i.e., of the nobility, the Bar Manuti. Because of Nabopolassar's background, the Neo-Babylonian Empire is sometimes called the Dynasty of Bit Yakin. The House of Yakin controlled the province around Ur and Ashurbanipal appointed Nabopolassar Prince of the Chaldeans at Ur. It is likely, then, that Nabopolassar was actually of Bit Yakin, though probably not the legitimate heir, as he refers to himself as a "nobody, the son of a nobody," i.e., not of royal birth. However, there are two economic texts which cite ancestors of Nebuchadnezzar as an "Ilubani" and a "Tabiya." If these are the princes of those same names, then Nebuchadnezzar and his father could trace their ancestry back to Nabunasir, who overthrew one of a series of Chaldean usurpers and kicked out their Assyrians overseers in 748 BC.

Nabubalatsuikibi—(a) Named "the wise prince" by his son Nabonaid; he is thought to have been a scholar. He was Prince of Harran and husband of Addaguppi. It is recorded that Nabonaid was Sumerian, but both his parents came from Harran in North Syria, and his mother was definitely Assyrian, the niece of the last king. So, for this to be true, Nabubalatsuikibi had to be of Sumerian blood, despite being Governor of Harran.

Narambel—(a) A general under Nebuchadnezzar, later, his rab shaq.

Nebuchadnezzar bar Nabopolassar—(a) Emperor of Babylonia from 605 to 562 BC. His name was literally Nebu-kadurri-usar, meaning Nebu protects the border/succession, but it was also a kind of title, meaning "heir," i.e., to the throne of Babylon. He was actually the second to carry this name, the first being of a long-vanished dynasty.

Nebushumlishtar bar Nabopolassar—(a) Brother to Nebuchadnezzar. Details of his life are sketchy, but it is known that he was second in line to the throne and that he did labor with his more famous sibling as a child hauling bricks for the temple complex of Babylon. There are also some references to him leading troops in some battles.

Nebuzaradan—(a) His name was literally Nebu-Seri-Idinnam, meaning Nebu has given offspring (seed). He was captain of Nebuchadnezzar's guard, the daggermen. The daggermen were fanatically loyal to the king and could be trusted even against plots hatched by the Chaldeans. After Jerusalem had been conquered, Nebuchadnezzar placed it in his captain's hands, who burned the Temple and reduced Jerusalem to ruins. By Nebuchadnezzar's order, he treated Jeremiah kindly and let him stay in Jerusalem (cf, II Kings 25, Jer. 39). In *Empire,* Nebuzaradan is the son of Arioch.

Necho II son of Psammetik I—(a) Pharaoh of Egypt from 610 to 595 BC, about fifteen years. Necho's queen appears to have been Chednitjerbone I, who was a Cushite princess. Necho's mother was the Great Royal Wife Mehtenweskhet, the daughter of Harsiese, one of the priests of Atun at On (Heliopolis), making Necho II be one-half Egyptian, one-quarter Lydian and one-quarter Ethiopian (The Great Chief of the West Necho I was married to an Ethiopian princess). Necho II was appointed pharaoh by King Nabopolassar of Babylon. After his appointment, he almost immediately rebelled against Babylonia. Marching through Judah on his way to Harran to help the Assyrians, he encountered the Judean army. King Josiah was killed in battle against him at Megiddo in 609. In alliance with Ashurubalit of Assyria, Necho tried to recapture Harran from the Coalition but failed. He stirred up trouble for the rest of his reign and died of unknown causes after which his son, Psammetik II, caused his name to be blotted out from almost all his father's monuments in Egypt.

Nehushta—(a) Daughter of Elnathan ben Achbor. She was Queen of Judah, wife of Jehoiakim, and mother of Jehoiachin. To gain her throne, she had her father deliver the prophet Uriah to Jehoiakim to be executed.

Nekhtu-Ra—(a) Master builder of Egypt, lent by Necho to Jehoiakim. Under him, Jehoiakim set about remodeling his city using Egyptian architecture.

Nergalniari—(f) Rab mag of the forces of Babylonia under Nabopolassar.

Nergalsharusar—(a) Nebuchadnezzar's recorder. (Not to be confused with the Nergalsharusar who was Belshumishkin's son, known to the Greeks as Neriglissar).

Ninnaramur—(s) The only so-called record(s) of Nabopolassar's queen(s) are recent concoctions, highly dubious and almost certainly apocryphal. Middle-eastern groups naming Persian or Assyrian princesses are attempts to rewrite history and create an integrated royal bloodline meant to link these ancient houses with modern personages.

Nabopolassar never visited the distant southeast corner of Persia from which a fictional Persian princess supposedly came. By the time the Sheik of the Chaldeans at Ur married, he was probably at war with Assyria and not a good candidate for marriage with an Assyrian princess. The timing does make it possible (barely), but why didn't the Assyrians record this princess or her marriage to a traitor? Why didn't Nabopolassar use such a marriage to legitimatize his reign? No, it is far more likely that the tradition that Nabopolassar's queen came from the streets of Ur is true. Her real name is uncertain, as is her fate.

Nitocris daughter of Necho II—(a) Second wife of Nebuchadnezzar, and sister or half-sister of Psammetik II. Nitocris, the god's wife had no children and meant for her niece, Nitocris daughter of Necho II to be god's wife after her. Nabopolassar invaded Egypt in 610 BC killing Psammetik I but allowing his son, Necho II to take the throne as a vassal of Babylon and taking Necho's daughter, Nitocris, as hostage to be married to his son, Nebuchadnezzar. Two hundred years later, when Herodotus visited Babylon, the people showed him various ruins and existing structures which were marked as Nebuchadnezzar's, but which they attributed to Nitocris as their most beloved queen. Many stories are told of her wit and compassion, and most are probably true. She is almost certainly King Belshazzar's grandmother and the queen that told this king to send for Daniel. No other possibility exists, the queen mother was dead, and all of the king's wives were already in attendance at the party.

Nitocris daughter of Psammetik I—(a) God's Wife of Amun. She was adopted by Shepenopet II, Adoratrix of the god Horis (i.e., high priestess, the Cushites did not have 'god's wives'). Shepenopet II was the sister of Taharka, the Cushite pharaoh, who was defeated by Assyria and pushed south, back into Cush. Shepenopet had already adopted Taharka's daughter Amondiris as her heir, but she was forced by Psammetik I to reject Amonirdis in favor of his daughter, Nitocris. It was this adoption that legitimatized his crown and that of his son, her brother, Necho II.

Nuranu—(f) An officer under Belnasir at Carchemish.

Pashur ben Immer—(a) He was a priest and Captain of the Temple Guard at the time of King Jehoiakim. He put Jeremiah in stocks by the Upper Gate (i.e., inside the gate) of Benjamin in the Lord's Temple. The next morning as he let him out, Jeremiah preached against him (Jer. 20).

Phineas ben Hilkiah—(s) A brother of Jeremiah. The Prophet Jeremiah may have had brothers. Jeremiah 12:6 says that his brethren were against him and attacked him, verbally or physically we don't know. The word brethren may mean brothers, but it could also mean family, including his cousins.

Potasimto son of Raemmaakheru—(a) General of Egypt under Psammetik II. Born in the small town of Pharbaetus, off the Nile delta, he appears to have been a nobleman (he and his father have surviving statues and his brother a stele). He was in charge of the foreign mercenary half of Psammetik's army. (Amasis was in charge of the Egyptian troops under Psammetik.) Potasimto's actual name was Padisemataui, but since his men were Greeks, he became widely known, even to the Egyptians, by this Grecianized form.

Psammetik I son of Necho I—(a) The first pharaoh of the Twenty-Sixth Dynasty, he was appointed Pharaoh of Lower Egypt by Assyria over eleven other Libyan princes who were rivals for the post. The story of drinking out of his helmet and so being chosen by the gods above the other princes seems to have convinced the Egyptians of the Lower Kingdom that his reign over them was ordained. Nine years later, he pushed the Cushites back across the first cataract of the Nile and forced Shepenopet, Adoratrix of the ousted Cushites, to adopt his daughter Nitocris I and declare her to be the new God's Wife of Amun. This legitimatized his reign over Upper Egypt, and so united the Two Lands. Psammetik I was killed at the Battle of Sais when Nabopolassar invaded Egypt.

Psammetik II son of Necho II—(a) Probably the son of Queen Chednitjerbone I, brother or half-brother of Nitocris, daughter of Necho. Pharaoh of Egypt, he reigned for a short six years during which time he was responsible for the construction of more monuments and temples than another pharaoh of his dynasty.

Raemmaakheru—(a) Father of General Potasimto of Egypt. He was a nobleman, overseeing large tracts of land in the data adjacent to the Fortress of the Milesians. *Empire* postulates that Raemmaakheru was a general under Necho II.

Ramose—(f) Son of Kaptah of Egypt and Marrat of Bit Amukanni. He was a spy for Nitocris, daughter of Necho and Chednitjerbone, queen of Egypt.

Sajaha—(a) Priestess of Esagila, First Seer to the King. *Empire* proposes that the Priestess of Esagila would have been synonymous with the Priestess of the Sarahu, and so, on the Akitu, she would also have played Lady Sarpenitum, wife of Marduk. Sajaha died in 562 BC. From a surviving bust, she was very beautiful. Sajaha wrote many treatises on her craft. Of particular interest is a writing in response to an enquiry by Nebuchadnezzar as to the meaning of his dreams. It is possible that this woman was behind many of Daniel's troubles since he usurped her authority on Nebuchadnezzar's orders. On the other hand, Nebuchadnezzar addresses her with great friendliness and familiarity, referring to himself while talking to her as "your old king." *Empire* assumes that she held her post from before the beginning of Nebuchadnezzar's reign, so was probably somewhat older than he was.

Samgunu—(f) A cousin to Captain Akhiramu of Assyria.

Sarduri IV—(a) 615 to 595 BC. One of the last Kings of Urartu. Very little is known about him, but *Empire* assumes he gained his throne as a toddler, because he reigned for twenty years, yet on his death, his brother, Rusa IV, last King of Urartu, inherited. That means Sarduri either had no children yet or that they were all dead. *Empire* chooses the first option. There is a discrepancy in the Urartu king list, however, where Sarduri III and IV are not even mentioned. It goes like this: Rusa III (620-609 BC) and his son, Rusa IV (609-590 BC). Weight should be given to the existence (and death) of Sarduri IV, because of the date of 595 BC. It was a very significant date in both Nebuchadnezzar's career and in the history of Jerusalem. Almost certainly this all would have been bad news for the Urartu and a change in rulership would be not at all unexpected.

Sarili—(f) An officer under Belnasir at Carchemish.

Saulius—(a) King of Scythia. It is not actually known if he was Arbaces' son, he may only have been a close relative, such as a grandson. He executed his brother Anacharsis for blasphemy.

Seraiah ben Azariah—(a) He was Chief Priest of God at the time of King Zedekiah. He was the grandson of Hilkiah, Chief Priest under Josiah and son of Chief Priest Azariah. He was arrested at the fall of Jerusalem and put to death.

Seraiah ben Neriah—(a) One of King Zedekiah's guard. He accompanied Zedekiah to Jerusalem with the tribute in his fourth year, and he carried a message from Jeremiah against Babylon. He was probably the brother of Baruch, Jeremiah's scribe. *Empire* assumes that Zedekiah would have found him the logical choice to appoint as Jeremiah's guard, but there is no historical proof of this.

Shadushushan—(f) Wife and widow of Belnasir, commander of Carchemish. She was a refugee of Anatho and resettled in Carchemish. Afterward, she became a lady-in-waiting to Amyhia, queen of Nebuchadnezzar.

Shallum ben Shallum—(a) Brother of Hilkiah of Anathoth, the uncle of Jeremiah the Prophet, the father of Jeremiah's cousin, Hanamel, who sold his field to the prophet and he was also the father of Maaseiah, the gatekeeper.

Shammua—(f) Father of Mishael, Asa, and Miriam. He was the cousin of Abda ben Sabaan, Daniel's father.

Shaphan ben Azaliah—(a) Personal secretary (Prime Minister) of Josiah. His name means "Rock Hyrax," a species of animal known for posting a guard over their colonies, rather like a prairie dog. Shaphan was the father of Ahikam, Elasah, Jaazaniah, and Gemariah—all of whom were royal scribes and elders of their people (Council members). He was the grandfather of Gedaliah, who was the governor appointed by Nebuchadnezzar after Jerusalem fell. He was also the foster-father and regent of King Josiah until he came of age.

Takhuita—(a) Queen of Egypt, The Great Royal Wife of Pharaoh Psammetik II, mother of Princess Ankhnasneferibre. She was the daughter of the high priest of Amun Mentemhe and the sister of his heir (also named

Mentemhe). As such, she carried the blood of the Priest-Kings who ruled before the Cushites. Takhuita was probably also the mother of Apries and Chednitjerbone II. She died in 567 BC and was buried in Arthribis, near Thebes.

Uriah ben Shemaiah—(a) He prophesied against Judah and Jehoiakim tried to kill him. He fled to Egypt. Jehoiakim sent Elnathan ben Achbor to bring him back. He was executed with a sword.

Uvakshatra son of Phraorla—(a) King of Media from 653 to 585 BC. He was known to the Greeks as Cyaxares and to the Babylonians and Assyrians as Umakishtar. Uvakshatra defeated Assyria with the help of Babylonia and Scythia. Herodotus says he reigned for forty years including the time of the domination of the Scythians, but virtually all historians agree that what is meant is forty years excluding the time of the domination of the Scythians. At the beginning of his reign, Uvakshatra was considered a vassal of the Scythians until 625 when he threw off their yoke and took sovereign control of his country. In total then, he reigned for sixty-eight years and, therefore, would have been very young when he first took the throne as he was still conducting military campaigns in person up until the year of his death!

Xiamara—(f) The mother of Shadushushan.

Zebidah—(a) Daughter of Pediah of Rumah. She was the second wife of Josiah and the mother of King Jehoiakim and King Zedekiah.

Zedekiah ben Hananiah—(a) An official of Jehoiakim's court.

Zedekiah ben Maaseiah—(a) Brother of Zephaniah the second priest. He was a member of the House of Prophets. He prophesied falsely for Egypt and against Babylon. He was burned to death by Nebuchadnezzar (Jer. 29:20-30).

Zephaniah ben Maaseiah—(a) Brother of Zedekiah the false prophet. Zephaniah was the cousin of Jeremiah the Prophet. After Second Priest Jehoiada's exile to Babylon, Zephaniah was raised to the office of the second priest. He was executed with King Zedekiah's officials in 586 BC. According to Second Maccabees, Zephaniah aided Jeremiah in hiding the Ark of the Covenant, the Table of Incense, and the Taberacle in Moses' grave on Mount Nebo. This was before the fall of

Jerusalem. Zephaniah supposedly also hid the ashes of the red heifer as well as the Eternal Flame in the caves beneath Jerusalem. Second Maccabees is known to be a colorful rewriting of history, but in support of this tale is Ezekiel's vision of the Glory leaving the Temple and coming to rest on Mount Nebo. Further support is lent by the copper scroll of Qumran and the "Treatises of the Vessels," both of which claim, probably based on Hebrew tradition, that at this time, a number of Levites and prophets buried or hid the Ark and other treasures.

APPENDIX II

Time, Calendars, Measurements

In most cases, *Empire* endeavors to use the appropriate measures used by the culture of the time. However, there are many instances where this could be a distraction, and in such a case, *Empire* will use modern measurements to move the storyline along more easily.

Hours and Days

The Judean, Babylonian and Egyptian day began at approximately 6:00 PM, known as moonrise. This arose from the ancient practice of watching for the New Moon to declare the new month. In this system, morning was at approximately 6:00 AM, known as sunrise. A whole day was known as an evening and morning, or moonrise and sunrise. Evening was divided into three watches of two beru (four hours) apiece which ran from 6:00 PM to 10:00 PM, from 10:00 PM to 2:00 AM, and from 2:00 AM to 6:00 AM.

The Persian and Median day began at midnight (like our modern day), and First Watch began at that point.

Babylonian	Modern Equivalent	Babylonian Alternative
1 day =	1 day =	12 beru
1 beru =	2 hours =	60 segments
1 segment =	2 minutes =	60 Babylonian seconds
1 Babylonian second =	2 seconds.	

The Babylonians measured time by clocks (clepsydra) which ran by a controlled flow of water or by sundials (gnomon) or by polos which were instruments which registered the shadow projected by a minute ball suspended over a half-sphere.

Judean	Modern Equivalent	Judean Alternative
1 day =	1 day =	24 hours
1 hour =	1 hour =	1080 parts
1 part =	3.3 seconds	

Egyptian	Modern Equivalent	Egyptian Alternative
1 day =	1 day =	24 hours
1 hour =	1 hour =	1080 parts

Weeks

A Jewish (Judean) week equals seven days and an Egyptian 'week' equals ten days, but a Babylonian 'week' varies in length, some with seven days, some with eight. There are four Babylonian weeks to a "moon" (month) which was 30 days long.

Months

The Jewish (Judean) and Babylonian calendars are very similar. Originally, the Israelites had their own names for the months, but generally simply called them by their number. The Israelites had two calendars, the civil calendar and the religious one, which was six months off and corresponded to the Babylonian calendar. The civil calendar is thought to have been the original calendar, and the religious one was adopted under Moses, by the order of the Lord, for the timing of the Passover. After the Babylonian exile, the Judeans tended to favor the religious calendar and renamed the months to more or less correspond to the Babylonian names. Only four of the old Israelite names for the months are known, and these are listed in square brackets, Judean (Jewish) religious months are in parentheses. The months are listed in their Babylonian and Judean religious calendar order with the Judean civil calendar numbering system recorded at the left. In other words, the Babylonians' first month was Nisan, which was the Judean civil calendar's seventh month. The Judean civil new year fell on the Babylonian seventh month of Tashritu while the Judean religious new year was the same as Babylon's.

Judean Civil	Babylonian	Judean Old	Judean Religious	Western
7	Nissanu	Aviv	Nisan	Mar–April
8	Ajaru	Ziv	Iyyar	April–May
9	Simanu		Sivan	May–June
10	Du'uzu		Tammuz	June–July
11	Abu		Ab	July–Aug
12	Ululu		Elul	Aug–Sept
1	Tashritu	Etanim	Tishri	Sept–Oct
2	Arahsamna	Bul	Marheshvan	Oct–Nov
3	Kislimu		Kislev	Nov–Dec
4	Tebetu		Tebeth	Dec–Jan
5	Shabaru		Shebat	Jan–Feb
6	Addaru		Adar	Feb–Mar
	Makarusha		Addaru-Sheni	

Seven out of nineteen years were leap years with the intercalendar month added. This was virtually equal to the solar calendar, with an error of only two hours.

The Egyptian calendar was quite different. At this time in history, it was no longer based on the cycles of the moon. Instead, the Egyptians used a solar year of 365 days, divided into three four-month seasons. This means that the equivalent modern date is always the same. For instance, Thoth 1, no matter what year, was always July 19. Their months were three weeks of ten days, or thirty days long. Five days were added at the end of the year for the birthdays of the major gods, Osirus, Horus, Seth, Isis, and Nephthys.

Akhet the season of the inundation ran from July 19 to November 15
Thoth (July 19–Aug. 17)
Paophi (Aug. 18–Sept. 16)
Athyr (Sept. 17–Oct. 16)
Sholiak (Oct. 17–Nov. 15)
Peret the season of the emergence (of the soil?) ran from Nov. 16 to Mar. 15
Tybe (Nov. 16–Dec. 15)
Meshir (Dec. 16–Jan. 14)
Phamenoth (Jan. 15–Feb. 13)
Pharmouthe (Feb. 14–Mar. 15)
Shemu, the season of the harvest (meaning low water?) ran from Mar. 16 to July 13
Pashons (Mar. 16–Apr. 14)
Payni (Apr. 15–May 14)
Epiphi (May 15–Jun. 13)
Mesori (Jun. 14–Jul. 13)
Epigomenal (Inserted)Days (Jul. 14– Jul. 18)

Years

In Israel and Babylonia, the years were counted from the year after the king in question ascended to the throne. For instance, March 605 BC was both the start of the twentieth year of Nabopolassar (though he had reigned 21 years) and the Ascension Year (or year zero if the Babylonians had recognized a zero) of Nebuchadnezzar. It counted back to Nisan 1, although Nebuchadnezzar's ascension would have been in Tashritu. According to this system, April 604 BC would have been the start of the first year of Nebuchadnezzar, though he actually took the throne in September of 605 BC.

Measurements

Babylonians measured distances in the length of time to travel on foot, for instance, a certain wall was known to be twenty-six beru long (two days and four modern hours) or approximately 270 km or 169 miles. This makes a beru equal to about six and a half miles.

Though in most cases to avoid confusion, *Empire* uses modern measurements for lengths, Babylonians, Egyptians, and Judeans measured lengths in cubits. One cubit was about eighteen inches. The Egyptians further divided cubits into hands and palms with each palm equal to the width of four fingers. A finger was segmented into three ro. Judean measurements were virtually identical to Babylonian:

1 Palm =	4 Finger Breadths =	3 inches
1 Span =	3 Palms =	9 inches
1 Cubit =	2 Spans =	1.5 Feet
1 Step =	2 Cubits =	1 Yard
1 Reed =	3 Steps =	3 Yards
1 Rod =	2 Reeds =	6 Yards
1 Cord =	10 Rods =	60 Yards
1 Parasang =		1.73 Miles
1 Beru =		6.5 Miles

These conversions are approximate; for instance, a reed actually was nine and eight-tenths feet. Parasang is a Judean measurement, Beru is Babylonian. Cords are Jewish, not Judean, however, and were added during the Talmudic Period, around 200 BC and so were not in use at the time of *Empire*.

Weights

Hebrew and Babylonian Common System

1 kikkar (talent) = 75.56 pounds

1 maneh (mina) = 1.26 pounds 60 manehs = 1 kikkar

1 sheqel (shekel) = 0.34 ounces 60 sheqels = 1 maneh

Babylonian Heavy Weights, used to weigh metals

1 Large Lion = 2.3 pounds

The "lions" come in sets of sixteen metal figures which diminish in size from about thirty centimeters to two centimeters in length. Following the "lions" are the "ducks" which are stone figures.

Egyptian Metal Weights

1 uten = 3.19 ounces

Similar to the Babylonian heavy system, Egyptians used metal lions and cows as heavier weights.

APPENDIX III

Gods and Goddesses

Ammonite

Molech—National deity of Ammon, he was the same as Milcom of Tyre. He was the Baal to whom children were sacrificed by immolation.

Assyrian and Babylonian

The square bracket indicates the old Sumerian equivalent.

Adod—God of storms, his symbol was the bull.

Aku—God of the moon

Anu—[An] King of heaven, chief of gods, but remote to humankind, father of Enlil and grandfather of Marduk, husband of Ishtar, his main temple was in Erech.

Ashur—Head god of Assyria. The King of Assyria was his high priest. His symbol was the winged disk. Some say he is never portrayed by the Assyrians as a human with divine attributes, but only as his symbol. This must be questioned since he had to be available to give his hand on the First of Nisan. His priests wore a stole over their left shoulder. Human sacrifice of prisoners of war, clad in lions' heads and skins, were offered to him. He was the Assyrian god of the sun and the forerunner of the Zoroastrian god Ahuramazda. The Assyrians were more gloomy and more religiously fanatic than the Babylonians. Hence, Ashur was more gloomy and serious than his father, Marduk.

Bel—(Lord) or Belu (He who rules). This was the name of the god who was the brother of Marduk but was generally used by the Assyrians to mean Ashur and by the Babylonians to mean Marduk himself. He was the hero of the gods and pretty much the same as the Canaanite god Baal.

Ea [Enki]—God of rivers, streams, canals, wells and all fresh waters that give life. Enki means "Lord Earth," his Semitic name, Ea, means House of Waters "The broad-eared one who knows all that has a name."

Enlil—God of lordship and dominion, son of Anu, father of Marduk. He was known as the Most High. His name means "Lord Air." Patron god of Nippur, where his temple was called Ekur, he was also the national god of Sumer.

Ishtar [Inanna]—Goddess of love and war, wife of Tammuz (and many others), her symbol was the lion, her planet was Venus.

Kingu—Son and consort of the dragon Tiamat. He was given the Tablet of Destiny to rule the universe by his mother. Marduk defeated her and then him, mixing Kingu's blood with the earth to create mankind.

Marduk—Son of Enlil. He was called Merodach in Judah. He fashioned heaven and earth out of the defeated goddess Tiamat (a female dragon) and mankind out of her slain consort Kingu. A gold statue of Marduk, shaped like a man and weighing three tons, was in the temple at Babylon. Marduk was the patron god of the city of Babylon and had seventy priests appointed to him alone. His temple was known as Ekua, also as the House of Bel. His planet was Jupiter; hence, he was seen as synonymous with Zeus of the Greeks.

Nabu—God of writing and education, son of Marduk, god of the city of Borsippa near Babylon. His temple at Borsippa was called Ezida. His provider (zaninu) was the King of Babylon. At times, he is seen as synonymous with Nebo.

Nebo—God of trading and fire, brother of Marduk. His planet was Mercury and like the Roman god, Mercury, was associated with commerce.

Nergal [Ninurta]—God of War, strongest of the gods, associated with the planet Mars. Also known as the god of the underworld.

Ninib—[Ninrta] god of gardens and the harvest. His planet was Saturn. Thus, he was associated with the Greek god with the same planet and with Cronus, god of agriculture.

Ninmah [Nin-menna]—Goddess mother of Marduk, called Queen of Queens, wife of Enlil portrayed as holding the hands of Nebo and Tasmit. Her temple, though small, was located directly southwest of the Ishtar gate and across the processional way from the old palace.

Nisroch—Assyrian deity at whose temple Sharuken (Sharuken) was assassinated. Nisroch is mentioned in the Bible under this name but is actually the Biblical Nimrod, who had come to be deified.

Rimmon—God of rain.

Sarpenitum—Marduk's wife.

Shamash [Utu]—Son of Nanna. He was the god of righteousness, the sun god, who lay bare the righteous and wicked, flooding the earth with blinding light. His hour of rule began at 6:00 AM. He was the patron god of Sippar and Larsa.

[Sharra]—Patron god of Umma.

Sin [Nanna]—The moon god. Sin originally was only the god of the crescent moon and Nanna was the god of the moon in all other stages. However, by the time of *Empire*, Sin had come to replace Nanna and the two were viewed as the same god. Sin was the god of the night, his hour of rule began at 6:00 PM. He was the patron god of Ur and of Harran. He could read into the dark future and knew the destinies of all.

Tammuz—The god associated with vegetation, flocks, and cattle. He was taken down to the underworld by force to take his wife, Inanna's, place so that he could not return to the earth.

Tasmit—Brother of Marduk, god of fate.

Tiamat—Goddess of chaotic waters, portrayed as a female dragon. Killed by Marduk.

Zagaga—[Zababa] God of Battle, patron god of Kish.

Egyptian

Amentet—Goddess of the dead.

Amun—Patron god of Thebes. Before the New Kingdom age, he was a local sun god, but when the Priest-Kings of Thebes came to power, he became supreme, usurping Ra. To appease Ra's priests, Amun became associated with Ra and was sometimes known as Amun-Ra.

Apis—The bull, worshipped in Memphis (along with Ptah). When a calf was born with Apis' distinctive markings, it became the Apis bull. Apis appears to be a title rather than a name. He could be synonymous with Kathaihemt.

Atun—The first god, from whom everything was made. His city was Awanu (Heliopolis).

Bast—The cat-headed goddess, her city was Pi-Beseth. Cyrus II defeated the Egyptians by having his men hold cats before them. The Egyptians wouldn't fight for fear of injuring the cats, sacred to Bast, and so they surrendered.

Hathor—Wife of Amentet, or Osiris. By the time of *Empire,* she has blended with Isis and is often called Hathor-Isis.

Horus—The falcon god, the god of war

Isis—Queen of the heavens. By the time of *Empire,* Isis has come to be identified with Hathor and is often depicted wearing Hathor's cow horn/sun disk headdress.

Kathaihemt—The sacred bull of Amentet and Hathor, possibly the golden calf of Aaron.

Neith—The earth mother, by Saite tradition, mother of Ra, patron goddess of the city of Sais. Neith is identified with Athena, and so, despite their xenophobia, the Saite dynasty felt a kinship with the Athenian Greeks. She is also seen as a goddess of war.

Nut—Goddess of fertility.

Osiris—God of the underworld.

Ptah—The scholarly god, the god of craftsmen, his city was Memphis.

Ra—The sun god, by some traditions, son of Amentet and Hathor, often represented by a simple disk. He was the head god of the pantheon, but with the Priest-Kings of Thebes, the New Kingdom age was ushered in and their sun god, Amun, became supreme. Ra was then identified with Amun as in Amun-Ra.

Median/Persian

The Medes seem to have had only one god, the Fire God, whom they worshiped, as did the Persians, from the mountain tops. They did not build temples and tended to look with scorn on those who did. The Persians, some time around Darius the Great, eventually adopted a different system, subscribing to the teachings of one of their mystics and became Zoroastrians, who are vaguely dualists: equating good with an equally strong evil. They then worshipped a god, Ahuramaza, and a goddess, Mylitta.

Philistine

Ashtoreth/Asherah—Wife of Baal.

Baal—The head deity.

Dagon—Baal in the form of the Lord of the Sea. He had a fishtail. The patron god of Ashdod.

Milcom—Patron god of Tyre, he was actually an Ammonite god (Molech). No other Philistines worshipped this deity. His temple was the glory of the city, but his worship was in form only. In truth, the Tyrians worshipped their money.

Scythian

Apia-Ge—Earth goddess associated with Hera.

Argimpasa—The golden goddess of love. The Greeks associated her with Aphrodite.

Goetosyrus—Te sun god.

Papaeu—Associated with Zeus

Tabiti—The great goddess. She was the most venerated by all the tribes. When Anacharsis attempted to introduce Greek worship into her rites, King Saulius, his brother, was obliged to execute him.

Thamimasadas—The patron god of the Royal Scythians.

Urania—The only god to have representation, a sword in brushwood. He demanded human sacrifice.

APPENDIX IV

Map

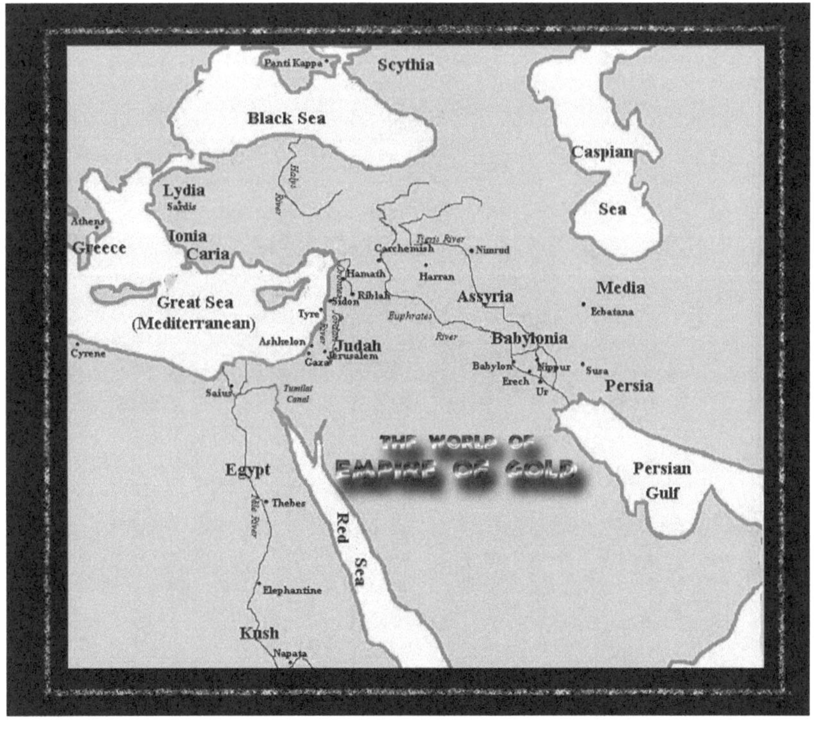

PARTIAL BIBLIOGRAPHY

Alexander, Pat. *The Lion Encyclopedia of the Bible.* Batavia: Lion Publishing Corporation, 1978.

Bury, J.B. *The Cambridge Ancient History, Volume III, The Assyrian Empire.* London: Cambridge at the University Press, 1925.

Buttrick, George Arthur. *The Interpreter's Bible: Volume 6, Lamentations, Ezekiel, Daniel, Twelve Prophets.* New York: Abingdon Press, 1956.

Fagan, Brian M. *Return to Babylon.* Boston: Little, Brown and Company, 1979.

Frank, Harry T. *Atlas of the Bible Land.* Maplewood: Hammond Inc., 1959.

Galvin, Dr. James C. *Daniel, a Life Application Bible Study.* Wheaton: Tyndale House Publishers, Inc, 1989.

Gordon, Cyrus H. *Forgotten Scripts.* New York: Barnes & Nable Books, 1993.

Harper, James. Great Events of Bible Times. Garden City: Doubleday & Company, Inc., 1987.

Hawkes, Jacquetta. *Atlas of Ancient Archaeology.* New York: Barnes & Noble Books, 1974.

Hawkes, Jacquetta. *The World of the Past.* New York: Alfred A. Knopf, 1963.

Jeremiah, David. *The Handwriting on the Wall.* Dallas: Word Publishing, 1992.

Layard, Sir Austen Henry. *Discoveries in the Ruins of Nineveh and Babylon, with Travels in Armenia, Kurdistan, and the Desert: Being the Result of a Second Expedition Undertaken for the Trustees of the British Museum.* London: John Murray, Publisher, 1853.

McDowell, Josh. *Daniel in the Critics Den.* San Bernardino: Campus Crusade for Christ, 1979.

McDowell, Josh. *Evidence that Demands a Verdict.* San Bernardino: Campus Crusade for Christ, 1972.

McDowell, Josh. *More Evidence that Demands a Verdict.* San Bernardino: Campus Crusade for Christ, 1975.

McGee, J. Vernon. *Daniel.* Nashville: Thomas Nelson, Inc., 1991.

Neuübersetzung. *Das Buch der Sajaha; Neunzehn Schriftsätze der Babylonischen Seherin.* Tempelhof: Self-Published, 1991.

Pope, John A. Jr. *Who's Who in the Bible.* Pleasantville: Reader's Digest Assn., 1994.

Rice, Michael. *Who's Who in Ancient Egypt.* London: Routledge, 2002.

Roux, Georges. *Ancient Iraq.* Cleveland: The World Publishing Company, 1964.

Russel, D.S. *Daniel.* Philadelphia: Westminster Press, 1981.

Sinclair, Andrea. *Colour Symbolism in Ancient Mesopotamia.* Melbourne: University of Melbourne, 2012.

Skinner, John. *The Expositor's Bible: Ezekiel.* New York: Hodder & Stoughton, 1923.

Studwick, Helen. *The Encyclopedia of Ancient Egypt.* New York: Metro Books, 2006.

Tenney, Merrill C. *The Zondervan Pictorial Bible Dictionary.* Grand Rapids: Zondervan Publishing House, 1967.

Thiele, Edwin R. *The Mysterious Numbers of the Hebrew Kings,* Grand Rapids: Zondervan Publishing House, 1983.

Thompson, Frank Charles, D.D., Ph.D. *The Thompson Chain-Reference Bible, New International Version.* Grand Rapids: Zondervan Bible Publishers, 1983.

Tippet, Frank. *The First Horsemen: "The Emergence of Man."* New York: Time-Life Books, 1974.

Turro, James C. *Old Testament Reading Guide: The Book of Ezekiel.* Collegeville: The Liturgical Press, 1961.

Walvoord, John F. *Major Bible Prophecies.* New York: Harper Paperbacks, Zondervan Publishing House, 1991.

EXCERPTS

Empire of Gold is a series of history books written in the form of novels. They cover the time of the Neo-Babylonian Empire and the Babylonian Captivity of the Jews.

Foundations

Excerpt:

Night fell on Nineveh. With it came the month of Abu.

Friend Tigris, the beautiful and bountiful, raged with uncontained fury. Three years of rain had swelled her level beyond anything previously seen in even the oldest grandfather's memory. The Tebiltu, running south from the foothills, scorned the manmade banks Sharuken had made for it and reclaimed its old wadi bed, flowing deep through the channel between the eastern wall fortress and the main city wall …

…the reservoir was far out of it artificial banks and the dam held back an awakening monster. This night's downpour had turned the overtaxed the sluice-gate runoff into a rushing falls. The torrent ate away at the barrier. This current, never envisioned by Sharuken's engineers, pushed and tore furiously at the superb but now inadequate construction.

Suddenly, inevitably, in one gushing burst, the dam collapsed, loosing the waters behind it … Mounting to a great surge, the wave rushed down the narrow valley and rose eighty feet high and was over five miles long. It annihilated everything in its path—trees, boulders, buildings. As if the force of the water itself wasn't enough, the wave now hurled debris and mud in its furious progress. Sharuken's old capital of Dur-Sharuken was directly in the path of the torrent. It was swallowed whole.

From Nineveh, the thunderous progress of the freshwater tsunami was almost unheard in the pounding of the rain. In the dark of a storm swept night, the wall of water closed on the wall of earth.

The great outer barrier of Nineveh was situated from northwest to southeast. It was made of loose gravel and rubble, all of which began to tremble. The watchmen on the battlements paused, wondering at the ominous shaking which grew under their feet. A small avalanche of pebbles, shaken loose from the barrier, rolled down into the water beneath. Peering into the darkness, the watchmen called to one another, but none could see the cause of the stirring in the blackness of the rainy night. A sudden wind—air pushed violently before the wave—hit the guards and blew several right off their feet.

"There!" A scream pierced the darkness and roar of the wind. Lightning flashed and lit the dark night, revealing a black mass against the skyline, blacker than the black of the stormy horizon, looming high where nothing at all should be. It was as if another city wall had somehow been built in an instant and was thundering towards them! The terrified watchman pointed and screamed again, *"There! There! There!"*

Jeremiah I: Prince of Babylon

Excerpt:

Topheth, the place of burning, that was what they called the fiery altars of the Baals and the unquenchable flames of the garbage heap of Jerusalem had appropriated the name. It was the picture of eternal damnation to the people of Judah.

Tongues of fire flickered before the prophet's face, casting eerie lights across his visage in the shadows of the city wall. The flames burned, attempting to devour the rubbish of the city which fed them. The rejected and outcast broken remnants of society were consumed here forever amidst the swarms of flies and the scavenging creatures which tried to gorge themselves on their share of the refuse before the flames could claim it.

Jeremiah faced hell and knew it could be avoided no longer…

Jeremiah II: Emperor of Babylonia

Excerpt:

Daniel had never actually seen Nebuchadnezzar before, and though he knew it, he was still surprised to see how young the king was. Only nineteen years old, Nebuchadnezzar wore a beard, but it was sparse, and though he was tall, he was slender like a boy, his shoulders not yet having attained their width.

Watching him, Daniel gradually realized that it was easier to blame a faceless evil, to hate someone he couldn't picture in his mind...

While Daniel stared, Nebuchadnezzar suddenly turned his head and looked directly at him.

For an instant, their eyes met, and the Suzerain faltered in midstride. To Daniel, it seemed as if lightning had struck him, and time stood still. The hubbub of the crowd faded into a distant hum, and the world around receded until only he and the king remained, focused and highlighted in crystal clarity. Dumbfounded, the Judean youth continued to stare. If he didn't believe in the Babylonian's concept of destiny before, this at least seemed to be something very like it.

"Ah, Lord God," he breathed, "what…"

He is Mine and you will bring him to Me.

Him!?! ME?!? In that instant, in the blink of an eye, Daniel felt his world turned upside down. *This* was the man who had invaded his land and left it in poverty by deporting its most productive citizens. This was the man who was responsible for his present state, the man who tore him from his family, friends, and entire life. This was the man who had ordered his mutilation and indoctrination into the very center of occultic paganism. The God of Israel wanted *him?*

The king, with a thoughtful look on his face, reluctantly turned back to his duties and walked on.

Daniel remained, shaken, and wondering what in the world, or outside of it, had just happened...

Jeremiah III: King of the Universe

Excerpt:

"…I do not understand the ways of the gods, but I do know that Enlil puts great value on the life of His prophet."

"Jeremiah?"

"Yes! Of course, Jeremiah! We are going to rob the God's house and tear it down, but He is the One who told us to do it. We are only obeying His commands. However, He would not look kindly on harm coming to Jeremiah.

"So the real reason why I want to put you in charge is because I can trust you enough to explain this to you. It is the most important order that I am giving concerning this city. Seri, when you have conquered Jerusalem, you find Jeremiah and look after him. Do it personally. Make sure he comes to no harm. Treat him however he asks, give him whatever he wants. And if he will, bring him back here to me."

"It will be my first priority, Lord."

"It had better be…"

Made in United States
Troutdale, OR
12/11/2023

15692207R10299